GW00792411

KIP FENN
REFLECTIONS

FOR ADAM

WITH THANKS
TO A AND B

EXTRACTS FROM THE AUTHOR'S DIARY
ON THE WRITING OF THIS NOVEL
CAN BE FOUND AT WWW.KIPFENN.CO.UK

PAUL K LYONS

KIP FENN
REFLECTIONS

PIKLE
PUBLISHING

First published in Great Britain in 2004
by
Pikle Publishing, Godalming, Surrey

ISBN 0-9548270-0-7

Printed and bound in Great Britain by
TJ International, Padstow, Cornwall

KIP FENN
REFLECTIONS

CONTENTS

For Guido and Jay, and Alicia

*Any questions/comments about Kip Fenn or his Reflections
can be addressed to Jay@kipfenn.co.uk*

PROLOGUE

'Reflections (2): The life of an individual written by the subject, generally in a looser, less formal way than an autobiography. First found in common usage during the early part of the 21st century to denote an autobiography written in a descriptive, impressionist style; later used more generally for informal autobiographies which combine professional and personal revelations.'

Encyclopaedia Universal (2098 edition)

I was born, at our home in St Albans, two days before the end of the century, on 29 December 1999. My father Tom tried, or so he said, to bribe the doctor into filling out a false date on the health authority paperwork so that Julie would be able to register my birth on 1 January 2000, but he refused. I am glad about this since, if I survive as planned until next January, I will have lived in three centuries. My mother, Julie, never told me why she decided on a home birth. I suspect Tom bullied her into it, because he knew there would be no chance of fiddling my birth date in a hospital. Nor was it ever explained why a doctor rather than a midwife attended my birth. I met him, the doctor, at an afternoon drinks party hosted by our family solicitor to celebrate his retirement. It was the day before my tenth birthday. I had never seen a house so full of Christmas cards. I was nibbling my way through a bowl of sweet nuts when a tall man, smelling of alcohol, edged up to me.

'I delivered you, boy,' he said without so much as a hello, and confident I would understand what he was talking about. I didn't. I looked down shyly.

'Dr Jessop. I delivered you, boy.' He repeated with such urgency I had to raise my head and respond.

'Thank you,' I said. This seemed to satisfy him and he lurched off to impose on someone else.

I lie here, all these years later, reflecting carefully back over my life, editing and dictating, editing and dictating to the wallscreen in front of me. I have a wealth of personal and more general material to help the process, not least a lifetime of email communications which, from my 20s, I collated and stored. One day they may be net-published along with this, the bare bones of a biography – or, more accurately, my Reflections – which I am preparing in these last months of my life.

You may have heard of me, Neil or Kip Fenn, thanks to my career within the United Nation's International Fund for Sustainable Development, the IFSD, (especially during the First Jihad War), or my modest efforts within an organisation called REACH in the aftermath of the Grey Years. You may also have heard of me in connection with my daughter Crystal, who fell victim to the suicide epidemic of the 2040s, or my son, Bronze, whose idiotic caper in the 2060s disrupted both our lives (his tragically more so than mine). Or, possibly, you may recall my name in connection with a sexual weakness, but which was, essentially, a private matter and should never have been exposed in public. I will not ignore the personally painful and embarrassing, but I hope other areas of my private life, for which I am thankful, will take precedence: my co-op children, Guido and Jay, for example, or my role in launching The Josephine Collection archive of 19th century photographs.

I should explain this thing Tom had about dates. He was born on 12 April 1961, the day Yuri Gagarin went into space. It was eight years later, on 21 July 1969, when he sat with his father, Barry, watching (on 'a dinky black and white') the live coverage of Neil Armstrong's walk on the moon that he realised the significance of his birth date, although he was shocked to learn that Gagarin had already died. By the age of 15, Tom knew more about the moon, the planets and rocket technology than most boys did about football or popidols. Unfortunately, his knowledge was generally undermined by a failure to be accurate with details (other than dates). He dreamed of studying aeronautics at university, but only managed to scrape through into a second-rate college course on business studies. In consequence of his enthusiasm, perhaps, and some talent for spiel, Marconi admitted him to their graduate training course on marketing, but he never made the grade. By 23, he had settled for a well-paid job selling oil field equipment.

It was a wonder Tom asked Julie to marry him, given that she was born on 3 September 1973, a nondescript day if ever there was one. The best he could do in later years was to talk about his wife as having been born in the year of Skylab, or to suggest she should have delayed emerging into the world by a few days so as to coincide with Jackie Stewart's retirement – motor racing being another of his interests. I like to think that love overcame that early obstacle to their relationship, although there was scant evidence of it left by the time I was old enough to notice. Julie, née Hapgood, came from an average mid-20th century family, one with traditional values, and traditional hopes. She had one older brother, Alan, my uncle. The father, Oswald, was a manager with the Central Electricity Generating Board, and the mother, Eileen, was a housewife and a teacher. After difficult years at school and college (not least because of Oswald's untimely death), Julie took up a teaching job in a large comprehensive school in Harpenden.

Tom found her one Saturday night in a tenpin bowling alley, slightly drunk, and playing on a fruit machine. The next weekend he took her to the British Grand Prix at Silverstone. Although Tom had a predisposition for exaggeration while Julie usually had an umbilical relationship with the truth, I am inclined to believe Tom's version of events that weekend. I do not suggest my mother lied to me, rather that her memory became distorted in order to accommodate her subsequent resentment to the man. She remembered how hot and bothered she was in the traffic jams during the drive, and how she hated the noise and the crowds during the race itself. Tom told me, though, that Julie had sparkled all day, like a shop girl taken to a palace, and that she had accepted his chancer invitation for them to spend the night together with undisguised enthusiasm.

Despite all that happened, my mother could never completely extinguish her love for him. There had been boyfriends before, but none had lasted. I do not think she fell for him as such, but rather that she made a decision to love him, as if he were a last chance, a last credit in that fruit machine, and once the decision was made, she allowed herself to fall. I can see her now, after his funeral, standing outside the crematorium in the sunshine. She is slim and frail, dressed in a dark grey suit, her hair clasped up in a silvery bun, and she is crying.

'I've met with him three times in 20 years, why these tears?' she asks me apparently puzzled. Behind her I can see my first wife, Harriet, with our children, Crystal and Bronze, all anxious to depart.

'Perhaps you are thankful for what was, and regretful for what wasn't,' I say.

'My little wise man, you, my little wise man,' she says for the first time since I was a child. I smile despite myself. 'No. It is that I am sorry for what was, but grateful for what wasn't.' This is so unlike my mother, never one for complicated or psychological analysis of behaviour, that I avert my gaze from Harriet who is now marching towards me, and look directly at Julie as if to ask for further explanation. Her tears have evaporated.

Writing in the Reflections mode means I am less constrained by time – although I wish to keep to a rough chronology – and I can embellish the facts more generously than in a formal biography with feelings and impressions. More importantly, I need not worry where failures of memory (especially in middle and later years) or records would otherwise leave me struggling to fill in certain obvious gaps. I am struck, for example, that I recall nothing about my own emotions at that funeral. This leads me to the more unsettling thought that my writing might be unduly biased in favour of my mother, or even, perhaps, in favour of Tom. But then it occurs to me that another advantage of the Reflections format is that I need not worry too strenuously about being fair.

I keep trying to find a beginning, but there isn't one. Did my life begin with birth, or with conception? Will it end with death? In a physical sense, the answers may be yes, but surely the least interesting part of my life is its medical record. Or should my beginning be confined to what I can remember all of a hundred or so years ago? Yet these are only memories of memories, photographically fixed and collaged (not dissimilar to a Henry Peach Robinson print), and re-photographed in my head, or digitally recorded and re-remembered in soft focus, or in the wrong colours, or …

I could call up from Neil the transcribed video recordings taken by Alan of me as a baby, or as a primary school child, but, to be honest, I can't be bothered. Meanwhile, I could introduce Neil, my personal digital memory store for more than 60 years. I was named after the astronaut, but the memory store was named after me, in a backhand gesture towards my father. I swapped my given Neil for Kip not long after he left my mother and me. It began as a school nickname. A teacher had caught me napping in religious studies, and Horace, that's Horace Merriweather, called me Kip as a taunt. Later, he decided Kip was a more suitable name for a friend of his than the dull Neil. Although he never took to the name Hip that we gave him, as I did to Kip, we became known for a while as Hip and Kip, he in the foreground, and I in the background. He died not very long ago, in the mid-80s. I remember thinking at the time how, in general, civil servants like me often age with more dignity than politicians like Horace who never quite become accustomed to living beyond the limelight.

I see I have not yet mentioned Diana or Lizette, with whom I came to know something of the love that people talk and sing and write about, nor even Arturo, the second greatest surprise of my life.

Chapter One

TOM, JULIE AND SCHOOL

'When every snowflake and every thumbprint is different, and we have no idea how to predict or control the formulation of their patterns, why do we still have the conceit to believe that we can fix and formulate the minds and characters of our children? Let us teach them with wisdom and humility not try and change who they are.'

The Snowball Effect or Parenting made Difficult by Julia Derwent (2006)

It is new year's eve 2019, a memorable night. I should have been at a college ball in London, and my father, Tom, should have been in Dorking at a marquee fest with his latest companion. Only my mother, Julie, was in the right place, in Edinburgh, after being pestered for many years by an old school-friend, Rachel, to visit her there. I was staying at the house in Godalming, my past home, over the holidays to recuperate, having badly sprained an ankle injury during a volleyball league match against the Richmond Reelers. Julie had wanted to cancel the trip north, but I insisted she go. Coincidentally, Tom phoned, not knowing where I was, to tell me he had been dumped by his girlfriend, and was on the M25. I told him I was alone at Julie's house in Godalming and suggested he come and keep me company. He arrived half an hour later.

I used the crutches lent me by St George's Hospital to hobble to the front door and back. Tom was as dapper as ever, even in his late 50s, wearing a dark blue overcoat and light blue scarf round his neck tied like a cravat and tucked into the lapels. He tried to hand me two bottles at the door, but when I declined for obvious reasons he put them down on the side table, next to an oversized picture of me aged 11 in school uniform.

'Do you know what the bitch did to me?' he said; and continued without waiting for an answer, 'she set me up, she bloody well set me up.'

'And you didn't see it coming?'

'Did I hell. Let's have a drink son and I'll tell you more.' But then he remembered he had left something in the car, and dashed out to return a few moments later with two large plastic boxes.

'Dad! One for my birthday and one for Christmas.'

'If you want.' He beamed, but it wasn't a smile that had flourished for seeing me, rather it was the one he wore as easily as his suit when he had some new toy or product to show off, or some new joke to tell. I worked my way back to the sofa, while Tom deposited the boxes, removed his overcoat, and disappeared to the kitchen to open one of the bottles and bring us both a glass of champagne.

'You'll have to sort out food for us too, there's some decent ready-mades in the fridge.'

'Later, later. So, how did you bugger up your ankle? Mmm this is good.' I told him as briefly as I could, knowing he would not be very interested.

'After jumping to block a smash, I landed on the foot of one of the Reeler's hitters, it shouldn't have been there on my side of the net – the goon. My foot and ankle and leg crumpled beneath me, and I was reduced to a shrieking mass of pain. The coach ice-packed the ankle for me, and then, after the game, took me to the hospital.'

'Did you win?'

'Yes.'

'And was that African chappy there.'

'No, Dad, Alfred's studying and playing in Manchester.' Once, and once only, my father came to see me play. I was about 15, and my school team had reached the final of the inter-school southeastern cup. We won, but this was of no interest to Tom. After the match, he wanted to know why I was always slapping hands with the black chap, and to remind me that Africans were a dodgy lot. There was a grin on his face, but I walked off in silent fury.

'Mea culpa. I'm a bit distracted, you understand. How's your mother?' Tom asked.

'OK. You could call her yourself.'

'I could. Neat place she's got, but then it ought to be, seeing as it cost me an arm and a leg.'

Within minutes Tom had emptied his glass and refilled it. He told me about Kerry, or was it Cherry – I forget, there were so many after Julie. This girl's brother was hosting a large marquee party to celebrate the birth of a child and new year's eve. Unfortunately for Tom, it was also a splendid occasion for Kerry to show off her new man – not my father. He was staggered at the depth of her hostility. Poor Tom. I watched his false smile transform into a grimace as he explained how she had taken exception to all the times he had talked about past girlfriends.

'What a bitch. She must have been a great actress.' He emptied his glass. 'All the way here, I've been trying to work out when exactly, in our three month relationship, she turned, and I've no idea, no idea at all.'

'Put it down to experience, Dad,' I said. This was one of his stock phrases, yet, already at 20, I felt wiser than him.

'Fuck experience.' I laughed, he didn't.

'What's that there, then?' I asked pointing to the boxes. I saw the weight lift from his brow, and a glint appear in his eye.

'Guess.'

6

'A new dinner service for Julie.' This was a joke, but elicited no more than a grunt. 'An Earthmate with Zeta gaming facilities?' I was never a huge fan of computer games, but I did know this had been an object of desire that Christmas.

'You wish. Better than that.'

'A model space station? I give up.'

'Scalextric. It was for Kerry's boy. I liked him. He liked me, but I'm buggered if I was going to give him 1,000 euros worth of two tier racing track and RC cars with programmable features and a computer console, after what she did.'

'No, I don't suppose you were. So what are you going to do with it?'

'Play with it. Now. With you.' He looked around the room. 'Could be bigger, but it'll do. I'll get us a refill, and then get us going. But first there's something else.' He opened the smaller of the two boxes and produced a battered but serviceable VHS player, which he deftly plugged into an adaptor and then into the old freestanding television. From his overcoat, he retrieved a cassette (the kind which, at the time, was considered collectable) and then set it going.

'A bit of nostalgia son. You won't mind if we keep it playing. You were two days old, I was 20 years younger, the world was in a happy mood. This is a non-stop recording of BBC 1 on 31 December 1999, from early evening through to the early morning. You, son, only saw about half an hour of this, when Julie brought you in to breast feed.'

'Where did you get it from, and, more to the point, why?'

'Bought it. A week ago, in a Jester shop. A whim.'

'It's a good idea,' I said.

The first programme which came on, while Tom was setting up the track, was a famous episode of Eastenders, but one I'd never seen. I was a faithful addict during my early teens, before the BBC sold the show for a fortune to William Caxton who used it to help launch the People's Channel in 2021. And, during that time I probably took in a few historical episodes on the repeat channels or in anniversary slots. Although Caxton slowly drained its quality, the most famous UK soap lasted into the 2030s.

Only after its demise, of course, did Eastenders become the classic it is today, beloved and analysed endlessly in English drama departments around the world. Gregory (one of my favourite pop-historians, brilliant but also often flawed) claims that, during the golden era of oil and chips, Eastenders became more culturally important in Britain than Shakespeare.

'It's coming back to me now,' Tom said as he crawled around the floor, 'I don't believe it – they haven't changed the connecting mechanism after all these years. You have to place one at an angle to the other and then wiggle it in.

What do you think?' I could see he had made good use of the furniture, for tunnels and bridges, and several pots crafted by my grandmother, for underpinning bends or for raised sections.

'I'm not covering for you, if one of those ceramics break.'

'They won't. Let's give it a go.' He reached into the box and pulled out some model cars. 'Do you want the silver Rhyme, the red Jaguar, the cream Princess – bloody hell, I remember those – or the turquoise Rigatoni Mini?' I may have mixed up the colours, but my memory of those model cars is surprisingly fresh.

'Which do you recommend?'

'Do you want speed or traction?' And so we played for an hour or more, stopping occasionally whenever he wanted to adjust the circuit, or to fill our glasses. He won every race, whichever car, whichever track, and I blamed my losses on having to keep one eye on Eastenders.

While eating microwaved lasagna and drinking a bottle of wine stored in the pantry for cooking purposes (the champagne having long since disappeared, largely down Tom's gullet), Julie rang. She didn't want to wait until midnight in case I'd gone to sleep. We wished each other all the best for the new year. I saw no reason to mention Tom's presence. It would only have upset her.

Perhaps Tom, fuelled by drink, had already lost his playful facade before the phone rang, but, as I manoeuvred round on the sofa to speak to him, he suddenly appeared all washed out, lost, empty, vanquished. Sitting there sloppily in the old armchair he had always used, his legs wide apart, I watched while his head fell forward as if asleep, leaving the loosened bulky knot in his bright red tie sticking out below his chin, and his arms, clothed in the well-ironed sleeves of his expensive shirt, sprawled out along the arm-rests.

'Dad.' It was only a word, to get his attention. But it was the wrong word, or the right one depending on which way you look at it.

'I'm not your Dad.' He said it without raising his bowed head. I thought I didn't hear what he said, and was about to say 'pardon', but stopped myself. The words and their meaning, nevertheless, filtered through into my conscious-ness; and then he repeated them anyway.

'I'm not your father. I can't be.' I said nothing. Everything had gone blank, but vividly blank, if that's possible. I kept on looking at him, and eventually he raised his head.

'Well, fucking say something,' he said. 'Well, fucking say something.' I'm very fond of that phrase. It might have come from Eastenders, except that the television was showing crowds of celebrants in Moscow, and, in any case, Eastenders was not then owned by Caxton.

I could make up the next bit, but the truth is I don't remember emerging from the blankness. I might have asked the primary questions, or he might have asked them for me, 'How do you know?' and 'Who is?'. Secondary questions, such as 'Why haven't you told me before?', came later.

This is what I learned that night. Tom was first alerted to his infertility during a serious affair in his early 20s with a 'busty social worker'. She was very keen to have children, but when she didn't become pregnant, she demanded they both get tested. When he came back with news of a very low sperm count, the relationship broke down. He told himself it was only a <u>low</u> sperm count, not a <u>zero</u> sperm count, and put it out of his mind. He went with a succession of weak women after that to restore his confidence, and eventually decided to marry Julie, who had youth, if not beauty, and was fool enough to have him. But he never told her. When she fell pregnant, after more than a year without contraception, he quashed any idea than she might have been unfaithful, and believed his own internal propaganda. My paternity was never discussed. As I grew up, however, without any physical characteristics similar to Tom (he was fairish, slightly built and of medium height, while I was dark, full-boned and tall), he allowed his suspicions to grow. Who knows whether he did this to justify his own infidelities, or whether his unfaithfulness escalated as a consequence of his suspicions. It was only on the brink of their separation that Julie hinted, in one violent argument, that Tom wasn't my father. Given Tom's insecurities in this area, which he had never revealed, this sparked further arguments. Julie, though, stubbornly refused to discuss the subject further. Long after the separation and divorce, Tom found himself unable to forget the matter. In order to get a DNA test, he forged my signature on the mandatory consent form, and acquired some of my hair. This was after the Bangkok trip and during my first year at university.

As for the who, Tom had no idea, no clue.

My memory re-engages about the time he is shaking his head and saying 'sorry' several times in a row. 'For what?' I asked mechanically.

'I'm sorry I'm not your real father, sorry for you, but much sorrier for me too. You're a fine son, the best.' This must rank as the nicest thing he ever said to me, and I was about to become emotional when he reeled out a rescue line. 'But heh, it's just as well you don't have my genes or you'd never have made it into the volleyball team.' I lay there uncomfortable but immobile on the sofa, while Tom eased himself out of the chair and left the room. The TV was showing crowds along the Thames, and firework celebrations from places further east around the globe.

I tried to think if I could recall any tall men from my childhood. There was only my uncle Alan, Julie's brother, but such a liaison was too horrible to contemplate. Moreover, although my mother was not religious she was morally upright. I may, youthfully, have wished Alan to be my father on occasions, especially when Tom was away so much or appeared disinterested in me, but

Alan's relationship with Julie was too honest, too straightforward for them to have hidden a secret. I could barely believe my mother capable of such a deception, one so deep and dark. But, at that moment, I had no doubt I would find out who my father was as soon as she returned from Edinburgh.

Tom re-entered the room some minutes later, more sober, more in control of himself, and proposed another game of Scalextric. I declined pleading enough was enough. I too needed the toilet so hobbled my way there. On the way back, coming through the breakfast room, I passed a photo of Tom, Julie and me taken when I was about six. I have it on the wallscreen now. I am in school uniform again (what would one expect with a teacher for a mother) and standing between my parents, but looking up at Tom, with something akin to love in my eyes. Julie is glancing down at me, and Tom, as usual, is staring forthrightly at the camera. How strange that I should be able to touch the very same emotion now, looking at this photo, that I felt then. Love for my father, love of my father, warts, Bangkok and all. It made no difference, I realised, standing there, held up by crutches, only 20 years old, that he was not my genetic parent, he was still my Dad, always was, and always would be. I told him as much then, and it felt good.

At about 11pm, we switched off the video, and flicked through various broadcast programmes looking for one hosted by someone both of us could put up with, which was not so easy. I vetoed any game shows, and Tom blocked any political or current affairs-type discussions. We finally compromised on a truly old comedy, *Some Like it Hot* with Marilyn Monroe, to lift our spirits. Since it was a film we both knew, we could let it fill the silences, or switch easily into the laughter, when our talk faded out. I wanted to know why Tom had not acted earlier to confront Julie or tell me. I did not get a straight answer, but I did come to understand, more or less. With Julie, he felt no responsibility: whatever his own mistakes, her deception had been the greater. As for me, I believe he was afraid of what it might do to our relationship, especially since it had gone downhill since the horrible trip to Bangkok three years earlier (about which I will have more to say later). As it happens, Tom's revelation served to re-establish our friendship, albeit an intermittent one, which lasted through to his death in 2038.

We fell asleep in situ, only to wake groggy and cold in the early hours. I told Tom he should take my bed, but he wanted to leave. He packed up the Scalextric and old video player, when I said I didn't want them, and ferried the boxes to his sleek car, I think it was a Ford Presumption, but it could have been one of a dozen, he was forever switching models. Rain had moved in overnight. We said goodbye on the doorstep under the porch, embracing awkwardly, and one of my crutches fell to the ground.

* * *

I spent most of new year's day 2020 searching through all Julie's private belongings for a clue about her infidelity and my paternity. Fortunately, she was a tidy, ordered person – a characteristic she pressed into me from an early age – and I was able to find her personal papers without much trouble. An old pine dresser in the kitchen held various papers such as bills, home accounts, tradesmen's flyers, job quotes and jumble sale notices. There was nothing of interest there. Nor was there much to find in the small oak desk, dominated by a dark green personal computer console, or in the three drawer old-fashioned wooden filing cabinet, both of which were tucked into the darkest corner of the lounge. Everything here was connected with her teaching work. I decided against checking the computer hard disk, despite the potential treasure of email correspondence, in case she had a security mechanism which might give me away, and require explanation.

I saved the white-painted desk in her bedroom until last. Here, where I spent several hours, I was extremely careful to ensure that every bundle of letters and email printouts (organised by correspondent, and with neatly printed copies of her own missives), every packet of photographs (labelled), and every diary (largely blank with only intermittent entries) were replaced exactly as I found them. I should note that I never saw any of the letters again (with one exception), nor any of her email correspondence except for some extended email dialogues between her and Alan, which I acquired after my uncle's death. Since I did not find any correspondence among the personal possessions I inherited from my mother, I assume she destroyed or lost them during her later years.

I discovered much about my mother that day, although, from this distance, it is difficult to untangle all of what I learned then from what I had already known, especially from Tom during the Bangkok trip, or from what I may have found out later. Also, whereas some of the information was pertinent to my search, some may have been stored and lain dormant, to be appreciated in conjunction with other events. I recollect, in particular how the letters to Alan, who lived abroad mostly, and the occasional diary entries, mostly in the period up to when I was 11 or so, revealed the depth of Julie's misery. While the journal entries were unrestrained, the letters told the same story in more coded language, a consistent tale of Tom's frequent trips away, his disinterest in Julie or in me or in any domestic business at all, and his ugly belligerence. Where he was brutish, she was sensitive, the subtext read, where he was cold, she was warm, where he was hard, she was soft. Oddly none of this was a surprise. I had lived with an atmosphere between them until I was 13, and my mother's written expression of the difference between the male and female character appeared rather normal. It was more shocking to realise that my mother saw herself as a martyr, and that she considered the self-sacrifice of staying with Tom as necessary for my well-being. She must have camouflaged this side of her character well, at least from me. Or, maybe, children have so many other daily petty grievances against their parents they never see the bigger faults. A year or two later, when I no longer felt the need to be so loyal to Julie, I recall Tom, in a pub, choking with laughter when I suggested she had a secret martyr complex. Not secret, he spat, but 'plain, plain as a bloody pike-staff'.

It was easier to forgive another fault that eked out of Julie's writing, especially in letters to an old friend who had given birth at a similar time to her but had then emigrated to Canada: an overly zealous anxiety about me. I had had glimpses of this when overhearing her talk about me to friends on the phone, but the letters and journal entries were stronger stuff. How strange it is to read about oneself in the third person. She wrote in great detail about my physical development, my behaviour, my progress at school, for example, as well as about my faults – disobedience, stubborn silences, insufficient effort. There was nothing unusual there, even at age 20 I could tell that, and yet she wrote with the intensity of an obsessive. I imagine this came from a deep sense of responsibility towards me, which I had never properly appreciated, and one she had never come to terms with – perhaps because she had chosen the wrong husband, or because her husband was not my father.

The first time the house phone rang that day I was already installed in my mother's bedroom, on her bed in fact, which was the most comfortable place for me, even though I had to hop backwards and forwards to the desk for each new bundle. But, as I had forgotten to bring the receiver upstairs, I was obliged to try and hop-rush down the stairs to answer it. On the way, I fell quite badly and bruised my thigh. It was Julie. She kept asking if I was well because I sounded so funny, so tense. And she asked, with that slight accusatory tone of hers, if I had a girl with me. I improvised well-ness, allowing her one more holiday day.

Of all the letters/emails to my mother, the most absorbing were those written by Alan. (Indeed, if anyone were to investigate the extensive files of my own correspondence stored on Neil, they would find the Alan Hapgood file one of the longest, the most easy to read, and the most stimulating. Not that emails have ever replaced the warm satisfaction of receiving a real letter sent by postal courier.) This was not only because, of all her correspondents, his life, spent working for the environmental organisation WWF, was the most interesting, but also because of his warmth and humanity, and the relaxed style with which he wrote to his sister. At this time, he must have been posted in Brussels or Geneva or another of WWF's offices, otherwise I would surely have seen him during the Christmas period. As I have said, he was a great, as in excellent, uncle, and he became a great friend, but since it was clear from the letters that Julie had never confided in him, there was no need to quiz him on this particular matter.

And what of my paternity? There was little to help me, except for this one sad handwritten (in green ink) letter, which alone was housed in its original envelope.

'Dearest Julie

How abysmal, how awful, how lonely these days. I can hardly bear to see you in school. You are so cold, so unfriendly. I'm not sorry for what I did, what we did, nor for who I am. Are you ashamed of me? Did you fall out of love with me in the space of one weekend? Did I do something wrong? Say something terrible? I know you feel something for me, you told me so. And I know you loved me in those nights, I know you did, I know you did, I know you did.

I love you. Love me again too.

Martin x'

I have this letter stored on Neil (during a subsequent visit to Julie's house, I conspired to copy it) and am looking at it onscreen now. The note is not so sad in itself but because, in one corner, my mother has written to herself 'I love you too Martin', and because several of Martin's words are smudged by, I imagine, a tear stain. I recall, also, that this was the one and only letter I discovered in my mother's entire collection with any romantic content at all, and that the single piece of notepaper had been much handled. The envelope was stamped January 1999.

In her 1998 diary, I found some further evidence. There was one entry in mid-November in which she complained about Tom's absence, and recorded her decision to accept an invitation to go to the theatre. The invitation was from 'a new young teacher with manners' who had, in less than a term, become 'a favourite with the Head'. My mother must have been flattered by the man's interest, and had justified responding because of her growing resentment towards Tom. A further short entry, at Christmas time, concluded with the simple phrase 'Martin rang'. The 1999 journal, a separate book with even fewer entries than the previous year, recorded nothing in March/April, round about the time I was conceived, except a bout of flu and depression which led to several visits from the doctor.

Despite the content and date of the letter, I was convinced that Martin had to be my father. I scoured the house to see if Julie had kept any school newsletter or prospectus from that period, but I couldn't find anything. I tried to project forward as to how, when my mother returned, our conversation would proceed, and how I might introduce Martin's name without giving away my illicit search. If I had been sufficiently angry this embarrassment might not have been a problem, but I wasn't: however large my mother's crime, I did not want her to know I had been rifling through her letters.

That evening, a Wednesday, I was taken out by some old school-friends. We went to the Mankind net pub by the river the other side of Godalming, and played MoonFusion for hours against a team in Seoul. We lost. I couldn't concentrate, and, that difficulty apart, I was hopeless at netgaming. All day Thursday I pretended to myself that I was reading a controversial book on the failures of the United Nations (which I did, eventually, use extensively for a mini-thesis), but in reality I was brooding, and becoming increasingly unsettled by Tom's revelation. I telephoned Alfred, on holiday from Manchester University, in Lagos, but chickened out of talking things over with him.

Julie returned on Friday night. It was still pouring with rain. She had rung the doorbell without thinking, I suppose, because she couldn't be bothered to find her key. By the time I had hopped my way through into the hallway, she was already inside, standing on the mat, a sweet picture: her glad-to-be-home-but-weary face, her damp glistening hair, fastened up as usual in a tidy bun, her overlong mottled green raincoat dripping, and a suitcase dropped down by her side.

'Sorry,' she said. And, for a moment, I thought she was apologising for her adultery.

'No taxis?' I asked rhetorically, knowing that, although both of us would normally walk from the station less than half a mile away, we would often buy a ride in bad weather or with heavy loads.

Half an hour later, we were sitting in the breakfast room where she had brought a tray of tea things. I listened to the details of her journey with curiosity, not duty, for she kept her anecdotes short and did not ramble. She was a good teacher, I am certain, one that holds an audience with confident and interesting delivery, as opposed to a poor one who holds an audience with discipline. But, all the time, I was thinking about how and when I was going to confront her. She's tired after the journey, I told myself, I'll wait until tomorrow. Then she quizzed me on what I'd been doing. I looked away, hesitated, said nothing. And then the words came out.

'Tom was here, he got drunk and told me something.' Words come out, we don't exactly choose them (not unless they are part of a prepared speech or presentation). And then we hear them, think about them, and then rally round to make sense of them with expressions, or more words, or actions. This was my brooding, jumping out of me.

'Tom was here, when, why?'

'He phoned for a chat, and when I said you were away, he said he was nearby and so popped in. That's all.'

'And?'

'And what?' I was afraid, trying to back away from the confrontation.

'You said he told you something.'

'Yes, sort of. It's a bit difficult. It can wait until the morning.' She had her elbows almost vertical on the table, and her chin rested in her hands. Her face was in the shadow created by her head from the ceiling light above. This was my mother, and I felt closer to 12 than 20. I looked away. Silence. I used silence a lot as a child. It was a defence against inquisition. Tom could never deal with it, and lost his temper. Julie, though, was more artful. She used patience, and soft-speaking, and, what? ... Yes, an expression which made use of a gentle encouraging nod, a slight sideways tip of the head, and raised eyebrows. I glanced towards her, saw this expectant look, and said the simple words I'd rehearsed.

'Tom says he's not my father.' The human face is a marvel. We train it to express so much, and yet it expresses so much else involuntarily. How can I explain the physical changes in that moment as I watched my mother take in my few words? A narrowing of the iris, as her brain switched attention from vision to thought, a tensing of the forehead, a drawing in of her cheek muscles, with a consequent loss of the slight smile she tried to hold in company. Certainly, the colour drained out of her skin, turning her very pale.

'Tom says he's not my father. I want to know if this is true, and, if it is, who my real father is.' This was another rehearsed statement. In my projection forward to this conversation, it was easiest to imagine my mother would say nothing immediately, and therefore to prepare a follow-up. I may have repeated the question too quickly, too urgently, for Julie then reinvigorated herself instantly, and responded sharply.

'He was glossy, he was talking tosh.' She got up and began to clear away the tea things. Denial. I had not expected a denial, and was momentarily phased. Could Tom have made it all up? Why would he do so? No.

'What else did he tell you?' she called through from the kitchen where water was running. 'Has he taken up Buddhism?'

I shouted back, not in anger yet, but loud enough so she would definitely hear me.

'He's had us – him and me – checked out with DNA analysis. It's 100% sure, Mum, a 100%.' I heard the water stop running. She padded back into the room, and sat down. I said nothing. I watched her thinking for a few minutes. I was in a state of high excitement, although I kept myself motionless and cool, waiting, fully expecting a momentous revelation. After a long silence, she spoke in a low distant voice, not to me, but to herself.

'I don't know, I don't know what happened. I had suspicions. But I don't know.' She got up again, heavily this time, taking the teapot with her.

The pitch in my own voice and language rose to follow her.

'You must know. It's not that fucking difficult to work out who you were sleeping with nine months before I was born. Or is it?' She stopped in her tracks, astonished to hear me use such language.

'I can't help you,' she said and walked out of the room.

I resorted to loud crude sarcasm next.

'So you weren't screwing anyone else at the time, you were completely faithful to Tom, and I was a miracle.' I collected one crutch and hopped after her. I stood in the doorway of the kitchen. 'Were you sleeping around, or weren't you? You must know, come on Mum, you teach sex education, you know how it happens. Who's my bloody father?' I wasn't given to swearing, or vitriol, or even anger most of the time, but on this occasion my normal behaviour patterns gave way to some combination of those I'd seen employed by Tom or Eastenders' characters. I stood there screaming while my mother, her back towards me, did the washing up.

I stopped soon enough. It was as though someone else was doing the shouting. I doddered back to the other room, where I sat down, and calmed myself. I considered whether I should ask her directly about Martin. Yet this was too risky. Firstly, she might simply carry on saying nothing; secondly, as I've said, I could not bring myself to let her know I had been through her private things; and, thirdly, my illicit behaviour could create a diversion for her and attenuate the righteous force of my demands to know the truth. I decided to make a more rational appeal. She returned to the table, looking at me with a rare sense of vulnerability.

'Mum, you can't not tell me. I have a right to know. Was there someone else?'

'Not really.'

'Not really?'

'There was a young man once, when your father was away, but, ...' she paused, appearing uncertain and confused.

'Yes,' I said encouragingly.

'But ... but I can't tell you any more. I don't know any more.' She paused again, having become vague and very distant. After that she closed up completely. Despite my insistent, but now calm, questioning, she would only repeat that same phrase, 'I can't tell you any more', with the strangest inflection on the last two words. Then she went to bed. I quizzed her again in the morning, but when she refused repeatedly to answer any of my questions about the past, or to acknowledge my right to the information, I left. I packed my rucksack (with some difficulty), called a taxi, and took a combination of trains and another taxi to get back to my Bermondsey flat. Tom rang while I was waiting at one station or another to tell me to go easy with Julie. It was just like him to be late with good intentions.

What did my mother mean by 'any more'? This taxed me for a long time afterwards. Did she mean she was not able to give me any further information, or did she mean that she no longer had any answers, that she was confused about the past. I never found out. Stranger still, I never discovered whether she even knew what had happened to her. She had certainly blanked out the truth in some way, but whether this was an involuntary unconscious initiative, or whether she deliberately pushed the information so far back in her mind and made the conscious decision not to access the knowledge, is hard to know. I incline to the latter view.

I am undecided whether to conclude this story now, or to leave it for another chapter.

***

A peppery omelette was brought in for me some minutes ago, and while eating I launched a database of early snaps that are now fading in and out on the screen. Some of these are so grainy, a tell-tall sign that they were scanned or snapped digitally in the period when computer memory was constrained by size and expense. They exude a glorious sense of generalised, not personal, nostalgia: I know who these people are, but they do not touch any live memories. Other photos from later on in my life are more meaningful in an emotional way, but they must wait their turn. For now, I might pause on one or two of these pictures.

Here are Tom and Julie outside a registry office. He is in a white suit, tightly fitted, with a compact pink rose in one lapel. He looks like a dandy. He may have had tendencies in that direction but, although a vain man, I thought of him as well-dressed rather than over-dressed. Perhaps, if circumstance had give him more freedom, he may have gone foppish. Julie is in a pink dress, and looks like a bridesmaid. In another photo, confetti is falling around their shoulders, and they are surrounded by family members. Alan, to one side, is looking amused and holding a box, from which a teenage girl is reaching for a further handful of confetti. Julie's mother, Eileen, is there on the other side. She was a stern but fair woman, also a teacher, and for many years the head at a large primary school in Reading. She was a keen potter. I never saw much of her. Tom used to tell me, when I was older, that she was more interested in her pupils and her pots than in her own children or grandchildren. She could never bring herself to approve of Tom, whose charm always fell flat with her. It is possible we saw her more when I was very young, but after our move to Guildford, and after her retirement to Parsonville, a custom-built retirement village near Bournemouth, she never came to visit us. As a family, we went to see her twice a year at most, although Julie alone went more often. Eileen's husband and Julie's father, Oswald Hapgood, had died of a brain tumour when Julie was only ten. There was also a distance between Eileen and her son Alan, which grew wider as they got older. Eileen was a traditional Tory: in her dotage she would reminisce about Margaret Thatcher, the Conservative prime minister in the 1980s. But Alan, despite her best efforts, went left, then green, and didn't start the journey back towards the centre until well into middle-age. My mother, by contrast, could never be bothered with politics, other than when it affected education policy.

Percival, Oswald's bachelor brother, stands at the back of the photo. He was a grey fellow. Oddly, he came to life when pulling crackers or playing tiddly-winks. In conversations, his contribution was often confined to nods and shakes. He tried to interest me in fishing once, not long after his retirement. I believe he spent time in a mental home. I remember his death, or rather seeing his dead body, the first one I ever saw in the flesh. I was 12.

Tom's father and mother, Barry and Evvie, are in the photo too, looking pleased with themselves; or is that relief in their eyes and smiles? I never knew Evvie, she died soon after the wedding. Barry emigrated to Malta.

Here is a favourite photo of Tom, Julie and me in Monte Carlo in May 2003. Tom is sitting on the bonnet of a bright red racing car, I am on his lap in bright red shorts, an orange t-shirt, and a baseball cap sporting the name Ferrari. Julie is standing next to us laughing at something Tom, or the camera holder, has said. She is wearing a light yellow frock, and a straw hat, and is looking her prettiest. This is how I picture her whenever I think of her as a young woman in the time before I had my own memories. She had this photo enlarged and framed; it was displayed in one room or other in the St Albans, Guildford and Godalming houses. There are two anecdotes about that holiday. I was told both of them a few times.

Julie's eyes would mist over when she looked at this picture – this is later, after Tom had left – and she would drift into a nostalgic mood.

'That was the best holiday we ever had, not because of the place or the weather, but because your father had never been more loving or caring. I had not been to Monaco, but he knew it well from business trips, conferences and exhibitions mostly. I was dreading the holiday, you were so young. I knew there would be multitudes of people and we would be pushing and shoving our way through the streets, amid the noise and smoke and smell of those noxious and obnoxious cars. But something magical happened. On the very first day he showed us around the botanical gardens with wondrous views across the town and beaches, and he held both our hands. As I was gazing at the succulents, the prickly ones, the curly ones, he was chattering on about the race as though my interest in it really mattered. He was the Tom I first knew, all childish and inspiring, all charm and innocence. The next day, the day of the main race, we negotiated the teeming crowds without any problem. He was determined you should have the best view of the race, and so he kept you on his shoulders most of the time. He bought us expensive ice-creams, took us to the aquarium, and played with you for hours on the beach. I remember – I know this sounds funny – falling in love with him again.'

I should note, although I'm racing ahead all of 80 years, that Lizette broke her hip in those very same gardens. It was a horrible injury which brought our retirement mini-journeys to an end.

Tom's story about the photograph was told to me for the last time that new year's eve when he came to visit while Julie was in Edinburgh. He saw the photo half hidden behind a pot on a windowsill in the lounge.

'That's a Ferrari, son. It came 8th – or was it 10th – in the 2003 Monaco Grand Prix. Do you know who drove it? Damn, neither do I. I forget.' He stopped to laugh. 'But how did I get the photo, that's the puzzle? You can't just wander around and sit on these cars – they cost millions.'

'No idea, Dad, how did you get the photo?'

'Oh I know you know, but it's worth the telling.'

'The re-retelling.' He snorted, and ignored me.

'After the race, it was heaving with people in every direction, all going back to their hotels and yachts. I didn't want it to be over, so we walked a kilometre or more – you were a great little walker, long strong legs even then – until we came to the track area with the grandstands and the pit areas. But of course we couldn't get in, there was a huge wire mesh gate and several two metre tall guards. Vehicles and pedestrians were entering and leaving constantly, and all were having their identity checked. Inside, one could see mechanics and drivers and advisers and owners and promoters milling around in the after-race milieu. I so wanted to be in there. I went up to the friendliest looking guard. I had to pull you hard because your mother was standing firm and holding onto your other hand. I had no idea what I was going to say.'

'Let me guess,' I said. He snorted and ignored me again.

' "Ferrari here," and I pointed at you, "is three years old and he's never seen the real thing." This was in my best Franglais. "We only want to have a quick look at the cars, five minutes that's all. We'll be back I promise. Look I could leave you my credit card, my bag…" There was a smirk of contempt on his face. And then, I'm not sure why, I said he could have my wife too. Julie looked shocked, as if it might not be a joke, but the guard smiled. Then he was diverted for a minute by a car leaving. As luck would have it, one of the passengers was old Limey Bimmerson from Exxon. I was embarrassed to be a punter and not on the inside of the show, but he leaned out the window, all friendly and smiles. "Hiya Tom, great race eh, Chet's down there somewhere in hospitality, this your wife? Hiya. Say hi to Harrison." Harrison was my manager at the time. And then the car whisked him away. The guard had witnessed the exchange, and came back over to us. He knelt down and looked you in the face. "What's your name son?" Good English. This would blow it, I thought. You said …'

Aren't parents the limit. At this point, Tom stopped and looked at me, so I could contribute to the pathetic story.

'Neil.'

'Neil. Yes, you little bugger – not so little now – you said "Neil", and I wanted to kick you across the other side of the road. Not that you could have known any better. Julie saw my face cringe, and bent down to gave you a hug. The guard simultaneously stood up to his full two metre height and laughed his head off. "I am so relieved," he said, "that your son is not called Ferrari; go on, but be back in ten." I bustled us through the gate before he could change his mind. Getting to the car itself was easier, we slipped under a rope, dodged round the back of a garage, and sweet-talked a mechanic. Even Julie was impressed.'

Here's another photo, more interesting in its way, for what it says – all too obviously – about my background. A group of mostly primary schoolchildren are standing/crouching together in several rows on a park lawn. All are wearing wellingtons and bright yellow pull-over bibs with black lettering saying 'Reading clean-up week'. Julie, a shy-looking 12 year old, and a lanky 14 year old Alan are the only two holding, what look like, walking sticks in front of them but which are surely litter guns. Between them, in the middle of the group and centre stage, is Eileen, in her prime. Eileen's dedication to clean parks led, possibly, to Julie's keen attention to green issues as a mother and teacher, and to Alan's career in environmental organisations. And the combined influence of all of them certainly affected the direction of my own career.

One more. It is a standard school photo. I am seven, though you could mistake me for eight or nine, given my height. I am wearing a dark blood-coloured school sweatshirt, and grey trousers. Across one side of my head is a wide white bandage, stretching from the middle of the forehead, skirting round the eyebrow, and down to the left ear. This was one week after the most frightening experience of my childhood (not counting Tom losing his temper with Julie or with me). I was cycling along a narrow dirt track near our house. When I came to a large builder's lorry which had stopped and was blocking the track,

I tried squeezing myself and my cycle between the side of the lorry and a hedge. I was halfway along when the lorry started to move. The rear wheel, which was huge, caught the back wheel of my bicycle and crunched it to the ground. I leaped for my life to the side, into a thorn bush, bashing my head on a thick branch stump, and tearing my clothes. Only after the cycle crunching did the driver spot something wrong in his wing mirror, although he should have checked before starting off. My wound did not ache that much, but it bled a lot, and looked severe. It is the feeling of shock afterwards I remember most, the fear of what might have happened. The driver shouted at me, as though it were my fault, but a foreman appeared. He proved to be a surprisingly gentle man, and walked me home carrying the cycle. Kudos came my way at school, and then, after Julie wrote a couple of letters to the construction company, a cheque arrived. Tom helped me buy a new bicycle – one with suspension.

***

I see I have avoided making a decision on when to finish the story about my conception. No longer. I have decided to do so later. These photos have put me in a different frame of mind, and I am thinking about my young life and schools, especially Witley Academic. My earliest memory, or the one I have fixed on as my earliest, is of a broken window, fear and Tom shouting. I do not believe I was ever hit hard, although Tom visited violence on me in other ways, chiefly by shouting and punishments which involved my muscles aching. Otherwise, I recall the feeling, not the face or personality as such, of a few playmates and teachers: Brittle Charlie who cried a lot; Quid who got his fingers stuck in bottles; Clarissa who came round to tea, because Julie liked her mother; KZ who knew how to find cricket balls at the recreation ground; and Mr Subramani, a teacher beloved by all (except my mother who may have been slightly jealous of his innate empathy with children, and my adoration of him).

Mr Subramani, who came from Birmingham (he called it Brimmingham for no particular reason), told us about the world. Some days he brought in a newspaper, showed us the headlines, and then explained how and why the news was important, but without talking down to us. This was the period when the conflict between the Christian and Arab worlds was only barely simmering, and when a general view prevailed that, so long as the United States and its allies spent billions on their war against terrorism, nothing as bad as 11 September could ever occur again. Years later, thinking back about Mr Subramani I came to believe he must have thought otherwise, he feared for humankind, and decided he would do what he could to educate for tolerance and understanding.

But, at the age of eight, when Tom found himself a new and better job, I was wrenched away from the school in St Albans to another one in Guildford, a commuter town south of London. There were good and bad things about the way that happened. We moved in the summer, so my 'forever' goodbyes at the end of the school year were lost among all the summer farewells. I would never see my best friends again, and I was inconsolable – until I saw several of them at the swimming pool two days later. There were lots of arguments in the week we moved, with all the packing and unpacking, but it was exciting to explore the new, bigger house and garden. There was an old rusty barbecue standing on the terrace out of view from any of the main windows. I acquired a box of matches, a potato, a frozen sausage and a chocolate bar. This makes me sick thinking of it even now. I used paper and a few fallen twigs to cook them. I didn't eat much of the black uncooked potato or raw sausage, but the melted chocolate dribbled down my clothes and gave me away. I blame this humbling experience on the fact that neither Julie nor Tom lavished enough attention on me in that manic few weeks. Worst of all, and hanging over me all summer, was the knowledge that I would be a marked boy at my new school, Boxgrove, since my own mother would be working there, as deputy head.

It was probably at this time – our move marks the most likely dividing point – that Julie withdrew from her intensive involvement in teaching me at home. I cannot testify as to what impact she had had on my education so far for I was too young. I do recall long sessions of reading, of writing, of talking about topics, and not being able to watch TV as much as my playground buds (did we call them buds then, I can't remember). There is laughter and fun in my memory of these times, but emotional colours of delight at achievement applauded and of disappointment at failures noticed are stronger. Julie could be stern, but I was always seeking the laughter and the smiles, and the only way to do this was with neat writing, correct answers, good work. (As an annex to this chapter, I am including extracts from Julie's emails to her brother. I am unable to provide much intelligence on my early life, or on Julie's role in my upbringing, so these extracts seem an essential addition to my Reflections.)

At Boxgrove, there was no Mr Subramani. I had 'grown-up' conversations with my mother about our relationship at school. She never learned to ignore me entirely, but she did her best. There was bullying of sorts. Without deliber- ately setting out to become a schoolboy guardian angel, I shamelessly used both my size and the threat of my connections to neutralise the bullies significantly. I became respected over time for never once actually enlisting my mother or any other teacher to defend myself or others. There were lessons and clubs. I competed in the pool with Josh, who invariably swam faster than me, with Little Manfred for top place in English, and with Veronica for bottom place in

Music. I played chess as if it were as simple as draughts with Big Manfred. A school trip to Snowdonia was all midnight feasts, rain, and queuing up to partner Josh on his netgames console. It cost over 500 euros, or so he said.

Tom was away as often as not, and when not, there were rows. Julie would end up crying and lock herself in the bathroom. I would rush up to Tom and punch his arm. He would push me away, onto the floor or against the wall. There would be a snort, a rude comment, and then he would bang the front door. Julie would re-emerge, with make-up on, and a smile. When I asked why Tom was so angry, she would never tell me. As I grew older she would generalise about how adults have complicated personal and relationship problems that can be difficult to resolve.

'But if you love each other and try hard enough, then you can solve them,' I would say naively.

'Yes, my little wise man, yes. I hope so,' my mother would reply. What I noticed, in retrospect, about my mother was that somehow she was getting bigger, stronger. Perhaps this was to do with a confidence in her deputy head position, or, perhaps, after marrying someone older, she was finally finding her own character, her own way.

'Yes, my little wise man.' A phrase I consciously repeated on occasions to my own children, but I'm sure never to the same effect as Julie with me.

At weekends, Tom had a knack of turning me against his interests. Cards. He knew so many different card games – from cribbage to canasta, from poker to piquet – and he made me play them all long before I was even able to hold a handful of cards in order. Mostly, he took control of both hands, and got very excited in explaining how they should be deployed. But, whenever he expected me to show skill or knowledge, I was a dumbo. I gave up trying very early on, he was too demanding. He had a particularly nasty way of calling me 'stupid' or 'idiot' that made me squirm. (Lizette, the last love of my life, whose final absence now gives me time to spend writing these Reflections, was a wizard at Melbourne Bridge. I tried to learn, I did try, for her. I enjoyed the complications of stylised bidding and back-bidding negotiations but I failed to rise above novice level, or escape feelings of tedium.) And, thankfully, Tom ensured I would never be very keen on cars or motorbikes or speed. He filled up winter weekends with non-stop sport on the screen (Julie never agreed to me having a television in my bedroom), and dragged me to motor races or rallies whenever the weather was clement. By the time he left, when I was 12, I had developed both defensive ('too much homework', 'a friend's party') and offensive ('I don't want to go – I hate motor racing') means of avoiding these day trips.

I say all this, yet surprisingly I loved him greatly and missed him whenever he went away. He brought me presents, that was one of his secrets. He was always telling me anecdotes about people he had brushed shoulders with in the oil industry, or places he had been, or some new theory he had read in magazines about space and space exploration. I don't believe I was ever interested in what he had to say, I simply wanted him there, talking to me. But the best times with him were the trips to the cinema. He was the movie industry's ideal punter: uncritical, star-struck, and unable to relax in his seat without a giant pack of rainbow popcorn.

I can define three stages in my relationship with Tom through our movie-going habits. While he and Julie were together, and I was but a child, he took me to the cinema once a month, from the age of about five, in St Albans, then in Guildford. After every film, he would ask me to compare it with the last one or two we had seen, and then give it a rating. As I grew older, I asked him for his rating too. There was one film, *Trumpet Boy*, to which we both awarded top marks. It made such an impression that it both haunted and enchanted me for years to come. I have never forgotten the plot and some of the visuals. The flick itself aged badly and only achieved cult, as opposed to classic, status. The director, a Mexican, Pedro Antonio de Malancas, known as Pam, having been feted in Mexico, was seduced by money to go to Hollywood, where he made *Trumpet Boy*. He was dubbed as a new Stephen Spielberg (the director of *ET*). I met Pam once – but I must attempt to maintain a semblance of control and chronology over the order in which I set down my memories.

I was ten when we went to the Odeon in Guildford to see ... I forget what. By mistake, or Tom's artifice, we settled in the wrong auditorium. No-one had checked our tickets on the way in, and no-one claimed our seats. When the film started and Tom pointed out that it was classified a 15 (or was it 14 by then?) it could have been a documentary and I would not have cared. *Trumpet Boy*, a computer designed and animated flick from beginning to end, was set in the near future on an island country, Reefland, in the Caribbean, with extensive poverty and ill-health, and rampant crime. The plot revolved around a group of teenagers who begged, borrowed and stole to set up computer and internet facilities for other teenagers. As the movement flourished across the country, so the confidence and ambitions of the teenagers grew. Along the path towards their, eventually successful, overthrow of the corrupt govern-ment, they faced – as one would expect – many physical, moral and emotional dilemmas. At the time, the computer generation of teenage characters was praised as impressively realistic, and the media was full of debate about whether actors were needed any longer. Within a few years, though, the films from that era were already looking wooden and crude. For me, Manuel, the 15 year old pickpocket and trumpet player, with long purple hair and a large brown mole on his cheek, who reforms, leads the revolution, and becomes president for a few weeks, was and is as real as any actor-performed film character I have ever seen.

Stage two – this sounds like a committee report – lasted until the Bangkok trip. After Tom left, and while I was living at home before going to uni, we used to meet once a fortnight, unless he was away, on Friday or Saturday and go to the cinema. I would sleep over at his pad in Bramley, and then return to Julie later in the day. This was the phase in which my own tastes matured, and I was able to persuade Tom to come with me to see films which were more serious or even subtitled. Stage three is all the rest of the time. As an adult, I never saw very much of Tom, but this mutual enjoyment of the cinema kept our relationship one notch above dutiful. It was not uncommon for me to receive an email inviting me to see such-and-such a film that same evening or the next, and for me to refuse because of work or family commitments. On occasions, if I saw an opportunity a few days hence, I would email him about a specific film, and we would meet, eat some popcorn, watch the film, and drink a beer after. He told me, not long before he died, that he wanted Vincent (Mush) Mallow to play him in a film of his life.

***

From Boxgrove in Guildford I moved to the private school, Witley Academic (situated approximately 12 kilometres from Guildford and six from Godalming) and not before time: by the age of 11 I had outgrown primary school in more ways than one. Tom was earning a good salary, so he could afford the fees, and Julie acknowledged that, despite endless rounds of educational reform, there were still some private schools in a class of their own. Witley Academic, one of the original Academic schools (there were to be 100 before the company was broken up under the Fuller-led coalition in the early 2040s), was not in the premier division, but it was in the second, and more importantly, it was nearby and I could get there on the train. Most of my buds moved on to schools in Guildford, and I wanted to go to one of those too; but I didn't, and, if I had, my life would have been very different.

Second only to nearby Charterhouse School, which we passed often and which was definitely a premier division school, Witley Academic was the largest school I had ever seen, even though it had been downsized from its 20th century incarnation as King Edwards when hundreds of boys and a few girls had boarded in addition to a large daily intake. Some of the buildings had been sold off to computer and service businesses, and some of the land had been transformed into a housing estate. Nevertheless, in my day it boasted two playing fields, its own full-size chapel, a large library, a swimming pool, a roomy gymnasium, language labs, well-appointed science and engineering laboratories, and domestic science kitchens. Every classroom was fitted out with computer terminals, and the pupils had their own lounge rooms, with special areas for different age groups.

Flip. I cannot think of Witley Academic without Flip coming immediately into view. Flip, aka Philip Liphook, was an inspiring history teacher, albeit one with a strong prejudice towards the ideal of European integration, who taught me for seven years. He wore a ragged beard, a black teacher's gown, and suede shoes with stains. Yet, despite his uninspiring appearance he managed to make a positive impression from the outset.

'I have one rule, and one only. Can you divine what it might be?' Sniggers and silence and more sniggers. 'Is it: no talking when I'm talking? No. Is it: never be late with homework? No. Is it: no drinking in class? No.' More sniggers. 'Well come on then.' I can hear him now, his voice booming through the room. 'Well someone ask what it is then. Yes, you, what's your name?'

'Horace ...'

'Speak up, you're not here to learn to be a mouse.' We heard this more than once or fifty times.

'Horace Merriweather.'

'Yes, Mr Merriweather.'

'What is your one rule, sir?'

'Thank you for asking, Mr Merriweather. Your name, by the way, opens up boundless possibilities. My rule is that I tell at least one joke every lesson.' More sniggers, a little wary this time.

'Now then, help yourselves to the exercise and text books in the corner. We must press on. The Romans won't wait for us, will they?'

Immediately after that lesson, I joined a loose collection of dazed pupils who were divided as to whether our teacher was a crank, an idiot, a fake, or all three. Horace was there at the centre of the argument full of very firmly-stated but wavering opinions. I kept my own counsel for a while and then sneaked off to find out the truth from one of the older pupils. I returned to the group bursting with the news that Liphook's nickname was Flip and that it was true he never failed to make a joke in every lesson. But my class-mates had moved on to telling jokes of their own, and no-one was interested in my news. Flip's rule or promise, whichever way you look at it, proved less difficult to adhere to than we had imagined. He did tell a lot of bona fide jokes. He would stop mid-sentence to say 'that reminds me of a joke', and then he'd tell it, and we would roar with laughter. Frequently, the joke would be linked in some way to the subject matter which led us to suspect it was all part of the prepared lesson, but equally frequently the joke would be related to the morning's news, or a question from one of us. There is no doubt he had a comic gift for timing. When the joke was over, he would give us 15 seconds to recompose ourselves before expecting perfect attention. And, usually, he got it. Even without the set jokes, Flip could never get through a lesson without making us laugh. His style was so full of quips, gentle facetiousness, sarcasm, mimicry and puns that it was a wonder we ever learned much, but we did. We loved him, and wanted to excel.

Forty years later, at the gala show and presentation to celebrate the school's 500th birthday in 2053, Flip was nearly as old as I am now, but he could have been 60 not 90. His beard and hair may have turned white, but who could tell the age of the man underneath. He was among a long line of staff and ex-staff receiving special medals from ex-pupil Terrance Spoon for their service to the school. I was in the main hall due to my friendship with Horace Merriweather who served, albeit briefly, in Spoon's inept mid-40s right-wing government (which followed on from the Fuller administration), and who had done much to aggrandise the anniversary programme. He saw it as a way to revive the flagging fortunes of the school. This event and others in the week-long celebrations were broadcast on Euronet Solar (which is how I come to have it stored on Neil, and am watching it now).

When Flip arrives on the stage, the audience in the Great Hall erupts with applause and then cheers. It is as though we have all stored up so much appreciation and thanks for the man and have not been given a chance to express it before now. The applause continues as we watch Spoon place a commemorative ribbon and medallion over Flip's head. The two of them exchange a few words. After several attempts, Spoon manages to quell the uproar by raising his open-palmed hands and moving them lightly backwards and forwards.

'That's an applause to die for,' Spoon says. A ripple of laughter. 'Should we give Mr Liphook, or Flip …' loud cheers '… the floor?' Louder cheers, which die down as Flip moves a step forward indicating his intention to speak.

'Not too many mice here today then.' Uproar. 'Thank you Mr Spoon, Headmaster, and thank you all. I take pleasure in seeing so many here today, I genuinely thought you would never survive in the real world – mollycoddled as you were in these buildings.' Laughter. 'Which reminds me of a joke.' A spurt of laughter, then a respectful hushed silence, and more silence. 'No it doesn't.' Said in a different way or with a lack of confidence, or without the wrinkled grin just visible under the white wiry hairs, this could be a bathetic statement. But it isn't. The camera pans around from Flip's face to the audience, and I can see we are all on our feet cheering and cheering again, as if it is the funniest joke we have ever heard. And, in its way it was.

'I was going to tell you the one about the history teacher who so loved his job and his pupils that at the age of 89 he couldn't resist coming back for one more fix of the old school. But I don't need to. You know that one and all the rest, and thank you so much. Until the next time.' Everyone is on their feet clapping. One camera rotates round again (there are many familiar faces) and this time I can see myself in the shot. Horace, who is seated a row in front, is leaning back, whispering to me.

'A1 star,' he is saying. 'No, A1 Star <u>plus</u> for Flip, there is nothing I enjoy more than seeing Terrance upstaged. He so, so hates it.'

That's Arturo next to me, he was already in his 30s, surprised to be there, and amused by the whole show. Why didn't Diana and Guido come? I forget. Diana and I must have already started to draw apart by then. 2053. Yes, that was the beginning of the end for us as a couple. I'll check the dates later.

Needless to say, Flip must have had a great and beneficial influence over my educational achievements since I excelled at history through the 16 exams and achieved a distinction in the 18 exams. He also ran a debating club and, for sixth-formers, the Brideswell Society (although Horace and I and several others were allowed privileged access to this before we reached the sixth form). The debating club, volleyball, the pool, homework in the library were among the activities that, most days, kept me at school long after lessons were finished.

It was through the debating club in the second year that Horace and I became firm friends. For several sessions in a row, all we did was listen to older pupils pontificate on subjects both interesting and deadly dull. It was only Flip's energy and encouragement that kept us coming. Then, about halfway through the year, he invited Horace and me to propose the motion 'Life will be better tomorrow' against two girls, one of whom was Gemma (who matured into a beauty and paired up with Alfred for a while). We set to our task with youthful enthusiasm, preparing and rehearsing our speeches as though our lives depended on it. I suggested we try and anticipate what the girls might say, so we would be better prepared for the concluding speeches, but Horace wanted to wing it. A good crowd turned up, our classmates and a fair sprinkling of seniors who came to mock. Horace, hands on hips to give himself maturity and more presence (hence the nickname Hip, like mine consciously similar to Flip), was fluent, witty and concise. By contrast, I was given to protective stooping, and verbose complicated arguments. We won by a close vote. On dissecting our performance afterwards, we came to the joint conclusion that it was Horace's inspired, but not entirely relevant, reference to hope that gave us victory: 'And what happened to hope. We are but teenagers, how can we not believe life will be better tomorrow?' We may have won that debate but we were wrong – so far as I can judge from today's standpoint. Yet, if Horace were here now and we were asked again whether we wanted to support or oppose the motion, I feel sure we would both, without hesitation, opt for the same stance again.

For the next 18 months or so Hip and Kip were often to be found together in the library researching on the net, or deep in discussion about some topic or other. Although we rarely lost a debate, sometimes it was too close for Horace's comfort. Criticism of my speaking style began to creep into our conversations, and this led me to object to his lack of depth and over-reliance on rhetoric. Witley Academic, as represented by Flip, inflated us without our knowing. But, whereas Horace's confidence was all brimming on the surface, mine was not. In the middle of the third year, I told Horace I no longer wanted to continue public speaking, but that if he could find a new partner who was happy to work in a team of three, I would do research and put forward ideas. There was no shortage of volunteers to pair up with Horace, but, to his credit (because I'm about to describe a debit and our falling out), he discussed with me who he should choose. Initially, Jeff Zimmerman was sceptical about the unusual arrangement we proposed but, when he saw the strength of our friendship and our commitment, he soon fell in with the plan. In practice, the system operated well: Jeff and I did the research, all three of us collaborated on the final preparation, and Jeff and Horace delivered the goods.

Now I must backtrack a year and reflect on a difficult subject. It was a Thursday. I had been messing around in the pool. I had changed, and was in a hurry to leave and catch my train. But, as I came out of the boys' changing rooms, I dropped some coins, one of which rolled across the corridor to the dead end wall next to the door to the girls' changing rooms. Two senior girls were chatting in the doorway, propping the door open. From my crouched position on the ground, I could see through into the dressing room. Several girls were half dressed or drying themselves with a towel, but one girl was entirely naked, standing upright and facing my way. I could see all of her except her head. This was the first fully naked girl – plump breasts and fair curly pubic hair – I had ever seen in the flesh. I froze. I stared. She walked forward a step, a beautiful step nearer, and as she did so she called to the other girls to close the door. One of them then turned to re-enter the changing room, which let the door swing free, and the other moved to exit. Momentarily, I was able to see the face of the naked girl, Melissa. In the same moment, before the door closed, she saw me. She did not blanch, or turn, or try to cover herself, she grinned, and the door shut. The girl remaining in the corridor then saw me scrabbling around on the floor for my coin and told me I should get a pair of binnocks.

That was the start. I have tried to analyse over the years whether my sexual preferences would have been any different if that episode had never occurred or if Melissa had shrieked and turned instead of smiling. Twice in the course of my life I have mentioned it to analysts of one description or another without the revelation leading to any firm understanding as to its relevance. During the following months, I overcame mighty feelings of guilt and embarrassment in attempting to achieve a repeat of the experience. The problem was invariably the same: the entrance to the girls' changing room was at the end of a corridor and there was no legitimate reason for a male to be there. On countless occasions, when the corridor was empty, I positioned myself strategically in a crouch outside the door, with a loose coin on the floor behind me. I moved as soon as anyone exited either changing room, or saw me along the corridor. Yet, even when luck was with me, and the first person to emerge came from the girls' changing room, I never had both a good line of sight and something to see. It was only when one of the girls in my own form, who'd never herself seen me anywhere near the changing rooms, called me a 'pervert' one day apropos of nothing in particular, that I woke up to the extent of my foolishness. I never entirely stopped hoping for another vision, but I scaled back my furtive spying efforts. Instead, I channelled my energy into bypassing the school filters on the internet computers which were designed to protect us from pornography and other undesirable material. I focused on the art-related netsites, particularly those linked to photographic galleries or magazines, which I found the most rewarding.

As for Melissa, I loved her, and lusted for her, but from a distance. She knew, and she knew I knew she knew. In the evenings, I was physically incapable of leaving the swimming pool, if she were there. I would watch her secretly, waiting for her to walk along the side. If we were to pass in the canteen or a corridor, she would straighten her back, push out her chest, lift her chin, and flick that long fair hair back to fix my attention, and only then would she look at me with such pride and power that I always lowered my eyes. I imagined a smile of satisfaction on her lovely face as she walked away. But this was not so. I know for sure, because, astonishingly, Melissa became my first lover, and she told me otherwise.

I explain all this because it needs explaining but also to demonstrate how clear I was in my own mind from the age of 14 or so that I liked girl's bodies and, by extension, girls. Horace, by contrast, developed a taste for lads. This appeared to happen to him without me knowing or suspecting. There was one day in the week, in the autumn term of our fourth year, when our last lesson was physical education. This meant that when the lesson was over there was no hurry to change. For some reason, Horace (who detested all sports except golf, and was never to be found in the gym or changing room outside set classes) and I chatted for longer than usual – no doubt about a forthcoming debate – before dressing. By the time we entered the shower room, it was empty apart from us. When Horace came so close he was rubbing shoulders, I moved away. When I looked round, I saw him holding his penis in one hand. It was erect. Maybe there were activities I had missed out on, but so far in my young life, I had not shared my erections with anyone, nor had I seen anyone else's.

'Give us a rub, Kip.'

'Get off.' Yet Horace was my best friend, and it wasn't easy to say no to him.

'Come on touch it, you'll like it.' I moved further away again, into the corner of the showers, and he followed. He stretched out one hand wanting to grab my penis. I pushed him way.

'No, I don't want to.' This was Horace as I had never seen him before. He pressed himself forwards, pinning me against the tiled wall.

'Come on Kip, what's the matter. You afraid.' He was trying to rub himself on my thigh. It may have been partly in jest, but I did not see the joke. I pushed him off and forced my way past him. I stopped before leaving the showers, and turned to say something, but he was too busy – with himself.

Horace prostrated himself before me, metaphorically that is, for days after, but I wouldn't listen to his protestations or to those of Jeff and one or two others who interceded on his behalf (without, I should add, knowing why). Our row, or rather my unilateral decision to end the friendship, was the talk of the middle school for several weeks. It took me months to recover. Horace was able to resume where we had left off as if nothing had happened. For my part, I was never able to fully trust him again. Looking back, I can see that it was only because I developed a respectful wariness of him that I was able to remain a close friend for so long.

***

Logically, I should move on now and talk about another important Witley bud, Alfred, and volleyball, but that's a happy story I want to employ as a bookend to this early chapter of my life. For the moment, I need to take the train six stops from Witley to Guildford, London Road station, and walk seven minutes to 121 Larch Rise. I usually caught a train around 6pm. Julie would know my schedule, and I would usually message her if I changed my plans. Occasionally, but not often, Tom would be at home when I arrived. Julie prepared supper for around 7pm, allowing Tom (if he was there) and I to catch Eastenders while Julie cleared up in the kitchen. This sounds unfair, but Julie preferred to keep the kitchen neat and tidy, especially during the week when we were all busy. She complained if we interfered. I did make her a cup of tea most nights, when she settled down to mark homework or listen to the radio. I'm not sure what Tom did around the house. He brought in more money than Julie, and he undertook handyman jobs when pestered. This was the general ordinary pattern for a year or so after I started at Witley Academic.

Shouting was not an uncommon occurrence in our house, as I've said, but things got worse in 2012 and came to a head in the summer of 2013. Tom had a short fuse. Julie had a way of moaning about petty things which were not important, and, as I grew close to adolescence, I developed a defensive habit of remaining silent, mute, which provoked and challenged both of them from time to time. The worst arguments by far, though, were those between Julie and Tom which ended with Julie weeping and locking herself in the bathroom, and Tom storming out of the house. Julie would tell me that he was out getting drunk. When these arguments occurred late at night, I would sense them first in a dream, with loud voices drifting through from far away and scaring me. Then I would linger for an unknown length of time, in the state between sleep and waking, desperately attempting to resist consciousness. As I describe this now, I realise the sensation is not dissimilar to that I used to have, as an aging man, of not wanting to recognise the signal of my bladder and the need to make the effort to rise and go to the toilet. (Now, in bed, I am permanently plumbed, without the fear of psychological or practical inconveniences, and so, when I wake in the night it is for other reasons.) As the volume of their voices – his crunchy, over-reliant on swear words, hers crisp, exasperated – ratcheted up, so I would bury my head under the pillow and press its sides into my ears. If a serious quarrel erupted during the day on a Saturday, I would travel into school; and, if on a Sunday, I would find a friend to visit. If I was lucky, Alan would be available.

I should mention my uncle Alan – Mr Abominable Snowman – at this point. Our moving to Guildford had coincided more or less with his temporary return to WWF's recently-expanded Godalming offices. He was always a busy man, never without a full diary, but he clearly had a soft spot for his sister and me, and so we saw him once every few weeks. Mostly, I enjoyed our walks on the North Downs, or along the Wey, or to the Waverley Abbey ruins or through some arboretum, with a visit to a teashop afterwards. Now and then all of us (including Tom) would take Sunday lunch in a pub. These meetings would often end in Tom and Alan arguing (I mean Tom arguing and Alan being calm and patient as ever), and me getting very bored. When Tom was away, Alan would come round and eat supper with us. More often than not, he would have a story to tell, about nuclear pollution in the Kola Peninsula, or developing the wetlands in Moldova, or a parrot in Borneo that had been saved from extinction, or the crooked empire of the oilserfs. There was a pattern to these evenings. While Julie cooked and prepared food Alan and I would talk, and then, through supper, the conversation would include Julie and start to lose me, so that as soon as I had finished my meal I would slip off to watch television. Then Alan would read to me for a few minutes before lights out. Later, once I was established at Witley Academic, it was not unusual for him to turn up at the school, and give me a lift home, or take me to his flat in Farnham, 20 kilometres away, for tea and cake and a chat. He also drew me into a team of volunteers which helped carry out environmental works on the marshy commons nearby. This was mostly cutting tree saplings, building and repairing board walks, and draining ditches. It was tiring work, to which I was not especially suited, but rewarding.

At the time, I did not know the underlying cause of the arguments between my parents, nor did I brood on them. In their own way, both Julie and Tom had tried to comfort me so many times when I was younger, that I no longer believed them. But I was not so numbed that I didn't cry, secretly, often. I would long for Tom to go away on a business trip, so the arguments would stop, and then I would long for him to come back, because I missed him. Unfortunately, I have no record of our emails from that time. It is my impression that we wrote a lot, and that this was fun, something I wanted to do. I rehashed Flip's shorter jokes and amusingly described the worst excesses of other teachers, and Tom talked of 'big deals' and 'big money' and 'very important people'. I would boast about his whereabouts to my friends ('my Dad's in China') and show them composite tourist pics (of him standing in Tiananmen Square, or climbing the Great Wall). Life was undoubtedly better when Tom was away: not only did I love him more then, but my mother and I got on so much better.

I do not wish to dwell too long on the summer of 2013. It was the time of the major Turkish riots in Germany and the shocking murder of the singer Vi Hoop by religious extremists in Utah. Tom's hopes of moving to Singapore or somewhere in the Far East was one open sore. Julie's wish to have a second child, and Tom's refusal to consider it, though, was the deep and underlying problem that had been festering between them for years. Both Julie and Tom confirmed this to me at different times and in different ways. I am sure Julie would have muddled through until I had gone to college but for Tom's increasingly brazen adultery. I suspect that Julie chose to ignore the signs, so long as they were not obvious. But that summer the evidence became far too strong, too pungent. Tom had picked up a venereal disease, which, under doctor's orders, he needed to tell Julie about. Then, a few days later, there was a nasty letter, a rant, addressed to Julie from Tom's current mistress in London. She had also been informed about Tom's problem, but naively, stupidly, she imagined Tom had caught the disease from his wife. However generously Julie assessed the situation – and I am using Tom's analysis here, the one he gave me on the Bangkok trip – she had no choice but to leave him.

That was a horrible, horrible day, the day the letter arrived, Wednesday 15 August. There was intermittent shouting and screaming, mostly by Julie. She wouldn't allow me to go out (presumably because she was already expecting to leave) and so I was forced to wear my earphones much of the time. Tom, in real distress, asked me twice to intercede on his behalf, which provoked an almost physical assault on him by Julie, for once completely aloof to what I might think of her. This in turn enraged Tom who began bellowing for his right to talk to his son. I went out to the garden, where I was embarrassed to find I, and the neighbours, could hear the shouting. Then it stopped, suddenly. An hour later, Julie and I were driving down the motorway to Parsonville. I think she hoped for sympathy from her mother, but she didn't get it. They argued non-stop too, only not in raised voices. One day later we were heading back to Farnham, to camp out at Alan's flat. Alan himself came and went for a few weeks, and then moved to Switzerland. I was more sad about my uncle's going away than about my parent's separation. We went back to Larch Rise of course. Before long, though, the property was sold. Julie and I moved to Godalming, and Tom rented a property in Bramley, five kilometres east of Godalming. (Some years later he bought himself a modern semi-detached monstrosity much closer to London, in Epsom.)

***

That summer was memorable for me in another far more positive way. In late July, before my mother's flight from Larch Rise, some of us from the Witley Academic volleyball club were recruited for ball collection and other duties at the European volleyball championships being held for the first time in the Guildford International Sports Complex. The two main auditoriums had been refurbished to provide championship grade courts (and changing rooms), comfortable seating and top-notch media facilities. There were three matches a day on each court for the mini-league phase during the first week. I fetched balls for two matches most days, and watched the third one. This was thrilling, not only because of the volleyball, which was of a standard I had never imagined (I was not yet so keen as to watch the sport on television), but because of the buzz of activity, the teams, the coaches, the support staff, the officials, and, most exciting of all, the media people.

I personally was interviewed by journalists from two broadcast companies, one from Croatia and one from Italy, about what it felt like to be a ball-boy at one of the most exciting matches of the year. It was a quarter-final between Italy and Croatia, and one of those titanic struggles that live in everyone's memory for years. At the time, I was standing too far back and was too focused on my job, watching and waiting for the ball, to follow the game and the drama closely, but so much was talked about the match, and written, that I soon absorbed the details: Italy lost five points because of a scoring error (almost unheard of at international level); one of the Croatians sustained a serious ankle injury; and there was a very rare disqualification (the referee finally lost patience with the Croatian captain who, having sought clarification after clarification of the umpiring decisions, would not accept the loss of a point that had given the Italians the fourth set and thus kept them in the game). There was also some of the most exciting volleyball you could imagine. The camrecording of that game was used for many years by coaches all over the world. How do I know? Because I was in it, and whenever in my adult life I met someone who had played volleyball at a high level, I would bring the talk round to Croatia-Italy 2013, and more often than not they would say their coach had shown it to their team. The recording has another place in my story, but I must come back to it at the right time.

How is it possible that after my whole life long, I can still sense a frisson of the excitement of being involved in that week. There were two rest days when I should have stayed at home with my mother but she was sulky and depressed because of the situation with Tom, so I lied to her about being committed to certain tasks. Instead, I spent the time watching the practice sessions, requesting autographs and then asking as many questions as players or officials or journalists would answer. I even knocked a ball around with one or two of the more easy-going international players. My one disappointment was not being selected to help with the final when Italy beat Spain, nor being allowed to watch in the auditorium, although I did see it on the live relay in the second auditorium. I did ball duties for one of the semi-finals (I don't recall who played, and I can't be bothered to search for the information). England, of course, disappointed. It was only 20 years later in Estonia, under the inspired and committed American coach John Buffer, that England finally made it to a European final. They didn't win then either, but it was a high for English volleyball.

All six of us (seven if you include our teacher/instructor) from Witley Academic that had been involved in the championship were deeply inspired to do better. Club nights became more disciplined, we started to spend time watching coaching films, and our instructor signed us up to play a number of friendly matches against other schools and groups. A year went by, we all got taller and slightly better; and then I recruited Alfred.

Alfred Ajose. He was a great man and a good friend. He died in Zanzibar during the Grey Years. I had an email from him the day before the accident, but I don't want to think about that one message now. I am remembering him as a young man of 13 at Witley Academic, one year younger than me, but eight centimetres taller. I had seen him in the playground, usually at the centre of a small band of other coloured pupils, and I'd heard he was the son of a Nigerian diplomat. He attracted serious attention, though, when he pinned a remarkable poster on the canteen noticeboard. It accused one of the teachers of unacceptable behaviour and of bad teaching, and it was signed. Alfred was immediately suspended; but, extraordinarily, he was reinstated without further punishment within a few days, and the teacher in question was dismissed. Later, I discovered that it had been the teacher's overt racism that had provoked Alfred into such risky action. Our headmaster must have been a wise man, for, having initially ignored protestations made by Alfred in private, he finally realised the truth of the matter; and decided that Alfred's actions had been more brave than subversive. Another pupil tried a similar approach a year or so later, and was severely punished.

It was a direct result of Alfred's notoriety that I found myself talking to him in the lunch queue. Because of his height, I suggested he join the volleyball club. To begin with, he proved awkward and gangly, as if unsure how to control his long limbs; and it took him nearly three months of training to gain a place in the team. I like to think that he persevered, despite being talented at many things and being much in demand, partly because he enjoyed training with me, but more importantly because I promised him he would be good. That I proved right about this was to leave him with an exaggerated impression of my intuition and foresight.

We both reached our full heights early. He achieved 190 centimetres, a useful size for a hitter, by the time he was 15, and I topped 180 centimetres, reasonable enough for a setter, by 16. For two years in a row, we won the national schools championship. My setting was certainly recognised as contributing to that success, yet it was Alfred's consistently accurate and uncanny hitting that took our team to the top. It was not only his practical skills that helped us to win, but also his captaincy. He knew instinctively when and how to be angry or sympathetic. He knew who would play worse if moaned at, but better if encouraged; and he knew who would raise his game if the fate of the team was suddenly thrust on his shoulders. Whereas our excellent coach taught and trained us, worked out our moves, planned our strategies, chivvied us along between sets and in time-outs, when in the thick of play on court, it was Alfred who gelled us.

And, as for the slapping of hands my father had referred to, that was how we expressed our joy at a good move, the combination of a good retrieve, a good pass and a good hit. Even as middle-aged men, departing from important meetings, Alfred, by then a more solemn person, and I would slap hands, perhaps in recognition of a result achieved, or more likely so as to revisit the intense pleasures of playing and of friendship in those days of youth.

EXTRACTS FROM CORRESPONDENCE

Julie Fenn to Alan Hapgood

October 2001

I must thank you for this computer. It has taken a while to get used to the new operating system, and the up-to-date software, but it's marvellous. Tom wanted to fiddle with it, but I told him sternly no – it's mine. He seems to have accepted that.

Will we never be rid of war. Everyone is waiting for the invasion of Afghanistan. I can't bear to listen to the news. I'd rather not write about it.

Neil has grown up so much in the last few weeks. He has such a range of facial expressions, and he can now use two and three word combinations. One of his favourite words is juice, he says it with such precision, it makes me laugh with joy.

Sometimes we sit together and say the alphabet. This has become a special game between us. He sits on my lap facing me. We look each other in the eyes. I say 'let's do the alphabet' and a smiling glint comes across his face. 'A', I say, and there is a long pause; he looks slyly at me, testing, watching, waiting; I say nothing and finally he says very softly 'A'. Then on we go through the letters of the alphabet, he can say most of them very well. If I say it loudly, he does too; if I whisper the letter, he whispers it too. When we get to the end, to 'Z', and we always do, for I never let him not finish, I give him a big kiss and we're both happy.

I was trying to think how I might possibly want him different, but he is perfect, adorable. Do all parents think this about their children? I can't believe so.

Alan, I don't like you being overseas in these turbulent times. When will we see you next?

August 2002

Tom and Neil and I have been in the Peak District for a week. I organised to stay at a B&B in Matlock Bath. The house was all pine, spick and span: pine furniture, pine doors, pine toilet-roll holder. The landlady gave us a front sunny room. Tom complained, accustomed as he is to five star international hotels. Breakfast on day one was a mite traumatic: I worried that Neil would spill egg down his front and on the cushion which the landlady had provided; I was concerned at the great fork he wielded in his left hand; and I worried about the volume of breakfast he stuffed away. But what a treat for him – chocoflakes, orange juice, egg, sausage and bacon, toast – all for breakfast. It's so long since you've been home, I bet you've forgotten the glories of an English breakfast.

On one walk we passed some lavender beds and I picked off a bit so we could all smell. Neil said, 'I like rosemary too; but I don't like black pepper'. When we saw a very old crippled man sitting on a bench by the river, Neil pointed to him and asked, in a very loud voice, 'Is he dead?'.

I have finally taught to him to shower, so that now he no longer cries when the water flows over his face. He grins and bears it. He does cry when soap goes in his eyes but I can easily divert him by asking him to shower my hand, or by pointing to his funny feet. Yesterday, he took Karshula (the name he has given to the panda you gave him) into the shower, which is a good sign.

May 2003

I haven't heard from you in a while, are you well? Is Monique in with a chance!

Neil has come along a treat. He is a beautiful child, with a charming spirit and an abundance of fun and joy in him. I think he is clever, but he has a general intelligence not any specific ability. He certainly displays a good memory and is already behaving in a conscious and calculating manner, mostly to the good. I must admit to being unbelievably in love: nothing has changed, tears come when I watch him sleeping.

Do you remember me telling you about the Peak District holiday? I have to pay for that now: Tom is insisting we all go to Monte Carlo for the Grand Prix. Why do I feel a headache coming on!

June 2003

All morning Neil was pretending to be a frog, and making strange frog-like noises. After lunch, he became a snake and is now crawling from place to place making sss sounds wherever he goes. Comfort toys have become important for him, and he invariably goes to bed with one of the pandas you've given him. But Karshula remains his favourite.

Yesterday, though, we had a difficult time. I became upset and angry because he wouldn't read something I knew he could. He tried to pretend he didn't know the words, and when I insisted he did, he started crying. Instead of comforting him, which I usually do when he cries, I shouted at him. And then, when I asked him to re-read some pages we had already covered, he suddenly couldn't read those either. And I got angrier. There is no doubt my behaviour was counter-productive. I was doing precisely the opposite of what I was setting out to do. Why am I telling you this?

Against all my expectations, we had a lovely time in Monte Carlo. How the rich do live!

I had a long talk on the phone with Mum. She's finally got a date for her hip replacement – October. It would be nice if you could manage a visit. She's become rather grumpy of late.

July 2003

I have stopped the reading lessons with Neil due to the difficulties I told you about before. They carried on, and his reading appeared to get worse. I have to make a real effort to remind myself he is not doing it on purpose in the way an adult does something deliberately. I must make it fun for him, or else there is no point. Meanwhile, he is proving to have an excellent aptitude for numbers so we do quite a lot of arithmetic and geometry. Before lights out last night, I showed him a photo of his nursery group. He names all the children and teachers for me. Then I ask him which of the children is the roughest, he says Jack; which of the children cries the most, Emile; which of the children laughs the most, Truman; and which of the children is the cleverest, 'me'. He chuckles. I read him a Noddy story. Minutes after turning the light out he is fast asleep.

August 2003

You wouldn't approve. I don't think I do. We went to the zoo last weekend. It was Tom's idea. Neil had a splendid time running from cage to cage and looking at giraffes, elephants, owls, flamingos, penguins and gorillas. We had a long chat about gorillas, and I explained how friends of yours were helping to make sure they could live safely in the wild. He was very impressed. But many of the animals looked in poor condition (emaciated, fur hanging off, apathetic) and the cages and pens were far too small.

I have been through the alphabet several times with Neil in recent days, and he now knows all the sounds of the letters, so I can say any one and he will say the right sound. Before a story this evening, I spelt out the sounds of C A T until he knew what the word was and then I said we were going to replace the C with an R, and we did the sounds until he got RAT and then we did the same with H and HAT. When I asked him if he could think of any more rhymes, he said 'BAT' straightaway. I am more and more convinced that the secret of good teaching, especially with really young children, is to keep their interest, to keep the subject fun. All these years, I've been a teacher, I suspected that was true, but I never really knew it. I do now.

Have you been reading about this Kelly business? I'm so confused I don't know what to think.

September 2003

We went to Malvern for a week. I hired a cottage this time, after Tom's complaints about the B&B. It was more work for me. One evening, we left Tom to watch the television and took a picnic up on the hills. It was such a lovely spot as the sun descended slowly in the west leaving its shine across the valley. Neil said it was like being in an aeroplane – The Malvern Aeroplane. And later he drew a colourful picture of it.

December 2003
I am glad you are coming home for Christmas. Will you stay with us for a few days, Neil would so love to see you. Mum is up and about, with a renewed lease of life. I pity her local Countrywide Campaigners group, she'll be launching all kinds of new efforts now.

Do you remember Thunderbirds and Dr Who. They are both showing again on television. Neil adores them.

September 2004
Neil has started school full-time, and he loves it. After his first day, I waited for him in the playground and when he didn't appear I walked into the classroom to find him hiding from me – he didn't want to go home. For a second, I felt acutely embarrassed.

September 2004
Neil became very upset this weekend because of Tom and I arguing and shouting. I am surprised how well he manages to exert pressure on us to make up. He moves from one to the other cuddling us, and if one of us refuses to do whatever we were going to do together (be it sit down to lunch or go out for a walk) he makes it very difficult to stay angry. Once, not this time but earlier, Tom was sitting down for a meal and I was getting the food out of the oven, and we had all calmed down. Neil quizzed Tom asking him, 'Do you think Mummy is a wonderful mummy?' I heard Tom answer, 'Yes, I think she is wonderful Mummy.' Then Neil said, 'But is she a wonderful Mummy to you?' Tom didn't answer. Then Neil said, 'But do you think she is a wonderful woman?' He said it so urgently, so sweetly, so tenderly, that I stopped what I was doing and gave them both a hug. He's growing so tall, I wish you were here to see him ... us more often. I've attached a photo.

October 2004
We are reading another Dahl story – The BFG. It is wonderful and captivates Neil. He has remembered and learned a number of good jokes and adores hearing new ones especially those that make a play on words which he understands. Here is his favourite from a new joke book I bought him yesterday: Who is the boss of the hankies? The Hankie Chief. He told and retold

the joke a dozen times to us in the car. Other favourites are: Where do cows go on holiday? Moo York. What do frogs drink? Croak a cola. And he made this one up today: Knock knock; who's there? Car; Car who? Karshula!

January 2005
Dear Uncle Alan – thank you for the wildlife book. I like all the pictures of the pandas. Have you ever seen bamboo? I have, in our garden.

January 2005
Neil's birthday passed in a feast of presents, activities, cakes and colours. He was a darling all day. Not long after dawn, he came into our bed all soft and quiet. When I asked him if he wanted to open his presents, he smiled coyly and said 'yes'. He started slowly trying to examine each one but after a while he found it impossible not to speed up, there was always another present to run and get: a construction set (racing car designs!), which is far too old for him; a Thunderbirds model to make; some clay modelling material (from guess who!); a box of magic tricks; and the book you so thoughtfully managed to courier in good time.

Yes, Mum came to stay over Christmas and was so annoying that when Tom shouted at her, I gave up a silent prayer of thanks. It's not only her sergeant major ways, it's the fact that she can't stop preaching to me about politics. It's difficult to know whether to blame the Tory party members like Mum, or the Tory party itself, but it seems to be so far to the right, it'll never find its way back towards the middle ground. Commentators are already predicting the Lib-Dems could do much better at the next elections, and that would be good for schools.

April 2005
Tom is away for three weeks, in the Far East I think. I don't care.

I have moved on to the multiplication tables with Neil and he is making good progress. I am anxious, not that he learns the answers necessarily but that he sees and knows the patterns, that he understands that seven times three is the same as adding up three seven times or seven three times. I have also been teaching him to count in twos and to understand the difference between odd and even numbers, both of which are different versions of the two times table. Why do I tell you all this?

Blair looks like getting back in. I won't begrudge him victory if does, though I'll vote for the Lib-Dems as usual. Mum's fuming, she thinks I, personally, am to blame for the failure of the Tories.

Guess what? I've been made deputy head, did I say. It means more money and paperwork, but slightly less teaching.

I was sad to hear you and Monique have split up, but I do understand how difficult the distance made things. Won't it always be a problem for you, unless you decide to slow down, settle down?

August 2005

We went on our own to Snowdonia this summer. Tom was away again. I loved being out and about on the hills. Neil is real trooper. He never complained once on our walks. When we came to forested parts, he was full of half-serious fears about ghouls and goblins, all stemming from the Tarquinade stories you read him last time you were here.

May 2006

While Tom was trying to mix a cocktail on the sideboard this evening, I was sitting at the kitchen table reading the news (dreadful floods in Eastern Europe – is this the kind of thing you've been warning about?). Neil climbed up on one of the chairs, and asked Tom if he could have a climb. He used to do this a lot, but he's bigger and heavier now, and Tom has been trying to discourage his toddler behaviour. A few days ago, Tom claimed a success in that Neil had climbed up onto his shoulders, Tom had remained absolutely lifeless and silent, and Neil had eventually climbed down out of boredom. This time, however, there was a twinkle in his eye and he was trying to suppress a grin. 'Don't look in my pocket,' he said to Tom. Tom turned to shrug him off, and Neil said, 'Oh darn it' or similar (he's full of family cartoon expressions such as 'yippee' and 'yummee'). Tom then saw that he had a mini-book in his trouser pocket and pointed it out. Neil played up to him with a guilty smirk. We all laughed when we twigged that his ingenious plan was to take a book up with him so he wouldn't get bored at the top.

Sometimes I love him so much I want to weep and weep with happiness, or take him in my arms and never let him go. Maybe that's why – you did ask – I cannot get too anxious about the absence of any real relationship with Tom. Don't be fooled by the cute domestic scene above. We had a row a few minutes ago.

January 2007

Mum gave Neil an expensive fountain pen for his birthday. He broke it within 24 hours; and when I got angry with him he went mute. I'd never seen him like that before. Later in the morning, he came up to me and said, 'Mummy, you know you said I was under a cloud, well there it is,' and he pointed above his head, 'and now it's raining, and now the cloud's gone away. Is that all right Mummy.' Sweet child. I made him write an apology to Grandma.

Is it really possible that peace will come to Palestine now – it's difficult to believe. We have had the hardest coldest December I can ever remember.

From Hungary to Russia! I loved your descriptions of Siberia (I have read them to Neil, and he wants to go. Beware, you're becoming a hero. He needs to see you more often or else the reality may be disappointing! So do I.) But are the environmental problems so bad, you make it sound heaven and hell all rolled into one?

March 2007

Neil continues to grow up into the most delightful boy. He has intelligence, strong features (at certain angles, he looks like you); he is sporty and competitive, but not too much; he is never bored at home and responds as well to being given things to do as to finding things to do on his own (mostly reading). Recently, he has learned to ride a bicycle and to tie his shoelaces (but not at the same time!).

I've been reading a fascinating new book called *The Snowball Effect or Parenting made Difficult* by Julia Derwent, an American Professor. I don't know how fresh the ideas are, but I've never read anything similar. She explains in layman terms what we know about the complex interactions between nature (genes) and nurture (environment), but then argues that early random influences – in the first year or two or three of a child's life – can have a much more profound influence than has ever been recognised. In essence, she argues that an event which appears benign in itself at the time can lead a child into behaving in a certain way, which then leads to the original event or pattern to be repeated and the reinforcement of the behavioural response – thus, the snowball effect. She cites fascinating studies of twins brought up together, showing how some develop very different characters, a fact which cannot be explained by their genes or their environment. She also sees a link between this analysis and several childhood development problems. She suggests, very controversially, that over-attentive parents can sometimes lead very young children into certain kinds of resistances, to foods, for example, or learning to speak or read, and that these resistances can then develop and enlarge, like a small ball of snow gently rolling downhill. She does, though, pull the analogy up sharp and insist that once formed a child's behaviour patterns cannot be broken up and remoulded like a snowball. Quite the reverse. The book only came to my attention because of the media furore, but I know from personal experience with Neil how close I came to forcing on him too much teaching at too early an age. God knows what damage we teachers do in class, although, according to Derwent, much of a child's character is already determined by the time he or she starts school (even if, according to the snowball effect theory, this might not yet be apparent), and any characteristics that are likely to change significantly during school years will do so in response to peer pressure rather than what teachers (or parents for that matter) do or say. She has quite a lot to say about this too.

I do go on so, don't I.

Your birthday is coming up, are there any books you need/want?

Oh, and I nearly forgot to tell you, Tom proposed we move to Singapore for a few years. Over my dead body, I said. He stormed out.

June 2007

I am making an extra effort at present with Neil's teaching at home. There have been personnel changes at his school which leave him less interested in class work. But he enjoys his home lessons. However, I will not be able to keep up this level of attention as Neil grows older, nor will I have the knowledge to keep his learning well directed. I am pinning my hopes on moving him to a better school, possibly next year, but we may also move if Tom decides to change jobs.

Have you ever been to Brazil? I can't remember. There was this glorious ten part series on the television. It's just finished. I watched it with Neil. The first programme on the Amazon hooked us, and then there were others about the Cerrado, for example, the country's history, and carnival (why are we so boring in this country, Neil wanted to know!).

We spent a lot of time on the commercially-oriented internet site, and, guess what, Neil persuaded me to order him lots of Brazilian posters. I helped him take down crinkled torn photos of the moon that Tom had pinned up years ago, and put up the new ones. But, by the next weekend, Tom had bought a huge poster of that Brazilian driver – whatever his name – who won the Grand Prix circuit last year, and another one of the car he drove, and helped Neil rearrange all the posters to make room for them. Neil tries to be fair about these things.

So, stranger, you are finally coming home for good. I'll believe it when I see it, when I see you, here.

October 2007

Uncle Alan. Mummy says you should be coming home by now. I hope you are not cold in Siberia. Mummy says you might be interested in my Dodge Book. 1) Get away from homework. Build a passage out of the window, and rope down. If there is no window try and burst the door in. 2) Excuses to teachers for not doing homework. I dropped it in the bin on the way to school. The wind blew it out of my hand. I did it, but when I turned it over it was gone. I used a piece of wood as paper, but Dad threw it on the fire. I suddenly went deaf at exactly the moment the teacher told us about the homework.

Next time you go to Siberia can I come, Mr Abominable Snowman?

Chapter Two
BRUSSELS, BANGKOK AND BRAZIL

The Lover's Triangle
First, there's me
Heroic, handsome, strong and gentle
Then there's you
Angelic, graceful, bright and loving
And then there's Dick
Cunning, interfering, mind-controlling Dick

The Ballad of Unwin Johns and other poems by Unwin Johns (2025)

There is a photograph on the screen now, the original of which I first saw in May 2020, a few days after Harriet had dispensed with my services, and several weeks after concluding the search for my father. It is not one selected from the database of 19th century prints which I personally owned at one time or another, but from the much larger database on Neil of prints which I have copied, from books, catalogues and netsites. I showed this photo to Jay, my youngest son, when he came to visit yesterday, and asked him whether I should write the story about Melissa. Either he had forgotten or I had never told it to him before. Consequently, I was able to rehearse what I intend write. He listened patiently and gave me his advice. Otherwise, he was full of gossip about the outside world, family and friends. As I lie here this evening, I am thinking about how much I love Jay, about how kind and generous a son he has been, and I worry that I won't ever have much to say about him in these pages, at least compared to my other more wayward children.

On the right of this photo, a pretty young woman, a girl, dressed in a white robe or sheet, lies semi-reclined on a chair, her head and shoulders resting against a large white pillow. Her dark shoulder-length hair is tucked behind an ear, and her eyelids are lightly closed. Her mouth is ever so slightly open. She looks neither asleep nor awake, daydreaming perhaps, or in a coma, or dead. Behind her stands a maidservant adjusting the pillow. She is bending slightly over the top of the girl but is looking above her head and across the room, towards an older woman, the mother perhaps, on the left of the photo, who sits directly opposite the girl. The older woman is wearing dark clothes including an oddly ornate bonnet, which hides all but the edge profile of her concave face, pointed nose and thin lips. She looks neither angry nor sad, but resigned. High curtains provide backdrops to these three people on either side of the photo, but, in the middle, where a cloudy sky can be seen through a sash window, there is the dark and featureless shape of the back of a man, the father perhaps. The photograph, a composite albumen print by Henry Peach Robinson from 1858, is called *Fading Away*. It was created from five different negatives, which goes some way to explaining how Robinson, in the High Art style of the time, was able to make the characters stand out from the photograph, thereby giving a similar effect to that created by the pre-Raphaelites in painting – but this is irrelevant.

There is another of Robinson's photos, *In Wales,* which I did possess for a while. Here it is, in the other database. It is less famous than *Fading Away,* but it too reminds me of Melissa. A smiling girl sits on a log or rock in long grass. She leans forward, elbows on knees with hands clasped together near the handle of a picnic basket. There is a pond in the background. She is wearing a shapeless white cotton hat, with the sides curled up, so similar to the one Melissa was wearing that day …

It is through Alfred that Melissa and I became friends. He launched a steamy affair with Gemma, a tall slinky brunette given to stretching the dress code more than most, after a Christmas dance. In the following months, he began to miss the occasional volleyball training session. Then, one Saturday, he failed to turn up for an important match, which we lost. Until that moment, none of us had yet come to appreciate how completely we relied on him for our success. Individually, several of us, including our coach, appealed to him not to let the team down again. I told him he had such a great talent, that to squander it would be a terrible waste. Subsequently, Alfred confided in me that he had been much touched by my appeal. Soon after, he was back at training and playing with full commitment.

He must have come to some arrangement with Gemma for, thereafter, she came to support our home matches and travelled with us to away matches. As the season was drawing to a close, in spring 2017, she brought a friend to one game – none other than Melissa. My play suffered, and I was substituted off court for two sets. This hurt my pride, yet her smiles towards me on the bench were simple and friendly; not even I could interpret them as a taunt. Thankfully, the substitute setter didn't fare too well either, and the coach put me on to play for the last and deciding set. As we lined up Alfred put his long arm around my shoulder and whispered in my ear.

'Concentrate, man.' Afterwards, Alfred, Gemma and Melissa sat around chatting in the school coffee-house for half an hour. I didn't say much. Not only was I disappointed with my own performance, but Melissa's presence and her warmth confused me.

Two or three weeks later, after a match, Alfred and Gemma organised for us all to go into Godalming for moussaka and retsina and then conspired to leave Melissa and me together. She was full of chatter and comment and sex appeal. But she also had an unnerving habit of starting a new topic of conversation while I was trying to respond to something she had already said. As I came to recognise this as a nervous habit, so I became more confident, and she relaxed in equal measure. On this first contrived date, though, Melissa did all the leading. She led the conversation, she led me to her home in nearby Busbridge (her mother and younger brother were away, with the mother's boyfriend), and she led me into her pink and yellow candy bedroom.

I do not recall what we talked about, I was still trying to fathom out why she liked me. Moreover, I was too intent on monitoring myself, trying not to say or do anything that might divert her interest, and debating with myself whether and when I should confess either or both of my twin sins: being a virgin and being condomless.

After closing the bedroom door, she went silent. She sat down on the bed (a lemon chenille bedspread), and I sat down next to her. I was shaking internally and externally, and my heart was beating as loud as the music in the Greek restaurant. I wanted to say 'I've been in love with you since I was 12' and 'I can't believe this is happening' and 'you are so beautiful', but every sentiment I considered seemed tacky or immature. Instead, I resorted to silence, a tactic that has stood me in good stead throughout my life in many different situations.

'You remember that time, the time you saw me?' I nodded. 'I thought about it for days and weeks afterwards you know.' She was very serious. 'I liked it. I liked knowing you had seen me. It gave us a special bond. Did you feel it too?' Then I had to say something.

'I watched you in the pool.'

'I know. I know. Whenever I saw you, I thought of you looking at me, and I liked it, I wanted you looking at me. But this is the weirdest thing, I wanted you looking at me naked.'

This was it, in essence, although I may have added an adult tone to her words. We kissed passionately for a few minutes, and then Melissa slowly took off her clothes. She stood naked in front of the bed, watching me watching her. I came in my trousers, and rushed off, red-faced to find the bathroom. By the time I returned, she had carefully rolled the chenille cover back, and climbed inside the sheets. Although I joined her in the bed, I knew the best part was over. My body was too big, my arms and legs were always in the wrong place; and I didn't know what to do, or when to do it. Melissa attempted to fit me with a condom (rather expertly!), but I remained too limp.

We were to have three more such encounters, every one split into two disjointed parts: foreplay and attempted copulation. It is my impression that we both preferred the former. Melissa's undressing and naked parading took longer and became more elaborate on each occasion. By contrast, my efforts in bed remained both gauche and gawky. I was getting the better part of the deal, and Melissa would surely have tired of me shortly. But fate intervened one very sunny June Saturday – the day of our final volleyball match of that season. Under orders from her mother, Melissa had been told to look after her 13 year old brother, Rob, and a classmate of his. This had unsettled Gemma's plans for a picnic after the match, but the two girls decided to proceed in any case, and to pack enough food for six. So it was that, around 4pm, we left the grounds of Witley Academic, crossed the busy main road, and walked the half mile or so along an overgrown footpath to Sweetwater Pond, and a flat grassy bank with a copse to the side providing shade.

Alfred and Gemma disappeared into the trees, and the boys went to mess around by the water, leaving Melissa and I to unpack the two picnic baskets, and then to lie quietly on the grass. I wanted to embrace Melissa, or touch her, but she had carefully and persistently declined my attempts to hold hands or kiss anywhere outside the privacy of her house. With one hand reaching over towards her, I shyly pushed the white cotton sunhat from the top of her head, and was thinking I might lean over to kiss her. All of a sudden the boys were screaming with laughter. I looked up to see Rob waving around a very long length of thick rod-like wire he had retrieved from the pond's edge on the far side where some builders' rubble had collected. He was splashing it in the water. A few seconds later, Melissa's phone rang. She stood up and walked the three metres towards the pond, to where her bag lay. At the same moment, Rob swished the wire over his head, as if it were a fishing rod, in order, I suppose, to create a bigger and better splash. The sharp end of the rod whipped into Melissa's temple. It stuck there for a moment, and then sprang out. Melissa fell to her knees and crumpled on the ground, lifeless. There was no blood, and, apart from the hole in her head, which could only be seen close up, there was no evidence that anything untoward had happened.

For an instant, I wanted to think Melissa might be play acting, but my mind couldn't hold on to that explanation for long. She had crumpled to the ground, too effectively, too realistically. As I moved over and knelt down by her body, I shouted out as sternly as I could for the boys to stop playing with the wire. Her face was lifeless, empty. I shouted out again, this time for Alfred. Within a few seconds we were all gathered in a circle around her. I think we all assumed she was dead. Gemma was the most active of us, bending over Melissa to see if she was breathing, and then dialling 999 on her phone. Strangely, Rob was the least emotional, he stood there frozen, just staring at the pond. Paramedics arrived in 20 minutes, the police in 30. Half an hour later, we were at Royal Surrey County Hospital. Melissa was not dead, but in a coma.

The parents of Rob's friend arrived first. Within the next 20 minutes my mother, Gemma's parents and a colleague of Alfred's father all arrived. It was some hours, though, before the police tracked down the mother of Rob and Melissa. By then, doctors, nurses and police had all talked to us. By the tone of their questions and the various discussions we half heard, there was no doubting that the adults understood this was nothing more than a tragic accident.

I never talked to Melissa's mother then, or ever, although I was to have two series of uncomfortable encounters with Rob later in my life. Poor boy, Melissa apart, he was certainly the most affected by the events of that afternoon. Subsequently, he became one of the 'losers' or 'inevitable costs' of the liberalised drug regime in the early 20s. I don't recall how exactly, but, in some way, the tragedy accelerated the trajectory of the relationship between Alfred and Gemma, which ended, either before or during the summer vacation period.

As for me, I recovered surprisingly quickly. I confided in Julie that Melissa had been my girlfriend, and allowed her to comfort me. I persuaded myself that Melissa would recover fully, a projection which clearly made it easier to get on with the rest of my busy life without feeling guilty. Initially, I took the train and bus to the hospital every week, staying only a few minutes. Yet this schedule soon slipped. Four weeks of that summer I spent abroad in Brussels, and, by the autumn, I was down to one visit a month. Melissa showed no signs of recovery, and no signs of dying either, and I simply became accustomed to the situation. Every now and then, I was arrested, so to speak, mid-phrase or mid-action by something triggering the memory of the wire whip arching through the air, slotting into the side of Melissa's head, staying there for a second, and then jerking out. When Melissa was transferred to a hospital in west London, my visits became less frequent. Later, once I was established at the London School of Economics, I made diary notes to be sure of not forgetting to pass by the hospital every two or three months.

And so, finally, for it has taken longer to tell this story than I planned, I come to May 2020 and Henry Peach Robinson's famous photograph. For me, it was a routine visit to the private room where Melissa lay, permanently. I planned to stay only ten minutes, and to read, as usual. That said, I was finding it difficult to concentrate because of a growing preoccupation with Harriet's offhand behaviour (a subject I shall come to soon). But this morning I had time neither to read, nor to get maudlin about my relationship with Harriet, for a consultant called me to his office. He explained, gently, that it had been decided, in full consultation with Melissa's family and various doctors, to turn off the life support systems within a week. I said I was sure it was for the best, and walked back to her room to say goodbye. She was propped up – similar to the girl in *Fading Away* – her eyes closed, her face white, her hair combed and shorter than before, and her life long, long gone. I kissed one cheek, said farewell, and left.

Half an hour later, after walking aimlessly the mile or so to Kensington, I found myself entering The Photography Place. The venue survived no more than 15-20 years, but, for a while, it was a lavish modern library and exhibition space dedicated to pre-digital photography. One gallery was showing a collection of Robinson's prints, including *Fading Away* (although not *In Wales*). The picture took hold of me in a barely explicable way. It seemed to catalyse my emotions about the accident, fermenting feelings which, though never fully expressed, were unleashed by the news of Melissa's impending death. I stood there, staring at the framed print, seeing Melissa, realising that I would never see her again; seeing her standing there in the shower room, laughing; seeing her prancing around in the bedroom, unbuttoning her blouse; realising, finally, I would never see her again; seeing her lying there on the grass, her eyes shut, her lips widening into a smile as she feels me sliding the soft hat from her forehead; realising, finally, finally, that I would never see her again; and seeing her there, lying silently among the white sheets and recalling the touch of my lips on her cheek but an hour ago; and realising, absolutely, that Melissa, unlike the girl in the photograph, was dead. Dead.

I cried for a short while, and then purchased a postcard reproduction of the picture. Odd and heartless as it may sound, the catharsis in front of Robinson's photograph served as a finale to my actions and feelings for Melissa (discounting Rob's several later re-appearances, and the occasional emotional refrain that would come whenever I saw a copy of *Fading Away*).

***

The end of the school year was always a busy time, and year six, which finished in July 2017, was no exception. The volleyball season had ended the day of Melissa's accident but, by then, I was heavily involved in the Brideswell Society (a forum for topical lectures). My responsibilities, initially confined to promotion of events around the school, had widened, thanks to Flip's confidence in me, to include direct liaison with speakers. Ronald Shuttleworth (who would shortly change his name to William Caxton) was our star speaker. He held the position of junior minister for communications in the second, and more successful (but not popular), Liberal Democrat-Labour coalition government. From my point of view, though, he proved to be a most difficult guest.

To begin with, Caxton's private secretary replied to the invitation I had written, in Flip's name, asking for a lot more information, about previous speakers, the school's population, and the expected audience size. A week later we received a curt rejection note; but then, a few days after that, Caxton himself telephoned Flip, said he had changed his mind, and offered to speak on a different day from that planned for the lecture. Flip agreed, and I was left with the task of rescheduling the programme. Moreover, Caxton offered one title for his talk, and then altered it with three days to go. He insisted on a named bottle of red wine and another of water, and on having a private room available should he need it. One of his secretaries informed me that the minister would not be available to answer questions after the lecture (because of time problems and the sensitivity of the issues), despite the very clear guidelines I had sent him for Brideswell Society events. Then, before I had a chance to ask him to reconsider, an email arrived, announcing that he would, after all, be prepared to answer questions for ten minutes. This was my introduction to the character who later rose to such heights and dubbed himself 'The man of the people'.

There can be no doubting Caxton's genius, although I'm not convinced any one biographer has yet managed to explain it adequately. I have reserved, in my mind, a part of the next chapter for Caxton, and for my – what shall I call them? – dealings with him, and so shall skip lightly over the day of the lecture itself. Suffice to say, he spoke passionately (although not convincingly to my young mind) about the need for freedom of speech, for open net access, and for minimum net regulation. Policing of the net had developed into a major political issue ten years earlier, but neither the weak first Liberal Democrat-Labour coalition nor the rag-bag Tory coalition that followed it had faced up to the problem. And this government, which was fast drawing to a close, had shunted the issue to one side. Caxton's views, which led to his resignation prior to the 2018 election, in fact fitted far more snugly with the subsequent Conservative Alliance administration that ruled our country so poorly through to the year I joined the civil service (don't blame me, my vote went to the Lib-Dems in the 2018 elections). But, by then, of course, Caxton's media empire had begun to flourish.

Two things struck me when Caxton walked into the foyer area where the headmaster, Flip and I were waiting to greet him and his two assistants (one old and male, the other young, female and attractive): his youthfulness, he must have been 30 or 31, and his short height, 165 centimetres or so. Those physical attributes apart, he bowled me over with his energy and intensity. After the introductions, he turned his babyish face towards me square on, his chin forward, his head angled upwards, a posture which gave him a permanent air of confidence and/or superiority. He never had any doubt that he was at the centre of a circle in which everyone else was on the circumference.

'You're Fenn.'

'Yes, sir. Neil or Kip Fenn.'

'I was mightily impressed with your organisation, the clarity of your emails, your responsiveness. Thank you.' He took a quick look around to assess whether anyone was pressing him to do something, before asking, 'What's your subject?'

'History.' Quick as a flash, he had a question for me.

'Who was the most influential politician in the 20th century?' I hesitated, went red, and looked over towards Flip.

'Don't look at me, mouse,' he said, but in a kindly way.

'Depends who you are, I might say Ghandi, if I was an Indian, or Mandela if I was African, or ...'

'But you're not, are you. You're British.'

'Yes, sir. And European.' I looked up and saw the whole group was waiting for my answer. Caxton glimpsed at his watch, a tiny gesture but one which provoked me.

'I won't say Hitler or Stalin because I can't choose between them, and, besides, I expect you mean influential in a positive way, so I'll opt for Jacques Delors, though I reserve a final answer until I have a precise definition of what you mean by 'influential' and 'politician'. Do you want me to say why?' There was a momentary silence, before Caxton gave me a slow soft clap, and a 'bravo'.

'No, I'll pass on the sophistry,' he said, gaining a chuckle from both his assistants. Before I could recover my composure, we were walking across the quad towards the packed main hall. Later that evening with Flip and others in the Chiddingfold Arms, I recounted the exchange to Horace, who earlier had petitioned Flip unsuccessfully to be included in the reception party. I don't think I had ever experienced Horace so transparently jealous of me.

***

A few weeks later I was on my way to Brussels, thanks, I am happy to recall, to Tom who otherwise had not played much of a parental role through my teenage years (apart from providing money, and taking me to the cinema). Earlier that year (2017), I had been advised at school to consider work experience jobs in the summer, and then, a few days later, I had gone with Tom to see the zany Italian comedy *Hold on to Your Boss*. Pacciotti went on to make better, more respected films, but never one so genuinely and ingeniously funny. Afterwards, in a pub by the Thames, I'd asked Tom if he could help me find a summer job. I didn't expect him to make the effort, let alone to achieve anything. He was good at promises, Julie commented more than once, but not at fulfilling them. On this occasion she was wrong. He messaged me (something he rarely did) one afternoon at school: 'Surprise in store. Collect you at gates at 5. Reply only if you can't do.'

When I saw him with a new car, a Retro Zephyr, I brushed off any expectations for myself. He drove us to a tea-house in Compton describing every feature of the vehicle in loving detail as if he were a car salesman. It was only when we were sipping cappuccinos and munching muffins that he did truly surprise me. It transpired that he had contacted a good customer of his in the London office of Euroil plc, an international oil/gas exploration and production company, who had then sent out a general email to colleagues. The manager for European policy/planning in Brussels, Sterling J Wood Junior, no less, had responded saying he would be undertaking a study exercise in the summer, and could do with some basic help. It would be database inputting mostly, Tom told me, some filing and research.

'But heh, what can you expect at your age,' he concluded.

In addition, Tom had established that I would have use of a company studio flat for no cost. Although my mother Julie expressed concern about me living away from home, and overseas, for four weeks, she had no legitimate objections – the euro, Eurostar, and the (failing) Euronet meant that Brussels was, in practice, down the road, or round the corner.

Altogether I spent three separate months working for Sterling at Euroil, a month that summer, a month the following summer, and a month in August/September 2020, at the start of the year I took off from university. I'm not sure what my original expectations of Euroil were, but the reality did not live up to them. On my first night, Sterling took me for an expensive fish meal in the St Catherine area of downtown Brussels. He talked, like my father, about the majesty of the oil industry, the riches it had brought to the world, and the constant need for vigilance against loony environmentalists. I listened mostly. I judged (rightly as it turned out) that there would be no advantage in trying to impress him with my own ideas or learning. I understood that I had cheap labour written all over me. Initially, the office was busy with 15 or 20 staff, but many of them, including Sterling, soon departed for vacation. I was left in the charge of Sterling's personal assistant, a middle-aged Flemish woman called Hilde. My main job was to revise a three year old directory of people in the various Union institutions and of interest to the oil industry. This meant trawling the Euronet and the wider net, emailing and phoning people, and, on my own initiative, redesigning the directory layout. In the evenings, I went to the cinema, walked around the sites and parks, or stayed at home to watch news or write emails. One weekend, I travelled to Holland to join Alfred at a volleyball tournament, and on another weekend Julie insisted I meet her in Bruges for sightseeing.

A year later, after my 18 examinations, the general pattern repeated itself. This time Sterling, who again took me for a meal and again disappeared on vacation within a few days of my arrival, really did have a study for me to work on. Earlier in the year, there had been simultaneous attacks by Muslim extremists on gas export pipelines in Algeria and Turkey. This had prompted the European Parliament to call for more emergency natural gas storage capacity in the European Union (EU) to be funded through an EU-wide energy tax, which itself would help to curb demand. The European Commission (the EU's executive civil service) had tabled a proposal in June which the oil/gas industry had rejected outright. In preparation for the lobbying that would take place in the autumn, my task was to trawl through European Parliament votes on energy taxation and oil/gas issues during the previous ten years to identify any Members (MEPs) who might have shown an inconsistent policy. Sterling and Hilde prepared a basic list of relevant laws and showed me how to find, from them, other relevant laws and resolutions. Beyond that, it was simply a matter of accessing the voting records and making lists.

Socially, life improved during this second trip. I went to the same annual volleyball event, but this time Alfred had pulled together a better team, and we won our mini-league; and winning is definitely more pleasurable than coming second or third. One night I went to a cavernous club, Noir Two, with the friend of a school-friend. He brought his girlfriend and a friend of hers, which made for a cosy foursome. My blind date proved to be a live wire, but too hot for me. I was too shy to ask for a date or to make a follow-up call to my original contact.

Unexpectedly, my uncle Alan showed up one day with a Czech girlfriend called Tamara. They took me to an Arab restaurant. We sat on the floor, ate with our hands, drank light tea and puffed on a waterpipe. They listened attentively to all my news, demonstrating, by their enquiries a genuine interest in me and my life. The rest of the time we discussed and argued about global problems, especially those concerned with oil and climate change. That was a special evening.

Otherwise, I spent too much time using the studio computer, discovering the allure of pornography. Although fluid communications were common, they were not yet universal. We had one such connection at home, but my private computer in the bedroom was an antique. In any case, Julie deliberately entered my room at all kinds of times, and for odd reasons, making any illicit activity difficult. During my first summer in Brussels, I had resisted the temptation of using the studio computer to seek out pornography, in case whoever maintained the machine might discover my trails. But I was a year older at the time of my second visit. Moreover, by then, I had been to Bangkok.

I see I have already referred to Bangkok several times; but, now I am here, at the point where I should expose Tom, I'm not convinced there is much to say.

In autumn 2017, Tom came up with the idea of taking me to Thailand for Christmas. He had a conference to attend, he said, and could trade in a business class ticket for two standard class seats. It would be a well-earned break for me, in my final year at Witley Academic, he argued, and was an opportunity not to be missed. Julie hated the idea. She and Tom argued furiously on the phone; and Julie employed her whole emotional armoury to persuade me not to go. All to no avail. None of my friends could understand Julie's arguments when I tried to replay them.

I have visited Bangkok a few times, yet that first extraordinary but excruciating trip stands out, like a neon light on a dark night, like a naked girl in a roomful of businessmen. There was the metropolis itself, a non-European city, with its US-style skyscrapers, Asian-style cycle rickshaws, appalling infrastructure and teeming human life. I had never seen human society so cheap, so dirty, so crowded, so colourful, so noisy, so animate. I recall, in particular, the magnificent Grand Palace with its radiantly coloured tiles and its many murals of town and country scenes; the exotic floating markets along the Chao Praya selling foods and flowers and artifacts which may as well have been transported from Mars for all I knew; and the drama/dance troupe we saw perform a traditional Thai legend at the New National Theatre. The story told of how royal brothers, wearing glittering costumes and tall golden hats, escaped from a sea giantess. Several singers and musicians, playing xylophones and small metal drums hung on a string in a horseshoe frame, accompanied the action. I observed a similar show in the new New National Theatre decades later, and I don't believe it had changed in any significant way.

The snake farm, located on the outskirts of the city, impressed me too. Tom was at his conference that day so I teamed up with a group of four Bristol University students. It was evident from their banter that they'd come to Bangkok as sex tourists and were only filling in time. We saw cobras, one enormous king cobra with its head held high, yellow-ringed snakes and vipers. The information has never been of the slightest use to me but I know to this day that the venom taken from poisonous snakes by squeezing the sides of their heads is injected into horses to incubate antidotes. Come to think of it, there must be more efficient ways of doing it now. And then there was the food. I had eaten Thai food at the Chiang Mai on Guildford High Street, but it was the street fare – pancakes with coconut, fried pork pieces and boiled rice, banana and sweet potato – which was so different, so exotic, so tasty.

For three of the six days, I had a fabulous time. Then came the fourth evening. Tom wanted to go to a night club and I wanted to go to the cinema. This sounds strange, but I was never a typical youth, interested in loud music and parties. Tom, who was fast closing in on 60, often acted and behaved younger than me. We had argued a few times already, but over minor things (such as the clothes I'd brought and my mislaying of the room keycard) but when I said I didn't want to go to the club he blasted my head off, perhaps because he was partially drunk, or (I worked this out later) because he had planned the experience in advance and was taken aback by my unexpected stubbornness.

'Fuck me if you aren't intent on spoiling everyone's fun. You know what you are, you're a boring old fart, and that's saying something for an 18 year old going on 14. Who paid for this holiday, anyway, who fucking organised it?' I took a deep breath, and gave in silently.

So far, I had avoided the extensive red-light districts. Tom had not steered me towards them in our walks together, and, on my own explorations, I had a strong sense that I shouldn't be interested in what was on offer there, and that the whole sex scene was sordid, dirty. The club Tom chose was not, by its location, obviously part of the sex scene. Neither did I twig the truth immediately on entering the place. I believed all the teenage girls dancing amidst the multicoloured flashing lights were genuine clubbers, and that the groups of men sitting in the shadows were their boyfriends or singles on the prowl. I began to feel uncomfortable when Tom suggested we step onto the dance floor as several other men had done. I rebuffed him tetchily – we had never gone dancing together before. When he insisted, and fearing a replay of his earlier rage, I followed him shyly but irritably. My mood transformed, though, when a pretty girl soon drifted into dancing with me. She was no older than me, but must have been 40 centimetres shorter. Apparently, she failed to notice I was awkward, tense, had spots on my forehead, and my cheeks were redder than the spotlight in one corner.

'American?' she asked.

'No, British.'

'My name, Choolee, you?'

'Kip.' She smiled and I fell in love. It surprised me, though, to see that Tom's partner was no older than mine. My innocence lasted only a few more minutes.

When we returned to our table, the girls followed. One of them immediately draped her arm around Tom; Choolee was less forthright but sat close enough to be touching me. A topless girl emerged under the red spotlight and rolled herself gymnastically around a stainless steel pole. I stared at her trying to work out what was happening. Then, when Choolee put a hand high up on my thigh, I went rigid. Some combination of confusion, anger and fear must have shown in my face, because a cheery-looking Tom tried to reassure me.

'Relax, relax, it's all part of your education,' he said.

It was a set-up which went horribly wrong. Tom, no doubt, had meant well, but had failed to allow for the normal insecurities of a young man, let alone the powerful nature of his sexual insecurities. I couldn't cope, I simply could not cope with what was happening. I froze emotionally and intellectually, which explains why I didn't race off into the night. After half an hour or so of doing nothing, saying nothing, Tom told me to go with Choolee. I allowed her to direct me through a curtain, along a dingy corridor and into a plainly decorated room with no more in it than a double bed. I do not know how long I was there, but whatever Choolee did (and she did a lot of things) an erection would not come. She remained friendly and smiling throughout, and never stopped trying. I came to realise later, thanks in part to Harriet's detached behaviour in the bedroom, that a diversion – a conversation, the television, almost anything – might have helped.

Choolee led me back to the disco room, kissed me on the cheek, and disappeared for ten minutes. She was back on the dance floor before Tom returned, beaming. When he asked me how it went, I replied with a meaning-less phrase such as 'fine, thanks', and when he pressed me, I said I did not want to talk about it. And, in order to forestall, further conversation, I thanked him for the experience.

This episode affected the rest of the holiday in two ways. Firstly, I used up all the rest of my free time separated from Tom in exploring the red-light district. I discovered I could enter a brothel to gawk and gape through a wide glass screen at a dozen naked or near naked beautiful teenage girls. They might be sitting and wriggling, or dancing and gyrating; whatever, the view was exciting, and free. But, then, for a negligible amount of money, I could buy the privacy of a booth with a one metre square screen and choose from a multitude of high quality porn flicks. A pack of tissues was available on the floor. For slightly more baht, I could watch, through a peep hole, a real live woman take off her clothes, and parade every bit of herself as though she was alone.

Secondly, Tom's behaviour, which clearly implied that he was accustomed to using prostitutes, gave me the right, or at least opened up the possibility, to question him about the failure of his marriage to Julie. I distanced myself emotionally from him, and felt older, wiser, and more determined to uncover the full extent of his guilt. Tom proved surprisingly willing to talk about the details (which is how I came to know as much as I did). Most of that which he told me had the ring of truth and fitted with what I already knew. It was a common enough story: in the beginning, the sexual side of their relationship was adequate (although Tom did all the running), until I came along, and then Julie lost interest and shut him out, Tom strayed, and there wasn't enough else in the marriage to keep them together.

On returning to the UK, my relationship with Tom remained strained. I did not see him for six months or more. He called to congratulate me on my exam results, and we then agreed to meet for a film and meal. This was the week before my second trip to Brussels. As I've said, that summer I spent too much time discovering the possibilities of a powerful computer and open access to the net, discovering, in fact, that the net was a voyeur's paradise. From then on, I was able to indulge this puerile habit without inhibition.

***

My consultant, Dr Rupert Lipman, came by a few minutes ago with a gaggle of doctors and Chintz, one of the nurses.

'Fine, Mr Fenn, everything is fine. We are re-tuning your pill menu slightly, think nothing of it,' Lipman pronounced. He looked over at the wallscreen, 'That's a pretty picture, where is it?'

'Copacabana,' I said, 'photographed in 1890 by Marc Ferrez.'

'Nice beach,' he remarked, none the wiser, and walked off followed by his entourage. Only Chintz remained.

'You mean Copacabana in Rio de Janeiro?' she asked.

'Yes. It was a wild and unpeopled place once.'

'Wow,' she uttered appreciatively.

'I own the original of this picture,' I bragged, knowing the boast would not mean much to her. But I'm running ahead of myself, I was only trying to jog my memory in preparation for what I should write tomorrow. No, that is not strictly true, I was drifting. This is a mammoth task I have set myself. It is so difficult to know what to write, what to leave out, who to mention and who to ignore. I should précis my early days at the London School of Economics (LSE) university, and move on as swiftly as I can to 2020, the period after Tom's drunken new year's eve revelation.

I had been drinking moderate amounts of alcohol since I was 15, I had voted for the first time that year, and I had spent half an hour with a prostitute, but my adult life only truly began the day I moved into the Bermondsey flat with Bartock and Philli, a couple from Matlock in Derbyshire, who had taken on the lease and advertised through the LSE noticeboard. Philli, like me, was aiming for a history degree, and Bartock, who later dropped out to start some venture or other, was studying commerce. Patrick, who took the other spare room, came from Belfast, and never ceased to keep us amused with tales of his attempted seductions. Philli suggested we should meet once a week for a meal which she would cook, so long as one of us brought a bottle of wine. It was a good idea in theory, but in practice there was never a night all four of us were in – or wanted to be in – at the same time. I never found much in common with any of the three, and increasingly became irritated with the size of my room, the traffic noise outside, and the inane domestic nattering of Philli and Bartock. After two terms, I moved into another larger flat, also in Bermondsey, with two friends from the international history department: Peter de Roo, a highly intelligent soft spoken Dutchman to whom I am eternally grateful for introducing me to Diana (my second partner); and, confusingly, another Peter, Pete Sampson, a formidable debater who ended up a professor at Keele (and through whom, coincidentally and decades later, I met my third partner Lizette). I became friendly with de Roo, even though he was doing a postgrad degree and was three years older, because of volleyball, and with Sampson because we were taking similar modules.

Student life was everything I had discussed with my buds at school and more. The social whirl, for which I was not best suited, carried me along to costume parties, pop and jazz concerts, pretentious arty happenings, cheap meals in newly discovered guzzleshops, and relationships on every level. I tumbled into two affairs at the same time, neither instigated by me. Dark and mysterious Trisha would make firm arrangements and never show, or turn up in the middle of the night weeping for no apparent reason, demanding that I hold her tight and long. By contrast, Annie, another history undergraduate, took a more serious view of life and friendships, which required much discussion about every aspect of our affair, not least my apparent impotence. I was as useless at sex as I was at deception, and I hoped they would both finish with me when they found out about each other. Instead, I became a war zone for two or three months (not because of any desirable attribute in me, but because I was a territory, any territory), until I could take no more, buried myself in the library and refused to answer any calls. Interestingly, though, of the two it was Trisha's self-centred egotism that came closest to rousing my natural sexuality, while Annie's determined attention to my problem – like Popsicle's later – failed miserably.

Volleyball remained an important part of my life until the second year at LSE – until I twisted my ankle in December 2019. At the summer tournaments in Holland with Alfred, I'd met some high-level players from London Docklands, a club which had won the national league three times in the last seven years, and had been invited to train for the second team. After much biking backwards and forwards to Rotherhithe, where London Docklands was based, and months of strenuous practice I did achieve selection. In my second season, during the autumn of 2019, I trained vigorously and performed well; then came the injury during a second team match against the Reelers. Although it had been exciting to train with some of the best volleyball players in the country (more than half of them foreign), I was not committed enough to stay with the punishing coaching schedule, and there was no chance of making the first team. Thus, I restricted my playing to the uni club which operated at a less competitive level, and where I was a bigger fish in a smaller pond. (By contrast, Alfred went on to greater things: he helped Manchester University, a rival of London Docklands, win its way into the national league; and, later, he played in more than 50 internationals for Nigeria.)

Whereas the social buzz sounded the loudest and always clammered for attention, it was the intense low-level hum of LSE's intellectual life which attracted me more. I gravitated naturally from the Brideswell Society at Witley Academic to the European Society at LSE with its lively debates and sponsored trips to Prague or Warsaw; I attended the Grimshaw Club lectures on occasions, and I took a keen interest in the Green Action group (although I sometimes felt frustrated at the juvenile level of its politics, and the silliness of its activities). It was to the Schapiro Government Club, though, that I was drawn most strongly. It had declined badly in recent years. A self-serving clique of quasi-fascists had staged a committee coup some years before my arrival, and the club had never recovered. But, I had enjoyed running the Brideswell Society, and the Schapiro was an opportunity to do the same thing and more, without any adult interference. I inveigled both my flat-mates – the two Peters – to help out.

To begin with, we simplified the name to Government Club (without Schapiro), and then set about finding controversial or interesting speakers. I contacted Flip who put me in touch with ex-Witley Academic notables. But one of our best early events, and the one which put the club back on the map (and more importantly brought in a flurry of subscriptions), came about as a result of an appeal to my uncle Alan. Amazingly, he delivered, so to speak, WWF's international negotiating director Ingrid Kallström. Not only did she speak with authority and humour on her topic, *Lobbying for Sustainable Balance*, but, according to Peter de Roo, she was 'drop-dead gorgeous'. I couldn't disagree. The two of us, Peter and I, had the privilege of taking her to the student bar for a drink; and the Government Club made front page news in the next edition of *The Beaver*, LSE's student paper.

In my second year, Peter dropped back to concentrate on his studies, but Pete Sampson and I, and a few fresh liberal faces we had recruited, took the Government Club to new heights. Its renewed popularity (and, not forgetting the status of the international history department professors) meant we could attract the occasional junior government minister and key figures from the European institutions (MEPs were always available!). I have no intention of trawling through our programme, even if I were able to recall it. I vaguely remember one excellent event which made the national media: a large audience justly booed the Conservative Alliance transport minister for his, only half-humorous, suggestion that students should travel less and study more for the good of the country. However, I do wish to mention, in passing, that Pete had an important influence on the club (and indirectly on me) because he was a mover and shaker in LSE's Net Society. This led the Government Club, in association with the Net Society, to present more events linked to internet and communications issues than might otherwise have been the case. For example, we bagged a top level European Commission official for one talk, and he explained frankly the political reasons behind Euronet's failure; and, on another occasion, we had difficulty keeping a straight face while Georgia's deputy ambassador justified his country's hosting of renegade net service providers (NSPs) with waffle about human rights and freedom.

***

But now I must move on again to more personal matters. I am trying to keep order – first my father, then Harriet, then Brussels, then Brazil. That will be more than enough for this chapter.

My father is easily dealt with. The doctor did it; the cad, or the rapist, whichever way you care to look at it. I'm not 100% sure, but I'd bet my inheritance to Jay on it. I had spent one year and one term at LSE by the time of that fateful new year's eve with Tom. For a while, I did wonder whether, if I'd returned to Bermondsey before that night and allowed friends to ferry me to a party, I'd ever have discovered the truth. I suspect Tom would have told me, eventually, one way or another.

I returned to uni that January uncharacteristically depressed. I worked solidly, as usual, and continued my various activities, but all too often I shut myself in my room seeking out diversion on the net instead of engaging with Pete and/or Peter. On occasions, I caught myself in a trance-like state during lectures, or, more dangerously, while cycling: a mile would pass by without me being able to recall the state of the traffic or whether I'd stopped at a junction. I made a series of querulous calls to Tom, without discovering any additional information. I visited Julie with the sole purpose of stealing a copy of the letter I've already mentioned; and then I tracked down its author.

If Martin Beale had no longer been a teacher, I might never have found him, but there was a trail, from colleague to colleague, a longish one, which, over several weeks, I managed to follow. I started at Julie's old school, where there was only one teacher who had been there more than ten years. I asked her for the name and subsequent workplace of the person who had been there longest when she started work there. This was the trickiest link in the chain. Three connections later I found someone who had known a young teacher ('who fancied himself a bit too much') called Martin Beale. He had transferred after three years to a larger primary school in nearby Wheathampstead. I phoned several schools and asked to speak to the longest serving teacher, and thus found that Martin Beale had moved on to a school in Bedford. I rang him there, and impressed on him the urgency of my mission, but without explaining what it was about. He agreed to meet on the Saturday morning and suggested the Ale and Coffee Lounge, not far from the central station. The Ale and Coffee Lounge!

Throughout the journey to Bedford I was preoccupied with trying to calculate the chances of Martin turning out to be my father. If he were, as I think I expected, then I knew I should be preparing myself for a pretence of interest in him as a person. But, if he were not, then I should be preparing myself for an anti-climax, a serious disappointment. But my mind jigged to and fro across the scant information available unable to reach any conclusion. I did not know what I thought, or believed, or hoped.

I saw him, complete with dark specs and a black duffel coat, entering the glass door, before he saw me. As he surveyed the Lounge and various shoppers relaxing on the large sofas, I noted a sense of disappointment nudging forwards into my consciousness. It originated, I worked out quickly, from his height, or lack of it. He took off his glasses, caught my eye, and walked over to greet me. We shook hands. He removed his coat. A waitress came and took our order.

'Julie,' he pronounced after only a short burst of fluff talk. 'I'd be lying if I said I remember her well. But I do remember her. Dark, not pretty but not plain either, fussy. You want to know if we had an affair, I can't think why else you'd trudge all the way to boring Bedford. Well, we did.' He turned his head from side to side to see whether the waitress was coming. 'And yes, I did know she was married. Her husband was never around, or so she said.' He peered over towards a corner where a group of children were being boisterous. How short a time it takes to dislike someone. Any traces of disappointment, engendered by a recognition that his modest height meant he was less likely to be my father, were truly vanquished by his undisguised aura of conceit. I didn't much care for the neat-cut beard either, or the ostentatious specs lying on the tabletop. I grasped the nettle with both hands, as they say.

'When did it finish, I mean when did your affair end?' He looked at me full on, so that I would be able to see a light dawning behind his squinting eyes. But I didn't believe him, he knew why I had come.

'Oh I see.' He spoke slowly, with a put-on drawl. 'You think I might be your father. How thrilling.' I tried to keep cool and reasonable.

'You had an affair at the end of 1998, I know that much.'

'And what does Julie say?' Oddly, I had not prepared myself for someone who might be prepared to lie or joke about the matter, and I hadn't thought through an answer to this question. I ad-libbed.

'She's dead; she died last year. Cancer.' This stunned him momentarily.

'I'm sorry.'

'I only want to be sure when your affair finished.' He looked at me again as if getting ready to tease me further.

'How old are you?' And then I realised that he knew, he absolutely knew I was not his son. How else could he be so flippant. In case he pressed his point, I prepared to tell him I was 19 not 20.

'Please, if you can, tell me when your affair ended. That's all I want of you.' The waitress arrived with our coffees. He sipped off the cream and licked his moustache.

'As far as I can remember, and it's a long time ago now, we only ever had sex two or three times all towards the end of 1999. I had to call it off after that. She was too uptight, and she kept coming to me in school time asking for another meeting.' Prick. I began to imagine his spotless duffel coat covered in café au lait.

'After you called it off, you never had sex with her again? Maybe she came on to you, for example, some months later and you were unable to resist the temptation?' (Did I really speak about my mother in that way? It is how I remember it.)

'No. And, besides, I always, always used a condom.' That second 'always' rankled deeply. I have never forgotten the sneering way he implied – intention-ally or not I didn't care – that he might have caught something from Julie if he had failed to take precautions. Inwardly, I was shaking with rage. I rose to my feet slowly, collected my coat from the side arm of the sofa, and threw a five euro note on the table to pay for the coffee. Then, as I was turning to leave the table and make for the doorway, I gave way – in my mind only, not in reality – to a display of soap opera emotion. I lashed an imaginary arm across the surface of the table swiping Martin's half-full cup of coffee and a bowl of sugar onto his lap.

Locating the doctor, William Jessop, could not have been simpler. He was listed in the St Albans telephone directory. Why did I seek him out? He was my only other option. I never considered him as a possibility for my father, but the fact that Julie had consulted him around the time I was conceived (according to her bare diary entries) opened up the possibility that she may have confided in him. One Thursday, the only weekday without a lecture or seminar, I rang his surgery and persuaded the receptionist to book me 'on a personal matter' for five minutes after his last appointment. It was a solitary practice taking up the ground floor of a large double-fronted house in Hemel Hempstead Road. Old and scruffy posters adorned the corridor and waiting room walls; grey wiry stuffing edged out of torn seat covers; a threadbare patterned carpet had lost its colour many years ago. I didn't have long to wait. As I entered the untidy consulting room, Dr Jessop busied himself with a computer screen and a few papers. I had prepared an imperfect pitch.

'Sit down, boy.'

'I'm sure you won't remember me, but we did meet once, when I was about 12, and my mother was your patient. I was told you personally delivered me at home. Apparently, my mother insisted on a home birth.' I tried an innocent smile. He carried on typing, barely looking up. 'This may sound a strange request, but my mother – that's Julie Fenn – died recently, and before she died she talked to me about a special friend she had in the spring of 1999. And I'm trying to trace this friend, though I don't have his name.'

'Why come to me?'

'This is the strange bit. In her agenda for the same period, she notes several appointments with you, and the one word 'depression', and so I was wondering if there might be a connection between this special friend and the depression. I put two and two together, and probably made five. It sounds dumb saying it out loud.' He looked up and over towards me with an aging face, ruddy and burdened by a heavily wrinkled forehead, not at all how I remembered him. I glanced down, in an attempt to maintain my ingenuous act. 'Is there a chance you could look in your records to see if there's anything you can tell me.'

'Don't need to. I remember Mrs Fenn, and she never mentioned any of her friends.'

'Why did she need to see you?'

'Depression, as you've said. Though you know as well as me, I'm not supposed to tell you.'

'I thought, since she was dead...'

'Well you thought wrong.'

'There's nothing you can tell me. Did you treat her?' He appeared to drift away in his thoughts for nearly half a minute. Then, when he spoke it was with an artificially bright tone.

'Hypnosis. Worked a treat. Now, boy, if that's all. I have to rush.'

That was it, the end of the trail. He gave me the clue, and left it up to me. He knew what he was doing. A few weeks passed before the whole story fell into place, thanks to Harriet. We had been dating for a month or so, and when one evening I opened up this unsettled bit of my history, she suggested the doctor might have used hypnosis to seduce my mother. She vaguely remembered reading about such a case, and proposed a newspaper archive search. Within five minutes, we had found the following article.

'Doctor acquitted of hypnosis rape – 15 March 2009.

A general practitioner was yesterday cleared of raping a woman placed under hypnosis during a home visit. Dr William Jessop, 48, from St Albans, Hertfordshire, was acquitted of raping Mrs X a 33 year old patient, who the judge ordered cannot be named, in November 2005.

The woman said in court that she been very stressed about her failure to re-establish sexual relations with her husband after the birth of their first child. Dr Jessop suggested hypnosis therapy, and, after one session in his consulting rooms, he visited her several times. On each occasion he administered pills to aid the hypnosis. She had no memory of sexual contact with the doctor.

When the woman gave birth to her second child in September 2006, she assumed her husband was the father. But, two years later, she saw a photograph of Jessop's own children in his surgery and was struck by the likeness with her son. Without her husband's knowledge Mrs X paid 200 euros for a paternity test, which proved that Mrs X's husband could not have fathered the child. Mr X discovered the truth, and the couple separated. Mrs X then went to the police.

Dr Jessop claimed that Mrs X had "thrown herself at him" after one session, and "very stupidly" thought it would do her harm if he refused. He denied that he had administered any pills. Ishmael Coulter QC, defending, brought forward expert witnesses who claimed it was impossible to be raped under hypnotherapy without being aware of it. Mrs X said, "I have no other explanation for what happened." '

What can I say about my response to this revelation? I understood, without any reservation, that Tom was my father and would continue being my father, and that my genetic father meant nothing to me. I reasoned, therefore, that I would be able to forget the matter and immerse myself again in work and my clubs, and spend more time with Harriet. Yet, my mind would not let the matter go. My thoughts festered around each of the three individuals involved. Should I confront my mother with the facts? Should I be angry that she had refused to face up to whatever it was that happened, her indiscretion, his rape? Should I be sympathetic and allow sleeping dogs to lie? Should I tell Tom? What good would it do? And should I go back to Dr Jessop for an EastEnders-style confrontation and force him to admit his guilt, his paternity?

No answers came into focus. No, no answers came into focus, not then, not ever. Instead, the questions agitated for a while, for too long, before slowly sinking into my subconscious. From there they took but occasional excursions to the surface, at different times during my life, without ever finding closure, as an analyst might say.

***

Rudy, Peter de Roo's son, came in to see me this afternoon. He's not been to Willow Calm Lodge before, and probably won't come again. He does not cross the sea to England very often, he said, but tonight he is playing his saxophone at a reunion gig with some old friends. He looked very tired, worn out. We talked mostly about Guido, my son and his friend, although I was delighted to hear news of Rudy's own son, Arnout. He's now in his 40s, a successful music producer, and father to two young boys. In my memory, though, he is but a toddler, a scamp, racing around with Jay at Guido's wedding.

It would be a pleasure to tune in now to Rudy's Coltranesque playing (Rudy gave me the broadcast coordinates), but I must press on to write about Harriet, Harriet Tilson. A whole lifetime later, my feelings and thoughts about her remain confused. I loved her. I'm sure that is true, when all is said and done. And, there is no doubt about this in my mind, she had a profound influence on who and what I became, possibly the most profound of any person after my mother. She also caused me much suffering. I am, though, clear about the difference between the emotional anger, with its sharp and short-lived pains, I suffered when we were young, and the intellectual resentment I harboured towards her later because of the way our children turned out.

Harriet was partial to making new year's resolutions, and the eve of 2020 was no exception. As on many other such occasions, she decided she needed more exercise, and would take up a sport. She started in January with basketball, gave up in February, and, on the advice of someone in the basketball club, tried volleyball. The LSE volleyball club had a system for involving beginners at the start of the academic year, but for the rest of the time, any newcomers took pot luck. In early March, Harriet showed up to a mixed training session, dressed in tight shorts and a bikini top, as if ready for a session of beach volleyball, knowing no-one, knowing not a move or rule, and perfectly convinced she was in the right place at the right time. Had she been prettier, one of the club's Don Juan's would have volunteered quickly to give her some coaching. Yet, somehow, it was I, still taking things easy with my ankle, who ended up talking her through the basics, and giving her practice with a ball. We all used to meet up in the bar after training, and Harriet bought me a beer by way of thanks for my help. She plied me with questions about my course, and told me all about her media studies degree. It is my impression that Harriet short-listed me that evening. She was single at the time, and looking for a partner; and she found me. She was tall, clever, serious and, superficially, strong. I was tall, clever, serious and weak. I do not mean to imply she was consciously looking for these qualities in a boyfriend; nor would I be able to explain how she knew so quickly that I might be suitably subservient.

Harriet never came again to volleyball but we met for lunch in the canteen a few days later. She decided the time and the place. Oddly, I recall that she interrupted my order at the serving counter and changed it. When I hesitantly challenged her decision to deprive me of my favourite meal, she launched into a three or fivefold justification of her action (health would have been one, changing routines would have been another, letting go control might have been a third). It all made sense. She usually made sense, in the moment, or, if not, it was difficult to see a lack of sense when she delivered so many different ideas in fast succession. She had a certain gift of the gab (which may have come from her actress mother or from maternal Irish grandparents), which is not to deny that, when she tried, she could also argue very logically about issues of the day.

Having quizzed me over lunch, she then asked if I wished to accompany her to a ball. This involved hiring a formal dinner suit (with Harriet's help), parading, dining and dancing with Harriet at the event itself, and then engaging in drunken sex of some kind at her flat in the early hours of the morning. After that, she treated me like a long-standing boyfriend, and acted as though we were a fully-fledged couple. It was good, and I fell for her completely. The over-riding impression I have of those early times with Harriet is of her intense interest in me, who I was, my family, my background, my interests. I only had to hint at an important unresolved practical problem, and she wanted the full story, and was bubbling with ideas to help.

This brief affair, which lasted less than three months, served – I can observe in retrospect – as a dress rehearsal for how we were to be later, only the performances at this early stage were bland, unpronounced, amateur. I allowed her to dictate my social life (apart from club activities) because she was good at society and socialising in general, and I put up only gentle resistance to her attempts to control all the little aspects of our times alone. Sometimes, they were amusing, in which case I negotiated for the hell of it, or else they were irritating in which case I ignored them. When Harriet sulked for hours over a trifle, I never for a moment imagined her mood was real or profound. I could usually win back her good favour by making some compensatory compromises. When I couldn't, then I would find myself distracted all day thinking about her, and about what I could have done, or should have done to please her.

Later, I was able to look back and see a pattern and how Harriet might have unconsciously expected me to be more submissive than I was. That was one problem, which may have led to our early separation. And then there was sex, or not.

During those two months, Harriet and I slept together regularly, three times or more a week, mostly at her flat. Yet it was hit and miss whether we would make love. We never kissed or cuddled out of bed, and nor did I ever make a pass at her. She took a business-like attitude. I believe it was vital for her to be in a couple as a way of earning social position, and sex was part of the job description. I don't think she ever expected to get much pleasure, nor do I know whether she ever did. If, after a few minutes of basic foreplay in bed, I didn't get an erection, she turned over, without a murmur, and went to sleep. Her disinterest in my performance, proved a useful aphrodisiac. I discovered that with a few drinks, a pleasant evening behind us, and the television on, I could put in a passable performance. This did not mean the sex was passionate or erotic by prevailing standards, but at least we did fornicate from time to time – much to my mental relief. Emboldened by this step towards sexual normality, I once tried talking to her about my impotent tendencies (not about my voyeuristic ones). She tried to listen, I must accept that, but she found it too difficult. I think it truly distressed her to talk or think about sex, or anything too intimate. Although her behaviour in the bedroom was unaffected by the confession, my insecurities returned with a vengeance. When Harriet finished with me – by email – on the pretext that she had no more time for a relationship because her exams were approaching and she needed to study 'twenty four seven', I partly blamed myself for being tactless. The tears I cried a few days later in front of the Henry Peach Robinson photograph, *Fading Away*, may have been more in response to this email, than to Melissa's final passing away.

***

Harriet's defection, Melissa's death, and the never-to-be-answered questions about Dr Jessop all conspired to seriously undermine my psychological well-being, and consequently my work. When the end-of-year exam and project results were posted, my personal tutor called me in for a 'private chat'. I also talked at length to Julie, and exchanged several emails with both Flip and Alan, before deciding to take a year off. Tom helped too, by contacting Sterling at Euroil who agreed that, after my usual month of working in August, he might be able to employ me on a more permanent basis.

For a third summer, then, I found myself in Brussels. Sterling did not bother to dine me this time, and Hilde foisted another boring database task on me. I remained at the company flat for only two weeks, then moved myself into a furnished one-bedroom pad in Ixelles. I signed up for a crash course in French, which led to some pleasant evenings out with other students. In order to overcome the tedium of the long office hours, I read, discreetly, through the Euroil archives. I started with those available on the company's employee site, where I located a store of public and not-so public documents (some of them written in the time of Euroil's predecessor companies): annual reports, outdated merger and acquisition studies, new market analyses, declassified techno-commercial field statistics and so on. I flicked through the titles of scores of such documents, and occasionally skimmed the conclusions. I dawdled longer over the environmental studies, not the location specific ones but those which looked at pollution problems more generally. For me, the most interesting sections – perhaps because of the influence of Ingrid Kallström's talk – were those dealing with the lobbying of regulators, and the counter-actions aimed at defusing the successful impact of environmental lobbyists. There were hundreds of documents related to the global warming issue, and I found a few case studies clearly written by oilserfs ('oil-is-still-the-future enthusiasts' as they became known – *Encyclopaedia Universal* informs me – in consequence of some highly successful Greenpeace advertising in the US during the period of the Alaska demonstrations). Some of these concerned the introduction of laws in Europe on unleaded and sulphur fuels in the 1980s and 1990s, the costly fight against banning the gasoline car in California, and a revealing story on how to ensure financial efficiency for decommissioning operations in Nigeria.

Among multinationals, Euroil, which eventually rose to challenge the giants Exxon and Shell, boasted a relatively clean reputation. Nevertheless, I had half-hoped to uncover a scandal, a buried secret, a forgotten illegal activity. This youthful zeal had several drivers. Firstly, there were the talks I had attended as a member of LSE's Green Action group. Secondly, around this time, there was a highly successful television drama series, which ran for several years, called *Charm*, after the name of the fictional multinational Charm. Many of the story lines concerned environmental or safety issues. Although different parts of the company with different characters were involved in each new plot, invariably the bad Captain Jake was skulking in the background trying to save the company money, helping a local manager to sack an over-conscientious employee, or bribing an official to open up a new opportunity. And, in the foreground, good Adam White was doing his best to clean up the unexpected and messy consequences of Jake's actions. Thirdly, I shouldn't forget Alan's subtle but persistent influence. He was always ready to polish every phone or email discussion with a green shine.

Having tasted the official documents on the Euroil netsite, I recklessly snuck into Sterling's office one lunch-time when Hilde, for some reason, had left a set of keys dangling from the filing cabinet lock. I rifled through several files and found one, benignly titled 'Future NGO campaigns' (NGO being short for non-governmental organisation) but with 'Confidential' emblazoned across the front cover and every page. I pulled it out, closed and locked the cabinet, and made my way to the print room to make a copy. Before I could replace the report, Hilde came back early from lunch. I was obliged to return to my desk concealing the original file. I waited, in a state of heightened tension, for half an hour before she disappeared to the toilet. I raced into Sterling's office. Thankfully, the key was still in the filing cabinet lock. I replaced the document, hopefully in the right place, and was exiting the room when Hilde returned. I flustered, I floundered, and I made some excuse about looking for a pencil sharpener. I imagined her glancing over my shoulder and seeing the other keys on the ring still swinging.

That night, in the privacy of my rented pad, I keenly looked over the prize: a copy of an NGO9 'Confidential Memorandum of Understanding' listing future strategy aims and, what I thought were, secret policies. For example, I knew, from my previous experience with Euroil, that the influential European Environmental Bureau or EEB (an umbrella organisation representing a hundred or more smaller environmental NGOs with the aim of influencing European Union policy) had been pushing for an EU-wide fossil fuel tax of around 10% (i.e. in addition to national taxes). In the confidential paper, though, I read about a campaign to lobby for a 50% tax.

It had been reported, earlier that year, that the NGO9 (the nine most important environmental organisations worldwide, including WWF and EEB) were planning to concentrate their actions and avoid unnecessary overlaps, but, as far as I knew, no detailed policy objectives had emerged. Yet, according to my document, there did exist an extremely detailed plan of action. I reasoned that Euroil must have obtained the paper from a mole, and that he/she worked in the EEB since the document had a faint EEB watermark running along the bottom of each page. It did not take long for me to decide what to do. I placed the copy, with a short note, in an envelope labelled 'private' and 'urgent, to be opened only by Alan Hapgood', and then put that in another envelope addressed to Alan at the WWF offices in Kiev.

My efforts were inconsequential. When I met up with Alan, months later, he explained reluctantly that, although the document had apparently been partially restricted (hence the 'confidential' tag), it had been deliberately leaked – long before I saw it – to governments and to industry.

How did Sterling discover I had been a member of Green Action? After catching me looking guilty in Sterling's office, had Hilde taken the trouble to scrutinise the LSE club netsite and the members' lists? I never found out. The day he came back from vacation he called me into his office and told me I would not be needed beyond the end of the week. I asked him why, and he told me that company policy prohibited him from employing anyone who was an active member of a radical environmental lobby group (I'm sure he made this up for my benefit). I tried to explain that Green Action, despite its name, was no more than a student talking shop. He shook his sterling silver-top head, and looked down at his papers. As I walked passed Hilde's desk, I made some comment such as: 'I'll be more careful where I look for a pencil sharpener next time.'

I spent only three days unemployed in Brussels before Lionel Wilcox MEP, took me on as a personal assistant. My incredible good fortune happened in this way. I had already developed an interest in the European Parliament, partly from the Euroil project I had undertaken two summers previously, and partly from my general interest in politics. I went straight from Sterling's office to my desk and compiled a list of the few MEPs who had given presentations to one of the LSE clubs. I also emailed Flip, asking him, as a favour, to give me the names of any MEPs who had spoken to the Brideswell Society in the last five or ten years. Flip replied overnight with four names, Wilcox being one of them. On my first day of unemployment, I took the long way round to the European Parliament's palace of glass, so as to walk in the bright sunshine through Parc Leopold. From the reception area, I rang the office of each MEP on my list, making the most of whatever connection I had established, and asking for a moment of the MEP's time. It sounds naive, but I got three interviews in two days. Two MEPs were friendly and helpful, but said they had no position available. Firey gave me five minutes at the coffee bar. When he asked what I knew about internet regulation, expecting me to shake my head, I was able to say something reasonably intelligent thanks to the talks Pete and I had arranged for the Government Club. Firey made a point of noting my lack of languages, my (young) age, and my inexperience, but he did, though, take a telephone number. The next day he called and offered me a temporary research assistant job. His offer: 'Long hours, a minimum wage, and a boss who shouts, or so they say.' My response: 'Sounds great.' I learned later that he had emailed Flip for a reference.

Firey, as he was known to friends and the press because of his red hair and occasional loud outbursts in committee meetings, had been an MEP since 2004, the year the first batch of ex-communist countries joined the Union. A Liberal Democrat, representing the southwest of England, he worked energetically, unlike some in Brussels, and made his mark as the rapporteur on the original Euronet Regulation proposal. Apart from a limited number of positions (such as committee chairmen, party spokesman, institutional liaison etc.), the best an MEP could hope for then was to be appointed rapporteur on an important legislative proposal. A rapporteur was responsible for writing a set of draft amendments, guiding the negotiations in committee, and then taking the committee's agreed proposals to the full Parliament for a final vote. Thereafter, the rapporteur was also partly responsible for arguing the Parliament's position in the complex negotiations between the Parliament and, what was then known as, the Council of Ministers (the Parliament and the Council being the two institutions jointly responsible for deciding on EU laws).

In retrospect, the Euronet came to be seen as both ambitious and innovative, even though its initial incarnation was castrated at birth by insufficient funds and political will (despite the Parliament's best efforts, led by Firey). It is not my task here to give a history lesson, but, as I became deeply involved in this issue for some years, I need to shade in some background. By 2005 or so, many politicians and several left-wing governments had begun to look more carefully than before at certain aspects of the internet. Various influential academic studies had emerged in a flurry which appeared to point, if not conclusively then with very strong argument, at the internet as a serious threat to the fabric of western society. As many had suspected since the start of the internet (my mother for one), it was demonstrated, by these studies, how the internet allowed criminal activity to flourish. The internet was a lawless land where terrorists, of whatever kind, could meet and discuss plans, where racists could congregate and reinforce each other's ideas, and where a flourishing trade in the abuse of human beings could be promulgated under the guise of international au pair agencies and exotic marriage or adoption bureaus. What concerned most Europeans, though, was the free availability of pornography, and not only soft-core top shelf images, but pictures and films of every imaginable and unimaginable type of perversion.

In 2006, the EU convened, in Prague, a world net summit. Although it was never so clear at the time, general acceptance of the unpalatable truth that the internet itself could never be wholly regulated clearly dates back to that summit. Within a year, the European Commission had put forward a proposal for an alternative net, the Euronet, requiring every net service provider (NSP) to be authorised and legally responsible for every Euronet address accessible through it. Guidelines were also to be laid down for Unacceptable Content, and NSPs were to be obliged to offer the Euronet separately from the internet. The laudable objective was to create a safe and reliable net, and one grand enough and important enough so that companies and citizens alike would be able to subscribe to the Euronet alone. The European Parliament strongly supported this approach. Unfortunately, several EU countries, not least those who had recently joined which did good business from hosting NSPs, watered down the proposal. They cut back the funding incentives to a quarter of that proposed by the Commission; they diluted the guidelines on Unacceptable Content; and they removed any obligation on governments to ensure the success of the Euronet. The Euronet was launched in 2011. By the time I joined Firey's office only 7% of European citizens used it exclusively, and, on best estimates, only about 1% of total net activity by Europeans took place on the Euronet. For example, when I signed up with an NSP at my Ixelles flat I was offered the Euronet alone for 20 euros a month (a legal obligation), or the Euronet and the internet for the same price. Historically, though, as I said, the Euronet came to be seen as far ahead of its time, and, indeed, the main forerunner of the regulated three tier net that has now been in place for 70 years and which we all take for granted.

At the fourth world net summit, convened and dominated by the Union in 2018, a consensus emerged for stronger and more effective action. The European Commission again tried to lead the way by presenting ambitious proposals. Firey, by now a big fish in the Central Group (which held a majority in the European Parliament at the time), was the natural choice for rapporteur. I had been taken on, in addition to his normal staff of two, a part-time secretary Bronwen, and his main adviser Brian Veitch, to help with the donkey-work. I was given a week of light duties to allow me time to read up on background and essential documents, and thereafter, for the whole year, through to the following June, I learned the meaning of hard work. But it was an enthralling time.

Bronwen, with a Danish mother and an Irish father, and an exquisite sense of the comic, was a laugh a minute. She had excellent administration abilities, and kept us all in order. I learned much from watching her operate. Moreover, I should note, she scared Firey. The first time he shouted her down (this is before I arrived), she wasted no time in clearing her desk and marching out. A grovelling apology from Firey, an increased salary, and a promise of never-ending respect eventually attracted her back. Brian, by contrast, enjoyed Firey shouting at him. It gave him a position of superiority, and usually led to Firey accepting some fine point that Brian had otherwise failed to get across. As time went by, I began to appreciate how well Brian would choreograph these arguments, leading Firey into, what would usually transpire to be, the right position. There was, regrettably, one unwholesome side to Brian. While studying for a postgrad degree in European politics at Humboldt University in Berlin, he had developed an addiction to salami full of garlic. People who knew him always chose to sit at a healthy distance, and those who didn't would shift uncomfortably on their chairs if Brian leaned too close. Bronwen plied him with mints, but he binned them complaining of rotting teeth. He never had a woman friend – to my knowledge – in all the time I worked with him, although I heard, years later, that he married a Polish journalist, and became some sort of adviser to the Euronet Agency (long after my involvement with it had ceased).

The Commission's plan contained a plethora of legislative ideas. There were further attempts to provide extra control over the internet's activities, by tightening the legal base for legitimate services providers, and by strengthening possible sanctions against countries hosting renegade NSPs. In addition, there was a major revision on the guidelines for authorised addresses on the Euronet. The key issue, though, was finance. The Commission argued that the Union should levy a tax, through the NSPs, on every customer, and use the income to fund a Euronet Agency. To avoid citizens subscribing in their millions to non-Union based NSPs, the Commission proposed an equivalent tax, to be raised through the telecom operators, on all access calls to NSPs based outside the Union territory.

Not only were these proposals highly political but they were all very technical. Firey's team, including me, spent the whole of that autumn seeking advice. We talked to companies, industry organisations, national and Union-wide regulators, consumer organisations, technical consultants. Often my job was to provide a half-page summary of a meeting with the key relevant points, or else it was to brief Firey, if Brian was away, on what questions/arguments to put before a forthcoming visitor. They both came to respect my way of simplifying issues down to core principles and consequently sought out my views from time to time. More mundanely, I was responsible for researching any and every whim of Brian's, and, in liaison with Bronwen, for arranging meetings and coordinating agendas. By the end of November, Firey and Brian had decided to propose a radical reshaping of the Commission's proposal, to divide the one Euronet into three: a basic Euronet, a business-oriented Euronet, and an academic Euronet. They confidently asserted that, despite the Euronet's less than glorious past, public finance and political backing was now ready to fall into place. Armed with Brian's dazzling and detailed analysis (smoothly transformed into a bullet-point presentation by me), Firey spent several weeks persuading his Central Group colleagues to support such a big change to the Commission's proposal. By January 2021, we had finalised a draft report and amendments for Firey to present before the Parliament's Communications Committee. It took six further months of discussions before the full European Parliament formally agreed its amendments to the Commission's proposal. But, as I will recount, the dossier subsequently became stalled because the EU's member states could not agree a position among themselves, and it would be many years before the new Euronet became operational.

A week after the final Parliamentary debate and vote, I left Brussels to return to London for ten days before flying to Brazil. Firey, Brian and Bronwen all tried to persuade me to stay on which would have meant abandoning my degree. I like to think, though, that they cared for me and if I had suddenly decided to stay, they would have been united in pressing me to finish my degree. In any event, I was assured of a (minimum wage) position when my degree was complete, if I wished to return to Brussels. Leaving Firey and his crew was tough enough, but there were other reasons I would miss Brussels. I thrived in the political atmosphere of the European Parliament, it was so full of important people, pretty women, characters of every nationality; and barely a week went by without one issue or another making media headlines and creating highly-charged gossip in the corridors. I recall listening to President Andrew McFeather make an absurd plea to the European Parliament to tone down its criticism of human rights violations in the US, vis-à-vis the Mexican immigrants, as if his very presence would be enough to influence the position of MEPs. He didn't last much longer. There was the day the Parliament voted, by two votes, to reject Turkey's accession to the Union. The vote had been turned by a German documentary, released via the net the night before, showing beatings of Kurds in Turkish prisons. The ensuing riots in Turkey against the government – for failing to gain EU membership <u>not</u> for the prison revelations – resulted in over 200 deaths across the country. For several days, the corridors went noticeably quiet as MEPs contemplated the consequences of their actions.

But best of all, I was there in March 2021 when the great African leader, Ojoru, then only 25 but already deputy president of Nigeria, delivered his historic mantra. Advance copies of a fairly standard speech had been distributed to the MEPs and to the press agencies, and the great chamber was only half full when he started speaking for his allotted ten minutes.

'In Africa, we are the most impoverished peoples in the world, we are the most uneducated, we are the most diseased. Why? Why is this? Why is it like this now? Why has it been like this for so long? Why will it be like this in the future? Why are your peoples so much less impoverished, diseased and uneducated? In Africa, we are the most impoverished peoples in the world, we are the most uneducated, we are the most diseased. Why? Why is this? Why is it like this now? Why has it been like this for so long? Why will it be like this in the future? Why are your peoples so much less impoverished, diseased and uneducated? ...'

By the third time round, the chamber had filled up with astonished MEPs, officials, visitors and me. We listened in total silence as he repeated exactly the same set of sentences 21 times, and by the end he was crying. He bowed, sat down and wiped his eyes. The European Parliament president remained silent for what seemed an age, then thanked him, and resumed normal business. The mantra was repeated on every newscast and in every newspaper around the world for days, and African issues were catapulted, overnight, to the top of the agenda in every international organisation. Ojoru, as is well known, went on to work tirelessly for African unity. He transformed the African Union and almost single-handed made it into a forceful presence within the United Nations. Alfred knew him well, and introduced me to him once. But, much later, he lost faith in the man, and accused him of having a god complex.

***

There is more I could say about my year in Brussels, but I am moving on – to Brazil. I had had a dream about visiting the country since as long as I could remember, so, with both money and time at the end of my artificial gap year, there was no good reason not to see it through. I will admit now, although I resisted the suggestion at the time, that I was influenced by the Hollywood flick *Gabriella* which had been released a few months earlier. It was a great movie, and became a romantic classic. It also introduced me to the 20th century Brazilian writer, Jorge Amado, and I defy anyone to read Amado's books and not want to go to Brazil.

I took advice from a Brazilian I had met at the European Parliament staff volleyball club in Brussels not to miss out on Recife. Alan insisted I visit an ex-girlfriend of his in Rio. Otherwise, I planned to visit Salvador, Ouro Preto and the Iguaçu Falls. I bought a detailed guide book for 40 euros, and an Earthmate V for 900 euros. (Incidentally, the Earthmate V was a beautiful machine, the first sub-1,000 euro machine of its type weighing in at only 500 grams which combined sophisticated computer, phone and net facilities, with a cam and Galileo services. The batteries could last for up to 20 hours and were easily rechargeable with solar power or, less easily, with body heat.)

As so often in life, the higher the expectations, the deeper the disillusionment. Bleary-eyed and jet-lagged I wondered aimlessly around Recife in a heat and humidity new to my experience. An intense disappointment filled me to the point of depression. Recife was no more than a big ugly city, dominated by concrete skyscrapers. Here was infinitely more squalor than beauty. I only had to walk a few metres from the tourist centres to be lost in a favela and be accosted by beggars or ragged urchins – the like of which I had not seen even in Bangkok – and to find alleys of pure garbage. And the only beauty I could see was of two kinds: the beaches, and a few tourist sites with preserved colonial – i.e. European-built – buildings.

Chiselled into a wooden plaque, hung on the wall above the reception desk in my pousada, was the well-known epigram: 'Brazil: the country of the future, and always will be.' In truth, the country had been making steady progress for nearly 20 years; and within another 30, by mid-century, it was to find itself a key member of the non-aligned group of 4/8.

Day two was no better. I received a message that my grandmother, Eileen, had died. This sad fact led me into several email dialogues with Julie and Alan.

But then, while resting my weary feet and drinking a cafezinho or three, my Earthmate, which I had naively placed on the table for a second, was snatched, in front of my very eyes, by a boy no older than nine. I raced after him instinctively, but he ducked and dived through the alleyways and I lost him within seconds. On my return, the barman shrugged his shoulders. I made my way to a telecoms office so I could phone Alan. I had to queue for access to a phone. As I began to wait, I thought if Alan or my mother wanted me to come home, I'd catch the next flight. But, after a few minutes, and by the time the phone was free, I realised I was actually terrified of being asked to return and attend the funeral.

On the third day, a breeze blew in from the Atlantic and brought a light shower. It refreshed my mood. I made my way to Olinda, and found the romantic images I must have been expecting: the baroque churches, exquisitely beautiful, the picturesque colonial houses (I rapidly let go of my prejudice against colonial architecture), and the sun-washed plazas with distant views of the sea. The following day I took a bus to Salvador. The journey lasted most of the day, but could have gone on forever for all I was concerned. I was sat next to the most beautiful girl I had ever seen. She was, she is, my Gabriella. I have her photo before me now on the screen, as she was then, 16 years old. Later, in London, I had an enlarged print of this photograph framed and it hung wherever I lived until Harriet gave it to a jumble sale. (I confess, here and now, that I confused the images of Gabriella and Conceição, who I shall come to, both in my conscious memory, and in my storytelling to friends.) Gabriella is standing at a petrol station, although there is no petrol pump or lorry cab visible because, subsequently, I airbrushed them out. She is wearing a loose, white tank top, barely covering her sharp full breasts with nipples erect behind the thin fabric, tight white jeans, with a lime-green belt and silver buckle. She is looking directly at the camera, brimming with innocence and temptation, her long jet black hair in front and behind her shoulders, but half covering the left side of her youthful, sultry, beautiful face. We talked in fragments of English and phrasebook Portuguese for the first stage of the journey, enough for me to be so bold as to ask to take her photograph at a service station stop. Back on the bus, we swapped places so she could sit by the window. The seats were comfortable and she soon dozed off, her body slightly twisted towards the window, and her head leaning against an air cushion she had brought. I did not fall asleep, or look out of the window across her. Instead I stared at her, which I could do without fear of embarrassment, at her face, but mostly at her tank top and the breasts behind them. As the journey progressed so one side of her top was pulled sideways incrementally, exposing millimetre by millimetre more of the flesh to the point of my being able to see, for the best part of an hour, her left nipple. This was sexual ecstasy without a climax.

I only mention Gabriella – rather than using these paragraphs to give some history of Brazil (with talk of Vargas, Tancredo or the future leader Neco the Prosperous) or to discuss deforestation and the plight of the Yanomami – because I was primed, as it were, as a result of that coach journey, to fall into the arms of Conceição. She was lounging with a group of boys in a bar round the corner from the cobbled Praça Pelourinho, in the centre of Salvador, where I had stopped for a beer before pressing on to try one of the cheap pousadas mentioned in the guide book. The group appeared lively, and I saw no reason to rebuff the friendly questions put to me in pigeon English. After a while, Conceição, who was very slim and dark and wore sunglasses, promised to find me a cheap place to lodge. I went with her, somewhat warily, to a pousada which proved both cheap and pleasant. When later she offered to show me around, I accepted. After eating and drinking too much, I allowed her to come back with me to the pousada and try – without success – to use her experienced hands in relieving me of my lust for Gabriella. I expected to pay her in the morning, but all she asked was to stay with me, to be my guide and interpreter.

To cut the story short, Conceição attached herself to me for a total of five days. She proved to be both fun and sexy, which, I suppose, is I why I didn't try harder to detach myself, though she proved a useless guide, and a drain on my resources. She giggled a lot, and she had this cute habit of giving me a childish wave whenever she left my side, even if it was only to go to the bathroom.

There is much in Salvador to detain the tourist, but I only wish to mention the sculptor Hector Julio Paride Bernabo (or Caybe as he was known) and his wood-carved panels in the city museum. Each one, inlaid with imaginative patterns of other woods, metals and ceramics, depicted an animal and some aspect of the macumba. Some six decades later, I was to see them again, in the national museum of modern art in São Paulo.

From Salvador, we bused to Ouro Preto, the fabulous town built on the back of the gold rush in the 18th century; and reconstituted in the 20th century with tourist gold. I like to believe Arturo was conceived when Conceição and I had sex on the squeaky iron bedstead in the traditional pousada near the Mine Engineering Museum. There was a spectacular sunset with the last of the sun's rays streaming through our window onto the bed. Conceição had succeeded in giving me a full erection which she then put to its proper use. I must have been overwhelmed with passion or gratitude or stupidity, for I neither worried about AIDS, nor about her getting pregnant. We were to copulate only one other time, but it was in a dirty hotel, which rented most of its rooms by the hour. Once in Rio, I decided it was time to separate. I contemplated ditching her furtively, but was too timid for such deception. Instead, I made up a weak story about wanting to spend time alone, and gave her more than enough money to return to Salvador. And, because she said she wanted to write me letters, I gave her my mother's address. I didn't have the gall to invent one on the spot. At the bus station, she waved goodbye, in her silly childish way, as if I would be seeing her again in five minutes.

Thanks largely to Monique, an ex-girlfriend of Alan's, I spent two glorious weeks in Rio de Janeiro. Originally from Tunisia, she had lived much of her life in France before working for WWF in East Europe. For several years she was in a couple with Alan, but then she moved to Rio to campaign on rainforest issues. She insisted I use the spare room in her tiny Ipanema apartment, and she introduced me to some of her younger friends. I played volley on the Leblon beaches, climbed Corcovado, danced samba at gafieras, bought trinkets at various markets, got drunk on caiparinhas, and engorged myself at churrascarias. Several times, I scurried off late at night to the Copacabana clubs, unsure whether I felt more guilty for enjoying the sex shows, or for having employed the services of a prostitute for a week. (I should note that, through a Brazilian friend, I came to understand later, long before Arturo appeared, that by British standards Conceição was less a prostitute and more a sort of good-time girl. That said, though, this epithet is also deficient because it does not allow for the small payments I made nor her temporary loyalty.)

Two blocks from Monique's apartment I chanced on an exhibition of Marc Ferrez's panoramic photographs from the late 19th century and early 20th century. At the turn of the century, when Rio was already a sprawling city, the old photographs showed Copacabana as a wild natural beach with only a couple of buildings set back from the sand dunes. Furthermore, although a cable car could take you to the top of the Sugar Loaf, there was no Urca suburb as now exists clinging all around the base of the Sugar Loaf and Urca hills, since the rock face plunged straight into the sea in those days. I purchased two large books with beautiful reproductions of Ferrez photographs. Somewhere along the way of my life, I lost them, but not before all the photographs had been scanned into Neil.

Monique also took me to stay for a weekend with charmingly bohemian friends in Parati (another colonial delight similar to Ouro Preto and Olinda, impressively preserved in Brazil's darker years with United Nations money) where I was spoilt with Brazilian delicacies, where everyone spoke English after dinner so I could take part in the conversation, and where I went scuba diving in waters as clear as glass. I experienced an unforgettable night at Maracana when Argentina beat Brazil in a world cup qualifier. I queued, jostled and pushed for four hours to buy a ticket (with the help and companionship of the porter at Monique's apartment building – if I'd been alone I would never have persevered). Over 100,000 fanatics squeezed into that stadium, and I saw it as a miracle of modern society that war did not erupt then and there around me, such were the passions of every individual, and the tensions and releases of tensions in the stadium as a whole. With heated arguments, fights and scuffles, and everyone moving aggressively through the crowds to get away, it was another miracle we escaped uninjured. And, before I flew home from São Paulo (an infinity of skyscrapers, a monstrous place then, and no less so when I went for the last time in 81), I visited Iguaçu, which involved long boring bus rides (no Gabriella diverting my attention, no Conceição making me laugh).

***

On my return, after family visits, I went to see Pete Sampson. Excitedly, he said he had signed up with Wilma Johnson at the LSE history department to do a PhD. Johnson was to become one of the department's most famous professors, not only through her warm media-friendly personality but because government after government called on her advice. She developed, according to Pete, a fresh approach to the analysis of modern history by following the geographical and chronological routes of religions and sub-religions and sidelining the role of nations. Pete, who painstakingly taught himself to read Russian, found her methods suited the study of Central Asia during the communist period, about which very little detailed history existed in English. He travelled extensively in the region during the five years of his PhD – part-funded it must be admitted by his family – and became something of an authority on the subject. His decision to remain at LSE was very good news for me, not least because he had stayed put in our old Bermondsey home, and was ready to take me back as flat-mate. Not long after I had reinstalled myself, Peter de Roo moved out to cohabit with Livia, a Cornish girlfriend, and we replaced him with someone whose name I cannot recall. I know we charged him a high rent so as to reduce our own. He was annoyingly good at word games, I seem to remember, so that Pete and I would conspire to beat him at speed scrabble, which we played very occasionally.

Although I had looked forward with anticipation to my final year at LSE, in reality I found it a frustrating and unsatisfying period. Student life felt stodgy and constrained as opposed to spontaneous and liberating; and there was a tired second-hand sheen dulling everything I did. Attending lectures, studying student texts, and writing essays were all tediously irrelevant compared to the work in Brussels. History itself, a subject once so enthralling to a teenager, thanks wholly to Flip, had become no more than a supporting act to the main show which I now considered to be international affairs, government and politics. I was granted leave to focus my degree dissertation on the origins of the European Union in reference to the history of inter-regional organisations, and this gave me considerable intellectual pleasure (not to mention an excuse for two week-long research trips to Brussels during which I was able meet up with Brian, Bronwen and others).

Pete Sampson had maintained firm control of the Government Club while I was away, and fully expected me to continue running it with him on my return. I did, but with far less youthful enthusiasm than in earlier years. There were, though, several younger members of the committee who more than made up for my absences. One of these was Tommy, a short tidy man of Indian heritage, who later worked for me at the IFSD. He was one of the most loyal, hard-working and enlightened individuals I ever knew. He fought ferociously, for example, throughout his life against religious or national prejudice in the Indian subcontinent. I recall him being drunk one night in The Madonna, after his first public contribution for the club, and telling me how he had been called TomTom at school, and how he used to stand around in the playground patting his head repeatedly.

My Brussels contacts proved a helpful network through which to find and attract high-class speakers, who served to pull in large audiences and new members with minimal effort. One evening we took over the wallscreen room to watch the launch hour of William Caxton's new free broadcast station, *The People's Channel*. Most commentators gave it no chance against the main channels (including the *BBC*, *Sky* and *Four* if I recall correctly) and the galaxy of other odd free channels that came and went as regularly as the seasons. We felt no need to take it seriously. In the debate that followed, for example, two political students parodied, with scintillating wit, the case for complete liberalisation of television advertising, especially to children.

There was one speaker we did not have to find – Triti Madan. She stands out for me, even more than Ingrid Kallström, as the most impressive thinker the Government Club presented in my time. In a short, friendly letter (addressed only to the 'President of the Schapiro Government Club, LSE, London'), she explained that she was the professor of international politics at the University of Mumbai, that she was coming to England to visit her daughter's family for Christmas, and that, because she had been a student at LSE and very much enjoyed the Schapiro Club, she would be pleased to give a half hour talk on her recent ('slightly controversial') work which had been published in major academic journals. We exchanged a few emails, to set a date and time. She attracted a huge audience thanks to Tommy, who made a special effort to promote the event. Our advertised offer of free mulled wine after the discussion might have helped too.

Madan, who must have been consciously and/or unconsciously inspired by the reports of Ojoru's mantra nine months earlier, quantified the extent to which civil unrest was growing and continued to grow, barely noticed by the

West unless Western civilians were caught up in an incident. Although governments worldwide and international bodies continued to blame religious fundamentalists, this was no longer a credible position. From one side – 'internal disorder' she called it – poor citizens were being inundated with western values, through multinational advertising, films on streetscreens and product placements on popular international radio broadcasts, and yet were utterly unable to realise any of the dreams being sold to them. From the other side – 'external disorder' – climate change had clearly begun to unsettle and disrupt both urban and rural populations in all kinds of ways (floods, hurricanes, earthquakes) thereby critically exacerbating the problems of governance in many countries with unstable politics.

None of this was new thinking, yet the traditional Hindu dress combined with the middle-aged motherly features and a crisply pronounced near-perfect English, gave her message such poignancy that we were transfixed in listening. But then she moved on to speak eloquently and forcefully on the need, not to double the flow of funds from the developed to the undeveloped world, but to increase it fivefold: at least to 2.5%, the level of Islam's Zakat. She suggested it was already 'very, very late' to consider a proper and adequate redistribution of wealth around the world, in parallel to the way that wealth is redistributed within a nation through taxation and government spending. The tides of resentment in the affairs of man, she said, are underestimated time and time again, and they are at times so huge that no dam, no army can ever stop them. Governments, peace organisations, individuals all stand for years and decades like King Canute trying to resolve the wrongs and resentments built up un-recognised for decades, or even centuries beforehand: witness Northern Ireland, witness Palestine, witness Kashmir. The same effect is happening in a global, less precise way, and only a substantial sharing of wealth will stem the rising tide of hostility felt by the poor of this world against the rich. Why not, she concluded, consider how much money you – the West – spend on beauty products, on pet food, or, apparently less decadently, on incremental medical research. So much of your medical research is taken for granted, unquestioned, yet what does it achieve? According to my detailed research, the average annual medical research budget of the United States improves overall life expectancy of an American citizen by five days. The same amount used effectively for health training or education or hospital infrastructure in India could increase life expectancy by five months. Ignore this reality, she said, and I predict 'endemic social terrorism'.

I had never heard the phrase before, and nor had any of my colleagues, but we would certainly hear it again.

***

Harriet came back into my life during the autumn. We had eaten lunch together once in Brussels, when she was visiting for some vague purpose, possibly to see me. On her initiative, we had had a long camphone conversation during the summer, swapping anecdotes about our lives. I welcomed both these encounters at the time, but afterwards I found myself thinking about her for days, and missing her high-octane companionship. She had messed up her finals, blighted by nerves or a personal problem she never revealed to me, and only scraped through with a mediocre degree. Nevertheless, she had a job in the print media, sub-editing for one of the Sundays. She liked the people and the kudos of working on a national paper, but the work itself bored her. Despite her best efforts, she had been unable to make the switch to a reporting position.

One Friday morning, while drinking a luke warm tea in the canteen, I received a message with the title 're: End of the affair'. She was asking me to meet her later that day at the 'usual place' and promising to pay. The 'usual place' was a guzzleshop called Mintoffs where we had snacked frequently during our short time together. Suggesting that she would pay was a joke since it was the cheapest halfway decent place to eat outside of the college. The message disturbed me, confused me, excited me. Why had she called it 're: End of the affair'? Was it a mistake, a joke, or a discussion topic? Harriet did not make many practical mistakes; nor did she joke very easily. The latter possibility seemed the most plausible. And was it our affair she wanted to discuss, or another affair, in politics, show business, film fiction, there were plenty around? Mintoffs was heaving, and sweaty. Some of its customers had got caught in a heavy downpour. Harriet was at a tiny table squeezed up against the mustard-painted wall, shifting a shoulder as she tried to avoid dribbles of condensation. She looked downcast, with wet unkempt hair, darker and less curly than when dry. I stopped for a moment, before approaching, and wondered if I was making a mistake.

Harriet did not beat around the proverbial bush. This is one of the many things I admired about her – her directness. Yet, in time, I came to realise it stemmed more from a lack of confidence than strength. Although happy to talk on a practical level about people's problems, she did not appreciate her daily life being disturbed by personal or intimate matters, such as difficulties in her relationship, or illness, or, as I was to discover, the complications of children. And so, when such a difficulty finally welled up to a point of needing resolution, she tried to get over it as quickly as possible.

With a vulnerable sheepish look, and while brushing her wet hair to one side with the back of a hand, she confessed that she had made a mistake. She realised, she said very plainly, that she loved me and wanted us to give our relationship another chance. Without waiting for any reaction from me, she went on to ask forthrightly if I still loved her too. I could smell bacon butties, which reminded me that we had yet to order. Did I love her? It was not a question I could answer spontaneously, honestly, passionately, in the way I might have been able to to Melissa, or dishonestly but lustfully to Gabriella had she asked. But, I don't believe she was asking me that. Later, after a little soul-searching, I understood better. In that moment, I think I knew instinctively that she was asking me if I loved her in the way she loved me.

'Yes, Harriet, I do love you.' What I meant by this was that I needed her, wanted her to be a part of my life, and that my life was incomplete without her. Romance and sex did not enter into the calculation of her question or my answer. Harriet required nothing further, all the rest was taken for granted. Instantly, we were an item again. That night we went to the cinema in Kilburn, and I stayed at her newly acquired mansion-block flat in West Hampstead. Once in bed, Harriet turned out the light and we kissed for the first time in nearly 18 months. Desperately not wanting to disappoint her, or myself, I directed my imagination to the picture of Gabriella in my head.

But I did. When she rolled off to the side, I thought she would fall asleep in minutes. Instead, she leaned across to switch the side light on, and then got up, naked, and walked around the room as if looking for something. I lay on my back and watched her. I watched her stretch to peer above the wardrobe, I watched her from behind as she bent over to look under the wardrobe, and I watched her stand in front of me not noticing that I was eyeing her up and down and smiling. Customarily, she wore a gown after the bathroom and so I had never seen her standing, let alone walking, naked before. She may not have been pretty but there was something very handsome about her face, and she kept her body fit and trim. Under the bedclothes, I was visited by a longed-for erection. Eventually, she pulled out, from one plastic bag underneath another one in the corner, a lacy bra. I could see her hands tremble as she tried to fix the clasp behind, and her body was all tense. She was nervous.

'What do you think?' she asked.

'I liked it,' I said, in the past tense, meaning the display, not the brassiere.

In the morning we breakfasted as though there had been no break in our affair at all. I was reinstated into Harriet's social life immediately. This had evolved since her student days, in terms of the quality of her dinner party invitees, food and conversation and with respect to her interests: she was on an opera kick that autumn, and had joined a swimming-for-fun club. Mostly, when together, we ate out or went to the cinema, and then spent the second half of the evening arguing about the acting/plot or menu/decor. In this way, we were great mates, inciting each other to increasingly irrational arguments. The only difference was that when we were with friends she behaved the same, and I closed up, preferring to listen rather than speak. We never had a problem with money, which – to hear the tales of friends – was a boon. She paid more than her fair share. This was practical since she had an income and I had debts. To show my appreciation of her generosity, I would buy her cheap but colourful flowers.

We never talked about intimate matters or feelings, so I never knew why she had left me, nor whether she had been in any other relationships. But we did confide in each other about our work and our hopes, and once or twice strayed close to language that implied a long-term future for us as a couple. There was also an unspoken assumption, especially in the way Harriet referred to 'us' in conversation with others, that we would live together one day soon, when I was no longer a student.

I should add that there had been no change in Harriet's bossiness. We settled further into a pattern, whereby I let her dictate our private life almost entirely. I told myself it did not matter, and that my partner's behaviour stemmed from an over-zealous care for me. I did, though, dislike it intensely if she treated me the same way in public, with friends or strangers in hearing distance. When this happened too obviously, I held my peace until we returned home, and then I let loose, raising my voice and letting out a torrent of abuse, half-consciously imitating Tom. On the whole, Harriet tended to ignore these outbursts, so I would leave and take the convoluted tube ride back to Bermondsey. Then I wouldn't answer her calls. Much as I tried to shut her out of my mind and concentrate on studying, I usually cracked within a few days. A long camphone conversation would ensue and we would be back to normal. I rarely lost my temper so crudely later in life with Diana or with Lizette, so, either I was provoked to greater extremes of anger by Harriet, or else I learned from her that such behaviour was counter-productive.

Whereas our first affair had lasted two months, this one survived for six. The morning after my post-finals celebration party, Harriet told me bluntly, as usual, that she had accepted a public relations position in Dublin. Dublin! She had decided weeks earlier but thought it best not to tell me for fear the news might affect my concentration in the run-up to the exams.

'And what about us?' was my inadequate response. I can remember the gist of the conversation, which did not last very long. We were sitting at the fold-down table in her narrow kitchen with toast and marmalade, and an over-sized plum-coloured teapot covered in blotchy scarlet elephants chasing each other round the curve.

'You'll get a job in Dublin, a good job. It'll only be for a couple of years. It's a great place. We'll buy a car and drive over to the west coast. I've got relations in Galway. We can rent a flat, and have friends come to visit. It'll be fun, exciting.'

'And my second interview?' I said calmly. Harriet had ignored this hurdle in her plans. I had been invited back for a second interview at Yorkshire House, where the government's Department of Communications was based. Having passed an exam, and been for a day interview conference, I was up for a junior grade post. Ironically, Harriet had encouraged me every step of the way, especially when I had expressed an instinctive reluctance to become a civil servant; I doubt whether I would have applied for the job without her encouragement.

'You never wanted the job in the first place. It's beneath you. Why jump at the first opportunity. You can't know what else might come along. A consultant will snap you up in Dublin for twice a civil servant's salary. Anyway, London's doing our heads in.' More often than not I treated these spontaneously-arrived assumptions – that my likes and dislikes, for example, matched her own – as amusing. A few times, though, they irritated me intensely.

'No. I'm not going anywhere.' I remained calm. I believed Harriet was joking or testing me in some way.

'You must, Kippy, you must come, or we'll have to end it.' That hit me in the face. She got up from her chair and started clearing away the table.

'I haven't finished.'

'You have.'

'I haven't. And I'm not going to Dublin. I want this job. You know I do. Why can't you try and get a similar job here?' I was trying to be reasonable.

'I'm going Kippy, and that's an end to it.' There was a firmness, and a finality about the way she spoke, that implied argument or further discussion would be redundant. Anger fired up inside me, and I wanted to shout, but words would not come. This was suddenly too serious. Instead I spoke with quiet bitterness.

'An end – to us, I agree. I am grateful that you had the decency to tell me to my face this time. Good-bye.'

I did a boisterous turn around the flat, collecting various possessions, mostly clothes, a few books, banging everywhere I went. I half hoped she would call me back into the kitchen and say 'let's talk about it', or 'we can work something out'. But she didn't. This time round, although I was personally stronger (and older), I was more severely wounded than before, suffering as I did from both the emptiness of losing her, and the bitterness of having been rejected.

To conclude this chapter of my life on a more positive note, I gained a good degree, three-five marks short of the best grade. I was offered, and accepted, a civil service post in the Department of Communications. I spent three sunny weeks in the Balearics, taking part in two beach volleyball tournaments, one with Alfred during his last European holiday before he returned to Lagos, and one with Peter. If Harriet visited my thoughts at night, during those weeks, they didn't disturb my sleep, nor my wild dreams in which the semi-fictional Gabriella was often the heroine.

EXTRACTS FROM CORRESPONDENCE

Melissa to Kip Fenn

May 2017

Mum and Rob away all w/e.

Tonight's Programme: Bill+Ben's 7pm; Rock 9pm; My Striptease Palace midnight or soon after!

Loving.

June 2017

Me/Gemma organising picnic after match. Stuck with Rob and friend, though, so they'll have to come. Bore.

Don't worry, we'll ditch them later. xxx

Alan Hapgood to Kip Fenn

August 2018

Thanks so much for your kind note. It was our pleasure, truly. You may have 'felt' awkward but you 'handled' the food as if a born Arab. Tamara was quite taken with you (as I am with her). After you'd left us at the hotel, she wanted to know why I couldn't find you a job at WWF. She thinks the oilserfs might get you for good!

Despite my fears, the meetings turned out to be more positive than I expected. Decision-makers will listen if you argue firmly and consistently, and back up your case with facts. After a stop in Copenhagen, we're back in Kiev now. There is so much work to be done, not only to convince the government to agree to our project, but to find and train technicians.

Keep in touch.

November 2018

Thanks so much for your note. I'm glad I was able to help. So, Ingrid gave a good show. I don't doubt it. Was any student bold enough to ask if being female and pretty helped open doors in the corridors of power? She has a stock answer: 'Doors open in different ways but it's what you do and say when you get in the room that matters.' Believe it or not she works so hard she doesn't have time for a private life. I took her out for dinner once – we're talking 12 years ago now when we were both working in Budapest and the flood problems were so severe – but she told me over the soup she didn't have time for boys. From all I hear, nothing has changed since. What a waste. And how's your love life these days?

Keep in touch.

September 2020

Remarkable document. Thanks. I'm not sure I should approve. For goodness sake don't get into any trouble.

Keep in touch.

December 2020

Many many happy returns for your 21st. I'm sorry I can't be there to celebrate with you, but we have composed (Tamara mostly) and acted (!) a modest ditty for you, as you'll see on the camclip. That's Zaborovsky Gate in the background in case you were wondering. Tamara says you must come to visit us. And – it goes without saying – I agree with everything she says.

And all the best for the new year (it sounds interesting and fun working with Wilcox – tell me more when you have time).

Keep in touch.

PS: Good news about your mother getting the headship, it's no more than she deserves.

January 2022

Thanks so much for your note. I do know Triti Madan. She has quite a reputation among the NGOs, it's only a shame Western governments don't take her ideas more seriously.

Have you read any books by the political scientist Chaminda Dharmasena. He's a professor at Colombo University, and is most famous for his studies on government responses to terrorism. Although he works in a very different arena from Madan, their general conclusions often echo each other. For example, Dharmasena argues, using costs and benefits calculated with his own much-lauded methodologies, that the largely military/security response by the US and its allies to 11 September was an international catastrophe, politically and economically, and that they only paid to store up trouble.

Keep in touch.

Harriet Tilson to Kip Fenn

May 2020, End of the affair

Kippy Darling, delete this as soon as you've read it, won't you. I don't want to hurt you, I love you so. But I have to stop seeing you. Exams in a few weeks. I need to be without distraction, focused twenty four seven. I've been keeping you from your work too. There are so many things we don't have in common (and some we do). It's all for the best. (Your mother never liked the sound of me anyway – or so you said.) The very best.

Maybe we can have lunch soon. Be good.

December 2020, Birthday

Kip Darling, where are you for your birthday? Are you in town? Shall I see you for martinis or zinis? You must celebrate 21, you must. You looked so well in Bruxelles mon cher. Call me, next time. OK. No excuses.

Happy Birthday. Have a great day. Bye for now.

October 2021, re: End of the affair

Kippy Darling, shall we meet for lunch, my treat. Usual place 12:30.

Don't be late.

Tom Fenn to Kip Fenn

December 2020

Son, it's a pity we can't get together this holiday/your birthday. It's been a difficult year for you and me in different ways. But, heh, things are on the up and up. At least you're not grounded with a mushy ankle like last year, and, you sound full of beans at work, with this Firey character. (Sterling's a prat, I agree. And no, I never did get any feedback about your leaving/dismissal – why should I have?).

I've a month in Indonesia during the spring (politics willing) (coincidentally finishing at the same time as the Bali Grand Prix), and a new girlfriend (Griselda – horrible name, lovely girl, tell you about her next time).

Lots of love, and love to your mother.

Horace Merriweather to Kip Fenn

December 2020

Sorry young chap, got there before you. I can report, confidently, there's no difference this side of 21 – all that key to the door stuff, reckon we get it when we're 14 these days. I'm madly jealous to hear you're working in the European

Parliament – some of us are still slogging our guts out at uni. One more year to go. Cambridge has a lot to answer for – it's very 20th century. Desperate to be out there, making waves. I've promised myself to get elected an MP by 25. Tindle's said he might take me on as a researcher in the Commons. And a while ago, I met Spoon, one of the most promising young Conservative Members of Parliament. We hit it off straightaway. He was a Witley Academic boy too, but left the year before we started. It wouldn't surprise me to see him brought into the government when Owen Perry shuffles in early spring. Must dash, Mother has recklessly promised me 100 euros if I can beat her at golf – weather permitting.

So, many happy returns Kip for the day.

Peter de Roo to Kip Fenn

December 2020

Kip. What no party? Pete says you're becoming too serious. All tangled up in the net. Ha Ha. He should be taking you clubbing. Have a beer for me, have five. And get laid, you wanker. Happy Birthday.

Chapter Three

Harriet, Caxton and the Net

'Integrity, loyalty and fairness, these are the qualities I have tried to bring to my personal and public life.'

'Unhindered access to information is essential to freedom, equality, and justice for all. Unhindered access to information for all is the key to a peaceful, democratic and progressive world.'

'Those who wish to control the flow of information, are those who wish to control our lives.'

A Man of the People by William Caxton (2029)

In general, I see visitors between 6 and 7pm in the evening or on Saturday afternoons, and, I prefer to see one person at a time. I set the pattern soon after settling into this sunset hospice, this halfway house – halfway between life and death. Jay comes most often, partly because I encourage his visits (talking with him tires me less than with anyone else), and, I hope, because he likes my company. Also, in the last few months, since his partner Vince Wells ran off with a holiday tour manager, he has been lonely. Most days I talk for a few minutes to Flora Pattison. She is roomed along the corridor, but, unlike me, can manage short spells in an Easy. I never bothered much with Easys, having moved straight from my last accident in a Swifty to this bed. Flora hums in, natters about the nurses and/or her pill menu and symptoms, and then hums out. She's so high-spirited, though, and so undemanding I don't wish to ask her to leave me out of her daily carrousel. She's scheduled her death on the same day as me, 31 January 2100, so I feel bonded to her in an odd kind of way.

And then there's Chintz. Ever since she asked about the Ferrez photo, she's taken to visiting me at the end of her shift. She stays until I say 'I'm tired now', and then kisses me on the forehead and leaves in an instant. I can talk to her, as I talk to Jay, about this book. They both help me put my thoughts in order; also, I can tell by their attention to my anecdotes how interesting they might be to someone other than me. Jay appreciates the family stories, the personal stuff; Chintz wants to know about famous people and exotic places. She's learned a thing or two about William Caxton, 'The man of the people', in the last few days. I seem to have been prevaricating, picking out the best bits with which to impress her, rather than making the effort to reflect on seriously, and write about faithfully, this bleak period of my life. Nevertheless, it's good to know a girl's smile can warm my heart – even at 99.

Because they made an effort to do so, many remember where they were or what they were doing when they heard about Caxton's assassination. It was the kind of fashionable fluff talk you could hear at young people's fiestas throughout the 100 year golden era of oil and chips. (Tom, my father, who was 18 months old at the time, claimed he could remember his mother Evvie shouting 'Oh my god' when seeing John F Kennedy shot on television. Although, under cross-examination, he would eventually admit he might have been told this later. About John Lennon's assassination, my uncle Alan always remembered his English teacher at primary school insisting on a minute's silence, and giving a lesson about the Beatles' lyrics. Peter de Roo, who had a teenage crush on Vi Hoop, was painting the family barge when the pop music on his personal player was interrupted with news of the singer's assassination.)

I remember where I was when Caxton was murdered (although I'm jumping a decade or so ahead here) for two reasons: because of the joy I experienced as I watched the giantscreen replay the moment over and over again; and because Diana demanded I tell her the full story. It was the first time I had told anyone other than Harriet. Part of it was in the public domain, but not my story, not my version. Perhaps his death had suddenly released me, or, perhaps I wished to impress Diana with uncharacteristic openness.

Diana and I had met only two weeks previously at one of Peter's festive gatherings, but this particular evening we were at Keizerskroon, a tulip palace restaurant, in the Dutch town of Zaandam. Diana looked radiant. She wore a long purple cotton dress, giving her a dash of added height (she was only a few centimetres shorter than I), and a dark red velvet bonnet slanted across her forehead half hiding a round, cherub-like face. I have a kitsch photo of us. Here it is now, exactly as it was then, on a large wallscreen. A roving photographer had ushered us over to a banked display of tulips in flower, a veritable rainbow of colours, and snapped us a few times looking self-conscious and stiff. He said something I didn't understand fully, but Diana translated, over-emphasising the last but one word: 'Put your arm around the lovely lady.' So I did. Diana bent her fleshy body sideways into mine (I remember the sensation vividly, for it was the moment I realised she – to use an old-fashioned word – fancied me), and the photographer said 'bravo'. Minutes later, the picture appeared on the wallscreen. There was a ripple of applause, one of many that night (and every other night), and I paid a small fortune for two large prints and for a copy to be sent me by email.

William Caxton, or WC as the British satirical magazine Private Eye dubbed him for many years, died instantly on Saturday 14 May 2033 at 5:13pm in

Moscow. It was 9:30pm our time when I caught a giant picture of Caxton's face on the restaurant wallscreen. I walked over to stand closer to a speaker so I could hear the commentary. One sequence showed the moment a bullet went through Caxton's forehead. Another showed a bearded youth, only five metres away in a crowd at the side of the street, holding a revolver with two hands out in front of his body, frozen for a few seconds, then rugby-tackled from behind.

Ten days later the assassin, Valentin Spichenko, bled to death in a Moscow jail. His wrists had been slit. In the weeks and years that followed, conspiracy theories abounded. One investigative reporter wrote a book, for example, claiming the Russian mafia had arranged the killing because a Caxton peep-hole or spycam had exposed, live on the net, one of their very best protectors, Georgia's home affairs minister. The man disappeared within hours and was never seen again. The author claimed Spichenko had told a guard he would never serve a prison term because he had very powerful friends. Another, frankly preposterous, theory claimed the UK's Special Armed Services were responsible. But I believed a simple explanation: an ordinary man had a mental break down and attacked the person he felt was to blame for his situation. Spichenko was a newly-qualified accountant with a young wife and a two month old child. His father had died six months previously and left him a substantial inheritance, but he had lost every last penny of it, and much more, by playing and betting on backgammon through one of Caxton's gaming sites.

I had met Caxton, he who was to become my bête noire, a second time (the first having been when I was at school) before I started work for the Department of Communications. He came to Brussels lobbying on the Euronet revision bill in autumn 2020. Bronwen ushered him and several assistants into Lionel Wilcox's office. He shook hands with Firey himself, then with Brian Vetch, then with me. Although I was 10-12 centimetres taller than him, I felt distinctly inferior.

'Ah, the tall young Fenn,' he said with alarming directness. 'I'm so glad we meet again.' He turned to talk to Wilcox for a second. 'We have both progressed since when you were a schoolboy and I was a junior minister.' We laughed with him for politeness. 'I'm glad you've opted for the Parliament. The European Commission might have been the more powerful institution in Delors' day, but no longer.'

I cannot say I wasn't flattered by the attention Caxton paid me. Nevertheless, I am gratified to recall that, subsequently, I was sufficiently sceptical about his character to allow myself to be wholly influenced against him by Firey and Brian. During the meeting they dismissed his anti-regulation arguments, and, once his entourage had left, they mocked him for being profoundly full of himself (and for being so short, but this only because they disliked him).

This second encounter with Caxton was not wholly a matter of chance, and, because I do not wish to be accused of avoiding facts that give succour to those who believe we make our own luck and our own misfortune, I should set the record straight. If I had not been so intent on name-dropping, my life might have taken a very different course. The truth is that I mentioned, somewhat youthfully and boastfully, to Brian that I had met Caxton before. Without this petty brag, he may not have suggested I sit in on the meeting; and, if I had not been there, it's possible Caxton would not have picked on me later to be one of his squealers. But I was, and he did. And I learned, from first-hand experience, that William Caxton was not a man who played by the rules, nor was he a man who bluffed.

Apart from countless biographies, not to mention his own early auto-hagiography, information about Caxton can be found in every printed and net encyclopaedia, so there is no need for me to cull more than a few cursory background details from *Encyclopaedia Universal*. Ronald Shuttleworth was brought up in a large, non-religious, Catholic family by a succession of nannies (his mother being too committed to the Girl Guides, and his father being far too busy managing the packaging firm inherited from his father); he won the equivalent of 15 million euros on the lottery when he was only 18; and, after spending a quarter of his winnings in two years, he had a sudden and dramatic (possibly drug-fuelled) conversion to maturity. He then bought and grafted his way through Harvard Business School. On returning to the UK, Shuttleworth settled himself in an estate near Tenterden, Kent, bought several local newspapers on the cheap, and joined the Liberal Democrat Party. In the media business, he developed a commercially-successful way of sprucing up the town-based newspapers in conjunction with information-loaded local websites. In politics, a readiness to use his money and his media for the cause soon won him friends and influence.

Why did Shuttleworth choose the Liberal Democrats? The historical consensus is that he adapted his apparent politics to the party which he thought would give him the easiest ride. He did not win a seat during the 2009 electoral reform election/referendum but, having done well in a tough constituency, he was eased into a safer seat which he won two years later. The weak coalition that took power in 2011 (the Conservative Alliance plus other anti-Europe groups) collapsed within 18 months, and Shuttleworth was elected an MP in the 2013 elections. In this, the third government in five years, and the second Labour-Liberal Democrat coalition, he was given a junior posting. He willingly withdrew from the day-to-day running of his burgeoning media empire and, otherwise, demonstrated a commitment to politics over and above business. In 2015, he was promoted to junior minister for communications. But, having bluffed and bribed his way so far, he was unable, or unwilling, to hold his tongue. Barely a week went by without Shuttleworth himself making the news for trying to edge policy, particularly on net issues, away from the government line. His resignation in 2017 was a spectacular affair, filling far more column centimetres than news about any other junior minister might have done.

Thereafter, he courted more media attention by changing his name legally to William Caxton. He shrugged off criticism from his family and politicians by dismissing it as nothing more than a 'stage name'. He let it be known that he had always admired the original Caxton for being a man of the people, and that he felt an affiliation with his fellow publisher not only because of Tenterden, where he was born, but because of their shared background in the textile industry (great, great grandfather Shuttleworth had been a wealthy mill owner). Within four years, the 21st century's very own Caxton had launched the Daily Truth newspaper and the People's Channel, both with integrated net services. As is well know, they became phenomenally successful, although the former before the latter.

Our paths crossed a third time on 15 October 2024 (the day after Hurricane Emma caused so much devastation in the Caribbean and the east coast of the US) and when they did, the European Union's Euronet legislation was the reason once again.

On joining the Department of Communications, in the autumn of 2022, I had been assigned to Alexander Duck, a lawyer by training, who acted as the British government's chief expert on European internet issues. The draft Euronet bill, the very same one I had worked on with Firey and Brian, had not made it onto the European Union's statute books: it had been stalled by an alliance of new member states (as they were known for convenience, i.e. the Central and Eastern European countries that became members of the European Union in 2004 and thereafter). No formal progress could be made (in those days) on draft legislation unless roughly two-thirds of the EU's states agreed on a text; only then could it proceed for final negotiation with its colegislator, the European Parliament. The new states did not favour the draft law and kept up a stream of objections to the proposed legal texts, but their main aim in stalling this and other significant proposals was to persuade the old states to maintain a high-level flow of funds to themselves, i.e. the new and poorer states, via the EU's financial perspectives and internal development policy.

During the years in which the draft law was stalled, there was a constant stream, from the European Commission or the member states themselves, of suggestions as to how to overcome each impasse. Every one of these required examination and analysis. It was my job to do this, and to make recommendations to Duck, who would then consult his masters before forwarding them to the UK's negotiating team in Brussels. At the June 2024 gathering of EU leaders in Warsaw, the Polish president, Walenty Czyzewski, skillfully negotiated a wide-ranging deal among the 30 odd European leaders which included agreement on the Union's long-term financial perspectives and on making a determined effort to finalise the Euronet Regulation. This was the signal for the lobbyists to start up in earnest again. No doubt Caxton's team was busy in Brussels, but it was equally keen on ensuring that the British government would take up its case and be pressing for the Regulation to be as open and liberal as possible. During my two years in the Department of Communications at Yorkshire House I had been involved in several meetings involving Caxton's companies, but the man himself had never been present. In advance of an important gathering of EU ministers due to make decisions on this dossier in November, though, he did turn up for a discussion with our junior minister. On this occasion, he paid me no attention whatsoever.

Two nights later Harriet and I (married and living by then in a mid-terrace house in fashionable Kilburn) were arguing about arrangements for the weekend when my phone rang. I went to my office room to answer it. William Caxton. The line was unusually crackly and he didn't identify himself by name, but I knew who it was. As best I can remember this is what he said.

'Fenn. That was a pleasure to see you the other day. I have a modest proposition for you. A simple exchange. Information for money. I need inside information on the detail, every last detail, about what happens on the Euronet Regulation after the ministers agree on the broad outlines next month. What a shame Wilcox is no longer on the case.' This was sarcasm since Caxton had been quoted in the press as saying he thought Firey's retirement in 2022 could be nothing but good news for the Euronet. I said nothing.

'As you know, the Council and the Parliament are about to start negotiating, I want regular reports.' There was a pause. 'What?' he said. I continued to remain mute, my heart was beating fast, and my head was all scrambled. 'I hear you asking about your reward.' I still said nothing. 'Fifty thousand euros.'

Although I had heard rumours about Caxton's unconventional methods, I could not believe this was happening. He stopped talking, and I needed to fill the silence.

'Thank you Mr Caxton, but no, I couldn't do it.'

As I spoke, I knew there must be more to come. He tried again to convince me to take the money. He assured me that extraordinary efforts would be made to ensure that the information could not be traced to me, and that my job and future would be secure. When I refused and threatened to put the phone down and to report the conversation, he turned nasty. He mentioned some debts we had accumulated at the time, and then, when that did not persuade me, he referred to Lola, my net madam of three years. I don't believe my relationship with Lola was, in any way, illegal at the time; and yet I did feel so ashamed of this secret that I was putty in Caxton's hands. He went on to explain in detail how he could expose the conflict of interest between my work on Euronet and my personal use of the net. Thus, under threat of public exposure in the Daily Truth, I did, shamefully, give in to his demands.

For the next year or so I told myself I was only passing on information that would be in the public domain within hours. In any case, I believed that Caxton's influence over a major legal text, which needed to be agreed by both the democratic European Parliament and a large number of European nations, could only be negligible.

***

I realise, though, that I have raced too far ahead and not explained enough about my personal life. Harriet did go to Dublin. After having lost my calm when she told me about her decision, I relented and proposed we see each other at weekends. She declined, and it was on her insistence that we broke up yet again. She resented the fact that I would not follow her to Dublin; plus, I am convinced, she never lost the feeling, deep down, that I wasn't good enough for her. After all, I was not handsome and I lacked character (how often did she tell me that over the years). Poor Harriet, she had been spoilt by her theatrical mother, Constance, and could never cope with being ordinary; and, although in some ways she was brighter than I, she lacked any ability to see herself truthfully or to think intelligently about who she was, and how she fitted into the world around her. It took me a long time to recognise and fully acknowledge this, blinded as I was by her social competence and extroversion.

For the best part of a year, autumn 2022 to summer 2023, we did not see each other, apart from one memorable lunch in Lewis's a few days before Christmas. I remember it because there were vast crowds in Oxford Street and long queues at the self-service restaurant. We argued the whole time about the immigrant hunger strikes which had just begun across the Union. They were to to dominate the continent's political agenda for months, and lead to 50 or more deaths. Harriet, taking an extremist view, said they should be allowed to die. I wanted her to understand about the long-term advantages to Europe of significant immigration and integration of cultures, and, therefore the need for softer more subtle controls. She insisted on the rights of democracy and of giving way to the insistent cry of citizens for protection from the ills of immigration and the crimes of immigrants. But what a pleasure it was to debate with her. She could argue, unlike so many of her friends, without losing a sense of logic.

When our intense debate came to a natural conclusion over some chinese tea brew (to counteract the duck fat in our meal, I was told), Harriet suddenly recanted.

'I think you're right, on the whole. I was only teasing. I don't want them to die.' I said nothing. I was thinking how much I had missed being with her. And then, as if she had not already done enough to recharge my feelings towards her, she added in a typical off-hand way, 'You know, Kippy, you're one of the most intelligent men I've ever met. I do miss you.' A few seconds later she was gone.

During the spring, we exchanged a few short meaningless messages, while I allowed myself to be dated by a girl called Popsicle (thank goodness I never met her parents) who, aptly, died her hair bright colours and wore jeans with neon flashes. We met at The Photography Place where I'd gone after work to see an exhibition of Irish stereo photographs from the 1860s. Some of the photographs had been mounted as large black and white prints, very slightly out of focus and in denial of the stereoscopic effect, but the exhibition also included a dozen or so stereoscopes placed strategically on shelves allowing one to bend over and experience the fully glory of the three-dimensional effect created by the near-twin prints (made from left-eye-view and right-eye-view negatives). I had my eyes glued to a scene called *Picnic by the Dargle* (possibly by Frederick Holland Mares). I did see the same photograph through a stereoscope again, decades later in Dublin, which might explain why I can recall the 3D image so well. Despite 250 years of technological development, however, I cannot reproduce the same effect on my wallscreen, and I must make do with this slightly out-of-focus reproduction to remind me of the detail. In the foreground, a group of ladies and gentlemen, wearing formal dress, are seated at a picnic table, looking at the camera, or drinking, or talking. They are all framed by a bower of trees. In the background, to one side, a river flows towards and past the picnickers. What I remember, however, is how the picture carried my eye: first to the front of the long picnic table, past an upturned top hat, and from side to side examining each face, bearded or bonneted, to the far end, and from there across the luxuriant foliage behind the picnickers to a cascade in the river set far back, and then down with the river widening into the foreground towards a darkish pool at the side, and, from there, finally to a second upturned top hat on an empty stretch of bench in front of the table, providing the visual clue to return to the other top hat and to examine the people again, this time more leisurely, and to wonder who they were, why they were there, and what I might say to them if I were sitting at the same table.

'Can someone else have a peep.' Having dallied in black and white on the soft and pleasant banks of the Dargle, I was rudely thrust back into the acute present, by a shrill voice and then, on turning round, by technicolour clothes. I stepped aside in mild shock.

'Wow.' She stood up after a few seconds and, finding me still there, started a conversation. 'Isn't it amazing that they could do this stuff so long ago. It makes you wonder what we've achieved in the last hundred years doesn't it?' It wasn't a rhetorical question, and so we ended up in the tearoom talking for an hour or so, before moving on to her pad nearby.

Popsicle, who made a living by photographing furniture for advertisements, proved a fun companion for a couple of months. More importantly she was instrumental in nurturing my interest in old photographs. But photography was the only thing she could take seriously; otherwise, she divided her time between watching soap operas on television and 'going out'. It didn't matter where, a club, a gallery, a cinema, anywhere. We were so unsuited, it was bizarre: I would no more introduce her to my work friends, than she would admit to her shallow arty/clubby friends that she was fucking (or rather not fucking) a civil servant. We only survived as a couple through to the spring because she saw my impotence as a real challenge. I gave way to her vain and utterly ineffective attempts to deal with it because I was lonely, and because I was becoming increasingly concerned about my growing reliance on Lola.

One day in late June … it must have been June because the football World Cup semi-finals were taking place in Venezuela, and the English media had gone mad with an Argentinian referee – I remember his name, Mendoza. He awarded a dubious penalty to Ukraine against England. Then, when the shot was half saved by Ibbotson, and the ball appeared not to cross the goal-line, Mendoza whistled for a goal without asking for cam-tech advice. The single score was enough to give Ukraine victory. One broadcaster mocked up a camclip of the penalty, replacing the football with Mendoza's head, and called it *On the Spot with Mendoza*.

One day in late June, Harriet messaged me: 'Kippy darling, You must come to Dublin. Come for a week. Come in August, I'll take holiday and show you round. You'll love this town and the country. Not the last week, though. Let me know soonest.' The sub-text was clear – she wanted to try again. And so did I.

Apart from seeing Harriet, and a visit to the splendid Liffy Theatre (a dense play about the 20th century troubles), the highlight of my week in Ireland was a trip to the Wicklow mountains. I'm not convinced we found the right picnic place by the Dargle river, but it was very similar to the one in the photo. We walked along the shingle in Bray, took an Irish cream tea in Enniskerry, and, at Powerscourt Falls grumbled together about the inadequacy of waterfalls in the British Isles (Harriet having experienced Niagara and I having been to Iguaçu).

There was one day when Harriet had to work, so I took myself to the National Library and, in the photographic print department, chatted amiably for more than an hour to an elderly expert on albumen prints.

Towards the end of the week, we were sitting in one of Bewley's coffee shacks talking about the delights of Ireland, when Harriet suddenly announced she was fed up with Dublin and her job and would be returning to London in the autumn. I responded with genuine delight. Although I tried to elicit a reason for the change of heart, she would not explain it. Instead, she suggested, as casually as if she were asking the waiter for another menthol tea, that we should marry and live together. It took a few seconds for the marriage proposal to sink in, and then another few to compose a response. Harriet stared at my eyes, as if daring me to be flippant, or to say 'hold on', or to argue. So I did none of those things. Instead I spoke meekly.

'That's a good idea.'

Later on, several times, I tried to quiz her on why things hadn't worked out in Dublin, but she would never say. Whether there was a man involved, or she didn't take to the work, or she had failed to establish a social life, I never discovered. Dublin's loss was my gain, or so I thought at the time.

Thus it was that, by November, we (as in Harriet) had decided on a duplex apartment in a terraced house on Torbay Road, not half a mile from her previous flat (which she had rented out while in Dublin and then sold for a reasonable profit). Tom gifted me 50,000 euros, which allowed my share of the deposit to equal that of Harriet's. Mostly, I let her organise the decor, and the fixtures and fittings, offering only token resistance here and there to expensive items. Over and above a sizeable kitchen, a lounge and our bedroom, there were two further rooms. I took the one downstairs as my office (but not before a major row with Harriet who insisted that if I was to have an office than she needed one too, which meant we would have no spare bedroom). In addition, there was a walled yard at the back which carried a patch of lawn and a few neglected shrubs.

In January 2024, Harriet began work as a public relations 'junior executive' for Mandrill Publications. (The company was sold to H.O.N. in the early 30s and subsequently submerged into the Caxton empire, but not before the megalomaniac himself had departed the world.)

In March, we married. It was a simple affair at the Marylebone Registry Office. I'll list a few of the people who were there, if I can find a photograph. Here's one. There's my mother Julie looking perturbed and flushed with Alan's arm around her shoulder. She looked old on that day, I remember, much older than six months earlier when I'd joined her and some friends for a dinner to celebrate her 50th birthday. It was Harriet that noticed my mother's distressed looks, she thought they were directed against herself. I thought they might have more to do with Tom's presence. He was there with an ugly girl in high heels. Horace took the role of best man (although, to be honest, I would have preferred Alfred, who sent a very touching camclip from Lagos). At the reception in a nearby brasserie, Horace embarrassed me with several anecdotes from our time at Witley Academic.

On Harriet's side, her wayward mother Constance was there with a husband (who Harriet flatly refused to talk to let alone consider as a step-father), as was her mother's father, John Tilson. He was in a wheelchair aided by a distant relation of hers that Harriet had never met before. Harriet liked John, her grandfather. She (and I sometimes) visited him in his Hertford retirement home once a month, and often took him out to visit show gardens or to sit and watch the anglers by the River Lee. I had a lot of time for John. He was born on the eve of the Second World War. After spells in the army and the hotel trade, he spent most of his life trying to run bars of one description or another. He was good at it (or so he said), but could never settle in one place. He told excellent tales about London in the 1960s (which is when he played happy families with Constance's mother), Sydney in the 1970s and 1980s, and Spain until the early 2000s when he returned to the UK for free health care. In addition to family, Harriet invited a variety of friends, but Yvonne – she with the thorny look in her eyes – is the only one I remember. Of my friends, there was Pete Sampson, Peter de Roo with Livia, by then his wife, and Phil Rumble (a work colleague who played in the civil service volleyball team) with his girlfriend Melanie Koper.

Two weeks later Julie told me about the tumour in her left breast, diagnosed only days before the wedding. With a combination of pills, surgery and radiotherapy, she recovered by the end of the year. Oddly, the illness helped Julie and Harriet bond; without it, they might never have softened towards each other.

I have not forgotten that I am backtracking, trying to give some shape to my life in the 20s, and to the part played by Caxton and his dirty tricks. I had been a client of Lola, off and on, since the year I'd spent in Brussels. Initially, I had balked at paying a premium for personal service, but I soon tired of trawling the net for photos or clips to arouse and satisfy my needs. For a modest fee, Lola, whoever she was and wherever she was, looked after me. To begin with, she provided a regular supply of high quality striptease clips. Then, inspired by Popsicle's passion for art photography, I became keen on black and white photos of innocent-looking girls caught in various states of undress by an apparently hidden camera. Lola had no difficulty in providing me with an endless supply. Surprisingly, she also had access to an excellent library of classic erotica, much of which I stored on Neil. Subsequently, I began to delve into the delights of voyeuristic camclips, despite worrying about how they might have been obtained. Lola reassured me they were all fake, and that I should 'just enjoy them'. She was good at her, or his, job. I assumed she was a woman, but she may have been a man for all I really knew. She was well educated and almost certainly British by the evidence of her writing. Apart from the obvious difference that we never met, our relationship was similar to one I might have had with a physical fitness trainer or therapist. I always felt she was interested in me, and would give thought to what I wanted and would appreciate, surely the mark of a successful professional. But, with Harriet's return to London and our marriage, I made a determined effort to forego Lola's excellent services.

Soon after settling into our Kilburn home, Harriet and I sank into a habitual pattern of sex once a week on Saturday night. Most of the time, I was able to function adequately, there being no pressure to seduce or perform, but there was very little pleasure in the act, neither for her or for me. And there was no question of any discussion or experiment. This was all the more disappointing because I could never put out of my mind the night Harriet had waltzed naked around the bed and shown off a lacy bra; I never stopped hoping I might witness that persona again. Within months (this is embarrassing to confess), I was back, secretly, furtively, getting ejaculation highs from the computer screen. My relationship with Lola, who remained attentive to my changing needs for over ten years until the day she net-vanished, was to outlast that with my wife. This is surely a comment on the 21st century or on me or on both.

Sex was not the only problem. Harriet had a habit of sulking for the most trivial of reasons. I viewed her behaviour as a remnant from childhood, and my behaviour as diplomatic coping. But, in fact, I was no more in control than one of Pavlov's dogs and would do my utmost to try and please her back into a good mood, at least in the early years. On a few issues, though, I did take a stance, and then, when it became apparent that the sulking had not worked, a big row would ensue. The very fact that I had allowed things to get that far, usually meant I was not prepared to give way at all. But, since both of us hated losing our temper, we both suffered afterwards to different degrees. I suspect Harriet deemed such arguments as a flaw in the marriage, and evidence that she had made a wrong decision in marrying me. This caused the kind of conflict in her psyche that she was poorly equipped to deal with. I do not know if inwardly she thought about these things at all, but outwardly her sulkiness took on a nasty tone. Whenever, after one of these arguments, I attempted to appease her, she would snap out some vicious comment, thereby subjecting me to a week or two of what can only be called punishment. Although such problems in our relationship became more complex later, especially with children in the frame, the basic pattern did not change.

***

After the dreadful phone call from Caxton and my weakling submission to his bullying, it did not take long to discover that my net service provider (NSP), a company called Velocity, was part-owned by Caxton's empire. In my files at Yorkshire House, I searched out a study of the European NSP market which the European Union's competition authority had undertaken in response to a notification, earlier in the year, of a takeover request by a Caxton-owned NSP for a German-based firm. It noted that the London-based Caxton Enterprises, directly or indirectly (through 27 different companies, all listed, including Velocity), controlled 32% of the mainstream Union-based market for NSPs. I can only guess at the rest: Caxton must have used an army of personally-appointed technicians whose job it was to collect and interpret information about key people whom he wished to manipulate. How many others were there? I had no idea. Most of Caxton's biographies steered clear of making any detailed accusations of illegal activity. One sensational book, published after his death, did quote extensively from an anonymous inside source who went so far as to call him an 'habitual blackmailer'.

The revised Euronet Regulation was finally agreed in April 2025, although there was a furious row before the location of the Euronet Agency was settled, at the Stockholm meeting of EU leaders, in June 2025. Since its inception, the Euronet had been run by an offshoot of the European Commission in Brussels, but the new Regulation legislated for a much grander Agency, independent of the Commission. Dozens of documents relating to this, and the siting of several other agencies, had crossed my desk. It was a multi-layered, multi-faceted auction between the EU's member states that had gone on for over a year. Every conceivable permutation had been touted by every interested party. Cardiff, Milan, Bonn and Warsaw were all on the short list. The Stockholm meeting was the EU's self-imposed deadline for a decision. A week prior to that meeting, *Reuters* claimed a scoop to the effect that Bonn would get the Agency. Chancellor Magdalene Kessler (who had come to public attention more than ten years earlier with vigorous criticism of government policy on immigration) denied the story immediately, as did the EU's leaders. But the Polish premier, Walenty Czyzewski, was not satisfied with these denials. He broke ranks and told the *Wall Street Journal* that, at the Warsaw conclave the previous year, he had been promised the Agency in exchange for his support for the overall Euronet legislative package. Fuelled by this evidence that such furtive arrangements really did take place in secret, the media went white hot, even though everyone with half a live brain knows that such deals are at the heart of politics. It was fun to watch from the inside and the outside. Warsaw won in the end.

Incidentally, it gave me enormous satisfaction to see the text of the final legislation crystallise with Firey Wilcox's three tier system firmly in place, substantial funds (paid directly by EU taxation) and sufficient legislative controls and remedies to give it a real chance.

Between October 2024 and April 2025, I spoke to Caxton's go-between, who called himself Carter, an average of twice a month. Having been advised not to change my NSP, Carter gave me access codes so we could talk in a way he assured me was secure. Fortunately or not, Harriet, who had fallen pregnant in early autumn, became too self-absorbed to enquire into why I had office calls at night. I did not like lying to her, and, at times, I wished she had quizzed me more intrusively, for I might have been tempted to explain all. I gave Carter the nitty-gritty of each Euronet meeting I attended, both important and unimportant, as well as any extra information I had gleaned from paperwork coming in from Brussels. At his insistence, I also outlined the forthcoming schedule of meetings so he would know when to contact me.

I did have the presence of mind to call Pete Sampson for help in setting up a discreet way of recording Carter's calls. He chided me lightly for only getting in touch when I needed something, and then for not bothering to confide in him about the purpose of my shenanigans. But, truth be told, he had become increasingly involved in academic life and had gravitated socially towards other potential profs, while my own free time was largely under Harriet's control. The effort was wasted. I was never able to manoeuvre Carter into mentioning Caxton's name, nor get him to provide a hint of why he, Carter, was interested in my information. If I said, for example, 'Are you sure, Caxton really wants to know all this detail?', Carter would answer me, ingenuously, 'Who?'. All the wrong-doing in these conversations was mine. On Easter Monday (soon after the Euronet legislation – the Agency's location apart – was finally agreed), a hand-delivered envelope, addressed to me, lay on the mat at the foot of the stairs inside our front door. It contained a bundle of 100 euro notes – 500 of them. The money itself gave me a slight buzz of guilty satisfaction, but it was far more pleasing to think that this distasteful episode in my life was over. Harriet was asleep, so I hid the envelope in my office. Thereafter, I withdrew two or three notes each week. (Fortunately, Harriet did not share my sneaky habit of looking through other people's possessions, papers and computer files.)

Caxton had clearly put much effort into lobbying on the Euronet Regulation, yet, at the final count, I could not detect any specific way he had affected the outcome, nor could any of my colleagues with whom I discussed the subject generally. Having lost the main battle for a free and easy regime to continue, his people focused on ensuring that the complex technical aspects of the telecoms world suited, or did not conflict with, the way his companies were developing their network systems and customer relations, about which I knew nothing.

That said, I do believe it was Caxton who orchestrated the great spycam scandal. Although it was never proved (and again no biographer was ever willing to point the finger directly), it had all the hallmarks of Caxton showmanship. If I am correct and it was him, then it was a rare error of judgement. He believed that exposés of public figures would lead to general outrage, and consequently make it awkward for EU politicians if they wished to support a tightening of the regulations, which might outlaw such important exposés. Caxton was right about the level of public interest, as magnified by the media, but he was wrong about the political response.

In brief, this is what I recall. During that winter, 24-25, the one in which the final and intense negotiations on the Euronet Regulation were taking place, there was a series of extraordinary live relays on the internet from secret cameras inside offices and homes of important/famous people. The spycams, it later transpired, were installed on some pretense (a gas leak, a telecom problem) by tradesmen who later could never be traced. It was not only advances in microcam capabilities that made this scurrilous activity possible, but in battery technology, meaning that such cams could be tiny and transmit data for a reasonable amount of time without requiring an external power supply. Although only a dozen episodes were seen on the net in this orchestrated campaign, a further 50 individuals (about half in the UK), out of the estimated millions who probably spent hours looking, were reported to have found illegal spycams in their homes or offices.

For each episode, a producer (sitting in Albania or Georgia or wherever) monitored the feeds from the cameras and, at the moment one of them contained something newsworthy, broadcast it live on the internet. Instant messages sent to key media around the world ensured widespread coverage.

The first episode led to the resignation (and subsequent suicide) of Johnathan Underwood, a High Court judge, who the world saw beat his wife in their bedroom. Only a few witnessed the two minute clip live, but it was repeated endlessly on news and net broadcasts for days and weeks with the netsite address visibly stamped into the clip. The second episode came three days later, by which time millions had signed up for an email alert of any new exposés. For seven minutes, we watched in amazement as three members of the Irish government sitting in cosy armchairs discussed the possible assassination of Sian Linton. Linton was a fierce campaigner in Northern Ireland against the pace of movement towards a unified Ireland, and had, by then, become a hero to many old people in the province who did not want to become Irish. It emerged later that the Irish MPs, all suspected of being Irish Republican Army (IRA) sympathisers 30 years earlier, had been secretly asked, by active remnants of the IRA, for their private opinions on the killing of Linton. The clip ended with a phone call, and one man, fear pulsating across his face, ushering the other two out of the room. The Irish government fell the next day.

This second episode resulted in all mainstream NSPs being persuaded to block access to the site and to any sites set up to replace it. This led many to sign up, almost overnight, to renegade NSPs, beyond the Union's frontiers. The five further episodes took place within about two weeks. Ted Ullswater, a hugely popular family comedian and actor, was caught at his computer terminal sifting through a collection of paedophile pornography. He ended up in jail, as did several company chairman who were shown to have hatched a stock market fraud. Some of these spycamclips did have a clear public interest element, but the purpose of others was less clear. There was one which exposed the illegitimate child of the BBC's chairman, another in which we saw an attractive young Labour MP begin canoodling with a man other than her husband, and a third in which we watched the daughter of the most senior European Union official involved with telecoms regulation mouthing off to a friend about her father and his racist views.

The public loved these scandals. The media loved them too, especially since the owners of the site and the spycams were anonymous and were in no position to enforce copyrights. Despite various legal and political actions to censor repetition of the episodes here and there, the media found ways to get round whatever restrictions were imposed, and rejoiced in doing so. Caxton, I feel sure, hoped these episodes would, one way or another, provide convincing proof that regulation should not be so tight that it would end up sheltering people from the truth. He miscalculated. The EU's member states and the European Parliament made no further liberal concessions at all: the agreed Euronet Regulation effectively legislated for three controlled nets – Solar, (open), Doré (business) and Sage (academic) – and tight NSP regulation. It also made telecom access to non-EU NSPs either very expensive or illegal.

Although recorded and edited spycamclips became a media staple, especially those legally obtained (or illegally obtained but with such powerful public interest they could not be ignored), it was only in the more liberal developing countries, especially Brazil and Russia, that live spycam broadcasts (such as the one that exposed the Georgian home affairs minister which may or may not have led to Caxton's murder) were witnessed on a regular basis for a further decade or so.

**

To return to more domestic matters, Harriet informed me of her pregnancy one evening in September 24. I arrived home from work and found her peeling potatoes in the kitchen. She spoke without even turning around to acknowledge my presence. I said something inane. Under Harriet's direction and in her social world, we transformed seamlessly into a couple who were expecting their first child. Apart from the constant shadow of Carter's calls and my feelings of guilt, this was a happy time for Harriet and me. She was rarely unwell, and she liked her work. We both enjoyed sharing our daily experiences in the evening. But, whereas I would simply listen to her accounts, she would become involved in mine, deftly exaggerating my own criticism of colleagues' work or behaviour and reinforcing the importance of what I was doing and how I was dealing with policy issues or departmental manoeuvring. Harriet was especially adept at advising me on how to deal with over-ambitious colleagues and on how to make sure my own position was properly valued by those above me. It is Harriet I must thank for my civil service grade promotion (she persuaded me when and how to argue for it), and for saving my civil servant's status after the dreadful Daily Truth business.

Crystal arrived on 25 May, within two days of the predicted date (and only a few weeks after I had received my payoff from Caxton). Harriet was not keen on ante-natal (or post-natal) advice, and we never discussed the consequences of her being pregnant nor did we make any plans together. Whenever the subject came up at a dinner party or with friends in a bar, it always surprised me how much she had already thought about, and planned for our child. After one scan, she told me, in an offhand way, that our baby was a girl. About three weeks before the nine month period was up, she finally took maternity leave, and used the time to convert her office into a baby room. She opted for Miss Princess wallpaper and matching cot, but I was not involved in the choice of decor or baby paraphernalia. Nor was I involved (and this did rankle) in the choice of name. A few weeks later, we purchased a fashionable and expensive sofa-bed for the lounge which we could use when Constance, or occasionally my mother, came to stay for a night or two.

It was 18 years later that I learned, from Crystal herself, how, as a teenager, Harriet had been enamoured of an author, very famous at one time, called Lucretia Quant. She had written several post-fantasy books with an anti-heroine called Crystal. On that same occasion, it was late summer in 43, I was delighted that my daughter wanted to see me, and optimistic that she might have good news, about a job perhaps, or a permanent boyfriend. However, I was perturbed that she wanted to spend our time together walking in the poorer areas around Paddington. To begin with, we talked backwards about things we had never discussed, her mother, our separation, and about Crystal's early schooling; only then did we talk about her current friends and her ex-boyfriend, Vidrio. I asked about her current situation and plans, and she began telling me about the notorious Pearl Worthington. I could and should have been wiser and seen her talk not as a willful teenage stunt, a poke in the eye to society, but as an agonising personal cry of pain. If I had, she might not have taken the Pearly Way only a few weeks later. No, that's fanciful self-recrimination, I am not convinced there was anything I could have done at that late stage.

Tom was abroad the day Crystal was born, but he sent a message of congratulation. He approved of the numerical date 25/5/25. 'Must be magical,' he wrote, making a slight quip against Harriet's mother. But he also noted, with dismay, that Martian Four was due to be launched only three days hence. (Poor Tom. He died while the Martian Six mission was still under way and without knowing that it would lead to one final mission, Martian 'Lucky' Seven, which eventually put Minty and Wayne Nolan on the planet.) Julie came to London to give Harriet a touch of motherly comfort since Constance was unavailable.

Why do the worst memories, the bad and the sad, always flick into one's thoughts far more often, far more easily, than the best? And why are they easier to write about, to define and to reflect on? Harriet and I had a difficult six months, more or less until she stopped breast-feeding. Crystal then slept through the night, and we took on a local childminder for five or more hours a day (so Harriet could return to work part-time and so we could socialise some evenings and weekends). I aimed to be a father by the equality book as they used to say, but Harriet did not want, nor could she suffer, my input or involvement in Crystal's caring. If I had concerns about her needs or wants, it was simplest to keep my own counsel. What I found most disturbing, though, was Harriet's mechanical responses to Crystal's bawling. She would try, in turn, a combination of the possible causes for the distress (the need for drink/food, winding, or a change of nappy) and if none of them worked, she would let her bawl until she fell asleep. I was not allowed to comfort her, unless Harriet deemed it the right thing to do. But, as I say, after that initial period of six months or so we settled down, and for a year lived in relative harmony. Every two or three weeks we were on the move with Crystal, whether to see Julie (and Alan if around) in Godalming, Constance (so long as her husband was out) in Canterbury, Harriet's grandfather John in Hertford, or friends wherever. We got on particularly well, I remember, with Phil and Melanie Rumble. They lived in a large apartment, bought by Melanie's parents, in Greenwich, and had a baby boy a few months younger than Crystal. They both, though, found it impossible to remain friendly after the Daily Truth article – a matter which I must soon get to.

It is possible that the fresh breakdown in my relationship with Harriet, which became apparent in January 27, was indirectly caused by the affect on me of new demands from Carter/Caxton. However, I do not believe my behaviour changed in any noticeable way. If I was partly responsible, it was Harriet that announced we had a problem; it was Harriet that proceeded to prove it by finding reasons for endless bouts of sulking and snapping criticisms; and it was Harriet that insisted, because I was causing the friction, that I see a therapist. I do not wish to over-use therapy language, but this was a denial of reality, a relapse too many, a power trip too far. I flatly refused to do any such thing. The truth was too obvious: having become diverted for a while by owning a child, Harriet had, once again, grown tired of me.

I proposed we both see a partnership therapist. Harriet was horrified at first, but when I continued to challenge her plan that I alone seek therapy, she reluctantly agreed. She chose Rosemary Acklow, on the recommendation of one of her friends (Yvonne I think). It was an uncomfortable experience. Harriet confessed, on leaving Acklow's Hampstead premises on one occasion, that she found the whole thing 'dirty'. She employed the word 'filthy' another time to describe a session in which Acklow had tried to broach the subject of our sex life. (Harriet had exclaimed definitively that our problems had 'nothing to do with sex'.) Most often, we simply sat in the consulting room answering questions and saying as little as possible. While I would spend long periods, journeying to or from work on the crowded metro or during some banal meeting, going over these discussions in my mind, I doubt Harriet gave them a moment's consideration beyond our own brief post-session comments.

With several months of inadequate progress behind us, Rosemary suggested we should install, in one or two rooms at home, cams and the necessary recording equipment so that we could 'review together', with 'the facts before us', what was happening in our relationship. Since the early 20s, cam-therapy had been fashionable: examples of couples willing to expose themselves filled the inside pages of life-style magazines, and minor film and sports celebrities found financial comfort in selling edited therapy camclips and camstills to the media. Some obsessed and very rich clients would set up a direct live link to their therapist so they could be honestly monitored at any time. I had learned about this in *GlobeOne*, the biggest selling Western political weekly. I had also read, I should confess, Julia Derwent's pop-science classic from the 10s, *Why Humans are Trees or the Hardships of Adulthood*, which took a massive swipe at the whole psychotherapy industry. In summary, Derwent argued that it was as impracticable for an individual to change his or her major behaviour traits as it would be for a mature tree to reconstruct its branches (or, I suppose, for a leopard to change its spots).

Neither of us would make up our mind about Rosemary's proposal. On the plus side, Harriet favoured the idea because it carried a degree of social kudos, and I secretly expected the recordings would show me in a reasonable light. Conversely, I loathed the thought of the extra expense we couldn't afford (in addition to the 1,000 euros a month we were paying for the therapy), and Harriet bridled at the possibility of sordid revelations. I think the reason we finally agreed to rent the equipment stemmed from our mutual trust of Rosemary Acklow, for she had somehow managed to keep a straight bat despite our various off-cutters, leg-spinners and googlies.

(This is an inappropriate metaphor, I know, but I have one eye on a corner of the wallscreen where England are doing well in the second of the triangular two day internationals against Australia and India being played at Lord-it Lords. Lord-it at Lords! What a crass advert the cricket establishment employed during the years when England slipped out of the five year Test League. I was diverted from writing earlier this morning as Flora revealed that her famous son, Barnaby Pattison, now dead, had bowled for England on no less than 53 occasions. She proudly rattled off his various impressive statistics before charging out mid-sentence to stop herself from boring me.)

Predictably, the money we paid to Acklow was wasted. To begin with, Harriet and I were too conscious of the cameras, which constrained our behaviour in the lounge and eating area where the cameras were located. (Harriet had refused absolutely to place one in the bedroom.) She and I would spend an hour or so prior to the sessions with Rosemary, speeding through the recordings in search of something suitable to show her, but for six weeks there was nothing remotely useful. Then, out of the blue, Harriet announced she was with child again. Almost instantly, she became better natured, more interested in me and my work; and she actively re-engaged us socially. The cam equipment contract was cancelled and we said goodbye, with feigned reluctance, to Rosemary Acklow.

It was Crystal's second birthday, a Tuesday in late May, at breakfast, when Harriet casually informed Crystal and me that she was pregnant. Crystal, whose broad uncomprehending smile was covered over by banana mush at the time, was more interested in the pile of presents waiting for her.

'I hope you don't mind,' Harriet said. 'It'll be a boy this time, I know it will. I did the test this morning. It must have been the weekend Mummy was here, which makes it five and half weeks. I was shocked when I saw the test result, but now I'm thrilled. Thrilled.'

'A lounge baby then,' I said light-heartedly to cover over my immediate lack of emotion at the announcement. Odd but true, we had better (less inadequate) sex on the sofa-bed than upstairs in our own bedroom (where Constance and Julie both slept when visiting). Maybe I should have tried to focus Acklow's learning onto that enigma.

'It's perfect timing. If we'd left it any later they'd be too far apart to play together when they got older. Crystal, you'll adore him. We'll have to move of course. Get somewhere bigger. How about Finchley, or Barnet.'

'Not yet. Can we finish breakfast.' Having been sidelined by Harriet over Crystal's nurturing, I was short on enthusiasm second time round.

'I don't want to tell anyone yet, not even Mummy.' She carried her bowl through to the sink, and on her way back stopped to wipe Crystal's face. She plonked a kiss on her fair head, and moved sideways to plonk one on me too, on the dark uncombed mess that was my hair. 'I'm sorry. Let's dump Acklow. Let's move on. It's a waste of money. And, anyway I think you're winning. The weather's looking reasonable. It's Southampton on Friday isn't it. Merriweather had better make it, or I'll kick his ass.'

Harriet. Harriet. Harriet. She could make me feel so bad, so un-able; and then, in an instant, she could turn me round.

***

Merriweather. After a full five year term in which the Lib-Dems had worked effectively with minority support from the Green Party, there was a long-awaited general election that very Thursday, and Horace, who was contesting a seat for the first time in the Southampton Test constituency, had insisted we come to a celebration/commiseration party on Friday. Before being selected by the local Progressive Party group, thanks in part to his friendship with the Member for Southampton Itchen, up-and-coming Terrance Spoon, one local paper had strongly objected to Horace on the grounds that he had no connection with the area. He responded immediately by buying, and moving to, a house in Totton, which was the venue for the gathering. Nevertheless, he retained the Kensington pad (which, conveniently for me, was near The Photography Place), as a useful London base, not only for scooting to Westminster, but for too many short-term love affairs with fickle boys.

Initially, Harriet had dismissed the idea of us making a weekend of it, and ordered that I should go alone, but, having announced her pregnancy at breakfast, by nightfall she had organised a weekend holiday, starting with Horace's party. It also included a day-trip to Cowes, a visit to my grandmother's memorial in the scented remembrance garden at Parsonville (at my request), and Sunday lunch with my mother on the way back.

Horace's commitment and hard work paid off. He was elected with a slim majority, lower than his predecessor who had retired, but better than the local polls had been predicting. He joined a larger group of opposition right-wing MPs than there had been in the previous parliament. The Liberal Democrats were again the largest party, but their leader, Adam Jones, found himself forming a government not only with the Greens (claiming no less than three cabinet ministers) but also – incredibly – the Republican Party. The Green Party, which had only been able to tinker with government policy during the previous administration, was to wield far more power in the coming years.

As for the coalition with the Republicans, it was widely known that Jones was not in favour of abandoning a monarchy, but that, during his previous five years as prime minister, there had been reports of tetchy meetings with King Harry. The Liberal Democrats and the Greens had a majority of 12 in the new parliament and some argued that Jones could have made do without the seven Republican MPs. He foresaw, though, that he could use the Republicans to make life easier for himself in Parliament, while, at the same time, sending a political signal to Henry that it was time to win a few friends and influence people. Jones did not concede to the one Republican demand – for a referendum on the monarchy – until the spring of 30. Even though there was a huge majority for keeping the King and all his trappings, and the poll effectively ruined the Republican Party, Jones was harshly criticised from several sides both for getting into bed with the Republicans, and then for allowing the referendum so soon. Some historians, however, believe Jones saved the monarchy for the next half century. Without Jones's forthright approach, the king might have followed in his elder brother's wayward footsteps; and, without the early referendum, the Republican Party might have continued to expand.

Jones resigned a few weeks after the vote, insisting there had been no link between his decision to call a referendum and to resign. In *Jonesy – The Autobiography*, he claimed that, from the moment he made the deal with the Republican Party in 27, he had a good idea of how he would handle the issue, since he knew the referendum would have to come in the second half of the parliament, and he wanted to resign before the next election campaign. Moreover, he claimed it was for the sake of the Party that he planned to deflect onto himself some of the negative public opinion stemming from the decision to call the referendum. His selfless act did not make much difference: in 31 the public were scared by the rise of the First Tuesday Movement, greedily interested in a revived Conservative Alliance (dominated by the Progressive Party), excited by the formation of Caxton's People's Party, and very tired of the Lib-Dems.

Returning to Horace's party, my old school-friend was on outstanding form. Having spent the day dashing from one interview to another and touring the constituency thanking various groups and helpers, he was ready to have a drink, and let his hair down with a few friends. Apart from Harriet and me (with Crystal obediently asleep in a spare bedroom, from whence you could see the famous Eling tide-mill) there were 30 or so others. Timothy, Horace's younger brother who was training to be an accountant, kept everyone's glasses full. Horace's agent, whose name I forget, left early, but not before having a large group of us in stitches with a stream of electioneering jokes.

Not all of Horace's nearest and dearest were there. His parents, who had been staying in a plush hotel, had flown back to their villa in Nice that afternoon. Neither was Horace's then partner present, having not been invited. I, and the Great British public, found this out a couple of years later from a kiss-and-tell article in one of Caxton's rags. It effectively scuppered Horace's chances of being given a junior minister position during the short Conservative Alliance-People's Party coalition in the early 30s.

Terrance Spoon (who was to be a minister in the 30s and prime minister for three short years in the 40s) dropped in to the party for a few minutes, no longer than he could remain the centre of attention. We all stopped our conversations to gather round him and Horace. Spoon asked us to drink to one of 'the youngest and certainly the brightest' of the new intake; and Horace asked us to raise a glass 'to a gifted politician who will go far, very far'. There was loud applause, but I slipped out of the room to check on Crystal. I gently tried to pull a thumb out of her mouth, but when she threatened to wake, I desisted. I wonder to this day if Horace had not pinned his banner so firmly to Spoon's rickety flagpole, whether he might not have achieved more than he did, despite the early setback caused by Caxton's scandalmongering.

***

But, before Caxton embarrassed Horace, he got me. More than 18 months after the first pay-off, Carter returned into my life. A phone call came in early January 2027. Carter said it would be to our 'mutual advantage' if we started talking again on a regular basis. The Euronet Agency in Warsaw was due to launch the three tier Euronet system a year hence, on 1 January 28. By this time, I had been given more responsibility to guide the policy and legislative interface between London, Brussels and Warsaw. Duck remained my chief, but his own portfolio of jobs had widened, which meant I often dealt directly with junior government ministers, or, by cam-conference, with high-ranking officials in the European Commission and the Agency. In late 26, the Commission put forward new draft laws affecting the launch and operation of the Agency and its regulated system. It was necessary, the proposal said, to close various loopholes that had come to light, and improve the efficacy of the already approved legislation in ways that had not been imagined earlier. In addition, the Commission finally put forward draft guidelines on Unacceptable Content.

Before concluding with the lurid details of my own particular involvement in the matter, I need to explain about Unacceptable Content. Within ten years of the internet being widely available and used in the home, there was already general concern that it could lead to unfortunate and unacceptable consequences for society. In some parts of the less-democratic world, governments were able to exercise a high degree of control over their citizens' access from the beginning; but in the free western world, where unfettered access had been championed from day one by those who had developed the concept of the internet, and where data privacy was of public concern, it was more challenging to prove the need for control, and consequently to set up effective regulation. The early Euronet had failed to expand, but damning evidence against the unregulated net continued to accumulate. This evidence took two main forms: the exposure of sites linked to illegal activities, such as terrorism, paedophilia, racism or human-trafficking; and sociological and psycho-sociological research showing how certain net activities (particularly pornography, gambling and netgaming) were undermining elements of society's social fabric.

Although there were, of course, several sides to every argument, by the late 2010s, the weight of opinion was beginning to coalesce around the view that, for example, the widespread, cheap and easy availability of hardcore pornography to young people, especially teenagers, was contributing to a worryingly high proportion of single and socially inadequate men, an acceleration in the breakdown of marriages and long-term relationships, and a continuing decline in the birthrate. The EVE movement, which expanded rapidly and became a very effective lobby during the debate on Unacceptable Content, emerged rather belatedly in response to the pornography explosion during the early part of the century. In some ways, the gambling issue was similar, since, as with pornography, the internet made it possible and very easy, for a large number of youngsters (impressionable and still developing their characters) to indulge in, and become addicted to, a habit which for many people, as the research shows, led them into life-ruining situations. And, with regard to netgaming, there were serious concerns about permanent psychological damage to some individuals (focused on a concept called 'general alienation' and, more specifically, on bursts of 'random violence').

There had been no attempt to define Unacceptable Content in the original proposals that Firey, Brian and I had worked on in Brussels. The European Commission's aim had been to win agreement on having a harmonised censorship regime (as an inevitable consequence of the regulated three tier system) but to leave decisions on the details of that censorship for the Agency itself to work out. By then, as I learned at LSE, it had become a standard practice of the Commission to try and draft legislation so cunningly that the most highly-charged political issues would be put to one side at the outset. Thus, the negotiating parties could focus their attention on the less complicated aspects, in the mistaken or naive belief that the contentious stuff might be left on the shelf forever. However, according to the strategy, which worked surprisingly often, once the framework legislation was in place, the pressure would build for better practical application and more detailed legislation; moreover, in the meantime, the EU's member states and their citizens would become incrementally accustomed to the new ground rules. At the time, it did not appear that the strategy was working in this case. The long delays in agreement on the new Euronet Regulation were partly caused by some countries awkwardly insisting on an early and clear definition of Unacceptable Content.

Ultimately, the European Union had only been able to adopt the new Euronet legislation in 25 because a decision on the details of what material the Agency would prohibit <u>was</u> deferred. The legislation stated that the operational and content guidelines for the business-oriented Euronet (Doré) and the academic Euronet (Sage) would be decided by the Agency's management board which included officials from the member states and the European Parliament. But, for the basic Euronet (Solar), which was to be an open net, guidelines for Unacceptable Content would be drafted by the Commission and then agreed by the Council and the Parliament. Working documents from Brussels, and policy positions from various member states about the issue, crossed my desk on a regular basis, but it was not until the draft guidelines were presented in December 26, that real negotiations (as opposed to Commission brainstorming sessions, expert witness symposiums, media punditry and political posturing) started in earnest. It was tough going, but the guidelines were adopted as EU law during 28 (leading, finally, to the actual launch of the three tier Euronet the following July, 18 months later than planned). Although, the guidelines were not as rigid as many, such as those in the EVE movement, wanted, they were much tighter than the FreeNet movement, in unholy alliance with privacy campaigners, had demanded. Furthermore, the fact that they existed at all meant it would become much easier thereafter to adjust them, tightening or loosening strands of the policy according to the winds of political and social change.

(Flora has just whirred in and out. She persuaded me to switch a corner of my screen back to the cricket. England scored 359 against the Australian/Indian bowlers, Australia were all out for 306 by the 45th over against the England/Indian attack, and India are now 323 for 7 with four overs left against the best of England/Australia with one substitution remaining. If England win, it will be their first ever victory in a triangular against these two sides at Lords, so Flora says. Crickatistics – a refined obsession!)

And so, back to Carter's phone call in December 26. I refused to talk to him. But, when I had cut him off a second time and he took such a bullying tone on

115

the third attempt, I feared he might turn up at our front door. So, foolishly, I listened to what he had to say. Either his voice had deepened over time, or else it was a different person. I didn't care. He asked for more of the same, straightforward information on the negotiations about, and progress with, the proposals on Unacceptable Content. He offered the same stick and carrot: exposure of my relationship with Lola if I refused to play ball, and, this time, 100,000 euros if I agreed.

A more practical, sensible sort of person would have closed down his Velocity subscription and chosen a non Caxton-owned net service provider. But, on receiving my first pay-off, it had seemed too much trouble, and, I suppose, I never considered I would be of any further interest to Caxton.

If I am honest (and I continue to write these Reflections trying not to compromise the truth in any respect), I do not believe the money swayed my decision, it was more the fear of my onanistic habits being exposed to Harriet, my mother, my colleagues and all – however harmless they were in comparison to much else around. Nevertheless, I did think the money would come in handy. By this time, Harriet had run up substantial debts, and was paying excessive interest rates on bank and credit card loans. She had never mentioned the debts, nor had I hinted that I knew about them. When she asked that the monthly sum I paid into her account for housekeeping be increased, I agreed without question. I also helped by paying whenever we went out or bought anything together, which had not been the case previously. As far as I could tell, from her paperwork (The Gold Rush and For Your Eyes Only were among the gaming companies I saw on her credit card statements), the debts began not long after Crystal was born. When Harriet returned to work at the end of her maternity leave, and during the 12 months that followed, she came close to clearing her debts. Then, not long before we started therapy, when she had become dissatisfied with me and her life, the debts began escalating again. I puzzled a lot about when and how she was finding the time or privacy to lose so heavily. Her computer was situated in a corner of the lounge, and it was rarely switched on when I was in the house. On most days, though, in the period I am talking about (after she had returned to quasi full-time work and when Crystal's daycare was shared between a nanny and a local kindergarten), Harriet was at home for an hour in the morning after me, and for an hour or more in the evening before I got back. Yet, when I returned from work unexpectedly early, she invariably appeared busy enough with Crystal. Given Harriet's general reluctance to discuss anything personal and her surly and uncooperative behaviour at the time, it was my thought that I might catch her in the act, and this would spur a confession. I never did. (Nor, I should add, did Harriet ever surprise me with my pants down, as it were, in the study. I needed a good 15-20 minutes in private time twice a week, and I usually chose late at night when Harriet was asleep.)

I did not seriously consider how I would explain to Harriet the gain of 100,000 euros, nor how I would manage to give a large part of it to her without admitting I knew about the gambling debts. But the thought of the money did, as I say, comfort me, for a while.

I gave Carter what he wanted for nine months. His calls came less often than before, but they still came. That summer Harriet confessed, but didn't want to discuss, having temporary money problems, so I asked Carter for a goodwill payment of 30,000 euros. He gave me 20,000, in cash. Months later, on Saturday 16 October, the day after Harriet's birthday, a stocky man with dark glasses and claiming to be Carter sidled up to me in Grange Park where I was watching Crystal in the playground bopping around on a funny spring chair with ears. He did not look at me, but stood by my side.

'We've had new instructions.'

'We?'

'You and me. I've been given them to pass on to you. The chief is very pleased with the way things are going.'

'The chief? You mean Caxton?' On the phone, he had never referred to any other person or to having received any instructions.

'I've 30,000 euros to give you right now, and the other 50,000 will be yours by the end of November, at the latest.' He paused. 'If.'

'If?'

'If we can … how shall I put this? … do a bit of nudging.'

A bit of nudging! Having reeled me in with relatively innocent (I had to believe that) information-gathering activities, Caxton now wanted me to try and influence the direction of UK policy, not on anything too obvious, too political, but on some techno-legal issues. I protested that I had no influence at all, but Carter knew well enough from our many conversations that my position allowed me to argue points of view and to draft possible responses to external suggestions. I tried to appeal to Carter's reason that it would be considered uncharacteristic of me if I were to start pressing too firmly on any particular issue. He said he was confident of my ability to ensure this would not happen. We stood there in silence for a short while. When Crystal stumbled on her way from the bouncy mouse to the climbing frame, I darted forward to help her get up and to flick off some wood chips that had stuck to the side of her coat. She tried to pull away from me, but, for a second, I wouldn't let her. I half twisted her body round so she would be looking at me, and so I could kiss her cheek.

'Daddy loves you,' I whispered.

'Very touching,' Carter said, with conviction, on my return to his side. 'I like kids.' And then he started to explain how this new stage in our relationship would work, and how it would involve me receiving, now and then, a few papers. I stopped him talking.

'Carter, I'm not doing this. I'm not going any further. You can tell Caxton, he's not getting another thing from me. I'm finished with this deceit. You can keep your money, and please don't call again.' I moved round to take the pushchair and wheel it over to reclaim Crystal from the climbing frame.

'You're making a mistake Fenn, I've seen what the chief does to others.'

'I don't care. I don't care.' I did care, but Caxton had misjudged how far he could drive this particular animal to his slaughter.

Carter tried to persuade me to change my mind by phone twice, although he was clearly constrained in what he could say without incriminating himself, and once more in person, again in Grange Park. Implicit in these conversations was the threat of exposure in the Daily Truth, not only of my relationship with Lola, but also my 'spying' activities, and Harriet's gambling problem (thankfully, Harriet was never to discover that anyone but me knew about this). Yet, I remained resolute to have no further dealings with him or Caxton. I would like to think that Caxton's demands had finally awoken my moral sensibility, and that I stopped being a spy because I wanted to do the right thing, behave in the right way. I suspect, though, that my decision was sparked by a catalytic conjunction of common sense with self-preservation. Had I gone any further, I would have been Caxton's forever.

For about one month, over Christmas, my birthday and into the new year, I lived in a state of near-happy delirium. Carter's calls stopped, and there was no media intrusion into my life whatsoever. As each day passed, I felt more sure that I had called Caxton's bluff and won. Harriet had taken maternity leave already in the middle of December. She was the size of a sumo wrestler, but, as when she was pregnant with Crystal, she was full of good humour and generosity. She positively enjoyed playing mother and housewife during this time. Our second child was due in the third week of January.

The call came on 4 January, a Tuesday morning before I had left for work. A high-pitched male voice introduced himself as a journalist from the Daily Truth. He said he needed an interview that very morning so I could put my side to a story which was of great concern to the General Public. I stood there, in my office room, stunned, petrified. I could sense my life crumbling instantly all around me in many different directions. My initial thought was to put the phone down immediately, but then I decided I should find out what the hack was planning to write. I considered calling Tom's solicitor who I had met once, but, in that moment, the issue was still a personal, private one and it seemed unnecessary to discuss it with a lawyer. So, I agreed to meet the journalist mid-morning in a guzzleshop more than a kilometre from Yorkshire House.

He was stocky, middle-aged, and had a face with rat-like features. I may have imagined the last bit. The interview lasted less than five minutes. He would not tell me where the story came from, and what was in it. I would not tell him when I last had sex with Harriet or other intimate details he badgered me for. Nor was I prepared to comment on the suitability of an internet porn addict being involved with government policy on internet policy regulation. I returned to work, informed my secretary that I was not feeling well, and made my way back to Torbay Road. Harriet was asleep on the sofa, and the screen was showing her favourite soother (slow-motion shots of seabirds in flight with Satie piano music on low). Crystal was at the kindergarten for the first time since Christmas. I sat down so I could watch her sleeping for a while. She looked uncomfortable, half propped up against the sofa's arm-rest, cushions pushed in to support her back, and her legs bent up and slightly apart. I understood so little about what made this woman tick that I had no idea how she would react. Nevertheless, I felt I had to make some attempt to talk to her about it before the story appeared the next day. I put on the kettle, made a pot of her favourite menthol tea, and brought a tray into the lounge. I switched off the media console, and gently woke her.

In an uncharacteristic emotional gush of words, I apologised for everything: for waking her, for deceiving her, for allowing this to happen so close to the new birth, for letting us both down, for bringing shame on our family. I begged her not to interrupt while I explained myself in full. With some effort she did keep quiet, but then she soon began looking away and shutting her ears, I expect. In conclusion, I pleaded, like a weasel, that I wasn't so bad because I had, after all, put an end to the matter with Carter before deserting my principles altogether; and, lamely, I suggested that getting my rocks off through pornography was hardly a capital crime. When, finally, I stopped, having only omitted the sordid details of my relationship with Lola (I fully expected these to be listed in graphic detail by the Daily Truth), Harriet grimaced. It was a horrible grimace. I sat there sheepishly, helpless.

The next day the article, with three photos (one of a Marilyn Monroe-type blonde bombshell), appeared on page five of the Daily Truth with a flash on page one. In addition, the story took a head position on the Truth netsites, and was distributed to 25 million subscribers around the world, via a free advertising-packed email.

I read the story first on the internet in the middle of the night. Then, before dawn, I went out and bought a copy of the newspaper. This was the only time I ever paid money for the rag. Although brimming with shame, especially at the thought of my family and friends finding out about this private behaviour of mine, I was very relieved that there was no hint of the information-gathering activities. I guessed, at the time, it would have been too difficult for Caxton/Carter to make accusations in my direction without implicating themselves either immediately or later were an official enquiry to ensue. At 6am, the phones started ringing so I put them on automatic. In those days, the privacy laws were as ineffective at prohibiting unsolicited pestering calls on personal phones as they were at protecting net data abuse. I rang my mother to give her the gist, and said I would speak to her later. I emailed Tom too, and suggested we meet at the end of the week. Harriet had dressed Crystal and given her breakfast. We ignored the doorbell rings, and, when I took Crystal to the kindergarten, I politely refused to talk to the reporters waiting in the street. By the time I returned, my wife had read the paper. She was in fighting mode. This was not a personal predicament I had to face alone, but a practical problem she and I would overcome together.

Over breakfast, we agreed there was no question of legal action, or any initiative on our part that might propagate the story. This meant no interviews of any kind (Harriet called her mother later and forced a promise out of her to keep mute, which was very much against her nature), and the immediate cancellation of any telecom services owned, or partially-owned, by Caxton, and their replacement, which was a pain to organise. Otherwise, our main objective was for me to keep my job. I took Harriet's advice on this. In a crisis, she was the perfect commander, my very own Churchill. She told me, for example, that humility was absolutely out of the question, as was any appeasement of my superiors. I was to take a firm line and stick to it, whether in conversation with my colleagues, or in any written memos to my seniors: the Daily Truth accusation concerned a personal matter and had no connection at all with my work or the way I carried out my duties.

I should acknowledge that Harriet never once made a snide remark or any comment about Lola (unlike my father), nor did she refer to my behaviour as debasing me or her or us. Some three months or so after Bronze was born, she restarted our regular bouts of passion-less sex on Saturday night as though nothing untoward had occurred to affect that side of our relationship.

A few follow-up articles appeared in different media, mostly in those owned by Caxton; but, within ten days, the journalistic intrusions had died out. Thus, by the time Bronze was born, on 25 January, our life had quietened down. Again Harriet decided on the name without any input from me. Gold was common for boys and girls by then. I thought it far too ostentatious and/or ambitious. Silver had a touch of class. The name Bronze was unusual, although it did become more common later. To my mind, it suffered from being the metal used for third place medals, and, as such, indicated lesser quality. At that time, though, Harriet had taken to the colour bronze and was buying knick-knacks made of the alloy. Most of all, she liked the sound of Crystal and Bronze together. Oddly, after our divorce, she declined to insist on the children taking her family name, Tilson (although Bronze did later). She had always disliked it, partly because her mother's full name, Constance Tilson, stuck on the tongue. Bronze was anything other than bronze, though, as a Mediterranean baby might have been. He was pale and thin. I couldn't help thinking 'poor little bugger' for arriving in the midst of all our troubles.

The media interest may have flattened out quickly, but I still had to deal with the fall-out at work, and among my friends.

At work, Harriet's strategy worked admirably. I ignored/resisted any suggestion that I should take the simple way out by seeking a job in the private sector. I declined paternity leave for fear that, in my absence, rumours would proliferate. Within a month of the article, I was offered a sideways move to the Industry and Technology Department. I decided to take it. Duck, who acknowledged my contribution to the section, was 'very sorry' to let me go. The same cannot be said of Phil Rumble. He cold-shouldered me in the Yorkshire House canteen; and, in advance of a long-planned inter-departmental volleyball match, he sent me an email, copied to the team members, asking me to step down 'to save the team's embarrassment'. On Harriet's cue, I resisted, continued to keep my head high and made no concessions to ignominy. When no-one else in the team backed Phil he found an excuse not to play. At around the same time, Harriet had tried calling Melanie, Phil's partner, to tell her about Bronze, but Melanie would not speak to her. That was the end of our three year friendship. More than a decade later, I ran into Phil at the retirement cocktail party of some high-level civil servant. He apologised for having been such a prig all those years earlier. He told me that Melanie, by then his ex-wife, had been a committed member of the EVE movement at the time, and had, he said, 'infected' him with her views. When I asked why we had never seen this side of either of them at dinner or during pushchair walks on Hampstead Heath and in Greenwich Park, Phil explained that, because of my work, he had always insisted Melanie steer clear of any related subjects. He went on to embellish his apology – needlessly and cringingly – by telling me that, when Melanie had walked out on him, he too had found plenty of comfort in the virtual world.

The Daily Truth article had no lasting impact on any of my other relationships. With few exceptions, if the subject was mentioned in conversation with friends, the discussion focused on the role of the media and the privacy laws. I never did talk to my mother about it any further. During one of the two weekends between the article's publication and the birth of Bronze, I met up with Tom, for the first time in ages, at a cinema bar. He found my troubles amusing and could not resist making the odd joke about Bangkok, and his own (non-virtual) sexual demeanours. I found him irritating, and was quite relieved when we were called in to the film. I think it was a new print of *Bus Stop*. If not then, we saw it a few months later. I remember because Tom leaned over at the appearance of Marilyn Monroe.

'There's Lola. Ha ha.'

A few weeks later, I tried to write an email to Alan encompassing both the news of Bronze's arrival and the Daily Truth business. But to someone as close as Alan, I couldn't make any sense of the latter without revealing the blackmail aspects, and I was not prepared to do so. It would be another five years before I told anyone other than Harriet, and that would be on the night of Caxton's murder.

Horace Merriweather was too busy being a good Member of Parliament to see me much in 28. He came to Torbay Road, self-consciously incognito with a scarf wrapped round the lower half of his face, to inspect Bronze. I went once to Kensington where we spent the evening talking politics. It was more than a year before we met in public again. I suppose he was right to be cautious, but I couldn't help feeling a mild sense of satisfaction when it was his turn to be laid bare before the public ('My MP lover hid me away'). I made a point of inviting him to lunch at a very public restaurant soon after the article appeared and while he was still being hounded. He did not take the opportunity, as Phil would do much later, to apologise for having ostracised me. I doubt if he realised he had done so. He was great company, and a good friend in other ways (especially as I never expected too much), so I did not take offense.

Thinking back on the whole degrading episode, as I have done from time to time during my life, it struck me as bizarre that our society, which had become so inured to sex in general, maintained such a taboo about masturbation. In the late 20th century and in the 21st century, it became common to talk about all kinds of sexual activities, to read about them in books and magazines, and for them to be flaunted in mainstream films and advertising, yet these were never, or very rarely, of the onanistic variety. Social scientists who attempted to understand this taboo by regarding it as one driven by evolutionary mechanisms to maintain the species, could not, in the same argument, explain Western society's near universal acceptance of homosexuality.

Needless to say my relationship with Lola did not end. Soon after changing my net service provider, I was back on line and thanking her for being discreet: I doubted not that the Daily Truth had sought her/him out and that the picture of her was a fiction. She sent me back a message confirming the absolute confidentiality of her client relationships, but thanking me in return, with a double exclamation mark, for the publicity.

I thought carefully before deciding to dredge up this matter here in these Reflections. I even discussed it with Jay. He could see no reason to mention that side of my life at all. I think, to be fair, he was simply embarrassed. I am sure the Daily Truth article was not much noticed in the wider world – after all it was only published because Caxton wished for revenge. As scandals go, it was distinctly minor, and it may have sunk into the mire of my unwanted and unremembered memories but for one thing. Years later, when I was important enough to be the subject of a few media profiles, the topic was often dragged into the interview, as a piece of unpleasantness that had to be dealt with, like a dirty nappy in the car, or a rotting mouse in the closet. And thus Caxton's intrusion became a blight on my life, one that I would have to explain to my partners and children in turn, and, occasionally, to important people who were trying to decide if I was a fit person to take on a particular task. My use of Harriet's strategy might not have persuaded journalists to omit that part of my life from their profiles, but it was sufficient to protect me against further prejudice in professional and practical ways. Ironically, by the time I had moved to Holland and become involved with the beginnings of the International Fund for Sustainable Development, I was already grateful to Caxton (about-to-be-deceased) for having inadvertently diverted my career.

There is one more consequence of the Daily Truth article I wish to mention. A few days before Bronze was born, I received a call in my office at Yorkshire House from the reception desk on the ground floor. A man, who would not give his name, wished to see me on a personal matter. When I asked if he was a journalist, the receptionist's voice descended to a confidential whisper and told me that my visitor looked very unkempt and distracted. It was Rob, brother of Melissa, my school girlfriend. The receptionist had not exaggerated. His unshaven face, wild hair, and torn, stained overcoat suggested he might have been living rough. He did not say so, but I assumed media coverage had triggered his memory and signalled how to find me. I took him to a nearby guzzleshop and bought him a late lunch. At first he remained surly, and made no attempt to tell me why he had sought me out. I asked questions about where he had been, what he was doing and whether his mother was well, which elicited scant information. I thought he might have wanted to talk about Melissa, but I was being too generous. It was money he wanted, money for drugs.

Neither Harriet nor I were given to helping those less fortunate than ourselves. We did not take in stray cats, for example, or worry about the homeless; nor, as we were regularly being urged to, did we help out at the old peoples' home round the corner from Torbay Road. But I couldn't turn Rob away. I called Harriet to explain the situation. Since she was in a happy pregnant state, overloaded with natural stimulants, she agreed to invite him to the house. We insisted he shower, lent him clean clothes, and gave him wine and food. He talked with a stutter and with his head bowed, and he often contradicted himself.

Much affected by his sister's coma, he had left school and home at 16, and moved to London. Under the liberal drug regime introduced by the Lib-Dems/Labour coalition in the late 10s, Rob had been drawn into the use of cannabis and other decriminalised substances. With a group of Scavengers, he learned how to get by without a regular job and to use harder drugs. Then he followed a heroin addict to Hamburg, where a crusading doctor put him on high doses of Solama. This stabilised him for a while. He held down a job for some months. Unfortunately the income helped him feed a growing, and illegal, chemical habit. He came back to England in 26 when his mother died. After selling the house she had part-owned and paying various debts, he had less than 30,000 euros. He moved back to London, found a pad with druggy friends, and squandered the money. Since then, he had been living on the streets, in turns angry, desperate, ill, and suicidal. He had enrolled on various rehabilitation programmes but never lasted the course. The police stopped and searched him regularly but never arrested him. All he wanted from me was money for more chemicals, to relieve for a few hours the unrelenting hopelessness of his life.

Rob made my problems appear negligible. He stayed the night on the sofa. Neither Harriet nor I had any idea how to help. We knew from the media, and from what we saw in the streets occasionally, that Rob was by no means an isolated case. In the morning, before he woke, I made calls to my mother and a couple of friends who I thought might know more than we did. I was given a few addresses and telephone numbers of rehab centres and recovery houses, and advised not to get involved. I didn't. We gave Rob breakfast, the contact details I had gathered, and 200 euros. And we said goodbye.

Only when he had gone and Harriet and I had reassured ourselves that there was nothing else we could do, did I allow myself a few still-strong nostalgic, pleasurable and sorrowful, memories of Melissa.

***

Chintz caught me this evening indulging in an old Movie Martyr flick – *Time and Sight*. The artist's name was familiar but she had never seen one of her films. Chintz drew up a lounge chair and sat down by the side of the bed and watched the screen with me in silence. At the sad bit, where Movie Martyr's mother goes blind (her editing is over-sentimental on occasions, but this in no way diminishes the acuity of her observations), I saw Chintz cry and somehow she reminded me of Crystal as a vulnerable infant, crying often.

Harriet was not a good mother. Have I said this before? She tried in fits and starts, but she never knew instinctively what to do; and, as often as not, she chose the wrong approach. When things were not going well, she distanced herself from the problem without letting anyone else (me, for example) deal with it. The problems with Crystal stemmed partially from Bronze's ill-health. As a child, as a teenager and as an adult, I can barely remember a time when Bronze was not complaining of some disorder or other. It is true that he was cursed with a body that did not function very well, but he never grew to compensate for that, instead his mental and physical life acted to exaggerate his misfortunes. I do blame Harriet partly. Unlike with Crystal, she pandered to his every whinge, scratch, cough and tear which only encouraged more whingeing, more scratching, more coughing and more crying. It started not long after he was born and went on, as far as I know, for most of his childhood and beyond. This was not only bad for Bronze, to my mind, but unfortunate for Crystal too. Harriet had never bonded with Crystal in the way mothers are supposed to bond with their children, especially their daughters, as happens in story books and breakfast cereal advertisements. Crystal was a job, a chore for Harriet, rather than a pleasure or a passion. The job was containable while Crystal was a baby, but became seriously troublesome when Crystal moved into toddler-hood. By the time Bronze came along, Harriet was ready to divert her attention to the new baby. Crystal became irritable and demanding which only alienated Harriet further.

During the summer after Bronze was born, we bought a 20 year old four-bedroom semi-detached house in Lacey's Lane, Willesden. That was the summer when the worst floods in modern history, driven by a cyclone and a tidal wave in Bengal Bay, killed nearly half million people in eastern India and Bangladesh. The world watched horrified as the death toll mounted day by day. When Alan first visited us in Lacey's Lane, he had recently returned from the area. He told horrific stories about how whole towns in the Ganges delta had simply disappeared without trace, how millions of people were lost and homeless, and how large areas of Calcutta looked like a war-zone. Alan blamed the United States for failing to back the Kyoto Protocol on climate change 30 years previously, and for refusing to support actively further measures beyond it. To his mind, because of that failure, the 2008 Delhi Annex and 2019 Hague Protocol came too late, and delivered too little. The floods all over the world, not only in the Indian subcontinent that year (28) were, though, to rekindle efforts on greenhouse gas control, and focus new efforts on climate damage response.

The Lacey's Lane house we (by which I again mean Harriet) chose was in reasonable decorative condition. Harriet was already back at work and did not want to live in a building site. I took the rear upstairs room for my office. From there I could glimpse a speck of green in Gladstone Park, which sported a more adventurous playground than Grange Park. Harriet and I talked at length about the advantages of a live-in nanny, but, thankfully (for I had no wish to live with a stranger), Harriet decided to manage without. However, I suspect that the succession of temporary nannies, childminders and childminding arrangements we employed did nothing to diminish our children's later problems. I blame myself as much as Harriet. With Bronze in her lap, she was less proprietorial over Crystal, and, if I had persevered, I might have been able to give our daughter more self-assurance. Unfortunately, she never showed much interest in me, and only ever wanted Harriet's attention. When tantrums didn't work, she became withdrawn, sullen and silent, sucking her thumb excessively and watching the virtually realistic cartoons for hours.

I seem to be drawing this chapter to a close on a down beat, so I shall delay writing about the end of our marriage – not that there is much more to say – until another day. Instead I plan to conclude what I have to say about Caxton here and now so as to ensure he does not muscle his way into any further chapters.

He was, without doubt, one of the most extraordinary public figures of this or any other century. Others have likened him to a youthful cross between Beaverbrook and Berlusconi, two larger-than-life characters in recent European history, from whom he said he learned a great deal. A key characteristic of all three men was that their ambitions could not be contained within commerce but needed a political arena. If Caxton had lived, who knows what his special combination of brilliance, populism and thuggery might have achieved. Not content with a media and telecoms empire that had become nigh on as large as possible under the EU's competition laws, and had coiled its tentacles around many enterprises in third countries such as Russia and China, Caxton set up his own political party. By no coincidence, he launched the People's Party, with great fanfare and a huge party at Wembley arena, on 1 July 28, the very day the new three tier Euronet went live. I received two invites to the party, one at work (signed by the campaign manager) and one at home signed by Caxton himself. It said, and I quote exactly: 'Bygones? – The People's Party could use a man like you.' How he had the time and the memory to keep me, a very minor pawn, so firmly in his sights, I have no idea. I took pleasure in tearing up both invitations, but regretted my actions when I saw the spectacular show broadcast onscreen. After his death, I also lamented not having kept the personal invitation as a keepsake.

The history books show well enough that the People's Party, and its supporting media, campaigned heartily with most other political parties (excluding the Republicans and Greens) for keeping the monarchy in 30. It then went on to win 50 or so seats in the 31 elections and to form a government in coalition with the Conservative Alliance, with John Lyndquist as prime minister. Caxton, after supposedly distancing himself from his commercial empire, was made minister for an expanded Department of Industry, Technology and Enterprise. Thank goodness I had already moved on to the Department of the Environment. Following his murder, the People's Party, which had been constructed on the foundations of the megalomaniac's money and ambition, imploded in slow-motion. The coalition government collapsed within months, but Lyndquist formed a new coalition, this time, to everyone's astonishment, with the Green Party, which had already spent much of the 20s in government allied to the Liberal Democrats. Gregory, the controversial pop-historian, has a lot of time for Caxton who, he believes, brought a welcome tornado of change into the European media industry, and provided an important brake on the ambitions of the regulators. Despite his great insight, I am not convinced Gregory knows as much about the man as I do.

As a final homage to Caxton, I am taking my last look at a reproduction I have on Neil of a collage created by the genius Tamson Bunting. At the centre is a camstill, as I first saw it in the tulip palace with Diana, of Caxton the moment after the bullet went through his head. Skillfully blended around the central picture are news and publicity camclips, merging in and out of each other, alternating in tones and tints, giving the impression, to me at least, of a complex powerful man with dark and grimy secrets. Zoom in on one eye in any representation of him, and you come out of another. Zoom in on the writing and the words transmute as you try and read them. For me, Bunting says more about Caxton in this piece than Gregory does with all his words.

Now also I am flicking through an archive of family snaps and clips from this period. There are not many as I was hopeless behind the lens, and Harriet only used a cam spasmodically. I realise that I have, inevitably, left out much of the detail from my life, our lives. For example, Harriet and I did a fair amount of travelling in the latter half of the 20s, although not often together. While I was at the Department of Communications and working on internet regulation, I made day trips to Brussels and two-day trips to Warsaw every few weeks. Three or four times a year, Harriet spent several nights in a major European city helping to promote Mandrill publications at a conference or a publicity event. I looked forward to her absences as they allowed me to pay more attention to Crystal and Bronze, not that they noticed.

Once or twice a year, we managed to get away together for a holiday. On the whole, these weeks were among the happiest of our times together. Harriet took a traditional view of how a holiday should be and therefore made a special effort. While on maternity leave, in the autumn of 25, we pushed Crystal's buggy around Florence and Rome, cramming both cities into one week. A year later, she decided we should go on an expensive club holiday to Morocco – not that we saw much of the country. The facilities for toddlers were excellent, as were the beaches. Harriet found some pleasure in tennis, while I hustled my volleyball skills.

And there was one holiday, to the Algarve, which has become my favourite memory of the four of us as a family. I recall none of the detail, but the character and sense of it became fixed in my memory by one photo. This one. We are on a sandy beach with unusual sandstone formations (arches and coloured layers) behind us. I can see the sea's edge, milky-yellow and then turquoise, to the side. All four of us are grouped together in the centre: Harriet, in a white t-shirt and white shorts, is cradling Bronze in her left arm; he has a khaki sun-hat protecting his tiny head. I am kneeling with Crystal. She is on my shoulders, also dressed in white with a pastel blue baseball cap. My hands clasp her ankles. Harriet has her right arm around Crystal's shoulder, and Crystal is holding, somewhat awkwardly, one of Bronze's hands. We have all been caught in a moment, unselfconscious, smiling and happy. Even Bronze looks as though life is treating him well.

NEWSPAPER CLIPPING

The Daily Truth (5 January 2028, page 5)

CIVIL SERVANT IN INTERNET PORN SHOCKER
Communications official caught in compromising position
The Truth about our policy-makers

Kip Fenn, a senior official in the Department of Communications, employs a personal net madam. Her name is Lola, and there is no type of porn she will not commandeer for him.

We do not wish to go into detail since the Daily Truth is a family paper.

What is wrong with this, we ask ourselves. On the surface, nothing. Long may Lola serve her clients, so long as she does so within the law. (And we have no evidence that Lola has ever done anything illegal.)

But Mr Fenn is no ordinary civil servant.

Mr Fenn is part of one of several teams of public servants involved directly with assisting government in setting policy concerning the net, and its regulation.

Important negotiations are currently under way in the capitals of Europe on net regulation. Would you trust Mr Fenn to be involved in deciding Unacceptable Content?

We at the Daily Truth are strongly in favour of a free regime. We argue for a strictly enforced worldwide ban on pornography with violence, children or animals. Lock up anyone who makes or uses such filth forever. Otherwise, leave us grown-ups free to decide for ourselves.

For all we know, Mr Fenn, with his perversions, might take this same view and help in our campaign. But we cannot keep the Truth to ourselves. And no more do we wish to rely on perverted officials. We want the government to make the right policy because it is right. We do not want to rely on individuals who might pervert the course of action, whether in the right direction or not.

Can Mr Fenn go on working at the Department of Communications? We don't think so.'

THREE PHOTOS
A photo of Harriet, looking very pregnant, taken in Torbay Road.
Caption: *'We feel sorry for Harriet – the loving wife. Mr and Mrs Fenn have one child, with another on the way.'*

A fake photo of Lola looking like Marilyn Monroe.
Caption: *'As a client for many years, Mr Fenn has been good business for Lola. Some estimates suggest there could be as many as 250,000 net madams.'*

A photo of myself exiting Yorkshire House (with the building name clearly visible above the entrance).
Caption: *'Would you trust Mr Fenn to be fair about how to censor the net?'*

EXTRACTS FROM CORRESPONDENCE
Kip Fenn to Alan Hapgood

June 2027
Thanks for your letter, and I'm sorry I haven't written for ages. Mum is well. She had her check-up recently, and everything was clear. When we saw her on Sunday (we lunched at the Barley Mow) she was very upbeat about her plans at Boxgrove for 'extending the definition of education'. She's been working on a pilot programme for years (I didn't know much about it), and now she's been given a bigger grant to expand on it.

I have news too. Harriet is pregnant AGAIN – only six weeks or so. She insists we keep this a secret (as you are in foreign parts, you don't count, but don't tell Mum). I should have been overjoyed at the news, but I wasn't. I feel a bit guilty about that, but Harriet didn't notice, and, to tell the truth, we had been having some difficulties. We saw a therapist. I won't go into details. Harriet's pregnancy, though, has brought us closer again, and I've started to become excited at the thought of a second child. Crystal's two now. In case you don't believe time is marching so fast, I've attached a photo Julie took. Doesn't she look a picture. She sucks her thumbs all the time, and has a tendency to talk gibberish for long periods. I imagine that's normal.

As I'm sure you've read, Adam Jones has agreed to form a government with the Greens (good news – your friend, Jill Asquith, may be our environment minister in a few days) and with the Republicans (I don't think many expected that). The Greens say the UK will now have to press the EU to accelerate the climate programme. I doubt Jones will have much choice.

Do you remember Horace Merriweather, one of my buds at Witley Academic. He and I (and, later, Jeff Zimmerman) were the top debating team for a couple of years. We've stayed friends since then. I'm not exactly sure why. He's a protégé of Terrance Spoon and has just been elected MP for Southampton Test. Harriet, Crystal and I went down there last Friday for a celebration party. On Saturday, we took the jetfoil to Cowes for a few hours. Harriet sailed a bit when younger, and was thinking we might take it up as a family. But her notions come and go as quickly as the wind changes direction.

And what's new with you, uncle of mine?

PS: While I remember them here's a couple of election jokes told me by Jekyll (Horace's agent when sober) and Hyde (a failed stand-up comedian when drunk).

1) Two friends are discussing politics on election day, each trying to no avail to convince the other to switch sides. Finally, one says to the other: 'Look, it's clear that we are unalterably opposed on every political issue. Our votes will surely cancel out. Why not save ourselves some time and both agree not to vote today?' The other agrees enthusiastically and they part. Shortly after that, a friend of the first one who had overheard the conversation says, 'That was a sporting offer you made,' to which the other replies, 'Not really, that's the seventh time I've done it today.'

2) 'Mummy, mummy, mummy, do all fairy tales begin with "Once upon a time"?'

'No, dear. Nowadays, lots of them start with "If I am elected …".'

3) Finally it's the day of the UK general election. An innovative portable-type electronic voting machine, much improved on the previous version, is being used across the country. Then, in one local village hall a machine breaks down. The returning officer arranges for a support technician to be called in. One hour later he arrives and, after tinkering around for a few minutes, manages to repair it. As he comes out of the polling station, a poll volunteer

asks, 'Well, is the machine fixed?' The technician thinks for a second, then before hurrying on to his next assignment, replies, 'Now, now, we don't like to use the f-word on election day.'

4) Have you heard the one about a man who walks down the street and is suddenly struck by a falling brick? 'What an outrage. You can't walk anywhere without a brick falling on your head,' cry the people who gather around. Then one of them notices the victim is a candidate in the forthcoming general election. 'What an outrage,' the crowd says, 'there are so many of these candidates there's no room for bricks to fall!'

Well, they were funny at the time.

Alan Hapgood to Kip Fenn

June 2027

Thanks so much for your letter. I haven't heard from Julie for a while, so I was glad of your news. I shall write her next.

Congratulations are in order. Do give my love and best wishes to Harriet. I know from my own experience all relationships go through ups and downs, so don't be disheartened. By having children, you've already taken a much more difficult route than I ever did. Crystal looks so pretty. I forgot her birthday. I was travelling until yesterday, but I'll send her a surprise soon. What about a Russian doll?

Horace, yes, I remember him. I came to watch you perform once. He was very confident and impressive in his speaking, while you were rather diffident and appeared to be in awe of him. I took you out for a meal afterwards. And what happened to Alfred, your volleyball bud? There was something very noble about him, he even towered over you.

Good for the UK Greens. Jill and I may have had our differences but that doesn't mean she won't make a good environment minister. Did I really tell you about our college flirtation (that was very indiscreet of me). It's not only in the UK that environment parties are making gains, I see it across Eastern Europe, in South America, and in some parts of southeast Asia. It's not surprising really, when you quantify, as we do at WWF, the rise in climate-related disasters of one type or another. (I'm sure I've told you, I've been working now for three years on a major report concerning the incidence of floods and related damage to homes, agriculture, etc.: when you take ten year rolling averages, the figures show a progression that is more geometric than arithmetic. The figures for actual loss of life are not so clear, but I fear the clarity will come.)

I'm back in Kiev now for a while. Keep in touch.

PS: Not to be outdone on the joke front, here's two golden oldies sent me by an American colleague.

1) In the beginning god decided to make the earth, but first he was under orders from CEPA (the angelically-staffed Cosmos Environment Protection Agency) to implement an environmental impact assessment. When he was ready, god appeared before the CEPA council. After some consideration, the council said it could see no practical use for earth since it was 'void and empty' and 'darkness was on the face of the deep'. So god suggested, 'Let there be light.'

This caused a further problem. One member of the CEPA council wanted to know how the light was to be made, and whether there would be strip mining, air pollution, nuclear contamination and/or defilement of the landscape with oilrig/windmill monstrosities. God explained that the light would come from a huge ball of fire. Nobody on the council really understood this, but, nevertheless, it was provisionally accepted, on certain conditions: no smog or smoke to result from the burning; a separate burning permit (to be awarded by a CEPA sub-committee); and, since continuous light would be a waste of energy, a halving of the burning time.

When asked by CEPA how the earth would be covered, god said, 'Let there be land made amidst the waters; and let it divide the waters from the waters.' No-one understood this either, nevertheless the Council decided that, before proceeding, god would be required to seek a further permit from IPBWM (the Inter-Planetary Bureau of Water Management).

The council then asked if there would only be water and land, which is when god said, 'Let the earth bring forth the green herb, and such as may seed, and the fruit tree yielding after its own kind.' The council agreed with this so long as all seeds were approved by UGA (the Universal Gene Authority). As to future development, god added, 'Let the waters bring forth the creature having life, and the fowl that may fly over the earth.' Here again, the council took no formal action since this would require a further approval by UGA.

The council was about to give its conditional approval when god explained that he needed to complete the project in six days. The council said his timing was completely out of the question since IPBWM and UGA between them would need 12-18 millennia, and thereafter CEPA itself would need a further few centuries.

On storming out, god yelled, 'To hell with it!'

2) President McFeather and his secretary of state are sitting in a zini lounge. A lady walks in and asks the barman, 'Heh, isn't that McFeather and Nielson?' The barman says, 'Yep, that's them.' So, the lady walks over and asks, 'Hi, what are you guys up to?' McFeather says, 'We're planning to invade Mexico.' The lady says, 'Really? Wow. What's going to happen?' McFeather

answers, 'Well, we're going to imprison all Mexican immigrants, bomb Mexico from the east coast to the west coast, and close down the three taco guzzleshops on Broadway.' The lady exclaims, 'Heh, why are you gonna close down the taco guzzleshops?' McFeather turns to Nielson and says, 'See, I told you no-one would worry about the fate of the immigrants or what happens to Mexico.'

Chapter Four
Diana, the IFSD and the FTM

Duke: In my world, we respect the law. You are part of my world. You will respect the law.
Iridia: I'm going.
Duke: You are not. It is not legal, it is not safe.
Iridia: I don't care.
Duke: I care. I am your father. You are only 14. It is my job to care.
Iridia: Then come with me, keep me safe.
Duke: That is a stupid idea.
Iridia: Why?
Duke: Why what?
Iridia: Why's it a stupid idea for you to come with me?
Duke: You are not going.
Iridia: I am. You can't stop me.
Duke: I can. I will.
Iridia: Come with me. I'm serious.
[DUKE LOOKS AT IRIDIA WITH ASTONISHMENT.]
Duke: Why?
Iridia: Why what?
Duke: Why should I come with you?
[IRIDIA TURNS SLOWLY TO THE WALLSCREEN WHICH IS NOW SHOWING THE FAMOUS CAMCLIP OF OJORU'S MANTRA. THE SOUND VOLUME STEADILY INCREASES.]
Iridia: To change the world.
[DUKE BURSTS OUT LAUGHING.]

I'll Change the World by Finbar Oakley (2030)

By the winter of 2028-29, Harriet had sunk into a depressed, sulky state that was impervious to my attentions and efforts to help. During the last year of that decade our life deteriorated bit by bit. She began to find Bronze as difficult as Crystal. We passed through periods of seemingly endless dinner parties and banal weekend visits, and others in which Harriet preferred working to being with us, her family. I was a buffer. When she was tired or busy, I organised the practical arrangements with childminders and transport to and from the kindergarten, and, when she wanted to take over again, I stepped back. We tried therapy together a second time (but without resorting to cams in the home this time round) on the pretense that the problem might be mine; and Harriet employed a different therapist alone on the pretense of improving her already successful life.

There was a respite in 2030 when Harriet managed to persuade her doctor to prescribe a course of the 'miracle' drug Solama. She had gone to the surgery for one of Bronze's problems, but had mentioned in passing 'a very mild depression'. Solama was only prescribed in this country for a maximum of six months with a lead-in and tail-off period at either end. (A few of the many who bypassed the law by changing doctors fuelled the suicide statistics that were to start accelerating in the 40s.) Solama worked for Harriet. She began an affair with a colleague at work which lasted as long as the drug did. She never tried to hide her actions, in the sense that she stayed away some nights, and never explained why. I accepted her behaviour because it seemed to be linked to a lighter and more carefree mood, which I felt was beneficial for our children. But when the Solama ran out, her affair must have burnt itself through, and once again she became impossible to please and chronically moody.

Towards the end of the year 30, I became seriously worried about Harriet's gambling bills. With so little to lose, since she was scarcely communicating and as gloomy and unapproachable as I had ever seen her, I took a decision to confront her about the debts. I chose a Saturday night, when the children were asleep. I pretended that I had been looking for something of mine in her drawers and found the bank statements. I spoke to her in a stern righteous tone, as Julie spoke to me when I was five, or in the way I spoke to the bullies in the playground when I was nine. I must have tried the tactic, one of few I possessed, on Harriet in our early days together, but no doubt she had quickly learned to disarm it. On this occasion, though, she made no attempt to counter-attack or to defend herself. I employed dramatic soap opera statements such as 'we have children now' and 'our very home is at stake'. I told her that, under no circumstances, could I allow this to go on. It was an all-or-nothing effort. She looked directly at me with horror or shock or both – in silence. When I ran out of sternness and righteousness, she sat there, deflated and quiet, her head bowed towards her hands in her knees. After a minute or two, she rose from the chair, left the room and went to bed.

I stayed up late into the night watching *Heart and Cold*, the second of the Sensations series which brought Movie Martyr worldwide acclaim. What she did, which no-one had done before in the mainstream film market, was to show, by filming her own life in excruciating detail, how awareness of self and acute consciousness could help one cope with life's excesses while, at the same time, enriching life's experience, whether good or bad. Somehow, she managed to provide each film with a personal story about herself, a member of her family or a friend, sequences of comic action to rival the great Charlie Chaplin, and bags of unexpected insights into the way we lived and who we were. Some critics hated her films. They argued that because she lived her life in such a way as to create the drama and comedy, her insights were not valid. Personally, I could see no difference between Movie Martyr's approach and that of the great travel writers of the 20th century who actively sought out situations which would provide material for good prose. I do not think it is a coincidence that I mention Movie Martyr here. For me, personally, the late 20s period was a nightmare and she provided some good honest commentary on what it was like to be human.

The next morning, Sunday, Harriet went out without saying where or when she would be back. I drove Crystal and Bronze to Godalming to see Julie. Harriet returned two days later but would not communicate. Christmas came and went in a sour domestic fog. In January, she announced she was going to live with her mother, by then single again, in Canterbury, and commute to work. I protested vehemently, not for myself but for the children. She ignored me, as she usually did, and for a month I was left to juggle the children's care arrangements and work (I had transferred to the Department of the Environment in Shropshire House the previous autumn but I'll have to return to this).

Then she came back and, in effect, threw me out.

By Crystal's sixth birthday, in May 31, we were divorced. I tried not to think about the fact that most friends and acquaintances would find a link between the failure of our marriage and what they had read or heard about in connection to the Daily Truth article. I settled down in a second floor pad with high ceilings in a Victorian house along Randolph Avenue, Maida Vale (a few minutes walk from Lords as it happens) and Harriet installed a nanny into my old office room in Lacey's Lane. I was surprised at how great a relief it was to be in charge of my own life. The downside was my separation from Crystal and Bronze. I had never been very close to them but, while we had lived in the same house, I had not recognised the reality of the emotional distance between us. This lack of a closeness mattered much more when we lived in separate homes. I saw them every weekend to begin with, but, as they grew older and more able to express their boredom with me, the schedule slipped and I saw them only once a fortnight. As time went by I thought about them often; and, even more often, I tried not to think about them.

As far as I know, from the day I forced Harriet to face the truth of her addiction, she never gambled again. My intervention did her no good. She did not seem to recover from that period in our life (I never saw her as happy again as when she was pregnant both times). Nor, I came to realise later, did Crystal and Bronze recover from our inadequate parenting.

***

Jay, by contrast, is a stable, affable fellow. The Jay co-op did a fair job, I'm pleased to say, not that I personally can claim much credit. He came in yesterday, later than usual, glossy from an afternoon session in a tavern with friends and some Australians they had met. He was rather taken, he said, by a young blond man who had made eyes at him, and then asked for a liaison. But the boy was nearly 20 years his junior, Jay confided, and would be heading back to Perth in a week's time. Besides, he added trying to convince himself, 'It was not sex I wanted but companionship.' I could sense, though, that Jay had been flattered by the attention and – with Vince's absence still hurting – wished to puff himself up a tad. I too felt flattered that my son, in his mid-40s, was able to confide in me about such a matter.

Before he went I showed him a few photographs.

Eduard Isaac Asser is not my favourite of the Dutch photographers (I prefer Pieter Oosterhuis and his glass stereographs) but he may have been the first to photograph the canals of Amsterdam. The few reproductions I have on Neil (still lifes, family portraits and views of Amsterdam) demonstrate a tight, formal sense of composition, constrained perhaps by the traditions of Dutch painting. I do admire this one, *Still life with dead chicken, grapevine shoots and pumpkin*, because of the way Asser composed the picture: the arc-like outline of the pumpkin is mirrored in the shape of one of the vine stalks, and in the curve of the breast of the chicken hanging down by one leg below the pumpkin and in front of the intertwined stalks and leaves; and the finger-like pattern of the bird's wings is similar to that on some of the vine leaves. Most of the photograph is dark grey, but for the chicken in the middle which is a bright white and the pumpkin and grapevine stalks which are light grey. All three elements also share a mottled tone. Evidently, for it was to be another 50 years before early in the 20th century colour photography was to achieve its initial success, this is a black and white photograph. Yet the bright orange of the pumpkin and the fresh green of the vine leaves ache to be recognised. Best of all, though, is the knife, barely perceived at first, which is stuck in the pumpkin, perhaps deliberately, perhaps carelessly, resting there, waiting for something – for someone to cook fowl and pumpkin pie perhaps.

Chintz came by a few moments ago with a copy of my latest medical report. When I asked her what she thought of this photograph, I had to explain that a pumpkin was not an American fruit but a tasty vegetable, from the same family as a marrow.

'A what?'

'A big courgette.'

'It doesn't look like a courgette, it looks like a melon.'

I am more fond, though, of this photograph by Asser of Keizersgracht. Jay said it lacks soul. I agree partly, but to my mind it is another deliberate still life. There are no people anywhere along the Keizersgracht, so the photograph may have been taken early on a summer morning. The water in the canal looks lifeless, and, if there are any barges, they are barely discernible under the distant bridge or beyond. But Asser takes me, the viewer, on the right hand of the photograph, down one side of the canal, past the church (Onze Lieve Vrouwekerk), past a dozen or so tall and handsome four storey houses, each with their windows at slightly different levels, to the bridge in the distance. The bridge itself cuts off the view of the street beyond, so I choose to walk across the three arches of the bridge hoping to reach the other side of the canal. But then, abruptly, before concluding my stroll across the bridge, I reach the edge of the photograph, and the end of my journey. Or do I? Although the water of the canal fills the left-hand side of the photo, Asser has not left me stranded. The dark mass of a treetop leans over into the top left corner, above the bridge, but much nearer the foreground. With the knowledge that the tree's trunk must be firmly planted on the left bank, marginally out of view, I can take that slight leap of faith at the end of the bridge and enjoy the walk back up the left-hand bank of the canal. Jay was not convinced. He did point out, though, that if all the people, scooters, bicycles and moored barges could be removed from the scene today, the very same picture taken, 250 years on, might not be much different. Yes, but only thanks to advanced, extensive and very costly dyke engineering.

What Jay did not know, until I told him, was that my tentative relationship with Asser (visiting an exhibition in Rotterdam and culling these photos from the net) started because of this very photograph of Keizersgracht, and not because of some expert appreciation of the artist. After moving to Holland in early 33 I had neglected my interest in antique photographs and it was only with a spring in my step wound up, if I can put it that way, because of a walk with Diana along the canal, that I set about trying to find the earliest photographs of it. There is a more soul-full and interesting picture (two photos, a stereograph) by Oosterhuis but it was taken at a different spot on Keizersgracht, and captures a scene across the water rather than along it. Jay preferred this photo to the one by Asser. He noticed the reflections in the canal and the way the real light and the reflected light forms a cross with the line of the street. I showed it to Chintz too. She spotted the difference between the two parts of the stereograph, as if it were a quiz in a journey book: 'Oh look, that cute Dickens street lamp has moved.'

I could lie here until my deathday revisiting my own collection of photographs or browsing through Portia, re-appreciating hundreds, thousands of these reproductions. The importance of the photographic record was not so widely acknowledged when I was a young man as it is today, although it became so by the 40s and 50s. I believe this was partly because digital photos did not entirely replace film photographs until the 20s and it took another decade for any sweeping cultural nostalgia for the old form to emerge. And when the nostalgia did emerge, it encompassed the whole 200 years since the origins of photography in the 1830s and 1840s. To my mind, though, it is only the photographs of the first 80 years that are so special. The moving pictures, when they arrived, in the 1920s, soon eclipsed ordinary still photos, and all other art forms, in their power to record and preserve the state of the world. Looking ahead a 1,000 years or more, we will be able to define our history, our culture, our geography, our dress codes etc. in three periods with reference to three main documentary tools: all of history up to 1840 through paintings, drawings and the like; a period of 80 years from 1840-1920 through still photographs (such as those safely stored by the great Daguerreotype Museum in Boston, the National Photography Museum and The Josephine Collection in England, the Rijksmuseum-Rotterdam extension, and Japan's Nikon Gallery and Archive); and all of history after 1920 through moving photos.

It is all too easy to allow myself to be sidetracked by these photographs, but I must move on.

***

The Department of Industry and Technology did not suit me. The European Union's research and development (R&D) budget was massive at the time, and I was one of many officials involved in various technical and bureaucratic positions all aimed at ensuring the UK got the best value it could from the European projects. In order to counter the R&D successes of the US and Japan, the EU's Member States had, over time, agreed to focus more and more of their R&D resources on technically-strategic goals instead of national political objectives. Because of my previous experience I was assigned to policy and planning for future programmes, which was better work than implementation and monitoring of current programmes. Nevertheless, I found my tasks tedious, and longed to be in a department which was important because of the issues it was tackling not because of the size of the budget. My less-than-glorious shift from the Department of Communications meant it would not have been wise to seek a further move in less than two years. Thus, it was only in the spring of 30 that I began actively looking for another position. After six months of increasing frustration, Horace rang, out of the blue, to suggest I contact Judith Singleton informally at the Department of the Environment. It transpired, as far as I could work out, that Horace had, on my behalf, been asking around among his colleagues in the House, and a junior minister had recalled that Singleton, head of the climate change section at Shropshire House, was in dire need of someone with EU experience and confidence, and with a head for complex policy issues.

I fell for Jude the moment I walked into her office: there were two Eugène Atget prints of Paris in the early 1900s, carefully framed and hung on one wall. Her desk was busy but not untidy (unlike many I'd observed which were examples either of unstable disorder or ostentatious emptiness), and she rose to greet me with a gracious smile and handshake. Her short-cut light hair and elegant simple trouser suit gave her a Scandinavian appearance. In time, I discovered she was ruthlessly efficient when necessary, in a very British way, an attribute which made her an excellent chair at meetings. At her prompt, I explained why I was anxious for a change. She outlined the job available. When her secretary rang through with a pre-arranged signal in case she wanted to close the interview quickly, she chose instead to order tea and biscuits, which allowed us another 40 minutes, five of which were spent talking about Atget. Subsequently, it took three months to move through the required civil service job opening and application procedures. By late October, when I was installed in a bright airy office on the third floor of Shropshire House overlooking one of the University College buildings, I had briefed myself intensively on the background and the job in hand.

Global warming, caused largely by a rapid growth in the emissions of carbon dioxide and other greenhouse gases, became an international political issue in the 1990s. It is generally accepted today that the world's efforts to prevent the consequences of climate change were, at best, marginally successful, and, at worst, without any effect whatsoever. Later, of course, the climate catastrophe of the Grey Years made any concerns over global warming utterly redundant. Many commentators, however, point out that the world's efforts in trying to deal with climate change led to alternative benefits, and that, in any case, nations often wasted resources through far less constructive activities, notably war. Personally, I believe the global warming problem concentrated the collective mind of mankind in a way that had never happened before, and thus helped it take a small step towards maturity – not that there haven't been several steps back.

Again I need to fill in some background which is readily available elsewhere, so I'll be brief. The UN Framework Convention on Climate Change was signed at the famous Rio conference in 1992 (the first World Summit on the environment) and set in motion a process that led to national and international commitments to control and reduce greenhouse gas emissions. First came the Kyoto Protocol by which most developed countries (but not the US) agreed to stabilise their emissions of greenhouse gases by 2010-12. Although the efforts were nation-based there were limited mechanisms designed to allow a flow of funds for investments into less-developed countries. Next came the Delhi Annex. Although signed in 2008, it was fraught with problems and did not come into force until 2017. Basically, it set the developed countries and some of the largest developing countries emission reduction targets for the year 2025. Furthermore, it put in motion a procedure for inter-governmental emissions trading, thus providing a crude mechanism by which the developed countries could buy progress towards their targets, and by which the developing countries could attract major investment. Although this had the distinct benefit of directing investment to where it could most efficiently be employed in reducing emissions, it also allowed the US, which had rejoined the process by this time, to continue prevaricating over any significant national measures.

My uncle, Alan, pointed out to me on more than one occasion that the US's position from Kyoto on set such a bad example to the rest of the world that the whole process was fatally undermined. He put it this way once: how could a rich and powerful ringleader who smoked like a chimney persuade the rest of his gang to give up cigarettes? The gang members tried, but, with the leader puffing away, many of them failed to put in as much effort as they might have done.

By 2010, the long-standing scientific International Panel on Climate Change (IPCC) had confirmed that the weather chaos across the globe and the related increase in human suffering (death, injury, loss of property and crops) was directly due to global warming, and that this was, as had been known for some time, partly caused by man-made emissions of greenhouse gases. Disturbingly, moreover, it had begun to suggest that, even if global warming was not progressing any faster than had been predicted 20 years previously, the impact of that warming on the climate system was becoming more chaotic than had been forecast by all but environmental scaremongers. It was one thing to have the media tell citizens each time there was a flood, famine or hurricane that it was caused by global warming, it was another to have scientists tell them that such events were going to become more frequent and more intense. The Hague Protocol, signed in 2019, was a last ditch attempt by the world to save itself from further expected havoc. As with the Delhi Annex, the negotiations were largely a battle between what the richer countries would do themselves and how much they would help the poorer countries to control their growing emissions. It was aimed at achieving certain objectives by 2035.

Theodore Roosevelt convened a world conference on natural resource conservation two centuries ago in 1909. An international conference in Stockholm in 1972, however, was the key moment in history when the environment became not only an international issue but one linked with the development of less privileged countries (i.e. those variously labelled developing or undeveloped). That same conference led to the formation of the United Nations Environment Programme (UNEP), and to the promotion of a concept called 'sustainable development'. The UNEP-organised first World Summit in Rio in 1992 not only agreed the Climate Change Convention but a global plan of action for sustainable development known as Agenda 21. Over the next 20 years, at Johannesburg (2002) and Beijing (2012), the international community toyed and tinkered with how best to promote sustainable development, linking it sometimes less and sometimes more with environmental concerns. At Beijing, the group of developing countries, forever known as G77 despite its actual number of members, launched a major campaign calling for a new fund for sustainable development. Opposition came from the US and Japan, and Europe was divided about the idea, so the G77 proposal ended up on the shelf for a decade. It was not until 2022 at the fourth World Summit in Lagos that an informal agreement was taken to launch, under the auspices of the United Nations, a major new organisation, to be known as the International Fund for Sustainable Development (IFSD).

Although the visionary Ojoru was not yet Nigeria's leader by the time of the Lagos World Summit, he played a crucial role in forging the IFSD agreement. His extraordinary non-speech to the European Parliament a few years earlier and the ongoing drought and famine in parts of West Africa had reminded the world it should not be turning its back on the region. And, in time for the Lagos meeting, Ojoru had miraculously persuaded the African Union, comprising nearly all African countries, to present a unified front, and to allow himself to be its chief negotiator. With the UN agreement in principle signed, Ojoru continued to lobby furiously throughout the 20s to ensure the IFSD would become operational as quickly as possible. He also pressed for it to be provided with sufficient funds to make a real difference and to be organised in such a way as to benefit the African continent in particular.

The IFSD, with an office in Abuja and a much larger operation in the Hague, was launched in 28. It was not as grand or as well-funded as Ojoru and many others had hoped, and there were critics a-plenty proclaiming it would make no more difference than other UN agencies had over the years. Yet, even as the IFSD was making its first grants, Europe (with strong pressure from the UK's green-tinged government) was already forging a plan to propose a substantial expansion. European leaders, meeting in Riga in June 30 (not long before my move to the Department of the Environment), agreed on the outlines of an ambitious plan to divert an additional 0.3% of the developed world's gross domestic product (GDP) to the IFSD to deal with, among other needs, the consequences of climate-related disasters, and the development and strengthening of infrastructure required to withstand future climatic disturbances. This was to be over and above the 0.7-1.0% of GDP already granted by most Western nations in overseas development aid (ODA) through multifarious channels. But, in addition, the European Union plan proposed four further incremental raises of 0.2%! The EU announced it would be seeking rapid approval for the plan and agreement at the fifth World Summit in Kiev in 32. It warned that its own commitment to raise ODA by such a huge amount (by as much as 1.1% to a total of around 2.0%) would depend on other developed nations making similar commitments. The EU gave itself less than two years before the Kiev World Summit to persuade the US and Japan and its own public as to why such apparent philanthropy was so urgent.

At the risk of sounding like a committee report, I should explain why Europe was intent on proposing a near-overnight 30-40% increase in foreign aid, and then a further 60-80% increase (a policy which would hurt its citizens' pockets in a less-then prosperous period). Firstly, the Bengal Bay tragedy in 28 and other major climate-related tragedies had demonstrated, in the most horrific way, the truth of the IPCC findings. Accepting this truth led to the inevitable conclusion that the developed world needed to make a more definite, reliable and sizeable contribution to deal with such disasters. Secondly, because of a steady acceleration in sporadic outbursts of terrorism, there was serious concern (in Europe more than the Americas) that the global relationship between the fairly static Christian world and the fast-expanding Muslim world was becoming unstable, and that the wealth gap between the two was at the root of this instability.

Thirdly, by the late 20s, the First Tuesday Movement had begun to scare the public and governments alike. On Tuesday 4 May 1927, the United Nations published a dry statistical report called *The State of Nations: a 50 year assessment*. With help from eagle-eyed non-governmental organisations, the media soon latched on to the headline message: between 1975 and 2025 the rich had got much richer and the poor had stayed poor. This proved to be a most terrible indictment of the efforts made by the privileged developed nations (not least through the UN itself) to help the undeveloped nations. Various demonstrations started up sporadically in cities around the world but soon coalesced, thanks to the net and the media, into the First Tuesday Movement (FTM). Within a year, there was no major capital city which did not see marches and demonstrations on the first Tuesday of the month. The FTM acted as a magnet attracting all kinds of disaffected and disadvantaged people as well as those well-off but with a conscience. (In London, Harriet and I were already burdened down with children and our own problems to be much affected by the FTM. Moreover, both of us were too straight, as they used to say, to join a demo.) In the early 30s, though, the FTM gatherings in hundreds of cities became characterised by rioting and purposeful anti-capitalist looting.

For many, the writing had been on the wall for decades: escalating climate disasters were a direct consequence of far too little action to control emissions; and escalating political and social disorder around the world, exacerbated by ever more severe floods and famines in the regions least able to cope with them, were a direct consequence of the rich nations having failed to share their wealth over the previous 50 years.

And this is where, after a lengthy introduction, I finally re-emerge into the story.

My main task in Jude Singleton's section was to facilitate UK input into the EU's plan for the IFSD. This involved liaising with other government departments (often through Jude but increasingly not) to crystallise the UK position; communicating this position to the policy group in Brussels which was negotiating and preparing the EU's position in advance of the Kiev World Summit (through a UK official in Brussels, or by attending the meetings myself); and reporting back to my masters on the outcome of relevant EU and international meetings. Despite having to liaise with a man called Rike Thomas (not Rik or Rick or Rikky but Rike as in Mike or tyke!) my opposite number in the overseas aid section of the Department of External Affairs and the frustrations of being engaged in complicated long-term international negotiations, I felt far more comfortable in the Department of the Environment than I had done in the Department of Industry and Technology.

Because I was living alone in Randolph Avenue and my only commitments to Crystal and Bronze came at weekends, I could work long hours and travel freely. Mostly I saw my children together every other Saturday, and I made an effort to vary our schedule. About once a month we would drive to Godalming and spend the day with Julie, exploring the open heath land or the North Downs. If Alan was around he would usually find time to join us. Much less often we met up with Tom at the zoo or an adventure park, but, if cold or wet, at the cinema. He brought my children gifts, and made them laugh. Once only did we make the trip across town to his home in Epsom, not the horrible semi-detached house, but another larger property he had bought with his new wife, Fragrance, an ex-secretary. When Tom had retired in 26, he had taken her to the Bahamas for a holiday, and they had decided spontaneously to marry there and then. I could not stand the woman, but they seemed to make each other happy.

Other Saturdays, I would impose myself on one friend or another for a few hours. In particular, though, I grew to rely on Miriam and Doug Turnbull who had two girls the same ages as Crystal and Bronze. Doug also worked under

Jude Singleton, dealing with chemical and industrial pollution policy. Since we didn't share any interests, I'm not sure why we became friends. Perhaps we thought and talked and operated at a similar intensity which led us naturally to seek each other out in the canteen at lunch-time, knowing it would be a simple uncomplicated encounter, free from innuendo and one-upmanship. His wife, Miriam took a while to warm to me, and, I feel sure, accepted my visits with Crystal and Bronze, who were not the easiest of kids, out of kindness.

At times I missed the long debates I used to have with Harriet (who became very business-like with me), but there were plenty of colleagues in Shropshire House (or in Brussels when I was there) willing to discuss, over a zini or pizza, the underlying purpose of bizarre drafting changes put forward by the Greeks or Norwegians. Unfettered by the need to hide my activities at home from anyone, my relationship with Lola flourished, as did my monthly bill for her services. Fortunately, a disturbing trend in my own tastes, for visual interaction with younger teenage girls (or composite equivalent), encouraged by Lola, was cut short by her sudden disappearance. She net-vanished leaving me stranded. My determined efforts to find connections as satisfying as those she had brought me failed miserably. Instead, I had to make do with a new net madam. I did this reluctantly. She sent me, formally and coldly, a copy of a standard Solar (the open Euronet) services form (with a summary of guidelines on Unacceptable Content), and required my e-sign. Within a month or two of Lola's disappearance, I decided I should make an effort to find non-virtual female company. I contacted old friends, joined a well-run singles dance and dinner group, and signed up anonymously to a few net dating agencies. I did get out and about more, but the more I did so, the more I realised how difficult it would be to find someone to be close to again.

**

Of the two years or so I lived in Randolph Avenue, I particularly recall the autumn of 32 because of several colourful trips I made all within the space of two months.

Tom called me one Thursday morning to tell me his father, Barry, who had lived in Malta since before I was born, had died, at the age of 91. He asked me to go with him to the funeral. I hesitated for a moment, thinking about the need to make rearrangements for Crystal and Bronze and a meeting on Monday morning which I would have to miss (Tom having proposed to stay an extra day). But I had not gone anywhere with my father in nearly 15 years, not since the Bangkok trip; nor had we spent more than a day together in all that time. On the aeroplane he reminded me that we had been to Malta when I was about four. Barry had invited us, and, reluctantly, Julie had agreed. I had no recollections of this at all. Julie had never talked about the holiday, nor shown me any snaps.

'What an effing week that was. We took one of those cheap flights from Gatwick. This was long before the air traffic reforms. Delayed five hours we were. You were suffering from fidgetitis and flu at the same time. Your mother was pre-menstrual. I was no less short-tempered than usual, and that was before we got there. We're not one hour at the villa when Barry starts laying into me about never visiting Evvie enough when she was alive. He calls me 'son' all the time which doesn't help. I try to stay calm, but when his Maltese wife – fuck knows what her name was – takes Julie and you to the bedroom, I start on about him never looking after her well enough. Maybe not then, but sometime during the week, I probably accused him of killing her by neglect. It was fun when we went out on our own, although I expect I gave Julie a hard time. I can't remember what we did.'

I paraphrase, but Tom's voice and some of our conversations remain remarkably fresh in my memory.

'Now the old bugger's died.'

'Where's he been living? And what happened to the nameless wife?'

'She left him when his money ran out. He caught lucky in the early 1990s with a specialised computer sales outfit. Made a cool three million selling it to one of the national retailers, and then retired to Malta. Spent it all ages ago. Been in a nursing home on the outskirts of Valletta for nearly ten years. A dull place. I've been twice, both times when he thought he was dying. He was bitter about the wife not visiting him.' He stopped, and turned his head. I was left contemplating what he said as well as the side of his face. Being middle-aged might have suited him, but old age was not treating him well; he could have been in his 80s not his early 70s. I felt sad to realise how ancient he had become.

'I don't want to go through that, I'll drink myself to heaven rather than spend one night in a home.'

And he did too.

Barry's nursing home, a modernish construction with 20 or 30 rooms, was located in Zejtun, not one of the island's prettiest places. The staff had arranged all the funeral details. Tom and I and the proprietor, a solemn charmless middle-aged matron, were driven in a shiny black hearse to a modest cremato-rium, part-owned, the proprietor was proud to tell us, by herself. Three others were present at the very brief service. We took a taxi back to the nursing home, where the matron had arranged for Barry's will to be read by her son, who was training to be a lawyer. Apparently, the will had been passed on from a high-class solicitor in central Valletta, when Barry stopped paying the annual charges, to the home itself. Tom hoped there might be instructions concerning Barry's ashes, but there were none. All of Barry's estate (precisely nothing) was left to the Maltese wife (she who had not bothered to turn up for the funeral). Tom needed a short time with the proprietor alone, so I sat on a wall outside in the sun battling with a horsefly.

Tom came out snorting with rage at the size of the final bill. Apparently, he had been financing Barry's stay in the home and his medical bills for many years (out of his own fat pension presumably).

'Nearly 4,000 fucking euros. Charges for undertaking duties, charges for the crematorium, charges for the solicitor – can you believe that? – and for various debts. That woman's a bloody crook.' Then, after a short pause in which I said nothing, there followed a routine we had developed over the years since the fateful new year's eve we'd spent together. Whether he said the opening line, or I did, it made no difference, because we both knew they were his words, and that, whereas once they had been used on me with alarming gravitas, they now served as a means for us to lighten our mood, to switch almost instantly from anything too serious to laughter and good humour.

'Well, fucking say something.'

'Put it down to experience, Dad.' On this occasion, it sounded funnier than usual for being so utterly inappropriate. 'And we still don't know what to do with his ashes.'

'Anything, so long as it doesn't cost.'

Tom realised he had forgotten to ask for a taxi. Having made a nuisance of himself with the proprietor he didn't want to go back in and beg a favour. So, in our dark suits, we walked through dusty streets towards the centre of Zejtun until we found a ride back to the hotel in Valletta.

The following morning we first returned to the crematorium to collect Barry's ashes, contained in a cheap casket. At Tom's insistence, we then went on a boat tour around the island. As the launch lulled in a pretty sea cave with colourful underwater flora, Tom leaned over the side, opened the casket and sprinkled Barry's ashes as ceremoniously as he could manage without drawing attention to himself.

'Goodbye you old codger,' he whispered with only a hint of regret. When we emerged into the dazzling midday sun again, I asked Tom what he would want done with his own ashes. I could have guessed his answer.

In the afternoon, as we sat in a small public garden sheltered by bougainvillaea-covered walkways, he revisited a few memories of his childhood. Later, over dinner we talked about Julie, and a moment came – I remember this distinctly – when I could have told him about her lover and about the doctor. I asked myself whether I wanted him to know, and whether he would want to know, and the answer was a resounding 'no' in both cases. If Julie had died first and Tom himself had grown old and maudlin and asked the question, 'Did you ever find out, son, who your father was?', I might have answered him.

The following weekend I spent in Manchester. Alfred, that African chappy as Tom called him, had returned to Britain a year earlier to do research and a postgraduate degree on 'New techniques in the analysis of the costs and benefits of international aid: application in two sectors (health and agriculture) and three countries (Nigeria, Tanzania and Sudan)'. We had met three or four times, mostly in London where he came often to see other friends. By that autumn, he had made excellent progress on the thesis. He had also persuaded his professor to let him teach a trial unit on bio-politics in sub-Saharan Africa.

On this particular occasion, though, I was invited to join him (and most of his volleyball club) to watch England play Belarus in a European Championship qualifying match. The game itself proved lifeless as Belarus, decimated by recent injuries, failed to offer England much of a challenge. But the result put England top of the mini-league, and almost guaranteed it a place at the championship finals the following May in Estonia. Alfred and I discussed plans to make the trip to Tallin, but they never materialised. This was a shame because England have never, before or since, made it to such an important final, or achieved top-three status in Europe.

Despite the dull match, though, it was a memorable day, not only because of England's success but because I timed out with scores of people I had played with or against in more youthful days. One of them introduced me to John Buffer, England's (then not yet legendary) coach. Alfred was much in demand. I hadn't realised until then how much of a volleyball celebrity he had become, partly because he had captained Manchester University so successfully for a couple of years in the early 20s, but more so, I would guess, because of his position in the Nigerian team which had won the African cup three times in five years. Gemma, as beautiful as I remembered her, showed up that day too. It surprised me that Alfred should have stayed in touch with her. She brought her husband, a musician of West Indian origin who sported dreadlocks platted with orange beads, and three boisterous children. Needless to say I did not mention my encounter with Rob; nor did Alfred, Gemma or I allude in any way to our dreadful shared memory.

Alfred may have won plaudits for his volleyball playing but, by the early 30s, he had not yet found his professional niche. Unfortunately, his father, who had been a successful diplomat in the 10s, lost favour and position with the change of regime that brought Ojoru in as deputy prime minister. Without friends in high places, even Alfred's top degree in political science had been no passport to power. He joined the army, trained as an officer and took his turn on peacekeeping duties in the restless parts of Africa. After seven years, he accepted the best civilian post he could find, assistant governor in a region of the country where ethnic disturbances were not uncommon. Given his experience in the army, the governor used him as 'a bucket of water to put out fires', Alfred said, whenever the fires (racial friction) threatened to spread. He hated it. However, instead of throwing in the towel, as it were, he worked assiduously and achieved results where and when he could. His success with the Nigerian volleyball team had allowed him to earn extra income for a few years by appearing in advertisements for a Brazilian car company. He also avoided marriage and saved ruthlessly. Which was how, in 31, he had sufficient funds to return to the UK and pay the uni postgrad fees.

Jumping ahead a few years, I like to recall that I personally engineered a meeting between Alfred and a Nigerian colleague, a personal appointment of Ojoru, who worked in Enterprise 35, and that this connection resulted in Alfred being appointed to a senior federal government job on his return to Nigeria after completing the PhD. From there, he went on to work directly for Ojoru in Abuja as one of his many, many advisers. Much later, I also found a place for his skills in the IFSD's Abuja office.

***

And now for something completely different (a phrase that has stuck in my head since Tom used it often during my childhood; it seemed to have a life of its own, as though it were amusing in itself). My third journey that autumn took me on a package holiday to Dracula Park in Romania. I do not think Harriet or I would ever have chosen such a holiday for our children of our own accord, but when Doug and Miriam told me of their plans and suggested Crystal, Bronze and I tag along, the idea somehow took hold. By this time, Crystal was already seven, and Bronze was a few months off five, and they were both comfortable with Doug and Miriam's girls (Lucy and Susannah). I expected Harriet to object, but she did not care. Crystal, on the other hand, had never been so enthusiastic about an idea of mine. Most children have a dream holiday preference for one of the mega-adventure holidays sights, such as Spain's Wild West, France's Disneyworld or Romania's Dracula Park. In Crystal's case it was definitely Dracula Park, but I had had no inkling of this. Miriam, though, who was closely attuned to her own children appeared to know more about my own daughter than I did, which is why we had been invited.

I have lots of snaps of that holiday, taken by snap-happy Miriam, and several good memories. The best are of Bronze laughing and giggling often, whether because Susannah was teasing him, or because of the excitement of the Transylvania helter-skelter or the giant Frankenstein puppet show. Although we spent most of the week in the park, as a group we did a day's sightseeing in and around Tirgoviste. Our guide to the famous ruins of Dracula's Palace told us, in gory detail, how Vlad Tepes, the real life Dracula, became known for his brutal punishment techniques. He relished ordering his enemies to be hanged, skinned, boiled, decapitated, blinded, roasted, hacked and buried alive (the list may have shrunk in my memory over the years). His favourite method was impalement on stakes, hence the surname Tepes, Romanian for 'the impaler'. Having won control of the region, with help from the Turkish, Dracula took revenge on the local nobles for having killed his brother. The older ones were impaled in the palace courtyard while he watched from a high tower above. The younger ones were enslaved to build a new castle at Poenari. Legend has it, the guide added, that Dracula returned to Tirgoviste in 1989 to drink blood from the bodies of the dictator Ceaucescu and his wife after their executions.

On several evenings, Miriam and Doug went out to eat alone leaving me to watch over the motel apartments and our sleeping children. In exchange, I was to have a whole day on my own to explore a bit further afield. Towards the end of the week when the day came, though, Crystal would not let me leave her. She had started out on the holiday friendly enough, excited with expectation, playful, similar to any other kid. But, after three days, Lucy had tired of Crystal's selfish demands (despite Miriam's instructions to 'be nice to Crystal') and finally gave way to a resentful crying fit. Miriam, having felt I was too lenient by far, finally lost her cool and gave Crystal a piece of her mind. Apologising to me later, she defended herself by attacking Harriet, who she had never met. I said nothing. As a consequence of this mid-holiday crisis, I decided to take my moody, thumb-sucking daughter with me on the day-trip, leaving only Bronze with the Turnbulls.

We took a bus to the Dracula centre north of Curtea de Arges from where one can look up and see the spectacular and forbidding Poenari castle built by the ex-nobles under the whip of Vlad Tepes. We could have opted to take the cable car that lifts the very young, the old and faint-hearted through the pine trees, but I decided we should walk the 1,500 steps. It took a long time. I carried Crystal on my shoulders some of the way, and for the rest we stopped every 50 paces so Crystal could rest. She appeared impervious to my irritation at her laziness. Once near the top, however, the stunningly gothic outline of the castle perched on the mountain top revived my spirits, and the narrow bridge across the gorge to the castle itself scared Crystal back into real life, into being there at Poenari instead of swamped in her own psyche. Inside, the thrill of peeking over ledges to witness the sheer drops kept her interest alive. On the way back, she repeatedly asked whether it was 'really really really true' that Dracula's first wife had jumped to her death from the south wall so as to avoid being captured.

I should mention one odd occurrence which may or may not have had a bearing on future events. Of the many rides and entertainments at Dracula Park open to seven year olds, only one had as many as three skulls (five being the maximum for teenage/adult rides) – the Vampire's Lair. On the last day, Crystal begged us to let her go on the Vampire's Lair one final time. Lucy and Miriam agreed to accompany her. The ride is little more than a modest roller coaster for 90% of its length. Then it climbs to a maximum height of about four metres and the shuttle car rolls downward smashing through an apparent rock face (a huge heavy material screen) into a dark custom-built cavern and an immense pool of blood (water dyed a frighteningly realistic dark red colour). The car then skims along the surface of the pool, spraying blood out sideways to splash several grotesque life-sized figures on the pool's edge. Carefully placed spotlights light up the faces of the figures, so you can see the blood dripping down. Never mind four or five skulls, the ride should have been x-rated. As chance would have it, on this last occasion, the car, with its 20 or so inhabitants, halted suddenly in the middle of the pool for no apparent reason. While Miriam opened a conversation with her neighbour about the possible causes or consequences of the breakdown, Crystal, somewhat waif-like, wriggled out of her harness, climbed out of the shuttle car and onto the rail board, which in this stretch was just covered in red fluid. She knelt down, and, with one leg, gingerly tested the depth of the pool. Discovering it was only a foot deep, she climbed in and started wading towards one of the plastic statues. Another child shouted 'look at her'. Everyone turned, and, for a moment, Miriam was horrified. Then, at about the same time, an engineer appeared from a corner of the cavern and saw the whole situation. He spoke firmly and carefully in English telling Crystal she was safe, to stay calm and not to move. As he began to stride through the pool to rescue her, Miriam, having realised there was no danger, pulled out a camera and took a flash photo of my daughter. I have it buried in Neil, but I do not need to view it now, nor do I wish to.

I can see her, a miniature figure, dressed in jeans and a pink blouse, her arms slightly splayed out to the side so as not touch the pool's surface, more than knee-deep in a flash-lit carmine sea. Later, Crystal reported she had wanted to know if one of the figures reclining on the pool's edge was alive, and Lucy had dared her to find out. Lucy denied this.

When I told Jay the story yesterday, he asked about Crystal's clothes and whether they had been stained by the blood-water. To my surprise, I remembered that Miriam had washed out Crystal's jeans with her own light-coloured trousers (which had been dripped on) and the red had come out much more readily than she had expected. Jay did ask to see the photo, but Chintz came in with my meal – tomato soup and basil soufflé dumplings – and I was able to ignore the request.

I wish Miriam had never taken that photograph, and I wish I had never given a copy to Crystal, and I wish Harriet had stopped her framing it, and putting it on display. The image became an icon, one which she employed for several years as a way of reinforcing her individuality and separateness from others.

***

At the Kiev World Summit, which took place during the late summer of the same year (32) before these various trips I have recalled, the world's nations with few exceptions agreed in principle to a major enlargement of the International Fund for Sustainable Development. Ojoru was a prime mover. He had not only strengthened the African Union, but, with much trepidation among Africa's christians, found common cause with the Arab world against the West. Moreover, his domestic and international successes led, during the early 30s, to Benin, Togo and Niger voluntarily becoming, as a result of referenda, part of a renamed Grand Nigeria Federation. (Incidentally, Ojoru also initiated and enabled a commercial and political alliance between Nigeria and Brazil, on the basis of many common characteristics, not least that the two countries dominated their respective continents and should therefore help each other practise leadership. This bilateral bond – forged between two great leaders Ojoru and Neco Corazon, or Neco the Prosperous as he came to be known later – proved surprisingly powerful over the decades. It helped both countries form a strategic grouping, with China and India, to act as a non-aligned counter-weight to the group of 13 industrialised countries and the Islamic nine. For Ojoru, the link with Brazil, and by extension with all of Catholic Latin America, had the additional benefit of demonstrating his ongoing balanced allegiance to the Christian minority in Nigeria.)

The Kiev agreement covered the following: a revised and more progressive set of principles for the IFSD, and consequently a much wider mandate; for most developed countries, a new and additional contribution based on 0.2% of GDP (i.e. 0.1% less than the proposed 0.3%), with specific smaller percentage contributions for some countries (such as those not deemed rich enough to afford a sudden 0.2% of GDP increase and for those already substantially more generous than the average); a commitment to further increases 'bearing in mind the proposal of the EU for four further additional incremental contributions of 0.2% of GDP and the very heavy burden this would place on the economies of some developed countries'; and carefully defined categories of countries eligible for different kinds and levels of aid. The media busied itself with cries of 'too much' or 'too little'. Right-wing pundits in the US predicted it would be the biggest waste of national resources since the Patterson education reforms. Left-wing analysts, by contrast, likened the Kiev deal to a worldwide Marshall plan which would invest US money with far better return than various 20th century endeavours such as the Vietnam, Korean and Cold Wars, not to mention the most inefficient and misdirected war in modern history – the war against terrorism.

For those who have lived as long as I or for those who have a cursory knowledge of history, it may appear odd that I pick out and highlight certain developments and not others. But I gave up being a historian on leaving the London School of Economics, and it would take someone far cleverer than I and with far more time to give a better balance and shape to world events. All I can hope to do in these Reflections is to flit hither and thither in my memory while endeavouring to keep a sense of chronology.

I mention the Kiev agreement specifically because it led directly, within the IFSD, to the formation of Enterprise 35, a group which aimed to bring about the practical application of the agreement by the end of 2035, and to my moving to the Netherlands to be part of the Enterprise 35 team. Jude, my department head, must have been involved in discussions while I was away in Romania, for she called me into her office immediately on my return. She needed to recommend someone to be seconded to Enterprise 35 for two or three years. I was her number one choice but, knowing my domestic situation, she was far from persuaded I could, would or should go. I had three days to think it over before she would need to consider other potential candidates. I put the offer to the back of my mind and worked solidly through the morning.

During my lunch break, I took a bus to Regent's Park and wandered round the boating lake. There weren't many people since it was cold and grey. I decided to consider the job from three angles: work, friends and family. I had discussed with Jude how the move might affect my civil service career, and she had said it was impossible to say. If all went well, it would do me no harm, and my willingness to accept such a big move on request would definitely count in my favour. If, as some suspected, the whole scheme were to become bogged down in disputes, directly or indirectly because so much money was at stake, it could prove tricky to extricate myself cleanly. On the whole, my ten years in the civil service had been rewarding. Even so, I had never escaped the feeling that my work, representing a single nation's interests, was parochial. My experience in the European Parliament had given me a taste of higher objectives. Enterprise 35 offered a chance to get back into an international arena.

Since my dating efforts had failed miserably and I remained very much unattached, there were no significant social obstacles to my leaving London.

Thus, I soon narrowed down the decision to one concerning my relationships with Harriet, Crystal and Bronze. I could foresee no hindrance to my travelling back to London every second weekend for a day or two (I should have known better), although I did perceive that my absence might make things more complicated for Harriet. This was because, after our separation, I had proved a useful stand-in for nanny coordination and other duties whenever she was ill or opted to travel on business. Moreover, as I would have no London base of my own and it would be impractical to rely on friends and family, I'd be obliged to utilise Lacey's Lane to spend time with Crystal and Bronze. Regrettably, in making my decision, I never considered my children's well-being, only how the practical arrangements might work in the future. In my defence, I believed they had grown so distant to me that nothing I did could have had any influence on their development. Our week together in Romania had not altered that opinion. Would their lives have been any less distressed if I had not moved so far away? I do not believe so. But then again, I'm fully aware of how capable I would have been of manipulating and moulding the reasons for my actions so as to justify what I actually did, and how those reasons would have been reinforced and set in concrete over time, so as to protect my psyche and, within it, an acceptable picture of myself.

I tried talking to Crystal about the fact that I might move to Holland, without eliciting any interest. Harriet proved supportive. She advised me strongly to accept the job, not for any selfish reason, I'm sure, but because she genuinely considered herself my career adviser. As for the practical aspects, she could not see any insurmountable problems. Bronze had started school that autumn, and the current nanny was reliable and helpful. There would be no problem in me using Lacey's Lane, and, with a modicum of planning, I could organise holidays to cover when she needed to travel. Julie proved less enthusiastic and worried about seeing less of me and her grandchildren. Tom thought it a great idea, and promised that Fragrance and he would visit regularly. As usual, I also sought advice from Alan, although on the professional, not the personal, side of things. Those working in non-governmental organisations, whether involved with development per se, the environment, or both were universally excited about the Kiev agreement, and Alan was no exception. He emailed: 'Go for it. Your talents need an opportunity; and Enterprise 35 needs you.'

By January, I had installed myself in a slightly cramped but well-lit third floor pad (with beautifully polished near-white wood floors) on Weissenbruchstraat, and Enterprise 35 had begun its work in earnest in a rented office a block away from the IFSD building. Pravit Krishnamurty, a brilliant Indian Muslim, only in his mid-40s, who had briefly studied 20 years earlier under Triti Madan, led a staff of 30, some from the IFSD itself but most of them seconded from various parts of the globe. Pravit reported directly to an executive board, made up of two IFSD vice-presidents and several elected foreign and environment ministers, which itself acted on the directions of a steering committee set up under the terms of the Kiev agreement.

Having talked to us all at length, Pravit quickly set about creating teams, team leaders and various programme tasks. Along with an Egyptian academic, who had once been a junior government official, and a maverick South African, I was assigned to a team led by Boris Kiselev, a 60 year old Russian who had already been with the IFSD for several years. The task given to our team was to examine the feasibility of the four further additional incremental contributions (each of 0.2% of GDP) by developed countries giving, as per the formal wording, 'due consideration to the heavy burden this might place on the economies of some developed countries'. Thus, I was not to be in the main stream – the heat of the battle, the eye of the coming political storm (as Brian Vetch had once, long ago, described our work on the Euronet Regulation) – of Enterprise 35's work but, for want of a better description, in the let's-write-a-fairy-story unit. I took the news badly, and confronted Pravit.

'I haven't decamped from London, moved across the water, and left my children 300 miles away just to sit around contemplating pretty scenarios for the future.' Firey, Brian and Harriet would all have been proud to see me so assertive, aggressive almost. But, truth be told, I had not yet taken my measure of Pravit, and he looked young, not that much older than me. The man smiled thinly, and shook his head ever so slightly as though recognising some mistake of his own.

'Where is the struggle for the future? What battle do we have to win?' His calm manner diverted me almost immediately.

'We need to convince the doubters that the extra money is absolutely necessary and can be spent wisely, or wisely enough; and we need to do so quickly. That's the mission of Enterprise 35.'

'Yes, I agree. But when you say "extra money", what extra money do you mean?'

'The 0.2% of GDP. It has been known for a newly-elected national govern-ment to increase a country's ODA by an increment of 0.2% but such a rapid increase has never been agreed across the board, nor have such large sums been channelled to one agency. That seems a big challenge; and I thought I'd come here to work for that.'

'Yes, I am happy that you did. You were very clear about it when we spoke before. You impressed me.' He paused such a long time that I had begun to think I should say something. 'But I see things slightly differently. To my mind, the 0.2% increment is a deal that's done – a done deal. Yes, yes, we have to wrap it up well with the fancy paper of political intentions, the strong twine of realistic, practical implementation details, the right address and correct postage. Meaning what? Hah, my flowery English always failed me at Cambridge. Meaning we have to address the package in the right way to the right leaders with the right weight to each. Yes. But that is not the struggle. I see the real struggle as the rest, beyond 35. To me the "extra money" you mention is not this 0.2% but the additional four times 0.2%, the 0.8%. Can we give wider international credence and power to the European Union's vision? Is it possible? Now that is what I call a challenge. And you Kip Fenn – such an unusual name, a pleasant one – do you want to be a packager or the man who devises the next parcel so astutely that we'll need our packagers long into the future. Hah, excuse my extended metaphor, it always goes on too long.' He paused again. His voice dropped to a confidential tone. 'Furthermore, I must confide, I may need you for higher things. Our Russian friend is dicky.'

Disarmed. In less than five minutes, Pravit had me completely disarmed and turned from a potential renegade into an Enterprise 35 devotee. If I harboured slight suspicions that he had achieved this through charm rather than sincerity, these were completely dispelled a year later when he chose me to take over as team leader. Boris, 'our Russian friend', had spent more time pursuing his private business than those of Enterprise 35 (we made progress despite, not because of, his leadership) and had, eventually, been recalled to Moscow. I suspect Pravit's threats to sack him finally penetrated the Kremlin's thick walls. The replacement, Ninel Horeva, far younger and more committed than her predecessor, became a valuable member of my team. I should mention that she made a simple pass at me one Friday evening, not long after her arrival. I then spent a sleepless weekend terrified that my refusal would undermine the new working patterns I had been striving to establish. But it was a redundant fear stemming from my own insecurity and inexperience. She was as bright as ever on the Monday morning, and, within a few weeks, had hitched herself to a Frenchman working in one of the other teams.

***

I declined Ninel, not because of a lack of attraction, nor because we worked together, but because, by this time, I had fallen in love with Diana.

For several months after arriving in The Hague, most of my weekends were spent either travelling back to London, working or shopping (equipment for my rented flat, a bicycle and a scoot-bike). I did find the time to meet up with Peter de Roo who, with his wife Livia, was living in Amsterdam. After concluding a postgraduate degree in energy economics at LSE, Peter had taken a post in a government agency providing advice to the environment ministry. Livia had completed a postgrad course in fabric science, and was working as a researcher for a large outdoor clothing manufacturer on the outskirts of Amsterdam. They had two children, Rudy and Ulla.

One Sunday, in late April, Peter and Livia invited me to join them on their barge moored at a pretty location not five kilometres from Alphen aan de Rijn, near a lake and a café-restaurant called Stoffers. Unfortunately, the spring weather broke the day before. Cold air and drizzle meant that by the time I arrived a small gathering had collected in Stoffers rather than on the lake shore. After greeting my friends, who gave me a general introduction, I sat down in a spare seat next to a woman dressed in two tones of green velvet. She turned to speak to me. This is where and when I first met Diana.

'You are English?'

'Like Livia.'

'She is Cornish.'

'It's not a separate country yet, I don't think.'

'But it should be. Scotland is a country, but it has no language. Cornwall has a language. It should be a country.'

'I see you've been a friend of Livia's for some time then.' She laughed. Her large hazel eyes, framed in a round cherubic face (I don't know how else to describe it) by a fringe of dark hair and two dangly silver earrings, latched onto mine with playful interest. I grinned back.

'A few years. I have a boat along the bank from Peter's. That's how we know each other. Well, it belonged to Karl, but he went back to Berlin, and I decided not to sell it.'

'And Karl is?'

'Karl was. Karl definitely was.' She had a very good command of English, although with a heavy but, to my ears, attractive Dutch lilt. For an hour or more, as we ate and drank, I let Diana monopolise me with talk about her work in theatre design and her enthusiasm for travel to faraway places. I told her briefly about Harriet and my children. In my limited experience, Diana stood out as an exotic creature, albeit one slightly older than me.

As the afternoon lazed on, Rudy, Ulla and a few other children, who had eaten at a separate table, managed to engage several of the adults in a game of Dump-the-Chump. I knew it well as one of the few games that would hold Bronze's attention for more than a few minutes. Diana proposed we walk along the river. The drizzle had all but halted, nonetheless she carried an umbrella to protect us on our way. She showed me Tic-tac-toe, a converted and motorised snik, beautifully painted. We sat in the narrow galley, drinking the coffee she had brewed and talking about the boat, and then about Karl Engelhard.

Somewhat naively, I can say in hindsight, I took it as a sign of friendship and intimacy that she opened up about her relationship with Karl. Over time, during the early years of our relationship, the barge, which was a permanent reminder of the man, became a constant if mild irritation. It was only after we decided to have a child together that Diana agreed, for symbolic reasons if no other, to sell the boat.

On the walk back to Stoffers, Diana suggested we meet for dinner a fortnight hence. She chose a tulip palace restaurant since I'd never been to one – which is how we came to be at Keizerskroon the night Caxton was murdered. We had drunk a bottle of wine between us, and Diana had rambled on at some length about Karl again, unashamedly (or provocatively whichever way you care to look at it) revealing fairly intimate details about the sexual side of their relationship. After the news broadcast, I began to explain why I hated Caxton, but I had not thought through where the story would lead. I certainly did not expect myself to go as far as confessing sexual frailties. But I did. I made a full and honest confession about Lola, and about the Daily Truth article. Diana listened attentively, encouraging me to explain more fully. She then asked candidly when I had last been naked with a real woman.

'A long time ago.' I felt as though I was at school again, standing outside the shower room waiting for the door to open.

'A long time ago is too long.'

Like Peter, Diana also lived in Amsterdam although in a very different part, next to the Noorder AmstelKanaal on Jan Van Goyenkade. Her flat, which filled the two uppermost floors of a five storey 20th century building, appeared a wonderland to someone as conventional as me. In the lounge area, exuberant masks and exquisite puppets jostled for space with Indonesian wood carvings and Nepalese weavings. In the large attic space above, which we accessed by climbing a steep ladder, model theatre sets (old, new and half-built) crowded part of the floor space, while framed and unframed photos of theatre stages covered the walls. Pens, paints, crayons, brushes, knives, scissors, tweezers, unused strips of coloured modelling clay, rolls of braid, coloured tapes and twines, jars of buttons and beads, tubes of glue and the rest filled a large set of mailroom-type shelves at the back of a wide, relatively tidy, work area. To one side, a glass desk backed by a sizeable wallscreen held a multicoloured keyboard and computer console.

'Welcome to the world of Diana Oostlander,' she said, before extravagantly removing her ruby bonnet and bowing towards me. 'And now, the bedroom.'

Back on the lower floor, this was a much quieter, calmer room suffused with a sweet scent of vanilla. A large bed, covered in a striking lacy or crochet-style cream bedspread, was placed by a wide low window, giving on to the trees that

158

lined the canal. To one side, on a small table, there was a vase full of tall apricot-coloured lilies. On the other, a huge palm in a square copper-glazed pot stood on the floor. A large mirror and dressing table occupied one corner of the room; a wallscreen (showing an abstract art soother) hung across another; and half of one wall was taken up with built-in wardrobes and cupboards.

'Welcome to the bedroom of Diana Oostlander.'

We returned to the lounge, and she offered me a joint. I hesitantly admitted I never smoked, so she poured us both a whisky instead. I was very nervous and stiff. I imagined that Diana was wondering if she had made a mistake. She fussed around for a while with the console, finally selecting a Louis Armstrong concert to play in the background on sound only, and then disappeared. I sank deeper and deeper into the silky cushions on the sofa, considering when and how I should say goodbye and leave. I may have been asleep or slipping into the music when I felt myself jolted. Diana had joined me on the sofa wearing only a white kimono carrying a trace of the vanilla perfume I'd detected in the bedroom. We kissed, and while we kissed she undressed me; and then she led me through to the shower. There she massaged me with soap, and encouraged me to do the same for her, but I was too tense, too impotent for an erection. Neither could I do much in the bedroom. Evidently, abstinence had not improved my ability to perform. When I tried to use inadequate words to apologise, Diana swore quietly in Dutch.

'Sex is for fun, for pleasure, don't go all English on me. What do you enjoy, what would help, what is your cup of tea? Don't be shy. English men, they are always shy, afraid the world will suddenly collapse when someone finds out they sniffed their sister's nickers once or caught crabs in a Manila brothel or bought a blow-up doll. Don't be shy with me, English man. You've done the tough bit – talking. What do you fancy? A striptease. I tell you I'm not very good, and I'm getting self-conscious about my flab. Or some porn. We have some good porn in Holland, maybe you have heard. Maybe this is why you are here.'

How can people be so different? How could Harriet be so different from Diana? How could I be so different from Karl. This plasticity of human behaviour has never ceased to amaze me. Professionally, I have met men and women of many different races and cultures. The religions, customs and patterns of behaviour differ hugely from country to country, and these are often emboldened in our mind by stereotypes. Yet what matters most in personal relationships, whether in a marriage or round the business table, is an individual's character, and this varies most from extreme to extreme <u>within</u> each race and nationality.

And as for falling in love, we understand little more today – give or take some inconsequential neuro-psychological science – than the great British poets Donne and Shakespeare did 500 years ago. Would I have fallen for Diana without the experience of Harriet behind me? Possibly, probably, given the chance? But, the converse is not true. Without Karl, Diana would not have looked at me twice.

I woke early, my mouth dry, my bladder full, and my head buzzing with emotions, memories of sensations, feelings of satisfaction and anxious projections about the future. I moved quietly through to the bathroom and then to the lounge, where I promptly fell asleep on the sofa. Before nine, Diana had dressed and made us both a milk coffee. We took a tram to Leidsestraat, and, hand-in-hand, walked slowly along Keizersgracht. The sun's warmth meant a light mist hovered over the canal. I remember feeling happier than I had for many, many years. At Leliegracht we cut across to Cafe't Smalle to scoff pancakes on the terrace. It was a restaurant we returned to often in the coming months, until a new owner cheapened the decor and food to attract more students. Afterwards, Diana made some purchases at the cute cheese and organic produce market that hung around the base of Westerkerk, before putting me on a tram back to Central Station.

I had meant to spend the Sunday working, but instead of returning to Weissenbruchstraat I walked a kilometre or so to the Mauritshuis near the parliament, thinking to divert my lively mind with the Vermeer classics that a colleague had recommended I see. It didn't work. I kept thinking about Diana, and particularly about how I should proceed to woo her, not wanting to be too keen, and not wanting to be too English. We had parted without another definite arrangement and I was worried she might perceive me as a one-off entertainment, a show that closed after the first night. On my way out, I noticed that a side room was dedicated to old photos of the Mauritshuis itself and the surrounding area. This gave me an idea. When I got home, I spent hours on the net educating myself about 19th century Dutch photography and downloading onto Neil a menu full of favourites. But it was the Asser photo of Keizersgracht (the one I have already mentioned) that I picked out to print and send by courier to Diana with a note thanking her for such a lovely evening, and promising to call.

A few days later I received, also by courier, an old French postcard with a crude sketch drawn using contours of red and green lines. In the envelope, curiously, there was a square of transparent red plastic. I have the postcard picture on my screen now. It shows a smiling man standing in the sea (right side) looking towards a young agitated woman on the beach (left side). She is dressed in a gown and has a bow in her hair. The card reads: 'Qu'à donc la

Baronne à courrir si vite?' (Why is the Baroness running so fast?) When the square of red plastic is placed over the left-hand side of the card, it has the effect of removing the red lines leaving only the green ones visible. The woman now appears naked. She has large breasts and a huge ass (not unlike Diana herself). A new caption says: 'Pourvu que l'on ait rien vu.' (Hopefully, nobody saw anything.) On the back, Diana had written, very lightly in pencil: 'Don't lose the red square English man.' Over the next few months, she sent me a collection of cards from the same set. And she also helped me find a way of copying them onto Neil: after scanning we used art software to separate out the red and green and to create a simple key command for removing the red. I must show them to Chintz later on.

Our love and friendship progressed at a measured pace. It took a few months for us to be comfortable with, and confident in, each other. Thereafter we found a routine which involved me spending part of every other weekend at her apartment in Amsterdam, and us meeting occasionally during the week, perhaps in Leiden for dinner or a film, or, if she was not too busy, in The Hague. I usually made the effort, for my pleasure as much as to support Diana, to be present at any mid-week opening nights, whether in Amsterdam or elsewhere. Occasionally, I would be travelling or too busy at the weekend in which case I opted to sacrifice a tedious trip to London rather than time with Diana. Harriet objected to my inconsistencies and would then make subsequent visits awkward for me. After a while, neither she nor the children noticed if I only showed up once a month. At times, Diana became feverishly busy, even at weekends, spending long periods in her studio engaged in camphone conversations, art work on the screen, or model building. Nevertheless, she would like me there in the apartment. So I would bring papers from The Hague, and read or write in the lounge; sometimes, if the weather was fine, I would walk across to Vondel Park with a report or a problem to mull over. Diana preferred to design for the theatre but, occasionally, took on festival and opera projects when they paid better. During her youth, she had often worked abroad, especially in Germany with Karl; by the time I met her, though, she had become tired of too much movement, and preferred to save her travelling for pleasure.

In the summer after my move to the Netherlands, I returned to England for two weeks, which was the minimum time I could negotiate with Harriet for being in charge of Crystal and Bronze. We stayed with Julie for one week making various excursions to the coast and adventure playgrounds. We saw Tom twice choosing the cinema for our entertainment both times. For the other week, I packed Crystal and Bronze off to an expensive camp while I visited friends and work colleagues. I also took two days for a stay in Bradford to explore the recently-expanded National Photography Museum (with which I was to have a closer association later in my life). This pattern remained similar for most of the 30s, although during one summer I looked after Crystal and Bronze in the Netherlands for two weeks, and, during another, Diana and I suffered a foursome holiday at a rented cottage in Devon. I hate to admit it, these were periods to be endured. Crystal took on a positively antagonistic attitude towards Diana, and, when reproved, slipped all too easily into a Harriet-type sulk, while Bronze lurched from one asthma attack to another with allergy rashes in-between. Assuming I stick to my outline plan, I will have much more to say about Crystal and Bronze in later chapters.

***

Diana and I took our first joint holiday, to Toulouse, in the autumn of the year we met. The following May, to celebrate our anniversary, we signed up for a 15 day group tour to the Andes. Neither of us had been away on an organised tour before, but with so little time (two weeks was the longest continuous holiday I could take) and travelling so far away, it seemed only sensible to make the most efficient use of it. We chose a British company recommended by one of Diana's friends, and were not disappointed by the guide or the itinerary: Lima, Cuzco, Machu Picchu, La Paz, Lake Titicaca, the Andes themselves. Subsequently, Diana employed an Inca motif for one of her play designs; and I added to my Ferrez collection by finding and copying a few early Peruvian photographs, such as those taken by the Courret brothers, Abraham Guillén and Martin Chambi, all roughly contemporaneous with, or slightly later than, Brazil's Marc Ferrez.

On that tour, Diana and I engaged with most of the other participants politely but as infrequently as possible. However, we did choose to spend free time with a Canadian couple, both journalists, from Montreal – Ike and Augusta Davidson. Diana and Augusta stayed in touch after the holiday, and, on Augusta's suggestion, we decided to use the same tour company for a similar activity holiday 18 months later to East Timor and the eastern islands of Indonesia. We were lucky to return alive.

There is much about that holiday which I could recall: the Hindu festival and the hot springs on Bali, strange green birds seen during a trek up Rindjani on Lombok, Ike's oddly aggressive tantrum over the mosquito spray on Flores, and our visit to the impressive mangrove plantations in West Timor developed to help with shoreline protection. My purpose, though, in mentioning the holiday is not to provide a travelogue but to lead up to 28 December 2035. We nicknamed the storm, which hit us that night, Cyclone Kip in honour of my birthday which began a couple of hours before the storm's eye. It was not officially recorded as a cyclone, nevertheless it did more damage to East Timor than any other disaster since the Indonesian army had sacked the already ruined country before its independence, more than 30 years earlier. Until global warming started messing with the world's climate, Indonesia had remained largely outside the cyclone zone. Two or three true cyclones had come dangerously close to Timor during the previous decade, but not to the extent of worrying the tour companies.

We lodged in large wood huts, built on stilts, 300-400 metres back from a delightful beach at Osolata. Although appearing traditional, the huts had been built solidly for tourists with glass windows and plumbed shower rooms. When planning these trips, I positively insisted on not taking the budget option, and even Diana, with more experience of travelling than I, would agree that the extra expense could be well spent. That evening, the 12 of us on the tour ate and drank well at a restaurant designed to cater for the tourists staying in the mod-con huts. As the meal progressed, so the wind outside grew in force. Our waiter even closed the shutters; and the restaurant owner told us, with a huge smile, that 'a beeeeg storm' was coming.

Later, Ike, Augusta, Diana and I all linked arms to walk back to our huts through the howling wind and rain. Diana proposed Ike and Augusta return to our hut, but they wanted to get out of their wet clothes and go to bed. Diana and I went to bed too, cuddling together more than usual, but nervously talking about our friends and the laid-back guide, and how good it would be to get back home soon. Suddenly, the door flew open and banged violently backwards and forwards. I had to drag a chest of drawers through the water (which had begun to puddle inside) to ensure the door stayed closed. By the time I'd dried myself and got back into bed, Diana was convinced the house was not only shaking slightly, but beginning to wobble. It felt sturdy to me, but I began to feel it might be safer if we got up and dressed. I collected our passports, money, phonepads and credit cards, placed them in a plastic bag, and put the bag down my trousers. When the eye of the storm came, and with it a peaceful silence, we both drifted off to sleep using sheets and cushions on the cane chairs. Less than half an hour later, I was woken with an almighty bang as a small tree crashed into the side of our wooden verandah. From nothing at all to full force, the storm came back within minutes. I suggested to Diana that we might be safer outside or at the restaurant which had concrete-built walls, but she nodded towards the door which I had barricaded, indicating it would be difficult to get out. Instead, we took our sheets and cushions and struggled to hide under the bed. We had only been there a few minutes when the house exploded.

I remember screaming involuntarily and somersaulting through the air, and simultaneously Diana screaming. Then I must have been unconscious for a few seconds. As I regained awareness, instinctively I lifted my head slightly but the wind was so powerful and carried so much debris (stinging sand, bits of wood) that I pushed my face sideways towards the sandy, muddy ground. I tried yelling for Diana, but had no idea how far my voice would carry over the howling and swishing of the tempest. I could see nothing through the darkness and I was unable to orientate myself relative to the hut or where it had been. Without moving my legs (I was afraid they might be broken and did not want to test them), I groped around with a hand until I caught hold of a heavy piece of wood (which proved to be part of the bed), and pulled this over my head for protection. I continued shouting for Diana until my throat went sore. I was terribly afraid that her failure to hear me or answer meant she might be dead or badly injured. I tried to think through where she might be or what might have happened, and whether there was any means of finding her. Even if I could run through the deadly wind, though, I figured I hadn't the faintest idea which direction to take. I also realised, after a while, that although neither of my legs were broken my left knee was injured and bleeding. As time wore on, the water level rose slightly and I began to shiver with cold. While the raging wind and flying debris continued unabated, I convinced myself that I must have been the lucky one and that Diana and our friends were dead.

I lay there for two or three hours, regularly shouting into the gale and peering into the darkness looking for movement or lights or the shape of a tree, before the wind began to lessen. Several times I thought I heard human voices but when I couldn't hear the same pattern again, I assumed it had been a noise mirage. Only with the first rays of light, and when the wind had quietened to nothing more than a strong gale, did I feel able to try and stand up and – with a very heavy heart – search for Diana. The gash in my knee stung viciously, and I gave momentary thought to the possibility of infection. But I had to find Diana.

She was no more than 20 metres away, uninjured and, compared to me, in relative comfort. She too had been thrown through the air but not so far. She had held on to a cushion, landed near the mattress and managed to crawl under it. Like me, she had undergone mental torment thinking I must be dead. A few metres away, where the hut had been, a single wall stood crookedly at an angle supported by fallen beams, broken planks and piles of crushed furniture looking not unlike a bonfire prepared for Guy Fawkes night. When I felt down inside my trousers, I was relieved to discover the plastic bag still in place. For a while longer, we lay together under the mattress hugging each other very tightly. Diana kissed me repeatedly as though needing to reassure herself of my living presence, and I couldn't help from saying to myself over and over again 'thank god' as if the words had meaning.

With more light and less wind, we made our way (I hobbling and Diana supporting me) along the debris-strewn walkway, manoeuvring over or round the roots and branches of fallen palms to where our friends had been staying. Although the verandah had gone, the structure of their hut had otherwise remained in tact. Inside, Augusta was shaken, but Ike, whose comic talents were not always appreciated (by me especially), greeted us (or me in particular) with this line: 'I thought you guys were doing something about this stuff.' Only then did he perceive the state we were in and the blood running down my leg. Augusta apologised for her husband and rushed me to the shower room where she had plenty of first aid paraphernalia.

Osolata, and hundreds of other towns and villages across Timor, suffered terrible damage as a result of Cyclone Kip. But, as far as I could find out from enquiries later, only a handful of people died as a direct result of the storm. Obviously, there was huge coverage of the disaster in the East Timorese press. The Indonesian media, though, was not so interested in the plight of the East Timorese people but in whether there might be a trend for tropical storms and cyclones to move west and hit Bali or Java.

In Dili, the following day, and on the plane home, and for weeks after, I thought often about how so much of the damage was local, to villages and local infrastructure, and I wondered how repairs and replacements would be paid for. I imagined that some individuals and small organisations would be clued up enough to seek compensation from the authorities, and that some aid agencies would provide assistance to others. But tens of thousands of individuals would have lost their homes, or their livestock, or their crops, or their possessions, and the vast majority of them would just carry on as best they could, more impoverished than before. I was no stranger to this issue: how to make aid work at a micro level across the globe in millions of villages and rural areas where the poverty, health and environmental problems were at their worst, as opposed to employing the easy option and depositing huge grants on bribe-fuelled inefficient governments willing to kowtow to Western demands.

Fortunately, I never had the wound on my knee stitched. It healed with a two inch scar, and, thereafter, I was able to embellish on my Cyclone Kip adventures whenever it was noticed by friends or family. The adventure firmed up our (or more accurately Diana's) friendship with Ike and Augusta; and, perhaps, it also strengthened my relationship with Diana.

Two days after our return to Amsterdam it was 1 January 36. But this was no ordinary new year's day. It was a Tuesday.

***

Since the influential United Nations report on the state of nations and the emergence of the First Tuesday Movement (FTM), only one new year's day had fallen on a Tuesday, and that, coincidentally, was in 2030, at the start of a new decade. From Buenos Aires to Nepal, from Paris to Manila, from Kinshasa to Oslo, cities across the globe witnessed some of the largest demonstrations in their history. In European metropolises such as Munich, Marseilles and Birmingham there were violent skirmishes between Muslim and Christian hooligans. It was estimated that nearly a billion people worldwide may have marched or protested against their government or multinationals or racism or pollution or poverty. That was the day, though, that led governments everywhere to take serious notice of the FTM: not only did the size and breadth of the protests scare the authorities, but some cities, especially in the developing countries, witnessed widespread looting and a significant number of injuries and deaths.

The FTM did not vanish thereafter, far from it; but, in the subsequent six years, there was no single Tuesday which brought out so many people on a global scale again. There were several explanations for this. Governments certainly succeeded by a variety of means (appeals/propaganda, firm prohibition announcements, far stricter controls, armed police etc.) in reducing the FTM appeal. A few countries with autocratic governments managed to stamp the protests out completely by imposing marshal law and shooting those who ignored it. Moreover, many of the demonstrators, having seen the extent of the unruly behaviour that day, decided not to march again. But, it was widely believed that the main reason for such a mass turnout on 1 January 30 was because of the conjunction of a first Tuesday with new year's day.

The movement itself had no concrete identity. It never had any formal headquarters, nor any leaders; coordination of meetings, marches and protests emerged organically through netsites or inadvertent signalling by the media. Authoritarian attempts to censor the net failed, and often backfired. At the command of the EU's member state governments, for example, the Euronet Agency looked into whether it would be possible to impose a ban on propagating FTM information through Solar, the open Euronet, but concluded it would be impossible to police. Where governments elsewhere did try, their efforts often proved counter-productive and led to bigger and wilder first Tuesday marches than usual.

So, on our return from Timor, the media was full of speculation about what would happen on Tuesday 1 January 36. Everyone who intended to be on the streets was, in effect, a potential FTM propagandist, and there was, therefore, no shortage of media material and advance publicity. In European cities, immigrants of all races and all colours were FTM adherents mostly because they felt, as the working classes had done in the first half of the 20th century, down-trodden; pensioners marched to the FTM tune because, for more than a decade, they had been cheated out of a comfortable old age; and youths were ready to use the FTM banner to protest about anything and everything unfair (unemployment, racism, war and gene technology to name but four targets). In the developing countries, where reasonably democratic governments had failed to silence the FTM, street spokespersons were anxious to rail against the riches of Europe, Japan and the US (especially their governments and businesses) and, like the youths in the West, wanted a fairer world; or else they wished to protest against their own poverty or lack of medicines or government corruption. Many of these would-be protesters could be seen in newsclips wearing the adaptable FTM logo, often with the middle T converted into a gallows hanging the dollar, euro or UN symbol.

Globally, the FTM attracted its biggest ever multitudes that day, and its worst. Looting and violence – Triti Madan's predicted 'endemic social terrorism' – was the norm, not the exception, in many cities.

In Amsterdam, as usual, crowds flocked to Vondel Park to hear spontaneous soap-box speakers, to sing protest songs and then to bring half the city to a standstill by marching to the Central Station. This time, though, the crowds were tenfold the usual numbers on a first Tuesday, and the marchers managed to cause a huge amount of damage on their way. Two children drowned in a canal. In London, the police used water cannons and plastic bullets to break up massive crowds which had dispersed from the official march routes. Nineteen people died from violence of one sort or another. In Paris, Brussels, Hamburg and many other European cities and towns, inter-racial clashes led to deaths, hundreds of injuries and thousands of arrests. In Cairo, Nairobi, Karachi, Djakarta, Mexico City the ransacking of multinational business premises was the worst it had ever been, and heavy-handed police may have killed up to 1,000 all told. In other cities such as São Paulo, Caracas, Moscow, and Seoul looting under cover of the city-wide chaos caused by the FTM resulted in billions of dollars of stolen goods and damage. Events that day led, eventually, to several requested interventions by the UN and European armies, not least the one that caused the Jamaica Skirmish in 37.

It was in the United States, though, that the most dramatic change between 30 and 36 was evident. The FTM had been slow to build in the US and Canada (partly because the late 20s and early 30s had seen a very slow recovery from recession and unemployment) but by 34-35 the FTM had taken off, fuelled, as in most other Western countries, by youthful disillusionment with capitalist ideals. The under-privileged masses, which in the US were the black and Mexican peoples, joined the protests on 1 January 36 in their millions, protesting partly for themselves but also against their government's arrogance in world affairs. The next day the headlines did not reflect the protesters' objectives but the rioting, looting, violent clashes and deaths. Of the large nations, only Japan and China remained relatively untroubled, but then they were among the countries to suffer most from the suicide epidemics a little later in the 40s.

New year's day 2036 day proved to be the FTM's zenith. Spontaneous first Tuesday protests continued around the world for many years but never again to the same extent.

***

The year 35 had come and gone without Enterprise 35 achieving its goal - a fact that had certainly provoked FTM protesters on new year's day 36. No-one, though, could blame Pravit Krishnamurty. He was a slave to the cause, and inspired most of his staff, including me, to be the same. The problem, inevitably, came from politics and the interplay of demands by various important donor or receptor governments. In the autumn of 34, there had been a follow-up meeting of world leaders aimed at transposing the Kiev agreement into reality. As a result, they had publicly promised to reach a conclusion the following November (35) in Vancouver. Secretly, or in the fine print of the preparatory accords, though, they had made so many contradictory demands that a deal looked doubtful. We all worked feverishly towards the Vancouver summit. Some weeks it appeared as though Pravit never left the (state-of-the-art) cam-conference room, having to listen and negotiate with so many different factions. There was less pressure on my own team because, whereas the others were engaged in preparing financial and legalistic detail for a formal agreement on how to spend the extra 0.2%, we had only to draft a set of recommendations.

Vancouver proved an embarrassing failure for the European proposal, the UN, and for the IFSD in particular, not because Enterprise 35 couldn't deliver, but because certain countries (the US, Germany, Japan, Russia, Nigeria and Brazil) were at loggerheads over several basic issues, and because of a serious stand-off between the Christian and Muslim worlds. A decision was stalled and a new summit scheduled for the following autumn in London.

I believe the United Nations would have reached agreement in London on the primary issues without the FTM chaos of 1 January 36 but, possibly, it might not have responded so positively to my own team's recommendations for future expansions. Under cover of the laborious and aggressive bargaining on details surrounding the committed 0.2%, my group had quietly beavered away with our hugely ambitious and optimistic plans to transfer four times as much money again from the rich to the needy. In this respect, Pravit proved to be an inspired strategist. While he consistently pandered to the IFSD executive board on the main issues vis-à-vis the initial 0.2%, knowing that its members were simply reflecting the views of their national governments which were, in any event, being played out at all the negotiating conferences, he managed to minimise their attention to the drafts of my report. Naturally, the executive board, and the steering committee did examine my team's work from time to time, and, at the summit preparatory meetings, we were always fully exposed to every nation's negotiators. Nevertheless, through Pravit's management, we managed to press forward in a kind of camouflaged ideological haze in which no rich nation wanted to be seen as anything less than beneficent towards the future well-being of the planet, so long as no real final commitments were at stake.

To divert for a moment to the personal, I wish to recall a particularly gruesome encounter with Rike Thomas, the oily man from the overseas aid section of the UK's Department of External Affairs. Not needing to contact him regularly was one bonus of my leaving the Department of the Environment, not that oily people didn't grease my Enterprise 35 office on a near daily basis. In private, Rike may have been an agreeable person but, somehow, he got up my nose more than most. When I was at Shropshire House, he would beg favours or ask for information, and demand to take me out for lunch or a drink in recompense. He gossiped continually, and had a childish name-dropping habit. He must have been good at his job, or how else would he have survived in it for so long. Unfortunately, after moving to The Hague I didn't lose sight of him completely because, on some issues, he was involved, as the UK's representative, in preparing the EU's input into the Enterprise 35 process. Prior to one meeting at our offices, he called to invite me to lunch. When I declined politely, he said he had a 'message' for me, and insisted on a private meeting. I gave way and agreed to a light snack at Jaspar's, near the gloriously nicknamed 'tits and penis' town hall. I ordered and ate quickly while Rike rambled on about how his wife's horse shared the same stables as a horse ridden by the wife of a cabinet minister; and how, unusually, he had actually been present at a meeting with John Lyndquist, the prime minister, and so on. I wasn't really listening until, through Jaspar's hum of banter, some words came into focus.

'... and, so you see, His Majesty's Government, HMG, your paymaster, is calling you to service. It's an honour really.'

When I got to the bottom of Rike's meaning, it wasn't so much an honour I uncovered but a threat. I was being leaned on to tone down the scale of Enterprise 35's ambitions. Rike suggested there might be a senior civil servant's job waiting for me 'back home' if I did as advised, but that if I was 'stupid enough not to listen' I would make 'a lot of important people unhappy'. My secondment to Enterprise 35 might be brought to a swift and unpleasant end, Rike warned. Even today, thinking about the snake makes me squirm. I never discovered how much he personally had elaborated on the 'message', but it was a clumsy and ill-judged manoeuvre. I knew the left wing of the Conservative Alliance could never have approved it (this Horace confirmed later by talking to his friend Terrance Spoon); and the Green Party, which was also part of the governing coalition, would rather have left the coalition than be involved in any attempt to weaken the IFSD. In short, the UK's finance minister, a Lyndquist loyalist positioned well to the right within the Conservative Alliance, had become alarmed by the latest draft of my team's report, and perceived a real danger that Pravit's tactics, especially after 1 January 36, might eventually lead to a yet bigger drain on the UK government's purse. One of his over-keen advisers had then worked up a ploy or two.

The main reason I mention this unsavoury episode is because I decided, as I was walking back from Jaspar's to the office, that I would, when the time was right, seek a permanent posting with the IFSD.

At the London summit, in October 36, the Western world agreed on all the myriad conditions and parameters for most developed countries to provide within three years an additional 0.2% in overseas development aid, half of it directly to the IFSD. The recipient countries, for their part, all made further commitments to deal with corruption and inefficiencies, to spread the incoming wealth to rural areas, to open up ownership and trade rights, and to tackle crime against foreign-owned property.

Astonishingly, moreover, the London summit participants signed up to a further total increase of 0.5% in two stages, raising the level by 0.25% each, starting in 39. While the wording on this was not as firm and committed as the Kiev agreement had been on the first 0.2%, it was still far more than most commentators expected after the Vancouver failure.

'What do you British say? Hah, I have it. Bingo,' Pravit whispered to me in a corridor when he knew for certain the content of the agreement. 'I believed, in my heart of hearts, there would only be one further increment of 0.2% – not so much work for the packagers. And now look how well the gods have treated us.'

The gods indeed. He might have been referring sarcastically to the world's leaders or to the fact that the 0.5% deal came largely as a result of growing religious (Muslim-Christian) conflict in Africa, Central Asia and Europe, which stemmed, the Arab/Africa lobby believed, from the odious inequality of riches. There is no doubt that the worldwide FTM disturbances at the start of the year contributed to the Arab/Africa cause, as did the escalating climate problems which regularly seemed to kill so many more poor people in poor countries than rich people in rich countries.

I am tempted to go on at length about the work my team did, and the content of the 0.5% deal, but this is a matter of public record and the UN's archives surely contain our final report delivered to the London summit. Besides, I have more to write about the IFSD in the next chapter and my role therein. Suffice it to say that the original European Union proposal to raise development aid by 1.1% in five stages (the initial 0.3% and four further increments of 0.2% each) had been whittled back to a 0.7% increase in three steps (an initial 0.2%, followed by two further increments of 0.25% each), but that, nevertheless, the Kiev and London agreements together constituted one of the UN's greatest ever achievements.

After the London summit, Enterprise 35 was disbanded, and most of the seconded staff offered permanent posts within a new 'future policy division' created to prepare the way for the next two expansions. I was recalled to Shropshire House for a meeting with the Department's most senior official and Jude Singleton. Rike Thomas's threat clung to me like an irritating boil that demanded squeezing but wouldn't subside, so I expected to be told I had let my country down and other disagreeable things. In fact, the reverse was true. My seniors had anticipated that I would want to stay on at the IFSD and were ready to entice me back with a grand lunch at Jude's club, and a significant promotion to section head (overseeing the environmental health of the country's waterways) within the Department. It would have been impolitic to refuse on the spot, so I said I would consider the offer. I took the opportunity, though, to gossip about Rike's dirty stick-and-carrot in the hope that the story might be spread round.

Half-jokingly and half-deviously, I tested the job offer on Pravit. He had been appointed director of the newly-created future policy division, and was in the process of devising its structure. He had already invited me to be a unit head, but I was still officially a British civil servant.

'Pravit, I've been offered an excellent post in the UK's Department of the Environment. Do you think I should take it?'

'I have been thinking about you Kip. Are you well?'

'Yes.'

'Are you happy here in the Netherlands?'

'I could be happy in London too,' I lied, thinking about Diana.

'And me. Am I happy?'

'I hope so. Enterprise 35 achieved more than you dared hope.'

'You know and I know it is not enough. It will never be enough. We can only do our best. But that is not why I am unhappy at this minute.' He looked very serious, almost forlorn. I couldn't tell whether he wanted me to speak, and there was a long pause before I responded.

'Why are you unhappy, Pravit ?' Suddenly and transparently, his expression lifted.

'I cannot decide who should be my deputy director.' A pause. 'The hints come from above and from the side, but I plan to make up my own mind, be my own man, as you British say. And then, finally when I make up my mind, the very person I have chosen – a highly intelligent thinker, a loyal colleague, a hard-working efficient administrator, and a nice fellow to boot – tells me he is leaving. If you can be happy in London, then, Kip, you must go. Yes you must go. Hah. You never know where you are with the British.'

Thus I became a UN employee, and stayed one for the best part of 30 years.

***

Flora has been absent for the last few days. I thought she might have had a relapse and been confined to her charpoy (which she insists on calling it, though her bed is nothing like one), but she just whirred in, and talked with such excitement I thought she might fall out of the Easy. She wanted to tell me about a stream of unexpected visitors (how does she cope with them?): some maharajah she had once known, and his daughters, visiting the UK; a great-grandson over from California; and the daughter of a niece who wanted to record her talking about her life history.

'I said no, no, no, my name's not Kip Fenn. And I dislike her intensely, she only suggested it because she wants me to remember her in my will.' And then, forgetting my low tolerance threshold, she prattled on about life in India with her husband, an expert in pharmaceutical manufacturing processes, 50 years ago or more. I closed my eyes until I heard her hum away.

And Tom slipped into my mind.

I want to conclude this chapter by introducing Guido, but before him, I need to give my father, Tom, a send-off. The last film we saw together was on my 38th birthday. During the afternoon we took Crystal and Bronze to one of the West End superscreens to see Aaron Lambert's *Marcella's Bullet*. There had been the usual commercial hype but, despite this, the film had attracted rave reviews. There were long queues to buy popcorn and to enter the auditorium. Unusually, both my children were content at the choice of film, and even I was interested to see what all the fuss was about (having missed the first Marcella film and only see one of Lambert's early adventure flicks). Marcella was billed as a modern female version of Batman, James Bond and Pacific Prince all rolled into one. Having inherited a fortune from her corrupt father (lots of flashbacks and opportunities for side plots), she had become a special private detective helping the unfortunates of New York gather evidence against their rich oppressors. In several of the stories (*Marcella's Bullet* and *Misty Marcella* for example), the International Police Authority persuaded her to close her Harlem office for a week or two and help them unravel a complex plot against the world, or capture some colourful villain. The formula worked splendidly, partly because Lambert was a genius storyteller, and partly because Lyra Hampton (who needs no introduction, even to youngsters today) brought intelligence, compassion, a touch of Irish humour and a cartoon sexiness to the role. Tom loved it. Crystal was inspired enough to forget to sulk afterwards and complain precociously about Marcella being nothing like a real person. And Bronze kept asking questions because the plot had been over his head. After milkshakes, we took the children back to Lacey's Lane; and then Tom and I went on to have an Indian meal in Willesden Green. He looked grey and tired; and he hadn't taken much care of his dress. He told me Fragrance had walked out on him and filed a legal suit for alimony. I guess, in retrospect, she killed him, she and drink. He certainly drank heavily that night – drank and coughed. I decided to go back to Epsom with him rather than stay in Harriet's lounge on the sofa-bed (the bad memories were overpowering) or return to Julie in Godalming. He fell asleep in the taxi, and I had to manhandle him into the house. The next morning, he apologised on his way to the loo, and then went back to bed. He was sleeping when I left.

A few weeks later, he called to tell me he'd had a heart attack and been admitted to Kingston Hospital. I took an early evening flight, and spent the night in Godalming. In the morning, Julie, who hadn't seen Tom for ten years but carried a dim torch for her ex-husband, wanted to come too. Tom was dozing when we arrived, but a nurse explained he had advanced cardiomy-opathy. A doctor advised heart surgery. We waited 20 minutes or so until he stirred. Once fully awake, he was in good humour; seeing Julie, though, gave him a shock.

'Bloody hell! Have I passed to the other side?' But it was said with a touch of the old charm, and he followed it up with warm words. I could see he was genuinely delighted to see her. He confessed that he had no intention of agreeing to any surgery. 'Never trusted doctors, and no intention to start now,' he said with conviction.

Julie drove the two of us back to Godalming, and then I borrowed her car to return later in the day and spend another couple of hours with him. He had become maudlin, morbid almost.

' "I see earth, it's so beautiful." They were the first recorded words spoken by a man in space. And then, in his statement afterwards, Gagarin said, "There was a good view of earth which had a very distinct and pretty blue halo. It had a smooth transition from pale blue, dark blue, violet and absolutely black. It was a magnificent picture." I've been wondering if life's a bit the same. Gagarin missed out the dark blue and violet, but me I've been there. And now I'm heading for the black.' He closed his eyes for a few seconds before slowly drawing out the familiar words, 'Well fucking say something.' But before I had chance to offer my usual rejoinder, he carried on with another Gagarin story, as if to cheer himself up.

'Did you know that in the official Soviet records there is no mention of Gagarin using a parachute ejection system, although he ejected at seven kilometres above the earth's surface to avoid the deadly impact of the capsule landing. The international aviation rules at the time stated that a pilot had to remain in his craft from launch to landing. Officially, he could have been disqualified from his record.' Tom loved this piece of trivia. 'He died, you know, before Armstrong got to the moon. I hope I don't go before Martian Seven.' I reassured him that he had many years to live. A taxi would be taking him home the following day, he said, and he'd be fine. It sounds corny, but I gave him a kiss on the cheek before I left, not because I didn't expect to see him again, but because he had appeared so sad, so vulnerable.

Four weeks later, his local doctor called me, as next of kin, to inform me that he had died from a massive coronary earlier that day. He had been sitting in his car about to go somewhere, and a neighbour watching from a window had seen him slump over the steering wheel.

The funeral took place at Croydon Crematorium. Wreaths, a few warm words and he was gone. Julie and I were the only two truly mourning. Harriet came with our children; Fragrance was there with a boyfriend, although she never spoke to me; and there were a few colleagues from Euroil. His will left bequests of 10,000 euros each to Crystal and Bronze, and the rest to me. After expenses and duties, and a negotiated deal with Fragrance, I inherited around 300,000 euros. I spent more than a quarter of it to launch Tom's ashes into space. The extortionately priced package came complete with an elaborately framed certificate and a three minute camclip of the moment the ashes were released into space (a view of planet earth behind). It was an irrational gesture for which I offer no explanation. Harriet thought it was madness, but Diana, who only ever worried about money in terms of the budget a director had given her, said I had surprised her — which was a compliment. I have the recording on Neil, and I've asked Jay to save it with all the rest of the family paraphernalia for future generations.

***

Guido. Here, on my screen, is a photo of him, aged but three weeks. He is wearing a bright blue all-in-one, centimetres too long for him in the feet. And here is one of the Guido co-op standing atop Peter's barge. It was Guido's fourth birthday, in December 42. Guido himself, who is perched on a raised hatch, is wearing a dark suit, a white bow-tie, and a top hat. (Diana loved dressing him up when he was young enough to put up with it.) Behind him, the four us – that's Peter, Dominique (Diana's younger sister), Diana and me – are all leaning slightly back in an arc and pointing fingers at Guido as if to say 'you're the man' or similar. I have a camclip from the same day of Guido making paper aeroplanes, and Dominique's two older children looking decidedly unimpressed. I do not like to view it, though, because it always brings Dr Jessop to mind. There is a moment in the camclip when Guido's face is at a half angle to the camera. The first time I saw it, I was reminded of someone, but I couldn't think who. The image of Guido stuck with me for days until I woke in the night startled by a dream in which I had gone to a doctor's surgery and seen a framed camstill of Guido standing on the doctor's desk.

But this is my favourite photo: Guido, at five and a half years of age, and I holding hands and laughing while running down a grassy hill towards the camera. It was taken, with Diana's camera, on the English South Downs by Veronique, Mireille's older sister, in June 45. I almost decided not to mention this photo now because it will be too complicated to explain, yet here I am delving back (or forward whichever way you care to look at it). Straightaway I should explain that Guido married Mireille, some 20 years later. Veronique and Mireille (16 and seven years old respectively at the time) were the daughters of Didier and Helene Rocard, a Parisian couple involved in the theatre, who were among Diana's closest friends. Veronique had recently arrived in Brighton for a long summer of English study, and Diana had arranged for us all to meet on the West Pier. On the second day, Veronique, Guido and I went for a walk on the South Downs, while Diana stayed behind to discuss a future project with a director at the famous Candyfloss Theatre. (This bit of business, which never progressed, having only been arranged by Diana to help us self-justify the brief excursion across the Channel.) Before Brighton, we had been to Southampton, where my old friend Horace Merriweather had won a fifth election victory. After making his first celebration party in 27 (with Harriet), I had missed the following three, and there was no pressing reason for me to go to this one in particular either, other than that Horace had especially urged me to be there. Perhaps this was because I had recently taken over from Pravit as director and the UK media had highlighted my appointment, or because he wanted to show off his recently-acquired grand house or his new (and discreet!) partner. (I should stress that, by then, Arturo had moved out of Horace's Camden Town pad… This is making no sense. I knew the photo would lead me places I do not yet want to go.) In any case, the timing of the journey was good for Diana and me. After Horace's party in Southampton, we visited Julie, who by then had opted to follow her mother's route and retire in Parsonville, before heading to Brighton for a couple of days. Driving on towards Dover, at the end of our short holiday, we heard on the radio that prime minister Terrance Spoon (of the Progressive Party which was still the dominant partner within the Conservative Alliance) had appointed Horace as minister for business. This was his first (and last) government job.

Viewing these photos, however, is a digression from my main purpose of introducing Guido. On returning from London in November 36, after the meeting with Jude, I announced the job offer to Diana as though I were seriously considering it (just as I would to Pravit a day later) – which I wasn't. Diana's immediate reaction was one of indifference; she wanted to talk about the weekend's arrangements. When I admitted, later in the evening, that I had no intention of going back to work for the UK civil service, she got angry with me for playing games.

'Go, stay, I don't care,' she said, barely containing an edge of spite in her tone as well as her words. This hurt, and I was left for days reassessing the nature of our relationship. It had been about three years since we'd met, and, I believed, we had established something firm and real between us. On the rebound from Karl, Diana appreciated my stability and loyalty, my grounding in the 'real world', and, I suppose, my intellect. Karl, a successful German theatre director who dabbled in film, had been instrumental in Diana's own creative development, but he had also abused her professionally once too often. In their personal relationship, he had played fast and loose with her love, and left her several times for young actresses. For my part, I adored Diana. Whereas my time with Harriet had been like a promised feast with nothing to eat, life with Diana was a rich picnic full of sumptuous tastes and unexpected delicacies – although not one without its ants and wasps to contend with.

Sex was one irritating problem, Karl was another. Sex had always been an important part of Diana's life and, with effort, we enjoyed each other. But we did not have the need or passion to make such an effort very often. Despite her liberal attitude to pornography, for example, it was only acceptable to Diana intermittently (whereas it remained a minor but regular part of my private life). Cannabis (which I would take occasionally) and drink helped, but even so Diana made the running. She grumbled about this, which led occasionally to me sounding off about being in Karl's shadow. Too many conversations ended with some reference to him, or Diana's past. Moreover, Diana was far less intellectual than Harriet so I missed being able to discuss my work in any depth. But, as I say, life with Diana was a glorious picnic. For her, though, life with me must have seemed quiet and placid, and a welcome relief from being caught up in Karl's nervy unpredictable domain.

Some weeks after the 'I don't care' argument, when I had already signed my new United Nations employment papers, I began to consider moving to a larger and better situated apartment. Thinking I could reassure Diana about my love and commitment to her, I tentatively asked if she had ever thought we might live together some day. Again Diana put the conversation to one side, not wanting to be diverted from some creative process or other. A few days later, though, a small package arrived at my Weissenbruchstraat pad. It contained a British postcard from the 1950s of a man sitting on a chair with a baby lying across his lap. Here it is on my screen. The man, who has a cigarette hanging out of his smiling mouth, is in the process of tying up the baby's nappy. On the floor stands an upturned red lady's hat adorned with a yellow ribbon. There is something dark and indiscernible inside the hat. Behind the man, a woman in a dark green dressing gown is screaming, 'Don't give me guff! You knew damn well that was my new hat!' On the back Diana had written in pencil, 'What's guff?' And the package contained a paperback entitled *Co-ops – a better way to bring up children?*. My immediate reaction was to imagine that Diana was pregnant but, after a moment or two, I realised she would not have told me this way. Instead, she was enlarging my question about living together into a much bigger one. Although she had never talked about it, I had no trouble in under-standing why she had not opted for motherhood (Karl). I had also noticed that, unlike some women of her age, she had not positively decided against having children. Most of the time I had found her neutral and unopinionated on the subject. I emailed her that same morning. If I embroidered my language a little, it was surely because I'd taken on some of her ways, some of her confidence in our relationship. I received a reply before midday.

Having made the huge decision to have a child at the age of 43 (in fact she was 45 when Guido arrived), Diana spared no effort in making sure everything functioned properly, if I can put it that way, during her fertile spells. When her first two or three periods came, she did not mention them; but, by the time of the fourth, she had begun to express disappointment and concern, which soon turned into anxiety, and visits to the doctor. I thought she was being unreason-able, but logic did not work well on Diana. Moreover, she had had two abortions when younger, and she knew several women who were unable to conceive.

Although I had agreed to the idea of a co-op for our child (when and if she became pregnant), I continued to suggest we look for somewhere to live together. Diana, who had wanted to wait until she was pregnant before making a commitment on this, changed her mind in the spring of 37. Her sister Dominique, with children herself, suggested it might help in some way to prepare her psychologically for conceiving.

By August, we had moved into a modern-looking three storey semi-detached house in Leiden, 25 minutes walking (less than ten cycling) from the train station. We had looked at older traditional properties, and if Diana had insisted on one or if we had found a house suitable for our joint purposes, we would have taken it. But this one, on Oldwijkgaarten, won both our hearts. It was part of a 12 house (six building) complex built around a large green with car parking terminals on its outskirts. To arrive at the front doors it was necessary to walk through the communal garden, past the complex's central wind turbine with a kids' climbing frame around the base. Each building, individually designed with silver-coloured solar energy glass (a precursor of s-glass) and charcoal grey absorption tiles, had two private secluded gardens (one for each dwelling) accessed from the lounge areas at the back. I could afford the mortgage for the house on my salary alone, so Diana opted to keep her Amsterdam pad and rent it out (in case things didn't turn out well between us). After two years, though, she sold it to the tenant, and took over part of the capital and mortgage base on the Oldwijkgaarten house.

Inside our new home, there was sufficient space to allow Diana and me separate areas: Diana took the two top storey rooms for her studio (with the door between them removed), we took a bedroom each on the middle floor, and allocated the third room to our unborn child. On the ground floor, I took the eating room as my office (we usually ate in the kitchen or, with guests, in the lounge). The private garden was – what shall I say? – petite, but had been carefully tended with mature fragrant roses, miniature fruit trees (apple and plum) and attractive clematis climbers on the border fences.

It is possible that Anders was conceived the first time we made love in the house, but, even if he wasn't, Dominique's advice worked, whether it was prophetic, salient or serendipitous.

But, life rarely offers such an easy ride. Eighteen weeks into her pregnancy, we already knew our child would be a boy. Diana had asked if I would mind calling him Anders as it was the name of her mother's father who she had adored as a child. I agreed, thankful I had been consulted. With this settled, we invited, on two successive evenings, Dominique and her husband Waltar Meijer, and then Peter with Livia. Both Dominique and Peter had already indicated they would consider it a privilege to be part of the Anders co-op, but we wanted to discuss it more seriously with their partners as well. I knew from the book Diana had given me that ours was the simplest form of co-op, not far different from the old-fashioned parents and godparents model. Nevertheless, by accepting a co-op role, Dominique and Peter knew they would be expected to make a positive contribution towards Anders' future. Should Diana and I separate for any reason, or if one of us were to die, then their involvement might have to increase substantially. Neither Waltar nor Livia admitted any objection to the commitments made by their partners, although Peter intimated later that Livia was not wildly enthusiastic about the whole concept.

Nor was I. Yet I didn't care. Diana and I were living as man and wife, and that was enough for me.

A week after these serious meetings with our friends, Diana began experiencing sharp pains. Within a further two weeks she had miscarried. There was a horrible scene in the bathroom, with blood and histrionics in equal proportions. I was unable to bring Diana any comfort. The external festivities (with Christmas only two weeks away) emphasised our sadness. A local priest organised a short simple funeral service in a nearby chapel. Only the four of us from the co-op were present.

As scheduled, I then went to spend the holiday period in England finding little consolation in seeing Julie or Tom or my children. Diana went to stay with Dominique and her family. Two months later Tom died. A month after that Diana fell pregnant again – against the advice of her doctor. Guido (a name with no significance) Tom Oostlander-Fenn was born, a healthy plump chap, on 22 December 38. Only then was the Guido co-op formed out of the vestiges of the stillborn Anders co-op.

POSTCARD PICTURES AND CAPTIONS
Diana Oostlander to Kip Fenn

May 2033
Without the filter
A woman leans over to tie her shoes; a bowler-hatted gentleman behind spreads his hands across her rump.
Caption: Oh! Quelles formes appétissantes. [Oh! What an enticing body.]
With the filter
A naked woman has turned round and is slapping the man in the face.
Caption: Zut! Ma femme. [Drat! My wife.]

July 2033
Without the filter
A portly man in a beach gown looks towards a bathing hut.
Caption: Que fais donc ma femme – elle est bien longue? [Why is my wife taking so long?]
With the filter
Inside the hut, a naked girl is embracing a young man.
Caption: Ça y est je l'suis. [Oh I get it.]

September 2033

<u>Without the filter</u>

An old dear sits on the beach looking out to sea.

Caption: Que fais donc ma fille, sous l'eau avec son cousin? [What is my daughter doing in the water with her cousin?]

<u>With the filter</u>

In the sea, a topless girl, with the perkiest of cartoon breasts, embraces a boy with an excellent leer.

Caption: Voilà!

EXTRACTS FROM CORRESPONDENCE

<u>Kip Fenn to Diana Oostlander</u>

October 2034, Last night

I've discussed the fabrics with you at length. I've contemplated all manner of projections on your screen. I've seen the model. And yet the final results left me breathless with surprise. Last night's show was wonderful. The colloquial Dutch was a bit impenetrable here and there, but it didn't matter I was too busy admiring your genius.

One reviewer says (I translate badly), 'It is impossible to imagine any other designer but Diana Oostlander doing this play such justice.' Another says, 'Although Van den Bossche's intelligent excursion into the heart of Dutch man and Dutch land makes this a great play, Oostlander's set with the Inca motifs lifts it into one of the very best of recent years.'

I agree.

<u>Diana Oostlander to Kip Fenn</u>

October 2034, re: Last night

Darling, I've got up so late this morning – the party went on and on. I wish you could have stayed in Amsterdam last night. I haven't looked for the reviews yet, but I could feel the success in the theatre. It was very exciting. And I want to say something. I want to say that part of this is because of you. We were together in Peru, and your comments on my work made a big difference. You think I dismiss you as a businessman with no art (except for a few old dirty photos!!!) and I make you listen and then never listen back.

But I do, darling – so there.

xxx

Kip Fenn to Diana Oostlander

January 2037, Guff

Guff means nonsense, humbug. Also, I didn't know this before I looked it up, guff means a smell or a stink in Scottish dialect. Actually, I'm not bad at changing nappies, and I can promise I would never misuse any of your hats, however out of fashion they were, and however infrequently you wore them. As for a co-op, why do I always feel you are not content to tint my traditional values, but want to dye them a new colour altogether. I'll read the book tonight, if I can control the buzzing in my head, and the pumping in my heart.

Diana Oostlander to Kip Fenn

January 2037, re: Guff

Darling, I promise you that all my red hats will be available for guff duty – so there!!! But I am very glad of your reply, I've been anxious since I sent the packet.

Kip Fenn to Julie Fenn

June 2033

I was delighted to watch you in that education promotional film. You were the star. But did I read somewhere that the Conservative Alliance is planning to prune back the Independent Education Authority because its ideas are too 'progressive'? Won't this undermine all Jones' efforts even before anyone can prove the IEA's worth? You look smart and kind, the type of head any school kid would want – except for me! I can't think why I had a problem with you as my deputy head. Now you've done the film, isn't it time for a book.

I should mention that I've met someone. She's called Diana, and she couldn't be more different from Harriet. She's a successful theatre designer, and a bit older than me, but attractive and fun and <u>warm</u>. I've attached a photo of us taken in a tulip palace (the same night Caxton was killed – good riddance). It's early days, but I really like her. See you soon. The second weekend in July?

Julie Fenn to Kip Fenn

June 2033

Thank you for your note and the photo. Diana does look very attractive. I hope things go well. I hope to meet her soon. (By the way, Harriet rang the other day and asked me if I would look after Crystal and Bronze for a week in the summer. Did she discuss this with you?)

Yes, you are right. I am very worried about this government. Unfortunately, the right-wingers are running scared and only see education in a 20th century kind of way. A reassessment of the IEA's role was part of the Conservative Alliance's manifesto, but it's a question of how far it can or will go. The Authority may have made some mistakes, and it's still learning, but it would be a shame to stop it now. It's already made a number of important additions to the curriculum: basic democratic/community responsibilities, sustainable development, the understanding of cultural/national differences, simple money management, news monitoring, and healthy/sensible lifestyles among others. They could make such a big difference to people's lives in the long run.

Alan was here for a few weeks. He says he's going to start work on a book about floods. I remember him saying the same things five years ago. But it was lovely to see him.

All my love.

Kip Fenn to Julie Fenn

January 2036

It was good to talk with you on the camphone last week. It was some trip, as you gathered. Diana says 'sorry' for dragging me to faraway places. It's true I would have been happy to spend the two weeks on Bali, but Diana has a need for adventure – she got her money's worth this time.

See you soon.

Julie Fenn to Kip Fenn

January 2036

Do you know there are children in my youngest classes who have never seen snow. I don't know if that is a good thing or a bad thing, but I decided it was time we had an assembly on climate change. I made you the hero of the day, explaining about your Timor adventure and about your work there in The Hague. I was also surprised to discover that out of 350 children in my school more than 10% claimed they had experienced an extreme natural event of some kind (mostly tropical storms, but also floods and earthquakes).

I can't believe how far things went on new year's day. I think teenagers and young adults are so sad and distressed at the moment. I feel it's our fault – teachers and leaders.

I'll see you next weekend, yes?

All my love.

Kip Fenn to Julie Fenn

January 2037

Do you remember telling me a few years ago about one of your teachers who had formed a co-op for her first child. A Dorothy maybe, I can't remember exactly? How is she and the child?

Julie Fenn to Kip Fenn

January 2037

She's still with me, one of the better teachers in the school. She has two children by the same man, both co-ops I think. I don't know much else. Why are you asking?

Kip Fenn to Julie Fenn

January 2037

Diana and I intend to take the co-op path. She really wants a child before it gets too late, and I want to have one with her. I don't think we'll get married. Here's the blurb from the back of a book called *Co-ops – a better way to bring up children?* by Caspar Melville Junior. Yes, he's American, but it's not a one-sided tract by any means.

'Co-ops, in a recognisable form, began around 2010-15 as an alternative model for raising children. The concept originated in the UK, but spread more rapidly in the Netherlands, Scandinavia and the US. Although no country yet recognises the legality of co-ops, both Finland and Norway are looking at the possibility of legislation. In the US, the Christian fundamentalist movement is too strong to allow for legal recognition but co-op arrangements have, nevertheless, won important battles in the courts.

The idea with a co-op is for a group of people, usually the mother and father (but not necessarily) and other relations/friends, to make a firm commitment to a child and his/her lifetime development and well-being. Thus, rather than a child being brought up in a family centred on the life and wants of the parents, he or she is brought up in a co-op entirely focused on his or her needs. Some sociologists believe the child co-op system is more suitable to a culture in which long marriages are now the exception rather than the norm, and in which individuals often choose to have children with different partners. Other experts believe the propagation of such ideas can only harm us by further undermining marriage, one of the cornerstones of Western society.

Lifetime studies, which began in the late 10s, have already begun to demonstrate that in many situations co-op children can be more popular, self-disciplined and successful in school compared to children brought up in traditional families. Far from accepting the ethos of co-op children uncritically, this book looks at the pros and cons, and how these might apply to individuals in differing circumstances.'

I'm not sure I could be an advocate for co-ops but, for Diana and me, it might be a good idea. Diana has no track record and I have a dreadful one, so bringing close friends into a co-op might help us both be better parents.

Any how, I wanted to give you early warning.

Lots of love.

Julie Fenn to Kip Fenn

February 2037

It's not for me to pass any judgement on your choices. Tom and I have nothing to be proud of – but you. Sometimes I worry so about Crystal, and about Bronze. I blame myself for much. But I can't see what any of us could have done or can do. Harriet tries, she does, I know. If they have problems, I believe it was in the chemistry between their genes, chance and the misfitting of you and Harriet together.

But Diana is a lovely lady and I've no doubt you'll make good parents together. And another grandchild is always to be welcomed.

All my love.

Kip Fenn to Julie Fenn

March 2038

I thought the funeral went well considering. Tom had become a sad man, and I don't think he enjoyed retirement at all. I was considering what you said, about being sorry for what was, and grateful for what wasn't. That's not like you at all, it's far too pessimistic a view. As you said in a letter earlier this year, how can we know in advance the way a thing will turn out. We do our best, that's all we can do.

But I'm writing to tell you that Diana, whose birthday it was yesterday, is pregnant and joyful again. In the summer or autumn, when you've retired, will you come and visit us?

Julie Fenn to Kip Fenn

July 2038

It's funny, but I think more about Tom now he's dead than I did when he was alive.

The school gave me a grand send off; I kept bursting into tears. I've attached a short camclip, although I'm a bit embarrassed by all the attention I was given.

To stave off the worst of retirement I've accepted a part-time (voluntary) advisory post with the Independent Education Authority. Now Ireland's reunification is finally complete and off the Westminster agenda, I'm hoping Garth Fuller's administration will refocus on domestic issues, and boost the Authority's mandate again. It might also do something about the stranglehold of the Academics.

I hope to have time to visit Leiden soon, or should I wait to the spring when the new baby will want to see its Gran?

All my love.

Chapter Five
CRYSTAL, THE PEARLY WAY AND PROMOTION

'There is no truth around me, not in love, not in charity, not in happiness, nor even in friendship. We are insignificant animals. Ants. We float around thinking we are gods, but we are no more or less than human ants, enslaved to selfishness, hope and money. We wallow in hypocrisy. I am suffocating. I write this book to breathe.'

No Reason to Live by Pearl Worthington (aged 15) (2041)

I know for certain I have one great grandchild. Her name is Maria Silva Magalhães. She is dark-skinned, so pretty, with mischievous eyes, high cheek bones, and thick glistening hair set up in a twig. She came yesterday, with her father, Juliano, one of Arturo's children, and her mother Eliane, who is from Recife in North Brazil.

Whereas most people might have trouble sorting out their family connections behind them, thanks to Arturo I have difficulty working out those in front of me, as it were.

Sometimes, on Saturday afternoons, I allow Chintz and others to make a special effort to transfer me from my fixed bed into a portable contraption so that I can be wheeled, preferably if the weather holds, into the gardens, or, if not, into the theatre room where some third-rate entertainer tries to raise the dead with comedy, magic or storytelling. The few times I've persevered through such shows it's thanks to Flora's creative and inspired heckling more than the quality of the entertainment.

Yesterday, though, it was a warm bright day, and I was taken out into the rose garden which is my favourite spot in early summer. Left alone for a few minutes, I closed my eyes, which was an odd thing to do: here I am, stuck in bed and in my room 24 hours a day, mostly communicating with a wallscreen or sleeping, and the instant I am brought out into the garden, I close my eyes. Sight can be too powerful a sensation. I sense more without it, the heat of the sun on my cheeks, the light breeze catching the edge of one ear, the fragrance of roses, and the chirruping of greenfinches in the laurel hedge or in the willow tree beyond. It is these sensations, more than any emotions towards Jay, for example, or Guido's children, or Maria, or surviving friends of mine, that cause me to regret the impending end of life. I mean no disrespect to those I love and those that may love me, rather that these sensations are a direct link to the essence of being alive, and thus draw attention somehow to what it must be like to lose that essence.

Since I settled here at Willow Calm Lodge, Jay has acted, with perfect generosity, as a coordinator for my visitors. And, since my death date was decided, he's cautiously contacted more distant friends and family with a view to encouraging them to make at least one visit during these final months.

To my knowledge, I have four grandchildren through Arturo (although I suspect there may be more). I never knew Arturo's first wife Edna, but I did meet their (or his) cloned daughter Alicia once. She disappeared in her late teens. I have, though, met his second wife Fatima and their three children, Ignacio, Juliano and Tina. Juliano is the only one of these three to have married and started a family. Of the whole clan, Tina, the youngest, is my favourite. She must be about 30 by now. When I saw her as a teenager she reminded me strongly of Gabriella (the composite Gabriella, part Amado character, part Gabriella on the bus, and part Conceição, Tina's grandmother). Jay tells me Tina may come to England in the autumn.

I am conscious of the fact that I have not yet even introduced Arturo adequately, so it is fortuitous I don't have much to say about Maria or her parents. Jay, who had sponsored their air fares (with my money), had also advised them that, given my condition, they need not stay long. Conversation was awkward since my Portuguese was poor, and their English was little better. When Jay was speaking, I let my eyes wander to watch Maria race across the lawn chasing after a ball. She tumbled over her own feet. This triggered in me another type of sorrow, not the self-pity I had touched earlier, but a contradictory one born of angst for the future. If Maria's world is going to be similar to the one I have experienced, suffering of some kind at a personal and a public level will never be far away. But then she scrambled to her feet, straightened down her bright pink top in a precocious way, and carried on running to kick and chase the ball. A few minutes later, she ran back to where we were sitting. I asked her to climb gently up on my lap, so Jay could take a camclip of us together.

On leaving, Juliano and Eliane each gave me a kiss on the cheek. Their kisses made me feel as if I were already a corpse propped up in a coffin. Having seen them out, Jay returned to the rose garden and asked if I wanted them to visit again at the end of their week-long package tour around the British Isles. Only if they must, I said.

'I liked them,' Jay volunteered.

'Me, too. I'm glad they came, really I am. I'm very happy to have met Maria, and to know she has seen me in the flesh, or what's left of it.'

'I don't think Ignacio will make it this year. As far as I can tell, he's devoting himself to local politics, in Pernambuco with Grupo Hijo de Jesus, the Son of Jesus group. His emails come with flyers about the movement. Did you know it has 20 million members in Brazil, 35 million in Mexico and nearly as many in the US? I'm only a click away from salvation.'

'Can I ask that you send Juliano one of the camclips, the one with Maria on my lap, and me brushing a hand through her hair. I bet she was grimacing.'

I let my eyelids fall, thinking I might catch the bird song again, or the scent of floribundas; but Jay was in a talkative mood.

'For a straight guy, Pa, you've created a right motley crew of kids, with one exception. Which is ironic.' I like that Jay calls me Pa. It was a tradition in his mother's family. Lizette called her father Pa while he was alive and after his death (she never talked about 'my father', only ever about 'Pa'). Jay went through a stage, in his late teens, when he thought himself too old for the familiar term, but he came back to it.

'Not ironic, if you follow the science of the matter and attribute this, er, "motley" gene to my DNA.' Jay, a good 15 centimetres shorter than I was before old age shrunk me down, but with more handsome facial features, is not my blood kin, no more than I was Tom's. Lizette was already with child when she and I fell in love, and it was partly because of my experience and influence that she agreed to the idea of nurturing Jay with me through a co-op.

'I'm not convinced a motley gene would be enough to explain Crystal's troubled life.' This was Jay prompting me, since he knew I had been planning to write about her and thought I might want to use him as a sounding board.

'No, not at all. A motley gene? I doubt it. Swathes of bad luck, definitely, for she was certainly caught in a cultural swirl; but, most important of all, incompetent, derelict parenting, mine and Harriet's.'

'It's a long time ago now.'

'Over 50 years.' I lowered my eyelids again.

'Are you tired? Do you want to go in?'

'Jay, I wish you'd find someone new. It's not as if you are as young as you were once.'

'What brought this on?' he asked. I kept my eyes closed lightly and began wondering if I could evoke any of the fragrances from the Taunton House garden. 'As it goes, I've heard from Vince. We're meeting next week. He broke his back two months ago doing some mad-fool stunt skiing in Austria, and now he's convalescing. He sounds repentant. You look tired, Pa, shall I take you in?' Jay asked again.

'I'm pleased. I worry about you living alone, being alone.'

'I'm OK Pa.'

'I know you are. But I've been remembering too much about Crystal; that weekend she came to Leiden, in May 43. Without the pill menu, the memory enhancers, I'd never be able to write these Reflections, and sometimes I wish

... I doubt if I should be doing it.'

'The visitors were tiring, you'll feel better later. You don't have to carry on, Pa, you can stop at any time.' Jay can be mildly patronising, but it's too late to fight it or change him. He means so well, and I wouldn't want to hurt his feelings. I let Jay wheel me inside. He stood watching as I was ably transferred back into my bed, and then, when I pretended sleep, he departed quietly. The medication may be helping my memory, but without Jay's support, his love, and his companionship I doubt I would have the resolve and the perseverance to make headway with these Reflections, too many of which are difficult, dark and painful.

***

Crystal dropped out of college when only 17. I had been given no hint of an impending problem, and the first I knew about it was a simple email from Harriet – this was in the autumn of 42 – telling me that our daughter had left home and was living with a boyfriend called Vidrio, an artist. The two were no better than Scavengers, Harriet said, and there was nothing to be done. I tried calling and messaging Crystal to no avail. When I flew to London a few days later, she refused to answer my requests to meet. By interrogating Harriet, I discovered our daughter had been spending most of her time playing intensive screen games or roaming the streets with graffiti artists. She had shown no interest in qualifications, and, since starting college the previous September, had threatened to leave home. Only the lack of money had prevented her. Then Vidrio came, and led her into the night.

Despite many emails to Harriet and to Crystal over the subsequent months, I learned next to nothing about Crystal's activities, until that is she turned up, unexpectedly, in Leiden a few days before her 18th birthday, in May 43. By then, Diana and I had been living in the Oldwijkgaarten house for nearly five years, and Guido was three and a half. These were busy, productive and mostly happy times. During Guido's early years, Diana had trimmed back her working life, but, when we entered him into pre-school, she re-integrated herself into the theatre world with gusto. I looked after Guido when I could, taking full advantage of the flexi-time laws (and over-working in compensation). When either Diana or I were away, we relied extensively on a caring and generous widow called Elly, who lived nearby and missed her own children. Incidentally, Elly's nephew ran an excellent local cheese and produce store.

Crystal materialised late on a Thursday afternoon. The previous night I had flown back from Washington, and, for various reasons, I was not due into the office until Monday. Diana was at a theatre somewhere, and Guido and I were in the Oldwijkgaarten common area showing our neighbours how to play cricket. I did not recognise the girl walking towards us. Dressed entirely in shades of grey, with a scarf covering her head, and a black material bag on her back, she could have walked out of a late 19th century photograph of gypsies I'd seen once. There was no smile of recognition, nor did she stop for a moment to allow a pause in our playful antics; instead she walked right to me, and, as if we were but acquaintances, put out her hand for me to shake.

'Hi Dad. I'm not too good. Can I stay for a day or two?'

I called Guido over to say hello to his sister, which he did dutifully before rushing off to collect the cricket ball and continue playing. I led Crystal inside, thinking we might drink tea and talk, but she only wanted to bathe and sleep. I called Diana to forewarn her, before going back out to find Guido screaming with laughter, and the cricket bat being used in a tug-of-war.

I have tried consciously over the years to hold on to the memory of that long weekend, for it is the best I have of my only daughter. I had taken Friday off work partly to attend an auction of vintage photographs at Swann's in Amsterdam, so I cajoled Crystal into accompanying me. On the train, she remained mute and self-absorbed, responding to my few questions with single syllable answers. Her ash-coloured headscarf, with its mottled pattern, vaguely resembled a moonscape, and I remember thinking my daughter might as well be on the moon. I distracted myself from anxiety by reading through the glitzy catalogue sent me from New York.

During this harmonious period of my life, and encouraged by Diana, I had assembled a very modest collection of vintage photographs and begun to educate myself on how to store and care for them. I paid three auction companies to send me their paper and digital catalogues regularly. I collected them with commitment, and often copied the larger reproductions into Neil. Only once or twice a year did I actually take part in an auction and make any purchases.

Crystal must have expected to see the old photographs themselves, because, having shown no apparent interest in our journey or its purpose, on arriving at Swann's she suddenly asked what was going on. I explained how the physical auction was taking place in New York, but that roomfuls of prospective buyers in Tokyo, Amsterdam, Milan and São Paulo were participating as if they were there in person. Huge wallscreens on either side of the Amsterdam auction room showed the item on sale from two different angles, and the central screen was fixed on the hammer-man. Bidders could either employ the traditional signal, with a waved hand which the intellicams would pick up, or utilise a keypad by each seat. It was a bit slow for some compared to a one-site auction, but pure entertainment for an enthusiast such as me: all those fabulous photographs, given a provenance, described in loving detail and displayed on the screens. Although prices were below the peak levels of a decade earlier, gasps erupted whenever the hammer went down on an item at over $100,000. I might have bought an E J Constant Puyo nude for around $1,000 but Crystal's presence intimidated me; instead I spent nearly $2,000 on three Japanese portraits, albumen prints by Felice Beato, each one hand-tinted. None were in the best of condition, nevertheless, I felt it was a good price. When they were delivered, a week later, I scanned them into Neil, and Diana used them to create and print out a special card for Crystal, a memento of her visit. I waited in vain for an address to mail it to.

We left the auction house on Prinsen Canal, ate a bagel and drank chocolate, and then strolled along Keizersgracht – all in silence. When we reached the stretch of canal in the Asser photograph, I started rambling on about the area and its importance to me, about meeting Diana, falling in love, and our first morning together walking hand-in-hand. And then, suddenly, as if a gag had been removed, Crystal began to chatter and prattle, barely stopping to take breath, much like her mother at times. Initially, she launched an attack on me.

'How can you do that, spend $2,000 in a moment, on a few bits of paper that mean nothing to anyone? Did you see that beggar on the bridge back there? $2,000 for what? Don't you know how hungry people are in Ethiopia, in Bangladesh? How ill people are everywhere, ill in their bodies, and ill in their minds? You could have given that money to the Red Cross, saved lives. It was obscene, watching you and all those others spend millions for nothing, on nothing. It's sick.'

But she wasn't talking directly to me, she kept her eyes sternly down focused towards the ground, while her head kept bobbing backwards and forwards as if trying to punch out, from inside, the obscenities she was talking about. I did not interrupt, I let her rant on about hunger and religious terrorism and injustice and disease and capitalism. After a while, she began to denounce the specific opinions of her mother or well-known politicians or her teachers, and to reveal a passionate support for the more anarchic ideas of her friend Vidrio. When she paused for breath and I asked her, very quietly, to tell me about Vidrio, she did.

Vidrio (Spanish for glass) was not his real name, but a self-appointed pseudonym. According to Crystal their affair lasted many months but had finished abruptly when, one morning, he had decided Berlin, not London, needed his art and talents. His life's work, I learned, was etching graffiti on glass, usually that found in expensive cars and shop windows. Glass etching had become a real urban problem at that time (one symptom of the endemic social terrorism in many cities) largely due to the availability of cheap etching/staining guns. Many countries had lightly outlawed the machines, yet they could be obtained easily enough. Yobbish youth culture (as typified by the Scavengers) tended to view glass etching as the fine art of graffiti skills. Poor Crystal, she saw Vidrio as a cross between Van Gogh and Vi Hoop, combining the artistic talent of the one and the passion for freedom from religious intolerance of the other. Who's to say she was wrong.

Intoxicated by love or poisoned by rejection, Crystal could not stop herself pursuing Vidrio by phone and email. I remember exactly the words she used when, as we walked around Paddington only three months later, I thoughtlessly enquired if she'd heard any more of Vidrio: 'He told me to fuck off. He said I was only his London fuck-chick, and I didn't know shit about art, or cock, or politics. And he'd never have looked at me twice but for my name. That's what he told me.'

We spent the rest of the Friday in Amsterdam (thankfully Dominique was able to cover for me by driving over from Utrecht to collect Guido from school), mostly walking and talking. She told me of Harriet's cycles of depression and boyfriends, depression and boyfriends, and recounted various tales about au pairs she and Bronze had put up with over the years. She had nothing favourable to say about her brother. When I eased the conversation around to her education and whether there might be any possibility of her continuing to study, she clammed up abruptly. Half an hour later, she leaned over an old iron railing and stared wistfully down at a barge decked out with flowers moving slowly along the canal. This led us on to find a tourist boat and to sign up for an hour long tour complete with an English-speaking guide. Afterwards, sitting in the quiet of the Begijnhof early evening, Crystal came round to asking questions about Diana and Guido and me. She expressed genuine astonishment when I gave a much simplified account of the IFSD and my work therein. For a minute or two, she looked at me with something akin to respect in her eyes. I was amazed too. How could my daughter have grown up, be almost an adult, and not know me, or who I was, or what I did? Unfortunately, there was no-one to blame for this but myself.

Diana and I swept aside most of our joint and separate plans for the weekend, so that I could spend as much time as possible with Crystal. On the Saturday, she and I took the train to The Hague, and I showed her round the IFSD building and my office. We stopped by the public relations department, where someone was invariably busy, weekdays and weekends, and I asked to be shown a promotion film for a recently-approved aid programme. I was keen to impress Crystal, not so much with my role, but with the fact that important efforts were always being made to help and support developing countries, even if this was not apparent in the daily media. However, she walked out of the screening before five minutes had passed. I guessed she could not cope (or did not want to cope) with the size of the funding figures or the scale of the works being undertaken, and preferred to allow a youthful prejudice against office buildings, full of nothing but paper, screens and computers, to extinguish any spark of interest in my work and the IFSD. We walked by the town hall, which didn't interest her at all, and stopped for refreshments at Jaspar's. As Crystal had withdrawn into herself again, I thought I might get back on her wavelength if I told the tale of how Rike Thomas had tried to threaten me in this very bar, but she yawned repeatedly and, apropos of nothing at all, interrupted to request we go to a games room. One of the waiters at Jaspar's directed us to Houdijk's, 20 minutes walk away in an area of town I had never visited.

In Houdijk's, a large basement café decorated in black and silver with aluminium furniture and grey terminals (Crystal was perfectly camouflaged), we waited half an hour at the bar for a table and a free terminal. Crystal may have tried to explain her favourite netgame of the moment, Final Oblivion, but her explanations went over my head. When I sat down to watch, though, my stomach churned. The object of Final Oblivion was to commit suicide, and to do so with a mission at one of many levels. The missions included the following: causing as much chaos and destruction against dark forces as possible; assisting an avatar with doubts about the ecstasy waiting beyond; and overcoming personal demons (the Pearl Worthington way). Crystal skillfully avoided other players' crazed suicides and psychological quagmires, and had clearly developed a real expertise at the game. In the corner of the screen, a counter showed that more than half a million people worldwide were playing concurrently. For the sake of our very recent and fragile friendship, I made no comment.

Later that day we returned to Amsterdam so Crystal could inspect Vondel Park, where so many FTM protests had congregated, and where, in recent years thanks to Dutch government initiatives, FTM festivals had become more popular than lawless marches.

Prompted by a further request from Crystal, this time to walk on a dike, Diana arranged for the four of us on Sunday to drive to Hoorn, north of Amsterdam, where a friend showed us around the pretty harbour. We made various stops on the way there and back, not least at Edam, and near Uitdam, where we fought the wind on dike-top foot and cycle paths. Spread across Ijsselmeer, we could see hundreds of modern yachts, windsurfers, parasailers, and the traditional sniks and skutsjes. Despite the apparently idyllic scene, large parts of the surrounding countryside had, in the previous 15 years, twice been devastated by storms and dike breaches. Many lives were lost on both occasions. Successive governments continued to insist that most areas remained safe, and to pour public money into never-ending improvements of the internal and external sea defenses. Nevertheless, large-scale regional evacuations, ordered and spontaneous, had become increasingly common. In the years to come, the sea would reclaim some of the land we could view that day, especially in Flevoland, the largest of the polders which the Dutch had so successfully exploited for more than a century.

I possess a few delightful photos from that day. There are several of Crystal with Guido and/or me, and one, taken by Crystal herself, of Diana, Guido and me. These are the pictures which are most deeply associated with my feelings of love for Crystal, the love that I had never been allowed (by Harriet or myself) to express, and of grief, and of guilt.

On the Monday evening, Crystal's last with us, we went to Dominique's house. Crystal and Dominique had met on the Friday, and Dominique had suggested we all come for supper on Monday. Having forgotten it would be Crystal's birthday, I had agreed. I suspect Crystal spent most of that day gaming, although she did return to Oldwijkgaarten with a few new clothes purchased with the money I'd given her. I left work earlier than usual, returned home first, and then drove the four of us to Utrecht.

Visiting Dominique and Waltar Meijer and their two lively sons, Jurian and Lukas, then aged around nine and eleven, was always a pleasure, their house being full of easy good humour, gentle activity, bright decorations and a multitude of house plants. Crystal did her best to relax and join in. For a while, before dinner, she helped Guido defend himself against the Meijer boys physical teasing (I saw flashes of a carefree childish Crystal), and she responded politely to Waltar's queries about her activities over the weekend. As a climax to the dinner, Dominique brought out a fantastic cake, topped with lavender-flavoured berries and 18 candles. Through a haze of chatter and laughter, Dominique asked Crystal to blow out the candles. Guido stood up on his chair and, so cutely, asked Crystal if he could help blow them out too. She stared at the cake and the candles and at Guido. For a second, no more, all the chatter in the room subsided, as if waiting for Crystal to answer Guido. But the sudden silence must have left her feeling exposed and scared for she shoved her chair back sharply, stood up and raced out of the room. Dominique followed but soon returned saying Crystal wished to be left alone.

We barely spoke on the return journey from Utrecht, nor the next morning. As Crystal and I left the house for the station, Diana, instinctively but thought-lessly, attempted to give Crystal an embrace and a kiss on the side of the cheek, but she shied away offering only a curt 'thank you'.

At the station, I too got a thank you, a softer one.

'Thanks Dad. It was good, wasn't it? I was afraid of coming. If you hadn't of been outside, you know, I might not … Guido's nice. He looks like you. And thanks for the money. I'm going now.'

'Take care Crystal. Thanks so much for coming, it was really nice to see you. Come again soon. Come any time, any time at all. If you need the money for the plane or train fare, just yell. And write, please please write.'

'I'll try. Thanks.'

I watched Crystal climb aboard the train with mixed emotions. Among them I recognised anxiety about her future. But also I felt relief at having been allowed to experience a humble shred of paternity towards her. As usual, though, I completely underestimated, or refused to face up to, the depths of Crystal's anguish. I would only see her one more time, and then she would be dead.

***

The days off work and Crystal's visit had already set my tight schedule back considerably. A pile of paperwork awaited me at the office after the Washington trip; and, by the weekend, I would be in Abuja, Nigeria's capital, for my third trip to the IFSD's African offices there.

I need to backtrack for a moment to put my working life in context. During the summer of 40, it had looked as though the world leaders, scheduled to meet in Djakarta that autumn, would not be ready to agree on detailed implementing arrangements for the second global increase in overseas development aid and expansion of the International Fund for Sustainable Development. Thus many of us in the IFSD were expecting a re-run of the Vancouver summit failure. However, a week before the Djakarta summit, anti-West and anti-Christian demonstrations flared up so violently across Java and Sumatra, but especially in the capital, that the meeting was hastily relocated to Oslo (conveniently for us). Parallel demonstrations across the rest of the developing and Muslim world were sufficient to persuade the recalcitrant Western leaders (led by the US and Japan) to relinquish their hardline nationalistic positions. The huge boost in development aid resources actually agreed at Oslo (i.e. the second stage 0.25% increase) allowed the IFSD to expand again, in The Hague and in Abuja, and with new main offices in Islamabad and Manila. Thereafter, we, in the IFSD's future policy division, continued working towards the third and final incremental increase of 0.25% (or, as it became known, the Next Step).

In my role as deputy director, Pravit exploited me as his organiser-in-chief for tidying up loose ends, or for modest liaison responsibilities with other IFSD divisions. And he employed me shamelessly whenever he felt a white face could achieve more than a brown one. 'We must work within the realities of the realities,' he would say confident of my understanding. I did not appreciate these tasks, and in the time leading up to the Djakarta/Oslo summit, in 40, I began to feel I had been sidelined. I watched unit heads, such as Ninel Horeva, press steadily forward and achieve tangible results. I also observed Pravit move from one crisis to another, using his considerable political and diplomatic skills to ease each team's work over apparently insurmountable barriers. By contrast, my own, often bureaucratic, input felt intangible and diffuse. On a few rare occasions, I failed to hold back my grumbles, but Pravit regularly managed to redefine or explain my role and assignments in such a way that I exited from his office refreshed with commitment.

Soon after the Oslo meeting, though, Pravit found himself increasingly involved in the IFSD's main business. This was because the agreement in Oslo had been bought at the expense of major compromises which created new and unexpected working complexities. As a consequence, increasingly during 41 and 42, he called on me, his deputy, to stand in for him as the head of the future policy division. Thereafter, though the demands on his time outside the division gradually diminished, he never attempted to reclaim the full power of his position.

In May 2043, a few days after Crystal's unexpected visit, I travelled to Nigeria. During two previous visits to the country, I had failed, through lazy planning, to catch up socially with Alfred. This time, however, work itself brought us together (as it would several times over the next few years). Alfred had moved sideways and upwards within Ojoru's administration and, by this time, had become a key adviser on certain agriculture and environment issues.

I had not seen Alfred in person for seven or eight years, not since he had finished his doctorate and returned to Nigeria. Yet such is the power of childhood friendship, even only intermittently refreshed, that I could barely keep a smile off my face during the flight in anticipation of meeting him again. And, at the airport, we greeted each other like long lost brothers. I had already agreed by email to put myself in his hands for the remainder of the day, Sunday, so first he drove me to my hotel and from there to a sports park in the city suburbs. Normally, on a Sunday night, he explained, he would be busy training the Capital Warriors for great exploits in the all Nigeria volleyball cup, but, in honour of my visit, the first and second teams had agreed to play a demonstration match.

'I told them it was necessary to show a great English setter how champion Africans play.'

'I don't need reminding how well Africans play, Alfred.'

'Ah, but you should see Sanfry – he's one of the best. He's made the Nigeria team already, and he's only 17.'

Unfortunately, Sanfry (short for Sanfrancissisi, apparently) didn't turn up that night, causing Alfred to spend an angry few minutes on the phone.

Nevertheless, the Capital Warriors put on a splendid display, and I told them so. Afterwards, Alfred took me to his modest home, a small, newly-built detached concrete bungalow, with a plot of long shaggy dry grass. He introduced me to his beautiful and very young wife, Fayola, and their two year old son Fela, named after the great 20th century Yoruba singer. Steering well clear of our own business which would start on the following day, we talked mostly about international affairs. Although I had seen glimpses of the old Alfred at the sports park, his personality had become more sombre than I remembered, weighed down, it appeared, by Africa's troubles. Some years earlier, a terrible drought had laid waste vast regions across the whole of the southern Sahara. All the affected countries (Sudan, Chad, Mali, Burkina Faso, and Nigeria's Niger state) were still dealing with the long-term consequences of the resulting famines, plagues and migrations. Alfred was intent on reminding me of past horrors, and present troubles. When I asked about his family and his wife and son, he brushed off such questions and wanted to know whether I approved of NATO (the New Allies Treaty Organisation which had evolved out of the North Atlantic Treaty Organisation) stepping up the terms of its treaty obligations with India. More specifically, he asked what I thought about the phrase 'a major act of aggression' by the Muslim states (which would define any NATO decision to become physically involved in protecting the remnants of Indian Kashmir). He believed that the United Nations should have done more, from the 20s, to tackle the growth of Christian-Muslim tension, and that Europe should have done more to curb US pressure within NATO for it to engage actively in religion-based conflicts. Every move by the US or Europe to bolster Christianity in Asia and in Africa, he opined, strengthened the Islam cause. In one particularly maudlin moment, before he took me back to the hotel, he turned prophet.

'The IFSD is swimming against the tide. It's only a matter of time before there's a real war. Five years or 20, it's inevitable now.'

I had come to Abuja with a briefcase full of tasks, but my main (and undeclared) purpose was to investigate why one stream of negotiations, led by our agriculture team, had stalled. The team leader, a German national (with a very French name), Louise Pavard, had repeatedly come to Pravit and myself complaining that Nigeria on its own and the African Union (representing almost all countries south of the Sahara) had refused to attend low-level negotiating meetings. She claimed the African states were asking for utterly unreasonable commitments on the share of funding to go to African agriculture. Moreover, she said, donors, such as the US and Australia, and recipients, such as the Latin American countries, had threatened to boycott any future discussions if the African states did not moderate their 'illicit demands'. The

African position was, apparently, further complicated by a re-emergence of internal conflict between, essentially, the Islam and Christian dominated regions.

All Monday, I sat through a meeting of the committee that liaised between the future policy division and the African Union secretariat. The future policy division's coordinators, based in Abuja, did most of the work. I intervened with explanations or potential solutions here and there, and everything proceeded as normal. Only when we came to the subject of agriculture did the meeting fall apart, mostly because the African Union's own representatives contradicted each other. I sensed, as it was my job to do, that something else was going on. Alfred, as an observer, remained silent throughout the meeting, and left before I could catch him afterwards. The next day, I was due at the Nigerian Ministry of Agriculture for a courtesy introduction to a new minister and for discussions with his advisers (including Alfred). However, before I had shaved, my phone rang. Alfred told me that my meetings had been cancelled, and that he would be arriving in one hour to take me on a guided tour.

A guided tour of Abuja University! To get there, we drove through a few respectable neighbourhoods, some dominated by residences and office blocks in the neo-Tropical style. These were generally free of traffic jams. Most of the journey though took us through areas typical of those to be found in many African cities: dense traffic, squalid and not-so squalid street shacks and semi-slums, unrepentant bustle and noise, and patchworks of colour in the midst of much grimness. However, Abuja was not as bad as Lagos, which, despite Ojoru's many advances (and the famous IFSD-funded 'golden' dikes protecting Lagos Island) had failed to lose its 'shitty city' status.

Life of all sorts – student traffic, games, teaching circles, snack sellers – teemed around the university buildings. Alfred began my tour at the tallest block, for teaching medicine. He showed me the well-stocked library, the lecture rooms, and the well-equipped laboratories, all supported by UN agencies. Then he showed me the artistically-furbished, but very different, Christian and Islam foundations, and explained that they were financed jointly by the federal government and the churches. A few other parts of the university appeared no poorer than a badly-funded European college, but Alfred's purpose was to bring me to the impoverished agricultural science and technology block, a concrete shell of a building with its rooms all empty but for a few broken chairs and tables. We stood outside in the muggy heat, and, finally, Alfred came to the point.

'Education, my friend, education. We need intelligent farmers, people who can read and write and understand money, and who know how to learn to look after their lands in good and bad times. We need farmers who are neither stuck in traditional ways nor taken in by Western salesmen, who can deal with suppliers and government agencies, who can read and research for themselves, who understand the importance of long-term sustainability, who can look ahead and manage their crops and animals with confidence and foresight. It's not that this building doesn't have the facilities of an Oxford college, you know as well as I that much of the teaching is done at home through the net. Yet this building says it all for me. We've had dribs and drabs of help from the UN for agricultural science and education; and there have been projects up and down the continent, but they've petered out, or collapsed in the face of financial and cultural difficulties. Our belief now is that these efforts have always failed because they've never been implemented on a large enough scale. The IFAD and Unesco have never had the muscle. There has been no momentum on this issue. Only the IFSD has the resources and the clout to make a difference. Yet, my friend, as you know better than most, education and training are not considered part of the IFSD framework.' A group of unruly students rushed by. 'We've tried before to get the IFSD mandate extended, but have been blocked at every turn. This time we're determined. Very determined. Now, come, I want you to meet someone. We must be punctual.'

Alfred drove us to the president's Palace. It took about half an hour to get there and another half hour to work our way through security and into an ornately decorated reception room. We waited a further hour which gave me plenty of time to examine the European-style portraits (I could only recognise Ojoru), the exquisite traditional hangings (batik-style), and the beautifully intricate wood carved sculptures and panels (by a famous 20th century artist called Lamidi Olonade Fakeye). Alfred refused to chat, or to confirm for whom we might be waiting. Then, he took a phone call, ushered me to my feet and guided me towards the centre of the room. Ojoru, surrounded by three assistants or bodyguards, entered the room in a gust. He came within a metre of where I was standing. He was slighter than I expected, and more human. I had only ever seen him in the flesh from a distance. I confess that I was slightly awestruck. All I had the presence of mind to notice was that his eye whites shone (like an actor's) and that he was dressed in a trim cream-coloured suit with crimson darts.

'Alfred has talked of you, Kip Fenn. He says you are a man of faith in people, and a man with foresight. I am glad of that. There is much to be done.'

'Yes, sir.' For several seconds Ojoru continued to peer into me. Everyone in the room remained motionless and silent. I debated internally whether to mention that I'd been there, in the European Parliament more than 20 years earlier, when he had delivered his famous mantra, but I felt too intimidated to speak further. It was as much as I could do to hold his gaze. Suddenly, he made a decision and put out his arm towards me. Instinctively, I stepped forward to shake hands with him. He had a very firm warm hold.

'Thank you for coming,' he said. Almost immediately he turned about and, with his entourage in perfect step, exited. Curiously, for a moment I thought not of Ojoru, but of Crystal's cold and formal greeting a few days earlier in the Oldwijkgaarten garden.

Over lunch back at the IFSD building, Alfred loosened up. He explained that if I could find a way of widening the scope of the exploratory negotiations for the Next Step (the third incremental increase in western overseas development aid) to include agricultural training and education, certain unreasonable African demands and differences might disappear. I thanked him profusely for the honour of being introduced to Ojoru, but protested that he was overestimating my position and responsibilities and what could be achieved at my level. Alfred thought not. He promised that a substantial and convincing plan, backed by academic research and intellectual analysis, would be forthcoming if and when it would be given proper acknowledgement and IFSD-backed circulation privileges. He also forecast that, if the idea gained legitimacy, the vast majority of beneficiary countries would gather in its support.

There were other meetings, and other business which I forget now, and a couple of meals out with Alfred (although his wife stayed at home with Fela). One evening, he persuaded me to borrow a pair of shorts and trainers, and knock a volleyball about with friends, including the tall, agile and smiley Sanfry, on an outdoor court near his house. The heat troubled me within minutes, the ball caught my left index finger badly, and then I fell, scraping a knee on the earth. I declared enough was enough and that my volleyball days had ceased long ago. Nevertheless, I did experience a buzz of pleasure seeing Alfred take so much enjoyment from the game.

On the flight home, I considered how I could achieve the mission that, in effect and thanks to Alfred, I had been given by one of the greatest men of the 21st century. It did seem an impossible task, especially since there had been previous failed attempts to enlarge the IFSD's aid framework to encompass education. Moreover, none of us at the IFSD were looking for new battles, and the entire future policy division was working towards an objective – the Next Step – that many sane and intelligent intellectuals and politicians thought could never be achieved. And, while Western national leaders steered clear of being too publicly negative or defeatist about the chances for the Next Step their opponents, international think-tanks, independent members of many parliaments, media commentators and others had no such qualms. Nevertheless, somewhere over the Mediterranean, an idea did emerge.

The following day I secured a late interview with Pravit who listened to my verbal report with patience. I had intended not to tell him about the encounter with Ojoru (after all nothing had actually been said), but then found I could not properly communicate the importance of the matter without doing so. I proposed that it was all a mistake, brought about because of my friendship with Alfred, and that it needed an older, wiser and more senior head than mine to find a way forward.

'Kip, you become trickier by the day. I do believe you are a tricky one, are you not?' Long pause. When he put such enigmatic questions, I usually found it best to remain silent. On this occasion, though, it was not the right tactic. 'Am I waiting forever then? All right, all right.' He was not in the best of moods, for otherwise he would have allowed us to saunter leisurely for a few minutes through the roles of master and pupil. 'My head is going to hurt tonight. Tell me your plan.'

And so I did. I have no wish to get bogged down in the nitty gritty of my working life, but, briefly, the plan (which partly succeeded inasmuch as any draft plan ever retained its original shape) was this. Firstly, it was necessary to deal with Louis Pavard, the team leader, who had repeatedly rejected all requests to circulate documents relating to agriculture education. She had refused to accept declarations on the subject citing the Next Step's mandate word for word, as if it were the Koran. Pavard was in the pocket of the German government which, most of the time, used its muscle to undermine the EU's generally positive approach to the IFSD. So, Pravit moved, through a German director of the IFSD board, who was not a closet nationalist, to replace Pavard with a younger more malleable and idealistic team leader. Secondly, Pravit and I began to propagate, through our respective contacts within and without the organisation, the idea that we should not be falling back on defensive positions for the Next Step but that, conversely, a new bold idea would help inspire support for it. And education – at least in terms of farming practices – was that idea. It was no longer feasible, we claimed, to believe real sustainable development of land resources would be possible without earmarking a very significant proportion of aid for teaching farmers (not a few hundred here and there, but tens of thousands, hundreds of thousands) how to profit from and, crucially, care for their land better. Thirdly, over the next six months, I travelled extensively to the capital cities of many Western donor countries, mostly those that were positively interested in seeing the Next Step succeed. At meeting after meeting with ministerial advisers (where I could get them), senior civil servants and all kinds of experts, I explained our current difficulties, our need for a new momentum, and the reason why a revision of the existing Next Step mandate was now being proposed. Often it was a thankless and dispiriting task, and, especially in the autumn during the weeks after Crystal's death, I lacked the necessary diplomatic energy (as Pravit would call it) to do the job effectively.

By the end of the year, however, doors began to open more freely, and a growing sympathy for our approach was evident at many of my follow-up meetings. In advance of the April 44 negotiating session in Mexico City, I took a gamble and attempted to coordinate a large group of donors who were prepared to ask for a revision of the mandate. In parallel, Pravit braved the IFSD board. There were all kinds of attempts to derail and block us (not least those stemming from other UN agencies, such as the IFAD and Unesco, involved with agriculture and education respectively). For the first three days of the Mexico meeting, I was apprehensive, believing they might have succeeded: some of the support I had so carefully fostered appeared to be drifting. But, while I had been arguing the case with the donors, Alfred's team had been hard at work too. When it became clear, on the fourth day in Mexico, that there was near unanimous support from the recipient countries for 'the role of education and training in sustainable development of agricultural practices' to be considered for the Next Step, more donors than I expected hesitantly pressed their green buttons. The opposition, suddenly isolated and spotlighted, fell away tamely.

For the next two years, until the second Djakarta summit (not relocated this time, thanks to highly controversial policing methods), 'the role of education and training in sustainable development of agricultural practices' became one of the main motors for the negotiations. It was during this period that Pravit retired suddenly for health reasons, and I was promoted to head of the division (after a period as acting head of division). It is possible that Pravit retired slightly earlier than he might have done so as to allow for my promotion prior to a change of government in Britain. Already in 44 it was evident that Fuller's centre coalition would not last a third term; and Pravit understood that a future Conservative administration might not provide the necessary behind-the-scenes national support for my promotion.

***

Before then, though, my heavy work load led to a series of conflicts with Diana, and the most uncomfortable period so far in our ten year relationship. In the summer of 43, Diana and I had promised (or casually planned depending on the point of view) to visit our Canadian friends, Ike and Augusta Davidson, in Montreal. So, when I declared, several weeks after the Abuja visit, that I would no longer be able to take a full vacation in the summer, Diana responded angrily. Following much discussion and argument about alternative arrangements, we decided that Guido and she would go without me.

As part of the same decision (and somewhat resentfully I judged at the time), she objected to joining me in London for a family-oriented weekend in early September, soon after her return from North America. My mother and her brother were the focus of that weekend. On the Friday, I went to Alan's book launch, and on Saturday Alan and I helped Julie celebrate her 70th birthday with a lunch party. I also spent Sunday afternoon (at the cinema) with Bronze, and delayed my return trip to the Monday morning so as to accede to an unexpected request from Crystal to meet up that evening in Paddington. As I've already disclosed (why is it so difficult to keep the chronology in order?) this was a distressing encounter.

Alan. I have all kinds of regrets about my life. Only stiff people, who live by imprinted route maps or hand-cuff themselves to pre-packaged religious models of being, can get to the end without regrets. Or so I like to believe. One of my regrets is that, over the years, I did not spend more time with my uncle Alan. He invited me to St Petersburg, where he lived for the last 20 years of his life, on numerous occasions, but somehow I never got round to going. He was one of the most intelligent and warmest and kindest of men I ever knew. Officially, he had retired from WWF in the late 30s. Yet he continued to work as intently as ever, not only as an adviser to WWF and others, but on his ambitious book. It took him more than ten years all told, and was finally published in September 43. *Floods: past, present, and future* (two atlas-sized volumes and a major netsite) gained immediate plaudits from across the world, and soon became a standard reference work. Not only was it full of geographical and scientific explanations, cultural anecdotes and detailed historical notes, but it was replete with glorious photographs and illustrations, albeit often of tragedies. For the next decade, until old age slowed him down, he enjoyed a certain amount of fame, travelling far and wide to give lectures based on the book and the information he had amassed for the netsite.

Alan had arranged for the book launch to take place in the same week as his sister's birthday, not only for his own convenience but because he thought Julie would enjoy a touch of reflected glory. The publishers, Universities Press Inc, in conjunction with WWF, had engaged the International Geographical Society in a marketing deal which included use of the Society's premises for the launch. A maxiscreen displayed a slick slide show, moving occasionally into camclip footage; large-scale photographs from the work and of Alan adorned the walls; and the books themselves had been piled up with architectural skill on publisher glam-stands. Constrained by looking after my mother, I managed nevertheless to talk with Anna Mastepanov (Alan's partner), Jude Singleton (my old boss from the Department of the Environment) who recounted a pleasingly awful anecdote about Rike Thomas, Matt Fortune (an influential

203

left-wing backbencher MP who, as a tireless campaigner for the IFSD cause, I already knew), and a sharp environmental journalist called Bobby Jespersen.

Part Danish and part American, Bobby had made a name for herself in Brussels by careful reporting on green issues for the *Wall Street Journal* and the *London Times*. She had written two books, one on European-US environmental policy conflicts, and another which analysed in detail how Europe had won the battle for the initial expansion of the IFSD. I knew she had excellent contacts in the IFSD, as elsewhere, but I personally had never spoken to her before. With a short squat body, far too much make-up, layers of odd clothes, and unkempt long mousy hair, she could have been 40 or 60. She was abrupt, almost rude in the way she interrupted my chatter with Julie; and she had no fluff talk at all. Despite this coarse outer shell, she had a gift for probing intelligent conversation and also for listening purposefully and attentively. While declining to answer a barrage of questions about progress on the Next Step, I did agree to grant her an interview later that autumn. No sooner had she bounded out of earshot in search of further contacts, than my teacherly mother deemed her an 'oddball', which was the best she could do to disguise her dislike of the woman.

I only mention Bobby because some years later she and I developed a useful synergy. Incidentally, she gave Alan's book a superb write-up.

After a couple of zinis and several short speeches, Julie and I took a cab to The Plains in Chelsea. Alan and his Russian partner Anna had invited approximately 30 friends to join them there for a post-launch late lunch. Julie sat next to a charming man she had encountered through Alan many years previously, and who lived in Ireland. (As a consequence of this re-acquaintance, the two of them became correspondents to the end of my mother's life.) Halfway through the meal, Monique, Alan's old girlfriend (who had looked after me so well in Rio de Janeiro all of 20 years earlier) appeared. She had missed the launch party because of a four hour security hold-up on the trains through the Channel Tunnel.

Having spent 12 years in Brazil, I learned, Monique had returned to Paris where her rainforest expertise was much in demand by international groups, including my own organisation, the IFSD. She had helped Alan on his book and was proud to show me, with exaggerated pride, her name listed as a key contributor. At one moment, she turned to watch Alan stand and affectionately embrace two people who were leaving.

'I love that man,' she said.

'Me too.'

My mother's birthday party, at the Dog & Pheasant in Brook, followed on Saturday. Here on my screen is the camclip recorded by Rachel, Julie's friend from Edinburgh, and sent on to me later. It is precious for being the last clip I have of Alan, Julie and me together. His friendly face is rounded by a trimmed white beard. He is laughing and raising a toast to his sister. Julie herself looks gloriously happy, and far from old. Harriet is scowling, and not communicating with anyone. She was invited largely to ensure the attendance of Bronze, so that, as a minimum, one of Julie's grandchildren would be present. And there I am in the camclip, making an effort to communicate with Bronze, whose face is covered in acne. I remember he wouldn't eat, and he complained about having to miss a religious march taking place in central London. I should have been grateful that Harriet and he came at all, at my request, but neither of them wasted much time being pleasant to Julie or me, and so I was relieved when they left early.

Later, I managed to spend an hour alone talking with Alan and Anna about the book, their plans and their life in St Petersburg. Anna spoke English moderately well and with an elegantly light accent. She must have been about 50 then. The two had first met in Kiev on a Ukrainian flood-relief project when she was 25, already with two children and a husband. Only later, after the marriage had disintegrated, and the two children had found high-paying jobs in far-flung corners of the Russian Federation, did she find Alan again. It was Anna who had persuaded him to slow down and settle permanently in St Petersburg. And, presumably, it was she who had provided a platform of domestic stability that allowed him to persevere for so long and complete the work on floods.

At the turn of the century, according to Alan's book, on average 1.5 million people were perishing each year as a result of floods; in the late 20s and early 30s the figure peaked at 3 million a year; and by the early 40s, had fallen back to around 2.2 million. Alan explained, in the book, how the turnaround had come about largely because the flooding cycles had increased to such a frequency that government policies and people themselves began to shy away from the most vulnerable areas. Furthermore, he showed how infrastructure investment, often led by the IFSD, had been instrumental in safeguarding important agricultural regions and many urban areas (there was even a sunset-lit picture of the Dutch-built dikes around Lagos Island).

**

We were not, though, living in happy times. While the cost in human life of flood damage may have been receding, other trends indicated that the golden era of oil and chips was fast coming to an end. Floods apart, man continued to be battered by increasingly unpredictable weather fronts with hurricanes bringing untold damage in a matter of hours, and droughts causing famines and plagues that lasted years. Religious conflict and intolerance were rising and arising day-by-day, and at every level whether in local communities or in the UN organisations. International affairs and diplomacy were often bogged down in efforts to bridge the growing religious divide. Many feared that NATO, its member countries under permanent verbal attack from the International Islam Brotherhood for Peace, was moving inexorably towards a defender of countries dominated by Christian peoples.

By this time, the First Tuesday Movement had already disintegrated into a patchy framework for religious protests, demonstrations and riots. Only the American continents, dominated by Christians faiths, were largely free of this particular affliction. Even there, though, in cities such as San Francisco, Quito, Rio and Buenos Aires young people occasionally demonstrated their anger against US arms being sold to so-called friendly regimes or freedom fighters in North Africa and the Middle East which just happened to proclaim secular or moderate religious objectives. Many ordinary citizens, faced with the growing chaos in the world and a belief that a decade of popular protest had achieved nothing, turned inward seeking spiritual or religious solutions. Cults of all types found new adherents, while traditional religions, in all their variants, swelled their numbers. This served to further exacerbate and polarise religious strife. According to the social historian Gregory 'a worldwide plague of pessimism' emerged, especially among those who could not find solace in imaginary gods.

There was one non-religious cult, the Pearly Way, which brought a most terrible despair to millions of families. Gregory's *Suicide in the 21st century*, published in the 60s, claimed that suicides worldwide increased from less than one million at the turn of the century (I am selecting these particular stats to allow a comparison with Alan's figures on flood deaths) to around two million in 40. By 43, this figure had grown to three million. It went on multiplying until it peaked in the late 40s at around five and a half million. My daughter was but one single individual in these vast statistics.

But a girl named Pearl Worthington was more than just another statistic. In 2041, her recently-published book, called *No Reason to Live*, won a major US award for its insight into youthful despair and tragedy. On live television, minutes after receiving the award, and while still on the presentation stage, she pulled a plastic gun from her bag and fired a bullet into the side of her head. Cameras caught each horrifying moment in close-up detail, and the camclip made headlines in all the media, from Beijing to Santiago and from Helsinki to Cape Town. A week later, *GlobeOne* magazine ran an in-depth feature on suicide, with three words on the cover: 'The Pearly Way'. Pearl's book became an instant bestseller, and was quickly translated into dozens of languages.

Across the world, but especially in Japan, Brazil, China, India, the US and the Scandinavian countries, unhappy men and women, young and old, followed Pearl's example, if not with a gun, then with pills or gas or by throwing themselves in front of metro trains or from tops of buildings and cliffs.

Pearl's mother, Xanthe Worthington, however, managed single-handed to turn what might have been a dreadful, but short-lived, fad into an appalling, tragic and permanent feature of our world. Xanthe, having started life as a call girl, amassed a huge fortune by marrying and outliving a series of rich and very rich husbands. Pearl ran away from Xanthe mansion (or wherever) when only 14 and never spoke to her mother again. The book, *No Reason to Live*, came to be seen as a suicide note, condemning society and the author's mother in roughly equal measure. Following Pearl's death, Xanthe spent several months trying out psychiatric programmes and psychotherapists, but emerged one day, with the appearance of a nun not a queen, to tell the media she had decided to use her fortune in remembrance of Pearl. With a team of amoral and greedy businessmen, software engineers and security personnel, she moved to the renegade Martinez islands in the Caribbean and set up hundreds of netsites in dozens of languages. Some of these glamorised the idea and practice of suicide, providing information on simple and effective ways to kill oneself, and making funds available for regional propaganda. Others offered free downloads for playing simple individual screen games. And yet others provided portals to the addictive netgames Final Oblivion I and II. Both of these were commissioned by Xanthe from a creative young game developer in Korea who later tried, ineffectively, to use his natural copyright (having sold the legal one) to close them down. Xanthe advertised the games widely, allowed the playing software to be distributed freely, and made no charge for involvement in the gaming universe. As the playing numbers increased exponentially, so her team worked round the clock to provide the necessary infrastructure in every continent.

It took Europe nearly three years, until 46, to place an effective ban through Solar (the open Euronet) on the Oblivion games (by classifying them as Unacceptable Content), but efforts to prohibit them in the US and at the UN level failed altogether. Xanthe herself died in 48. It's possible she was poisoned by one of her employees, but the facts were never established. Thereafter, her associates fought among themselves, and the mini-empire quickly fell apart. By then, though, Xanthe's bitter and vindictive objective had succeeded all too well. Even in the Arab world, which suffered least from the cult because of the strictures of Islam, there were increased numbers of suicide bombers, disease-spreaders and fire-raisers, all ready to appease their anger and find glory wherever and whenever they could. In India, China and Southeast Asia there were epidemics of those dying slowly from hunger or quickly from earth burials. Mostly they were protesting against low pay, inhuman working conditions and poverty. In Catholic Latin America and Southern Europe, the suicide statistics were dominated by those eager to get to heaven and experience oblivion. In Northern Europe and the US, we had them all: the oblivion seekers, the nihilist black-hole-and-outers and the Pearl copycats who used suicide to protest, whether against their lovers, their family or society. And, across the Western world of course, there was an explosion in the numbers of those ready and willing to make a quick easy escape from the trials of old age (plastic surgery sags and other cracked-mirror syndromes, pension failures, or body/brain dysfunctions).

Crystal killed herself on Wednesday 23 September 43, only three weeks after she and I had walked through the streets of Paddington. She was found by a friend called Donna at a Scavenger's house in Streatham, South London. She had cut her wrists and was lying in a bath of blood and water. A note, in her handwriting, said only: 'All is annihilation, all is oblivion. I do this entirely on my own, and of my own free will. Crystal.' An autopsy found her stomach full of prescription pain killers and mood calmers. This, and evidence from the distraught Donna, were sufficient to convince the coroner that Crystal had taken her own life. She was cremated in Croydon at the same crematorium as her grandfather, Tom. While the sun had shone for Tom, it only rained for Crystal. Apart from Diana and me, there were a handful of mourners: Harriet and a manfriend, Bronze, Julie and three odd-looking acquaintances of Crystal. We all went our separate ways soon after it was over. I did attempt to exchange a few words with Bronze, to establish how he was coping, and whether he needed anything. He had become a fervent evangelical Christian by then, and believed his sister had done the right thing and gone to a better place, and that, therefore, there was nothing to grieve for.

'R. I. O., rest in oblivion, Crystal,' he said to me without a trace of irony.

My relations with Diana, which had been under strain since the summer, deteriorated during the journey back from London. On receiving the news about Crystal's death, she had been sympathetic, and generously agreed to accompany me to the funeral. On the train journey to London, she had allowed me to grumble, as I had done in the early days of our friendship, about Harriet. But Diana had a selfish streak (greatly tempered, I should add, by being a mother) which I never wished to acknowledge, let alone stand up to. During the return leg, Diana's thin shell of forbearance towards me crumbled. I was probably re-living the weekend Crystal had visited Leiden, or re-dissecting our walk and conversation in Paddington, when Diana snapped. I do not believe it was anything in particular I said, rather that she had waited until a nearby passenger moved so we would not be overheard.

'It's no good going over it again and again. She's dead. She was unhappy, and now she's dead. Bronze is right, she is in oblivion.'

'I don't believe in oblivion, you know that.'

'You left her a long time ago, it's your fault, it's Harriet's fault, it's the world's fault. What is done is done. Let it go.'

'No.' I felt offense. 'She was my daughter. She lived in pain. She died before she was even an adult. Whose fault is that? You want me to deny she existed, stop thinking about her, stop talking about her, forget about her altogether?'

'Yes.' This stark word stunned us both into silence. I felt she meant it literally and turned away towards the window. The request (or was it a command) felt threatening, not in itself, but because it meant I might have to re-evaluate the person who had made it, and from there, possibly, reconsider why I was loving her. It was easier to contemplate the rain battering the glass, and the rivulets streaming from one side to the other. It took Diana a minute or so to continue her meaning, and to try and deflect her apparent callousness. 'Yes. Yes, stop thinking about her for now, stop talking about her. Please, for me. Not to forget her. Remember that you ruined the summer, that you are working too much, that you are always travelling. You want Guido to become like Crystal.' Instantly, she realised she had gone too far again. She apologised verbally, and physically too, by taking hold of my hand. Silently, I made yet another resolution to control my working hours and be more available for Diana and Guido. Yet, as with previous efforts, it was soon forgotten – for this was the time I was busy on my mission for Alfred, Ojoru and Africa.

Before leaving the subject of the Pearly Way I should add that I, personally, knew at least five other individuals who committed suicide in the 40s. They were: a Russian IFSD employee who had been caught trying to blackmail his line manager; a Japanese civil servant who negotiated in the IFSD committees on conditions and funding for solar energy and who had been passed over for promotion; an actress acquaintance of Diana who had been screamed at once too often by a director and who had never got over abuse by her parents; the mother of Waltar Meijer who was suffering from multiple sclerosis; and Rob, the brother of Melissa.

Rob had found his way to the house in Lacey's Lane several times in the 30s, evidently seeking the kind of financial handout we had given him once before. On each occasion, according to Harriet's emails, he had stated he was looking for me, so she had given him my address in Leiden and a few euros. He finally caught up with me one weekend that same summer (43) while Diana and Guido were in North America. He arrived with Imogen, a woman ten years his junior who acted like his self-appointed social worker. He had changed beyond recognition from our last meeting, about the time of Bronze's birth in 28.

Physically, he looked much tidier than when I'd last seen him, although his unbearded face carried several shaving nicks, and his suit would have fitted a taller, fatter man. Mentally, he reminded me of a dull and doltish teenager, one devoid of character. The nervous and shy Imogen explained that Rob had talked of making this trip for so long that she had finally consented to organise it and accompany him. They stayed for one afternoon only (thankfully), during which we took a short walk around the Leiden sights, and ate ice cream in the touristy Mars Bar (one of Guido's favourite places) on Nieuwe Rijn. Rob struggled to talk at all, so Imogen raised the topic of Melissa for him. Rob's memory of that fateful afternoon had become so distorted or muddled up with other memories, I learned, that Imogen did not even know for sure whether he had had a sister, or how she had died. So, while sitting on a bench by the quieter Oude Rijn, I described, in as much detail as I could remember, the picnic at Sweetwater Pond and what had happened subsequently. Rob's eyes quietly watered as I told them of my final visit to the hospital and hearing of the decision to let Melissa go.

Imogen put her arm around Rob. I was touched by the friendship of these two. But that is all. I had travelled a long way, and, at this busy time in my life, I had no spare emotions. Imogen and Rob were intruding, and I was being polite. At the station, Imogen thanked me profusely once, and then again when I gave her 200 euros. Six months later I received a short letter from her informing me that Rob had died from a deliberate overdose of heroin. She explained that he had not been an addict for more than five years but that a chronic kidney disease had flared up and left him in pain, so he had decided to take the Pearly Way.

My own attitude to suicide has undergone several revisions. When young I believed in a liberal euthanasia policy, such as that evolving in several European countries, and I would not have argued against an individual's choice to relinquish his or her mortal coil (so to Hamlet-speak). Harriet, whose extended family, both present and past, had been scarred by more than one suicide, led me into several prolonged debates on the subject during our time together. She believed that condoning suicide was problematic because of the impact on friends and family, and because individuals rarely remained suicidal for long. I allowed myself to be persuaded. Over time, I suspect, Harriet's views hardened and she became fervently intolerant of liberal views on suicide, which may or may not have affected Crystal's course.

In the weeks and months after Crystal's death, I deflected the pain of the grief and the guilt, as many other parents of suicides did, through anger. The media was full of debate and comment about Xanthe Worthington, her netsites and games, and the various offshoot cults she had fostered. Most governments considered laws and initiatives to try and curb the escalation in suicide attempts (for every successful one there were several failures which put enormous strains on health services, and caused psychological traumas among relations and friends). And, everywhere, the Pearly Way was a topic of intense discussion in families, at dinner parties and at workplaces. My anger switched easily to and fro between Pearl/Xanthe Worthington and the media which did so much to propagate the Pearly Way ideas. For two or three years, I took the view that any legal opening for euthanasia had been wrongly allowed and that any such laws had opened the floodgates, allowing citizens to deny their citizenship, and abdicate their responsibility to families and communities alike. Diana, who did not usually have any firm views on major political or social issues (nor did she much enjoy discussing them), expressed surprise when she heard me pontificate these views. It was only in the late 40s, when Diana and I witnessed the pain and struggles of Dominique and Waltar with regard to Waltar's mother's illness, that my moderate liberal opinion returned.

Even today, 50 years later, thanks in part to the Pearly Way epidemic, I had to go through an endless rigmarole before getting official approval for my own death date.

Horace said once, during a school debate on the phenomenon of suicide terrorists (this may have been an argument I personally originated, but I only remember Horace speaking it), that one of the best arguments against anyone, including a desperate religious fanatic, committing suicide was that life is full of surprises, possibly good ones. If Crystal had held on for a few further weeks she would have been presented with a fully-formed, fully grown half-brother – Arturo – and who knows what influence he might have had on her.

***

For me, Arturo turning up so soon after Crystal's funeral seemed akin to some god's crass attempt at providing a replacement or compensation; it was as if Crystal's tragedy had entitled me, unknowingly, to a ticket in a lottery of miracles, and I had won a dubious jackpot. The first time I saw Arturo he certainly looked a million dollars, as they say, with his light tan-coloured skin, short wiry bleached hair, a bold handsome face (with mauve lipstick and purple-dyed eyebrows in the re-invented he-fem cat-walk style popular at the time), and an immaculate shiny two-tone jacket and pressed trousers. It transpired that he had gone to Godalming and charmed my address out of Julie (without so much as a call to me to check if it would be all right). He said he was the son of a friend from Brazil and wished to surprise me, which, I suppose, was no deceit. While Arturo lacked other qualities (I could mention integrity, morality, decency) he was not short of charm.

It was a mild but overcast Sunday in October, Diana had taken Guido with her to Theatre Stadsschouwburg in Amsterdam to monitor work on the set of a play she was designing, and I had spent the morning at the IFSD office in The Hague. I returned at about 2pm, and was strolling through the communal gardens thinking about what I would eat and drink when I saw a jazzily-dressed young man sitting on one of the benches. His gaze followed me to the front door, and, as I was turning to close it behind me, I saw him approaching. I waited.

'Mr Fenn?'

'Yes.'

'My name is Arthur. Your mother give me this address. I wish to talk to you.' His English was adequate – in the present tense.

'And my mother is?'

'Excuse me.'

'My mother? What is her name and where does she live?'

'She live in Godalming. She call herself Julie, naturalmente.' He smiled. He looked harmless, and carried no bag (containing potential weapons), and so, mildly curious, I let him in. I led him through to the lounge area at the back of the house, and offered him tea.'

'Coffee, do you have coffee? I wish to drink coffee.'

'Coffee it is.' I went through to the kitchen to put the kettle on. 'Where are you from Arthur? You sound Spanish or Portuguese from your accent. It sounds familiar.' I spoke loudly so he could hear me in the other room.

'Brazil. I am from Rio.' And when he said the words 'Brazil' and 'Rio' he said them in the way of his own language, which I did then recognise as Brazilian Portuguese. This was a further clue to what the man might be doing in my house, but it only took me as far as thinking he could have some connection with Monique, who I had run into at Alan's lunch six weeks earlier. I took the coffee and biscuits through to the lounge, sat down opposite the man, and poured out a cup for each of us.

'It is pretty here, artistic,' Arturo said.

'My partner, Diana, is very artistic.'

'And that?' He pointed to a poster-size portrait of me temporarily hanging on the door to the kitchen. It was no likeness, except for the long legs and lanky body.

'That's by Guido, our son. He thinks I'm three metres tall.' I kept wanting to say 'so, Arthur what brings you here', but he continued to edge in, asking questions with his broad lipstick grin.

'You have a son. How old?'

'Five in December.'

'Five. Do you know how old I am?'

'No.'

'I am 21 last April. I finish my degree, in biological sciences. I finish it quite young you know, and I get a top mark.'

'Congratulations.'

'Where is Guido today and Diana?'

'In Amsterdam. They're coming back soon. I don't mean to be rude, but why are you here, Arthur, how do you know my mother or me, how did you get my mother's address?'

'You know Brazil.' It wasn't clear whether this was a question or statement.

'Yes, I've visited Brazil, but Arthur why are you here?'

'You have a good time in Brazil?' Now I began to feel impatience, and saw no alternative but to show it.

'Arthur, please answer my question or I will have to ask you to finish your coffee and leave.'

'Naturalmente, Mr Fenn, but please my question, then I answer.' Arturo's smile vanished, and he suddenly become intent.

'Yes, Arthur, yes, I did have a good time in Brazil. I liked Rio very much.' And I waited. Arturo looked around the room. There was an expression on his face, and he carried a look that made no sense, no sense at all, and for a moment, until he spoke, I began to feel wary, under threat.

'Conceição. You remember Conceição?' And still I would not tune in. I have been trying to think how to explain what was happening in my head, and the best I can do is to compare the process to that of trying to find, but only half-heartedly, a radio station on the long-wave receiver, moving through bands of low-level interference, crossing louder bands of hissing and static, and making no serious effort to find the correct wavelength where sound and information could be heard and understood crisply.

Hearing the name Conceição provided a moment of relief, for, at least, the mystery was explained. But then I realised that if this Arthur had come visiting on the strength of his relationship with a woman I'd long forgotten, I had absolutely no interest in him or his business with me.

'Vaguely, very vaguely. I met her briefly. I hope you haven't come all this way to tell me something about Conceição, because, quite frankly, I wouldn't be very interested.'

'Excuse me.'

'I mean … I'm sorry, I remember the name, but I don't remember her at all. It has been a pleasure to meet you, but I do have things to do. So, if you don't mind.'

'She is my mother.'

'I see.'

'She dead, died, two years ago.'

'I'm sorry.'

'Of AIDS.'

'I am truly sorry.' I was beginning to long for the return of the supercilious mulberry smile.

'I am, was 19. The compensation pay for me to carry on my study. Is more coffee?' I poured him another cup from the coffee pot.

'Please take your time, I'm going to phone Diana.' I went upstairs to call her in case she was close to arriving home. When I returned to the lounge, Arturo was standing by the kitchen door and examining Guido's poster.

'I am born in April 2022, you know. April 2022 is nine months after July 2021. Do you think I look like your mother? I think I have her nose, but your chin.' And back came the smile.

All the hissing, all the crackling, all the interference vanished. In an instant I was digitally tuned in despite my very best efforts to flounder around on long wave: the man was claiming to be my son. A true Eastenders moment, if ever there was one in my life, only there was no emotion within me to guide my words or actions. Instead, with Arturo's comically alien face staring at me, waiting for some acknowledgement, I fixed on doubt as my way forward. I asked him how he knew I was his father, when Conceição must have slept with other men before and after me. He pulled out a piece of paper from the inside pocket of his jacket and passed it over to me. It was a certificate declaring that Arturo Fenn Magalhães was born on 10 April 2022. He said that Conceição had told him it was a question of dates and possibilities, and that there was only one possibility. She would not have put my name on the certificate without being certain that I was the father. And why hadn't she contacted me before now, if only for financial support? Because she did not want my help or involvement. She recognised it had been her mistake, and she had no desire to interfere with my life; also I was far away. And why then had Arturo shown up now? Because he wanted to know his father, and to study in England, and to see Europe. His backpack was at the station, and he didn't have much money.

Naturalmente, I told Arturo he should stay for a few days while we find out more about each other. I insisted, and he agreed without question, that we should take a DNA test as soon as possible. (This proved my paternity. It would be dishonest of me to deny that, in the few tense minutes waiting for the result, I did not entertain a hope that the test would prove negative, and that I would be able to cast out the stranger from my life without remorse.) But, from that mild October day in 43, Arturo became a part of my life and stayed one, intermittently, for more than 35 years until his death in 79. Indeed, through his varied offspring, he remains so, as witnessed by the visit of Maria a couple of weeks ago.

Flora, bless her. She has more life than all the staff (except Chintz) put together. Not long after observing me with Maria in the rose garden, for example, she rattled into my room demanding to know who she was. No sooner had I told her, than she launched into a never-ending eulogy about her own <u>seven</u> great grandchildren. Since then she's been hyperactive, visiting too often and staying too long. I confessed to Chintz this evening that I might have to ask Flora to cross me off her touring list. But Chintz hinted that she was not as fit as she appeared, and that too many others inmates had already shut their doors on her. When Chintz asked if I had any good flicks lined up for viewing, I got out the popcorn (metaphorically speaking) and launched Joaquima's *The Last Great Puppet Show*, a film based on the 48 Barcelona World Puppet Festival.

***

I suppose, from the standpoint of my emotional response to Arturo, I could have shut the door on him, even though he was my genetic son, not with a slam but with firm and persistent pressure. And yet I didn't, I left it open, wide open. Perhaps if he had arrived before Crystal's death and the guilt and pain I felt about that, I would have been less accommodating. Perhaps not.

Superficially, Diana tried to accept Arturo's presence with reasonable humour, and my invitation for him to stay with good grace. But she was not one to hide her feelings for long. On a near daily basis, I sensed her communicating that she resented his existence, his presence, and his ongoing residence, especially given my frequent absences (abroad on IFSD business). My relationship with Diana was already under strain, and Arturo only served to exacerbate the effects of the distance between us. I did not blame her. She was probably being more tolerant than many a partner might be under such circumstances. On the plus side, Arturo proved a reliable and trustworthy guardian for Guido, relieving logistic and time pressures on Diana and me. He played with Guido more empathetically than either Diana or I could manage. He was polite, and charming, thanking us for meals and the loan of our various vehicles. On the downside, he was chronically untidy, regularly asked for money, and used the house as if it were a hotel. I signed him up for English language lessons. I tried to get him a part-time job in the Mars Bar or similar, but the immigration laws had been made watertight, and only a few quasi-legal enterprises, which never survived long, would risk employing those on tourist visas. By the end of November, his presence was proving too great a strain on our small family.

In early December, I sent him on ahead to London, with all the relevant paperwork, to organise a British passport. He stayed in a cheap hotel. I followed a few days later and the two of us went to my mother's house. By then, Arturo and I had altered the past to make it more palatable for Julie: I had had a holiday romance with Conceição, a student, and she had recently died from cancer. I let Arturo improvise in response to more detailed questions. Over the course of a long weekend, and daily train trips into the capital, I introduced Arturo to various people, not least Harriet and Bronze (that meeting was a gaggle of laughs, though I had forewarned them with a letter) and the Turnbulls.

After Dracula Park, Doug and Miriam Turnbull had never invited me on vacation with them again, but they had remained friends. I was accustomed to dining with them whenever I visited London, initially with Bronze or Crystal until they reached their teenage years, and thereafter on my own. The daughters, Susannah and Lucy, had matured into attractive and active young women. Susannah had gone through an anorexic phase while doing her 16 exams, and Lucy had finished her 18s and was studying at a music college. I guessed they might find Arturo interesting and/or amusing, but Miriam, with the insight of a protective mother, saw danger. She kept our visit short, and brushed aside my suggestion of a meal out or a visit to the cinema.

It was Horace, perversely, who resolved the dilemma of what to do with Arturo. I knew my son wanted to study genetic engineering at a British university the following year, and that, until then, he needed to concentrate full-time or nearly full-time on improving his English, but neither he nor I were clear as to where he should do this. We had discussed various alternatives, but I had hoped that one of my friends, such as Doug Turnbull, would offer to help him settle in London. By the Monday, my last day away (I was due to travel somewhere on Tuesday evening from Amsterdam), I was no nearer deciding what should be done with the boy. I'd arranged to meet Horace at the Houses of Parliament, partly because he had contacted me recently wanting my news, and partly because I thought Arturo might like to be taken inside and shown around by an MP. Arturo had dispensed with the lipstick at my request, but he looked no less alluring. Once inside, and in Horace's hands, so to speak, Arturo piled on the youthful charm. In the guest's Tea Tavern, Horace announced, for I had not known this, that he owned a third storey studio in Camden Town, in addition to the Kensington apartment and the Southampton house. It had been inherited from his parents. They had died within a few years of each other and left Horace and his younger brother Tim several properties which they rented out. A year previously Horace had taken the Camden studio back from an unscrupulous agency, and lent it to a struggling artist. That artist had now gone overseas and the flat was free. True or not, it was Horace's story. Arturo could have it for six months at a nominal rent, he said. I tried to intervene, to thank him, and to say we would discuss the matter and get back to him, but Horace was talking to Arturo, and Arturo was responding with enthusiasm. If I, personally, had any doubts about what Arturo was getting himself into, I did not have any that he thought he knew what he was doing. I can't put my own mind about the matter clearer than that.

Arturo returned with me to Leiden to collect his backpack (and a second bag we gave him to carry the new things he had bought). On the way we discussed finance. I offered to pay the rent and the education fees, but he would need to work to cover his living expenses. Apart from the English lessons, I insisted he enroll in a local college and work towards two university entrance exams. If he passed them with a reasonable grade and achieved a university place, I said, I would pay his fees and cover his accommodation expenses for up to four years.

I hoped life at home would improve with Arturo's departure. For several weeks, it felt as though it had. I made a conscious decision to preserve the Christmas holidays for Diana and Guido (and I paid for Arturo to fly home for two weeks, so as not to feel obliged to invite him to stay again). But, no sooner had the year 44 started than I was travelling again, and working all hours in the run-up to the negotiating session in Mexico (which I have already mentioned). There was a brief respite after Mexico, when Diana, Guido and I managed a week-long holiday on the island of Rhodes in May (which was entirely overshadowed by the news of the terrible earthquake in San Francisco), and a holiday with the Rocard family in Italy during the summer. Then, from the moment I became director of the future policy division in October 44 to the final Djakarta summit in December 47, work took me over completely again. There were a few breaks, such as the one to England in June 45 to Brighton and to Horace's party in Southampton, but they were usually short and rushed.

Diana and I did not have many serious rows, but one argument stands out in my memory. In early February 46, I was labouring 12-14 hours a day in preparation for another negotiating session, this time in Cairo. Diana was working towards a big show in Antwerp. We had our diaries and schedules and Guido-caring responsibilities clearly planned out in advance, as was always necessary whenever Diana was in the final stages of a project. I was due to leave for meetings in Geneva on a Tuesday afternoon. Diana would be working in Antwerp that day and evening but would return by 10pm. Elly, our dependable childminder, would collect Guido from school, take him to her house for supper (where he played with a daughter of Elly's neighbour), then bring him to Oldwijkgaarten, put him to bed and wait for Diana. On Monday afternoon, Elly left a message to say she had contracted a chest infection and would be unable to collect Guido the following day. She was excessively apologetic, as if mindful of the trouble her illness might cause. Diana and I began arguing over who should make the calls to find covering arrangements. Under normal circumstances, Diana would do this. She was more social, she was better on the phone, and she had a much clearer idea of who might be able to help. On this occasion, though, she demanded that I do it, and would not relent. Unkindly, I wondered if she already knew that neither Dominique nor Peter from Guido's co-op (who were usually willing to help out if they could) would be available. Peter's wife, Livia, did assist a little by offering to collect Guido on the Wednesday. I phoned two alternative childminders we had used in the past, but neither of them were free. I contacted other friends, and I even walked round to some of our neighbours in Oldwijkgaarten (which was embarrassing since we did not have that kind of relationship with them). When I returned and told Diana, she was furious and blamed me for not having asked the right people, or for not having asked them in the right way. And she insisted I would have to delay my flight to Geneva until the morning. I said that was impossible because I had important meetings. I suggested it would be much easier for her to come back early from Antwerp than it would be for me to postpone my flight. Although I was annoyed by Diana's lack of logic, and unable to fathom out why she was making such a big issue out of it, I wasn't surprised, since we had had similar niggly arguments on many occasions. This one, though, would not end. Our voices got louder, and we swung from Dutch to English and from English to Dutch. Diana accused me of being a workaholic, of not caring for Guido, of not supporting her in her work, of following the same pattern as I had with Crystal. I defended myself by arrogantly trying to take the moral high ground and implying that my work was more important than hers – much, much more important. I called her attitude selfish and egotistical. I might be a workaholic, I admitted, but at least I was working for a worthwhile cause not a vain one.

'Nothing will stop me going to Geneva tomorrow, nothing,' I shouted.

'Don't bother coming back,' she screamed. Never before had either of us let loose a thought that implied there could be an end to our relationship. The argument came to a sudden halt when Guido, in his Oink jamas, came bursting in to ask that we stop shouting, and that we kiss and make up. He was crying and demanded a family cuddle. Diana bundled him up in her arms, and took him back to bed. I went to my office to do the work I should have been doing earlier.

A week later, the play – Angelika Stockmann's *The Children's Land* – opened to excellent reviews. Stockmann was certainly one of the best German playwrites of the 21st century. This play, which had been a great success in her home country two years earlier and which had been translated into several other languages including Flemish, helped develop that reputation. Classically structured, and Ibsenesque (or, more accurately, Oakleyesque), it tells the story of the battle for a piece of land, situated in a housing estate dominated by immigrants, earmarked for a children's playground. Unrelentingly, Stockmann strips down the characters of the planners, the developers, the officials, the immigrant campaigners, the religious and altruistic do-gooders and so on to reveal the upper, middle and lower orders of hypocrisy. Only the children are left unblemished.

Given the distance of Antwerp from Leiden, Diana suggested I not accompany her to the opening night, but that we make an evening of it, with Peter and Livia, on the Saturday. Diana's set was impressive. She had managed to create a central waste ground space which cried out for the promised playground. In each scene where adults met to argue with, or bully or bribe, each other for using the plot of land in some other way, there was a symbol of adult recreation (such as a cycle exercise machine, a punch ball, or a carpet golf strip) nearby, while across the stage, a child would be kicking the inevitable tin can or throwing stones.

We did not get back to Leiden till one in the morning, but it was a good night out. It might have been better if, when I opened the programme, I had not seen that Karl, Diana's ex, was listed as the play's director. Peter noticed too, and asked after the man who had been his 'barge neighbour' years earlier. Fortunately, he was not in the theatre that night, thanks, I have no doubt, to Diana's planning. I did not want to think about Karl's reappearance in Diana's life, or why she hadn't told me he was directing the play. Nor did I confront her about the omission, the deceit.

The next day, Guido, Tom's spirit and I, along with the rest of the world's population except Diana, sat glued to the screen watching Minty and Wayne Nolan walk on the surface of the planet Mars. (And, nearly two years later we again united with most of the earth's population to wait tensely for the Martian Seven module to return safely into the earth's atmosphere. As is well known, the craft's power had been exhausted in the last desperate navigational adjustments, and the scientists, with all their billion dollar computer facilities, were unable to predict if the module would burn up or land the orphan brothers safely in the Pacific Ocean. The Nolans – what heroes!)

***

Life as a team leader and as deputy director had been a doddle compared to that as director. In one obvious sense, the success of the Next Step and the third expansion of the IFSD was in my hands. It depended on the way I handled the people I met and how I dealt with the paperwork on my desk. The responsibility was on my shoulders. But, when all the wheeling and dealing was done and dusted, I personally made a negligible difference to the 47 Djakarta deal, the Djakarta Settlement as it came to be known. The IFSD board, and in particular its director-general, monitored every significant step we took; and, ultimately, the world's nations decided for themselves how far they were prepared to negotiate on every detail. The plain truth is that by 47 the world was teetering on the edge of a global conflict essentially between the Christian West and the International Islam Brotherhood for Peace (IIBP). The IIBP, already under the influence of Imam Al Zahir, had begun talking about the need for the rich to pay Zakat – meaning that the West should be contributing a full 2.5% of their GDP in aid to the developing countries not only 1.5-1.7% (which was approximately what the percentage would be for the top rank richest nations once the Next Step negotiations were concluded and implemented).

By this time, all international negotiations, whether in the UN agencies or at the world group summits, were constrained by the need to keep peace. And the only effective way to keep the peace was for the West to bribe the East, the rich to bribe the poor, especially the Muslim poor. Thus, no-one any longer believed the West would renege on its original offer of a third big increase in overseas development aid, it was more a question of how the aid pie would be sliced up, or, in other words, how much the West would give in to the threat-ening demands of the Islam nations. The US strongly backed Catholic Latin America and was the most hawkish voice in NATO (by then the umbrella for most of the developed world's armed forces). Japan lobbied for its Far East neighbours, both Muslim and non-Muslim. Europe, as usual, was dominated by doves and tended to take a middle ground, but it also insisted on fair play for all countries, which meant providing the most support to the most needy countries, i.e. those in sub-Saharan Africa, many of which had not yet aligned with the IIBP (thanks largely to the continuing effectiveness of the Ojoru-led African Union).

Last night I showed Jay a panorama photo of all the heads of state at the Djakarta summit. I pointed out a few of the historical names he would recognise, not least Terrance Spoon, the GB Conservative prime minister at the time. Ironically, he was wielding one of the widest smiles (viewable on enlarge-ment). I explained that while the Garth Fuller-led coalitions, between 37 and 45, had actively supported the IFSD and pressed for the Next Step, Spoon, who brought the right wing back into power in 45 thanks to coalition support from the newly formed Christian Faith Party, attempted to stone-wall the European policy (like Lyndquist had done in the mid-30s). This was one instrument in his tool box of policies designed to convince a domestic British audience as to the strength of his commitments on fiscal prudence. I caught a 'so what?' expression on Jay's face, whose disinterest in history has been tested by my anecdotes on many occasions.

So what? In the spring of 46, my friend Horace Merriweather, minister for business in Spoon's government, had taken time out from a busy European tour including The Hague to invite me for lunch at my choice of restaurant. This was a low moment for me personally because of the friction with Diana. Moreover, the IFSD had recently been rocked by the uncovering of various fraudulent activities. None of these, I hasten to add were in my division, but the problems inevitably put a spotlight on the organisation's administration and the size of its bureaucracy rather than on its many excellent works. They also provided ammunition for opponents of the Next Step.

I chose the quiet Indonesian restaurant Lake Toba (which, despite several changes of management, served me well for decades). It proved to be an appropriate venue since Horace's prime motive was not social but to quiz me about the current situation on the Next Step and progress towards the Djakarta summit scheduled for the following year. In particular, he endeavoured to extract information on any vulnerable points in the negotiations which the GB might be able exploit to dilute the financial impact of the Next Step on European countries. This is my interpretation, but when – in a teasing light-hearted way – I accused him of such deviousness, he protested his innocence with inappropriate vigour. As minister for business, the Next Step negotiations were way off Horace's patch, but Spoon must have decided it would be worth trying to exploit Horace's friendship with me.

Jay showed little interest in this explanation. His thoughts had been diverted. What he really wanted to know was how things had worked out between Horace and Arturo. The honest answer is I never knew, not exactly. Once Arturo had installed himself in Camden Town and his regular allowance was in place, I heard from him less than once a month; and I was generally too busy to respond to his emails, or to enquire further as to his well-being. Besides, my own role in the situation did not bear much scrutiny. If the two of them did engage in a mutually beneficial arrangement, then I, who was paying only a nominal rent to Horace (on his insistence), was, in effect, pimping my own son. I did discuss the situation with Diana on several occasions: when Arturo and I returned from London, and later when Horace's name cropped up in the occasional email from Arturo. Her attitude never varied. They are grown men, she said, let them get on with their lives. This I do know. Arturo lived in Horace's flat not only through to the summer of 44, but for the first six months of his time at Imperial College. It was only a few months before the British general election in 45 that he emailed me a new address, in Kentish Town.

Thereafter, Horace's name was never mentioned again. I saw Arturo a couple of times year, when I was visiting London, and once when he came to stay a few nights as part of a holiday round the Benelux countries. I believe he had a fling with Lucy Turnbull, although neither of her parents, Miriam and Doug, ever referred to it. I did not volunteer the information (nor that Arturo might have been sleeping with a Member of Parliament at the same time). In 48, Arturo graduated with a good degree in bio-engineering. He returned to Brazil where he joined a large, but highly secretive, organisation called O Futuro, or, in English, The Future.

As I say, I was only ever an administrator. I oiled wheels to help the political trains run a little more smoothly, and I greased the points to help those same trains avoid collisions. If I personally made any more specific contribution over and above this, it was through the Ojoru mission which I'd undertaken as deputy director. Following the decision in Mexico to widen the mandate, our objective, as first proposed to me by Alfred at Abuja University, took on a life of its own and did in fact become a key element in the Djakarta Settlement. Perhaps I am being too modest. The final documents contained scores of drafting subtleties that, over the years, I had prepared and proposed to the chairmen of negotiating sessions. Then again perhaps I'm not, for they also contained text proposed and discussed and negotiated by thousands of other individuals.

In many ways, the Djakarta Settlement (for the third incremental increase in rich-to-poor overseas aid) was a more advanced agreement than its predecessor, the one fixed at Oslo, which had been modelled on old methods and patterns of aid that had been creaking at the seams for decades. Without getting bogged down in detail, one of the many improvements (to my mind) in the Djakarta deal related to how tightly and directly the donors controlled the purse strings. It became far more difficult than hitherto for nations to tie their aid to trade deals or political considerations (other than a set of clearly stated conditions relating to war, terrorism and human rights). Moreover, it allowed for much more wastage and inefficiency to occur before project funds became blocked and Western-trained troubleshooters were aerohovered in. If I am to claim any other slight influence over the agreement, it must be in relation to this latter aspect. During the 40s, there was a growing body of research and analysis, from the least developed African and Asian nations, which demonstrated clearly how inefficiency, bribery, wastage were cultural norms and could not be eradicated over night, or in one generation or two. By continuing to impose impossibly high standards on project implementation, Western donors and their agents (whether companies or non-governmental organisations) had often acted as the final arbiters over what actions, projects, initiatives the recipient countries needed (as opposed to wanted). And, as a broad generalisation, these actions, projects and initiatives tended to fit well with what expertise or equipment the Western nations wanted to sell, and with their domestic politics. I pressed my staff to be aware of the importance, especially to the most undeveloped nations who often had the least effective negotiators, of this issue; and when it came to preparing drafts for negotiating sessions, I paid special attention to the clarity of the language for certain types of amendments!

After the Djakarta Settlement, it took a year for the IFSD to expand once again. A new director-general, appointed in 48, overhauled the entire structure. The future policy division, which had had less than 100 staff, was disbanded. In 49, I was appointed director of the environment division, one of the top seven posts in the organisation, accounting for over 700 staff employees (400 of them in The Hague), and over 1,000 additional contracted personnel around the world. It was responsible for nearly one quarter of all the IFSD's outgoing funds.

***

And so – as a finale for this chapter – to Barcelona, May 48, where and when Diana, Guido and I spent a most happy two weeks staying in a large apartment with the Rocard family. Didier Rocard and Diana were old friends having studied for a short while at the same theatre school in Berlin. On returning to Paris, Didier began working as an actor, but his inventive imagination and ability to motivate others soon led him on to directing plays, especially large open air spectaculars. And then, for one reason or another (about which I was never clear), he diverted out of mainstream theatre to run a puppet theatre. At about the same time, he married Helene, a childhood sweetheart from their home town of Arles. To many, including Diana, it had seemed a strange match at the time. Outwardly, Helene, an accountant, appeared far too conventional and harnessed to a world of numbers and business, while Didier was an artistic explorer living in a world constrained only by his imagination and ability to self-promote. By the time I met them, which must have been during my first year with Diana, no-one could doubt the success of the partnership. Their differences and different worlds had not led to them drawing apart, making different friends, having different ambitions (as Diana had expected). The reverse was true, their partnership, their love and friendship, or whatever one might call the rare magic they possessed, had guided them into an exciting and successful venture which lasted more than 20 years: the publication of a series of works called *Le Monde Fantastique de Marionnettes*. Each 'work', which focused on a particular historical or geographical aspect of puppetry, was 'published' as a largish crafted wooden cube containing a collection of objets d'art: a replica puppet, a lavish book, further miniature puppets, photo-posters, and an uncopiable memory story for a screen show full of texts, camstills and camclips on the particular puppet topic. Initially, the works were published in a single limited edition of 500 and sold for 500 euros, but, for later works the limited editions number rose to 1,000, and the price to 1,000 euros, making each one a million euro enterprise. A few years ago, I saw a Rocard original, not in the best condition, sell in auction for 7,000 euros. Didier designed the packages and employed the artists, and Helene managed the projects, organising the finance, printers and manufacturers. For the first two works, she demonstrated an astute instinct for marketing and promotion. By the third one, though, marketing was no longer necessary since demand had begun to exceed supply (opening the way for other companies to make good money producing similar but lesser products). Diana had three Rocard originals on show in our Oldwijkgaarten house, with the main puppets cleverly self-supported above or in front of the attractive cubes. One of them, the first of the series, Diana had been given in lieu of her help in designing the box; and the other two she had purchased at cost price.

But I digress. In the autumn of 47, Didier had invited Diana to work with him on a large well-funded school project within the framework of the annual World Puppet Festival in Barcelona the following spring. He had been offered a fancy apartment in the old quarter, and, after various on-off discussions, it was agreed that we would all go for a full two weeks (though it would mean our children taking one of them off school). I warned Diana that if the Djakarta summit unexpectedly failed to deliver, and a new one was convened for June, say, I might not be able to take time off. Diana suggested, with a naivety I found both endearing and disturbing, that I make sure it did not fail. I obliged.

There were seven of us in the apartment. The Rocard girls, 19 year old Veronique and ten year old Mireille, took the attic bedroom with its one window view across the roofs of old town Barcelona; nine year old Guido made himself comfortable in a tiny box-room; Helene and Didier took the master bedroom, with an excess of mirrors; and Diana and I had the most charming room, L-shaped and decorated with rococo-light wallpaper, a style we thought had faded out in the 30s. Soon after arriving we decided communally to confine eating to the large kitchen, and project work to the dining room, which left the, thankfully spacious, lounge for, well, lounging, entertaining and entertainment. We used a potpourri of English, French and Dutch to communicate, which was no problem for the five of us adults, but Guido and Mireille had to communicate in pokes, tickles, signs, surprisingly proficient mime and schoolgirl English.

Didier, who made several preliminary visits, arrived a week in advance of the rest of us. Until his show was over at the end of the first week, he worked from dawn to midnight. Diana had been supplying ideas and designs by email, and also contributed her time for the first half of the holiday; only thereafter was she able to relax. Indeed, for the initial week we were all involved in the project to one extent or another. To explain briefly, Didier was using a school and upwards of a 100 children to create what I can only describe as a public hide-and-seek game. It involved giant puppets (twice life-size, each with two children inside) and extraordinary drapes and material/paper creations to transform the school buildings and infrastructure. All three of our children made definite choices to take part for the three days of performances, while Helene and I were more than happy to help out with whatever preparations were required of us. It was a blissfully happy time for me, a make-believe world far, far away from the IFSD and all its tensions and responsibilities. Some evenings (more often when Didier's show was over), we fought our way through crowds along the Ramblas, always finding something new to examine in the artisan stalls displaying puppet-related artefacts, toys and books. Then we would stuff ourselves with paella or tortilla, and drink too much wine before allowing (or not) Veronique to bully one or more of us along to a late night (and by extension vaguely adult) plaza show or pop house or sound/light multiscreen extravaganza.

During the second half of the holiday we formed groups varying in size from two to seven to explore Barcelona and to see as many shows as possible. We were guided so expertly by Didier and Diana that we had the good fortune to be present at live performances of four out of the five shows that featured in the famous film *The Last Great Puppet Show*. (The film was originally going to be marketed as *The Greatest Puppet Show on Earth* or similar, but Joaquima changed the titled after the organisation, that had fostered and developed the festival for 15 years, became subject to an ugly commercial takeover. The change in management led to many great puppet groups and theatres boycotting the 49 event; and, thereafter, the festival never recovered its status.)

Didier's *Les Géantes Invisibles* was one of the five shows immortalised by the film (there is a brief interview with Didier, and Diana is also credited), so was the Raluy Puppet Circus, which had captivated Guido when we first saw it in Amsterdam, and a Czech group's light-work puppets performing *The Unbearable Lightness of Being*. Most spectacular of all was the Ecuadorian firework puppet theatre which drew tens of thousands of people to the beach for two performances only. This latter came out least well on film. Oddly, when watching the movie with Chintz a few nights ago, she enthused over the one show in five I did not see: *The Hollywood Stars and Strippers!*. The metre-high string puppets were manipulated traditionally by hand from a team of operators hidden in a lowered ceiling, but each puppet contained one or more semi-camouflaged screens which intermittently showed clips of old entertainments (*What the butler saw!*, Charlie Chaplin, Blue Toons) all coordinated perfectly with the puppet movements and their stories. Hilarious and exhilarating.

It is thanks to the Catalan, Joaquima Ferrer i Germa, the inspired director of *The Last Great Puppet Show*, that these magnificent shows have been partially preserved for so long. It is also thanks to Joaquima that I met one of my childhood heroes, the Mexican film director Pam (Pedro Antonio de Malancas) who had made the movie *Trumpet Boy*. I do not recall why he was in Barcelona, perhaps he was giving a keynote speech, or involved with one of the shows, or on holiday like me. Despite the demands of her filming schedule (although, in fact, large chunks of the movie were not actually shot during the two week festival), Joaquima hosted an illustrious party at her Sant Cugat villa some 30 kilometres from the city. She was a large lady, and larger-than-life, one of Catalunya's most famous socialites. When asked by interviewers how she managed to find time for all her many activities – film-making, socialising, media appearances, affairs (being 50 and large had not diminished her appetite for young men) – she usually answered with some variant of 'by eating instead of sleeping, and screwing instead of dreaming'.

We were all invited to the party because Joaquima had been working with Didier and Diana at the school filming *Les Géantes Invisibles*, one of the shows that did have to be filmed during the festival. We all squeezed into Didier's hired Siberian and drove out to Joaquima's villa. It proved to be a fabulous place for the children to explore, with its exhibition rooms, wild gardens and dolphin-shaped pool. And there were many interesting people there. I distinctly remember feeling myself colourless, exotically inadequate. Diana was radiant, a partial theatre celebrity in her own right, dressed in a verdant green silk lounge-gown, and usually at the centre of a mini-crowd. I didn't see Didier and Joaquima for hours, so I assumed they had disappeared to talk business; and Helene was a consummate party animal, as comfortable and relaxed with strangers of any type, as she might be in the bath. I sat down on a bench near the pool to watch the children splashing and screaming. With hardly a movement or a noise, an old man sat down by my side. He must have guessed I wasn't Spanish, for he spoke in English, but with a Latin American-type accent.

'You know the Portuguese word saudades?' He didn't wait for an answer. 'These days, I am full of saudades for the time when my children were young. I watch these ones here – are they yours? – and I am jealous of their fathers. My youngest boy now is 18. Once I was a god to him, and now he knows everything more than me. Everything. I love him, I love them all, but it was best when they were young. Before then, in the past, they made me feel young, now they make me feel old.'

I pointed out Guido and his girlfriends, and asked the man how many children he had.

'Three wives, three sons and two daughters. All of them a great drain on my resources.'

We sat in silence for a few minutes until an American woman, in her 30s, her bare legs and arms pinked by the sun and/or the wine, rushed over to our bench. She had recognised the man next to me, and wanted to add his autograph to several others she had collected that afternoon. Thus, I discovered the man was none other than Pam. When he had shooed the woman away, in a kindly fashion, I let an aura of peacefulness around us, enhanced somehow by the children's play only a few metres away, return before speaking.

'But you know a good deal about youth and being young yourself. I was ten, my son's age, when I saw *Trumpet Boy*. No film before or since, spoke to me as that one did.'

'A lucky chance. A constellation of fates. A booming film industry, a producer with more money than sense, a genius writer who later killed himself with drink, a computer graphics team that caught a leading edge of technology and then, despite the film, went spectacularly bust, and a headstrong director with too much fame, too much power and a belief he might do some good.'

'A potent brew.'

'It is not that I stopped wanting to improve things, in the way my mother never stopped trying to improve me ... But, how shall I say this? You know, it is as though whatever I do takes me one step further back, never forward. My steps get bigger, more deliberate, more carefully placed; my shoes get more expensive, but I am always moving back, further back, losing sight of what it is I wanted to do, what I wanted to achieve ... what I wanted to achieve.'

At this moment, Guido came rushing over to me shouting, in Dutch, 'Daddy, Daddy, watch me do a back-flip.' We watched him back-belly-flop into the water, and Veronique stand over him saying, in French, 'not like that you silly boy', and Mireille try and push her sister into the water for being so rude to Guido. Pam then turned to me, as if it had suddenly dawned on him that he was talking to someone in particular. He had a dark weathered, leathery face but, I thought, it was furrowed by too much thinking not weariness, too much action not age. He offered me a large hand and introduced himself, thus allowing me to explain who I was, and why I was there. And, on his enquiry, I told him about my position at the IFSD. This had the unexpected effect of prodding him out of the nostalgic backward-looking mood, if I can put it that way, into an active forward-step seeking mode.

I would be lying if I said I could recall the progress of our subsequent conversation. I like to imagine that the basic idea for United Artists International Forum was mine, but when I attempt to recall the logical progression of our conversation, this does not make any sense. It was Pam who, in the autumn of his life, was seeking fresh and worthwhile endeavours, not me; it was Pam who said he had already been thinking of offering his voluntary services to one of the UN agencies if he could dream up a suitable project; and it was Pam who belonged in the film world, bridging the gap between artists and businessmen, and who must have already discussed a hundred such ideas with a hundred colleagues. But it was me who, very simplistically, wondered why there wasn't some way of using the power of film and other art media (theatre, novels, pop music) – which for 50 years or more had created pervasive trends and fashions – to teach people certain universal basic ideas, about health, disease, safety, environment, energy use or human rights. It was me who questioned why big name directors had not used their blockbuster films to try and counter the Pearly Way epidemic, for example. And it was me who brought up the subject of broadcast soap operas and how they had been effectively employed, in developed countries as elsewhere, to deliver social messages, and who confessed that, even in my 40s, I could recall powerful episodes of Eastenders dealing with immigration and sex issues.

Somewhere along the way of this conversation, which continued as we walked around the garden to fill our glasses and find the tapas table, we came up with the concept of an independent agency, altruistically funded by wealthy artists, that would exist to provide carefully thought-out and structured opinions on how films, music, painting, theatre, literature could advise human behaviour for the good. We quickly arrived at a possible working arrangement for such an agency, whereby contributors would, in effect, hold a share of votes proportional to their contribution (with a maximum and a minimum), and this board would appoint independent thinkers, with a salary and a three or five year commission to consider how specific art forms could potentially deliver important messages of various types. Some organised internal procedure would lead to final opinions, which would then be published and thus be available for artists, producers, directors and writers to take up and use with confidence if they so wished. In addition, the board could be responsible for setting a general agenda for the types of opinions to be drawn up: defining which sectors should be targeted and in what form, and how detailed or general the message should or could be.

We were deep in conversation when Guido came to tell me that the others were waiting to leave. It was the night of the firework puppets on the beach, and everyone was keen not to miss them. I was disappointed to leave since Pam had become excited and was bursting with enthusiasm and ideas. He took one of my hands and cupped it in both his, and promised me our conversation would lead to a step, a real step forward; and that one day he would be at my door asking for funds. For the best part of two years, he worked like a trojan on the idea that had been conceived that afternoon in Joaquima's garden. As a highly respected elder statesmen of the film industry, he was a man who could open doors and help raise millions for charities simply by endorsing certain ventures. Where Pam led, others were sure to follow, so, when he decided to set up his own charity, there was no shortage of backers and sponsors. But Pam wanted to get the structure right. He took his time, and consulted widely, beyond the frontiers of the movie business into other art sectors. He and I engaged in an extended email dialogue, several long camphone conversations and cam-conferences, before he was ready to ask for IFSD money and support, something which would give the organisation, by then already called United Artists International Forum, credibility on a global scale. Even as, or especially as, environment director, I was not able to wave a wand and support projects simply because they were my personal favourites, however insignificant the requested funding. Nevertheless, there was a channel through which mini-scale finance could be donated to – for want of a better word – speculative ideas targeted on our main policy goals. And, with my advice, Pam had prepared an excellent proposal detailing the kind of environment-related practices (of interest mostly in the developing countries) that could very easily be propagated in certain kinds of movies. We leaked, to trustworthy journalists (lunch with Bobby Jespersen was always a pleasure), elements of the plan that we thought would play well in the press, and then I took the idea to the IFSD board. To my surprise, the board members loved it. I think they imagined themselves already on the invite list to Hollywood and Bollywood premieres. It did mean, though, that for five years United Artists International Forum (UAIF) (as led by its chairman Pedro Antonio de Malancas) was largely tied down to the elaboration of opinions on sustainable development issues. But, since a surprising number of the UAIF opinions were taken up by screenwriters and directors, sometimes on the level of advertising product placements, and sometimes more integrally in the plot, the IFSD's seed funding clearly demonstrated the principle could be made to work. As with most charitable international organisations, the UAIF went very quiet during the war years. Thereafter, it slowly expanded again, in the movie world and other artistic sectors. Today, the UAIF's status is as high as ever, and its opinions generally attract much art-world and media attention.

Finally, I should mention that Joaquima had a minor role to play in Guido's story. Her film captures a short scene in which two adults remove a large white bull-like costume from over the tops of Guido and Mireille who then move to one side. The adults demonstrate how the upper half cleverly concertinas up and down to hide/reveal the giant's head. At the same time, Guido is turning his face towards the camera. Mireille turns too, but to look at Guido; and then all of a sudden she pecks him on the cheek. An embarrassed Guido grimaces and wipes his face with the back of his hand. Years later, Diana used a large camstill of the cheek-pecking moment, and had it framed for a wedding present.

Inspired, I believe, by our love of Guido, who was as problem-free a child as one could wish for, Diana and I occasionally mulled over the idea of extending our family. With money for the best modern monitoring and caring techniques, determination, and a modicum of luck, Diana could surely have given birth in her late 40s. As time went on, we also considered adopting. But it was not to be.

For years we had sunk into a pattern of occasional love-making, depending largely on whether Diana could be bothered, and whether I felt strong enough in myself to let her be bothered. (How strange that sounds, I'm not sure I can explain it any better. With my own sexual needs easily fulfilled in private, I suppose, I became less and less willing to put myself in the position of being even partially responsible for arousing any desire in Diana that I might not be able to satisfy.) On domestic and social levels, the relationship worked well. Most of the time, I never felt any compulsion to discuss my daily working life: the endless difficulties with people, the intricate policy issues, the political emergencies, the bureaucratic nightmares. In the evenings, it was a relief to fall into the lively and cultured atmosphere of our home, where Diana's world governed. On a social level, there was more democracy: I had learned that if I was not too demanding and kept my requests to a minimum, Diana would, without complaint, accompany me to important formal events. Also, with regard to our friends, who were mostly artistic types, there was rarely any tension. I could natter for hours about the future of Flemish theatre or the importance of Tamson Bunting's collages or the beauty of Gustave Le Gray's 19th century photographs. Besides, although they were largely Diana's friends, many of them were not as religious as Diana about their art, and, if they were, they usually had partners eager to talk about anything other than the theatre.

Without the sexual connection, though, there was a void between us. Occasionally, as I say, we reconnected emotionally, and this had led us two or three times to discuss raising a second child together. This happened for the last time in Barcelona towards the end of the two weeks; but, once back in Leiden, the subject was never raised again.

EXTRACTS FROM CORRESPONDENCE
Crystal Fenn to Kip Fenn

June 2043

Thanks, it was good. Made me feel lots better.

I'm with Donna now, and she's cool. Should be OK.

Looking for a job. Say hi to Guido. x

June 2043

Thanks for the emails. You shook hands with Ojoru; my Dad has met Ojoru. That shines.

Saw Mum yesterday. Shouting. Bronze has done exams and gone to Wales with churchy friends for two weeks. I don't think Mum wanted him to go, so I don't know where he got the money from. You?

No Dad, thanks for offer, I don't want handouts. I start work Monday. Screen work (scream work), data-matching. I'm trying, it's going to be OK.

How's Guido, Diana? x

July 2043

Sorry I've not been writing. I wasn't good. It's the bad things. I wrote them down in a list. And then I wrote down the good things. I can't tell you where I am, and my phone's gone. I went to sleep but Donna woke me up, and ... well I'm OK.

July 2043

Thanks Dad, for the letters and money.

But the problem's in my head. One minute it's like I'm in so much pain, and then it's the world in so much pain, and then me again.

I can't stop any of it.

July 2043

Dad, I'm good, it's going to be OK. I've moved on. I'm not with Donna any more, but Kingston. He's rancid. And ace.

I said I would try and write, you see, and I'm being good.

July 2043

No Dad, I can't tell you where I am. It's good. I'm good. Kingston's kind. (NO, he's not a druggy! Rancid means cool.) He understands about the pain. He listens.

September 2043

Sorry Dad, I'm not good. Can't come to Aunt Julie's. Give a hug from me.

September 2043

Dear Dad, are you here tomorrow. I want to tell you something. I should be OK.
I'll wait by the flower stand, outside Paddington Station at 6:00.

September 2043

I don't want any more emails like the last one.

It's a good thing. Don't you see. It's action, not inaction. Kingston's gone,
but I'm good.

Don't tell Mum any of our conversation. Please.

Arturo Magalhães to Kip Fenn

January 2044

I am so grateful for the journey home. You are kind man, kind father.

I saw the children of the sister of my mother, and many friends.

I stay in Parati for Ano Novo.

And now I am in Horace's flat. It is very cool. I am so lucky.

Muito obrigado.

March 2044

Thank you for your email. I am studying very hard. Imperial College have
agreed to my application, but I must pass the English exam. I am doing an extra
exam in English: molecular biology.

At nights, I work in a pub. I like it. English drunk people are funny.

Um embraço.

April 2044

Thank you so much for the money and the e-cartoon from Diana. On my
birthday night, I went to a club in the End West (foreigner joke) with friends
from my English class (I am good student, top of the class), and last night
Horace took me to a very fancy restaurant. He is funny, I like him. Very serious
and very English and pompous and very silly. He told me when to watch the
screen, and I saw him speak in the House of Commons. Important people are
the same as everyone. I like it.

Um embraço for my generous father.

May 2044

Today must be a bad day for you (Crystal's birthday), so I just wanted to say hello, and tell you how grateful I am for all your help.

I am doing well in English. Yesterday I went out with Lucy. She is very sexy girl. I like her.

Um embraço, and remember me to Diana and Guido.

June 2044

Thank you for the card of Colossus. I see my brother is growing up fast. I'll come to visit you for a few days in July, if this is OK. And then I'll go with Lucy for two weeks to Scotland and the Isle of Skye. Would it be too bad to ask my father for some extra holiday money?

Did you know I have a relation (a two cousin) in San Francisco. My aunt tells me he is OK, but it is the same as a war was there. He knew a family crushed. The Americans always appear so invulnerable, don't you think, and this reminds us they are human.

Um embraço.

PS: Horace took me to see Peter Grimes at Covent Garden last weekend. Why are you English people so sad?

October 2044

Congratulations on your promotion. You are the right man for the job.

It is very exciting at Imperial College. So many clever people and professors. I am so happy to be here. And it is all thanks to you.

Um embraço, and one for Guido, tell him he's a dude.

PS: It is one year since you are my father.

February 2045

Apologies, I haven't written for a while, I was very happy to go home at Christmas for beach and sun, but I had a lot to catch up with when I got back.

I must tell something that happened, because I know Horace is your friend. He came round a few nights ago without calling. Usually he calls first. And I was with a girlfriend. He got very angry. I can't stay here much longer.

I'm going to find a pad with some friends, and I will apply for a student loan, to help pay. And then I will work all through the summer.

Um embraço.

February 2045

That is very kind. I am grateful. What would I do without you.

April 2045

Thank you very much for the birthday present. You are a very generous man, a generous father. I am getting accustomed to my pad-mates in Islip Street: one more Brazilian studying genetics; a very tall American girl who wants to create and then marry a bio-robot; and a Portuguese girl who loves to cook for us all and studies music theory. I like it here.

Um embraço.

Chapter Six

GUIDO, BIO-FESTS AND AL ZAHIR

'If Europe had stood firm and NATO had approved [the US] resolution for a nuclear strike, many Christian and Muslim lives would have been saved. The war would have ended, not in the appeasement of evil, but in victory for the forces of good. Al Zahir would still be burning in hell as I write; instead, the devil is amassing arms for a new assault on the free world. I have no doubts about this.'

Life's a Gamble by Steve Tarbuck (2065)

For most of Homo sapiens' history an individual could count himself very lucky if he survived for 50 years or more. By the middle of the 21st century, though, it was possible to hope – if you were rich or had managed to secure a reasonable life-long pension – that your life was only halfway through. When people greeted me, on my 50th birthday, with the usual medley of comments implying I had only reached the halfway stage, and that life would be as long in the future as it had been in the past, I laughed or smiled and tried to avoid a disdainful reply. Centenarians were already ten-a-penny (one of Tom's expressions) by 2050, but I could not see myself growing that old. And, even if I could have done, I would have had no desire to spend decades doing little more than managing my health and monitoring my funds. Besides, although we all tried to live and work in the belief that the world would become, with the right policies and enough effort, a better place, there was scant evidence to support such convictions.

Perhaps if I had known I would live this long, I might have stopped to take account of the mid-life moment. But I doubt it. For most of my days, I've had too many external preoccupations to waste time in self-examination. There was that uncomfortable period of cam-psychology or cam-quackery, as some called it, with Harriet, and later, after the break-up with Diana, I took a helpful course in musical psychotherapy. But even in retirement I kept fairly busy, thanks in part to Lizette (who was also responsible for the idea of writing these Reflections and thus for keeping me occupied in extreme old age, beyond my dotage).

In retrospect, I can confirm that in many significant ways my life was more than half over by 29 December 2049. The drama, joys and despairs, the achievements and disappointments, the important events and meetings of a life stand out, as it were, as if they were extraordinary buildings in a dark landscape caught by the sun. But the sunlit memories from the first 50 years of my life far outnumber those of the second 50. And, although there have been many dramas, joys, despairs, achievements, disappointments, events and meetings in my post-50 years, they came after earlier experiences and so rarely registered in the memory as firmly; thus they seem to catch less light, to glisten less. An independent biographer might, however, put more emphasis on my later achievements (within the International Fund for Sustainable Development and during the war years) since I worked at a higher and more important level than I did when younger. Furthermore, there was nothing insignificant about my relationship with Lizette, which filled up much of the second half of my life. But, to put it another way (and to mix and match my metaphors), change and movement in one's early years create memorable landmarks while routine and habit in later years are accompanied mostly by dull visits to old monuments.

Thus, and I do wish to explain this, the chapters dealing with the latter half of my life may – although I can't be sure at this stage – be blander than those already gone by; and the reflections to come may be more artificially selected than those I have already recorded. For instance, to start this chapter, I am going to visit, as briefly as I can, two fifty fiestas, Diana's and my own, even though I went, sometimes on sufferance, to other parties which, in their own way, might have been more memorable. For the year 49 alone, I could write about the UN-sponsored reception in a tulip palace to celebrate Indonesia's centenary at which Diana and I were forced to lie on the ground by a protester brandishing what turned out to be a toy gun, or Peter de Roo's barge extravaganza which indirectly led Guido and I to buy our own barge. Also that year we went to the Rocard ball in Paris and Amy Mistral's Third Man centenary event in Amsterdam, both of which would certainly have featured in Diana's Reflections had she ever written any.

Diana decided years in advance that she would celebrate her 50th birthday by hosting a bio-fest. As happens so often with cultural trends, bio-fests emerged in the alternative artistic world, and then became popular among celebrities, which in turn led everyone else to try and emulate the idea. But there were bio-fests and bio-fests. At one end of the scale, Hollywood actors would hire bio-fest contractors to manage a package deal, including netsite broadcasts, books and, occasionally, high-cost ticket entry for strangers (although attempts at staging bio-fests outside the home, as an exhibition, never caught on). At the other end of the scale, A N Other would put up a couple of 20th century photos of his grandparents and play childhood camclips on the screen and call it a bio-fest. Diana's bio-fest fell somewhere in-between the two extremes. Personally, I could not help thinking such demonstrative displays of self were mostly vulgar, a dressed-up way of bragging, of swaggering. I could, though, forgive Diana and other artists this vanity, since bio-fests were often no more than another means of self-expression.

Diana used up much of her spare time over a period of months in preparation for the occasion. Guido and I became fully involved a couple of weeks before the (Easter) weekend of her birthday, in April 47 (this was the year before our puppet festival trip to Barcelona). All the rooms in our house, and most walls and surfaces in those rooms, were given over to some aspect of Diana's life. Our bedrooms and Diana's studio became exhibition spaces for the models and designs of her most successful shows, demonstrating her early, middle and later periods respectively. The screens in each area carried sequences from the plays themselves and from broadcast interviews with Diana about her work, while printed reviews, praising her sets, had been enlarged and posted nearby the relevant models. Various awards, certificates and trophies (some dating back to school and college and some more prestigious) were on display. Guido had been given a fairly free hand to prepare a mini bio-fest for his own room, since Diana felt that he was an extension of herself. Nevertheless, she tried to guide him and this led to a few loud arguments which Diana, gracefully, let me adjudicate. In my office, we covered the walls with photos of Diana's friends, going back as far as her primary school, but trying to make sure there would be at least one picture of everyone who had been invited. The bathroom was decked out with paraphernalia she had kept from Tic-tac-toe, the barge she'd once owned and shared with Karl. Since Karl had been such a large part of Diana's life, I was quite relieved to see his presence confined to the bathroom. The hall, dining and large lounge areas downstairs were taken up with family and domestic photos and mementoes, along with the very best of Diana's own framed photos and designs (mostly theatre related), and the most treasured art works acquired from friends (such as the Rocard puppets). In the lounge, the big wallscreen showed a silent loop of family photos and camclips. Photo-collages and Guido-drawings of Diana, Guido and me dominated the kitchen.

The bio-fest spread across the whole weekend, with family and neighbours mostly visiting on Saturday, and friends coming on Easter Sunday. We hired a mini-marquee (with heating fan) which was easily attached to the back of the house and accessed through the lounge door. Diana had wanted to solicit friends to look after the food and clearing up, but I insisted on hiring help for both days. We put food and drink for the adults in the marquee, and for the kids in a couple of tents in the front common garden area. Both days went smoothly – with two exceptions. On Saturday we had the garage roof crisis: Guido confidently led two girls, younger than him, across Oldwijkgaarten to the garage area, up some stepped brickwork and a wall, and onto a roof. Once there, the girls refused to follow Guido down. Tears, rescues, and recriminations followed in succession but were then soon forgotten when Guido promised to make the girls a paper jumping frog each. (While other boys had been learning to play football, Guido had nurtured an interest in origami!)

And on Sunday we had the Anders crisis. This is Diana's story more than mine, and replete with names that I will not use again, but Jay was moved by it when I told him a few days ago, as we all were at the time. To recall this accurately, I need to play the camclip someone helpfully took of the bio-fest exhibits.

The photos displayed along the hall from our front door start with Diana's parents Powles and Neeltje Oostlander, both of whom were long since dead. Powles had trained as an architect, become diverted by architectural history and ended up as curator of a local history museum in Utrecht. Neeltje, too, assisted Powles at the museum, but not before she had spent most her life working as a nurse fitting in different kinds of jobs around her child-rearing responsibilities. Next on the wall are Neeltje's parents (Diana's maternal grandparents), Anders and Claudine van der Klein. There is one photo of them standing outside the Utrecht house, the same one Dominique occupied for much of her life (which is a long story in itself although it had a happy ending, inasmuch as Dominique and Diana never fell out over the inheritance), and another one of them at a flower market. There is only one photo of Powles's parents (Diana's paternal grandparents), Eduwart and Maartje, but two of Powles's sister, Saartje (Sarah) and her English husband Anthony Nash, both with Liam their son. This is because Diana knew that Liam, her cousin, would be flying over from Bristol in England for the bio-fest. He proved to be a most interesting man. On inheriting a water pump business from his father, he had eschewed the chance of making millions by selling the manufacturing plant, and instead used the regular profits to invest in research and the development of cheap and ultra-efficient filter technologies. Whenever it was possible, he had opened up the patents for his designs and techniques through, as it happens, an IFSD-sponsored technology-transfer netzone. But this is a complete digression.

Anders and Claudine had four daughters, of whom Neeltje was the oldest. On the bio-fest camclip I can see there are several photos of the daughters together and some of their offspring. Two of Neeltje's sisters (Diana's aunts), Betje and Kaatje, were alive at the time. Then, in the dining area, there are the photos of Powles and Neeltje's children: the four Ds. The oldest was Demeter, known as Dimi, then aged 59. She had married young, gone to live in the north of Holland, and worked as a family doctor her whole life long. Emulating her mother, she too had four girls (plus several grandchildren, perhaps the girls who got stuck on the roof). Dana, in her early 50s by that time, had emigrated to New Zealand when young, married, and was running a local chain of pharmacies in Whangarei. She sent Diana a camclip of herself and her husband riding horses along a beach, which we found quite bizarre. Diana was the third daughter, and Dominique the youngest. The bio-fest camclip shows all kinds of photos of the four Ds, with and without Powles and Neeltje, as toddlers, juniors, teenagers and adults, some funny, some beautiful and some enchanting. Many, but not all of these, had been sent to Diana by Dimi who kept the largest collection of family memorabilia.

All the photos were much admired during the Saturday, but it was not until the following day that the festivities were disturbed by Helene's discovery. The Rocard family had driven from Paris for a few days holiday in Leiden to coincide with the bio-fest. Helene was a hobby genealogist, which might or might not explain why she examined Diana's family photos with more zeal than most of us had done. During the afternoon, when the kids were taking advantage of the spring sunshine, and the adults had settled into conversation cliques, she noticed, among the half dozen photos of the four Ds as babies, photos of five different children. At first she assumed Diana had mixed them up and included a cousin or nephew with Neeltje's offspring. She called in Diana, who admitted that she could barely tell the difference between the babies' faces, but, on closer examination, agreed that one of them did look more boyish and different from the others. Dominique (who, with Waltar, was present on both days) was summoned next. She could shed no light on the matter. The three of them went to Diana's room and computer to examine the store of photos that Dimi had sent. The toddler in question had been clearly labelled, by Dimi, as Dana, but when they looked at other photos of Dana, there was no resemblance. After a camphone conversation, Dimi promised to have a closer look at the archive. While waiting for her to call back, Helene, Dominique and Diana came to find me. I was refereeing a volleyball free-for-all in the garden. They were showing me the photos and explaining the mystery when Dimi rang to say she had found one other similar printed photo, but there was no name attached. And so Diana called Neeltje's sisters. The youngest, Betje, who had been there on the Saturday with her son, was suffering from an early form of senile dementia and her memory was very unreliable. Kaatje, however, who was immobile but happily ensconced in a nursing home near Arnhem, was still very alert. She solved the mystery immediately, without any fuss. Before having Dimi, Neeltje had given birth to a son, but he had died from meningitis when only about 18 months old. It was a great family tragedy at the time. The boy had been called Anders.

Initially, Diana was angry because this important piece of family history had been kept secret. She forgot her guests and the bio-fest and made several more calls, to her sisters and her aunts, accusing each of them in turn of a conspiracy of silence. But Kaatje was clear that Neeltje had made the definite decision not to talk about Anders or to remember him in any way, and so there was never any reason for her, Kaatje, to do otherwise.

Suffused with guilt, for having chosen such a doomed name for her first child, and for not remembering our own Anders in her bio-fest, Diana's mood shifted from anger to despair. She broke down. We all tried to comfort her in different ways, but it was Dominique's idea to re-assemble the Anders co-op (since we were all there) that provided the necessary healing balm. Taking a photo to record the co-op took longer than expected since we could not agree on whether to smile or look sad. Eventually, serious won the day, and Diana prepared and printed the photo out on her high-spec machine. She then juggled the pictures on one of the lounge walls to make room for it. It was a cathartic experience for Diana. Thereafter she never referred to her bio-fest but only to Ander's Day.

***

My own 50th birthday party, two and half years later, was also memorable for different reasons. Most years, we either got together with Peter de Roo and his family (and/or others) for a meal on 29 or 30 December, or subsumed a birthday celebration into some theatrical new year's eve party or other. But, for my 50th, Diana decided we should mark it more deliberately. I suspect she felt this was necessary, despite my protestations, because we had all put so much effort into her own bio-fest. We chose the afternoon of 1 January so our gathering would not clash with new year's eve (new half-century's eve), and because it was a Saturday.

In contrast to Diana's Day, this was no bio-fest, and there were no theatrics, unless you count Imam Al Zahir's new year message, which I shall come to all too soon. But it was a very special day, simply because of who was there. Not ever before or after were so many of my friends and family all gathered together in one place.

It was the only time, for example, that all three of my children met together: Guido had just turned 11; Bronze was about to turn 22; and Arturo was already 27. Since Arturo had been back in Brazil for more than a year (and, thus, was taking no money from me at all), I offered to pay his fare and living expenses for two weeks over the Christmas holidays. But the three boys had nothing in common – except me, and these staged photos that I have on my screen now. I don't believe they developed any brotherly bonds, or ever sought each other out in life. Here is Bronze, smiling but still managing to look miserable, and Arturo with a face full of mischief. They are kneeling down slightly apart, and Guido is standing on tip-toes in-between them. All their heads are at roughly the same level, making for an awkward looking picture. There is another photo, even less elegant, of all four of us. Both these photos make me feel sad. They do not remind me of the one day when we were all together, which was, as I say special, but of the fact that, on a personal level, my life has been chaotic and defective.

All our regular friends were there, including the Meijers and the de Roos, as were several neighbours and a few colleagues from the IFSD. My uncle Alan and his partner Anna Mastepanov came from St Petersburg, bless them. They stayed for several days, which allowed me more time with Alan than I'd had since I was child. He looked weary, but had lost none of his calm or wisdom. I must have spent half our time together enthusiastically seeking his views on various issues (as if I were 12 again and he 40) that had already crossed my desk as the IFSD's new environment director. I also attempted to persuade him to take on light duties as a paid advisor for my department. Whether Alan was interested or not, I never found out, since Anna firmly vetoed the idea.

My mother, against the advice of doctors, made her very last trip overseas. Bronze, dutifully, drove her. It was a strain for both of them and for me. Bronze and I had nothing to talk about. He didn't seem to trust me, and my questions only ever elicited meaningless replies. I let him lock my office for an hour so he could use the screen to join in prayer time with his church; and, later, Diana caught him preaching to Guido. During the journey over, Julie reported to me, Bronze had revealed details about his current life, details that I would not have discovered otherwise. On leaving college with an inferior degree in sociology, he had worked for a religious marketing company. After nine months he had got bored and left (although Julie, reading between his lines, thought he might have been sacked for prolonged illness, whether imagined or not). A period of unemployment followed until he was recruited by an organisation called the New Crusaders, and given a place in a hostel near Newbury. He was working as a net-recruiter, and learning Arabic. Life was 'a bliss', Bronze had told Julie.

Also from England came Horace, already by then a cranky backbencher (Spoon's coalition had fallen early), with his partner of several years; Miriam and Doug Turnbull, who were back together after Miriam's sorry affair with a family friend; and Pete Sampson with a new youngish wife (Clarity) and one year old baby (Joan).

Furthermore – and this is partly for Chintz, who wanted to know the other day if there were any famous people at the party – I should mention Oakley. Although he had a Christian name, Finbar, he was universally known as Oakley. Diana worked with him years earlier when Karl directed the German productions of two his plays. He was about ten years older than me, and had emerged as a formidable playwrite around the time I was leaving school. While other writers were stuck in a 20th century time warp churning out self-obsessed material about their failed relationships with people or drugs or possessions, Oakley opened up a new and rich genre of theatre: the theatre of international politics. He was far from prolific, producing only one play in three or four years, but the majority of them proved to be masterpieces. Many imitators followed, but few managed to equal his ability to blend the political with the personal and create dramas that resonated so loudly with people's concerns for their own backyard and the world beyond. Angelika Stockmann, who Diana also worked with, was one of Oakley's more successful followers.

Oakley came to live in Amsterdam in the 30s. He and I met, thanks to Diana, at a press night. Thereafter, Oakley initiated several meetings (lunches in The Hague mostly) because he wanted to research some of the mechanics and politics behind the IFSD's work. At his request for a contact in West Africa, I put him in touch with Alfred. Consequently, we are both thanked, recognisably but anonymously, in the play script for *Pilgrimage to The Hague*. This is one of his most controversial plays, and the only one to tackle religion head on. It tells the fantastical story of three African men – one Christian, one Muslim, one a believer in tribal gods – who go in search of financial salvation for their peoples. Oakley wrote it in the early 40s, round about the same time I was working on the Alfred/Ojoru mission. But that does not necessarily mean I would know why he elected to use the IFAD, the UN's agricultural aid agency, to thump home messages about corruption, inefficiency and bureaucracy!

After *Pilgrimage to The Hague* was finished and throughout the 40s, Oakley and I continued to meet once a month. This was usually at his instigation, for I rarely initiated any social contact with anyone. But I soon came to look forward to our lunches. We rarely talked about anything other than the main political issues of the day, but, whereas I dealt with the world's ills in the way a doctor deals with a patient's pain, he seemed to feel the ills himself. I guess it gave it him some relief to analyse and diagnose the causes of the pain with someone in the medical profession, if that makes any sense. Over time I came to love him for his combination of intelligence and humanity. He hated being a celebrity, nor was he the slightest bit flattered or interested in the theatre world's sycophants. He never married, and as he got older he found socialising more and more onerous. He accepted my invitation on 1 January 50 not because he wanted to, for by then he was already finding any kind of festive gathering uncomfortable, but out of friendship for me, and because I'd never made any such demands on him before.

Oakley's last play, produced in London in 53, bombed, as they say. One cruel tabloid writer said that Oakley had finally 'vanished up his own varnished arse'. In truth, even before the war, the middle-class public had long since grown tired of being reminded of the world's troubles, what with the FTM riots, the climate disasters and the suicide epidemic. For more than a decade, they had been flocking to farces and musicals. Oakley never wrote another play, and he himself never recovered. He returned to England in the mid-50s, bought an isolated cottage on Dartmoor, and lived as a recluse until grief – grief for mankind – drained all life out of him. I believe he may have suffered more than those wounded and killed in the war that he, personally, had failed to prevent.

I had not planned to write about Oakley in this chapter. But, now I have, I should record that I did try to contact him several times over the years; and once, because he would never respond to my calls and emails, I borrowed a friend's car and drove to the cottage. It was a pretty enough house, in a charmingly wild location, but neither the gardens nor the property itself showed any signs of maintenance. I hammered on the door for several minutes before Oakley answered it. He looked the part, an anchorite with long hair and a beard down to his chest. But I was not welcome. He spoke to me as if I were an annoying nosy neighbour, saying he was busy and had no time to invite me in. Come again another year, he said, and closed the door in my face.

Because Oakley turned his back on society and culture, the middle classes, the artists, the intellectuals, the media all in their turn rejected and ignored him for the best part of 20 years. The few biographies published during his life, largely failed to reveal the man or to assess confidently his worth, which is not surprising since the authors had no access to the man or his papers. Ironically, it was not until his death, in 63, that his reputation as one of the most important playwrites of the century began to solidify. Chintz, who in common with most youngsters these days, studied Oakley at school, would be pleased to know that my excellent medical care, and thus my ability to be writing these Reflections, has been made possible, in part, by the royalties from *Pilgrimage to The Hague*. Oakley left clear and unambiguous instructions in his will that I should inherit all the rights for the play, and that I should use the income 'not for humanity for which I can do nothing, but for a human man, a man that was my friend'. I have much appreciated the additional income (and Jay will benefit until the copyright runs out), but there was an unexpected bonus to the inheritance. For more than 30 years, I've had biographers of all types, whether students or heavyweight academics, seek me out for information, and this has allowed me some slight influence over their feelings about, and opinions of, the great writer.

***

And so, to conclude these specific recollections of my fifty fiesta, I must unfortunately move on to Imam Al Zahir's 'new year message for the United States, the Europe Union and their NATO allies'. The first signal was a call from Tommy Chowdhury on my phone. Seconds later, Oakley darted into the lounge urging me to switch a newsfeed onto the screen. So as not to disturb the party, a group of us went upstairs to my bedroom where we watched a live broadcast from Esfehan, Iran. Most historians came to consider Al Zahir's speech that day as the starting gun for, what in the West we now call, the First Jihad War.

By this time, Al Zahir, Iran's effective leader since the late 30s, had spent more than ten years trying to unify the Islam world. Early success came through Iran's United Brothers Treaty with Iraq and Pakistan, which effectively defused the chronic friction between the two main Muslim camps. This he managed, *Encyclopaedia Universal* tells me, largely because of his status as a Hujjatul Islam ('a living proof of the reality and the veracity of the message of Islam') which allowed him to be seen as transcending the differences between the Sunni and Shia. Then he set about uniting the Arab nations in the International Islam Brotherhood for Peace (IIBP). In response, the Christian world became increasingly two-faced: it kept a diplomatic smile fixed on the laudable stated aims of the IIBP; and it concealed a strategic grimace at the IIBP's success and growth, especially as Arab governments turned fundamentalist and less tolerant of non-Muslim minorities or neighbouring countries, and more willing to abuse international rules, whether on issues of trading, immigration, the environment, armaments, crime or whatever. As they had always done, European and other NATO member countries gave preferential treatment to the more moderate governments within the IIBP whenever it was politically acceptable to do so. Most of the time, however, Europe, with its many divided interests, looked to the United Nations to find compromise solutions wherever possible. An increase in development aid and the expansion of the IFSD was one of the few areas where compromises and progress had been found over the years. It is also worth recalling that, throughout the 40s, there was an unholy alliance between the US and the Russian secret services which intervened regularly to undermine the most fundamentalist Arab regimes, and to fund opposition and underground parties favourable to the West, and that these actions were consistently opposed by senior United Nations representatives and by most leaders in Western Europe.

In the late 40s, Al Zahir and the IIBP extended their ambitions and influence beyond the Middle East and North Africa. A preliminary step was Turkey, which had tried to dance with Europe so many times and been jilted once too often. Then came Indonesia. Supported, bribed and armed by the West, a secular government had held on to power for one year after the summit that agreed the Djakarta Settlement, but it had then fallen to a popular coup led by Islamic fundamentalists. Within weeks, Indonesia's new leaders signed up the country to be a full participating member of the IIBP, inclusive of mutual defence treaties. Furthermore, by the late 40s, and since Ojoru's complete retirement from politics in 47, the countries of sub-Saharan Africa had begun to fall under the influence of Al Zahir.

There was no doubt that Imam Al Zahir's rhetoric had been hardening, albeit slowly, over the years. But he knew how to talk to Western leaders, how to deal with the Western media, and how to explain away, to the millions of Muslim followers, his apparent friendship with the West. Up until new year's day 50, whenever doubts were raised publicly about Al Zahir's long-term aims, whether by archbishops, popes or the leaders of right-wing political parties in the Western world, commentators were obliged to admit that there was no real evidence that the man was anything other than an enlightened leader of the Muslim peoples. If the IIBP was challenging the Western invented and regulated institutions this was not, in itself, reprehensible from an objective point of view. If the IIBP was legitimately encouraging and helping Islamic-run states, this may have been unpalatable for Washington, Tokyo and Brussels but why shouldn't the IIBP countries help each other, the independent commentators asked. And, if Muslim communities across Europe were gaining in strength and demanding proper representation at every administrative level, then this too was but equality at work. Nevertheless, it was not only American nationalists and Christian zealots that feared the future, many people in Europe especially, on both the left and the right, were not blind to the direction of world events and the lessons of history.

Al Zahir picked new year's day because he knew it was a traditional time for Western leaders to deliver their own messages, and he chose the late afternoon to ensure coverage across Europe and the US. Here are some quotes from that famous speech.

'Islam is the guardian of human rights and nobility. Islam is the religion of justice, freedom, salvation, wisdom and knowledge. Islam is the religion of life. Islam is the religion of innovations and new ideas. Islam is the religion of civility, science and development. Islam is the religion of logic and rationalism. Islam is the religion of sacrifice and tolerance. Islam guarantees and protects ethical precepts and moral decency. Islam is the religion of unity, fraternity and world peace. ... Those who try to depict Islam as a religion against human rights, civility and security, are launching the most ignominious lies and accusations against our religion. These tactics are intended to justify the brutalities committed against Muslim nations and peoples. ... The Eastern and Western regimes speak with untrustworthy tongues. ... In the Name of Allah, the All-beneficent, the All-merciful, we reject unity with those that would oppress us, those that would seduce our youths, steal our food, take our wives, slander our beliefs, and with those that would be rich when others are impoverished. ... The officials of Islamic states, be they in legislatures or executives or judiciaries, or armed forces or anyone who is working anywhere, must overcome their weaknesses. The way to ensure prosperity for our nations and peace for the world is through the Koran. ... Mohammad, the Messenger, and those who are with him must remain firm against the unbelievers. Did he not say: "I have been ordered by Allah to fight with people till they bear testimony to the fact that there is no God but Allah and that Mohammed is his messenger, and that they establish prayer and pay Zakat. If they do it, their blood and their property are safe from me." ... A new horizon is opened, where from we are able to see more visibly, hear and understand better the way to eternal salvation. The blossoms of knowledge and Islamic fraternity, and divine guidance flourish and appear before our eyes. ... We have struggled for 20 years and still the rich in the West are unbelievers, and still they rule some of our precious lands, and still they refuse to pay their Zakat. In the name of Allah, Islam is the religion of Jihad.'

Apart from other expletives muttered under the breath of those collected in my bedroom, a collective gasp went up at the word 'Jihad': since becoming Iran's leader, Al Zahir had never been heard to utter it in public. But we had no time to comment on this, for he went on to inform the world that the IIBP would, within the next few days and 'after 100 years of conflict', be considering a request from the Kashmir liberationists for a final and decisive offensive against the last remaining India-held territories. This simple statement lightly disguised two messages: within the IIBP, Pakistan had finally agreed to an independent Islamist Kashmir state, and, secondly, the IIBP nations were willing (never mind the 'request' terminology) to declare war on India alongside Pakistan and the guerrilla organisations fighting for Kashmir's independence. And we all knew this meant NATO – which only months previously had celebrated its centenary – would be obliged to respond in support of India.

There was no quick fix for my mood that day, as there had been for Diana's on Ander's Day. Even the Marc Ferrez print that Diana gave me as a birthday present could not lift my spirits. When the last of the guests had departed or retired, I spent a few minutes alone in my office. I was tempted to tune into the BBC for some analysis on the Al Zahir speech, but then I saw the book-sized package on the shelf, still partially gift-wrapped. I had deliberately left it there and not prepared it for the cool storage because I knew I would want to re-examine its contents. There were many things wrong with the (175 year) old gelatin print. The photo itself was over-exposed, the print was flawed with flecks, and the corners were bent and cracked. But it was a genuine Ferrez. Diana never told me how much she paid, but it would have been over 1,000 euros. It wasn't a picture of a deserted Copacabana beach (I would have to wait nearly 40 more years to get my hands on one of those), but it was a Ferrez, and I had longed for one since the early days of my interest in old photographs. This photo (it had no name) showed a man sitting on the ground, between a track and a creek, by a small thin-trunked tree rising up, at a crooked angle, into, and silhouetted by, a cloudy sky full of dark foreboding clouds. My eye wandered across the postcard-sized photo searching for some artistic merit, but, as there was none, it kept returning to the man seated on the earth. I could barely see his face, the detail being lost in the darkness of the print, but, I thought, he was weighed down with thoughts. It was a magnificent possession, especially when I contemplated the fact that this fragile item had once been in Ferrez's very own hands. Yet it was a depressing picture: the black clouds, the morose man, the half-fallen tree. I carefully placed it between two acid-free transparent membranes, inside a sealable transparent bag, and then inside another sealable but opaque pouch. The whole thing then joined dozens of others in the specially-designed cool storage trays on top of one of my filing cabinets, to be removed and touched only rarely in the years to come.

Diana was already asleep when I went to bed (Julie was in my bed, and Bronze was sleeping in the lounge). I kissed her lightly, lovingly on the cheek, not wishing to disturb her, but she drifted back to consciousness. I said thank you for the party and for the Ferrez; and I told her dark clouds were coming.

Having already delved into my photo databases to remind myself of the Ferrez, I am tempted now to access Portia and look through some of the very earliest war photographs, all dating from approximately 200 years prior to the First Jihad War: Hippolyte Bayard's haunting images of the French Revolution, Roger Fenton's gentlemanly look at the Crimean War, Felice Beato's artistic pictures taken during the Indian Mutiny and the Second China War or Matthew Brady's documentary photos of the American Civil War (not forgetting the most famous early war photograph of all, Timothy O'Sullivan's *Harvest of Death*). But I must resist the ongoing temptations to be diverted by history or antiquarian photographs and proceed with my own story, such as it is. I've promised myself to complete this manuscript by the end of the year, the end of the century, and my time is running out.

I have had a rush of visitors in the last few days. Lovely Josephine came on Monday, bustling as ever with news of the Collection, her fund-raising activities, and of mutual acquaintances. She brought a large bunch of roses (flame-coloured) which, later, Chintz carefully arranged in the over-speckled vase that dominates the windowsill in this room. Then, on Wednesday, by coincidence or not, Belinda came, offering me gossip of a more mundane kind about The Josephine Collection museum and about herself. On Tuesday, Irene and Yewla, two of Jay's cousins (Lizette's nieces), came together. I like them both very much, but not together. They have visited before, on their own, and then I could cope. They're all the same, these media creatures, they seem to live in a faster (and dare I suggest shallower) river than the rest of us.

***

In early 50, I was still coming to terms with the tasks and responsibilities of my position as environment director; and the IFSD itself was still re-establishing itself after the Djakarta Settlement decisions and the shake-up created by the new director-general. I spent most of the day following my fifty fiesta, a Sunday, on the phone with IFSD advisers and various other colleagues (not least Alfred whose star had unfortunately fallen with Ojoru's departure from power in the late 40s). Much of that working week I sat in emergency conferences, with my staff, with the IFSD director-general, with internal and external UN committees, with the main financial donor countries and with the representatives of some very anxious recipient countries and regions. Despite all the feverish activity, and the sketching out of dozens of horrible and not-so-horrible future scenarios, information on which to base practical decisions was hard to find initially. Before long, though, Pakistan stated it no longer would claim Kashmir for its own, and was prepared to mobilise all its armed forces to fight to give the region nationhood once and for all. Several leaders of Islamic states issued statements supporting Pakistan's 'decisive move' to bring stability to the region. By April, the IIBP nations had agreed unanimously that, unless India acceded to an independent Kashmir, they would go to war 'for peace'.

During these months I tried to focus my time and energy fairly across all my tasks, but Kashmir was in the news every day; and, almost every day, there were new elements to discuss or decide on. Luckily or not, depending on which way I look at the matter, I had Tommy Chowdhury running the Kashmir desk. We had become friendly during my final year at uni through the Government Club, but then lost touch. After a miserable period working for a multinational in Lahore, he spent time with Amnesty International before moving on to run an independent information netsite about Kashmir. The responsibilities of a wife and children drove him to find better-paid work. Given his skills, he had no trouble getting a post with the IFSD as a project manager. In the early 40s, he was assigned to the climate response division; he then moved to the poverty alleviation division. Not long after my appointment as environment director, I poached him to come and work for me. He was much relieved to get back to analysis and to using his intelligence for preparing policy advice instead of sifting contractor proposals and monitoring project performances. What Tommy did not know about Kashmir, its history, politics, organisations, was not worth knowing. And, given the chronic troubles in the entire region, successful project development and implementation in the area relied heavily on detailed and local policy advice.

Already as a student, Tommy had decided to disguise his heritage so that no-one knew if he came from a Muslim or Hindi background. His surname was no definitive guide, and he adamantly refused to claim a particular faith. Personally, I never observed any bias in him to one side or the other. He did not care about the territory, but only about the people whatever their nationality or religion. Because there were never any pat solutions, his private views on the political situation changed as the century wore on. He had once thought, for example, that a repartitioning of the region between Pakistan and India would be the best solution. Then he had come round to accepting the Chinese plan for a jointly-administered protectorate (though this was much opposed in Washington). Tommy believed an independent state would be the best outcome in the long run, yet he also understood the costs of getting there, and of holding independence, would be very high.

During that year, 50, Tommy moved heaven and earth to provide me with the detailed arguments for maintaining IFSD funding and projects in the Kashmir region. It was a great asset to have someone so knowledgeable about the subject; but it took extra time to manage him and the passionate approach he took to the job.

By the spring of 51, the matter was out of our hands. It had been decided at the highest level. The IIBP pronouncements had led to a series of emergency summits between the three major international groupings (I've checked the encyclopaedia to ensure I get this right): the G13, representing broadly the biggest and most important industrialised countries (US, Japan, Germany, France, Italy, GB, Canada, Russia, Spain, the Netherlands, Australia, Ukraine and Korea) most of whose armed forces were largely united through NATO; the I9, the Islamic nine, representing the largest and most important of the IIBP nations (Iran, Indonesia, Turkey, Saudi Arabia, Algeria, Pakistan, Egypt, Bangladesh and Morocco); and the non-aligned four (China, India, Brazil and Nigeria), which at times expanded to eight (with Mexico, Thailand, Vietnam and the Philippines). All kinds of international deals and fixes were proposed, some in secret, some in public, but Al Zahir played his cards – the demands for Zakat from the West, and a string of territorial claims – as efficiently as a poker player with a rigged deck. He did not want to win, he wanted war. At times, it appeared the IIBP was on the verge of some compromise with the G13, but then it would become clear that Al Zahir had simply been trying to stir up conflict within the G13 and between it and the non-aligned countries, especially China. In early 51, one G13-I9 summit broke up in disarray, and a subsequent one was cancelled. Meanwhile, the main IIBP nations suddenly all signed non-aggression pacts with China, thereby tacitly approving its claim to the Indian state of Ladakh, north of Kashmir. Immediately, orders came down from on high for all IFSD (and other UN) activities connected with Kashmir to be frozen, and all personnel in the region to be withdrawn.

Tommy was devastated. Unlike most of us, he had continued to believe that a war in the region could be avoided. Because we all hoped any conflict would be over shortly, with as few lives lost, and as little damage to the region's infrastructure as possible, I kept him assigned to the Kashmir desk producing daily, and then weekly bulletins. But as the war moved through the usual stages, from smart bombing to peace talk attempts, from random bombing to peace talk attempts, from air battles to peace talk attempts, and to the inevitable ground and guerrilla war, so Tommy became increasingly unstable, and emotional. If my secretary stalled his calls, he would come storming into my office, his spiky black hair all disarranged, spectacles in one hand, papers in the other, with some vital piece of news which was of no relevance to our work at all. Having persistently failed to follow my advice or that of a senior personnel officer to take holiday, he disappeared without notice. I waited a few days for him to contact me, and then I called his wife, Tamarind, a deeply serious woman who had often worked as a volunteer for one of the Dutch religious tolerance organisations. She told me Tommy had gone to Amritsar, India, to the Red Cross base there to replace an operations manager who had been killed on a mission. When I expressed anger at his failure to inform me, Tamarind defended him, saying he was a man of many divided loyalties, and that he had not wanted to let me down. The next day I received a short email in which Tommy apologised. He explained that he had been going mad pushing paper, and doing nothing. He sounded like someone who had been let out of prison. I called the personnel department immediately and pulled rank to ensure he was given an immediate six month sabbatical (three of them on full pay). Thankfully, he had been with the IFSD long enough to allow such a leave of absence. He came back after five months, shell-shocked, far less driven, more stable, very grateful to me, and more than ready to play his part in keeping our work going in those areas of the world where we could make a difference.

Al Zahir's forces, as they were often called by the media, continued to make slow advances in Kashmir, winning territory through the attrition of men. Indian nationals were dying at ten times the rate of NATO soldiers, but it was the NATO deaths and the prospect of losing the Kashmir war that, finally, in early 53, led the US hardline Republican President Steve Tarbuck (who had taken over the White House from the Democrat Betty Arklington in 51) to press for the nuclear option. There was much head-banging, especially between the European leaders, before NATO made two class C nuclear strikes on military-dominated towns in Iran and Pakistan, killing a total of 21,000 civilians and military personnel. As is well documented, this action played right into Al Zahir's hands. Intelligence material had indicated the IIBP alliance would fall apart if faced with the realities of nuclear devastation and this claim had been crucial in convincing the European doves to accept the class C strikes. However, it transpired that the intelligence material was not only flawed but wrong in almost every detail.

The two nuclear bombs led the IIBP to set in motion immediately a series of devastating suicide bomb missions on Tel Aviv and – horrifyingly for those of us safe and cosy in Europe – on Constanta and Athens. It announced Turkey would be sending more armoured troops to the Kashmir front. It called to arms terrorist warriors lying low in the more hawkish European countries. It further restricted oil and gas supply to NATO members. And, worst of all, for this is what many in the world had feared, the IIBP declared the rich West had left no alternative but for an extension of the Jihad into other areas where unbelievers were suppressing the Islam message. Three weeks after the nuclear missiles, Al Zahir pronounced that the IIBP had received (i.e. had agreed) requests for military support from the Islam Liberation Front in Mindanao, from Sudan to support the Muslim rebel movement in Chad, and from Uzbekistan and Kyrgyzstan for border disputes with Kazakhstan.

What Al Zahir pronounced usually came to pass. From halfway through 53 the conflict between NATO and the IIBP escalated rapidly. As with the Cold War 100 years previously, open wounds and hidden sores of the conflict could be found across the world's geography. Although in Europe we were largely free of any direct experiences of the war, we quickly became accustomed to a new level of terrorist alert, to seeing and dealing with racist tensions (some countries demanded oaths of allegiance from Muslim nationals and expelled non-nationals), and to a steady stream of dead youths returning home in body bags. Moreover, the anti-war movement flourished, and this led to some of the largest protest demonstrations seen since the First Tuesday Movement peak two decades earlier.

NATO found itself neutered by an inability to use its most destructive weapons, and the IIBP ratcheted up the pressure. Every week, there was talk of fresh attempts to solve one crisis or another, or to find a global solution, but the IIBP's demands continued to escalate, always to a level beyond that which the Christian nations were prepared to give.

For the first two or three years (this was in the period when the war was confined to Kashmir) I was able to make a reasonable contribution in my new position as environment director. Apart from Tommy, I established a good team of policy advisers and heads for the regional departments. I should mention Ninel Horeva who was never given sufficient backing from Moscow to get a top posting herself. She sat comfortably at my side, so to speak, for many years, and provided invaluable advice on Ukraine and the Russian sphere countries. And there was Chidi Naiambana, a shiningly intelligent Nigerian ex-diplomat that Alfred, through Ojoru, had managed to parachute (meaning the normal channels were not followed) into the IFSD. He was tall, although not to Alfred's standard, with thin gracile features and long fingers which he wiggled around when trying to make a point. In addition, I redesigned the organisa-tional structure of the whole division, so as to allow us to channel our energies efficiently into the new priorities which had been established by the Djakarta Settlement.

I did, though, spend too much time on infighting, a chronic disease of the UN, and a speciality of the IFSD which had grown so large and powerful at the expense of other international organisations. Two times, once in the 20s and once in the 40s, the world's major management consultancies (different ones each time) had clubbed together in an altruistic mission (taking several years) to help streamline the UN system. On each occasion, the recommendations were only partially implemented due to entrenched interests and the growing political divides which led to increasing levels of distrust at all levels. In partic-ular, the UN's failure to reform the agricultural agency (IFAD), in the late 30s, meant it had become no more than a political tool for certain countries. The situation had resulted (partly thanks to Alfred and me, as I have recounted) in the IFSD moving into the same policy territory as the IFAD. And, like it or not, the Djakarta Settlement had turned the IFAD into little more than an advisory arm for the IFSD – and like it, the IFAD did not. Much of the IFSD's responsi-bilities for sustainable agriculture and training/education for same fell under my command. The IFSD director-general and the UN Secretary General washed their hands of the whole dispute, and so it was left to me to find a way of breaking down the barriers between our two organisations. Pravit Krishnamurty, who I wrote to now and then seeking his wisdom, commented: 'Well, my friend, you know it is all reaping and sowing. Not much has changed in 10,000 years.'

I took no pride in the task, nor did I employ any special skills. I simply persevered with calm patience, and used any opportunity to expose the IFAD's intransigence and failings. In this, the journalists Bobby Jespersen and Ike Davidson (who had moved to Brussels to cover, among other things, the NATO command side of the war) proved useful. After a widely publicised but unwarranted counter-attack on me, the IFAD's chief retired early, and his replacement (who eased out several obstructive deputies without much difficulty) proved more willing to cooperate.

**

Although Diana and I recovered some stability in our relationship, around the time of the Barcelona trip and for two or three years thereafter, my IFSD promotion and the global conflict brought with them new personal tensions. It is possible that, without the war, we might have stayed the course through to old age. I make this assessment in retrospect, and only after reading writers such as Gregory who have never been short of a theory or two to put us mere mortals in behavioural boxes. Gregory rehashed a theory on how war was responsible for leading individuals into more short-termism ('decisions driven by passion rather than consideration') but this can only partially explain, if at all, Diana's decision to leave me in 55.

As Guido moved into his teens and no longer needed to be looked after by us or Elly, so our time and logistic problems evaporated. Nevertheless, Diana liked me to be around, to be there in the evenings and weekends to discuss ideas, to consider some new design, or to accompany her to an opening night; and she became increasingly intolerant of my absences. I too was growing old and more selfish and less tolerant, and I became less able to cope with her egotism. Moreover, for years I had never acknowledged any frustration concerning her disinterest in my work or international politics. Yet, soon after my promotion, it began to rankle seriously for the first time; and then, with the war preoccupying my working day and all my spare thoughts, this frustration took on a life of its own. Thus, despite my best intentions, I slipped back into old habits of working late at night and on Saturdays.

And on Sundays, I gravitated to spending most of the day with Guido, tinkering about on Ginquin. Peter do Roo had grown tired of my idle musings about buying an old boat and learning how to repair and rebuild it, so on the day of his barge extravaganza in 49, when I was a touch glossy, he provoked me into accepting an offer for him to find us a boat. Both he and his son Rudy promised to help with advice and contacts, and Guido, who really enjoyed using his hands, was very keen on the idea. Within a few months we had acquired a small and shabby motorised skutsje, along with a mooring less than a kilometre from Peter's. It was Guido's suggestion to rename the barge after our cat, Ginquin, who had died months earlier. (We were given Ginquin in the mid-40s by a couple, originally from New Zealand, living in Oldwijkgaarten who then moved to the US.) Initially, Diana approved of the project wholeheartedly and took part in our plans and helped with a few of the early tasks, but before long she lost interest. The first year also tested my resolve. Even with Peter's support, we were way out of our depth. The boat had to be dry-docked twice (the second time because I had failed to deal knowledgeably and efficiently with the professionals at the yard). Moreover, we ended up employing various tradesmen (mechanics and fitters, for example) although I had imagined we would persevere with much of the work ourselves.

In March 53, Diana went to Berlin for three full weeks, the longest she had ever stayed away on a job at one time. Guido, at 14, was already highly responsible and could be trusted to get on with his homework and prepare his supper if I wasn't home. If he knew I was going to be late, he would sometimes go to a friend's house. We lived well in the house together, albeit in a practical way, very quietly and humbly, yet, whenever Diana was absent for more than a few days, we tired of the novelty quickly and missed her presence acutely. As it happened, she was away when the IIBP bombers shocked the world with the retaliation suicide bomb raids on the two European cities. This led Guido to insist on a reassuring camphone conversation with his mother (we didn't usually bother with the camphone), even though she was only 500 kilometres away, while Constanta and Athens were 2,000 kilometres away on the other side of the continent.

After Guido had gone to bed, I went to Diana's desk. It was only later that I worked out my motives. I had seen a painting in the room where Diana was sitting during her conversation with Guido. The style was similar to a picture, painted by Karl, Diana had owned. I had first seen it hung in a cabin on Tic-tac-toe. It was stored somewhere in our Oldwijkgaarten house. The visual clue must have unconsciously triggered some anxiety I had kept buried for years, probably since the night we went with Peter and Livia to see the Stockmann play in Antwerp. With no particular motive, I flicked through a number of files in her cabinet: financial receipts, supplier account statements, project proposals, reviews, business letters and so on. I did feel guilty about this especially as we had always respected each other's privacy, and knowing she would be horrified if she discovered I had trawled through her papers. What I really wanted to do was to look at her emails. But, if I switched on her computer console, she would surely know someone had used it in her absence, and neither Guido nor I would have any reason to do so. It took me 24 hours to decide on the details of an elaborate excuse to use if necessary, and then I returned to her computer. Thus it was I learned she was working and staying with Karl in Berlin – and had done so before.

I have not seen Flora for more than a week. Chintz says she's had a relapse and the doctors are worried about her condition.

'She was flying too high, anyone could see that,' I said.

'Don't understand much, me, but I do know it's tough to get the pill menus right, every person's so different, and their metabolisms shift and change with the weather and the food and the company. And then some want more than others. It's more luck than judgement. That's what I think. But don't tell.' She has such a twinkle in her eyes.

'I'm doing well, I hope.'

'You? You'll be here forever, you're the fittest one in this place. You don't look a day over 50. What you got on the movies tonight darlin'? Anything I might enjoy?' she asked in a mock cockney accent.

'Chintz, don't you have a boyfriend to go home to? It's none of my business, but I'm worried what might happen if you hang around us dead folk too long?'

'Loving's for those needing heartache. You should know that, watching all those Movie Martyr flicks.' She turned away to check the display on a monitor, and then turned back. 'But if I had had just one sweetie same as you, a couple of years younger maybe, I might've put on the white.' Later, when her shift was over she returned and we watched a very old film called *Niagara*, with Marilyn Monroe playing a deceitful wife.

Which put me in the right sort of mood to try and record my conversation with Diana. I collected her from Schiphol Airport on a Saturday afternoon, and drove home in near silence. Guido was out but had left an origami bird for Diana with the message 'welcome home' written inside the beak. I started speaking in Dutch but soon switched to English. Yet even in my mother tongue, I was unable to find adequate words or phrases to communicate the anger I felt and the sense of betrayal.

'You've been with Karl.'

'So what?'

'You've been with Karl, staying with him, and this is not the first time.'

'So what? It's not your business?'

'Not my business? You spend three weeks in Berlin, working with your ex-husband, living with your ex-husband, screwing your ex-husband, and it's none of my business?'

'Yes, it's none of you business. I'll work where I want to work, I'll stay where I want to stay, and I'll screw who I want to screw. All right, English man, are you happy.' Diana flew out of the room and up to her office, where she soon discovered my own deceitfulness. She stamped back down into the lounge to find me by the back doors staring into the garden, my fists and teeth were clenched.

'So, now you are a spy, a dirty grubby snipper,' she paused, it would have been funny at any other time, 'no, I mean snooper. That's what children – humans who have not grown up – do, they snoop in other people's belongings.'

There was no protection against my shame about this, all I could do was let my rage ride on.

'And what do adults do? Lie, cheat, slip off whenever they can to fornicate behind their partner's back. Very grown-up. You know what I've been thinking about this last week, since I found out? About that big row we had six or seven years ago when you were working in Antwerp. That was about Karl wasn't it, you wanting to be with him. It's been going on since then hasn't it. Or longer. Is it longer?' And, as I was saying the words, the worst scenario was dawning on me. 'Did you ever stop seeing him, did you ever stop screwing him?' Diana dropped down into one of the lounge chairs and curled up, as she did sometimes when upset, but never before as a result of me being angry.

'Make some chocolate please,' she whispered.

So I made hot chocolate. This is the person I was, who I had always been, and who I would always be. I was not one of those Hollywood or soap opera husbands who, when discovering they have been cuckolded, unleash violence on their surroundings. I made hot chocolate. By the time I came back with the drinks, Diana had dropped her defenses and become meeker than I had ever known her. Although it was possible to construe her story as an attempt to blame Karl, I understood this was not her intention. She was trying to make sense of the situation for her and for me. Yes, she had worked with Karl on four plays, starting with the one in Antwerp, and each time she had fallen back into his arms. She had never planned to, or wanted to. Before accepting each commission she had sworn to herself not to get involved, and she had made him promise – very touching this – not to try and seduce her. But he was her first serious love, and it was as if he held a spell over her that she was powerless to resist. Once working together, and in each other's company, Karl had broken his promise and re-unleashed her passion for him; and she had been weak, unforgivably weak.

After the confession we talked for a long time. It was the most earnest, honest and loving conversation we had had for many years. Diana promised she would never work with or see Karl again. I believed in the sincerity of the promise, but I doubted whether she would be able change who she was, any more than I could change who I was.

***

In June that year (53), and on the back of a series of meetings, I spent five days in England. I met up with Arturo, who was in London to speak at a commercial conference on advances in human cloning. This was the first time I had seen him in the flesh since my fifty fiesta. In only a few years, he had matured from playboy student to besuited scientist, yet was as beguiling as ever. Given his respectable appearance I invited him to accompany me to the 500 year anniversary celebrations at my old school (once called Witley Academic). I had planned to take my mother, Julie, but she was not well enough to go. On our way there, Arturo and I talked about the latest developments in the war, his girlfriend Edna (who was shortly to become his wife), Guido, and his work. Once we arrived, and prior to the main event, Arturo was content to wander around on his own leaving me to meet up with old school buds. Horace Merriweather found me soon enough and we circulated together enjoying the occasional exuberant cry of 'my word, it's Hip and Kip'. When Arturo suddenly appeared with a huge grin, Horace went as white as a sheet, especially when my son pressed a kiss on his cheek.

It was a great occasion with several highlights, not least the short performance by the 30s popidol, Gold Spencer, one of Witley Academic's most famous sons, and, as I have already recalled, the tumultuous applause for our old history teacher Philip Liphook. After the main presentations, Arturo left to return to London under his own steam. Horace and I spent the early evening with others from our Witley Academic cohort at the famous Greensand Retreat near Chiddingfold, courtesy of Jeff Zimmerman who was a member. Jeff lived nearby in a palatial mansion. He had made a good living as a corporate lawyer, but, in so doing, had become overly dependant on material possessions. As previously agreed, Horace and I drove (in Horace's sleek two-man Darkstar!) south. First to Winchester to dine at one of his favourite taverns, and then to Parsonville, where he dropped me off at Julie's before heading on to his Southampton house. We had much to discuss, not least what had become of so many of our old friends, but I wish to recall only one particular topic.

As a right-of-centre politician, albeit one closer to the centre than many, Horace was opposed in principle to taxing the rich heavily to give to the less well-off, whether at home or far away, and this had naturally led him to a chronic scepticism towards the role of the IFSD. When in government, as one of Spoon's lackeys, his scepticism had apparently hardened into a policy of obstruction against its operational enlargement. But, by this time, Horace had been a backbench MP for some years, and a liberal tendency had begun to show through his conservative front. Moreover, the war was affecting him deeply. When our conversation moved round to my current preoccupations, I expected the usual teasing cynicism and challenging criticisms of our work at the IFSD. Instead Horace was full of genuine interest and questions. He even came close to explaining (if not apologising for) his past attitude. Much as I appreciated this mellowing of his politics, he knew as well as I that the IFSD had already been badly weakened by the war, and its future role looked very uncertain. Unkindly, I thought it was typical of a Tory to pretend sympathy for a wounded opponent, so long as the sympathy did nothing to help that opponent's recovery. However, his conversion, if I can put it that way, did have consequences, inasmuch as some years later Horace helped to protect my position within the organisation (although whether that was a good or bad thing for the IFSD is for others to judge).

I had forewarned my mother I might be late, so she had organised for a key to be left at the Parsonville reception/security centre. I crept into the bungalow very quietly, but she heard me anyway. I spent a few minutes by her bedside, before retiring, and then stayed with her until the following afternoon. The retirement village was well serviced with doctors, nurses and carers, so long as you had the right insurance policy package, which she did. Mostly, we talked about the past and especially my teenage years when the two of us lived together in Godalming, and about Alan. I also went on at some length about Guido, his various theatrical exploits, his all-average school reports, and about our working together on Ginquin's renovation.

From Parsonville, I used a combination of taxibuses and trains to arrive at Chapel Chorlton in the Midlands, where Pete Sampson lived in a pretty lane-side cottage nearby an oak wood. Pete's ex-wife had held on to their previous house in Stoke-on-Trent where I'd stayed several times over the years, while Pete himself had set up a new home with Clarity and their daughter Joan. Pete had done well. As professor of modern history at Keele University he had managed to expand and improve his department bringing it onto a par with the best in the country (except for Oxford and Cambridge, 'the impregnable bastions of excellence, a work of history themselves' – Pete's own assessment). It attracted substantial sponsorship from commercial sources, and occasionally advised Britain's foreign ministry. Clarity, who was 15 years younger than Pete, had unknowingly followed in his footsteps, studying with Wilma Johnson at the London School of Economics. She had then gone to Keele to do a doctorate under Pete on the history of Kurdistan. Her father, a Kurdish intellectual, came to Britain during the early years of the century, married a Welsh lass in Chester, and brought up his only daughter with a good command of the Kurdish language. Pete and she had had a very brief affair while she was his student. They had come together seriously only after Clarity's father had died, when she had finally shed her fixation on all matters Kurdish, and gone to work as a lecturer in Pete's department.

In my honour, Clarity convened a dinner party on Sunday night, which is how I first came to meet Lizette, one of Clarity's friends.

During my short stay in England, I saw the Turnbulls, and caught up on their news. Years earlier Doug had taken over as head of the section (from Jude Singleton) and then moved sideways to another department (after a spat involving the Spoon government environment minister). Miriam took much pleasure in telling me about the progress of her daughters. Lucy had become an accomplished violin player and been taken on by the London Symphony Orchestra. Susannah had gone into publishing and married her boss in a whirlwind romance. A grandchild was already on the way. They also told me, with some concern, that my son Bronze had been in touch recently. They hadn't seen him since he was a young teenager, but he had called them wanting phone numbers for Lucy and Susannah. Both daughters had then reported back to Miriam that Bronze had attempted to recruit them to the New Crusaders.

***

Bronze. I also met up with my son that visit. He had been too busy to see me until the Tuesday evening, so we met then, at a Scandinavian beanplace he suggested (I forget its name). He arrived half an hour late, and did not apologise. I barely recognised him. He had cut his dark hair short and sported a tidy beard. He wore a cream jacket (school blazer-like with an insignia on the top pocket), a dark polo neck sweater, and well-pressed white flannel trousers. Overall, the impression was of a holiday camp entertainer. The New Crusader look, I learned on making enquiries, had been chosen deliberately to appear amusing and thus unthreatening, which was useful, in different ways, both at recruitment and official levels. It did not last. A point came, later that year, when the New Crusaders claimed to have established 500 churches in Great Britain and to have signed up over a quarter of a million members. When the media stopped describing the uniform as 'comical' preferring to use adjectives such as 'sinister' and 'ominous', it was discarded rapidly.

Until that evening, I had heard almost nothing about the New Crusaders. Bronze had joined the church more than three years previously, but, on the very few occasions we had met or spoken since then, he had never wanted to talk about it or much else. This time, though, he did. After working on a volunteer basis, recruiting and training recruiters for the New Crusaders, and being paid scarcely more than pocket money, he had recently been taken on as a full-time employee. He worked under the admin department with a small team of computer experts setting up, or helping purchase, whatever systems the organisation needed. Mostly, he said, he was moving around the country providing networking advice and expertise for newly-acquired church buildings. Each one had to be technically adapted so that the screens, member consoles and payment pouches for smart cards (at the entrance and at the sitting booths) were all directly connected to the central networks. Enthusiastically, Bronze explained how cleverly the whole system functioned to ensure members paid well for the privilege of membership (church attendance, nurture groups, Crusader counselling, beneficent personalised messages – they went on and on).

What troubled me most was not Bronze's allegiance to a church. He was far from alone in needing a religious framework to give his life meaning, and god was a preferable route to salvation than the one Crystal had chosen. No, it was his allegiance to this particular church, as he was describing it, that made me uneasy. The New Crusaders claimed to be a Protestant church, loosely affiliated to the Church of England neither particularly high nor low. Its beliefs were rooted in traditional interpretations meshed with ways of dealing with modern insecurities and political realities. I paraphrase Bronze's way of putting it. In particular, the New Crusaders believed it was necessary to stand up for Christian beliefs in a very uncertain (and un-Christian) world. The New Crusader organisation criticised other Christian churches for not taking a strong enough stand behind the one true god, and for their appeasement talks with infidel religious leaders. It called for the World Council of Christian Churches to launch New Missionary Endeavours; and, according to Bronze, it had announced a plan to send a preliminary wave of its own missionaries to countries considered on the verge of falling to the false prophet Mohammed. Bronze took my silence for approval and, having finished his salt-free lentil bake (or similar, Bronze's dietary demands changed with the weather), became exuberant and indiscreet.

'This war is brilliant.' Yes, my son actually said this. 'This war is brilliant Dad, it's opening people's eyes to what is really happening in the world.'

'And what is really happening?'

'The devil has stepped out from the shadows.'

'The devil?'

'Yes, and his henchman Al Zahir, and his troops.'

'His troops?'

'Muslims.'

'You believe Muslims are the devil's troops?'

'Don't you? What is the Jihad but a war to kill off the true God. At last now, good people, Christians everywhere can see the truth, there's no hiding the devil's intentions. The New Crusaders believe in action, not inaction.' He paused for a moment, looked round to check that we were not being observed, and then whispered a few words which I recognised as Arabic. 'It means, I am a New Crusader.'

'Why Arabic?'

'I shouldn't tell you but my nurture mother has promised ...'

'Nurture mother?'

'Oh she's wonderful, an adviser, a counsellor, not everyone chooses to be part of a nurture group – but it's worth every cent. Any how, she says that if I learn to speak Arabic well enough, I could be chosen for mission work.'

'And that's what you want?'

'If it's my calling. Right now I'm needed here. There is so much to do. You'll be hearing a lot more about the New Crusaders in the near future.'

White citizens across Europe, especially in those countries with sizeable Muslim populations, flocked to the New Crusaders and its sister organisations. By and large the bulk of its members came from other Protestant denominations, but the church also drew in new adherents to the Christian faith, and it converted lazy non-denominational Christians into fervent believers. Mostly its members were attracted by the church's willingness to take a firm and definitely right-wing political stance. The bigger it got, the more legitimate it seemed, the more members it attracted, the more money it had, the more power it wielded. By the mid-50s, with the Jihad war having spread to a dozen different arenas around the world, the New Crusader Church was claiming over ten million members in Northern Europe. It had a turnover, in Great Britain alone, of 100 million euros, all declared and above board. Its public relations department was as professional as that of any multinational business, and its spokespersons and leaders could regularly be seen and heard on the media. It was a very slick operation which exploited a real hunger for spiritual food with political substance; and it had a significant influence nationally and internationally. Nationally, the New Crusaders campaigned for a tightly-monitored register of all aliens and first generation immigrants from Muslim countries, never mind the financial and social cost. Indeed, the New Crusaders helped stoke anti-Muslim sentiment whenever they could thereby contributing to a steady rise in violent religious clashes. Internationally, the New Crusaders lobbied for a complete block on Western aid to Muslim nations, severe sanctions against all active IIBP members, a massive build up of NATO military forces in the war zones (using conscription if necessary) and a willingness to employ nuclear bombs to end the war quickly. Although these objectives were never met, they did sway public opinion and politicians, more in some countries than others, and thus affect, slightly but noticeably according to historians, NATO's policies.

***

In the IFSD, as in most other UN agencies, the war took its toll on our ability to function. As each new front of the war evolved, so our operations in that area had to close down and retreat. Furthermore, while religion-based animosities were uncommon within the organisation itself, they often erupted in the various committees of experts, civil servants and lower level politicians, through which our policies, operations and projects were developed and approved. This hindered our effectiveness even in the areas without conflict. Over time, the IIBP nations became deliberately obstructive. In order to balance the stoppage in funds to Muslim areas, their representatives constantly sought ways of stalling projects in Christian areas (South America being a favourite target).

By 55-56, the other IFSD directors – how can I put this? – had lost the will to fight the IFSD's cause. They went through the motions, but there was little incentive to strive against the current: the highest level UN authorities, other international groupings, and governments were all preoccupied with military matters, diplomacy or terrorism and civil disorder. For some reason (perhaps my break-up with Diana, a matter I shall come to shortly) this was not the case for me. I worked longer hours than I had ever done before, and I expected my staff to do the same and ensure the ethic passed right down the line to our secretaries and office boys. Many a project could be saved by the right combination of persistence and pressure on the budget release mechanisms, for example, or the contractor insurance policies. Moreover, there was plenty of mileage in the basic quid pro quo system, it just took time and effort and cross-departmental communication (which I was very keen on). Because there was a war under way, this did not mean that water desalination plants, irrigation projects, flood-prevention drainage, solar roofing, sustainable agricultural training programmes and so on, were no longer needed. If anything, the reverse was true, the world needed a commitment to sustainable development more than ever. In my division, we would not let a project go until the door was slammed shut and bolted. I record this, not to brag, but to provide an explanation as to why I might have made enemies.

I should explain that all personnel at my level within the UN system were officially, in theory, appointed on merit. In practice, though, due regard was given to nationality. My own appointment at director level (as Pravit Krishnamurty's replacement in 44) had depended not only on the director-general wanting me (thanks to Pravit's recommendation), but on there being a suitable opening for a British subject, and on a nod of approval from the British government. Incidentally, someone within the centre-left Fuller coalition (the British administration at the time) had given me this nod on the basis of affidavits from, among others, Jude Singleton and Matt Fortune MP. It was good to know one's friends. Had Pravit stepped down a year later, it is far from clear whether the right-wing Spoon-led government would have backed my promotion. Although director of the environment division was a bigger job in every respect than director of the future policy division, officially it held the same UN rank, and thus switching from one to the other had not required so much political fuel. In any event, Spoon and the Conservatives had returned to the opposition benches by then.

Given that my appointment could be considered, loosely, a political one, it meant my removal could be effected through political manoeuvring. In 56, the British electorate threw out the coalition of Liberal Democrats and European Socialists that had opportunistically held on to power for eight years, and it ended up with a coalition which included the Conservative Alliance (led by the suave Paulina Worcester), the European Conservatives and the Christian Faith Party. The latter vehemently denied any connection with the New Crusaders or what it termed 'policies of the far right' (one of which, incidentally, was to close down all IFSD operations in Islam-dominated countries). Nevertheless, it did manage to position itself closer to the New Crusader ideas than any other political grouping, and therefore catch most of the New Crusader votes.

In early 57, not long after I had returned from a gruelling trip to Bangkok, Phnom Penh and Vientienne, I was suddenly faced with a plot (no other word suffices) to remove me. The first I heard of it was from Tommy, who had a good bush telegraph line to the British civil service. One of his friends had a colleague who worked as an adviser for the minister of finance. The new British government, the rumour went, was keen to see the IFSD undermined, and easing me out would help this cause. I might have been flattered at the idea of being considered so important, if I wasn't so fearful of the consequences for me and for the IFSD. Very charitably, Tommy reaffirmed his loyalty to me, and, in effect, appointed himself my campaign manager. Both Ninel Horeva and Chidi Naiambana rallied round, and proved themselves loyal colleagues. Within days Tommy had set up, through his operational level contacts, an information network across the world. We know, he advised me, that most of our clients appreciate your loyalty to the IFSD and your determination to keep things moving, so we need to ensure they make noises here and there in your favour. And we also know, he added, how determined Worcester and her chums are to remove you. Tommy said he would do what he could at his level, but suggested I call in favours among relevant European and American politicians. Even one or two might make the difference, he said. And he advised me to work my British connections to the full. So, under cover of IFSD business, I went to London to meet with several friends and colleagues I hadn't seen for years. Some promised to put in a good word where possible, others saw no immediate future for the IFSD.

My most important contacts, though, were Matt Fortune and Horace Merriweather. Matt, a podgy genial family man with bushy sideburns but no hair on top, offered me his support eagerly. He suggested taking soundings with a view to forming a group of IFSD-friendly MPs. Horace, too, positively enthused about taking up my case, which heartened me. As a Conservative, he could be more influential with this government than Matt. Moreover, Horace had made a name for himself, not so much because he had been a minister, but because of his speaking ability. His voice was much sought after by campaigners of whatever ilk; and, caring less and less about the party whips, he had supported some unlikely causes. As we spoke, he was already looking through his diary to see what parliamentary debates were forthcoming and how he might use one or other to weave in a mention of the IFSD, and to promote the idea that the work of the British environment director reflected well on the British government. Before leaving the Commons zini bar, I called Matt in his office and asked him to come over and meet Horace (they only knew each other by sight). I wasn't sure they would get on, but my worries were in vain. Between them, they did a remarkable job in establishing a linkage between the plot to dislodge me and wider issues to do with the war. As a consequence, those who might not have raised a finger in my defence under normal circumstances were willing to do so as a means of opposing the excesses of the Worcester government and the right-wing Christian fanatics.

On my return (and therefore long before I could know how well Horace and Matt might do), I dined at Lake Toba a couple of times, once with Ike Davidson and once with Bobby Jespersen. Tommy and I had employed the services of the division's press team, but it was only geared up to deliver factual operational news. The most we could do with the IFSD's own facilities was beef up my profile, with quotes and photos, in the press and media packs that went out on a regular basis. But with Ike and Bobby, the situation was very different. They were able, if willing, to deliver articles that could be very influential.

Lunch with Ike was a trial. To be honest, I had never taken to the man. In the early days of my relationship with Diana, when we went on holiday together, I had found him boorish. In particular, his humour, which had endeared him to Diana (and to his wife obviously), struck me as crass and very North American. But, I suppose, because Diana's friendship with Augusta had seemed more important than my coolness towards her husband, I never allowed my feelings to show transparently. After the disastrous holiday in East Timor, Ike and Augusta came to stay with us once in Leiden, but I excused myself from most of Diana's social arrangements on the grounds of some work crisis. I'm sure there were arguments about that, as there were about the summer trip to Canada in 43, the one I never took with Diana and Guido. In fact, Diana returned from that holiday, her first visit to the Davidson home, less convinced of Ike's charms and with stories of his over-drinking and rudeness, both of which had grown in parallel to his reputation as a news journalist. A few years later, so Diana told me, Augusta kicked him out. In the early 50s, he was posted to a top job in Brussels. From there, he had called Diana and me trying to inveigle himself into our social world. But, having learned more about him from Augusta post-separation, Diana had declined to return his calls. Nevertheless, there remained a personal connection between us, which both he and I had employed to our professional advantage several times since his Brussels placement. I had personally briefed him on issues by camphone, and, once, we had met up for a drink when I was in Brussels.

With Ike I had to spell everything out, not because he didn't understand, but because he knew I was asking a favour and he wanted me to squirm (or that's how it felt). I had told him on the phone when arranging the meeting that any conversation would have to be 'off the record', but I did not press for him to acknowledge an understanding of this condition. Moreover, during the lunch itself, the one thing I failed to spell out was the importance of not implying that I had, in any way, been a source for the story. I saw no reason to do so, given the obvious sensitivity of my position and the fact that I had mentioned the condition on the phone. Also, it is probably true, I felt some awkwardness because of our friendship and did not want offend him. Three days later, Ike's syndicated story appeared in several US news media. It quoted me extensively (although Ike had not, to my knowledge, used a recorder or made many notes) with the headline 'Influential British IFSD director sacked?'. In Britain, the Sunday Telegraph took Ike's story, firmed it up with a few extra calls to prejudiced contacts in the coalition government, and bulked it out with old photos and, yes, spurious facts from one particular Daily Truth article, many many years ago. Ike's stories horrified me. For several days, I believed what he had written. I thought my career was over. The only good thing to have come out of that lunch was that I never had to meet with, or speak to, Ike ever again.

By contrast lunch with Bobby was easy and entertaining. I looked forward to her stories and rarely disagreed with what she wrote. On this occasion (the day after lunch with Ike), she saw the picture I painted very clearly, and understood instantly she would not be able attribute any information to me or the IFSD. Nevertheless, she was prepared to publish something helpful to me personally, on the basis of our long-standing 'fruitful relationship'. I suggested she call Horace if she wanted more on the politics, and Tommy if she needed testimonials from further afield. A few days after the Telegraph article, the London Times published an excellent analysis piece by Bobby. It drew attention to several dubious practices by the Worcester government aimed at undermining certain UN activities by stealth (its attempts to remove me being just one of these). She also insinuated the British government was prepared to halt all payments to the IFSD if it could find a good enough reason. Bobby's article went a long way to repairing the damage Ike had caused (or I had caused indirectly by dealing with him so inexpertly), and proved very helpful to the endeavours of Horace and Matt. Indeed, about three weeks after first hearing about the plot against me, Horace phoned to say he had been given assurances that my position was no longer under scrutiny by certain individuals in the government. In any case, he said, they said they had only be 'vaguely looking' at 'the IFSD situation'. I called Tommy to my office immediately to tell him, and to thank him profusely for all his energetic work on my behalf. He was delighted at the news and my gratitude.

***

By the time of these events in 57, I had already been separated from Diana for nearly two years. Surprisingly, after her three week stay with Karl in Berlin during March 53, our life together improved. Our sex life took a brief turn for the better as Diana tried to compensate for her guilt by making more of an effort again in the bedroom; and, in the summers of 53 and 54, we enjoyed two-week holidays at a rented villa near Grasse in the south of France with Dominique, Waltar and their youngest son Lukas. Although several years older than Guido, Lukas happily partnered him on day trips down to the coast to flirt with girls on the beaches. During the autumn of 54, Diana and I slipped further back into our chronic daily pattern of working long hours and rarely having much time for each other. As the war widened out from Kashmir and I became increasingly consumed by it, Diana was no more able to discuss international developments or politics or my work than she had ever been. And her betrayal with Karl lay in the background, always tempting me to make more of any disagreement or tension than I had done in the past.

In the summer of 55, Guido went to Paris to spend six weeks with the Rocard family: two weeks with Didier working (unpaid) on a community show; three weeks (paid) working with the *Le Monde Fantastique de Marionnettes* production team; and one week on holiday with Mireille. The Saturday after Guido left for Paris, Diana called me into the lounge for a talk about 'something serious'. She began by apologising, and by telling me how determinedly she had tried to be a loyal and loving partner. But, she said, it was no longer working, and she had decided, therefore, to go back to Karl. She had been thinking about it for some months, and her decision had not been taken lightly. When I protested, as one does, about the effect such a separation might have on Guido, she calmly asserted that he was old enough now for it not to matter too much. She had figured it all out. She would go to Berlin for the rest of the summer, then she and Karl would rent a flat in Amsterdam. Guido and I would continue to live in Oldwijkgaarten until Guido finished school the following year; then we would sell the house and share the proceeds. She wanted no income for herself, but suggested, since I earned much more than she, that I subsidise Guido until he was in full-time employment. I was shattered on the inside, yet there was nothing for me to say. I made no scene. I certainly did not plead for her to change her mind. I recognised the situation as a done deal, and that I had been excluded from any negotiations.

Rather cowardly I thought, Diana wrote to Guido in Paris to reveal her plans to him. Immediately, he called to see how I was. He offered to come straight home, which would have been a great sacrifice, but I told him I was fine. He then called Diana who tried to clarify herself on the camphone, but she broke down in tears. Guido told me this; and, on my request, he gave me a copy of her letter. As far as I was aware, Guido had not known of Diana's lengthy liaison with Karl, and therefore the news had come as a shock. On the other hand, I think that for years he had sensed an imbalance in the relationship between his parents, and had known that I was more in love with Diana than she was with me. I believe this had led him naturally to respect her for persevering with me, but also to love me marginally more than he might have done otherwise.

I was deeply hurt in different ways by Diana's departure. There was the loss of companionship. Although we argued at times and we talked about important things less than I would have wished, Diana was great company, she was involving, and full of fun and imagination. Life without her was dull. And I missed her touch, in the sense that when we weren't being tetchy, she was physical with me, as she was with most friends. There was also the psychological damage that comes with rejection, I suppose, which I cannot define in any detail. I understood that I ought to feel resentment and/or some anger, but when such feelings did arise, they were soon ousted by anxieties about what problems might be waiting for me at the office.

Our lives evolved much as Diana had commanded, but with one exception. Diana had planned, without telling me straightaway, that she would carry on using her workroom in the Oldwijkgaarten house during the day, travelling there from Amsterdam several times a week. In theory, I had no objection to this plan. Guido and I did not need the space; it would save Diana renting a workshop; and it would mean she would be around some days when Guido returned home from school. In practice, though, I soon found it impossible to cope. Returning home from the office, sometimes early to prepare food and eat with Guido and sometimes not, there were often unexpected reminders of Diana: her odour mixed with a vanilla-ish perfume lingering in the hallway, a fresh batch of foods in the kitchen, or design pads left in the lounge. Other times, I was disturbed because I noticed that she had taken a bundle of books from the shelves or a decorative item (replacing others to even out the space on the windowsill for example) or a practical implement from a cupboard she thought I would not need. Initially, I let these hints of Diana, these trails of her movements, pass over me as meaningless, but I over-estimated my ability to deal with them. I became increasingly depressed, without knowing why.

On the recommendation of Peter and Livia, who had both been very kind and supportive since Diana's departure, I put myself in the hands of a 'musical psychotherapist' – Eva Stibbe. I persevered for 20 weekly sessions, and, in that short time, was helped more than I expected. Firstly, Eva showed me how Diana's regular visits to the house might be contributing to the depression. Subsequently, she gave me the wherewithal to confront Diana, and, eventually, to insist she move out completely. Secondly, she introduced me to the therapeutic and meditative powers of classical music.

Astonishingly I had reached the age of 55 and been to no more than a dozen concerts, and those I had attended were usually part of some diplomatic function or other. I had no idea which orchestras I'd seen or what programmes they'd played. Moreover, and more to the point, I had never sat down on my own and done nothing else but listen to a symphony or concerto. Diana's tastes veered from smoochy schmaltz to smoky jazz, but mostly she listened to music because it was linked to her projects. As Guido grew up, his musical tastes matured from teeny pop to teen pop to pop, all of which needed the volume turning down (and, preferably, off). I did occasionally put music on to play, but it was invariably on my return from some corner of the world where I had been given a sample of the local musical heritage. Few of these odd sounds appealed to any of us, so they were usually passed on to Guido's school or a charity shop.

In the musical therapy sessions, Eva obliged me to remain inert and to listen quietly to different pieces of music. To begin with, she would let complete tracks finish, and we would discuss what I had been thinking about as they played (she trained me rigorously to divert my thoughts away from anything to do with work, which was hard, but achievable). As the therapy progressed, she would switch the music off suddenly and insist on knowing in great detail about whatever had been going on in my head at that moment. If there was nothing, she would peer at me steadily and smile as if trying to work out whether I was lying or not, say 'good' or 'excellent', and start up the music again. Matters linked to my own depression and Diana came up regularly for seven or eight sessions, but once I had dislodged Diana from the Oldwijkgaarten house, my mind freewheeled more expansively over the past. When the music stopped, I told Eva about Bronze and Crystal, or my photographs, or about Melissa and my sexual initiation, or about my father. Before long, though, I grew tired of the game, and could see it only as a self-indulgence, one I did not need to pay good money for. Instead, I spent time buying, downloading and storing on Neil high quality recordings of, among others, Bach, Mozart, Williams and Zanichelli. I also bought a Supremely Comfy set of blindfold and headphones, and became hooked, as they say, on my own personal music self-help sessions.

That winter, after Diana's move to Amsterdam and while I was still living in the Oldwijkgaarten house, my mother's health went downhill fast. She was well cared for in Parsonville, but, with no other relations nearby, I felt obliged to journey over to see her once a fortnight. I called each night on the camphone (except during an extended trip to China in November) to check on her after the visiting carer had gone. Early in the year, she was hospitalised for a few weeks with a severe bladder infection. One doctor thought she might die, so I messaged Bronze (who went to visit once), and, on one of my trips, I brought Guido with me. I contacted Alan too, who came as soon as he could from St Petersburg (without Anna who was unable to get away). By the time he arrived, Julie had recovered and been sent home in the care of a part-time nurse. Alan himself looked far from strong. He had shrunk in size, and flesh had fallen off his face leaving a bony lean visage behind the white beard. It was good to see him, albeit briefly. For some reason, I did not mention to him or my mother that I was no longer with Diana. I preferred not to give them any cause for concern on my behalf. It was a relief, therefore, when Alan declined my half-hearted invitation to return with me to Leiden for a few days. Alan stayed a week by Julie's side. He knew he was saying goodbye, for he told me as much in an email later.

My mother died during the night between Saturday and Sunday 14 May. I had left the camphone connected, as I did when I was most anxious about her. Early in the morning I watched the nurse arrive. She said 'hello' to the cam (having seen it was online one way and knowing it would be me at the other end) before moving to the bedside to check on my mother. I saw her feel for a pulse, examine her eyes, and then tense up as she steeled herself ready to turn and face the cam again to tell me my mother was dead. I waited to speak to the doctor, who came within half an hour, and then set off once again for England, this time by car knowing I would want to bring back some keepsakes. It did not take long to clear out the bungalow, distribute her things, bury her body, tidy up the life that was my mother. Everything works very smoothly and efficiently in Parsonville when someone dies.

I used to try and visit her memorial in the Parsonville remembrance garden once a year. Now I rely on a few photos. Here's one of my favourites again, from Monte Carlo in May 2003. Tom is sitting on the bonnet of a red racing car, I am on his lap wearing a baseball cap that says Ferrari. Julie is standing next to us laughing. She is wearing a light yellow frock, and a straw hat. She looks so pretty.

My mother died, and the world seemed to be dying with her too.

**

The following summer we sold the Oldwijkgaarten house. Guido, who had lived his whole life there and had many friends in the neighbourhood, was saddest about this. As Diana had predicted, he elected to go to Amsterdam University (after toying with the idea of the European University in Brussels), and decided to focus on drama. For a while, therefore, he moved into the large house Diana and Karl had bought together. I saw him once a fortnight on average. He either came to stay in the modern (and expensive) eco-roof apartment I had bought on Van Hogenhouckstraat in The Hague (not five minutes from the apartment I had once rented on Weissenbruchstraat), or else we would meet in Amsterdam for a meal and a film. When the weather was fine, we would take Ginquin out for a gentle cruise to one of the lakes or to a barge festival, or to visit other barge hobbyists we had met over the years.

My new life as a bachelor was lonely and depressing. I stayed long hours in the office, usually for no additional benefit. When at home, I watched news programmes, thought about the next day's tasks, or listened to music. My stomach filled out a centimetre or two, my hair receded and turned a fetching shade of ash grey. If obliged to walk up several flights of stairs, I panted. Yet, despite these signs of aging, my colleague (and subordinate) Ninel Horeva made a second pass at me, some 20 years after the first. This time I had no cause to reject her. Although she too had taken on more flesh and needed dye to keep the grey out of her hair she was still an attractive woman.

Ninel had always been good company (for a Russian!). I admired the way she never took life too seriously, as though the world really was about to end, but was able to work with commitment and verve. As one of my deputies, she was responsible for overseeing policy and programmes in the whole Russia/Central Asia region, an area much caught up in the Jihad war. On leaving a reception (organised for some dignitary or other), we bumped into one another at the cloakroom collecting our coats. She proposed that since it was early, and we were both alone, we go to a nearby bar. There we drank more, and laughed a lot about how sad our respective private lives were. It was Ninel who recalled, without any shame, her original proposition, and then asked if the timing was any better these days. I did not catch her meaning, and so she put her proposition more forthrightly, which left me flustered and speechless. But she made light of the whole situation and, faced with my hesitations, promised everything would be fine. In my defence, I was fairly glossy, and could think of no good reason to rebuff the advances. We took a taxi to her apartment in Delft where she gave me a further drink and led me to a bedroom with a four-poster bed and scarlet drapes. I stood there gormless, stunned like a fox caught in the headlights of a lorry. Suddenly I was so sober, so horribly aware of my sexual inadequacy and psychological insecurity that I could no more have coped with any stranger's bed, let alone one adorned with satin sheets and scarlet drapes, never mind that it belonged to one of my key members of staff. Ninel disappeared into the bathroom to shower, and returned wearing only a towel. I was sat, upright, on the bed as if in a trance. Ninel laughed, although not unkindly, pushed me over on top of the bed and proceeded to remove my clothes. And when, not many minutes later, she discovered why I had become so serious, embarrassed and stiff (although not in the right place), she cackled theatrically, which made me laugh, and consequently eased the torture.

As promised, Ninel made everything fine. From a drawer in a bedside cabinet, she took out a vibrator (a bigger thing by far than, in the best circumstances, I could have created) and instructed me on how to employ it. The distraction of following strict instructions and doing so with some success helped me relax and lose myself in Ninel's sexuality. For a few days, I worried how this night of mechanical passion would impact on our working relationship. But it didn't, not at all. So, when I received a private email from her with the one word 'Tonight?', I answered 'Yes'. Thenceforward, in this manner, we would arrange to meet, have dinner and sex about once a week. After two months, though, the emails stopped. She never told me why, and I never asked, and our working relationship carried on unperturbed, as evinced, a few months later, by her staunch support during the attempt to depose me from my job. Thereafter, occasionally, when I saw Ninel talking to colleagues I wondered if they too had experienced the four-poster bed.

By the late 50s, much of the UN system, including the IFSD, was close to collapse. As the tensions of the wars infiltrated our negotiating committees, so initiatives, projects and programmes of all kinds and at all levels were stalled or cancelled. Most large donors, such as Japan, the US and the European Union, progressively froze all their overseas development aid to Muslim countries and many more besides, citing the costs of war and severe economic depression. Contractors and all non-staff personnel were disengaged as soon as their projects ran out of funds or came to a standstill for some other reason. But, beyond that, a lack of administration funds began to choke the life out of us. Every few weeks I had to take decisions on which staff to make redundant. And those of us that remained were no longer working for the good of mankind, but simply to keep the IFSD functioning. My division had remained the most effective for the longest but, by 58, there was little I, or my skeleton department, could achieve.

Retirement was not an option. I had no more wish to stop working than I had to expire. I did consider stepping down, and trying to find another role for myself, but concluded, gloomily, that I had invested too solidly and exclusively in my work for the IFSD, especially having called in so many favours to hold on to the job a year or so previously. Ironically, it might have been better for me personally to have allowed the British government to bully me out of the IFSD in exchange for something else, something different. Moreover, I had been foolish to sacrifice so much of my life to the organisation and to my high position within it, meaning that, following my separation from Diana, I had very few friends and an impoverished social network. Most depressing of all, I recognised that there was no-one, not even Peter de Roo, with whom I could discuss my own personal problems and situation. Thus, in my own way, I was as closed off from society as my old friend Oakley.

Regrettably, I was not able to diminish my own despondency by comparing it to the suffering of millions in war zones and immigration camps beset with disease and poverty, nor by reminding myself that further millions were losing their lives, their homes, their loved ones because of climate change catastrophes, while I continued to sleep in a dry comfortable bed, and eat good food, and wash myself in clean hot water.

Then, suddenly in March 59, as is well known, the First Jihad War came to an abrupt end (in the sense that the IIBP and NATO stopped fighting each other, although of course the so-called left-over wars carried on regardless). We had all grown so accustomed to the media telling us about 'fresh peace talks' or another G13-I9 summit or an 'intervention' by this or that peacebroker, that we barely paid much attention. But, in 58, there had been a very significant escalation of the war when the IIBP's forces turned their full attention to Israel, as though they had been biding their time, and this had been their target all along. The NATO countries rallied to Israel's defence, although not very effectively. For most of the decade, they had already been sustaining financially and politically expensive campaigns in Kashmir, Central Asia and West Africa among other war zones, and their citizens were losing patience. The US, still led by President Tarbuck, tried to bully NATO towards the use of class B nuclear strikes as a last resort. Because this was acknowledged to be such a high risk strategy, it became known as Tarbuck's Gamble.

Sadly for Tarbuck, the Spanish government collapsed within weeks of suggesting it might support the US policy. Although there was a deep-seated fear in Spain of a new Moorish invasion, it was nowhere near as strong as the people's revulsion for weapons of mass destruction. Thereafter, the governments of most European countries, many with large Muslim populations, constant civil unrest and extraordinarily high levels of opposition to the use of nuclear or biochemical weapons, refused to back the US. Consequently, NATO found itself back-pedalling trying to hide its impotence with long declarations of threat and intent and offers of compromise. Israel, too, lost its nerve when faced with Al Zahir's threat to use every last IIBP atomic bomb in retaliation if Israel employed one single nuclear weapon.

Tarbuck's Gamble failed, and NATO members and affiliates began secret negotiations with the IIBP, China, the Philippines and other involved countries. A Peace Treaty was signed in Singapore on 25 March 59. China took over the north Indian state of Ladakh; Kashmir was declared an independent Muslim country (but later united with Pakistan after a rigged referendum – causing yet more bloodshed when the nationalists refused to accept the decision); the whole of sub-Saharan Africa shifted noticeably towards Mecca (with several secular governments giving way to Islamic administrations and new constitutions); and the Philippines agreed to an autonomous Islam region. According to *Encyclopaedia Universal*, the NATO group members achieved the following: peace (which was politically much more important to them than to the IIBP members); a confirmation of the primacy of the UN system (the Peace Treaty was subsequently enacted through UN declarations); the continued independence of Israel (although Palestine did make a significant territorial gain); and a limited increase of development aid by rich nations to poor nations up to 2% (not as much as the 2.5% Zakat demanded by the IIBP). (Although, the IIBP had demanded a bias towards Muslim countries in the distribution of this aid, it knew this would never win acceptance in the UN and so gave way during the elaboration of the complex donor/recipient formulae that underpinned the funding of the agencies, such as the IFSD.) Furthermore on the NATO side, Russia was appeased by the agreements that Uzbekistan and Kyrgyzstan signed with Kazakhstan.

It took a while for the UN declarations to be concluded, but once they were, I began restoring my division's staff levels, restarting projects and programmes, and negotiating new arrangements. I expected personnel changes at the highest level, but I didn't care to think about my own future. I'd done enough of that in the last year or two. I kept my head down and paid no attention to UN gossip.

In early autumn, Tommy came into my office one day to ask if I'd heard a rumour that I was being considered as a possible replacement for the director-general (who we all knew was on the way out). I told Tommy not to listen to tittle tattle. Instead, we discussed how quickly he could get a team to Srinigar to help the new government plan its aid programme tenders. When the phone rang, my secretary, MarySue, told me to hold for the private secretary of the British foreign minister (within the recently-elected centre-left government led by Charlie Venables). Tommy moved to leave me alone, but I gestured for him to stay. Would I, the lady asked, allow my name to go forward for the director-general post. I muted the phone for an instant and told Tommy 'not tittle tattle'.

He gave me a thumbs up sign. Months later, after a horse-trading international summit and various high-level meetings within the United Nations system, a basket of new agency chiefs were decided, not least my own appointment as executive head, director-general, of the IFSD.

EXTRACTS FROM CORRESPONDENCE

Diana Oostlander to Kip Fenn
(freely translated from the Dutch original)

December 2049

It is no hard thing to be 50!!!

Can I suggest my English man that you get up on your feet, turn around, and clamber up that tree (you see it has been placed at a slant to make it easy for you). If you climb high enough, perhaps you will be able to see faraway, beyond the hills that block any normal view, towards those views of a wild and empty Copacabana Beach. Views that are, frankly, beyond my bank account and, no doubt, that of the IFSD too.

It's a small flawed thing; a small flawed token of my love.

Happy birthday. xxx

Diana Oostlander to Guido Oostlander-Fenn
(freely translated from the Dutch original)

July 2055

I have bad news. I should have told you in person but it has been a difficult time for me, and I thought it might be easier for both of us if I were to try and write to you first. I am leaving your father, so that I can return to live with Karl. We will rent a flat together in Amsterdam, and, during your last year at school, I hope you will be a constant visitor at the weekends. Perhaps, then, you will want to go to Amsterdam University and you could live with Karl and me. But that is for the future.

This is a hard thing for me to explain, and I want you to be clear that this is nothing to do with your father (or, of course, you), it is to do with me, my needs, my desires, but most of all my weaknesses. I can be a very selfish person, and for this I am very sorry.

It is possible that I have never stopped loving Karl. He was my very first love. He is a theatre director, a gifted one. We worked and lived together for many years. He was/is not an easy man, and he hurt me many times. But, we are both older, and I am certain now that we want the same thing.

This war is a terrible thing, and may get much worse. I do not know how to explain this properly, but I feel as though Karl and I have a common purpose in the way we are, and especially in our work. Now, I am going to Berlin for the rest of the summer, and we will prepare a show for the protest festival in September.

You must have sensed that I have no connection with your father in this way. He is a good man, a great man perhaps in his work, but I cannot share in this greatness, and I know he finds that difficult. He has grown distant recently, and I hope my move away will not distress him too much. But, in any case, I can rely on you to be a friend to him. You and he have established such a good connection in these last few years.

But I will be coming to Oldwijkgaarten often, to work in my studio many days during the week. We shall see each other all the time as before.

Let's talk on the phone when you've received this.

Give my love to Helene, Didier and the girls.

Very much love.

Chapter Seven
LIZETTE, BRONZE AND RESIGNATION

<u>The Photograph</u>
I was (said fixedly)

<u>The Clone</u> *[an extract]*
...
I am (said hesitantly)
I am (said confusedly)
I am (said doubtfully)
I am (said disbelievingly)
I am not
I am not (said hesitantly)
I am not (said confusedly)
I am not (said doubtfully)
I am not (said disbelievingly)
I am
I am (said hesitantly)
...

<u>The Retiree</u>
I am (said tiredly)
I was (said resignedly)
I was (said regretfully)
I was (said questioningly)
I am (said amazedly)

I AM poems by Kolin Delvreux (2065)

I have a photograph of Giuseppi Garibaldi on my screen. It was taken in 1860. Two hundred years later, I saw an actual albumen print (made from a glass negative) at an exhibition in Paris. Naturally, I bought the catalogue so that I could copy all the images onto Neil. This particular photo is a three-quarters portrait, set in an oval cameo style. Garibaldi must have been about 50 at the time. His body, posed with left hand on hip and elbow pointing out, is subtly framed by the slight shadow lines of a jamb and window frame behind. He has a beautiful soft face: a large forehead with receding hairline, hooded eyes intently looking towards the camera, and a thick tidy greying beard. He wears light trousers, a dark shirt (which, because he was famous for wearing a red shirt, the imagination sees in colour as much as the orange of the pumpkin in Asser's still life), and a neckerchief. Hanging down across his shirt, there is a simple chain attached to something heavy (presumably a watch) in his shirt pocket. And, in the only acknowledgement of a military or leadership role, the right hand grasps a sword, held by a harness to his belt, which takes a near vertical line down in front of his legs.

When I first glance at this picture, I focus initially on Garibaldi's face, drawn in by the intent gaze (in which I see not only concentration but serious-ness, wariness, curiosity), and the warmness of the visage as a whole. After some time (for I want to dawdle and examine his features in detail) my eye eases down the line of shiny buttons on his shirt towards his hand and the hilt of the sword, and then along the edge of the sword to reach the bottom curve of the oval, before moving back up again to take in more detail, the nonchalant elbow, the sagging pocket, the neckerchief, and the exquisite way the whole portrait has been emphasised by the vertical and horizontal lines behind.

But it is not only the aesthetic qualities that make this one of my favourite photographs. Despite leaving any serious interest in history behind in the class and lecture rooms of youth, I have always had a soft spot for Garibaldi. This is thanks to Flip, my school history teacher, who was a devout European. Frustrated by the strictures of a course focused on British history, every now and then he would randomly slip into a lesson information about his favourite continental characters. He had a lot of time for Luther I recall, Peter the Great and El Cid, and for the people who built the European Union, such as Robert Schumann and, a hero of his, Jacques Delors. For some reason, I also remember Portugal's Marquis of Pombal, and the Dutch leaders Lamoraal Count of Egmond and his contemporary William of Orange. Horace and I, though, had a particular reason to take up Flip's attachment to Garibaldi.

Once, and only once in my time at Witley Academic, Flip organised a debating contest between our history department and that of Charterhouse (another eminent public school in west Surrey). It was an important occasion, held in the Great Hall, with hundreds of students in attendance. There were three debates for different age groups. We were in the middle group, but this was before Jeff Zimmerman joined us, and when Horace and I were Hip and Kip. Our particular motion read, 'Garibaldi was a great European', and we were given the task of defending it. We thought we had drawn the lucky straw since it would be far easier to argue that 'he was a great European' than 'he was not a great European', but we soon realised this interpretation of the motion focused too much on the adjective 'great' and not enough on the noun 'European'. The other side would be able to argue he was a great Italian hero, thus putting the onus on us to explain why he mattered beyond the Italian nation state.

I am becoming sidetracked here, reflecting on events that should have been contained in and by the first chapter. And yet, lying here, so many years later, I continue to be startled by how strong, how potent these early memories remain. It is as though I can touch the rapture of those times, especially in the debating victories I shared with Horace, and the volleyball wins I shared with Alfred.

To move on swiftly, we won the debate. I should refresh my patchy knowledge (half-remembered from Flip's teaching and Pacciotti's great Hollywood bio-flick with Vincent Mallow as Garibaldi) from *Encyclopaedia Universal*. In May 1860, Garibaldi landed in Sicily, then ruled by the king of Naples, with a volunteer force clad in bright red shirts and known as the 'one thousand'. By the end of June, he had conquered the island and set up a provisional government. He then crossed to the Italian mainland and, by taking Naples itself, paved the way for the establishment of a kingdom of Italy with Victor Emmanuel as king. Garibaldi, the encyclopaedia says, was a great patriot, a truly honest man, and one possessed of great political and military skills which he devoted to the nationalist cause. Prior to the debate, I came up with the concept that nationalism had to be an essential precursor to internationalism, or, in this instance, Europeanism (although Flip must surely have helped me with this). Horace delivered the arguments we developed from that idea with stunning panache. Flip's two other teams lost to Charterhouse, but we were victorious and, very properly, the toast of Witley Academic for a day or two.

Chance took Gustave Le Gray, one of the great artistic photographers of the 19th century, to Sicily in 1860. His business in Paris was failing and so he decided to join the author Alexander Dumas on an expedition, aboard his luxurious ship Emma, to Egypt. They stopped in Sicily where Dumas became involved in Garibaldi's cause (to the extent of fetching him arms), and Le Gray took stunning pictures of Palermo in the aftermath of Garibaldi's conquest, including several of barricaded streets. Dumas records in his book, *On board the Emma*, the following exchange with Garibaldi (as reproduced in the Paris exhibition catalogue, English language edition).

Garibaldi: 'Do you have a photographer with you?'

Dumas: 'The best photographer in Paris – Le Gray.'

Garibaldi: 'Well then, let him photograph our ruins. It is only right that Europe should know what is happening here: 2,800 shells rained down in a single day.'

Dumas: 'We shall photograph all this, and you too, in the middle.'

Garibaldi: 'Why do you want to photograph me?'

Dumas: 'Well, I have only seen you as a general; and, really, you do not look like yourself, I would prefer you in your own clothes.'

Garibaldi: 'Do what you like with me. As soon as I saw you, I knew I would be one of your victims.'

And Dumas goes on to record in the same book, how Le Gray spent days making 'magnificent photographs' of the ruins of Palermo and how he (Dumas) planned to send them to Paris 'for exhibition'.

Which leads me back, conveniently, to the spring of 2060, and the exhibition at the Musée d'Orsay in Paris where I first saw the portrait of Garibaldi in an original print, and the other magnificent Le Gray originals; and to Lizette.

***

As I have recounted, I met Lizette during a dinner with Pete and Clarity at their cottage in Chapel Chorlton in 53. We did meet again, I can't remember exactly when (I seem to have no email correspondence that would help me pinpoint that second encounter). It was definitely after I had separated from Diana; and Clarity's daughter Joan was six or seven. I remember I was taken for a day trip to the Peak District, which included a walk along Dove Dale (or Eagle Dale in George Elliot's Adam Bede, a favourite of Clarity's), a kitsch well-dressing fair at Youlgreave (the main objective of the journey), and afternoon tea with Lizette at her house near Leek. I recall only that she was very welcoming, served an excellent cake (using figs from a crooked tree that curled round the corner of a stone outhouse) and was curious about my work.

During 59, Lizette changed jobs, moving from Keele University to the European University. She then contacted me to suggest we have dinner the next time I went to Brussels. I was flattered, but faltered in my response, or lack of it. Several months later, in early 60, Clarity wrote to congratulate me on my appointment as director-general and to pass on details about Pete's achievements or Joan's progress, as she did sometimes. She also urged me to get in touch with her friend, Lizette, who was not finding Brussels easy. Thus, one very cold February Tuesday, we met at the famous Fish and Chippy in the St Catherine area of Brussels. The restaurant had been called Jacques in my Euroil days, but, after several name changes, it had became Jacques – Fish and Chippy even though the original Jacques was no more. Unusually, the place was half empty; yet it was still surprisingly animated and the windows were all steamed up.

Lizette Sanderson, I learned, was born in 2018, just four years before my oldest son, Arturo. Her father, Mervyn Sanderson, had been a civil engineer, a builder of bridges. Wendy, her mother, like mine, had been a teacher but one who worked mostly with disadvantaged children. She had two brothers, one older (Samuel) and one younger (Mercurio). In response to her father's various jobs, the family had moved about a lot when she was young with stints in Southern India, Cambodia and the Philippines. But, by 28, the scale of social unrest around the world, especially the growth of the First Tuesday Movement, and concerns about the children's education (Samuel was only a year or two away from his 16 exams, and Mercurio was ready to start primary school) led the Sandersons to return permanently to the UK. The family settled down in Bristol. Lizette did well at school, with high grades in her 18 exams, and won a place to study materials science under Professor Jean Hunter at Nottingham University. By this time, Hunter was already a celebrated scientist, although it would be a further decade before she was awarded a Nobel Prize for chemistry. While a postgraduate student, Lizette married a trainee lawyer named Clint Tuohy. They moved to Stoke-on-Trent. She took up a research/teaching post at Keele University, and Clint joined a law firm in Newcastle-under-Lyme.

That first evening together, in the fish restaurant, Lizette looked attractive but slightly older than her 41 years. Dressed all in black, a polo sweater and jeans, she wore light make-up except for an excess of kohl around the eyes which contrasted too strongly with dyed-blond wavy hair. She smiled often but it was a smile constrained by a small mouth and thin lips which tried to keep slanting upper teeth concealed. She was not a beauty (she said so herself on numerous occasions), but she was 20 years younger (and nearly 20 centimetres shorter) than me; she was slim (much slimmer than Diana, who was heavily built and expanded over the years); she talked with the sense of a scientist; and she came across as a practical, down-to-earth woman, with lots of warmth. Most important of all, though, she appeared very interested in me.

At her request, we arranged to meet again the following day, for an early supper, so that I could catch the last train back to Holland. This is when I told her about Diana, and when she told me about Clint. He had disappointed her, she said. Having planned to go far in politics, he had settled for petty squabbling as a councillor on the Stoke City Council and a job dealing with wills and property conveyancing. While at Nottingham they had had similar dreams and ideals, she said, but time and reality had driven a wedge between them. She had other disappointments. The materials science department at Keele University had been impressed by her Jean Hunter association, and been all too willing to allow Lizette to continue the research line taken in her doctorate thesis. But it had proved to be a dead end, she confided. She was unsure whether this was because of the limitations of her tools (having been unable to attract sufficient funding for state-of-the-art equipment), or because Hunter, with many neophytes at Nottingham, had ruthlessly guided her towards a line of investigation she wanted closed rather than one with real potential.

In the first year of the Jihad War, Lizette took stock of her life and found it wanting. She left Clint, and moved to the house near Leek which she shared with another woman, an administrator at Keele University, called Rhoda

Jackmann-Ives. To fill up the non-working part of her life, Lizette took to gardening ('a mild antidote to chemistry') and short-term sex affairs (as encouraged by the also recently-divorced Rhoda). And she set about considering how she might escape, perhaps to revisit the exotic places of her childhood. It had taken years to make a move (partly because of her parents' chronic ill health), and then, when she did, it was no further than Brussels. She had proved herself no less lacking in initiative than her ex-husband, she concluded rather dejectedly.

I told her she was talking nonsense, and that she had been very courageous to come to Brussels. Notwithstanding difficult early days at the European University I predicted that her Brussels life would improve. I must have remarked that Guido had toyed with the idea of taking a degree there, and then rambled on about missing him and planning to go to Paris shortly. Which led to Lizette saying how much she wanted to visit Paris again, and to a suggestion (I'm convinced it came from her, though she denied this in the years to come) that she join me for the weekend. So, in March 60, we rendezvoused in the French capital. Arriving late Friday night, we took separate rooms in a high-class pension in the Montmartre area. Part of the Saturday I spent with Guido, while Lizette went sightseeing. She returned with a chalk portrait of herself. That night we slept in the same bed, unmemorably, I'm happy to report, because Lizette did not want to make love.

This was the start of an affair and a friendship that would last, with ups and downs, the rest of our lives. The next morning we caught the metro to Concorde and strolled, arm-in-arm, through the Jardin Des Tuileries, along the Seine, across the Royal Bridge to the Musée d'Orsay to wonder at the photographs of Le Gray, and the Garibaldi portrait in particular.

A first 'down' occurred all too soon. Two weeks later Lizette came to The Hague to stay with me for a weekend. After showing her round the city during the day, I had thought we would eat out somewhere special. But with Amsterdam planned for the Sunday, we both decided to stay in on the Saturday evening. In any case, it became apparent, Lizette wanted a serious talk about our relationship, which was better conducted in the privacy of my home than in a restaurant. After our successful weekend in Paris, a series of intimate emails, and a pleasurable day together in The Hague it was clear that something was troubling her. She asked a lot of questions about my children, all of which I had mentioned but, until then, without much explanation. Then she wanted to go to the bedroom and make love, as if to reinforce the bond we had already established without sex. But I was unable to perform. Perhaps I was intimidated by her tales of promiscuity. Lizette thought I simply did not find her attractive. Later, I learned that her affairs had not served to reinforce her self-esteem, which had been the idea, but to undermine it. Thus, in the moment, in the bedroom we (I can use the plural pronoun because we discussed it later) were suddenly caught by a shock wave of alienation, a complete loss of confidence in each other and in our relationship. It was as though a spotlight, that had the power to illuminate self-awareness, had suddenly caught us in the wrong place at the wrong time with the wrong person.

In order to overcome my own feelings of inadequacy, I blundered into various apologies and half explanations. I also tried to reassure Lizette that I found her attractive. She appeared entirely unconcerned by what I had to say. We re-dressed and returned to the main room with its large window and the night cityscape view. And then, standing by that window, with a mug of Ceylon tea in hand she told me she was 14 weeks pregnant and that she could not, would not have an abortion. Sheepishly, hesitantly and anxiously, she looked over towards me to see how I was taking the news. I waited, without thinking about the confession, to hear the rest. I feared the news would get worse, and she would reveal an involvement elsewhere. She turned to look out across the city's lights.

'I don't think I can tell you who the father is.'

'That helps,' I said. 'That's very helpful.' She put the mug down on the coffee table, and returned to the window hugging herself.

'You sod. This isn't easy Kip. I'm here. I'm telling you. I'm trying to tell you.' She continued to face away from me.

'Maybe you could explain why you can't say who the father is?' My tone was sarcastic, edging towards irritable, I suppose, as I began to take in the full meaning of what she had told me. At this, she spun round defiantly.

'I called you four months ago, more than four months ago. You promised to contact me. Why now, why after so long?'

She turned back round to face the darkness of the window and the night beyond. 'Why don't you think you can tell me who the father is?' I asked the question more softly, more genuinely this time round. I waited. I had been standing too, but now I flopped down on the sofa, weary.

'Is it going to matter? I mean do you still want to go to Amsterdam tomorrow? Will you want to see me again?'

'Not if you're involved with someone else, no, I don't believe I could deal with that.' She swivelled round sharply again.

'No, of course not, of course I'm not seeing anyone else, how could you think that? It was a mistake. A stupid mistake.'

I am recalling the dialogue as best I can, condensing maybe, or improvising. But, from Jay's point of view, this is the worst that was said. And knowing how much both Lizette and I have loved and cared for him, he has no hang-up about his conception being 'a stupid mistake'. Indeed, ever since he's known this snippet of family history (which came a dozen years after being old enough to appreciate that I was not his genetic father) he's employed it mercilessly for the sake of argument or humour. So I've no compunction about mentioning it here.

From my point of view, Lizette had eliminated the worst possibility, but there remained two reasons for the enigmatic silence: either she did not know who the father was because, after arriving in Brussels, she had continued to sleep around (making me one of a sequence, and one yet to be consummated); or, she did not want to tell me, which, in a different way, signalled danger.

'You haven't answered my question, is it going to matter to us?'

'I don't know, Lizette. How can I know. I like you. I like you very much. But I don't know. Only time will tell.'

'Thank you.' Then she came over to the sofa and sat down next to me, linking her arm through mine.

'When we walked through that garden in Paris, past the magnolias and the witch-hazels, it felt good. Holding on to your arm, I felt warm and happy and safe – though I knew already I was pregnant.' She paused and pressed my arm tighter through her own. 'I went back to England for Christmas, to see Ma and Pa, then to Chapel Chorlton for a few days, and then to Leek for new year's eve. I part own the house and use a tiny bedroom to store stuff. Rhoda had a party, as she does, to which she invited Clint. Oh this is so complicated. You need to know that after Clint and I separated, Clint and Rhoda had an affair. No, even that's not the full truth. They slept together once while we were still married and living together, although we had separate bedrooms by then. I didn't mind, it helped with the decision to split up, and, besides, Rhoda had asked my permission, although Clint never knew that. I rented for a while before moving to Leek, and that's when Rhoda and Clint screwed around some more together. When they gave up, they stayed friends, as I did with both of them. You'd have to know Clint to understand. In public he's professional and competent, but in private he's a child, needy and compulsive, always wanting to be liked and promising to make up for any shortcomings tomorrow. At the same time, he nags for favours, often for company, and especially for sex. He has no self-respect in this regard. But he's lovable. I loved him for years; but I grew tired of it all. We got back together once, in 57. I was very depressed, and he had suddenly been discarded by his second wife. I had Rhoda screaming in one ear about how it had taken me five years to get him out of my system, and I was screaming at myself in the other ear. Yet I let him plead me round to giving it another try. He was so desperate to get back together, he said, and he had changed.' She stopped talking for a few seconds. 'You must know how stupid we women can be. Three months I fooled myself into thinking I might have exaggerated our earlier marriage problems, and that I would never find a man who loved me as well as Clint. And then I woke up, again, and told him enough was enough. I felt guilty, and more depressed than ever, for a year or more. A whisky would be nice. I'm still trying to tell you. I'll get there. But it would help if you could talk a bit, about Harriet and Diana, and, well, how you managed in the bedroom department. I mean four children, it doesn't sound like you had much of a problem to be honest.'

I laughed, poured us some alcohol, and did as she asked. But, as before, I felt as if she were far away, not paying much attention. I wondered if she was using the time to sort out how she was going to tell the rest of her own story.

'I'd like to blame Clint. I'd like to say I had too much to drink on new year's eve, and he seduced me with flattery and neediness. But that's not true. I hope you appreciate this, you sod, I hardly know you, and here I am baring my soul. I decided consciously, early, to let him come on to me. But this wasn't a weak decision, as in the past, but a strong one. You have to know I felt that I'd escaped, that I was a new person, and that there was no danger any more of going backwards. But I'd been nearly six months in Brussels without a fuck, and I wanted it easy. And ... shit ... even that's not the whole truth. I'm trying here Kip. I'm really trying.' She held out her glass for a refill, and waited for me to return to the sofa so as to snuggle into me tighter than before.

'The truth is ... I'd given up hoping for a real relationship. Rhoda hadn't forewarned me Clint was coming. When I saw him there that evening, I decided not only to let him come on to me, but to throw caution to the wind, throw the dice, and see if I could get pregnant. So, you see, it's my ex-husband's child. And, before you ask, no, I haven't told him yet. And, yes, of course I should.'

She felt so tiny, I tightened my embrace around her shoulders, and awkwardly kissed the hair on the side of her head. She was crying, so she didn't turn to kiss me back. Instead she slid down so that she was nearly horizontal across the sofa and her head was in my lap. I used one hand to brush aside her hair slightly, and the other to stroke her cheek with the back of my hand, and then the back of a knuckle to wipe away her mascara-streaked tears. Her eyes were closed. For a few moments we remained very still, suspended in time. I wasn't thinking about her or her story, I was simply enjoying our closeness. Then Lizette slowly wiggled her head slightly, rubbing an ear into my crutch, and, on sensing my arousal, continued. Deftly, she turned over on her stomach, undid my trouser belt and fly, and gave me the kind of lip service I thought only prostitutes performed in cars. Afterwards, I worried, thanks to years with Diana, about Lizette's pleasure, but she did not want to make love as such, and confessed to being glad that we had not had intercourse earlier.

'You'll need some space, Kip, to decide what to do with me. It's not only me, it's me and a child, and, now that I've managed to tell it all to you, I don't want there to be any misapprehensions. If we're right for each other, and I hope we are, there'll be plenty of time for affection, tenderness and other pleasant things.'

Affection, tenderness and other pleasant things. I've always remembered her saying this. I do not know if she invented the phrase spontaneously, or had culled it from a book, but if she hadn't already won me over with her genuineness and honesty, then this idea that a life together could be full of affection, tenderness and other pleasant things won me over completely.

***

Chintz came in a few minutes ago, bringing with her a bowl of fruit sponge-balls (mixed flavours). I was crying. She had never seen me crying before. I told her I was thinking about Lizette, the last love of my life. After all I've gone through in writing these Reflections, revisiting the emotions connected with Melissa, for example, or Harriet or Crystal, it seems so strange that I should be brought to tears by this simple memory. Chintz asked to see some photographs of Lizette, so I promised to search one out, but I'll do it later. For now, I need to press on and record a difficult period professionally.

At the time, I did not consider the Peter Principle (which states that employees tend to be promoted beyond their level of competence) might apply to me and my own promotion to director-general of the International Fund for Sustainable Development (IFSD). In retrospect, though, I came to see, as much as one can, the truth behind my appointment. I read and heard a range of opinions at the time; there are some articles on Neil, but I can't be bothered to seek them out or re-examine them now. Most commentators focused on the fact that, as a career UN official, I was an unexpected choice, and that only two years earlier the previous British government had made a half-hearted effort to oust me. It's true that, by this stage, the director-general of the IFSD did not have as much power over his agency as earlier chiefs had done, nor as much as other agency chief executives (whatever their title, each agency had a different structure). Nevertheless, the IFSD, although it had suffered along with the whole UN system during the Jihad War, had re-emerged at the turn of the decade (in consequence of the Singapore Peace Treaty) as the funnel through which the largest portion of development aid would continue to flow. Many an ex-diplomat, or ex-minister, or even ex-prime minister from a smaller country coveted the job, and there were plenty of secretary generals, presidents, director-generals and executive directors of other agencies that wished for elevation. As with all such high-level appointments, mine followed a huge amount of behind-the-scenes bargaining much of which I never knew about. With all the irrelevant positions and manoeuvres filtered out, it came down to this: there was no consensus on three or four prime candidates, but there was an unholy alliance of IFSD members willing to support Britain's proposal to place me in the position. Why unholy? Because half of them, having witnessed my commitment and achievements as director in the early years of the war, believed I was the man to defend and promote the Fund through thick and thin; and the other half wished to attenuate the Fund's effectiveness by appointing someone they believed would be ineffective in the top job. At Singapore, the Western powers may have been forced to agree to further share their wealth, but that did not stop a number of them employing a range of tactics (including, apparently, supporting my appointment) to slow down implementation of the decisions. How they could predict that I would not manage well in the job is beyond me, yet they were right.

I collected a good team of advisers, that was the easy part. I'll mention three in my cabinet. I took Tommy because he wanted to stay with me, and his insight into the never-ending political problems of India and Central Asia was invaluable. I persuaded the much younger Chidi Naiambana that I could not do without his expertise on sub-Sahara Africa, and that two or three years with me would assist not hinder his own promotion prospects. (It didn't. Many years later he made it director-general himself.). And, thanks to Tommy's ear-to-the-ground, I unearthed Eduardo Villalonga, a brilliant Bolivian lawyer languishing in an IFSD backwater where he'd been closeted after falling out with a vindicative supervisor years earlier. There was MarySue, my English secretary who dealt directly with my other personal staff. I had 'inherited' her from Pravit Krishnamurty when I took over as director of the future policy division, and, apart from three extended breaks to nurture two children and a sick husband, she had stayed with me ever since. What she lacked in humour and tact, she more than made up for in efficiency and loyalty.

As director I had remained in touch, just, with the nuts and bolts of the division's work (the planning, the programming, the projects). I felt, rightly or wrongly, that I could see, albeit dimly, the end result of my negotiations, actions and decisions. But this was not the case as director-general. Consequently – I can only say this in retrospect obviously – I spent too much effort and time trying to control and influence the directors (about nine in all), who were not so much below me in the hierarchy but to my side. As a director I had not understood this intrinsically, I had simply enjoyed my autonomy and fought, usually with success, against any interference. Mostly, though, the IFSD's earlier director-generals had been of the hands-off variety. I was a hands-on chief. At best, I might have helped guide the weaker or more inexperienced directors, at worst I certainly drew other more experienced directors into unnecessary conflicts, thereby absorbing too much of their valuable time. I do not wish to dwell on these failures, but I will give one example, pared down to its basic components.

Liu Xiangjun, a crusty, tallish Chinese man about ten years younger than me, had taken over my job as environment director. He had held a similar high-level position in the World Bank but, earlier in his career, had been an academic (a professor of sustainable development at Harbin University), an environmental policy planner, and, for a short time a deputy ambassador in Hungary. By 61, I had become frustrated at how slowly the IFSD was returning to normal operations. As the chief executive, I should have been able to do something about this. Barely a day went by when I didn't try to devise ways of speeding up our activities. It came to my attention that Liu's department appeared less dynamic than most others. Instead of focusing on the restart of many important projects which had been stalled by the war, using the special streamlined procedures I had instigated, he had decided to revisit and re-evaluate each one. By insisting on fresh contract and approval procedures for every project, he was adding a minimum of one year to their implementation timetables.

Did I pick on Liu because, as his predecessor, I had been in charge of developing these particular programmes and projects? Lizette thought this might be the case; as did Liu who told me as much in private when I was making a last informal attempt to push him along. Then I issued an Information Note to the relevant directors, which everyone knew was targeted at Liu, ordering work to continue with minimum delay on all stalled projects and programmes. Since I had played a formal card, it should have been the end of the matter, but Liu decided to challenge my authority publicly. He wrote an unprecedented Information Note Response and distributed it to the other directors. Foolishly, I would not let the matter drop; and, shamefully, I made use of one his deputies, my ex-assistant, Ninel Horeva, in order to accumulate ammunition for further assaults. Ninel had coveted the environment director job herself and then, having failed to win it, resented her new chief. She helped select and exaggerate various lethargic practices in the environment division which I then used to question Liu's competence. Meanwhile, though, he presented the results of a study, contracted months earlier, presenting the dangers and inefficiencies of restarting projects without a full reassessment. He was right. I had been blind to the extent of the problems caused by, for example, the loss of local staff and expertise, damaged or stolen equipment, and the unavailability of original contractors. The spat only wounded me, but it did for Ninel. Liu got shot of her as soon as he could, and I was in no position to interfere. She chose to leave the UN system altogether (although this was not necessary) and work as a lobbyist, with a huge salary, for a large Russian consultancy organisation.

Instead of interfering downwards, I should have been doing more hobnobbing sideways with other UN agencies, and upwards with the Secretary General's staff and the General Assembly members, and more moving around the globe promoting the public face of the IFSD. And, if I had wanted to make the IFSD more efficient, I should have done it by a careful reorganisation of its structure and determined efforts to make life easier for the directors, not by trying to do their jobs for them.

Would I have been a better director-general if I had taken over at a less demanding time? I like to think that the odds were stacked heavily against anyone managing to guide the IFSD through that particular five year period. The Jihad War was only just over. The Singapore Peace Treaty promised to deliver more worldwide equality than mankind had ever known and a long-lasting peace (though there were many doubters on this latter pledge). It also increased the UN's power, under carefully circumscribed conditions, to pull together an intervention army, and to intervene within sovereign states or to control border conflicts. But the Jihad War had cost many lives, resulting in devastated families; and it had cost many trillions of dollars and euros, which had left most of the developed nations suffering their deepest recession of the century. Recovery was expected. Nevertheless, European and US middle-class citizens, however sympathetic with the plight of those less well off, were resentful about having to pay higher taxes, initially for the war, and then for increased overseas development aid. The UN's authority and position in the world had been preserved and enhanced by the Treaty, but there was a considerable downside in terms of public support and understanding of its work.

This public support did not recover in the short term, and when the UN was torn apart again a few years later by the Second Jihad War, it plummeted further. Today, thirty years later, I am pleased to say, the UN has fully re-established itself. I hope it will go from strength to strength in the 22nd century.

Indeed, I am inclined to believe there is some truth in Zoe Bergmann's simple and powerful theory that we will only ever be able to rid war from the face of the world when the United Nations, or similar, can establish a governing body with the biggest and most powerful army in the world. She says it may take a 100 or 500 years, but history shows a slow, if uneven, progression towards such an objective. Bergmann grew up in Vienna when the First Tuesday Movement, at least in Europe, was at its most idealistic. Her Jewish parents, both artists, brought her up on a diet of pacifism and FTM marches, and had a perfect right to expect her to develop traditional left-of-centre views. But, as a teenager, she rebelled and turned against them. She rejected a place at Linz University to join the then nascent European army at one of its bases near Trieste. For four years she trained as a soldier, and then as an officer, but all the while studying in her spare time. She waited, so her autobiography says, for a taste of combat, which came when the UN asked the army to help resolve a civil war in Jamaica (the Jamaica Skirmish), before leaving military service and winning a place at Heidelberg University to read history contexts and international politics.

It was only in the 60s, during the war, that Bergmann became a darling, as they used to say, of the English media, which often set her up against Gregory. They were both essentially historians, among the best of their generation, and they were both roughly the same age, but the similarities stopped there. She was quiet, controlled and forceful in the way she answered questions or argued in media/public debate; he was often loud, outrageous and long-winded. Whereas Bergmann's theories were the tips of icebergs of her research, it was not unknown for Gregory to make up a theory while on a live broadcast, and then spend six months putting together the research to back it up. Which is not to say that his intellect wasn't razor sharp, or that he wasn't (most of the time) an important social commentator.

In short, Bergmann based her theory on the mechanism known as 'survival of the fittest', initially employed by Charles Darwin to explain the drivers for evolution, but since adapted and used to understand other phenomena. However, although there had been attempts to weave Darwinian ideas and politics together, she was the first to do so coherently and to back it up with such a large amount of evidence, drawn from geo-historical analyses, that Darwin himself would have approved. She argues that for millennia, certainly since before Homo sapiens developed agriculture and civilisations, man, as opposed to woman, has been more disposed genetically to be aggressive. Early on, man needed to be aggressive to survive, to mate and to ensure his genes were passed on to the next generation. If he wasn't aggressive enough, then his genes didn't survive. In other words, and to put the survival of the fittest model the right way round, to be here today, a man's or woman's distant male ancestors are likely to have been aggressive. (This is a gross generalisation – the theory at its most rudimentary – but I only wish to mention the basic idea.)

In the period leading up to civilisation, to larger societies and to nation states, aggressive genes remained extremely useful for individual survival, wealth accumulation and mate choice. But these same genes meant that certain individual men in these societies accumulated far more power than most others, to the point of becoming rulers; and then, in continuing to express their aggressive genes, these rulers sought to extend their wealth and territory by taking over the wealth and territory of other rulers. Thus, Bergmann's theory goes, the powerful 'survival of the fittest' mechanism explains the tendency for aggressive people to rise into positions of power. But more than that, it explains why only strong societies survived, since weak ones were over-run by strong neighbours. Precisely the same principles have continued to apply up to recent times, she says, noting in one of her books that even in the 100 years after Hitler and Stalin, during the golden age of oil and chips, there were more than 500 wars, whether civil, border or international.

Despite these statistics, Bergmann says, the settlement and security of sovereign states, the integration of regions, the rapid growth of trade and multinational companies, and the growing importance of international organi-sations all meant that it did become more difficult during the golden era for aggressive out-of-control leaders to maintain their power bases. Moreover, democracy as a political system combined with the widespread use of democratic principles was so successful during recent prosperous times that many (intellectuals, politicians, ordinary citizens) thought it would be able to overcome the aggressive gene effect and man's historical tendency to war. Not so, says Bergmann. It has taken me far too long to arrive at this point, and it would have been quicker to use a summary from *Encyclopaedia Universal*.

Bergmann's key argument is this. She says the usefulness of the genes which dispose man to be aggressive lose their usefulness within stable democratic social systems based on equality and liberty, while other genes which express themselves in softer more feminine characteristics, and especially through women, tend to become more widely accepted, thereby influencing the society as a whole. This softening of one society as a whole, ultimately makes it vulnerable to another society which has not allowed itself to mature democratically (using Bergmann's terminology). By bunching themselves together for the best part of a century most of the rich mature nations ensured, with artful politics, threats and bribery, that the worst ravages of the immature and aggressive nations and groups were focused on each other. But this strategy was never going to work forever, not while a large proportion of the world remained poor, under-developed and without the influence of strong democratic principles. It was inevitable that some new aggressive empire (i.e. the male-dominated Muslim sphere, as led by Al Zahir) would arise and challenge the developed world for its riches. There can be no end to such a cycle, Bergmann claims, until a world government has sufficient authority to distribute wealth, and until it has a large enough army to act as the world's policeman. Only then can democracy thrive; and only then will the expression and the advantages of man's aggressive gene diminish and fade away.

This was far from a populist theory when presented in the 70s. It attracted considerable opposition from many different quarters, and Bergmann was mercilessly lampooned in the downmarket media (encouraged by Gregory's cheap ridiculing of her). But she marshalled her research so carefully, and her books were so well documented that the historical and political establishments could not vanquish her ideas, however doggedly they tried. While many intellectuals believed the theory reeked of hopelessness, because they could only see into the short term, I was of the opposite view. I believed her when she claimed mankind was moving forwards, albeit very slowly and jerkily, towards a time when a peaceful world could be possible. I suppose I was predisposed to believe in Bergmann's prediction because the United Nations and its evolution was such an important line of evidence in her argument, and I had spent most of my life working for, and believing in, the UN system.

I tried, on many occasions, to persuade Lizette of these ideas. As with others of her sex, though, she got stuck emotionally on the suggestion that, if societies were strongly influenced or dominated by women and women's ideals, they would be weaker than nations dominated by men. For some reason she would not or could not see beyond this basic principle to the more subtle of Bergmann's points that, given a chance, societies choose to 'mature' by becoming more feminine, and that, ultimately, male aggression and blundering will lose out to female gentleness and wiles.

***

As director-general of the IFSD I did do plenty of globetrotting and hobnobbing with power and money brokers, although, as I've said, not as much as I should have done. Half the time, I felt as though my role was little more than chief public relations officer. Not only did I have to present and promote our work around the world but I had to do so to the IFSD boards, the UN's General Assembly and other institutions. Life in this regard was not made easy by the fact that, after much negotiation, the world's leaders had decided that Ojoru should be brought out of retirement to take on the role of Secretary General. He was not, though, appointed for his administrative or management abilities, which had once been formidable: it was widely known that, in the later years of his political career in Nigeria and leading the African Union, he had become increasingly autocratic. No, he was chosen because of his geopolitical colour. Unfortunately, as Secretary General his imperious style had consequences. It led to the upper echelons of many parts of the UN system developing a bloated bureaucracy. Thus, to give one small example, a two-sentence command from one of his many personal advisers calling for a report into the under-represen-tation of Gambians in UN staff and contract positions would lead to excessively burdensome administration tasks and a huge waste of resources. Which is not to say that Ojoru was not the man for the job, if anyone could have avoided the Second Jihad War, it might have been him.

Incidentally, my friend Alfred might have been in Ojoru's cabinet at the UN headquarters (giving me a useful listening post in the higher stratosphere) if he hadn't burnt his bridges with the man. When Alfred thought Ojoru was a spent force, in the 50s, he spoke his mind to the media and to biographers, criticising his former president for behaving 'like a dictator'. Mostly I sensed (largely from letters written in the 40s) that his criticism was kindled out of a disappointment that Ojoru had been corrupted by power, and, as a result, had not achieved as much as many, including Alfred himself, had hoped. Alfred also told me later (in confidence, which I am now breaking) about an unbelievable incident during which Ojoru had demanded Alfred lick his shoes.

Travelling was a pain. I had done relatively little of it as a director, choosing, as often as possible, to use the cam-conference facilities to get business done. But the ceremonial (which is how I thought about them) duties of a director-general included many activities which could not be done via a screen: opening new IFSD premises, launching IFSD programmes, singing the praises of the IFSD to the presidents of donor nations or multinationals, and enthusing staff in all four corners of the globe. Very occasionally I looked forward to a trip, such as the one to Brazil in February 62, but this was only because it would give me a chance to catch up with Arturo, and to revisit Rio.

I delegated most of the research and planning for this mission to Eduardo, since it had been his notion originally and since he would be travelling by my side. The main priority was for me to be seen opening a new IFSD building in Brasilia. Further, I was scheduled to attend a series of meetings with the IFSD staff, two Brazilian ministers, a collective group of non-governmental organisations (NGOs), and the regional Latin American Community Organisation (LACO). In addition, Eduardo planned for me to fly to La Paz so that I could personally launch a multimillion programme for the Andean countries aimed at reviving traditional craft skills, particularly weaving. The concept for the programme had been tried and tested in other regions of the world, and had proved highly successful in terms of employment, local community integration, and attracting tourism. Eduardo had convinced me that my visit to La Paz would go a long way to reviving the IFSD's reputation in the area, and would serve to persuade the (somewhat reluctant) Bolivian government to promote the schemes. About a week before we were due to leave, I received a communication from Ojoru's office suggesting I cancel the La Paz extension to my trip. When I asked Eduardo for an explanation, he shrugged his shoulders. I requested Chidi, who had the best line into Ojoru's cabinet, to find out more. Later the same day, he came to my office, his fingers wiggling more than usual. There was a human rights issue, he said, which another UN agency was trying to deal with behind the scenes, under much pressure from Amnesty

International, and it had caught the ear of one of Ojoru's advisers. Eduardo argued strenuously that it would do more harm than good to cancel the meeting, and went so far as to accuse Ojoru's adviser, a Peruvian, of trying to sabotage my visit simply because my itinerary did not include Lima. I weighed up all the information I had been given, and struck La Paz off the agenda. Unfortunately, this decision seriously undermined my relationship with Eduardo, although, because he chaperoned me on the tour with good humour and professionalism, I did not realise it at the time.

Of all the IFSD offices I ever visited the one in Brasilia, designed by a Petrópolis School architect, was the most striking. South America had been largely untouched by the physical devastation of the Jihad War. It had suffered an economic downturn, caused by the general global economic recession, but not as badly as elsewhere. More IFSD projects had continued uninterrupted in this continent than in any other region of the world, although this was not many given the general disintegration of UN decision-making structures. Brazil's great leader, Neco the Prosperous, had originally planned to redevelop and rebuild the derelict aeroplane of Brasilia (originally, in the 20th century, the capital city had been socially planned and engineered in the shape of an aircraft), but it took another 20 years, through the 50s and early 60s, for the work to be implemented. The new IFSD building formed part of the redevelopment in the Jardim Botanico sector. It was twenty stories tall, slightly concave on all five sides, with lime-green and lemon-yellow glass panelling and IFSD logos etched into each of the wavy solar window-hoods.

My discourse, given on a large raised terrace overlooking the botanical gardens themselves, was well received. Eduardo had culled parts of it from presentations given on similar occasions. Other speeches were given by the mayor of Brasilia, the government's foreign minister, and the LACO executive director. When the speeches were finished, it was my task to smash the magnum of Brazilian champagne against the Harkness Cylinder. I'd done this enough times before to know the form, but I rarely knew in advance exactly what each Cylinder would deliver. On this occasion, it was scores of self-inflating green and yellow balloons, three self-inflating tethered flags (the IFSD, Brazil, and LACO), and remote triggers for day-time fireworks to sparkle above the rising balloons, and for samba music to start up. There were whoops of joy from the crowd of invitees and IFSD employees, and then, as had become customary with the use of Harkness Cylinders, I presented the (unbroken) magnum to one of the (pre-chosen) lower-ranking employees who worked in the building.

There was nothing remarkable about the occasion, except that my son Arturo was in the audience. This was the only time, as far as I can remember, that any of my children saw me perform an official function. Previously, by email, I had suggested to Arturo that we meet in Rio, because I would have more free time there. But he lived and worked in Goiânia, which was much nearer to Brasilia than Rio. So, I had asked Eduardo to organise a special pass for him to be admitted to the IFSD function. Only after the balloons went up did I catch sight of him at the back of the terrace, smiling widely and raising a glass towards me. We did not speak more than a couple of words together through the buffet lunch, such was Eduardo's zeal in introducing me to as many notables as possible. But, for half an hour, between the official end of the building launch event and my first meeting of the afternoon, I was able to sit alone with Arturo in a peaceful library room (used only for meetings, but lined with books that had been placed for wall decoration). For a few minutes I let Arturo flatter me, about my appearance and my IFSD performance. He asked about Lizette and Jay (who was a walking 20 month toddler by this time). And then, without missing a beat, he said it must be odd to be a father and a grandfather at the same time, to have a son almost the same age as a granddaughter.

'What granddaughter?'

'Alicia, naturalmente.' He was smiling. Sometimes with Arturo you could find yourself smiling back without knowing why (even on the camphone) but this was not one of those occasions.

'Arturo, who is she? Who is Alicia?' I began to suspect he must have a newly-discovered daughter from a past relationship. Like father, like son.

'What you think about cloning?' I recall that his English had deteriorated, but his grin was no less supercilious.

'Are you going to tell me about Alicia?'

'You tell me about cloning, your opinion.'

Despite countless questions by email, and shortish conversations by camphone at Christmas or on his birthday or mine, I knew next to nothing about Arturo's life, other than that he had married Edna, a cute black girl from Fortaleza in 55, and that his own success had grown with that of O Futuro, the company that employed him. I should have known about O Futuro, but I didn't.

'No, I'm not.' My free minutes were ticking away. 'Stop playing games and tell me about Alicia.'

'OK, but remember I try to warn you. OK. She is my daughter. She is cloned from me. Edna was infertile. She agreed. She is four years old.' Cloning female daughters from male parents, using two different sperm to gather the X chromosomes, was demonstrated successfully in the 20s, and the technique had gone commercial in the 40s. But, even in the 50s, it was considered a more risky procedure than same sex cloning.

'FOUR!'

'Yes. If you want, we go tonight to Goiânia, to my house, and you meet her. But not Edna. She is gone away. We can go in my plane. It's easy, one hour. I bring you back late tonight or early morning.'

I read (in one of Gregory's books) that there were many similarities between the tone and extent of the political and moral debate about abortion in the 20th century and the debate on cloning in the 21st century. The content, though, was very different. At the international level, the Europe Union, the US and most other Catholic and Muslim nations negotiated, during the 10s and 20s, very basic objectives through a UN Convention on the Limitations of Human Cloning (and, in time, this did lead to the broad-ranging Agency for Genetic and Cloning Techniques). But some very large countries, including Brazil, China and Russia refused to accept the harmonised objectives, and instead nurtured social welfare and commercial cloning industries. The European Union and the US went their own separate, but similar, ways, developing far more detailed rules than those at the UN level. In practice, these outlawed human cloning, except in very exceptional circumstances, until such a time as it could be proved that the techniques led to a risk of infant mortality no greater than under normal birth conditions. As a requirement of the same rules, the policy and the risk rates were to be re-examined once a decade (this point was agreed between Europe and the US).

Experience accumulated in the countries with cloning industries and this helped the pro-cloning lobby elsewhere not only to gather and present real scientific evidence for the decadal reviews, but to put forward scientific, humanitarian and commercial justifications for a legitimate development of their own cloning activities. Nevertheless, by the 50s and 60s, the pro-cloning lobby in Europe and the US had failed to make much headway. One reason for this was the strong link created, by many anti-cloning politicians and religious leaders, between cloning and the suicide epidemic in the 40s. According to Gregory, a statistically higher proportion of suicides in some countries were early clones from the 20s, although, overall, the numbers were comparatively low. Moreover, he pointed out that millions had been affected psychologically by the very idea of cloning, and that while some of these people had harnessed their anxieties into passionate campaigning, others had found it undermined the value of life and their belief systems, whether religious or moral, to the point of mental implosion. It's also worth noting that Pope Maria spoke strongly against cloning in her first Christmas Day address in 52.

Personally, I was completely opposed to cloning, as were the majority of Europeans. I could not be moved by the stories of couples that had lost their only child in the war or as a result of tragic accidents, or of young women who had been unable to conceive because they were victims of crimes. I understood all too well that the world was full of tragedy, but, for me, it was a question of priorities. Even as a young man, I never approved of the billions of dollars and euros that were spent on cloning research or on other medical techniques designed to improve, ever more incrementally, the well-being of rich Western peoples, while poverty, inadequate drainage and water supplies, and impoverished inoculation programmes in many parts of the world meant that the life-expectancy gap between the US and, say, Sudan continued to increase not decrease. In this belief, I was much influenced by Triti Madan, the Indian professor who had delivered such a powerful lecture to us at the London School of Economics.

Arturo was waiting for me with a taxi at around seven. It took less than 30 minutes to drive to the airport, past many colourful and luminescent Petrópolis School buildings, to board Arturo's Amazonia light-jet, a six-seater silvered plane. It was fuelled, I knew, with the aviation biofuel Vivido, one of Brazil's most important export success stories of the previous 30 years or so.

During the flight, I questioned my son, initially about his work, and then about his reasons for cloning himself to create (how horrible that verb sounds in this context, even today) Alicia. He told me that O Futuro manufactured medical equipment, including the sophisticated devices used for animal and human cloning. Moreover, it owned a subsidiary, in Goiânia, which operated at the high end of the human cloning market. It did good business, mostly for rich Americans and Brazilians who had failed to conceive through normal channels or simply wanted to avoid the trauma of childbirth. Since concluding his degree at Imperial College (the degree I had funded), Arturo had worked for O Futuro in developing the commercial human cloning business. He had kept this information from me, he said, because he suspected I would not approve. I did not.

Arturo lived in a large modern villa, complete with a swimming pool, stables and a field for two dappled horses. Several staff were present on our arrival. One showed me to a room so I could shower and put on a new shirt Arturo had provided for me, another brought us caiparinhas, and yet another discussed, with Arturo, the meal we would have later. After rejoining Arturo on the marble terrace overlooking the pool, a woman named Luz, who looked as though she had stepped out of a men's lifestyle magazine, brought Alicia to meet me. There was no doubting she looked like Arturo, in a babyish, girlish sort of way. But, however much Arturo had rigged her genes, she was still my granddaughter, and I was predisposed, if not pre-programmed, to want to love her. This was the awful dilemma about human cloning: an individual (or a nation) could oppose the idea, but once a cloned individual existed nothing other than normal decent human emotions (or laws) could be deemed appropriate in dealing with that individual. Moreover, for most of us, it was hard to keep up any serious level of chastisement against those who had cloned themselves because ultimately this would reflect on the innocent children. Today, there are still those who are violently prejudiced against cloned individuals and their parents, but, thankfully, they are dying out (literally, since most of them are old).

I have a camclip of the two us together taken by Luz and sent to me by Arturo a few days later. Here it is now, the picture is grainy because Luz must have had the cam on the wrong setting. It starts with a view of tiny Alicia, wearing dark jeans, a red tank top and long pink hair, leading giant me by the hand along a broad marble hallway to her bedroom, which is strawberry coloured and servant-tidy. From there, the camera follows us to Alicia's toy room, complete with an English style doll's house, dozens of dolls and a sophisticated console for the wallscreen, and then through a side door to an enclosed paddock where a shiny grey pony is galloping around. Alicia is jumping around shaking her head, her pink hair flying from side to side. She is shouting (in Portuguese): 'He is my Angel. I want to ride. Can I ride?' The camera swings round towards Arturo, as if looking for an answer to Alicia's request. Arturo puts a smile on for the camera, and tells Alicia it is time for bed. I had forgotten, until seeing this clip again, how Arturo looked then: tall, very erect and admirably slim, smartly dressed in perfectly pressed trousers and shirt, both in creamy silk or silkette. On both wrists he wore chunky loose gold bracelets; a large gold medallion hung around his neck. Most striking of all, he had dyed yellowy-golden hair (short and curly), eyebrows and lashes. On the IFSD building terrace he had stood out, as if the sun shone for him alone, which, I guess, is why I had noticed him at the back of the large crowd.

I did ask what had happened to Alicia's mother Edna, suspecting she might never have agreed to the cloning and had left because of that. But Arturo reiterated – and I had no reason to disbelieve him – that she was unable to have children. So then I asked how they had decided which one of them should be the clone parent, and which procedure they should follow. It was as though I had pulled a gun on him. The warmth in his face was dismissed in an instant, giving way to a powerful vicious look I'd not seen before.

'It was my way, naturalmente; I did not want Alicia to have the same problems. The ones Edna had. And, it was my company, my work. It had to be my way.'

'Then it must have been tough for Edna, being a stepmother.' I struggled to comprehend the implications of Alicia having been cloned. Although friends and colleagues had talked about the cloning experiences of people they knew, I'd never come up against the reality of cloning gene-to-gene as it were.

'The truth is she died of a drug overdose, the day before Alicia's first birthday.'

'Poor her. Poor Alicia. You've kept a lot from me.' It was a stupid thing to say in the circumstances.

Arturo apologised for not flying back with me to Brasilia. We embraced stiffly next to his jet on the runway of a private airstrip not far from his villa. He promised he would send a copy of the camclip and that he would contact me the next time he was in Europe. I thought about Arturo and Alicia on the journey back to Brasilia. Arturo's villa had been fitted out with expensive decor and furbishings but it was all superficial allure, reeking only of money and vanity. I had always thought, or hoped, there was more to my son than had appeared on the surface. As a younger man, his charm had seemed to give him substance, but in middle-age it hung on him like the loose gold bracelets around his arms. I realised that I had come to despise him. It was not solely because of what he did for a job, or what he had done, because, in the context of a life spent working for a company such as O Futuro, a desire to clone his own child did not seem so outrageous. It was because of who he had become.

But, as for the sweet lively Alicia, I had the pleasant memory of her miniature hand in mine, leading me confidently through the house, eager to show off her doll's house and pony. Yet it was impossible not to wonder what would become of the child, so motherless and spoilt.

It was not until I was back in the hotel (the Corazon) at about one in the morning that I checked through the day's messages. A whole 12 hours earlier, Anna Mastepanov had requested I call her immediately. She answered on the first ring as if she had been holding the receiver in her hand. I tried to apologise for not having replied earlier, but she was distraught and speaking fast. Alan had suffered a massive coronary the previous night, gone into a coma, and had died during the late morning. There was nothing that could be done for him. I offered to switch on the cam, to allow us to be more personal, more intimate, but she declined. Instead, she talked without stopping for several minutes, faster and with a more pronounced accent than I remember. She told me how he had been so well in recent weeks, how they had spent a month over Christmas on Corfu (from where, I realised, I had received my last ever communication from him) with some friends, and how the 'damn bloody cold' had killed him on their return. She said that he had talked so often about me, it was as though I were a regular visitor to their home. But this was too much for me to bear. I had to stop her flow and apologise for never having visited in person, and, bizarrely, I found myself trying to make excuses for this, as if there could be any. My outburst had the effect of calming Anna down. She tried to explain that this was not my fault at all, but hers because she should have persuaded Alan not to be so shy of pressing me to come.

'He loved you, like his own son.'

'Did he? I loved him like a father too. I only wish ... I only wish ...'

'It's fine. He lived well. He did good things. He was a precious, precious man. Now we must warm ourselves with his memory.'

It was Anna who eventually brought the conversation round to practicalities. She told me when the funeral would be, and insisted, knowing where I was, that I should not interrupt my important mission nor fly halfway round the world for the funeral. I considered what she had said for a few seconds, and then agreed. It would feel so wrong, I told her, to make such an effort to go there now he's dead, when I never made a tenth of the effort when he was alive. I said I would write and asked that a few of my words be read at the funeral.

I slept fitfully that night, disturbed less by his death (he was, after all, in his 90s) than by my own self-pity and self-anger at never having made the journey to St Petersburg. The next morning, over breakfast, I told Eduardo the news. He offered me his condolences, but was anxious to know whether he would need to cancel or re-arrange any of our forthcoming meetings. When I reassured him that I had no plans to cancel any appointments, a sharp memory suddenly shot into my consciousness. It was of the email I had received, in 21 during my student holiday to Brazil, which informed me about the death of my grandmother, Alan's mother, Eileen. What I recalled so vividly was how the news of her death had struck me with fear: fear that I would be summoned home and my Brazilian adventure would be curtailed before it had begun.

***

Jay and Vince took me out to the garden yesterday, Saturday, the first time for many weeks. Not to the rose garden, for it was busy with too many children visitors, but to what Flora refers to as the 'twut' (as in two hut) garden. It has been such a wet summer, but the fuchsias, which remind me of Lizette, are in good colour ('dripping crimsons, purples, violets', she would say). The hibiscus plants are also doing well. There are so many scattered through the gardens, I suspect there must have been a gardener in generations past who had a passion for them. Vince is walking again, and full of praise for something called the Alexander Technique which he is employing as a way of restoring order to his body. He wanted to explain in detail but Jay, who has been following the evolution of this chapter with some concern, had another agenda. To begin with, he told me that Guido and Mireille would be making a rare return visit to Holland from Ecuador in late October (no news could have brought me more joy), and that, therefore, Vince and he had decided to take a two week holiday overlapping the same period. Then, using Vince as an unwitting adjudicator, he asked why, in my Reflections, I had fast forwarded to 62 skipping entirely over his own birth. Even though he knows full well I'm not following a strict chronology, I can understand why he jumped to that conclusion: in our discussions of the last few days, I've been preparing myself to press even further ahead and tackle the events of 64.

I reassured Jay he was not being left out (to murmurings of approval from Vince: 'Better not, or you'll have me to deal with.' I do like Vince, but where was this loyalty six months ago?) How could I leave Jay out? He's my anchor. Without him I would have drifted away many moons ago, leaving not a whit, not a jot, not a single reflection.

While I struggled with the elevated role at the IFSD, my relationship with Lizette flowered. We met most weekends, when I was not away, mostly in The Hague, since she had more time for the travel. Occasionally I trained to Brussels and we went from there to a high-class hotel in Ghent or Leuven to pamper ourselves during an overnight stay. We spoke every night on the camphone. At Lizette's suggestion, we both installed camphone facilities in the bedroom so we could chat from our beds. As we became more relaxed with this system, so we began to natter while preparing for bed. Thus, by accident (or Lizette's wiliness) we developed a pattern of pleasuring ourselves voyeuristically. To an outsider, this might seem a one-sided arrangement, to my advantage, but Lizette enjoyed pleasing me and watching my pleasure. Moreover, she had her own ways of achieving sexual satisfaction while on the camphone. Best of all, though, our virtual sex enhanced the real thing at weekends. Now that I am in the late afternoon chapters of this book (misconstruing the old cliche), I may not stray again to matters intimate, but this is one happy ending: sex in my sixties and early seventies was the best I ever had. Thank you Lizette (with apologies to Jay for saying a little more than he called for).

In July 60, when the European University semester finished, Lizette came to live in my apartment on Van Hogenhouckstraat for six weeks before returning to England. Then she went to the Midlands to see her friends and undertake some emotional negotiations with Clint, and from there to her Ma and Pa in Weston-super-Mare. She gave birth to Jay in a local hospital, and, having taken maternity leave, remained for the rest of the year at her parent's spacious bungalow. It was during that winter, when baby Jay was first taking in the bright lights of the world, that the lights went dark for his GrandPa. Having suffered from a form of muscular dystrophy for many years, Mervyn Sanderson finally expired from pneumonia. (Only later did I learn that Lizette had, many years earlier, organised a genetic profile for herself and Clint so as to ensure any children they bore would not inherit her father's disease or any other testable genetic weakness. This knowledge, it transpired, was another factor in Lizette's semi-conscious decision to have a pot-luck fuck with Clint.) Because of various complications, not least the baby and the dying father, I only met up with Lizette twice during this period. Once when I flew to Bristol and we stayed in a hotel there for two nights, and once in Brussels when she needed to check on her apartment and carry out some administrative duties. She was distraught on this occasion, because, despite special payment, the building concierge had let her tub fuchsias, which decorated the glassed-in balcony overlooking Parc de Cinquantenaire, dry out and die. Soon after settling in at the bungalow in Weston-super-Mare, though, she had a private camphone installed in her room, so we were able to talk as regularly as before; and I was able to monitor the baby's progress. In January 61, she returned to Brussels, found an excellent creche for Jay, and resumed her life, and pattern with me, albeit one more constrained than previously.

The three-way relationship worked surprisingly well. Lizette was eager to put my paternal experience to good use, and to balance it against her own maternal (and, to my mind, overprotective) instincts. I adored Jay as if he were my own child, which was fortunate because Lizette had decided that it would be better for him if Clint played no part in his life. We had many discussions about this, especially in the context of my suggestion that we form a co-op for Jay. I proposed that we should find some way of including Clint. Lizette could not be persuaded. She knew, she said, he did not want a child, and that he would make a lousy father. We thought about Lizette's brothers and Rhoda for the co-op and rejected them too. Mercurio was, apparently, feckless, and had embedded himself with the Notek movement, and Samuel was too caught up in his own family and work. Rhoda, Lizette argued, would only be a bad influence. In the end, we agreed to form the Jay co-op ourselves, just the two of us, and we went so far as to use the Dutch legal framework for co-ops, which had proved itself relatively stable. This required us getting Clint's written approval, but Lizette had no trouble in obtaining it.

During 62, Lizette made regular weekend trips to Weston-super-Mare because of her mother's deteriorating health, and, whenever I was available, she would come first to The Hague to drop Jay off before flying to Bristol. I have very fond memories of wheeling him in his chair through Westbroek Park to the playground, and reading the Sunday papers while watching his antics on the clambering frames and tussle-jumpers. Towards the end of that year, Lizette's mother stepped over the edge, deliberately, to follow her husband to a better place.

It was not until 63 that Lizette, Jay and I, in our personal life together, had a trouble-free year. We took a substantial joint holiday during the summer, to a gîte near Poitiers in France; but little stands out from those weeks, except a feeling of relief at leaving work behind, and an equally strong sentiment that serendipity had brought me Lizette. Two events that same year, though, are worth recording.

In the spring, Anna Mastepanov came to visit for three days. She was on her way to Brussels, Paris and London to commune (I can't think what other word to use) with people important to Alan. The week before her arrival, a large trunk of Alan's things were delivered to my apartment. There were all the papers, storage disks and personal items he had specified for me in his will, plus a number of mementoes that Anna wanted me to have. She was a lovely lady, older than me in years, but younger in spirit, full of bright but controlled enthusiasms. We spent most of one day going through the papers and items. Inspired by these, Anna talked at length about his passions, achievements and friendships, and about their life together. And, on the second day, we looked at the many photos and camclips on her personal digital memory store, accessed through the net. There were surprises.

For more than 30 years, Alan had donated a minimum of 10% of his income to a health clinic in a small town in Bangladesh. He had visited it often, and knew many of the people there. Anna, too, had been on three visits and was full of stories about the lives of the characters in the camclips and about how the clinic had served not only the town's health but its economic well-being.

At one moment, Anna saw me drifting away in my thoughts, looking wistful, and asked me why. This was the difference between Alan and me, I said. He had helped on the ground, with people, real people, getting his hands dirty, spending his own money, risking his own life, sacrificing his own time. And I thought, but did not say, that he had done and lived while I had only done and lived by proxy. Anna cut short my maudlin self-pity to tell me that Alan's view was the complete reverse.

'It's easy to help, he used to say, but few can help – like Kip does – when it comes to the big picture. He was very proud of you,' she said. 'I would hate for you to forget that for one minute.'

Another surprise was that Alan had an adopted son, a Czech man called Karel. There were photographs, but no camclips, of Alan together with a woman called Tamara (who I had met once in Brussels) and Karel as a child, and of Karel alone at different ages through to adulthood. Anna knew little of Karel's history. Tamara, it seems, had been very keen on adopting a deprived child, but then, soon after the adoption, she had fallen out with Alan and run away. He had never had any contact with either of them since then, except that occasionally a photograph would arrive by email. Subsequently, I searched all through Alan's records and his few personal jottings but there was no correspondence to or from Tamara (which shows he must have carefully edited his files in good time before dying) and no explanation of why he had never told me or my mother about Karel. On our third day together, Anna and I strolled around the city. We talked about Diana, Guido and Lizette; and then, tearfully, she left to continue her pilgrimage of sorts. She was heading for Paris next, to see Monique.

If I were to trawl through my own papers, I might find other events that year more worth recording that the short trip I made to the world volleyball finals in Munich. Fortunately, these are only my Reflections, and I've long since demonstrated that I have no intention of documenting my life or the world around in any rigorous way. One morning, in autumn 62, MarySue called through to tell me that she had a very strange person on the line. He insisted on talking to me personally, MarySue said, but refused to say what about. He said his name was Sanfry and that it was personal and important. There was something about the name Sanfry which rang a bell, and so, against my better judgement, I told MarySue to put him through. As soon as I heard the word volleyball, I remembered who he was. Alfred had kept me informed of his progress over the years: starting with the Nigerian team aged 17, he had become its captain at 20 and led it to a world championship triumph in the early 40s. Now, as president of the World Volleyball Association (WVA), he was calling to ask if I would present the trophy to the winning team at the world cup finals in May 63. Because such an event was beyond my usual public appearance portfolio, I hesitated slightly. But then, when Sanfry explained the details of another duty I was to perform at the same time, I accepted the invitation with alacrity.

Alfred. Alfred. Alfred. To my shame, I had forgotten about him recently. I spoke to Chidi as soon as I had finished the conversation with Sanfry. He had no recent news either, so I asked MarySue to track him down. On the phone, I heard the voice of a resigned man. I learned how resentful he was of Ojoru, how his wife Fayola had left him for a richer man, and how his son, Fela, had become a banker, 'a greedy man'. I discovered that he was working in public relations for an agricultural exporter, biding his time until he could afford to retire and go to live on Zanzibar. He had bought a plot of land there many years previously, and wanted to build a house. Later the same day I talked to Chidi again. Within a month, we had created a place for him as a special adviser in the IFSD's Abuja office, not I hasten to add out of charity, but because we knew he could be an excellent interface between The Hague and Abuja offices, and between the IFSD and the Nigerian administration.

I did not see Alfred in person until the Munich volleyball finals. I sent him a return plane ticket, with an option to travel on from Munich to The Hague for a few extra days (which he did not use). I persuaded another of my old volleyball buds, Peter de Roo, into accompanying me for the weekend. It turned out to be a fantastic trip. Alfred knew many of the people there, but even Peter and I (long-since aliens to the volleyball scene) found several long-forgotten buds from the summer contests of our student days. We watched four matches, two semi-finals on the Saturday, and, on the Sunday, a youth cup final (the US versus Brazil) and the world cup final (Nigeria versus Russia). I sat with Sanfry and all the high officials of the volleyball association, while Peter and Alfred sat a few rows behind in seats that Sanfry had secured for them. During the youth match, Sanfry talked throughout; he wanted to explain his personal debt to Alfred, and then to reaffirm how much he had done for Nigerian volleyball over the years. After I had awarded the trophy to the winning youth team, and its members had left the arena, I was due to deliver a short speech and hand over a WVA annual award for services to volleyball. Earlier, I had arranged with a technician to use the big overhead screens to show a camclip I'd given him access to. I began by asking the 10,000 audience to humour me for a minute. The technician launched the clip, and I spoke over the top of it.

'Fifty years ago, Italy beat Croatia in a European cup quarter-final that was held in Guildford near my home town in England. It was universally acknowledged to be one of most exciting games of volleyball you could ever wish to see. Italy went on beat Spain in the final, and then to reach the finals of the world championship two years later.'

The camclip froze, and my 13 year old (grainy) self filled the screens. I paused for effect. My heart was thumping so loud I feared the microphone would pick it up. I had grown used to public speaking, but this was personal, not work, and I had not adequately discounted for the difference.

'This is me, ladies and gentlemen. And you can see, by my showing it today, how proud I am of my appearance as a ball-boy at that famous match. It was the day that volleyball entered my soul.' (Chidi thought 'soul' was more appropriate than my suggestion of 'heart'. I should say that Chidi assisted me in drafting the speech, which was kind of him for it was not official business. He had a gift for speech-writing, and knew how to enliven my dull drafts, to spice them up, while keeping to a style that suited my way of speaking.)

'I was so fired up by those European championships that, not many weeks later, while waiting in the queue in the school canteen, I waylaid a boy I didn't know.' I stopped to turn and look at Alfred to see if he had understood where this was going. It had been Sanfry's decision to keep the award a secret.

'Perhaps things have changed but, in my day, talking to someone you didn't know, from a different year was taboo. And the only reason I spoke to this boy was his height. I knew he would be perfect for our volleyball team. We soon became good friends. He went on to captain our team and lead our school to its greatest sporting triumphs. I may be exaggerating, but then who cares about football or athletics.' I was worried about this line, but Chidi, who knew nothing about volleyball, understood what specialist audiences enjoy. It drew a great applause, and I was glad we kept it in. I went on to list Alfred's achievements in Nigeria, and Nigeria's achievements in the world, not only in terms of success on court, but in terms of encouraging other developing nations to nurture their sporting talent. I then closed with the following words.

'Forgive me if I have drawn a straight line from my recruiting efforts in the school canteen to the presentation of this award today, but you all know the achievements are his, and that I have been but a bedazzled bystander. And I cannot end without saying, in all honesty, that I would not be here today, presenting this award, were it not for a lifetime of this man's friendship and support. So you can understand why I am overjoyed to present the 2063 WVA award for services to volleyball to my great and dear friend Alfred Ajose.'

Alfred made his way down from behind us and manoeuvred himself onto the walkway in front of where I was standing. I didn't shake his hand as I had done with the captains of the youth teams. Instead, we instinctively slapped palms in our accustomed manner, to the delight of the crowd; and only then did I pick up the trophy and present him with it. He turned and bowed elegantly to the crowd receiving a huge ovation, and returned to his seat. No sooner had I sat down, emotionally drained, than the presenter came on the loudspeakers to introduce the teams for the world cup final. Sanfry chattered throughout the game, probably to divert himself from the pain of seeing Russia defeat Nigeria by three sets to none. I didn't mind the dull match because it left Alfred's award as the climax of the day.

***

Now I should move on from this high point to a very low one. In September 64, during a routine visit to Belfast, I was kidnapped. It was the second most physically dramatic episode of my life, second only to Cyclone Kip. Though it concluded as no more than melodrama, it was to lead to my resignation from the IFSD. The timing could not have been worse (to mimic one of the media's most beloved expressions) as I was due to be in Paris a few days later for the wedding of Guido and Mireille. I arrived by jet without any delays in Ireland's second city, installed myself at the O'Hilton, and completed two separate meetings with ministers and their officials, one of which included lunch. My schedule then allowed me a free half an hour in the hotel room to make calls. From there I was due to find my way alone (my assistant having gone on ahead) to the adjacent O'Hilton Conference Centre to deliver a keynote speech to an important gathering of international environmental NGOs, many of whom worked with the IFSD all over the world. While on the phone to MarySue, there was a knock on my door. A waiter presented me with a tray containing a teapot, cup, milk and biscuits. I protested mildly that I hadn't ordered tea, but, while trying to concentrate on MarySue's messages, he walked in and deposited the tray on a table. I thanked him as he left. I know I finished my call, drank the tea, and looked at the text of my speech. After that I recall nothing, nothing at all. I learned later, from the police, that I had been given an illegal mental anaesthesia drug, and that two captors had walked me out through the back staircase and the hotel's rear entrance, while successfully using beaked caps to hide their faces from the surveillance cams. Apart from the rest, which I am about to record as succinctly as possible, it was terrifying to experience one of these hypnosis drugs for myself: to realise that I could have been persuaded to do anything, while appearing compos mentis, and yet remember nothing.

I recall waking, feeling very groggy, and finding myself in a shoddily furnished basement room with one high window of frosted wired glass, a table, chairs and a heater. I didn't know if it was the same day or the next morning. My watch, phonepad, identicard and cashcards had all been removed from my suit pockets. I was lying on a threadbare sofa with one hand cuffed to a metal backplate. My head hurt. Water and biscuits were in reach on a rectangular plastic-wood table. I desperately needed the toilet. I assumed I had been taken hostage, but had no idea why or by whom. Why would anyone kidnap me, and in Ireland, such an unturbulent place? I shouted out for help. No-one came. I drank some water, and the ache in my head eased. I thought about my conference speech and felt sure I must have been missed; then I thought about Guido and his wedding on Saturday; then I debated whether to urinate through a gap in the cushions onto the floor behind the sofa (I was desperate); and then I remembered the tracer in my ear.

Whoever had kidnapped me, they were not top-notch professionals or else they would have made allowances for the possibility of a tracer. They could have put me in a deep bunker, or dressed me in a metal fabric jump suit with metallic ear pads (earlobes being the most common location for tracers), or questioned me and cut the tracer out without causing a serious wound. Being taken hostage was a chronic risk for all those travelling into the less stable parts of the world. Mostly rich businessmen and politicians were snatched and ransomed, but there had been two top UN officials abducted in the 50s. As a consequence around 300 key UN staff were offered tracer implants. I became one of the chosen when I took over as the IFSD's director-general. Each tracer had a unique code and could be identified through special equipment, controlled by a carefully vetted commercial company, based on the Galileo satellite system. (Such tracers were widely used for other purposes, by police and prison services, for example, to keep track of undesirables, and by ethologists to monitor animal migrations.)

I tried to calculate what should have happened. When I failed to show for the conference presentation, my assistant would have returned to the hotel, checked with the management, checked my room, and then called MarySue. Not finding any note or message as to my whereabouts, the Irish police would have been contacted, and they would have begun an enquiry within, I calculated, two hours of my disappearance. That would have been at about 4pm. Meantime MarySue would have gone to my desk to find an envelope she knew was there to be opened in such an emergency. She would then have called the special UN elite security group, which in turn would have contacted the upper echelon of the Irish police. That would have taken at most another 90 minutes, say two hours. I was, therefore, fairly sure that by 6pm somebody somewhere should have known where I was.

I shouted again. This time the door opened and a tallish man came in. He was carrying a gun, and wearing a black hood with large eyes holes, a bomber jacket and scruffy jeans. A youthful male voice asked me what I wanted, and I said I was desperate for the toilet. He went out of the room for a few moments, and, when he returned, unlocked the cuff, and led me a few steps through the door to a filthy smelly bathroom, where I was able to relieve myself. He then escorted me back. I tried asking questions but was told to 'shut up'. I was re-shackled to the sofa, this time by both wrists. The youth left the room, but two minutes later was back again. He put a blindfold around my head, and then another person entered. This new person, another man but with a croaky false voice, told me the plan. I was to make the calls necessary to ensure that one million euros were transferred from the IFSD bank account to a given private account – by midnight. I laughed. I laughed, and was slapped vigorously across the face. It was shocking. The second man shouted angrily 'leave him'. My face stung. I could not remember being hit since I was a child. I felt very, very vulnerable. I decided to measure my words, and my laughter.

'I laughed because I can no more get one million euros from the IFSD than I can one hundred,' I said with a controlled voice having filtered out the anger and the fear. 'It doesn't work that way. We have 200 financial staff, a financial director, a budget committee, an oversight committee, an auditor, bankers, financial control procedures etc, I never see a cent.'

'You could if you had to. Call the financial director. Tell him it's an emergency. Do it. Do it now.'

'I can't. The financial director would laugh at me. He'd say it was a joke, and if I insisted he would call security. He would know something was wrong.'

'What the fuck now?' the young man asked the other. It was a farce I realised.

'Shut up, I'm thinking.' This time the second voice was less strange, less disguised. I recognised it. Bronze!

'I can get you an absolute maximum of 10,000 euros of my own money, now, on the phone. I can transfer it wherever you want, but you have to promise to let me go immediately and get out of here now.' But it was not enough for my stupid, idiot son.

'One hundred thousand euros and it's a deal. You go free and unharmed. No negotiating. If you refuse, we hurt you, until you agree.'

'I can't do it. The bank has rules and I'm limited to how much I can withdraw by phone in any one day.'

'Fuck you, you're lying.' This was the first man again. They questioned and threatened me several more times, and then I lost patience.

'Look Bronze, I know it's you. This is ridiculous ...'

The youth interrupted.

'Fuck me, how does he know who you are?'

I told him.

'Fuck. This is weird.' I could feel him trying to come to terms with this. Bronze too was stunned to realise that I'd twigged his identity. The two of them then engaged in a loud argument. When, after a few minutes, I heard a very loud knocking from the floor above, I shouted over the top of them.

'This is ridiculous. The police know where I am. I have a tracer.'

'What's that?' the youth screeched. I explained. This sent him into an excess of fury and expletives, until he crashed an ornament to the ground, and raced out of the room. He was caught, I was informed later, exiting from the back of the house. Bronze left the room too for a few minutes, and I heard that he was communicating with someone far off, but not what was being said. He came back, and took my blindfold off. I barely recognised my son. I had only seen him three or four times in the last ten years (his choice not mine), and since the last occasion, he had put on much weight, clearly evident through his heavy overcoat, and let his hair grow long and unkempt. He looked ill, with a yellow tint to the skin on his face, and dark rings around his eyes.

'I told them I'd kill you if they came in.' He showed me a gun, presumably the one the youth had brandished earlier, now in the pocket of his coat.

'Why did you do that?'

'Shut up.'

'Let me walk out freely now before this gets out of hand.'

'It's too late. We stole a car, and the gun, and we injured a hotel porter who tried to stop us.'

'Nevertheless, it'll go much better for you, if you let me loose now.'

'I can't do that.'

'Why?'

'Shut up.'

He did let me go, but not for half an hour, during which time he bared his soul, in a quite extraordinary way, as if he were in a priest's confessional. Initially, he remained silent. I asked him to remove the cuffs so that I could sit comfortably. I promised I wouldn't leave until he said I could.

'Bronze, why are you doing this?' I asked. The question caused him pain, visibly so, and led, a few seconds later, to a wheezing fit, followed by a confession. I cannot pretend to remember his words sufficiently well, all jumbled up as they were, to reconstruct the monologue, as I have for the dialogue above. But the gist of what he told me in a nebulous way was this. He was tired of serving the New Crusaders, giving his all and getting nothing back any more. The organisation repeatedly promised he would be sent out on a crusade, a mission to set up a Christian church in Iran or Tunisia or Tajikistan (he very much wanted to go to Tajikistan). Whenever he questioned the duration of his self-paid training or asked the leadership about the schedule for his mission, he was told there were no funds at present. And yet he had witnessed hundreds of crusades, planned and implemented, many of them by recruits who had joined the New Crusaders years later than him. Tired of being passed over (and, presumably, exploited, but that's my word), he decided to raise his own funds for his own crusade. He acquired sketchy details of my trip to Dublin from an exchange of emails which had begun with my invitation to Guido's wedding. The kidnap plan was hatched with a young friend he had recently recruited to the church, and who had underworld connections. (I discovered later these 'connections' were his father, from whom the gun had been stolen.)

As his soliloquy continued, punctuated by frequent bouts of wheezing and half choking on his medical throat spray, I came to understand how much Bronze was burning up with bitterness. He felt bitter towards god for not dealing him a better hand; towards the church and his work colleagues for not acknowledging his self-sacrifice; and towards his mother, whom he saw as infrequently as me, for never having loved him. He even savaged himself for messing up friendships. I thought I was being left off the list. I could hear the police loudspeakers penetrating the basement room asking for a response. There was frequent rapping on the outside of the room's one window. Telephones chimed in the distance. In his last few minutes alone with me, he admitted, finally, to hating me. He cited my having left Crystal and him alone with their mother, and my failure, like Harriet's, to love him properly. I came to realise that for most of his life he had dismissed the relationship with his father as unimportant and irrelevant, but that recent developments had steered his psyche towards identifying me as being at the root of his problems. One of these developments, no doubt, was my involvement with Jay, about whom I'd written often. More immediately, my obvious delight at Guido's forthcoming wedding may have sent Bronze over the edge.

I feared the police would make an inappropriate armed break-in, so I walked over to Bronze, put my arm around his shoulder, took the gun, shepherded him out of the room, and up a set of stairs. At the same time, I shouted, as loud as I could, that we were coming out. Outside, a street of sad-looking terraced houses (in a town called Birr, central Ireland) was full of police vehicles, ambulances, and armed police wearing protective suits. Bronze was arrested and taken away in a police van. I was driven to Dublin, with a high-ranking policeman called Tyrone Lopping, in an un-marked police car. On the way, I called my assistant and MarySue.

There were so many varied ramifications of this ridiculous episode, I will not try to pin them all down, nor do I wish to dwell on them.

As it was in my interests and those of the security services to avoid any publicity, I discussed with Lopping how this could be done. But it couldn't. He could vouch for the police under his command, he said, but not for the ambulance crews, other sundry officers or the bystanders. Furthermore, there were reporters at the NGO conference that would be making enquiries. Then I asked another question: would it be possible to keep it quiet about Bronze being my son, since he had taken Harriet's name, Tilson, not mine?

By midnight, having been subject to two hours of close questioning, and having called everyone I needed to, including Harriet and Lizette, I was back in my hotel room watching the breaking news on the kidnap and release of a UN high official. Because the whole ghastly event only lasted a few hours, it was already old news by the next day, and the story was confined to the newspapers' inside pages. For about 24 hours I lived in hope that the relationship between Bronze and me would not become public. It broke on the second day, I don't know how or why. My office and private phones were inundated with calls. I gave my journalist friend Bobby Jespersen a detailed exclusive and asked her to make clear that I would never be talking about the matter again in public. She was most comfortable with political reporting, and usually steered clear of human interest stories, so I hoped she would not delve too deeply into my personal history. Accepting the interpretation I gave her, and in sympathy with it, she was happy to portray Bronze as a cult victim rather than someone with criminal intent.

Neither Bronze nor his partner in crime were given bail by the Irish author-ities, even though I employed an expensive lawyer. I did not attend the trial six months later. They both pleaded guilty and were sentenced to ten years incarceration. After a year at Mountjoy Prison in Dublin, Bronze was transferred to Highdown Prison in south London, which made life a lot simpler for Harriet who, surprisingly, visited often and acted like a caring mother. I visited rarely, once every two or three months. It was a trial of duty. Bronze and I never re-established, or should I say established, any worthwhile relationship. During my hour-long stays we talked of trivial things, about prison life, about Harriet, and about his efforts to convert fellow inmates. He never asked about Guido or Jay, and I never mentioned them. He died in 66 from a punctured lung sustained during a vicious fight. His assailant, a convicted killer, was later found guilty of Bronze's murder.

Until he took me hostage, Bronze had been so distant, so minor a part of my life, that I had successfully shunted him beyond my emotional horizons. I had stopped thinking about him, except for occasional emails and very intermittent encounters, and I had almost stopped caring for him. So, in one way, his desperate ploy worked, for afterwards, barely a day went by when I didn't wonder about him, when I didn't have to cope with feelings of guilt and inadequacy. I would think of him when I was in the lift, or on the toilet, or waiting at the station for Lizette and Jay to arrive, or in the middle of a meeting.

And, without doubt, he not only wiped the shine off my happiness the following Saturday, but stripped the veneer too.

***

I had no involvement in the preparations for the wedding. Didier and Helene Rocard, a wealthy couple long since, insisted on paying for everything; and any parental involvement on Guido's side was handled by Diana. My only job was to liaise with Guido's half-brothers. With Bronze I must have tried too hard, but with Arturo I did not try at all. Guido had no particular interest in Arturo, especially after I'd informed him about the Alicia situation, and so I took responsibility for not sending him an invitation.

There was a huge row between Mireille and her parents over the shape and style of the wedding. I know this because Guido kept me fully informed thinking he might need me to intervene. Guido, obviously, sided with his wife-to-be, but Diana aligned herself with the Rocard parents. The problem arose because Didier wanted to 'produce' a wedding, a theatrical event, which Diana would design. I've no doubt it was a generous, loving offer from both of them. Mireille was as plugged into the theatre world as her parents and Guido, and, at first, the idea did tempt her. But when Didier began talking about possible themes and ideas, Mireille's toes caught a chill. Guido advised her to talk to her father immediately, but she prevaricated, unsure of what was right, and afraid of disappointing him. To cut a complicated story short, Mireille left it far too long before deciding. By which time, Diana and Didier had launched various initiatives, not least negotiations for a venue. They were not prepared, therefore, to drop the whole thing because of Mireille's cold feet. They tried to talk her round, to bribe her, to threaten her. The more they argued, the more Mireille realised, to Guido's relief, that all she wanted was a simple quiet church wedding. It was only later that I discovered how close Guido and Mireille came to running off to marry in Corsica. According to Guido, their decision, a year or so later, to go to live and work in Ecuador had much to do with Mireille needing distance from her father.

The Rocards may have called it a simple quiet church wedding, but few others would have done. The church – scouted and bought for the day by Didier – was opulent with gold and silver ornamentation. Diana had ensured it was further adorned with the wildest, most exotic flowers you could imagine. And then, as if that was not already enough colour and splendour, there were 100 or more friends and family most of them theatrical and dressed up to the hat. Rudy, Peter's son and Guido's best man, and Guido stood at the head of the aisles on one side, with a portly cleric (heavily made-up as if more concerned about the camrecording than his appearance in the flesh). Guido wore a brushed silver knee-length jacket, and silver-white trousers. He looked like a prince; but an image of fat Bronze with unkempt hair and a wheezing cough would not let me go.

While we waited for Mireille and Didier to enter the church and walk down the aisle together, a choir sang quietly, and an elaborate organ was played by someone I could not see. Lizette, Jay and I all sat in the same pew as Diana and Karl (various introductions having been made earlier outside the church). Opposite, on the other side of the aisle, sat Helene and Mireille's sister Veronique with her partner Yves Lafont (the then famous footballer-poet). Behind us, the other two members of the Guido co-op, Peter and Dominique sat with their respective partners Livia and Waltar and various very adult-looking offspring. There was also Arnout, a fidgety five year old, Rudy's son (and Peter and Livia's first grandson) who later, at the reception, linked up with Jay for mischievous expeditions. If these had been Guido's Reflections, Rudy, a gifted saxophonist, would have been a major character. He and Guido had played a lot together as children, on and around Peter's barge; and, as students, they had employed our barge Ginquin to take their girlfriends (Mireille in Guido's case) on holidays through the Dutch and German waterway systems.

I might have been thinking about Karl, having never met him before that day, or wondering what Diana and Lizette were making of each other, but I wasn't. I was thinking of Bronze. Mireille, when she arrived, looked ravishing, in a tight cat-suit made of the same brushed silver as Guido's jacket and a long flowing white muslin train. Together, Mireille and Guido belonged in some yet to-be-written futuristic fairy tale with an enchanting beginning and, I hoped, a happy ending. Bronze, for his sins and mine, belonged in a prison.

Didier had apparently compromised with Mireille over the wedding service. In return, Mireille and Guido had let Didier and Helene have their wish with respect to the reception. It was the biggest social function the Rocards had hosted since the ball in 49 which had been given to celebrate a milestone in the fortunes of their puppet artwork company. I thought – ungenerously and unkindly – the wedding reception was no more than another Rocard promotion. Guido confessed to knowing only a fraction of the people present, and not being interested in any of them. I tried to remain at a dining table, quietly talking with Lizette, Peter and Livia, or catching up with Dominique's news. Yet we were constantly interrupted. I was the father of the bridegroom, which meant Mireille and Diana kept trying to drag me off to be introduced to every Tom, Dick and Hamlet. More than that, though, I had become something of a celebratory in the last few days, first with the kidnap, then with the revelation that it was my 'other son' who had done the kidnapping. People were naturally curious, and, given the world in which they inhabited, their curiosity was not tempered by any care or respect for my feelings. I am being unfair. Both Didier and Helene were very likable characters, and they had produced two very eligible daughters. I was glad for Guido. He had made an excellent match. But, by then, I had become easily irritated by those in the theatre and art world. Thinking back, I believe this was a consequence of my relationship with Lizette. We talked often about my work, and more generally about politics, science, culture. Life had been different with Diana. Yes, she was brilliant, but she had only been able to maintain that brilliance, like many artists, by focusing exclusively on her own world. I had followed her there, onto the stage, as it were, as an observer, a friend, a patron, but by the time of our son's wedding I had already drawn far away, and was no longer so easily taken in by the scenery and spotlights. Not then, but now, I wonder whether I resented in some way Guido's decision to follow Diana into her world.

***

That year, 64, was 'one helluva year' for me (as Betty Arklington famously said of 51 before losing the US Presidency to Steve Tarbuck). Not only did I lose Bronze and Guido, in different ways, but I lost my job too.

As I have tried to indicate, I neither enjoyed being director-general nor was I very good at it. I had unintentionally alienated several of the directors, I had shirked my duties as an ambassador, and, worst of all, in response to the

Singapore Peace Treaty and subsequent agreements, I was failing to make the institution respond effectively and efficiently to its renewed and extended responsibilities. Personally, I do not think this latter failure was even half my fault. The UN's General Assembly had been much inflated (puffed-up in fact) by the terms of the Peace Treaty, but elsewhere in the UN system, which included many agencies large and small, problems of policy, politics, diplomacy had been hindering actual operations. The world and its nations and their disputes were taking a long time to recover from the Jihad War. Some thought this was natural, others that the underlying tensions had not gone away and were ready to resurface at any time. Our experience in the IFSD gave weight to the second opinion. We blamed our problems on the distrust between nations, between Muslim and Christian, African and Asian, southern and northern Europe, and Europe and the US. And the difficulties did not ease. Unfortunately for me personally, some smaller UN agencies recovered more quickly than the IFSD, and thus our apparent stagnancy began to attract close scrutiny. Then came the incident in Dublin, and a fiftyfold increase in requests for interviews with, and profiles of, me personally, every rejected one of which was a potential nail in my professional coffin.

In early November, Eduardo Villalonga asked for a private interview. Since the Brasilia trip, our professional relationship had stalled, I would say. I had no reason to fault his work or his advice, but it only ever went so far, he never put himself out for me, nor did he inspire me with confidence. In short, I expected more from the members of my cabinet than he gave. This said, it was a shock to hear him threaten me with resignation. He had followed the media as closely as I had. He had taken his own soundings, and read his own runes. If I did not resign within two weeks, he said, he would. Eduardo, himself, could not have brought me down, but his private threat was clear evidence of my soon-to-be untenable position.

I took Tommy for lunch at the Lake Toba restaurant. I wanted to break it to him gently that I was not prepared to fight this time round. I had no more to offer, and it would not be fair to start a battle I did not think I could win. The very fact that my own son had caused a major security alert for the Irish authorities and for the UN system was sufficient reason in itself to resign. I tried to explain how I had hoped the media frenzy would die down quickly, or that there would have been some measure of support for my position forthcoming, at the very least, from British heavyweights. Now that it was obvious that such backing would not come voluntarily, it was time to go. Tommy tried to hide the relief that showed on his face. Faithful Tommy. He never was any good at hiding his feelings. He had, it transpired, spared me the worst of his bush telegraph intelligence.

Although the UN's chroniclers have judged my last years harshly, thankfully none have gone so far as to blame me personally for the Second Jihad War. This may sound like a fanciful notion yet there are radical historians who believe the second conflict was caused, not by the rich-poor divide, or the Muslim-Christian divide or by Al Zahir's power-crazy ambitions to become Islam's second most important prophet after Mohammed, but by the United Nations and its leaders, not least Ojoru. A better organised, a better functioning, a better led UN, they say, could have averted the war. Dreamers, every last one of them.

There was another reason for my deciding to resign which I did not reveal to Tommy. I can be certain I am not inventing this now, in retrospect, because, at the time, I had an argument with Lizette over the matter. The simple truth is that I saw (and feared) war coming again, and I did not want to be there when it arrived. Lizette refused to believe I could act so selfishly, or that I would capitulate simply because I saw a tough road ahead. Perhaps she sensed echoes of her stamina-less husband Clint, or perhaps – this is another ungenerous thought – she did not want to lose status (she certainly enjoyed being taken to official functions). Because she had not witnessed the full extent of my commitment to the IFSD and its objectives during the early 50s I searched out a few favourable press clippings. I also recounted the story of how Tommy and I had campaigned to preserve my position when I was still only a director. Above all, I stressed, I would not have considered resigning then but for the daggers that were already unsheathed and being sharpened.

Officially, I cited old age and ill-health as the reasons for my resignation. I was granted a grand retirement party, at which several long-standing colleagues delivered kind words about my contribution to the IFSD. I have a vivid recollection (which unfortunately has tainted my memory of that party) of Eduardo being unctuous, a side of him I had never observed before. I received many cards and messages of goodwill, including one from Pravit Krishnamurty (who was to die within the year): 'It is not so bad in the grandstand, my friend, you can twiddle your thumbs, shake your fists, and shout "bloody fools" out loud.'

Lizette's flat was too cramped to accommodate me for more than a few days at a time. I tried to think about my future, but I refused to discuss this with colleagues and well-wishers who contacted me with offers and half offers and rumours of offers. I told them I needed time. Neither the thought of staying put in The Hague, or moving to a place in Brussels appealed much to me.

I spent some time with my antique photograph collection, then, after ensuring I had high quality prints of my favourites and copies of them all on Neil, I put the whole lot up for sale at Swann's. The auction did not take place until the late spring in 65, months after I had left the Netherlands. I cajoled Lizette into taking a day off, arranging a friend to collect Jay from school, and travelling to Amsterdam so that I would not be alone when my treasured possessions went under the hammer. My photographs, quaintly sub-titled in the catalogue 'The collection of a gentleman', took less than 20 minutes to sell. Lizette, who had only seen individual items, was humorously outraged to discover that a good third of the collection was erotica.

Over Christmas/new year the three of us floated around England. We stayed with Samuel and his family, then we opted to use a London hotel for two nights so that I could catch up with Horace, the Turnbulls and others, and visit Bronze, and then we ended up at Rhoda's house for my birthday, with a new year's eve celebration at the Sampsons in Chapel Chorlton. It was during these travels, feeling very rootless, that I decided I would return to England and buy a house somewhere near where I had grown up, in Surrey. This caused friction with Lizette, who was troubled by my decision to move further away from, not closer to, her. I sold the eco-roof apartment on Van Hogenhouckstraat, and shipped a small volume of furniture and a large number of books and papers into storage at Guildford. By the spring I was spending several days a fortnight being shown around a bewildering array of Surrey properties. I had no real idea of what I wanted, and so I would store up a handful of possibilities and wait for when Lizette could join me to trail round them again.

In-between times at Lizette's flat and in Guildford, I visited friends. Oddly, I saw more of Peter and Livia after having left the Netherlands than I had in my last years living there. Both of them had done well in their respective, and unusually straight-lined, careers, allowing them to take early retirement. Livia, after extended maternity breaks and several unpaid sabbaticals, had eventually become a director of the company she joined not long after arriving in the Netherlands as Peter's partner. Peter himself had served his country well, choosing to remain an energy research and policy analyst, focusing for many years on the development of the hydrogen economy. He was one of the key scientists who had helped the Netherlands remain one of the greenest and pollution-leanest nations in the world. Since retirement, Peter and Livia had moved out of Amsterdam to a rural retreat, not far from Leiden or Alphen aan de Rijn, near where they still moored a barge. Livia was finally fulfilling a lifetime ambition by designing clothes for her old company; while Peter was opting to take on the occasional freelance consultancy work for commercial firms to bolster their retirement funds. Guido and Mireille had moved into a pad near Pigalle, characterful but tiny (bought outright by Didier as a wedding present), and, although they were both always very busy, I was invariably made welcome. Horace's house in Southampton was too far from the Godalming/

Guildford area to be a good base for my house hunting, but, nevertheless, I went there often to talk politics, politics and more politics. Nothing much else interested my old friend. Once politics had been his only mistress in the search for power, now, past his prime, he was one of her many vassals.

In June, I found a property in Tilford, a pretty village with a slanting cricket green, east of Farnham. Built of brick in the 1930s with part hung tile elevations, and a mature vine pinned to a solid trellis across one half, Taunton House was one of the prettiest properties I'd been shown. It had a huge lounge with sunlight streaming in on one side in the morning and the other in the afternoon, four bedrooms (one in the attic), and a refurbished kitchen. The energy and waste systems were all ultra-modern. The electrics and electronics had been recently upgraded, and the decorations were first class. Even the half acre garden, with its two oaks, had been loved, with shrubs a plenty, fruit trees, and a vegetable plot behind a low stone wall. This was it. I had been looking and prevaricating too long. In order to win Lizette over, I employed old negotiating tricks: I under-promoted the house so as to let her find its charms for herself; and, I set it up against other (admittedly cheaper) properties which had no charms. The strategy worked better than I had hoped. Having long since resigned herself to my resolve to buy in England, Lizette approved the house with undisguised enthusiasm; and then, during the three months it took to buy, she decided to terminate her contract with the European University and, until such time as she found her next job, to live with me in Tilford.

EXTRACTS FROM CORRESPONDENCE
Alan Hapgood to Kip Fenn

January 2062

We've escaped the bitter cold of St Petersburg for a rare holiday. Anna has a cousin called Akilina here in Kerkira, in the north near a village called Velonades. The name Akilina means eagle, and the lady does have a broad generous wingspan, but there's nothing remotely predatory about her. She owns an estate villa, and runs a large olive tree plantation. They are beautiful trees, the olives. Have you ever been here? I mean with time for yourself, not with your IFSD collar on; I remember you going to Rhodes once ...

When you first see the ancient gnarled trees – single-trunked but also, so unusually, double and triple-trunked – layered down the hillside, they draw you in, into a darker and darker stillness, into an Escher-like maze; it's as though they are woods that might be haunted with Tarquinade's ghouls or Narnia's evil spirits. They say that old men become children again, and I wonder if that is true. If we could but return to the simple world of our childhood imaginations, where truth and courage and loyalty could see us through the darkness to the peace and truth beyond.

Akilina is busy now, at this time of year, with her workers collecting up olives from the ground nets. They use the olives primarily for local power generators, but about 10% go to a restored traditional mill run by (not very hardline) Noteks to produce eating oil. And very flavoursome it is too. But Akilina gets less than half her income from the olives, the rest comes in subsidy from the island government to maintain the groves. Officially, the subsidies are payments for farmers to be ready and willing to providing emergency irrigation when necessary, so as to preserve the island's environmental heritage. Unofficially, as everyone knows and Akilina certainly acknowledges, the olive groves are subsidised because they draw tourists to the island.

Anna (whose love I do not deserve – I confess this to you only) is out sightseeing, and I am meant to be writing a few letters. Yet I am caught with the image of the forest, as the poet Robert Frost said, 'mysterious, dark and deep', and I find myself thinking back to my early days, childhood days playing hide-and-seek with Julie (and always winning), and to your childhood (reading you the Realm of Tarquinade – do you remember it?) and to your teenage years in Godalming, those special times we spent together.

I'll be back in St Petersburg by the middle of January. It would be good to see you this year or next!

Keep in touch.

Kip Fenn to Anna Mastepanov

February 2062

No news could have saddened or touched me more profoundly than that of Alan's death. He was not only an uncle to me, but a brother and, at times, a father. And more than that, a wonderful friend.

Your sorrow must be great also – to lose such a friend, such a partner in life – but I've no doubt he's left you with a store of memories which will sustain you through this difficult time.

When I was but a toddler, Alan gave me a cuddly toy panda. I called it Karshula. I was about 15 when Alan asked me – I've no idea why – what had happened to it. I didn't know and didn't care. I relived this exchange in a dream 40 years later. I saw Alan's face, as it was then impressively open and optimistic, stonily refusing to laugh at my natural adolescent insouciance for all things childish. The dream came after a post-conference day trip from Hong Kong to Chengdu to visit the panda research and cloning centre. During our walk through the Panda Park, Karshula had come to mind, and, absurdly (for I was with other high officials talking about some big funding project or other), I caught myself thinking back, trying to remember what had become of it. That same day after the visit but before the dream, I emailed my mother Julie to ask if she could remember. The next morning, after the dream, she emailed me back – I was in a transfer lounge at Hong Kong airport – to say Karshula had gone to a kindergarten in St Albans, before our move to Guildford. I had thrown it out of the window once and left it to rot in the garden, and my mother had rescued it. Yet more absurdly, I recall being thankful that I had asked this question while my mother was alive (she died later that same year). Alan would want to know – I never bothered to tell him while he was alive – that Karshula had found a good home.

I tell this silly story only because it gives an idea of how firmly Alan is embedded in my life, in me. Although he was often overseas, I always felt he was there, round the corner, at every stage of my life, ready with a kind word, generous with advice and contacts, regularly sending me books, and, best of all letters, richly embroidered with stories of his friends and his environmental endeavours. One period stands out, though, when I was in my young teens. He lived in England, then, near my mother and me. My own father, Tom, had gone away – or so it seemed – and Alan had come in his stead, to spend hours chatting about politics, and history, and religion, world events and, inevitably, green issues. At the time, I considered there was nothing unusual about this, but, knowing more about teenagers now than I did then, I realise how very patient he must have been. And kind, and wise, and generous ...

In his last letter to me, only a few weeks ago, he said this: 'If we could but return to the simple world of our childhood imaginations, where truth and courage and loyalty could see us through the darkness to the peace and truth beyond.' I am sure that Alan is there now, somewhere, basking in peace and truth, for no man other deserves to be there if not him.

With love and sorrow.

Chapter Eight
JAY, WAR AND THE GREY YEARS

'Once or twice a year a mighty wind in the Out-There blows up a sand-fog which lasts several days, and then I peer trance-like into the swirling depths and imagine. I imagine that when it falls still there will be green pastures and fields with sheep and cows, and hedges and trees as far as the eye can see. And perhaps a river with stepping stones. Or else I imagine there will be a mountain scene with a hamlet in the foreground and a forest of pine trees in the background. These are pictures from the story books of the Long-Ago. It's hard to accept that once such scenes were common in our world, before the greyness in the sky, before the great and terrible drought, and before the Domes. But when the sand-fog settles, there is only sand in the Out-There, sand and more sand.'

Beyond by Lucretia Quant (2018)

M y decision to return to England and purchase Taunton House seemed a good place to end the previous chapter, even though, in consequence, it covers fewer years chronologically than other chapters. Despite a self-imposed deadline of completing this book by the year's end, I stopped writing for a week in order to read over material stored on Neil, to refresh my memory on the traumatic events of the late 60s and early 70s, and to talk with Jay. He does remember being aware of the Second Jihad War through his primary school years, but has no clear recollections of it. By contrast, he has vivid memories of images, taken by aerohover cameras and imaging satellites, of the eruption of Toba. And he has no difficulty in identifying the Grey Years as coinciding with his early years at the Witley Academy of Excellence (my old school Witley Academic, long since renamed) – the classroom never quite warm, the swimming pool unheated, and his hands and feet often frozen during sports or while waiting for the school bus on winter mornings.

Now that Jay has entered the story, so to speak, he is more self-interested than before so we talk at length about his childhood, his mother, his friends, his activities. Unfortunately, this means that his advice about what to include and what not to include in these Reflections is not as objective as it has been.

But it is thanks to Jay that I have decided to elaborate on my reasons for resigning from the IFSD. When I explained about my fear of the onset of war, and my remembered conversation with Lizette, he quizzed me.

'I don't understand why you didn't want to be there when the war arrived? I don't feel you've explained this well enough. From what you've said, Ma thought the same.' I closed my eyes, and thought about how to answer him. I could have said: I was tired, I'd had enough, and I had no stomach to fight to keep my job, when the job itself, already a nightmare, was going to get worse; and besides, as I have already explained, I would certainly have been pushed out if I'd not resigned. But I didn't. There was more to it. There was more to the reason why I would have been ousted, and consequently why I resigned before that could happen. And so, despite Jay's sudden protestations that I was looking weary and should sleep, I told him. Perhaps, while composing the previous chapter I forgot (the pills may not have been working as effectively as before) or perhaps I deliberately skimmed over the truth. In either case, I've decided I should correct the error. The end of these Reflections is in sight, so if I were now to bypass verity – when I've endeavoured to stick to it as carefully and objectively as one person can – I would undermine much of what I've already written.

The messier truth is not that difficult to uncover. I had, throughout my years at the IFSD, consistently tried to ensure that the conditions under which aid was provided were as loose as possible. I am not exactly certain when or why I developed the conviction that this was necessary. Alan influenced me in a general way when I was a schoolboy, but it was Pravit Krishnamurty who probably affected me more directly. I was also much affected by the many ideas and proposals we came across during my early IFSD years in Enterprise 35. Although I had friendly arguments about and around this subject over the years – in the office, meeting halls and zini bars – there was no recognition by my peers or political masters of my disposition on the issue (I doubt I could have defined it myself), not even when my position as environment director came under threat. As I hope I made clear earlier, my power as an administrator over policy was never significant, and, at most, my influence to change or direct it was never more than marginal. Nevertheless, as I said, I do believe I had some (as opposed to no) influence. At the policy level, this might have come through the way my team drafted proposals or put forward suggestions for negotiating compromises, or through the informal advice we gave occasionally to representatives of smaller recipient states when we thought they were being outmanoeuvred by the heavyweight donor countries. And, at the programme and project level, we sometimes tried to derestrict (very slightly) the conditionality on contract terms to allow the money to be committed or released more quickly and/or to be used more flexibly.

One of the arguments put forward by those who considered it necessary to shackle all aid with the tightest of conditions and contracts was to ensure that the donated funds were not willfully misused to support, in any way, the ability of recipient countries to develop police state or military capabilities. Six months before I resigned, the US administration had published a report demonstrating how, in the run-up to the First Jihad War, several IIBP member countries had misappropriated large amounts of UN aid and used it to build up their military structures. The aid may not have been employed directly to buy arms, yet it had helped with the costs of apparently benign but, in fact, military-related training, supplies and infrastructure. In a final section, the report suggested that since the end of the war this trend had begun again in earnest. Indeed, it warned, certain countries were exchanging experience on how best to exploit the UN and others. No fingers were pointed at any individual, but the report was highly influential, especially with those reluctant about the Singapore Peace Treaty.

It is certainly possible that this same report undermined my confidence at the time, and thus led me, subconsciously, to give more weight to other reasons for resigning. I certainly took due account of it more consciously when, some years later, I began preparing an important theoretical exercise on the future of the UN about which I will have more to say later. But, even in retrospect, how can we really know the truth of things. Maybe, in some slight way, I did assist those countries which wanted to abuse the aid mechanisms; but then how could this fault in the system be gauged against the benefits a more open/flexible approach brought other countries whose ability to implement development programmes was significantly improved by not having to follow Western strictures on scrutiny, deadlines and other red tape.

The first unmistakable sign that Al Zahir had only paused for breath, as it were, in order to allow the IIBP countries to regroup, rearm and reconsider objectives, came when a Brazilian journalist, Se Lobo, was captured in Mozambique, and then escaped. His scoop made headlines around the world. A conflict between Muslims and Christians had been under way in the country for decades. It began as a guerrilla operation by a marginal group of Muslim fanatics, but escalated when they won hold of a northern corner of the country bordering on Lake Malawi. Prior to the First Jihad War, the IIBP had funded the Muslim group modestly and secretly, then, during the war, it had stepped up its backing with air support and troops. When the group had occupied nearly half the country, NATO moved in to help defend the secular (but Christian dominated) government. The dispute should have been settled by the terms of the Singapore Peace Treaty, which gave both the IIBP and the NATO countries six months to withdraw troops, military advisers and use of their hi-tech satellite eye equipment. Moreover, the Mozambique government had promised to amend the country's constitution to provide more autonomy for Muslim-dominated regions in the north. However, with ongoing guerrilla activity, the government had dragged its feet. This was one of the left-over wars. It was a fundamental part of the Singapore Treaty that neither the IIBP or

NATO affiliates should interfere militarily in such conflicts. The journalist Se Lobo discovered that there were hundreds of Syrian and Algerian personnel directing, organising and supplying the Mozambique guerrillas. The government had claimed as much but its claims had fallen on deaf (or closed) ears.

Soon after, in 66, other left-over wars flared up, as if Se Lobo's article had been a starting gun. Each one was brought to the United Nations. The most interested Western countries and groupings protested vehemently at violations of UN resolutions (those which had implemented the Singapore Treaty) but without much consequence. In a rare interview granted to the Western media, carried by *GlobeOne*, Al Zahir called the violations 'minor infringements', and said they would be dealt with. 'Peace is our aim,' he declared, 'and peace is our destiny.' Al Zahir's position as leader of Iran, the IIBP and Muslims across the globe had strengthened considerably since the First Jihad War. *GlobeOne's* front cover portrait made him appear elderly, thoughtful, benign, and the article itself served to provide, for want of a better description, the Al Zahir appeasers with much fuel. Fortunately, I was never in a position where I had to make any decision which would lead our armed forces into a battle and to our sons and daughters dying, but if I had of been, I'm sure I too would have opted for appeasement rather than give any excuse to restart the Jihad War. And, if we had not appeased – by allowing Syrian and Algerian troops to multiply in Mozambique without reply, for example – would it have made any difference. I doubt it, not in the long run.

In 67, things only got worse. The Second Jihad War, the history books say, began in May 68 and came to an end in 71, but this is only half the truth. There was already much turmoil under way long before May 68: the Islamic terrorism and riots in Europe; the rapid escalation of left-over wars where agreements on paper meant nothing in practice; and the emergence of armed Islamic groups in previously peaceful countries and regions, especially in West Africa. And, at the end, there was a cease-fire in 71 but no settlement until the following April, and this only dealt with very major issues. The fear, poverty and hunger of the Grey Years may have helped bring the war to an end, but it did nothing to assist the peace. Today, three decades later, the Christian-dominated rich nations continue to live in fear that a new Al Zahir will appear one day, unify Muslims everywhere, and set light to the fragile truce now guarded by a stronger, but still very flawed, United Nations.

***

In Tilford, a quiet corner of sunny Surrey, Lizette, Jay and I were well insulated from the terrors of war. There was a mosque nearby, but the local Muslim population was surprisingly well integrated. Most of the mosque members were loyal British subjects and opposed Al Zahir's Jihad. One of our near neighbours, Dr Sami Abd al-Jabbaar claimed Pakistani heritage. He was a consultant at Guildford hospital, an official at the local mosque, and regularly featured in the *Surrey News* because of his prize-winning vegetables. Jay played with one of his two boys; and I saw him occasionally whenever we were leaving from, or returning to, our homes on foot at the same time. He never lost an opportunity to condemn the latest terrorist outrage in a European city or IIBP military exercise.

Lizette was fortunate to find a well-paid teaching post at the Farnborough Science University. Jay settled in easily to the middle-sized primary school across the other side of the village. As for me, premature retirement did not suit. For all my adult life I had been faced with busy-ness: people, meetings, papers, deadlines. Now I was spending much of the day alone, in the small office we had had built at the back of Taunton House. For the first and frustrating year in Tilford I attempted to write a book called *The IFSD Years of Expansion* for the same publisher that had handled Alan's work. But I had no will to do the necessary research nor could I find a coherent view or analytical framework to give the book meaning. I had taken no advance, nor signed any contract so, bit by bit, I let the project evaporate. I took up bowls, which I played once or twice a week, weather permitting. It was refreshing to join in the petty squabbles and friendly (and not-so friendly!) sparring, to swap inane remarks about the terrors of the war or the conflicts on the parish council as if they were of equal importance, and to mull over, for hours afterwards, shots made, both good and bad. I spent much time in the garden, usually under instruction from Lizette. And, for Lizette, I read countless books on the art of bridge, in all its variants. I managed to better my technique and learn the conventions, but not my ability to memorise and mentally sort cards, which was more important. Thus, I never improved to the point where Lizette wanted to partner me in competitions (did I ever really want to?). In frustration, and because being a mother didn't leave her that much free time, she eventually stopped badgering me and decided to put her hobby aside for a while. For my own pleasure, I would tune in live whenever there was an important auction of 19th century photographs, and watch it through from beginning to end, drooling over the old images on the screen.

Whatever my daily activity, I looked forward to mid-afternoon when I would stroll through the village to the school to collect Jay, and then, on the return, dawdle slowly back across the green, stopping perhaps at the local shop to buy Jay an ice-jet in summer or a sherbet-dinger in winter. There are dozens of episodes I could recall from Jay's early school days, but this one stands out as well as any other; it was the first time I realised Jay had his own life, his own secret world. During the walk home, I would quiz Jay about his day. He was never very attentive to my questions or responsive, and I was lucky if I caught a snippet of information, about the lunch menu, a special lesson, or another child being told off. On occasions we would walk back from the school with other children and their parents. If the weather was clement we would stop at the playground by the river. One time, when Jay's buds had left, and I was pushing him round on the roundabout, I asked who he played with at school. He told me he was a bit sad. A bit sad? I asked him to explain several times but without result. I reported the conversation to Lizette who suggested he himself might not know why he was sad. Then, later, when I was reading him a story in bed, in his attic room, I asked again about being sad at school. This time he was more forthcoming.

'She makes me sit down, and takes off my shoe. And she doesn't give it back. Until later.' With further gentle questioning I discovered that a girl called Lindsay had taken Jay's shoe several times and each time this had resulted in Jay crying. Lizette and I had assumed Jay was happy and untroubled at school, and so this news – extracted with difficulty – came as a shock. Lizette wanted to approach the school, but I argued we should help Jay deal with the situation on his own. Lizette cautiously gave way and delegated the problem to me. I explained to Jay that Lindsay's actions were definitely wrong, and that, if she took his shoe again, he should seek the assistance of an older child, one who would help. If Lindsay threatened or hurt him, he should report her to a teacher. I have no idea if the advice worked or not, for Jay never talked about being sad again, at least not in relation to life at school.

Jay has pointed out (!) that this is a dismal anecdote, and that I should balance it with 'a nice one' from his early school years. I am happy to oblige. On his seventh birthday, in late September 67, Jay was sent a box of simple magic tricks by Lizette's brother Samuel and his family. One weekday soon after, when the school was closed to pupils for some reason, and Lizette was away all day at work, Jay kept pestering me to show off the tricks. I suggested he save them and put on a show for Lizette and me that evening. For the rest of the day, he beavered away in his attic room, interrupting me in my office only rarely. Once he came to give me a ticket, complete with seat number, code and tear-off section. When he heard the front door, he raced down the stairs to give Lizette a ticket too. At the appointed time, we went together to the top of house. On the door to his room he had pinned a sign saying 'Jay's Marvellous Magic Show'; and inside he had arranged two chairs with seat numbers. Jay himself was hiding in the toy cupboard. A mock deep voice said 'take your seats', and then he appeared, cutely dressed wearing a bow tie and a plastic make-it-yourself top hat which had come with the magic tricks box. This was no static magic show, for the magician needed a member of the audience for each trick, which meant we were both up and down every few minutes choosing a card, closing our eyes, or waving a wand that went limp if we didn't hold it right. We laughed and laughed (except when he lost his props or made a mistake, in which case we pretended not to notice). After each trick we clapped and Jay bowed. When, at the end, we demanded an encore, and explained what we meant, he looked crestfallen at not having any more magic to give us, until we explained it was perfectly acceptable to do his best trick a second time. We applauded enthusiastically again, signalled for Jay to retire from the stage to his toy cupboard, and then departed the attic-theatre. Ten minutes later, Jay came downstairs looking very miserable.

'I feel very sad. I've worked all day and now it's all over.' Sweet, sweet boy. Lizette cuddled him. She wanted to explain about how enjoyment should be sought from the work itself not the result, and how the best cure for sadness was to start work again on the next thing, but he wouldn't listen.

For a couple of years, our lives were complicated by Clint Tuohy, Lizette's former husband and Jay's genetic father. While Lizette had been in Brussels, Clint had considered Jay out of reach, and had abdicated interest and responsibility. This had suited Lizette and me, and had allowed or encouraged us to form the Jay co-op without him. Once back in England, though, we went on a visit north to see Pete, Clarity and Rhoda, and, during that trip, Lizette took the trouble to call on Clint. Thereafter, her ex-husband began transferring funds to Lizette's bank account for Jay's maintenance and, at the same time, demanding access. Lizette returned the monies, and tried, via camphone, to persuade Clint that, after six years of minimal contact between him and Jay, during which time I had effectively taken over as Jay's father, contact with him would only confuse the child. Lizette thought she would be able to reason him round, but she was wrong. His interest in Jay grew to the point of a fixation. He turned up in Tilford, one Saturday lunch-time, uninvited. We treated him hospitably. But after showing him round the village, and taking him for a walk along the river with Jay, we expected him to go. He didn't. He wheedled and whined, and begged to stay the night. Lizette wanted to kick him out, but I couldn't agree. In the morning, Lizette found him playing pick-a-stick with Jay in the lounge. Later, after breakfast and after we had finally got him out of the house, Jay told us that Clint had asked to be called 'Dad'. Lizette was so outraged by Clint's behaviour that she called him immediately, and screamed abuse down the phone while he was driving north. After that he turned up regularly, every few months, always uninvited, always unwelcome and always apologetic. He was never allowed to stay the night again, but, if it was possible, we did let him spend a couple of hours with Jay. Between these visits, there were arguments, threats and counter-threats. Clint demanded more regular access, and indicated he would take legal action. Unfortunately, the Dutch co-op laws, which might have given us some protection in the Netherlands, were not valid in Britain. Lizette counter-attacked by suggesting she might send anonymous letters to the local Stoke media about the unacceptable behaviour of one of its upright citizens and councillors. From Clint's side, I should add, we also received streams of apologies, promises and presents. The whole situation was horribly messy. Lizette and I spent far too much time discussing it between ourselves, and Lizette spent yet more time moaning about Clint on the phone or by email to her friends Rhoda and Clarity.

In autumn 67, Clint vanished from our lives. We learned, from Rhoda, he had formed a new relationship. We assumed it had become convenient for him to forget about Jay. Some years later, when that relationship broke down, Clint again tried to impose himself on us and Jay. He started with phone calls and emails, but when he turned up on our doorstep, we would not let him enter the house or see Jay. Lizette warned him to stay away or she would seek legal advice. Jay can tell his own story about Clint, in his own time, if he can be bothered – I've given him too much space already.

Lizette was a demanding mother, expecting much of her son. This was partly because of her insecurity about the paternal side of Jay's upbringing, in particular Clint's intrusions. But her own background also played a part. From what she told me of 'Pa' and 'Ma' they had been committed parents, never prepared to accept second best. Clearly, the approach had worked with Lizette, and with her elder brother Samuel who had become very successful as an engineer (tidal turbines), but not with the younger brother Mercurio, who, for whatever reason, had opted out of mainstream society. Perhaps, also, the escalating war exaggerated Lizette's disposition in some way. Whatever the reason, she tended to push Jay academically, providing only occasional effusive praise when he produced excellent work, and criticising him regularly for modest or poor work. At times, when she was being overly harsh or pressing him too far, I tried to intervene, but in this aspect of Jay's upbringing, his education, she would not be swayed by my opinions. Certainly, there was little in my track record to inspire any confidence in me as a parent: during the first year of our time in Tilford, I was still making occasional trips to visit another of my sons in prison.

Instead of intervening I observed quietly how Jay learned tricks – not magic ones – to avoid being assigned harder and harder tasks, or being the target of higher and higher expectations: how to pretend he didn't understand what was being asked of him, how to ask sweetly for help over and over again, and how to underplay his own knowledge or ability. As he grew older, so Lizette became partially wise to these games, which caused plenty of strife during Jay's teenage years. I sincerely believe this had no long-term negative effect on Jay's intelligence (I'm on dangerous ground here), but I suspect it did divert him away from Lizette's beloved science subjects, towards less academic ones such as drawing cartoon characters and designing impossible worlds on the computer (and then giving us virtual tours), although this was already later on.

***

I say my interest in writing a book on the IFSD petered out, but this was partly because, after about a year in Tilford, I let myself became involved in other, more engaging projects. I agreed to join a team of retired WWF campaigners to take a close analytical look at ten large recent programmes conducted for or with one of the UN agencies, to see if any lessons could be learned, not on the policies themselves, but on the procedures for winning project funds, for collaboration and for implementation. In addition, I took on two non-executive directorships, one for a large environmental consultancy, Greenwell-Plasset, and the other for a subsidiary of Euroil which made and marketed a synthetic aviation fuel, a competitor to Vivido. Greenwell-Plasset paid me only a modest wage which I balanced against the idea that I might have some beneficial influence over their activities. Euroil, though, rewarded me very well and demanded little in return. I had no doubt I was being paid because my name and former position enhanced the company's international credibility, but as long I was not asked to do anything unethical, or vaguely unethical, I didn't mind. In fact, during a preliminary lunch with Euroil people, at the Greensand Retreat (which had been completely refurbished in the Romaine Riche style, and looked and felt more luxurious than ever), I drew such a collection of smug smiles of self-satisfaction when I told them I had once worked for Euroil in Brussels as a young man (but without any details!), that I decided there and then to give them a rough ride. I spoke frankly, controversially even, at the meetings I attended, and soon became more trouble than I was worth. When my three year contract expired, no-one offered to renew it, and I had no time to ask why.

In April 68, Guido and Mireille came to stay at Taunton House for a week. They brought presents for Jay and expensive chocolates for Lizette. I joined them on various explorations, to the South Coast to see the old docks in Portsmouth and to promenade in Brighton; and to London to see some of the best shows I had seen in a very long time. This was at the same time as the IIBP's unexpected missile attack on Rhodes, the one which wiped out a European Army base, and led to the formal start of the Second Jihad War. On one day, we took Jay out of school and went to Alexandra Palace, which had 15-

20 years earlier been the greatest museum on interactive broadcasting history and technology in Europe. Jay and I watched the same 30 minute holographic movie *Jungle Journey* that I'd first seen with Diana and Guido on a trip to London in the late 40s. Guido, who had oversold the place to Mireille, spent most of the day criticising the lack of investment and innovation. On our return, I received a message from Tommy, who was still at the IFSD (and with whom I corresponded occasionally), informing me that MarySue's son, Conrad, had been killed in Rhodes. She and I sent each other new year cards, but otherwise had not communicated for ages. I had known Conrad slightly, and MarySue had talked about him often. Once, Guido and I had met MarySue and her son while shopping in Leiden. Conrad was a young teenager at the time, and Guido only seven or eight, but, for a few minutes while MarySue and I chatted, the two boys joined forces to admire the ultra-cycles and cycle paraphernalia in a shop window.

I was under the impression that Guido and Mireille had come for a break, but Guido's mood was not as light as usual, and both of them prevaricated whenever I asked about their plans and projects. After supper one night, Guido took me for a drink and a manly chat in the village pub, the Barley Mow. We bought a bottle of English rosé wine (why do I remember this?). As soon as we had settled down at a corner table, he told me the news he'd been holding back all week, the news he'd come to Tilford to deliver.

'We've decided to go and live in Ecuador, in Quito. There's a theatre there waiting for us. Teatro Sucre. Our names are already etched into the crumbling facade.' He paused, waiting for my reaction, but I didn't say anything. 'We met a man, an entrepreneur, called Felix Rico Montechristo. He was in Paris, he came to our show. Some people call him Felix, others Rico. He's Ecuadorian but his mother was American. His main business is managing celebrities ...' and here Guido listed half a dozen names of footballers and singers who he thought I might recognise but didn't. Then, still trying to build a credibility bridge between Felix and me, he mentioned that he managed the Ecuadorian volley-ball team, and in particular, its captain Carlos Mallastro. I did know of Mallastro because he had led the Ecuadorian team to a place in the quarter-finals at the 63 world cup in Munich, and, only last year, to a semi-final place at the world cup in São Paulo.

'Felix has bought a dilapidated theatre in central Quito, and wants to refurbish it, make it glorious again. He wants us to manage the artistic side. We've accepted. We're leaving at the end of May.'

I knew they had been to Quito some months earlier, but I had no idea it was more than a holiday. Mireille had studied European literature and literary traditions at the Sorbonne, but then demeaned herself (this is the assessment of her father, Didier, long before the wedding) by becoming a stage manager. Guido, after completing his degree in Amsterdam, went to Paris, partly to study mime, and partly to be near Mireille. After realising the limits of his acting ability, he reluctantly gravitated towards the same occupation as his mother, theatre design, for which he had a real talent. A year or so after the wedding, the two of them discovered, to their own surprise, how much they enjoyed working in tandem on the same productions. Subsequently, in-between separate regular paid assignments, they teamed up together to direct and design small-scale adventurous plays with low production costs and in which actors would perform more for love than money.

'How long are you planning to stay?' I asked. Guido drank swiftly, looked away and then back at me.

'Two, three years. We have no fixed plans. But we'll come back, to see you and Mum, of course, and Mireille's parents.'

'It's so far away,' I said. Confusion and sadness must have shown on my face, for Guido went on quickly, wanting to explain.

'And far away from the coming war. It's not that we're afraid, but that we want no part of it. We feel it has nothing to do with us, with our lives.'

'I'm sure many people feel that way in France and in England and all over Europe, but they're not emigrating to another continent. France, Holland, Britain, they remain among the most safe, cultured and sophisticated places on earth.'

'I know. We know. It's not the only reason. It's a great opportunity too. We could never hope to run a whole theatre in Paris, not for years and years, and certainly not without the help of Didier. And to be honest, Mireille is sick of him trying to help her. She falls for his offer of money sometimes, and then is too ashamed to tell me. That's not all, he talks secretly to friends and colleagues in the business, and encourages them somehow to give her work. Then halfway towards a production she finds out, and it's too late to extricate herself. He's suffocating her, us. And Helene is becoming impossible too. She keeps discovering new distant relations, holding dinner parties for each one, and insisting – really insisting – on us being there so she can introduce us. She's uncovered dozens of relations in her own family, Chastrain, and twice as many Rocards, all within a train ride of Paris. Family is so important, she says. She's become obsessed.'

'I didn't know things had got that bad. I haven't had any contact with them, Does your mother see them?'

'Not much, I don't think Karl has time for them any more. They used to get on when they were younger. Now, they're too rich for him. He despises anyone with money. I don't see Mum either.' Guido didn't need to tell me. Several times over the years he had confided that he positively loathed Karl, mostly I think because of his influence over Diana. 'And Karl and Mireille have a mutual aversion to each other.'

'I can't imagine anyone not liking Mireille. She's so pretty and thoughtful. Lizette was delighted with the chocolates ...'

'She won't accept Karl's brusqueness or arrogance without a challenge. He hates her telling him off. I watch Mum put up with the behaviour, but Mireille won't.'

'So you're running away from family as much as from war, I hope that doesn't include me.'

'Mireille adores you, you know that,' he said, pointedly, jokingly, leaving himself out of the response.

'What did your mother say?'

'We haven't told her; she's next.'

'And Mireille's parents?'

'They're last.'

'So I'm the dress rehearsal.'

'It was Mireille's idea. We thought it would give us more confidence if we had your blessing.'

'And was it Mireille's idea that you should talk to me alone, man to man, down the pub?' I didn't wait for him to answer. 'This Felix character worries me. Won't you be completely dependant on him once you're out there? And neither of you speak much Spanish.'

'We've been studying night and day. And Felix is cool, we've discussed this a lot. He's a true patron. He paid for our trip, he's offered us good long-term contracts, and he's shown us a delightful villa we can rent cheaply. He loves our ideas for the theatre. We're going to make it the most important playhouse in the country. If we stay in Paris we could work for 20 years and not be noticed and, even if we were, we'd never stop worrying that Didier was pulling strings behind the scenes.'

I gave him my blessing, which is not to say I wasn't sorry about them moving to another continent or concerned about the risky enterprise. To my shame, I suspected Guido and his wife, having been introduced to famous actors and writers during their brief lives, were seeking a short cut to eminence. I underestimated them both.

***

A few months after Mireille and Guido had departed for South America, I became involved in a project – thanks to Horace, or so he claims – which was to preoccupy me for several years. Horace was one of our most regular visitors, rarely a month went by when he didn't stay over on a Thursday or Friday night; now and then he came on Sundays too. He had found a route through from London to Southampton, passing nearby us, which took him only half an hour longer than on the toll roads, and saved him from paying the high charges. Horace was not a poor man, despite devoting his life to the House of Commons, because he and his brother Tim had successfully developed a smallish property business. Yet he had a compulsive hatred of road tolls. Horace did not oppose them publicly for that would have been no different from opposing taxes in general, but he was often the first critic to appear on the media whenever a hike in tolls was announced, whoever was in government.

I was always happy to see Horace. Lizette tired of him at times. If he was droning on about a topic of the day, usually the war and the policy of the British government towards the latest developments, she promptly told him to change the record or to shut up and let someone else get a word in edgeways. He never took offense. When she was annoyed by him, though, she would suddenly disappear, to the garden or the bedroom. Then Horace, often glossy after too many drinks, would drift into airing a grievance or rehearsing an argument or statement he was hoping to make in the House, and I would drift too – but into sleep. I should say that Horace was a polite guest, ever considerate, and always ready to take us out to eat. He regularly sent us invitations for events in London (which we rarely accepted). Jay called him Uncle Talk-a-lot, although there's was nothing remotely uncle-ish about him. He had no idea how to converse with Jay.

Sometimes, though, he would bring Tim, his younger brother, who did communicate well with our son. Tim had divorced years ago, and his three children had long since gone their separate ways. He missed seeing them regularly. Tim and Horace were similar in appearance with their medium-height, spectacles, and wispy regenerated hair. But Tim was fatter all round, with a large paunch, puffy cheeks and a second chin. Strangely, it was Tim who was the more active of the two, having played golf and done some sailing in his time. Horace kept surprisingly lean, without ever taking up a sport or control-ling his diet. Whenever Tim drew attention to this difference between them, which he did regularly (why, I never understood), Horace claimed, one way or another, that it was mental activity that had kept him thin, thereby implying the opposite was true for his brother. This enraged Tim, who had spent his life far removed from Horace's intellectual world, mostly using his accountancy skills to market country estates, and also to run their joint property business.

During one of his stay overs (before I lose the thread of this narrative entirely), Horace mentioned that he had lunched with Matt Fortune during the week. The two politicians had remained friendly since I introduced them to each other in 57. Matt had retired from Parliament and gone to work part-time for the London branch of the European Institute of Politics and Diplomacy (EIPD), which was one of the most important and respected cross-border think-tanks in Europe. Matt had told Horace about an ambitious study on the future of the United Nations, and that the EIPD was still considering who should administer the project. At this point in the conversation, Horace claimed, he had proposed me. Later, though, Matt said my name was already on a draft short list.

Without knowing it, this was the work I had been waiting for. The EIPD's illustrious 50 year reputation had not been won by shadow boxing with governments or other institutions over issues of the day, or by responding to requests from the European Union (which had provided its funding for many years) to investigate a particular topic, both of which it did regularly, but by involving the highest calibre politicians and diplomats to launch debates on big questions, on the controversial subjects of tomorrow. Ten days after Horace's visit, I received a call from Matt himself inviting me to the Institute in Cavendish Square. A week later, when I was ensconced in his office, he explained in detail about a major study on the role of the UN after the war. It would investigate whether there was a case to start again, with a fresh model. The working hypothesis would be that the UN had served well for 100 years, but that its failure to avoid the First and Second Jihad Wars was a sign of terminal failure. Would it be possible, the EIPD wanted to know, to combine the experience of the UN with that of the European Union (undoubtedly the most successful regional integration model in history) and find a new way forward for the world in the 22nd century. The study was to be called *World Union – thinkable or unthinkable?*. He briefed me on how it was to be planned and implemented. I listened intently. My role would be that of administrator, organising and overseeing a group of 30 prominent political characters, 'wise men', through from beginning to end (three years in all) and liaising with the EIPD. Yes. I said yes. Matt, genial as ever and with sideburns so bushy and white he could have materialised from a Dickens novel, thanked me profusely.

Initially, during the early stages of the project in autumn 68, I was obliged to travel to a large number of meetings in Brussels and other European capitals (and to arrange ad hoc Jay-care for the first time since being in Tilford), which was a pain because journeys, whether by train or plane, took two or three times longer than in normal circumstances due to the heightened security arrangements, and security alerts. Once the study proper was under way, I was able to manage it partly from home and partly from the EIPD office in London which provided the necessary secretariat and cam-conferencing facilities. I organised for our wise men to be provided with a library of background documents. These included the two important, but much over-looked, analyses carried out decades earlier by management consultancies; several documents from my term in the IFSD's future policy division; numerous papers and reports that various UN agencies had produced on their own future; and whatever papers/books we could track down that had already been written on the subject of world government.

The wise men elected Dr Luigi Costa, by dint of his seniority, as their chairman. He had been a prime minister of Italy, and there were only two other ex-prime ministers on the panel, both from countries smaller than Italy. In my opinion, he was not the best man for the job. He had been a pedantic leader, safely honest and bureaucratic, but short on charisma and inspiration. His main claim to posterity came during his first stint as Italian prime minister, in the 40s, when he had been one of the loudest voices in Europe advocating the Next Step and propelling a strong European input towards what became known as the Djakarta Settlement. Certainly, he was one of the most internationally-aware leaders Italy had produced in the 21st century.

More than half of the wise men approached their task with determined objectivity, while the others let politics dictate their opinions. Most of this latter group had held high office, and, although retired from the political front line, retained constituencies (if not with voters then among colleagues within their own parties) which needed servicing to one degree or another. A few of this group, which included Costa, could see no further internationally than the politics of the ongoing war, so every idea they offered, every opinion they put forward, every bit of text they drafted was tainted in some way by their positions on the war. Fortunately, these individuals did not all pull in the same direction; moreover, Costa's position as chairman gave him no extra weight, so long as the others were vigilant enough not to let him exert undue control over their opinions. It was my job to ensure they were vigilant, and to keep the wise men's thoughts firmly focused on the long term and not on the present or short term. Thus, I often found myself in conflict with Costa. He would ring me up at all times of day and night, demanding to know why I'd distributed this or that document or why I'd drawn conclusions from a meeting or a round-robin of opinions which ignored his position. Other times he called to discuss the most minor of changes to a draft agenda simply to tailor it to his preferred shape. I dealt with him firmly and fairly. When necessary, I reminded him of our respective roles: his was to be a wise man, to think forward, strategically, imaginatively; and mine was to implement a framework in which he and his colleagues could do this to the best of their ability.

For the best part of three years, this job kept me lively. It diverted my attention from ruminating too long on daily reports which told of an ever increasing number of military campaigns, bombing raids, destruction, death. I was again in contact with important and interesting characters, many of whom I'd met, or heard of or read about in the media. It felt like a useful task and, therefore by extension, I felt useful. Prior to the EIPD study, Lizette had begun to worry about my lack of employment and so, when I started, she was content to see me busy again, even though it meant I had to travel and be away from home more often. She relished me confiding in her about the clashes between the wise men, whether because of character or policy; and she took my occasional requests for her opinion so seriously that she would think about them for days.

What did we achieve? *World Union – thinkable or unthinkable?* is available on the net, and through any good library, so there's no purpose in my reiterating it in any detail here. Also, as is evident, there is no World Union today, and the United Nations is extant, with much the same basic underlying structure as it has always had. Nevertheless, the aim of the report was to launch a debate, and this it definitely achieved. The European Union, for example, having largely bailed out of the UN in the 70s as a consequence of the Jihad War, deliberated carefully over the ideas in our report. It set up an analysis group and produced several major policy documents. Eventually, though, it lost its nerve (or saw sense, depending on where you stand) and decided to re-support the UN model.

Now, as I dictate – with next century optimism filling the corridors of power – very serious consideration is again being given to major changes in the UN system: a more powerful General Assembly; a complete overhaul of the structure of the agencies to provide greater coherence; better coordination, and clearer lines of accountability towards the General Assembly; and, as we proposed 30 years earlier in the EIPD report, a virtual parliament to provide a degree of democratic control over the General Assembly. We calculated that a world parliament would need no fewer than 4,000 members, with only one physical plenary session a year hosted by countries in rotation. Otherwise plenary debates and votes could, with the right technology and safeguards, be adequately conducted on the net (we produced a supplementary report on how this could be done). To prepare for virtual plenary sessions, 50-60 special committees could function in a virtual way but with more frequent physical meetings at permanent bases in selected locations. Crucially, the report suggested, each member of this visionary parliament would be made respon-sible not only for representing his/her constituency to the parliament, but for representing the objectives and achievements of the parliament to his/her constituency. Any voter who did not know what the world parliament did, the report proposed, should be advised by the UN itself through the media against voting for the incumbent member. I only mention this last point because it was the single good idea (to my mind) that Costa brought to the report. He had suffered during his political career, he told me repeatedly, because he had been unable to transfer his enthusiasm for the objectives of the UN or the European Union to his public, and consequently he had never reaped sufficient applause at home for his achievements internationally. He had always wondered why this was, and how individual citizens could be made more aware of their responsibilities beyond municipal and national boundaries.

***

Flora died yesterday. Chintz told me. She came last night when her shift was over. I asked the standard question: was there any suffering, any pain? The answer was no, it's always no. Pain is what I personally fear most. If the doctors and the plumbing and the pills cannot keep the pain away, I'll not be able to sustain the will to hold on and finish this book. Flora's going makes me feel especially vulnerable since, coincidentally, we had both planned to die on the same day. I too could expire at any time. I might not wake up tomorrow. Conversely, if I feel as well on 31 January as I do today, there'll be pressure – in my head and from Jay – to postpone my deathday. But so long as I have completed these Reflections, I am determined not to falter, not to change my mind. The euthanasia forms I signed require two doctors to agree that my condition is one of 'rapid deterioration'. I only need to stop popping the pills for that to happen. It's what people do, people like me who wish to move deliberately and considerately to their end, people like me who insist on keeping control of the inner light switch until the last.

To cheer ourselves up Chintz and I watched Amy Mistral's classic 60s thriller *Zola's Loop*. Over the years I've experienced all the possible plot sequences, so I let Chintz decide on Zola's timeslip factor at the three choice junctions. She opted for a route which led Zola through a very early film called *The Third Man* (references to which appeared in many Mistral movies). Afterwards, knowing how much Chintz enjoys my gossip, I bragged about having met Mistral and been present at her infamous Third Man centenary party. And then I rambled on about Babashkin's remake of *The Third Man*. Vadim Babashkin, unknown in the early 80s when he made the film, substituted war-torn Karaganda in the final months of the Jihad conflict for Vienna in the aftermath of the 20th century's Second World War. Some thought the film was the arrogant conceit of a young man and overly stylised, others (including myself) that it was a worthy homage.

Kazakhstan was indeed torn apart by the Second Jihad War. At the outset, it was generally thought, *Encyclopaedia Universal* explains, that the IIBP's aims in the Europe/Central Asia region were only to install an Islamic Republic in Kazakhstan, and to support Azerbaijan's territorial claims to part of Armenia. The occasional missile attacks from Turkey, Algeria and Libya on military bases in Greece, Spain and Italy respectively were judged to be no more than an attempt to keep the European nations focused on their own territory, and to ensure minimal support for Russia in helping to defend Kazakhstan and Armenia. The US, having been chastened by its unprofitable and costly involvement in the First Jihad War (not to mention the political lessons of Tarbuck's Gamble), and under the leadership of the mealy-mouthed President Paul Kidderminster, declined to involve itself in any of the main IIBP-led conflicts in Europe, Asia or Africa. Kidderminster and most of the US administration believed (or wished to believe) the IIBP's statements of support for the long-standing (but fragile) Palestine-Israel peace treaty, and did not want to pull any trigger that might switch Al Zahir's attention towards Israel. NATO, which had been through more formations during the 21st century than a zylovex, required its members to help each other under clearly defined and varied conditions. Only in late 69, when Turkey and the IIBP, after weeks of sustained bombing, invaded Cyprus, then Rhodes, both of which fell easily, and then Crete, did the North Americans (US, Canada and Mexico) finally agree such conditions were met. Their military strength was employed to reinforce the Mediterranean coastal frontiers of Portugal, Spain, Italy, France and Greece. But, while this was happening, Turkish troops moved into eastern Bulgaria, as ever with IIBP campaigns, 'to liberate repressed Muslims' and to bring 'peace for all peoples'.

We had no idea at this point where Al Zahir and the IIBP would stop, or where they could made to stop. Every day our screens brought frightening images: the extraordinarily flamboyant displays by IIBP nations of their weaponry; hundreds of thousands of Muslim troops, all in disciplined formations (reminiscent of Russia and China during the 20th century Cold War, historians said) across North Africa, in north and west Turkey, in Azerbaijan, Uzbekistan, Kyrgyzstan, all ready and willing to die for the Jihad cause, for Allah; and scenes of chaos where IIBP missiles had found their way through the NATO defenses, missed their military targets and killed dozens, or in some cases, hundreds of Spanish or Greek citizens. But we heard nothing of other major conflicts in Africa (civil war in Nigeria for example) and in the Far East (including a massive uprising in the Muslim Xinjing province of China). Al Zahir, himself, could be seen day after day repeating the same ideas: 'Peace is our aim, peace is our destiny. Christian nations must share wealth with their Muslim brothers;' and (a particular favourite of mine), 'The IFSD is but a petty bribe, a dummy to our mouths – now we demand what is rightfully ours.' Some commentators began speculating that if Bulgaria and Greece were to fall, the

'IIBP hoards' could trample through the Balkans; and this might give them the confidence to take the Moorish route through Southern Spain; Sicily could fall too, and Sardinia. Many of these same analysts urged, once again as they had done a decade earlier, for NATO to use its superior nuclear and 'ultimate weapon' capability. Yet no single leader across the Christian world came out in favour of such a strategy. The simple, awful truth was that all European airspace could not be guaranteed all of the time, despite NATO's technological superiority, and the IIBP would, one way or the other, be able to deliver nuclear and/or biochemical weapons. If he chose to, most Europeans believed, Al Zahir could kill 100,000 if not half a million civilians somewhere – whether in Spain, Portugal, Latvia, Ukraine or Finland – in one strike.

With Europe becoming the focus of the war itself, so political and social strife multiplied across the continent. The media was full of stories about families torn apart by bereavement or injury, or because one sibling had chosen to fight while another campaigned for demilitarisation, or because some members had fled to Australia or Canada and been branded cowards. Violent clashes between peace protesters and those willing to fight for freedom became commonplace, in the workplace, in pubs, in suburban streets, and during weekend protest marches. Worst of all, though, was the breakdown caused between Christians and Muslims. Distrust spread like a plague, and wherever ignorance and fear took hold, so racism and victimisation followed in its wake. The vast majority of Muslims in Europe, as with the vast majority of Christians, agnostics and atheists were fair minded people who did not want this war or support the actions of the IIBP. But there were a few Muslims that did. Either they felt oppressed or unfairly treated, or else they agreed with Al Zahir's philosophy. The most fanatical ones worked secretly, as terrorists, helping to promote fear and panic in the most unexpected of places; others worked to encourage and finance the peace movements. European governments, depending on their politics and their national situations, reacted differently; but all of them went further than they had in the First Jihad War to monitor Muslim individuals and communities.

***

Our neighbour Sami was a very reasonable man. His paternal grandparents had emigrated from Pakistan to England in the last century. His father had won a scholarship to a good medical university, married a mixed race girl (half English, half Indian) and become a successful geriatrician. Sami himself was an orthopaedist, working with the national health service, and had married an English woman, Iona, with no trace of foreign blood. Despite this history, and despite the fact that he practised, with Iona who had converted, a popular

338

Westernised form of Islam, he was obliged to register at a regional centre set up for the purpose. He had to sign a form affirming his support for the British government and denouncing any connection with Muslim terrorism or illegal propaganda. It was degrading, he told me. Moreover, as he and all Muslims knew, this registration process was an empty gesture, a sop to warmongers and fear-spreaders, since only signed-up members of mosques or other Muslim organisations had to register, and no terrorist or political agitator would let him or herself appear on such lists. Fortunately, for Great Britain, which recovered relatively quickly from the war and the Grey Years, we had more Muslims of Sami's ilk, willing to keep their resentments low key, and ready to work patiently for the good of the community as a whole, than many other countries.

I was fond of Sami, but not of Iona. Lizette had no time for either of them. She judged them smarmy, socially competitive and materialistic. As a consequence, Lizette tried to dampen down Jay's friendship with their son, David (who went to a different school), because she thought he was a bad influence. For about a year they were forever scampering around together, but then it was Jay who dropped David, under pressure, I suspected, from his non-Muslim buds at school. In the late summer of 69, though, two incidents led us to give our neighbours more consideration.

One weekend at the village playground, Lizette witnessed a vicious assault on David by Lindsay, who, by then had moved on from primary school bully to teenage terror. Jay had not come home in time for supper, so Lizette went to find him at the playground down by the river. David was lying on the ground and Lindsay was screaming verbal abuse and lightly kicking him at the same time. Jay and a friend of his were calling – not very urgently – for Lindsay to stop. Two other children were laughing. Lizette intervened immediately, established that David was not hurt, and attempted to censure Lindsay. She ambled away laughing.

Ten days later, Sami came to see me very early on a Saturday morning. He appeared distraught, face unshaven and grim, hair uncombed and shirt sleeves loose. His vegetable and fruit garden had been vandalised in the night. I was still in jamas, but he insisted I come immediately to inspect the damage. Elaborate cane frames for beans and raspberries had been crushed to the ground; various green vegetables had been kicked apart and trampled on; and marrows, pumpkins, aubergines and melons had all been sliced into pieces. He was hoping I might have heard or seen something in the night, but I had not, nor had Lizette or Jay, or any of our other neighbours. Later the same day, Sami came over to discuss if we thought he should go to the police and/or to the local newspaper. Lizette was adamant that he should certainly go to the police. She argued that if nothing was done, the hooligan would continue with impunity.

Sami, though, was cautious. Whether the attack was racist or personal, he did not want it to lead – deliberately or by accident – to any escalation of racial tension in the village. I tended to agree with his approach, and he went away having decided to take no action, other than to spend the rest of the weekend trying to rehabilitate his garden. When Sami had gone, Lizette let the full extent of her anger show, not only against Sami, who she suspected of cowardice, driven by his or Iona's determination not to lose face in public, but against me for giving him moral support.

There would be no more to these two anecdotes were it not for a conversation I had with Jay a few days ago.

'Did Sami Abdi ever find out who did it?' Jay asked.

'Dr Abdi. Is that what you called him? Sami Abdi? No, I don't think so. Although the same thing happened again the next year, didn't it. And then, when we lost the sun, he gave up. It was Allah's will.'

'I knew.'

'You knew what?'

'I knew who it was, who messed up Abdi's garden.'

'How? Who was it?'

'She told us herself. It was Lindsay Durring, the primary school bully. She's the one who stole my shoes. She also knifed open my bag once, stole other kid's lunch money, and started a cannabis cabal in the bicycle shed. She wrecked the bowls green once ...'

'I don't remember. Was I was away?'

'She used a mechanical device to churn up holes in the grass. We laughed when she boasted about it at school, partly because she was a good entertainer, and it didn't sound that serious – sorry Pa – but most of all because we weren't the victims in this instance. She calmed down a lot for a period, during one school year, the year before the incidents with David and Sami's garden. We had a teacher, I forget his name, who had a lot of time for Lindsay, encouraged her comic side, and listened to her long after others had got tired of her lies and exaggerations. He only stayed a year at Tilford. After that Lindsay went from bad to worse. Later, while at secondary school and during the Grey Years, she burnt down the village hall. It was the night before the Ramadan play. You must remember that.'

'Why didn't you tell us any of this at the time? Especially about Sami's garden?'

'I don't know. I might have been afraid, or I didn't think it was important. She was caught for the village hall arson, and went to a junior prison. The mother and a younger sister moved away. I don't think I ever heard of them again.'

'You should have told us.'

'We thought the whole village knew. Poor old Sami Abdi, I think he loved his vegetables more than his children. David used to tell me he wished he had a father the same as you ...'

'Me?'

'Yes, collecting me from school, reading me bedtime stories, defending me against Ma.' He said it casually, as though he were referring to a third person. I closed my eyes to savour the idea that Jay had thought of me so well, even back then when he was a child.

'I didn't know you set me up as a role model for your friends.'

'I had to as it goes. When you came to collect me from school, they all called you my grandad: "Look Jay, there's your grandad." '

Surely, this was sufficient punishment for relishing a false pleasure, but Jay hadn't finished ruining the moment.

'Lindsay nicknamed you Wrinkle Man.'

'She should see me now.'

***

Lizette did lose her temper at times, not only with Jay when he refused to understand a simple precept from science or maths, or when he dodged out of working, but with me. She and I rarely argued over practical arrangements, as Diana and I had, but over points of principle, politics or morality. The argument over Sami's garden was such a case. More often than not, it was my laid-back, laissez-faire attitude rather than my actual position that infuriated her, to the point of shouting. I'm not sure I can explain this properly, since it sounds bizarre. I used to say to her that a lifetime of public service meetings was enough to trim the passion off any individual, but this alone could incense her. I think she felt that if she got angry with me, I would get angry back; but, when I didn't, she got angrier still as if any lesser reaction might undermine the justification for her original exasperation. Then I would compromise on the point we had been discussing, and this infuriated her further. During these (short-lived and, I must stress, infrequent) episodes, I was often to be found – apparently – without a backbone.

After we had been in Tilford a few years, there was a period when Lizette's temper shortened significantly and became more personal. I thought the war might be to blame. It had recently veered towards Europe and was thus the subject of daily debate. Yet, Lizette's anger seemed to stem more directly from Jay's less-than-perfect performance at school or my continuing involvement in the EIPD study, which meant I was away and busy far more often than I had been hitherto. I did not say anything or draw attention to the problem; I hoped it would go away. And it did, almost overnight.

I was aware that Lizette was bored with her job, and longed to return to research. I had said we should move if she could find a good position somewhere else in the home counties. She was reluctant, not only because she was happy with our plan to send Jay to the Witley school when he reached 11 and did not want to disrupt our lives, but because she loved Taunton House. I did not, though, make the connection between her job dissatisfaction and her erratic moods. One day in February 70 Lizette returned from work, radiantly happy. She had been to the hairdressers in the morning, which invariably lifted her spirits, and she had a bag full of shopping with knick-knacks for Jay and me. She also had an announcement. There was a research/lecturer position falling vacant at Surrey University in Guildford. She would apply for it, she predicted, and she would get it. Our lives improved appreciably from that moment, apart from a tense month when, because of the draconian government cutbacks in public spending, there appeared to be a doubt over funds for the position. Notwithstanding her excitement, it was an awkward move for Lizette, involving a loss of seniority, a cut in pay, and a return to research in an area for which she had no particular expertise.

I cannot claim to understand in detail what she did at Guildford, but it was linked to the efficiency of collecting electricity from plastic glass. Lizette's boss, Professor Sidney Jensen, who had spent his entire career devoted to photovoltaics, saw no reason why every window on earth shouldn't produce electricity. It was only a question of cost and efficiency. I knew from my experience at the IFSD that photovoltaic windows were near standard in buildings above a certain size in cities with plenty of sun where electricity supply was expensive. I also knew that, with time and effort, they had become cheaper, more efficient, more reliable and easier to install. But this was a long way from Jensen's dream. Lizette's role, as I understood it, was to work on the molecular mechanisms by which the photovoltaic film-covered plastic glass created and transmitted electricity in low light conditions. This entailed creating new forms of the photovoltaic film, through micro-biomolecular manipulation, and then testing each one for a range of properties. Promising variants – I usually heard about them – were then given more substantial tests. It sounded laborious, but Lizette enthused about her work, and she soon became very fond of Jensen and her other colleagues. Then, of course, after the Toba explosion, the research became much more important. Jensen's team never made any substantial scientific breakthrough, not while Lizette was there, but it surely contributed to the sum total of knowledge, which itself led (not during the Grey Years alas) to a rapid expansion in the use of, the now generically-named, z-glass.

We – Lizette and I and the people we talked to – took only cursory notice of Toba when it first began to splutter. Not only had there been dire warnings about the volcano for years, but the first big eruption had to compete, news-wise, with the following: NATO's withdrawal from western Crete; a NATO air-raid on Istanbul which resulted in nine aircraft shot down; a mosque explosion in Marseilles killing a group of 35 Muslim schoolchildren; and an Intent missile deliberately aimed at Cathedral Sainte-Marie Majeure in Toulon, on a Sunday morning, killing 200. There is no doubt that, at this time, in September 70, the IIBP was still on the attack, winning the war, and Europe was very much on the defensive. The Turks with the help of Iranian, Syrian and Iraqi forces had won substantial territory in eastern Bulgaria and eastern Greece. Constanta, Bucharest, Sofia, Thessaloniki, Malta were all subject to regular attack. Several Greek islands were already under Turkish and/or Egyptian occupation. Russia was finding it equally difficult to help Kazakhstan defend its large land mass, and had all but given up on Armenia. It was also considering a major strategic retreat behind the Caucasus leaving troublesome Georgia to be divided between Turkey and Azerbaijan, or so the media reported. The US had finally entered the war a year earlier and inflicted substantial damage on the aggressive states in several arenas; mostly, though, it had helped stall, but not necessarily prevent, assaults by the North African nations across the Mediterranean.

Most historians thus agree that the Toba eruption saved parts of Europe from a Muslim future. They are divided as to how much territory they believe the IIBP forces could have conquered, and as to how far the ambitions of Al Zahir and the IIBP went (depending on the extent to which they believe the writings and retrospective claims of various Islamic leaders at the time). There is no dispute among them, however, that Al Zahir intended from his earliest days in power to win Israel back for the Palestine people, and that his strategy of duping NATO (not Israel itself, which never trusted him) into believing otherwise was all too successful.

Only when it became clear a few days later that upwards of 100,000 people had died immediately and many more were still dying as a result of the initial explosions in the Toba caldera, did we all begin to pay much closer attention to the media reports. The images were terrifying: the isle of Samosir disappearing into the sky as gigantic plumes of rock and rubble and ash (a 30 kilometres high mushroom cloud); the waters of Lake Toba flooding out across thousands of square kilometres of Sumatra, wiping out hundreds of villages and those inhabitants that hadn't managed to escape; and the airfalls destroying property and crops across Sumatra itself and the peninsula of Malaya, and killing unfortunates in cars hit by falling boulders, or caught in collapsing buildings. And that – as is common knowledge – was only the start.

The modern world knew about war, had coped with it throughout its history; nations, societies, and cultures had survived and grown stronger as a result of its terrors and horrors and tragedies. But it knew nothing about a catastrophe on the scale of Toba, a volcanic eruption more powerful than 1,000 class A nuclear bombs, the media said. Humankind had no experience, no relevant history, no cultural memory to draw on. The five months of permanent night in most of Southeast Asia and the Indian subcontinent led to a minimum of 100 million deaths mostly from hunger and disease, but also because of the violence that came with an epidemic of robbing, looting and marauding. Some countries managed better than others, depending on the strength of their economic and political alliances with the richer nations. China, which had made no friends during the First or Second Jihad Wars, and which, because of the prevailing winds, caught the worst of the short-term full darkness, suffered very badly.

Before the full extent of the disaster became apparent, Al Zahir was able to maintain his war in Europe and surrounding areas. But the volcanic aerosols having settled dark night on a fifth of the world's population for several months spread out through the troposphere worldwide, reducing daylight, initially with a haze, then with the equivalent of cloud cover. When signs of determined protest against the costs of the war began to surface in the Muslim countries, the IIBP decided, once again as it had during the first war, to focus all its forces on Israel. It consolidated gains in Europe, and eight of the Brotherhood's nations turned their full air and missile power on the Jews. Because of the nuclear winter already descending on the world and because it was ready to fight to the death, Israel used three nuclear bombs (two class C and one class B) on Lebanon, Syria and Iraq. Syria responded in kind, destroying Haifa. Muslim troops stormed in from Egypt, Jordan, Syria and Lebanon. The US made a token effort to help Israel, but would not employ its nuclear weapons. In any case, it was heavily occupied in Europe, and becoming preoccupied with its own domestic situation in response to the loss of sunlight.

Opposition to Al Zahir's war continued to grow with massive domestic protests from Rabat to Islamabad: Muslims everywhere were scared, and they wanted their governments to attack problems of crop failure, water contamination and disease, not Christians or Jews any longer. In December 71, some 14 months after the Toba eruption, the IIBP finally agreed to a cease-fire and to begin peace negotiations. Four months later, on 15 April 72 in Colombo, NATO and the IIBP signed a territorial treaty which is no less controversial today than it was then. More than half of Israel (which had already lost land in the First Jihad War) was divided up between Syria, Lebanon, Jordan and Egypt. Turkey took small bites out of southern Bulgarian and eastern Greece. It also retained Cyprus and Rhodes (and other sundry islands). Crete became a divided island administered by NATO and the IIBP (and, evidently, has remained divided between independent Crete and Turkish Crete, mirroring what happened to

Cyprus in the 20th century). Georgia and Armenia held on to their independence, while Russia, Turkmenistan, Uzbekistan and Kyrgyzstan all accrued territory in Kazakhstan, and an Islamic Republic was installed in what was left of the country.

The future of the United Nations took more than another ten years to resolve (as did sundry other NATO/IIBP-provoked disputes around the world).

Although these tumultuous events of history are common knowledge, it is difficult to make sense of our own lives without some reference to them. On the other hand, given their impact on our world (international and local) and the suffering they caused, it feels wrong to skim over them so lightly. But I continue to try and hold fast to my own Reflections.

***

Apart from the comfort and joy of having each other, Lizette and I were fortunate in so many ways. We benefited from being in Europe, which was relatively rich and technologically capable of dealing with the worst of the Grey Years. Further, we were fortunate for being in Great Britain, which was even better equipped than much of Europe to cope with adversity. In line with most countries, we had food rationing for many products, price controls, specific laws against greed (what strife they caused), and strict regulations on vehicle use. But, as a nation of gardeners, we the British (but not Sami) took on the challenge of finding edible plant species and varieties that would grow in chronic low levels of light (and with lightly acidic rainfall). Almost nothing green and edible grew without artificial light, but the effort helped with morale. As a nation of hobbyists and enthusiasts, we also found it easier than our European neighbours to re-adapt to traditional do-it-yourself house maintenance (Notek books were never so popular) and to the barter mentality of car boot sales. Even more significantly, our country relied less on solar energy than many others, having invested heavily in tidal and wind energy which maintained a good level of electricity production throughout the Grey Years.

In addition, Lizette and I were both lucky for being employed, meaning we were well paid (enabling us to maintain a reasonable lifestyle) and we had work to keep us occupied. While the relatively modern Farnborough Science University closed down altogether because it was starved of funds, and most of the research programmes at Surrey University were also frozen, Professor Jensen's department, in which Lizette worked, survived. I too was busy. In spring 71, I had taken on a new task, overlapping the EIPD study slightly. London was chosen by the European Union to host a new and swiftly-established agency to administer Rapid Emergency Aid for Countries seriously

Hurt by climatic disturbance (REACH), and I had been asked to manage it. I presumed my experience and reputation at the IFSD was ample qualification, and my work on the EIPD study had kept me visible. The job sounds more important than it was, otherwise I doubt it would have been offered me.

I should explain what REACH did (though Jay found my explanation convoluted and warned me not to bother). Soon after the start of the Second Jihad War, the United Nations, which had only partially recovered from the aftermath of the first war, imploded again. By the end of 68, the European nations had withdrawn a large proportion of their development aid contributions to UN agencies such as the IFSD. Thereafter, and during the war years, these same funds gravitated towards military and defence uses. However, with the darkening of the skies and the consequent humanitarian crises around the world, most rich countries began to restart modest national aid programmes. The European Union, though, wished to make a more obvious and visible contribution, at least until such a time as new agreements re-legitimised the UN agencies. Thus it was decided to set up REACH: a temporarily-constituted agency to use funds which might otherwise have been apportioned through the UN, 'for rapid assistance where urgently required in order to save lives'. Initially, and until the cease-fire was agreed, the funds were only to be allocated to projects in areas not affected by the military conflict.

But REACH was given a very tight mandate and an inconsequential budget. The British government donated office space near London Bridge, in Pickle Herring House. My main tasks were administrative, to get the agency functioning, to install procedures quickly and efficiently, to find the necessary staff (80 at its peak), and to ensure the available money was spent, and spent wisely. In a few cases, it was possible to employ people I respected and who had been made redundant by the IFSD. Furthermore, I enquired to see if there was any chance MarySue wanted to go back to work, but the war, the greyness and especially the death of Conrad had drained all the life out of her. I made the mistake of calling by camphone and was shocked to find her looking shrunken, and 20 years older than when I had last seen her.

Mostly, though, I needed to employ experts with experience of managing emergency aid, since I had so little myself. For my deputy, I took on Jean-Michele Olivier, a Belgian recommended by experts in Brussels. He proved to be a wiry, tense and surprisingly vain man. His mother, I learned over time, had been posted to the Belgian embassy in Tunis, where she had been seduced by the owner of her rented apartment. She thought the relationship would last, but, when it didn't, she returned with baby Jean-Michele to Brussels and married a civil servant colleague. When I first met him, Jean-Michele was about 40. He had spent most of his career working with various agencies, in

346

every link of the aid chain, and most recently with Water Aid in Milan. He had divorced an Italian wife and was willing to return to Northern Europe. Being somewhat temperamental, he was easily upset and only worked well (and tirelessly) when he felt he was being appreciated. Some colleagues found him amusing, others intently irritating. Initially – I confess this freely – I wondered if I had made a huge mistake by accepting him on my staff. But the reverse was true: REACH never achieved a great deal, but what it did achieve was largely thanks to his know-how and ingenuity.

Jean-Michele had a real talent for being able to assess potential aid allocations, their realistic value in terms of human lives (both senses of the word), their viability, and potential problems. And, for the important challenges, the ones we believed in, he could imagine and conceive an efficient, often imaginative, pathway through from idea to implementation. When other staff, government liaison officials or enactor agency chiefs occasionally complained to me about his manner, I would sympathise lightly and expound on his abilities, as if he were an artist of some kind, to whom one needed to show tolerance. I recall my uncle Alan complaining in his letters about prima donna colleagues, and wishing they would all grow up. I don't mind, he used to admit, if they've got something real and tangible to give. Despite his waxed moustache, Jean-Michele had a lot to give, and his heart was in the right place. So long as his vanity was in tact, he would spend 24 hours a day if necessary on the shop floor, so to speak, tying up every last loose end to ensure a consignment of water, food, fuel, medicine or tents would make it through to the planned destination.

Lack of sufficient money aside, prioritising was our biggest headache. Each day we received informal and formal requests for funds. We had adequate procedures but this did not stop European governments trying to bypass the rules, or desperate developing countries pleading for more scraps from Europe's table, or members of our own staff being moved to tears by media reports of disasters-in-the-making and preparing own-initiative plans. I found it easiest, morally and practically, to stick rigorously to the selection rules we had established. Where this left equal choices – which often happened – I relied on Jean-Michele to advise and influence the selection committees.

Jean-Michele became a regular visitor to Taunton House, and would stay over from Saturday to Sunday (although never if Horace was expected – they only met once which was enough for them to establish an instant antipathy). Initially, Lizette had disliked his pompous demeanour, and, after his first visit, asked me not to invite him again. But I talked about him and his invaluable assistance so often that she grew curious enough to want to give him a second chance. As she warmed to the man, so he became more comfortable in our house and more interested in us and our lives, which in turn led us to appreciate his idiosyncratic company. He was a very handy man to have around the place, as comfortable with electrics and basic electronics as he was with carpentry. He often went out walking on his own, usually across the greensand heaths which remained attractively covered in heathers and bracken during the Grey Years. Jay, by then well and truly into teenagerhood, found him patronising and comical; but he too changed his opinion in time.

During the last of the lost summers, in 73, when he was 13, Jay suffered a severe bout of depression. We did not know whether this was a genuine SDD/CDD (seasonal/climate disorder depression) or not. He endured various tests, including those for melatonin and serotonin deficiencies, but the results were inconclusive. The medical establishment had not fully accepted SDD, with critics citing the ability of an individual to affect his or her own neurochemical levels by eating a good meal, sex, sport or watching a movie. In the media, sceptics called it 'scarce-dollar depression'. Lizette was a sceptic, believing that effort and work and activity was the way out of any depression, especially during the Grey Years when the whole population was chronically depressed. It's my belief, though, that she pressed him too hard on his school work, and then, when the doctor proposed he might have SDD, she became yet more demanding, driving him further into his own personal greyness. She may have been able to browbeat him to working more when he was younger, but as a teenager her efforts were counter-productive.

It was Jean-Michele who rescued Jay. He had heard Lizette moan about Jay's lethargy more than once, and he had remembered Jay talk idly of redecorating his bedroom. One weekend morning, he asked Jay to show him the attic room and to explain what he might wish to do with it. Then they sat down for several hours with paper and pencils and a ruler. By lunch-time, Jay was excitedly showing us a plan to refurbish the room with a custom-made stilted bed and desk space, a larger screen on one wall and Live wallpaper on another. Lizette was stunned by Jay's apparent change in mood, and when Jean-Michele promised that he and Jay would undertake the whole project together without any outside help she offered up no objection. For the next few months, Jean-Michele came once a month and worked busily with Jay the whole time he was here. In-between visits, Jay regularly emailed his new friend seeking advice on an interim task or putting forward new suggestions. Once the room was finished, Jay claimed it was the most stylish in the house, and possessed real 'Jay-space'. He went so far as to organise an opening ceremony, with a ribbon across the door frame, a bottle of wine, and a short speech thanking Jean-Michele for all his help. The Belgian, beaming from one edge of his moustache to the other, took a slight bow, and magically produced a party-sized Harkness Cylinder. When Jay flicked the coloured crystal apart with a finger, it released a spray of glitter, and a dazzle balloon playing one of Jay's favourite pop songs. Jean-Michele. There was a touch of the Harkness Cylinder about the man himself.

Jay's imagined or real SDD never returned. Unintentionally, the way events transpired, we were able to return the good deed. Despite his visits to Taunton House, we knew very little about Jean-Michele. I had never been to his apartment near Clapham Common, nor had he talked much about his private life. It was as if he did not have one. But there was a moment when his guard dropped. We were in the office, both tired and downhearted after failing to secure an increase in our budget allocation from the European Parliament. The other staff had left for the day, and Jean-Michele was moaning about the world in general, and REACH's impoverished budget in particular. Then suddenly, as if struck by a lightning existential crisis, he said it would all be easier to bear if he wasn't so lonely. I asked him what he meant, but he dismissed his own remark and my question as irrelevant. I relayed the comment to Lizette, and she suggested we invite Jean-Michele when other friends were visiting rather than when they were not. Of her friends, though, only Rhoda was single, and Lizette would not have wished Rhoda on her worst enemy.

In October 73, around the time of Lizette's 55th birthday, Pete and Clarity came to stay for a few days. Pete had retired by this time, and was keeping busy by writing course material. Clarity too had left the university and was working, mostly from home, as a researcher and presenter for the BBC's Kurdistan news network. Their visit was timed to follow on from a conference meeting Clarity was attending in London. At that conference, Clarity befriended a Russian woman called Raisa who worked as a translator for the BBC and others. At Clarity's request, we invited Raisa to join us all – including Jean-Michele – for lunch on the Sunday. By late afternoon, our two single guests appeared to have bonded, and it was no surprise when they then made the necessary calls to alter their pre-arranged rotor transport so as to travel back to London together. Thereafter, we saw far less of Jean-Michele. When I asked if we would see him at the weekend, he replied saying he was busy. When I asked if he was busy with Raisa, he made a flamboyant hand gesture as if to wave away my question. I could never pin him down, and he continued to keep mum about his personal affairs. It is only because Raisa stayed in touch with Clarity for a few months that we knew the two of them had fallen in love. That Christmas, and at Lizette's insistence, I urged Jean-Michele to bring Raisa to Taunton House but he declined politely.

If I am now focusing too much on the personal, it is because the only way any of us could cope with the mayhem across the world and all around us, was by turning inward, to our own families and friends, for solace.

***

Over 800 million people died between 70 and 75, from drought, starvation and disease mostly. It is estimated that a further billion died later, prematurely as a direct a consequence of the Toba eruption (many from lung cancers and other respiratory diseases caused by the polluted air). The gross national product of the world fell by one third, with much of it reverting to economic standards prevailing one hundred years earlier. Europe and North America suffered proportionately less than most other regions, at least in terms of physical human death and suffering, which is all that really mattered. Not to Gregory, though. He wrote about the psychological trauma of the rich Christian nations. He suggested there was 'a correctional downshift in expectations of seismic proportions'. Such downshifts are as inevitable as hills on a hike, he said – if I recall the oddly-reversed metaphor correctly – but it is better for an economy (or more accurately for the individuals within that economy) to walk up a steep hill for a short time (short-lived but very deep depression as with war and the Grey Years) and walk down a shallow hill over a long period (sustained growth) than the reverse (a long period of recession with a short boom).

As I say, Lizette and I coped reasonably well with the Grey Years. The same cannot be said for those afflicted with real or imagined acute SDD, Gregory's psychological downshift, or CDCB (circumstance-driven criminal behaviour) many of whom had to be to locked up for the safety of the rest of us. The British police force nearly doubled in size during the early 70s, absorbing men and women from the armed forces. The prisons, correctional institutions and cloisters for those with brain dysfunctions were all overcrowded; new ones were created in a hurry, often in unsuitable premises. Harriet, the mother of our two dead children, was sent to one of these temporary cloisters, and died there. I'm not sure why or how. She had married a second time. Her husband, from whom she had recently separated, tracked me down, and asked if I wanted to go to the funeral. I expressed my sorrow, and apologised for not being available.

If I shed no tears over Harriet, I did over Alfred. One day, in November 72, I received a warm and informative email from him. A few days later, before I had had a chance to reply, I received another email from his son, Fela, informing me that Alfred had died in a road accident in Zanzibar where he was living by then. A drugged-up gang of youths had stolen a service vehicle and taken a joy-ride; they killed seven pedestrians, including Alfred, before crashing. Since one of them had a gun, the police shot them all. I phoned Fela. This kind of thing is happening all the time, he said, especially on the east coast islands of Zanzibar, Pemba and Mafia where rich Africans like to retire. It was bad enough during the war years, he added, now it's anarchy. I told him what a great man Alfred was and how much I had loved him. I could hear Fela's voice, on the other end of the line, full of emotion, trying to tell me he wished he had not been such a stubborn child and listened to his father more when he was young. Fela had disappointed Alfred initially, that was true. He had rejected public service and sought material happiness; but, eventually, he had turned his early banking career to good use by going to work for the West African Development Bank, a benevolent institution set up during the Ojoru years. I told him each man has to find his own way, and that Alfred's pride in him had shone through in all the recent letters to me.

There was no question of me flying to Zanzibar for the funeral, given the cost of, and restrictions on, international movements, but I promised Fela I would take part by camphone if he opted to allow a private broadcast. He didn't; but the service was recorded and I did receive a camclip a few days later. There were only a dozen Zanzibar friends in attendance. It was a sad end which I do not wish to dwell on.

Instead, I prefer to see Alfred on the volleyball court, taking three long elegant strides towards the net, rising high into the air (so high that his finger-tips could touch the gym roof cross-beams, so my imagination sees him) and swinging his arm to hit the ball gracefully yet so forcefully and accurately that the opposing team has no chance of a return. Or else, if I must see him as an older man, I recall the time in Munich when I handed him the trophy, his vigorous black face for a moment serious and then bursting into a smile full of humility and pride and warmth and friendship.

I said goodbye to other friends during the Grey Years. Matt Fortune died of a broken heart (in both senses) not long after his wife succumbed to a cancer. He left one son, Oliver, who has followed Matt's path into politics. MarySue, who like me had returned to England to retire, never fully recovered after the loss of her son. It is likely she was one of the victims of the government's policy on rationing of medical care for the aged. (Incidentally, my increasingly eccentric friend Horace was campaigning against his own party on the issue. He did this despite the fact that most sensible people across the political spectrum recognised the need for public service cutbacks in all but a few areas, such as law and order.) In distant St Petersburg, the cold dark weather sunk into Anna Mastepanov lungs, but not before she had written asking if I would carry on the regular donations to Alan's health clinic in Bangladesh. She made me promise I would go there once. I never did. But Jay has already taken over the responsibility from me. He will, I'm certain, make the trip there next year. (He has also promised me, I should add, to seek out a real or email address for Karel, Alan's adopted but estranged son, so as to send him a copy of this book.) And I lost the Turnbulls too, although in a different sense. They cashed in all their chips and emigrated to Australia, from where they sent me a couple of letters. Then we lost contact.

During the Grey Years, efforts to rehabilitate the United Nations and its constituent parts were doomed to fail. The world and all its nations were in double shock, recovering from the Second Jihad War and the mega global disaster caused by sustained low temperatures and light levels. Even the European Union, which despite more than a century of unsteady progress had remained the world's most successful example of regional integration, became unstable and threatened to fall apart at the seams. It may well have done if the skies had not begun to clear in 74.

The first time we saw the sun in nearly three years, Lizette's brother, Mercurio, was staying with us in Tilford. Once a year, he would leave his Notek community in Pembrokeshire and do a cycle tour of the south of England, passing by various family and friends. Jay adored his strange, long-haired scruffy-looking uncle, and anticipated his visits with mounting excitement. Lizette was more cautious, she looked forward to seeing him, but anticipated arguments, many of them stemming – this is my personal assessment – from her inability to accept his Notek way of life.

The Notek movement emerged during the 40s in North America then spread to northern Europe. Pop culture histories say the 30s was the decade in which individuals exploded with anger protesting for change, and the 40s was the decade when they began searching inward trying to cope with the hatred and violence they had seen in the 30s and with economic and technological stagnation. The world had appeared on the edge of a dangerous precipice in the mid-30s with the universal excesses of the First Tuesday Movement protests and riots; but it was in the 40s that the deeper and more consequential problems began to evolve, particularly with the intensity of religious activity, both alternative and mainstream, and cults of one form or another (the worst of which, of course, was the Pearly Way). But there were also many benign cults, including the Noteks, which flourished during the introspective 40s. The not very original name 'Notek' was coined by a Canadian news organisation to describe a group of art students at Vancouver University who were expelled because they refused to work with computer technology and submit their work electronically. They had been inspired by a Californian writer called Chuck Harris who argued that the insidious spread of electronics into every part of our lives had led individuals to feel they were no longer in control. If our cars, our plumbing, our lamps, our toys went wrong, he said, we used to be able to mend them, now we can't – there's a chip in everything, and who knows how to mend a chip. He railed against all aspects of life which involved electronics, but was particularly angry about, and opposed to, the way the electronification of the media and communications had created vacuous virtual communities at the expense of physical ones and 'human human relationships'.

Over three decades, many different types of Notek communities sprang up all over the world, not only inspired by Chuck Harris, but drawing on naturalist philosophies stemming back to Lovelock and Vernadsky in the 20th century. Many of them were small and relatively private, and most were benign. Those that tried to impose their alternative standards on others, did not last long. For some reason, perhaps because the British had a tendency towards cultism, Great Britain had – and obviously still does have – a flourishing Notek population. During the 60s and 70s, amid much anguish at local level, Noteks managed to buy into whole hamlets and then villages, and turn them into Notek communities. Old churches were converted into book libraries and meeting rooms, around which the communities revolved. In time, and not before a national election had been won and lost over the issue, the law found a way of dealing with these communities, allowing them to pay reduced taxes in return for reduced services. As the communities became more widely accepted, so they attracted some important intellectuals; and, there seems no doubt, the laudable Church of Moral Atheism originated within the Notek movement. More prosaically, among a basket of social innovations, we must thank Noteks for the Mildew – not that I can person-ally recommend the sinuously wild dance, having never tried it myself. Nowadays, it is not considered an easy life in one of these Notek villages, and some of them only survive through tourism, which is frowned on by the hardliners.

At this time, immediately after the Grey Years, in the mid-70s, there might have been half a million Noteks in Britain, but not all of them lived in communities, and the figures were inflated by those claiming support for Notek ideas but unwilling to give up their phones or screens. It was ironic that many people turned to the Notek philosophy during the Grey Years: while electronics had helped the world become far more resource-efficient than it had been in the 20th century, the sun – an icon of the power of nature for the Noteks – had disappeared. Although I argued at length with Mercurio about this, I was prepared to acknowledge the Noteks had some beneficial influence on our society. When Lizette joined in these friendly disputes, however she became exasperated at the childish way Mercurio refuted my arguments. He was able to rile her, in a way that her equally lightweight students at Guildford could not (or so she told me). As his older sister, she felt responsible for him in some way. Moreover, she was angry that he had two children, aged ten and four at this time, who she had not met in person. He had never invited us to Pembrokeshire, and he had certainly never cycled with them to Tilford. On top of these frustrations, she also worried – rightly and ultimately wrongly as it turned out – about his influence on Jay.

As the nearest being to a sun worshipper we knew, Mercurio was the right person for the occasion. Although we had no specific information about when the sun might break through, we'd been told the day was not far off. For months, there had been media reports of celebrations across the globe, and in recent weeks there had been a few in northern Europe. That particular morning there was a cold and very blustery wind, but it was breaking up the cloud cover and giving brief glimpses of clear sky. Mercurio wanted us to bike to nearby Waverley Abbey, a 12th century ruin and beauty spot. I protested against the venture, claiming my arthritic ankle was too painful to cycle, but both Lizette and Jay were so enthused by the idea and refused to go without me, that I finally agreed. It was only about three kilometres and the pain in my ankle was not that great, especially if I pilled-up and we rode slowly. I expected the place to be deserted, as it always was during winter and cold weather. But there were hundreds of families there, some with picnics, some with flexiscreen camphones and many with what appeared to be umbra-lighters. Jay, who was our only link with the day-to-day fashion and trends of the young, explained they were not umbra-lighters (which no-one would need in daylight), but new-fangled umbra-viewers, with transparent filter material specifically for looking safely at the sky and enhancing the cloud shapes and light densities. Jay managed to borrow one from a school-friend for a few minutes, so we all got a chance to see the essence of the sun behind the clouds. It was two hours, during which time the crowd numbers trebled, before the shy sun finally gave us a glint. It may have been shrouded in a heavy veil of haze but it was, most definitely, sunshine. We were all on our feet, some standing on the ruined Abbey walls, waving umbra-viewers and hats and scarves and shouting whoops of joy. Mercurio fell to his knees and gave thanks.

With the sunlight, hope returned. People everywhere began to rebuild their lives, their communities, their nations, and their international institutions. Evidently, I was most interested in the last of these. No-one doubted that the world needed a United Nations system, but what kind of system. Most citizens in the richer developed countries opposed the idea of sharing too much of their wealth through a bigger stronger United Nations (as they always had done), but their leaders recognised that a new world order could not go backwards from the best of what it had been before the First and Second Jihad Wars, and that it would have to compensate for the alarmingly uneven death toll of the previous five years. In 74, when the Islamic countries joined the preliminary conference on the future of the UN, they were still dominated by Al Zahir. His position had been weakened during the Grey Years, yet he had retained sufficient power to hold the IIBP together, and to present aggressive demands. That conference and subsequent ones disintegrated amid chaotic claims and confused counter-claims.

The truth was plain to see: a quarter of the world insisted on doing business through Al Zahir, and the rest of the world, but especially the American and European allies, would not trust any commitment or offer he might make about the future. After all, he had started two world wars and annihilated half of Israel. In Russia and Europe, there were deep resentments over Kazakhstan and the Greek islands respectively. The Catholic world had been told by Pope Maria that Al Zahir was the third modern incarnation of the devil, after Stalin and Hitler.

How strange it is that the Israeli policeman, Noam Livnat, is as notorious as Al Zahir himself. The former killing only three men and himself, and the latter responsible for the deaths of hundreds of thousands (without calculating how many fewer people might have died in the Grey Years if five trillion euros and incalculable other resources had not gone up in smoke during the two wars). Historians agree that Al Zahir would eventually have been displaced within the IIBP, but that Livnat's revengeful deed accelerated the UN's rehabilitation by three or possibly five years. In the year after the assassination, the IIBP splintered into factions and this allowed less tainted, more acceptable Islamic leaders to present themselves at the international negotiating tables.

***

Yesterday, Chintz and I watched Flora's funeral on my screen. It didn't take place here, as mine will, but 250 kilometres away at a crematorium in Liverpool. There's a garden there with a family memorial containing the ashes of, among others, her mother, father and one son, the one that played cricket for England. Months ago, she showed me a picture of the stone vault, and expressed impish impatience at the time it was taking her to get there. The chapel room was full, and the traditional Christian service mercifully short. Flora was described as a woman who had lived a very full life, who carried joy around with her wherever she went, and who would be greatly missed by many grandchildren and great grandchildren.

'And by us,' Chintz added sadly. 'She was the life and soul of this place,' and then, thinking this might offend me, continued 'but you're the life and brains of this place ... and my movie master.'

I was far away, trying to imagine the scene at my own funeral a few months hence.

And this morning, as if telepathically understanding that I needed cheering up after yesterday, Tina arrived. She came alone, not wanting to wait until the late afternoon when Jay would be free. Previously I had only seen her in the flesh twice. Once in the 80s, when Lizette and I did a mini-tour of South America, and once about ten years ago when she spent a northern hemisphere summer travelling around Europe. Tall, sultry and sexy, Tina had inherited the looks of her grandmother Conceição and the charm of her father Arturo. I had warmed to her as a teenager and a young lady, but now I'm disappointed to find her copying too many of her father's superficial characteristics: swathes of make-up, gaudy clothing and an excess of jewellery. Her black hair, once shoulder-length and free, was tightly pinned together with a woven double chignon, and decorated with silver clasps. Also, I found her allure had become more deliberate with age, more sticky if that makes any sense – but maybe this is me being paranoid. It is impossible not to suspect that Jay's endeavours to encourage these doubly-distant relatives are succeeding only because they hope I might favour them in my will. (Jay knows most of what remains after my excess medical and hospice bills are paid will be his, although Tina, Inti and Maria will receive token endowments.)

Tina's English is adequate, nevertheless talking with her was tiring. She told me about life as a hairdresser in Belo Horizonte, where she lives with a boyfriend she met on a holiday in Rio, and about her aim to become a fully-qualified child nutritionist. She has been studying in night classes for three years and is about to take an exam which will, if she passes, qualify her to work in a health practice. She had little news she wanted to share about her brothers, or her mother Fatima. She became most animated when talking about samba. I knew she was a good dancer, and that this took up a lot of her spare time. But I did not know, until she told me, that she belongs to one of the premier samba groups in Belo Horizonte and is responsible for coordinating the headwear and hair design for the carnival parades. As with all samba groups, Tina said, hers is already preparing for the February 2100 carnival.

'I send you how to watch carnival here on the screen. I will wave for you.'

'How will I know it is you?'

'OK, I will send you picture first, of me, in costume, then you know it is me waving. I wave like this.' She waved, and giggled, and for a moment I saw Conceição.

EXTRACTS FROM CORRESPONDENCE

Guido Oostlander-Fenn to Kip Fenn
(freely translated from the Dutch original)

March 2069

After six months, it is still a struggle. We've had to put back the schedule for opening Teatro Sucre until September. Everything, and I mean everything, takes twice as long as expected. This week, finally, I've been able to meet with the upholsterers to finalise the material for the seating. This should have been done before Christmas, but Felix insisted we use a particular company, and for weeks they were too busy, and then Felix wanted to look over the samples but he was away, and then Felix ...

What I actually want to tell you, but I find it so embarrassing is that for three months – sorry if I haven't written since your birthday – Felix has been trying to seduce Mireille. Felix doesn't only adore the theatre, he wants drama around him, everywhere. He started quietly flirting with her and – well you know what she's like – she didn't take it seriously, just rebuffing him tactfully. Then he became more overt, which upset her, because she had to be more obviously resistant. At this point she told me, and said she could deal with it. But he carried on with direct invitations for a quiet dinner, or a weekend at his Salinas villa; and then, when she continued to refuse, he began applying pressure, saying we might have to move out of the house soon, or that the money for the theatre might run out. We needed to be flexible, he kept saying. I got so angry I wanted to return to France. But Mireille viewed it as no more than a difficulty, one of many we would have to face. I went to confront him, to tell him to leave Mireille alone – I felt so stupid. He laughed at me, and said he only wanted her once, to taste her once. And he asked me why it was such a problem. Didn't we trust each other? Hadn't we had sex with anyone else before? And then Mireille and I discussed it. We discussed her sleeping with him, one time. I mean it happens. You know it happens. You must know how it feels. (Sorry to be so direct. It makes it a lot easier knowing how happy you are with Lizette. I hope you don't mind.) But it was different with Mum, I suppose, because she wanted Karl. And then we (Mireille too) thought that, with half the world engaged in war, we were being so stupid, childish. We should have known from the beginning there would be a cost, that fairy godfathers don't exist. I bet you knew, I bet you thought Felix Montechristo sounded too good to be true. We did too, we just didn't want to acknowledge as much to each other.

I doubt I would be telling you this if Mireille had paid the price, or if we had decided to come back. But we made up our minds to fight, to let him evict us from our home, and to let him completely starve the project of funds before we gave in. He did neither. As soon as he realised Mireille would prefer to let the theatre fail than give in to his demands – not in the end for emotional reasons, but because she didn't appreciate being toyed with – he stopped his bullying. He laughed it all off as a game.

So, what I'm trying to say is that we've grown up a bit, but we're no less determined. If anything, we're as excited by the whole thing as before we came. We love the language, the country, the city and the people (I'll tell you about some of them another time).

Love to Lizette and Jay.

PS: Didier and Helene are coming for two weeks. They say they'll be visiting twice a year until we return! And Mireille's sister, Veronique – did I tell you she works now for a Swiss media firm making documentaries – has persuaded the company to let her make a low-budget info-flick about the Teatro Sucre project. She's coming soon too, and then again in September. If the film ever transpires, I'll send you a copy. In the meantime, here's two camclips, one of Mireille dealing with the carpenters, and another of me on our terrace thinking of less stressful days (evenings spent making cardboard cut outs for drama club, or Sundays aboard Ginquin).

August 2070
Back safely. Thanks for taking us to the airport yesterday. It was good to see you and Lizette and that scamp Jay, even if for such a short time. Didier's death was such a great shock to Mireille, I think the only way she can cope is to be extra busy again (shades of Helene), and we have so much to do here. Will write more in a few days. Take care.

May 2071
We've had to close the theatre. It was inevitable. There's no audience. Felix – bless him, apart from the odd flaw, we still love him – has run out of charity. And the government is passing emergency laws which would have shut us down anyway. I thought we might return to France or even England (from what you say), but Mireille wants to stay. The money from Didier's will has finally come through. After his death last year, two women with no connection to each other – I find this shocking – made a legal claim against the estate. One had a 15 year old girl, and the other a nine year old girl who they claimed were Didier's natural daughters. They both said Didier had been funding the girls' education. Helene hired the most expensive lawyers, and a couple of private detectives. In the end, though, once the DNA tests were forced through, the claims were dismissed. Half the money has gone to Helene, and a quarter each to Mireille and Veronique. I think the idea is that Helene will make provisions for Veronique's children and ours if we have any (!?!). Mireille wants to use the money (and the money from our flat in Paris which we've sold) to form a theatre group and go on the road, to travel round the country performing for free in villages and towns; and in Peru and Bolivia as well. If we live frugally and only employ a maximum of six players, we think we can do this for four or five years before the money runs out. Will the darkness last that long? We'll be dead by then, from exhaustion. Mireille believes it's our mission to take a 'rainbow of entertainment' wherever we can.
     I hope all is well with you and Lizette, take care.

358

September 2074

Mireille is pregnant. I am allowed to tell you now. Five months. Inti, a boy, should be born in January, all being well. I wonder how many others around the world celebrated their first sight of the sun as we did!

Thanks so much for your letter, and your news.

We have stopped travelling – at last – and, while we're waiting for Quito to want its grand Teatro Sucre up and running again, we've started a community theatre to work with the psychological victims and the schools and the unemployed. We're hoping that within a year we can find a way of covering our costs. Helene's given up arguing for us to come back, and will be visiting as soon as she can. She may stay for a while and help with the finances.

When will you and Lizette come, and my little brother? He can't be so little any more. We would so love to see you. It has been a miserable time, and now it is possible to imagine the future again.

Take care.

April 2075

First we had Helene here for weeks and weeks and weeks, now we've got Mum worshipping at Inti's altar – and he's only three months old. I've attached several new camclips, more tomorrow.

Lots of love.

Take care.

Doug Turnbull to Kip Fenn

January 2070

We are here in Sydney. After some months of renting, we bought this place (see pics). We can scoot to the beach in ten minutes (Miriam is there now doing group exercises), or be at the grand old opera house in 50. The skies are blue, and the sun shines as if there were no tomorrow (I won't mention the flies). The views across the harbour are breathtaking.

Lucy may come and live out here too. She's split up with her man (a cellist – a tosspot) after ten years, and the doctors have lost control of the rheumatism in her shoulder. She can play well enough, in short spurts, for teaching purposes, but not for performance any more. Susannah is expecting again, her third. She and her husband are staying in New York. He's climbing up some media empire hierarchy. I don't suppose Miriam would have wanted to emigrate if they had remained in blighty. We see them once a year. Funny isn't it how you get lots of grandkids from one daughter and none from the other? How's your crew, Lizette and Jay, and Guido, and that strange man Arturo?

359

As soon as this damn war is over, we shall expect you for dinner – as usual!

PS: I heard from Jude Singleton the other day. Would you believe it? She's still working – must be in her 80s – acting as an advisor to a think tank on war damage and environmental recovery. Rather her than me.

October 2071

Glad to hear you're back in the saddle. Rather you than me. Wasn't the pet licensing authority in Pickle Herring House, or has it moved? Can't be many people taking on pets these days.

Miriam wants to go 'home', but we can't. It's all too complicated and expensive. Back home the cold and damp was normal most of the time, but here it's worse, it feels sharper for being so unnatural. The Aussies aren't coping very well. You'd think in such a big country with so few people we'd be able to avoid the food and energy rationing ... once they did battle with surfboards and cricket bats, now they fight in queues.

Nor are we coping well. Lucy's moved in, but she blames us for coming here in the first place. Miriam blames me for the same. Although it was her idea (seriously she thought the sun would make her young again).

I go out to the glasshouse to do battle with the aphids which multiply as fast as humans are dying across Asia.

Alfred Ajose to Kip Fenn

November 2072

The beaches on the east coast here in Zanzibar have seen turbulent times, but at low tide they are wide and white and flat. You can watch the old women collecting seaweed, but there are no tourists floating around in scuba gear, any more, no kids building castles, no glamourpusses, no urchins selling fizzes and wiches at extortionate prices. It is a melancholy place, like your beach resorts in winter – like all beaches everywhere now.

I was walking along the sands today thinking about many things, but much about you my old friend. Is it acceptable to call you 'old friend'? I feel old. Do you? All that volleyball has prematurely aged my bones, my joints – and for this I blame you. It would be unfair, though, to blame you for the cold, heavy weather which seems to make all aches, including the ones in the head, worse. How can anyone not feel old in these days.

What do you think when you hear the news? I listen (for I cannot watch) for hours on end, and then I go to the beach to feel the sand between my toes, which is the only thing that takes me out of the present and back to a time before there was a weight on my shoulders. What do you feel?

What do I feel, you ask? I am too impatient to wait for you to ask. There is pity and sorrow and anguish. But these are feelings I've had for most of my life. I've suffered with my fellow Nigerians, whether they've been suffering from disease, from crime, from famine or civil war. I've never stopped crying. Can I feel more now that millions are dying?

But I do feel more. Something different. Something terrible. And there is no-one to whom I can tell this but you.

I am filled with anger and resentment. I am bursting with it. Are you not?

You and I both have struggled our whole lives long, in different ways but with one aim, to combat inequality and make the world a fairer place. We have had two enemies, always two enemies, man himself and nature. But it felt like we were holding our own, if not making progress, and mitigating the worst of what man and nature could do to us.

And now this all. First man finds a way to wipe out every advance we ever made; and then nature spits in our face as if to remind us how petty our efforts have been, how pathetic they have always been.

But where is my anger to go? To whom shall I address my resentment? Should I turn towards Sango (the Yoruba god of thunder and lightning) before I die?

Meanwhile, I go to the beach and feel the cool sand beneath my toes ...

Fela is coming soon, for two weeks. He has business in Dar es Salaam and will travel here after. I was too harsh a father. I see it only now. And he repays me with a love and respect I do not deserve. He has become a good man, and kind. I wish him many sons, many sons and many daughters.

And to you old friend, I send my warmest greetings, wishing you and your family a peaceful and safe way through these dark years.

Chapter Nine
ARTURO, NOTEKS AND OLD PHOTOS

'On waking, the first thing I see is the wallscreen with the time, a message for my wife from her daughter, and a sunrise scene from Tahiti. As I move through my house, the temperature and lighting are just perfect. I go to the john, where the bowl 'knows' when and how long to flush. In the jacuzzi room, the water flow is controlled by a sophisticated central heating/plumbing system (and my razor has an automatic 'bristle thickness sensor'). In the kitchen/dining area, the stove, the fridge, the freezer, the dishwasher, the garbage processor, the breadmaker, the microwave, the mixer, the toaster and the coffee-maker (did I forget one gadget or ten) are all computer chip controlled to a lesser or greater degree. The lock on my front door is activated by a chip; as are the gate to the garage and the lights along the drive. My car has 137 computer chips controlling everything from battery state to traffic density information and seat angle. At work I use a keyboard, screen and phone, all completely reliant on computer hardware. In the office gym, even the traditional weights are in-chipped to provide display information. In the evenings, I don't lumber around the house being useful, mending our son's bicycle for example (the gears, suspension and lights are dependant on electronics) or seeing to a faulty window latch (it's hooked up to a sophisticated thief alarm). From morning to night, I've not used one appliance or piece of equipment that I could mend if it went wrong. On retiring, I find my wife in the bed. She's in-chipped too, for medical monitoring and hormone flow, but at least I can still fix her mood – some nights anyways.'

Out of Control by Chuck Harris (2049)

It is difficult not to believe that the Grey Years should be classified as the greatest catastrophe in human history. Certainly man himself, by means of war, never created as much devastation. One well-known historical demographer suggests the plague in the 14th century may have wrought a similar amount of damage proportionally; and a cohort of scientists give considerable credence to the idea that an eruption of Krakatoa and the subsequent climate disorder in the 7th century was so devastating that it affected human civilisation more profoundly than the Grey Years have done so far, or will be seen to have done a century hence. Whether true or not, more people probably died prematurely as a result of the Grey Years than the sum total of all the world's population at any one time up until about 250 years ago. Looking at the figures, a simple calculation shows that approximately a million people were dying each day during the

Grey Years (or more accurately during the Grey Years and the subsequent year). Surely, every individual on the planet was affected (except the mentally ill and young children); and yet they all – we all, Homo sapiens – carried on about our lives as best we could, concerned as ever with our own shelter, food, energy, mating, parenting, working and socialising.

During the Grey Years, Lizette and Jay and I had kept our heads down, so to speak, working hard, living quietly, making a daily commitment to watching the news, and trying – if not always succeeding – to acknowledge our relative good fortune. Thereafter, with the return to a more normal climate, not much about our personal lives changed in 74 or 75. In the village, as everywhere, there was more obvious leisure activity outdoors. Local working parties formed to clean up the landscape (removing unsightly dead vegetation and planting new trees and shrubs), and we joined these whenever we had time. Lizette was an enthusiastic member of the Tilford Propagators whose main objective was to keep the working parties supplied with young plants, whether propagated at home (or should I say in the home) or bought with funds raised from charity events.

The Tilford Propagators had another source for their seedlings. In 72, and at Lizette's instigation, they took over, from an absent-but-willing landowner, a derelict commercial greenhouse. They repaired the structure and installed s-glass units, and then, rather than using it to grow their own produce, set up a parish species databank, with the aim of being ready for the day when regener-ation could start. One of the group, a gardener by training, wrote about the project for a media outlet, and the concept took off more widely. It probably did more good keeping people busy, though, than in helping to restore the countryside. The earth contained plenty of dormant seeds and rootstock ready to sprout anew, and these tended to do so much better than the transplanted seedlings, which were easy prey to hungry, and fast-breeding insects. Damn it, nature will have her way, Lizette would say tetchily before explaining why some planting or other had failed. Underlying these petty complaints at nature I detected in Lizette a deeper and ingrained antipathy towards biology and biologists (although not, obviously, to hobby gardening and gardeners), although she would never admit this overtly. I imagined it was a bias that came with the territory of her academic discipline, after many years of education, training and peer involvement in materials science. Theoretically, all biology had long since been reduced to chemistry; and biochemistry had been a major discipline for over a hundred years. Nevertheless, biologists worked at the level of living matter, trying to control nature but willing to live with it, while chemists were incessantly trying to break matter apart and recreate it from scratch.

Today, 25 years on, a botanist or a dendrochronologist would be able to tell that something terrible had happened to the countryside around Tilford in the 70s but not many others. The last time I was there, in the mid-90s, the day the sale of Taunton House was completed, all was as lush and beautiful as it had been during my teens: the triangular green (still sloping, still a venue for cricket matches), the banks along the river Wey by the old bridge, the playground nearby, the pretty track to Elstead, once used by the monks of Waverley Abbey, a millennium earlier. In the 10s and 20s, Julie and I, or sometimes Alan too, would take the car to Elstead on a Sunday and walk through to Tilford for lunch at the Barley Mow, or to Tilford and then walk in the reverse direction to Elstead for lunch at the Woolpack. I loved that route, through the wooded edges of Hankley Common, with its surprisingly-high embankment above the Wey, views across the flood plain fields, and the oak tree with its hanging rope from where, with a leap, I could swing backwards and forwards above the river, or, in summer, jump for a swim.

Here on my screen is a nostalgic camclip of that rope swing, one taken by Horace, he who never dared to jump on the rope himself. There are two boys whose names I don't recall, as well as Jeff Zimmerman and myself, all playing the fool. We must have been about 15. I am fully dressed (and shoed) and swinging on the rope dangling above the middle of the river. I can't get any momentum to swing back, despite my writhing efforts. I must have miscalculated how much movement I needed to return to the raised river bank, or, more likely, one of the others had blocked a safe landing. The whole gang is laughing. After a minute or so I let myself fall into the river. There is much applause. Here's another bit of the same camclip. Horace must have lent the cam to Jeff for the rest of us are racing around trying to pull each other's trunks off. Horace is making a particular effort with mine! And, a few metres away, an old couple are trying to have a quiet picnic.

Under cover of the screaming antics on the screen, Chintz has crept into the room, and is giggling too.

'He's a sweetie.' She thinks the boy trying, unsuccessfully, to hide his privates is me, but it isn't.

Not all of nature recovered as quickly as that on the lush banks of the Wey, especially in areas of the world which had been most acclimatised to strong sunlight and high temperatures. Genera, thousands of them, which had taken millions of years to evolve, were wiped out in a few short years. Their ecological niches were filled by aggressive, quick-growing, quick-breeding species. In much the same way as the efforts of the Tilford Propagators were less than successful so were most of the many and varied grander schemes, in the 70s and 80s, designed to re-strengthen species, or in some cases reinstall vanished species from scratch, through DNA databanks or re-creation schemes licensed by the Agency for Genetic and Cloning Techniques (AGCT).

The AGCT was one of the first UN agencies to become fully functional again in the mid-70s, after the Second Jihad War, and in the last of the Grey Years. It required relatively insignificant levels of funding, and the disputes tended to be more agri- or bio-technical than political. But, at the same time, most of the UN's other institutions, including the IFSD, were starved of funds and, effectively, in mothballs. Debate about a new world order had been under way at the highest level since the end of the war. Some statesmen went so far as to say there was no way back for the United Nations, and it was not uncommon for commentators to mention the EIPD World Union study. While the international negotiations on the UN continued to be hampered by the Christian world's distrust of Al Zahir, Europe and North America were visibly considering other options. Soon after Al Zahir's assassination, though, in 76, the Islamic countries made clear their determination to negotiate seriously and quickly for the resurrection of the United Nations. With the world so needy, and so many institutions all ready and waiting to be brought out of mothballs, it became clear there was no realistic possibility of starting again from scratch.

Once the international negotiations began in earnest, they were neither very speedy nor transparent, which resulted in the European Union prevaricating over an extension of the mandate for REACH. When, finally, we were given a three year extension, to 79 (by when it was expected the EU would be ready to funnel its funds again through the UN agencies), we had lost six months' worth of operations. I took the EU's decision-making delays in my stride, but Jean-Michele could not relax. He would come into my office, close the door carefully behind him so as not to be overheard by my secretary, and rant about the failings of politicians. At project level, Jean-Michele had infinite patience, and would work through whatever problem, whatever hold-up until it was sorted; yet, oddly, he was hopeless at coping with the drawn out political processes of those above him, especially when the decisions they were making affected his work. The best way to deal with him in this mood was to let him rant and say little in return.

Several years later, when REACH was winding down, he did come once with Raisa to Taunton House, for a garden dinner party. While there, he moaned to me about having failed to secure a future position at a higher level. It was as if he'd come to visit with the sole purpose of quizzing me about this. I did not prevaricate. I advised him he would be better off sticking to a job not too far removed from the operational level where his best talents lay. He looked at me suspiciously, marched off to find Raisa, and left soon after. As Jean-

Michele suspected, I had replied to discreet enquiries about him from various selection boards without whole-hearted praise of his managerial abilities. Since I was convinced his skills would be wasted if he moved too high up the ladder, I did not feel guilty about this. When the REACH office in London was closed, Jean-Michele went back to Italy with Raisa, where they married (we were invited to the wedding but did not go). We lost contact with them after that. Much later, I heard on the grapevine they had two children, and Jean-Michele was doing an excellent job running Italy's national agency in charge of emergency humanitarian aid.

**

During the Grey Years, and through to 75, everyone moved around far less than hitherto, not only was energy so expensive but there were tight and complicated restrictions on private and business vehicle movements (not least through the rotor arrangements). We ourselves rarely went beyond the confines of our work and home areas, and others, even regulars like Horace, came to see us much less often. By 76, though, transport had become marginally easier, and Horace began to reappear on our doorstep every now and then. On one occasion, in early summer, he brought Tim, his podgy brother, who we hadn't seen for several years. Although the active part of their joint property business had stalled during the Grey Years, they still owned and rented a score of buildings. They argued a lot, and Horace usually tied Tim in knots. I bet, Lizette would say, they squabbled as children; they love it. This particular visit, Tim appeared anxious and sullen. He sought, as soon as he could, a private conversation with me. I took him for a walk, through the village to the bowling green. In short, he was asking my help to persuade Horace against standing in the next election, due in the autumn when the National Coalition's five year mandate expired. According to Tim, Horace's health was deteriorating, and, by supporting increasingly bizarre causes, he was making a fool of himself in Parliament. I was not convinced that Tim's appeal was motivated by real concerns, and suspected some deep-seated, perhaps unconscious, sibling ploy to get one over on his older brother. It was true that Horace wheezed a lot, but then who didn't at 75, and that his political comportment had declined. I had seen media reports of Horace being suspended from the House of Commons for several days as a result of bad language against a Green Party MP. Nevertheless, he continued to lobby tirelessly for policies that would benefit his constituents. Moreover, among his 'bizarre causes' was one I could not help but approve of: he campaigned persistently for Great Britain to lead the march towards a new international order, and regularly cited the EIPD study on World Union.

366

Later that day, while Lizette and Jay took Tim over to see the Tilford Propagators' glasshouse, I sat in the garden with Horace. We drank a light refreshing Wiltshire wine he'd brought with him.

'Made by one of my constituents in the late 60s. Larry. Amiable man. Went bankrupt in 71. Had no choice but to put his land in the hands of the Department of Agriculture. From vineyard owner and sophisticate to farmer and muck-raker. Damn good wine though. Looking for investors to start the vines again. When he gets the land back. I'm considering. What do you think? Not as warm as it used to be. Could stay cooler. What do you think? Half the experts says the Grey Years have done for global warming and we're on the brink of an ice age, and the other half pontificate about faster climate change. Giving money to Larry, be like playing the lottery.'

'Tim says you're thinking of standing again.'

'If they'll have me. Selection committee's meeting next week. May invite me to continue, may not.' He said it with conviction as if he had no idea what might happen. 'What do you think, you've got your ear to the ground: warmer or cooler? vines or no vines?'

'I don't know Horace. Sounds risky to me. Hot or cold, people always need houses, but vines won't always grow. I thought you'd be ready to step down now, give some other likely lad a chance.'

'If the committee'll have me, and the voters want me, I'm still that likely lad.'

'You didn't even like Southampton when you were selected back in the 20s.'

'Long time ago.' His clipped delivery, which had become more exaggerated with age, softened and slowed down. 'Be 50 years in 77. Fifty years an MP. That would be an achievement.'

'Is it 50 years? I didn't realise. I remember the party the night of the election. I came with Harriet and Crystal ... Harriet had just told me she was pregnant again...' I sunk into my own memories. The names of Harriet's children only had to flit into my consciousness for a second, and it was as though someone had knocked all the air out of me, and then dipped me in a wash of sadness. (Incidentally, writing these Reflections has helped me come to terms with the fates of Crystal and Bronze, although nothing can ease my regrets.)

'A real achievement. I'd be only the third person in history to serve 50 years as an MP in the British Parliament – that would be something to put on the cover...' I was not listening, instead I was wondering, for the thousandth time, if there might have been a course I could have taken that would have led to less anguish in the lives of Harriet, Crystal and Bronze. Horace stopped talking, and then restarted, insistently.

'What else does Tim say? Let me guess. Thinks I shouldn't. Bad for my health. Making an ass of myself. Thinks I should stop before I'm remembered for the wrong things. Let me tell you something about Tim ...' Horace's phone rang and he answered it. I probably went inside to urinate, it's what I usually did when there was a break in conversation. When I returned, he repeated the question.

'So, what does Tim say?'

'He is worried about your health. I can see why.'

'No affordable lung transplants yet.'

'And, yes, he does think you're past your sell-by-date. I'm reserving judgement.'

'Big of you.'

'How many times has the Speaker expelled you from the House now?'

'Lost count. He's a fool.'

'Who?'

'The speaker.'

'Why don't you tell him,' I said facetiously.

'What do you want me to do? Tidy up my diaries. Won't be a pretty sight.' Diaries! Now he certainly had my attention. I had no idea he kept a diary.

'Diaries?'

'You didn't know?' He knew I didn't know because he had never told me. 'I've a publisher ready and waiting; he's legally bound to keep it a secret until I say so. Won't publish till I step down.'

'When did you start? Why have you never mentioned this?'

'About 50 years. Only political, not much personal – except where personal is political. Didn't need to write personal, Caxton did that for me.' Having spent but a few years in government, and only as a lesser minister, I could not imagine there would be much of political interest in Horace's diaries. 'Never told anyone. Not Tim. Not boyfriends. You're the first. People clam up if they know you as a diarist; they keep you out of the inner circles. Good advice from Tindle when I office-boyed for him. Told Spoon once I was thinking of writing a diary, he said, "Don't do it. Don't ever do it. Is that clear." I'd started long since. I took his advice to heart, and never did do it – tell anyone that it is.'

Having failed to win me over to his cause, Tim tried a playful attack on his brother over supper, appealing to Lizette's common sense, and expecting Jay's support simply because the boy preferred him to Horace. But what started as banter descended into a full-scale row. Lizette screamed at them to stop and sent them out of the room, in the same way she used to deal with Jay when he was six and misbehaved. Jay found it all most amusing. But it was far from that. The brothers fell out for six months; and we never saw Tim again at

Taunton House. Sadly, Horace did not achieve his 50 years in Parliament. He was reselected without difficulty, and, although right-wing parties were expected to lose seats in the forthcoming election, there was no real threat to Southampton, or so he said. But, about four weeks before the election, he suffered such a serious coronary thrombosis that he was obliged to stand down. Ironically, the Progressive Party chose a candidate nearly 50 years younger in his stead.

I went to visit Horace several times at a private hospital in Southampton, while he was recovering, and then later before and after his heart surgery. During one of these visits he explained that Tim had been anxious for him to retire from politics so that the two of them together could wind down their business (which, apparently, would take more effort and time than simply keeping it ticking over), and then retire fully, possibly abroad. If Tim thought Horace would leave Britain, he must have been prematurely senile.

***

A few weeks after the visit by Horace and Tim, and during the last ten days of Jay's summer holiday, we made our own journey, to Pembrokeshire, and then, on the way back, to Chew Magna in Somerset. It would have been very inconvenient to use public transport so we took our Toyota Ishfreel despite the cost of fuel and tolls (although the much-hated not-full-occupancy tax supplement had been scrapped by this time). I loved driving the Ishfreel, a saloon I'd bought in the late 60s which served us well enough for nearly a decade. It was the quietest car I had ever owned, but more than that it reminded me of the petrol-fuelled vehicles I had driven as a young man, the ones which had razor-sharp acceleration. Since 71, the hapless machine had only been used as a rotor bus for trips to the station or school or supermarket, and hardly ever been allowed out for a run on the motorway. This holiday was Lizette's idea, and focused entirely on her family, so driving the Ishfreel again was my private source of pleasure. Although I was happy to visit Samuel, Lizette's older brother in Chew Magna, I was less sure about the trip to Stackpole Haven, the Notek community five miles south of Pembroke. Jay thought we were making a long overdue friendly visit to Mercurio, Lizette's younger brother, with no ulterior motives, but Lizette's aim was for Jay to witness the harsh uncomfortable reality of Notek life (although she was also very curious about Mercurio's children).

To my mind, Lizette had long since lost any control over Jay's behaviour, his plans or his hopes, but this did not stop her trying to affect them (nor did her intelligence and a good basic understanding of psychology). I doubt she would have advised any other parent to behave in the way she did towards Jay.

It was as though an emotional drive displaced her intellect. Jay, though, had learned well how to bluff and how to pretend he was listening; and he had perfected the art of underplaying his own knowledge about anything and everything. Whereas once he had used this technique to avoid being faced with genuinely more complex tasks, he now used it to maintain a secret, smug power over Lizette. When she tried to push him to do better on his maths or science course work, he would feign ignorance in the face of her expectations. Then he would pretend confusion at her exasperation, and, within minutes, they would be arguing without knowing about what. Whereas I had had some influence over Lizette's behaviour towards Jay while he was young, I had none left by this time.

Jay had taken the 16 exams earlier in the year, and achieved modest results. Lizette was not satisfied with his progress, and regularly made disparaging remarks about his grades, as if, somehow, this might spur him on to do better next time. One of Lizette's greatest fears was that Jay would drop out of school, something he could legally do at 17 (along with drinking, smoking and voting). Partly inspired by Mercurio's annual visits, Jay had developed a schoolboy interest in the Noteks, and often, at the pitch of his arguments with Lizette, would threaten to run away and join a Notek community. Lizette knew no more about what went on inside the Notek villages than I did, and what little we did know came from Mercurio (although Lizette discounted anything positive he said) and the media, which loved to expose Noteks as living way beyond social and cultural norms. Nevertheless, she felt informed enough to judge it bad (plagued with the deadly sins of sloth, lust, greed, pride, not to mention poverty, ill-health and inadequate hygiene) and that the sooner Jay saw the reality of Notek life, the sooner he would throw off his childish impressions.

We spent Saturday evening/night at Hereford with an old school-friend of Lizette's, arriving at Stackpole Haven around midday on Sunday. It was a surprisingly ordinary-looking village, similar to other rural hams planned and constructed in the 20s and 30s. A pond, a church-library, a grocery store and a pub called The Last Elm all clustered around a large oval green. Children were playing in one area of the green; groups of people seated at benches by the pub were eating and drinking; and bicycles were parked haphazardly all over the place. Lizette and Jay were both disappointed in their different ways, although I had no idea what they were expecting. A group of girls sitting cross-legged on the grass were busy knitting. When I asked for directions to the address we had for Mercurio, one of the girls, about 15, naturally pretty with long seaweed coloured hair, a spotted blue t-shirt, knee-length jeans, and bead bracelets on both arms, answered.

'Rio? You want my dad, he's over there, in the pub. We prefer it if you leave the car outside the village lines. Didn't you see the signs?' And she returned to concentrate on her knitting.

'Yes, sorry, but I didn't know where we would need to stop. We'll drive back and park now. In the pub you say? And your name is?' One of the other girls said something, and they all burst out laughing.

'Who wants to know?' she said. And they all sniggered. 'Friend of Rio's are you?'

'Yes. Sort of.' There was another whispered comment and more laughing.

'Yewla. My name's Yewla.' This time I heard the whisper, 'It's the tax men.' And they laughed again.

I returned to the car, pleased with my discovery, and pointed out the girl called Yewla, Lizette's niece, Jay's cousin.

A few people looked up as we entered the pub, but not Mercurio who was one of a group in the far corner playing chess. Jay noticed there were no screens or lottery machines. He said the place had the appearance of a heritage inn, and went to investigate the board games and books stacked on a dresser by one wall. Lizette and I observed Mercurio from behind until he became aware of our presence. I expected him to be horrified or perturbed at our sudden and unexpected arrival, but he wasn't phased at all. He expressed more delight than surprise, and calmly introduced us to the rest of his chess group.

We had made no arrangements about where to stay, thinking we would take advice on a nearby hotel from Mercurio, but the community had a guest house which was free that night, so Rio – as everyone called him – said he would take us there. On the way across the green, we stopped to say hello again to Yewla and her friends. This time she put her knitting down, stood up and came to give each one of us in turn, including Jay, a two-cheek kiss. Jay went bright red. (Jay to me a few days ago: 'You're making that up, I wouldn't have gone red.')

The cottage, a 19th century stone bungalow, was clean and tidy, and decorated with hand-woven fabrics, enamel artwork and ceramics. Mercurio helped us to carry the luggage in. Mercurio, Jay and I then left Lizette alone in the cottage for half an hour, to unpack and freshen up. We took the Ishfreel to a parking bay, and then accompanied Mercurio to a nearby farm where he needed to explain why he would be absent for a couple of hours. That afternoon he was due to service a harvester, he said, but it could wait until later. I had had no idea he was mechanic (why had I never asked?). He serviced and repaired all the community's farm vehicles. Jay was intrigued because he had thought the Noteks lived without all technology. Mercurio explained how there were many different kinds of Notek community, some purists refusing to use tools or appliances that had been made with modern electronic or computer-aided technology, some only rejecting technology invented within the last 50 or 80 or 100 years. Most, though, as with Stackpole Haven, chose a boundary before the electronic age, rejecting all use of chips, but with specific well-defined exceptions where electronic technology helped to preserve the environment or natural resources (s-glass for example). Mercurio said most Noteks liked to talk about their communities as celebrating and preserving sustainable human cultures including many technologies, and not as communities which rejected human development.

From the farm we returned to the guest house to collect Lizette before moving on to a pottery, which filled a large extension at the back of one of the brick buildings. In 50 years, it hadn't weathered anywhere near as well as the stone guest cottage which was four times as old. Mercurio introduced us to Esos his six year old son, playing in a sandpit with some friends, and Esos's mother, Andrasta. She was no older than 30, but her very thin visage and huge sunken eyes gave her a haunted look. There were a hundred pots, glazed and unglazed, all over the workroom floor, and she was trying to reorganise them to make more space on the storage shelves. Jay asked if he could try his hand at one of the pottery wheels. Andrasta, far from pleased at the intrusion, glanced at Mercurio as if to ask whether the disturbance was truly necessary; he winked, smiled and gave her an encouraging nod. As I watched Jay make a mess of the slippery clay, I had a sudden flash memory of being taken once by my grandmother Eileen to a pottery on the south coast.

From Andrasta's workshop, Mercurio led us to another similar building but without an extension. It appeared to house several adults and children, all of them busy with play or work of some description. Here Mercurio found Yewla's mother, May, much older than Andrasta but more comely, if I can use that old-fashioned word. May was not only Yewla's mother, but a member of the Esos co-op, thus indicating more of a pattern in Mercurio's affairs than he had hitherto suggested. Indeed, to my mind this was a very different Mercurio from the one we saw at Taunton House, more thoughtful, more interested in our good opinion, more robust. It was as if, in the past, he had deliberately exaggerated all the aspects of his life that he knew Lizette would despise.

Mercurio continued to guide us round (farms and workshops mostly, and a Notek shop on the main road some distance from the village centre) and explain about his life. I found the place remarkably ordinary, if somewhat quaint. I did notice the Notek community land looked cared for (and less damaged by the Grey Years) than other rural areas we had passed through, but then it was well known that Noteks nurtured their land well. This was one reason why, over the decades, they had been able to argue for and win special legal status. Jay was unusually enthusiastic with his questions, especially about

Yewla, schooling and leisure activities; Lizette remained oddly quiet, confused or annoyed by Jay's enthusiasm.

When Mercurio left us to return to work, Yewla and a half-brother, Almond, offered to show us Stackpole Quay and the beach at Barafundle Bay. I declined because my ankle had swollen up, but Lizette and Jay went, and gave me a full report later. That evening we congregated at Mercurio's house which, we discovered, he shared with Andrasta's sister. There were a dozen others, including Andrasta, May and her current partner, Mercurio's children and Almond. A large trestle table had been set up in the garden. Andrasta and her sister had prepared a splendid meal: a gazpacho-type soup, cold duck and many salads, and a 'delicious strawberry-filled ice-cream'. I am using Jay's memory here. We talked about this a few days ago, on his birthday, before he left on holiday. He enthused particularly over the ice-cream: 'A few years later, when I dropped out of Reading to join that Notek community in Cumbria, I expected to be eating that delicious strawberry-filled ice cream every day.'

Over supper and with the help of a potent elderflower wine (this I remember), Lizette's quiet manner gave way. Perhaps she had herself been bewitched by the peacefulness and harmony of the community and wanted to remind herself why life in the real world was real, or perhaps she was determined to try – for Jay's sake – to show up some faults in the Notek way of being. She began by asking a variety of seemingly innocent questions, but soon took on a more goading tone, grilling Jay and his friends about the community's economy. Before long, she was in full flurry claiming that if everyone were to become a Notek there'd be no science, no research, no development, no progress, no future. But she misconstrued the indulgent mood around the table, believing our hosts were not taking offense, and went so far as to accuse the Noteks of being no better than parasites, who were only able to survive because they fed off a developed and responsible society. Andrasta was the first to crack. She got up in a fury, collected Esos (who had ice-cream round his lips), and stormed off. At that moment, I too thought Lizette had gone over the top, especially given the gracious way Mercurio had received us.

Yet it was Lizette who suffered. Mercurio himself looked thoughtful and said little. He let his friends enjoy a deserved and sustained offensive against Lizette, using their well-rehearsed, almost religious, arguments. What is the point of science? of research? Why do we need development and progress? What do we have to hope for in the future? In what actual specific definable ways have electronics made life better? Why do we need camphones and computers and chips? What does your life have that ours doesn't? Why should man live to 95 rather than 80? Why has the world fought two abominable wars which utterly wrecked its ability to cope with a natural disaster – an inevitable natural disaster? How is life different now – really different in its essence – from 100 years ago, or 200 years ago?

The basic Notek philosophy counts on the following ideas (among many others): there is a natural limit to economic progress and to man's ability to enjoy wealth; capitalism has done well to get Western societies to this natural limit, but thereafter expectations of lives improving endlessly are counter-productive and damaging; wealthy nations should seek not seek 'sustainable progress' but 'sustainable balance'; and excess wealth should be fairly shared with those less well-off.

Lizette did her best to argue about how science should and could improve medicine, agriculture, energy efficiency and environmental protection, but the Noteks knew how to respond. They were not opposed to science and research itself, but to nine-tenths of it which was wasteful and unnecessary. In a fully-committed Notek society there would be sufficient funds for useful science, research and development. Lizette became increasingly irritated at not being able to score any useful points (not that Jay was listening, he'd long since been taken inside by Almond, ostensibly to look at paintings) and would have gone on for much longer, had Mercurio not intervened. He offered an olive branch by stating that Lizette's area of research, as far as he understood it, was the kind supported by the Noteks. But Lizette would not stop, her tongue loosened by alcohol, and so, eventually, Mercurio's patience evaporated. Why, he wanted to know, had Lizette never visited before now. Lizette's stock answer was that she had never been invited. I had always supposed this was true. Mercurio revealed that he had begged Lizette many times when they were younger, in their 20s and 30s to visit, and she had regularly scorned him and his invitations. Lizette looked extremely uncomfortable, and suddenly very tired. She glanced down into her empty glass, and then back up at her brother.

'Well I'm here now aren't I.' This was said with attempted defiance. 'Well I'm here now aren't I.' The second time the words carried a mixture of apology and sorrow. I was dumbstruck by the new information (Lizette had clearly deceived me about the relationship with her brother) and the change in her demeanour.

'Yes you are,' Mercurio said. 'Yes you are.' Then someone filled all the glasses again, and Almond suddenly appeared and said he was taking Jay to see the children's treehouse in a wood nearby. I leaned close into Lizette, put my arm through hers, awkwardly, and whispered so no-one else could hear.

'You were very brave to come here, and to speak out. It's as though you were prepared to be shot down in enemy territory. I didn't realise before but you've come here for a reconciliation, and in a moment, this moment it has been achieved. It wasn't that painful was it?' She nodded, meaning I know not what, and clutched my arm tighter. When I asked if she wanted to go, she said no.

I decided to divert the focus of conversation by asking about the prayer that had been said before supper: 'For what we are about to receive may our children, and our children's children, and our children's children's children be privileged to receive, amen.' This is how and when I first heard of the Church of Moral Atheism. It was a church, I understood, in the broadest sense of the word (any body professing a common creed) based on an understanding, a hope and a belief. The understanding was that god never was or never would be and that therefore we, human beings living in a complex society and world, must be responsible for ourselves, our fellow man, our fellow creatures, and the environment in which we live. The hope was that our children would have good lives, free of hunger, danger and disease. And the belief was to be in a fixed moral code acceptable to all humankind, only this had yet to be elaborated. The Church was a new fad, we discovered, which had been spreading through the Notek communities and elsewhere for several years. A few social academics and philosophers had written papers about the movement, Mercurio explained, and the International Notek Confederation (much larger and more important than when it was originally formed in the 50s) had launched a major study to define a moral code for the church that would be acceptable to a two-thirds majority of Confederation members.

We remained at Stackpole Haven for a further two days. Lizette and Jay did more exploring while I sat for hours in the pub talking with members of the community or reading in the library. Surprisingly, Lizette fell in love with her brother again. This was the first time, she confessed, since he was 11 when, in consequence of some huge grievance, she had relinquished her role as his guardian angel.

On the Wednesday, we drove to Chew Magna, to Samuel's three storey mansionette 'at the opposite end of the Sanderson family spectrum' as Lizette put it. The property came with a long drive, large well-manicured gardens, and several outhouses (a conservatory, a play room, an office). Samuel and Lynn had three children: the oldest Saul who worked with his father in their tidal engineering consultancy firm; Irene, who had travelled a lot before the Grey Years (and had visited us in Taunton House), worked as a journalist on women's magazines in London; and Mahonia, who continued to study architecture at Warwick University. All three lived away from home, although Irene was visiting at the same time as we were, and Saul lived nearby with his wife and baby son. Despite the rich trappings, Samuel and Lynn were hospitable and down-to-earth, and not at all pretentious. Again, I had been slightly misled by Lizette, who, I realised, could only see the members of her family through a magnifying glass.

Samuel was semi-retired, so both he and his wife had time to lead us on various trips. Lizette wanted to go to Weston-super-Mare, to lay flowers by her parents' memorial stone, and Jay went for a swim on the beach. Another time, Irene took Jay and Lizette out in the family skiff on a nearby lake, while I lunched with Samuel and Saul near their offices. Sanderson Engineering Consultancy Services, they told me proudly, had helped on tidal barrage projects in 47 different countries. The business had been healthy before the Toba eruption, but now, with post-Grey Years investment, they were overwhelmed with opportunities. This meant the firm would be able to expand rapidly if Saul wished.

They did not have to sell the technology to me. For 30 years or more – since the advances in systems durability and safe materials with long-term resistance to marine growth – we at the IFSD had promoted the exploitation of tidal turbines as a reliable and regular source of electricity for coastal areas. And yet, surveys said, we had not come close to fulfilling 10% of the potential demand for this kind of technology, even in those regions which fell well below the recommended minimum UN per capita power-consumption ratings.

I knew full well that Samuel had grown tired of the travelling and extended stays away from his family required by many of the company's contracts in the past, nonetheless, I decided to sing the praises of the UN's Wisdom Force. During its early heyday, in the 50s, there were nearly a million retired citizens from wealthy countries working in and for developing countries. The basic idea was that retired professionals of whatever ilk – engineers, surveyors, geologists, architects, teachers, doctors, software programmers, company managers – volunteered for terms of duty, of one to three years, with no other purpose than to transfer their knowledge to those less well off. The programme had run aground during the Jihad Wars, in common with many other UN functions, but was rebuilding itself in earnest. Although only minimum pay was provided, the programme's popularity stemmed from the way it made the voluntary contracts sound as pleasurable as a holiday: five star accommodation, excellent health and safety care, domestic help, a social network, and part-time hours to suit.

That same evening, at my suggestion, Liam Nash joined Samuel, Lynn, Lizette and me for a gourmet meal at The Wild Salmon in the centre of Bristol (Jay having opted for a film at the nearby superscreen). Liam, Diana's cousin, had stayed in contact with me since our first encounter at Diana's bio-fest. Apart from intermittent emails, we had met half a dozen times over the years, usually at his instigation, and usually for a lunch in London. Because he lived in this same area and worked in a similar industrial sector, I thought he and Samuel might get on (although there was a ten year age difference). But I had an ulterior motive. Liam, having retired some years earlier (and buried his wife), had signed up for a term of duty with the Wisdom Force, and was heading out to Namibia to help plan and build a new water filter manufacturing unit.

The five of us got on well. Lizette gave a more detailed report on our trip to Stackpole Haven, and we spent much of the time debating the pros and cons of Notek values. Liam and I ganged up against the Sanderson trio, all of whom were prejudiced against Mercurio. Lizette may have undergone a reconciliation with her brother, but her long-held views about the fundamentals of his way of life had not changed. Like me, though, Liam appreciated what the Noteks had achieved and what they were aiming to accomplish. Also, unlike the others, we were both willing to acknowledge that the Noteks had had a beneficial influence on our society, our culture. It was not until the waiter was serving coffee, though, that I managed to bring the conversation round to Liam's forthcoming venture to Namibia.

The following day we set off to return to Surrey. All in all, the tour had been a success, working out much better than I'd expected. Lizette had got tetchy with Jay now and then, but this was nothing unusual. She and I, though, did have one row on the way home. I was driving, Lizette was expounding on the great benefits of material science, and Jay was listening to music through his earphones (the Rainbow Sharks, he informed the other day, his favourite band for many years).

'You and Liam, last night ... defending the Noteks. I agree they could survive, but not at that comfort level. It's the energy provision that makes the difference and they wouldn't have so much if it wasn't for the s-glass, the polymers that make wind and water turbines so efficient, and h-fuel storage technology. And to subscribe to the notion that you can cherry-pick your science and research investment ... It's fatuous. Scientific development and invention doesn't follow prescribed patterns. If it wasn't for pure research into materials and matter, Liam's filters would be a hundred times more expensive, Samuel's turbines would still be stuck – literally by marine growth – in the pilot project development stage, and your great IFSD would be the International Fund for not-quite-so-Sustainable Development.'

I changed the subject.

'What do you think ... will Samuel consider the Wisdom Force?' There was silence for a few moments, and then Lizette erupted.

'You did it on purpose. You invited Liam, so as to encourage Samuel. I don't believe it. You sod.' I said nothing. 'I don't want my brother going off to some god-forsaken place halfway round the world, dragging Lynn with him. I can't believe you did that.' Lizette stormed on. She was particularly cross at the fact that I hadn't discussed my 'devious plan' with her beforehand, which was 'very uncharacteristic' of me. I did not mind being called devious, but I hated the idea that Lizette liked me being predictable, so I argued back – definitely not the right thing to do. Our raised voices, apparently, made no impact on the Rainbow Sharks, for Jay never removed his headphones once.

Three years later, in 79, Samuel and Lynn went to Lima, Peru, so that Samuel could help train Peruvian engineers to build their own highly efficient and low-maintenance tidal turbine units, instead of importing them from Japan, Italy or Britain. He took a one year contract initially, and then extended it by a further two years, which is how they came to be there when Lizette and I undertook our tour of South America in 81.

***

On our return from the west country, I went immediately to an orthopedic specialist at Guildford Hospital. For years he had been treating the severe rheumatoid arthritis in my left ankle, and for years the pain and discomfort had grown progressively worse. I had survived so far through a combination of painkillers, a surprisingly comfortable ankle bandage-brace (thanks again to Lizette's beloved material science), and a micro-surgical reconstruction which miraculously helped enhance the joint for nearly two years. I also employed a walking stick and special shoes. This time the specialist proposed a second, more complicated (and costly) bio-engineered joint reconstruction. He promised it would give me a minimum of five years pain free hiking. I agreed. But, within 18 months, I was once again in agony. Late one afternoon – it must have been September 78 (Jay had not yet left for Reading University) – I was hobbling back from the bowls green, when I bumped into Sami. He wanted me to inspect the quality of his cucumbers (purple) and the size of his marrows (enormous). Now that rationing had come to an end, and Iona was no longer concerned that growing their own food might indicate hardship, Sami was keen to start exhibiting again. I hadn't been in his garden for years and the ostentatious fortifications took me by surprise. He confided that he used the security lamps to extend natural daylight, but that this was not illegal (energy use restrictions had not been fully lifted by this time) because they were only powered by energy collected from the s-glass on his own property. Most of this energy, he said, came from a huge new L-shaped s-glasshouse. Inside, he showed me an exotic array of tropical vegetables (but, oddly, no fruits). I thought Sami's efforts at excess gardening were eccentric if not absurd (certainly compared to Lizette's hobby gardening and the purpose-driven organic horticulture in Mercurio's community) but, nevertheless, I praised his efforts.

Which goes to show how a little hypocrisy can take you a long way – literally. After applauding his okra, cocoyams and dazzlingly-coloured chillis, he was ready to let me leave. But, as he unlocked the side gate, I needed to hold on to the fence to ease the pain in my ankle. He insisted on taking me inside for an examination. I gave him a brief medical history of my ankle and told him the name of my consultant to which he replied, 'Oh my god'.

Stupidly, I had allowed myself to accept treatment until then without doubting the advice of my surgeon. According to Sami, the reconstruction surgery on my ankle had been a waste of time, money and pain. There was constant pressure for doctors, he explained, to choose the least-cost option, regardless of whether this led to higher costs in the longer run, whether these costs were paid by the state or by the individual. It was ever thus, with the state trying to minimise short-term costs, and the medical establishment insidiously (or subconsciously if the word can be applied to an establishment) trying to maximise its income. What I needed was a new ankle, Sami said. It would be five times as expensive as one micro-surgical reconstruction but would last ten times as long. More importantly, he added, it would give me much greater mobility with far less discomfort.

'Go to the surgeon, ask for a second opinion or referral, to me at St George's. I'm so sorry that I haven't paid more attention to your discomfort before now. I never thought to ask. It's so very rude of me. We can do it half on the health service, or more, so it won't worry your insurance too much.' Iona had come into the room with a tray of drinks and edibles. I thanked him and her profusely. Although I did get myself referred to Sami within a few weeks, it was some months before I could undergo the necessary surgery. In the meantime, Sami's prescriptions and an improved ankle bracelet helped me control the discomfort. The new ankle, when it came, transformed my life: gone was the constant threat of pain day and night, gone was the routine of pills and cold-presses, gone was the ankle brace, gone was the stick, and gone was my chronic reluctance to leave the house or office to do anything at all. It was a magnificent ankle with, I guess, 85% of the movement of the previous one before it went bad. The monetary cost was high, even discounting the health service share, but there was an additional price to pay: not only was I obliged to inspect and applaud Sami's vegetables several times a season, which I didn't mind, but Iona took advantage of her husband's good samaritan neighbourliness and added us to her dinner party guest list, which Lizette did mind.

I should admit that I had no qualms about taking advantage of the most recent advances in bio-engineering despite my personal belief that Western societies had spent and were spending far too much money on medical research (and many other things besides). Politicians often find themselves in deep water when their private lives are put under the microscope; but I am no politician, and I have no psychological objection to classifying myself a hypocrite.

I spent the spring of 79 becoming accustomed to the way my new foot felt, and revisiting various walks around Tilford, especially my favoured hike across to Elstead (although it took a while before I could manage the whole distance one way, with a bus ride home). It was in this period that Lizette again became occupationally depressed. The year before, the year Jay left home, she had applied to take over as Sidney Jensen's departmental deputy, which would have given her more managerial responsibility, and allowed her to hope for a professorship in the future. Sidney, however, opted to bring in a younger woman, Olive Norrington, with an exceptional research track record. Lizette felt slighted. She made an effort through 79 to look for a new position, knowing we would be free to move anywhere as soon as my contract with REACH expired, but most of her applications were half-hearted. She went to two interviews, and was offered one position, in Norwich, but turned it down. By the end of that year, she had come to terms with spending the rest of her working life at Guildford University, a decision partly eased by a growing respect for Olive, who had (Lizette grudgingly admitted) enlivened the department.

***

I, on the other hand, could not come to terms with my situation. REACH's mandate (and my job) terminated in December 79 (administration of the ongoing projects was transferred to the European Union executive in Brussels). Surely my life was not over. I was 80, and relatively fit, all the way down from the mind to the ankles. (It would have been churlish to complain about the mild symptoms of rheumatoid arthritis elsewhere in my body which, with my ankle clear of pain, had become more noticeable.) Lizette was not insensible to my octogenarian angst and fears about retirement. She stepped up our social arrangements with trips to the theatre in London, more visitors at the weekends, and, inevitably, more tasks in the garden and bridge practice. It was around this time that Horace's book, *Reflections of a Political Lightweight*, was published, and that Lizette first proposed, half seriously, I write my autobiography and call it *Reflections of a UN Heavyweight*.

Incidentally, Horace's book was a racy read. Not only did he reproduce as much printable Parliamentary scandal as could be squeezed into the story of his own career, but he had one truly newsworthy tit-bit which catapulted the book into the bestseller lists. He revealed – to much astonishment – that he had had a brief affair with Terrance Spoon. The same Terrance Spoon, now deceased, who had been married with four children, and had been prime minister for several years in the 40s. Unfortunately, the book and the revelation turned Horace into something of a media darling; he was able to make more of a fool of himself in broadcasting studios than he would have done if he'd still been an

MP in the House of Commons. A newly-constructed heart certainly ensured his zest for attention continued unabated. At Taunton House, Lizette rarely bothered any longer to help me entertain him which meant I alone had to cope with his garrulous turns.

When I looked back on my life then, I realised that apart from a tedious period at the Department of Industry and Technology in the 20s, I had been very fortunate in the progress of my career. I had never had to struggle to find jobs, they had found me. I decided, therefore, it was finally time to be more proactive, to tout around for any modest employment. I drew up a list of people I could contact, and I tried to draft what I might say to them. This proved far from easy. I had never been good at keeping in touch with colleagues, and so there was no way to disguise a communication as having any purpose other than canvassing. 'Hi, how are you? By the way, I'm not doing anything at the moment. If you hear of any opportunities coming up ...' Ridiculous. I couldn't do it. The most I could do was mention, in the normal course of social contacts, my distaste for retirement.

In the summer of 80, I received a surprise call from Jude Singleton. Lizette and I had just returned from a week in the Midlands staying with Pete and Clarity, to find Jay camped out at Taunton House. A year earlier, he had dropped out of Reading University (having scraped into a course on 'The Information Interface' a year before that) to join a Notek community in Cumbria, and this was his first visit home. Lizette lost no time in losing her rag. She was shouting when my phone rang. Jude Singleton, who was around ten years older than me, must have been in her 90s. We had met occasionally while I was working for REACH in London Bridge; and we sent each other new year cards.

'Have you heard of Josephine Lock?'

'No.'

'Let me ask you another question then. How's your interest in old photos?'

'You know I sold my collection before leaving The Hague. But I follow the auctions onscreen, and I've been known to trek into London for an exhibition. It's one of my only pleasures these days.'

'Self-pity, that's not you Kip.'

'No, I've put it on, like a hat.' She laughed. 'So who is Josephine Lock?'

'Josephine Lock, née Shuttleworth. The only child of Ronald and Deborah Shuttleworth, later known as William and Deborah Caxton. Caxton left Deborah a very rich woman. She squandered some of it, but soon learned – with the help of a second husband who died in the 60s – to handle the power and guide the Caxton assets. She passed away last year, and left over a billion euros to her daughter. Josephine, who's about 60 now, was married to a

Captain John Lock, but he too died years ago. There are several children on the scene who take up some of Josephine's time, and for whom a chunk of the inheritance will be earmarked. Much of the rest of her time and money is dedicated to various charities. But she has one abiding personal obsession – old photos. She already has a large collection, which is curated on a freelance basis by one of the specialists at Bradford. But now she has this money, she wants to do something big, something very big indeed. Are you there, Kip?' The shouting between Lizette and Jay had escalated, and I moved out to the garden to avoid any of it getting through to Jude.

'I'm here, Jude, all ears. How do you know this Josephine?'

'Green Aid. We both sit on an advisory panel. She's a special person, exceptionally humane and giving. She's spent most of her life working for charities of one sort or another. She's very attentive, with a tendency to become involved. Overly so. It's only with the help of tactful assistants she manages to get through a hectic schedule. I think it's a reaction to her father. It's as though she believes the very worst things written about him, and is trying to make up for his moral corruption with her own life. The photo thing, that's different, it's a private passion. A weakness, she calls it.'

'And she wants to do something big with this weakness?'

'She wants to starts a new museum on the origins of photography, here in London. In collaboration with Bradford if possible, but competing with it if necessary. She's proposing a generous budget: for a property, for acquisitions, for staff and for investing to provide a secure future for a minimum of ten years. But that's not all. She plans for the new museum to launch and lead an international project to create a single portal providing simple and efficient access to the world's most important early photographs regardless of their owners. She dreams of being able to switch on her screen and within seconds being able to use one portal to find any photograph over 200 years old by date, by artist, by subject, or by location along with a relevant encyclopedic-type commentary. And ...' She paused.

'And?'

'And, she's thinking of involving you.'

'Me? Why?'

'If it was the museum alone, she could pick any number of experts from here or abroad who would jump at the chance of such an opportunity, but the portal will be a different matter entirely, involving sensitive negotiations with historic photograph libraries around the world, and Josephine sees the two projects as integrally linked. She wants someone with your administrative and diplomatic experience to oversee the whole scheme and there aren't many like you, with time on their hands, and with such a detailed knowledge of old photographs.'

382

'She knows a lot about me?'

'From me, I'm afraid. Although not, of course, about your personal dealings with her father. You'd be paid, but not much. Not because she can't afford it. This is my interpretation, of course. She imagines you having ... wants you to have, the same passion for the project as she does. Do you want to meet her?'

The front door crashed as Jay left. After putting the phone down on Jude, I felt dazed and elated.

Four weeks later, I travelled by train to Tunbridge Wells from where a skinny youth with ear-rings and a dappled jacket drove me (in a Duo which took ages – I've always hated the Duos, with their minimal leg room) to Caxtonbury, a beautiful 15th century manor house, complete with moat, near Cranbrook. This is where Josephine lived when not in London. I was nervous throughout the journey, scared that I might not like her and that, if there was no chemistry between us, or that my earlier dealings with her father somehow interfered in our business, she would look elsewhere for someone to realise her dream. But Josephine created her own chemistry with people. We had already spoken several times on the phone, and she had researched me thoroughly. She wasn't at all how I had imagined her, a media celebrity elaborately made-up, with chic clothes and shaped hair. She wore a long hanging tan shirt over dark red slacks and appeared surprisingly small. There was no disguising of age in the flesh on her face, but nevertheless she had girlish cheerful features, and radiantly piercing eyes, which seemed ready to hypnotise. At a distance you would never tell how much energy she packed into that fragile body; close-up she was a controlled fire-cracker, not one that scares but one that enchants.

I spent the afternoon at Caxtonbury (a name which had been imposed on the property by Caxton). While being shown the gardens, Josephine talked about her father, who had died while she was still a teenager. She had come to the conclusion, many years ago, that he had been an astonishing man, astonishingly clever and astonishingly awful, but he had never deserved to die so young. I mentioned my earliest meeting with him, when he was a Shuttleworth and I was a schoolboy, but not my later encounters. Thereafter, neither of us mentioned her megalomaniac father again. We ate lunch with a quiet middle-aged man named Leo Vaughn, who helped Josephine store and catalogue her prints and negatives; then the two of them showed me a sample of the collection. Stunning. Josephine had upwards of a hundred rare early photographs and glass plate negatives, from the 1840s, and a thousand more from slightly later. Most of the rarest and important photographs had been bought, at very reasonable cost, from a French institution which, in desperation, had sold off some of its treasures during the Grey Years. Josephine was bubbling over with excitement as she tried to talk me through her different holdings, explaining the provenance of each print, or amusing me with an anecdote about its purchase. Leo was run off his feet, doing all the work, removing fragile prints, metal daguerreotypes and glass plate positives from their storage, giving them to me to examine and then returning each one to its proper place. I do not remember exactly what she showed me that day, but there was one of William Henry Fox Talbot's prints called 'Pencil of Nature' (not in good condition), a remarkable daguerreotype of Siberian workmen taken by J P Alibert, some beautiful Le Gray photos, and a Hippolyte Bayard albumen print of barricades in Paris (which reminded me of a Le Gray photo of Palermo after Garibaldi's conquest). I also recall several particularly appealing French stereoscopic daguerreotypes of reclining nudes, which were similar, but earlier, than the stereoscope prints I had owned. Josephine would have kept us both there until midnight, but Leo, who was heading all the way back to Bradford where he worked, had to leave after a couple of hours. He said he wanted to tidy up first, and suggested Josephine and I retire to a more comfortable room to discuss what they had nicknamed the Project.

Josephine and I talked non-stop, in the garden over tea, then in the drawing room (where all walls were covered in a patchwork of framed reproductions of old photos), and through a delicious supper (the cook doubled as a waiter and appeared happy to do so). While drinking coffee, the dapple-jacketed youth interrupted us to ensure I was taken back to the station in good time to catch the last train to Gatwick with a connection to Guildford. Over the next few weeks, by email and phone, we prepared a simple plan of action, which I then wrote up as a proposal and she discussed with her legal and financial advisers. I was to manage the whole project in two overlapping programmes. In one, it would be my task to prepare a detailed operational plan (with a budget breakdown, objectives, staffing levels etc.) for the museum, which, when ready, would be brought to a project development board set up and chaired by Josephine. Subsequently, and with the board's approval, we would purchase a property and appoint a curator who would handle the museum's furbishing, launch and operations. Josephine and I (and other advisers we chose) would buy the stock for the museum. She saw no reason why we shouldn't start this immediately, since it would be a long and stealthy task finding potential collections to purchase. The second programme would also involve me preparing a detailed proposal on how to approach the complex task of realising Josephine's dream of a single portal for the world's most important 19th century photos, getting it approved by the project development board, and then implementing it myself.

My retirement landscape no longer looked flat and barren.

***

For several days in a row now, I've had the pleasure of Guido and Mireille visiting in the afternoons. Today they have gone to Paris for a week, and then they'll be back in London for a few more days. They look middle-aged now, but they were still young people when Lizette and I visited them in 81. I couldn't say when the change took place. Although I communicate with Guido in Dutch by email and on the phone, when together with Mireille (the two of them are usually inseparable) we speak in English since Mireille's Dutch is no better than my French or Spanish. Where Guido hesitates over a word, Mireille completes his sentences for him. They are a sweet couple, but I do not feel close to them. They enquired politely about my progress on this book, though they both share a disinterest in the past or their families' heritages. Guido has never asked to see any of the chapters, and, when I've emailed him queries about our life together in Oldwijkgaarten, he's replied pleading a faulty memory.

Their son, Inti, is a waiter and a would-be movie actor. He studied drama in San Francisco. Mireille and Guido thought he would return to Ecuador, and are disappointed that he's decided to settle in the United States.

Mireille and Guido themselves are on the road half the year, touring all over South America with their famous Grupo de Teatro Quito. Whenever they have a new show start-up, Guido gives me net access rights so I can watch the broadcasts if I choose. Over the years, I have made attempts to tune in. I can see the theatres are full, and the audiences enthusiastic, but I don't watch for long. Theatre is meant for the stage not the screen, and in any case the flow-translation, which works well for business and basic communication, never gets close to interpreting theatre language adequately. I stuck with one of their shows, an adaptation of Amado's *Gabriella*, through from beginning to end, and it was fantastic, although, to my mind, it owed more to the 21st century film than the 20th century book.

I did see one of their plays for real, before they started Grupo de Teatro Quito, and while they were still in charge of Teatro Sucre. This was on the grand tour Lizette and I undertook in April 81. We were away six weeks in all, an exhausting six weeks, but one I could never have done without Lizette's companionship (and Sami's wonderful ankle). Bel, as in Belinda, who the Project had employed as a general purpose dogsbody and who worked out of Josephine's office in Soho, London (part of her extensive apartment), organised the itinerary for us. Although I did have Project business in both Lima and Rio, and thus her help with travel arrangements would have been partially legitimate, I paid her overtime out of my own pocket. Bel was as bright as a button and as sharp as a pin, and managed to buy us some government-controlled permits for the Galapagos Islands. Most people booked up two years or more in advance to visit the famous islands, but she discovered a special broker who dealt with permit returns and cancellations and was authorised to re-sell them. We went to Quito, then to the Galapagos Islands, followed by Lima, Cuzco, São Paulo and Rio. I could fill this chapter with details of the journey, but will restrict myself to a few highlights.

Six year old Inti was one such highlight. This was our first physical encounter. Content to have his own audience, he never stopped performing for us. Already at the airport he gave us a one minute show, a dance and a poem in Spanish, on the moving walkway. At the colonial-style house in the San Marcos quarter, owned by Guido and Mireille, Inti showed us the tiny amphitheatre, with seating for four, constructed in the corner of the elaborately tiled patio. There was a weatherproof screen there, and a cam connection. I recognised the place, for Inti and Guido had used it to talk to me by camphone. Inti looked not unlike Guido did at that age, but there was none of Guido's diffidence. I never once noticed the boy slope off to his room to do something on his own. He wanted to be with the adults and involved in their activities. And there was plenty of activity in the house. It seemed as though the phones were always ringing; and there were people coming and going all day, not only those connected with the show, but neighbours, or those who had worked for the community theatre during the Grey Years. Guido and Mireille had long planned to take a week off during our visit, but, because of the late switch in our schedule to accommodate the Galapagos Islands, we ended up arriving when they were much tied up with a production. Nevertheless, they made us feel very welcome. Our bedroom, although cramped, had been brightly decorated with a floor vase containing a large bunch of bird of paradise flowers. They reminded me of Diana.

Guido and Mireille were immensely proud of Teatro Sucre, not only of having restored the building and theatre in 69-70 (with Felix Montechristo's money) but in re-resurrecting the theatre as a going concern during the previous three years. Many of their shows were the talk of Quito, and consequently a sell-out. They knew how to choose the best touring groups, from as far afield as Europe, and they had a talent for putting on their own spectacular shows. The one we saw, *De Aqui Hacia el Sol*, a musical about the Grey Years, had been written by two local writers. It was designed and directed by Guido, although Mireille, as the co-producer, had also taken a hand in the direction. I thought it an exciting show, even without fully understanding the text, while Lizette judged it simplistic and over-cinematic. The story revolved around two families, rich Catholic and poor Quechua, with organ music employed effectively for the former and panpipes for the latter. What I remember most, though, was the dazzling way each aspect of the show moved progressively from dark to light and from grey to colour (I'd never seen Electralon material used so effectively).

I had been to Quito twice during my time at the IFSD. The old centre was a joy to wander around, with its craft shops, indian markets and trendy eating places; and it was certainly no trial to revisit the Baroque churches with their gold-rich interiors, although Lizette was more impressed than I by the religious relics. But I had not been to the Galapagos Islands. My expectations were so high that I couldn't fail to be disappointed, not by the islands, and definitely not by the tortoises, the iguanas, the boobies, but by the way we were led around like sheep, our every step ordained and monitored, and by the way the whole place felt like a wildlife zoo. I did, though, understand intellectually that these very restrictions were necessary to enable I, and many other tourists, to experience the islands' treasures. The park for giant tortoises, along with a UN-licensed cloning centre similar to one I'd seen in China for pandas, was interesting, as was the Galapagos Island Survival Foundation Exhibition which explained how the islands had coped with climate change excesses (updated to include the Grey Years) and sea level rises. The Foundation had been set up and supported for many years with IFSD money. The best part of the week was three days sailing around the smaller islands on a modern Brazilian-made ketch. We searched out sea lions, penguins, tropic birds and the waved albatross, and ate lobsters, crab, small tuna and goat all caught by our skipper and his son.

In Lima, we stayed with Samuel and Lynn, both of whom had fallen for Peru in a big way. Lynn rambled on incessantly about the Inca civilisation, while Samuel appeared genuinely happy with the work and the opportunity to pass on his learning. He hadn't realised, he said, that he would end up becoming involved in investment decisions, by dint of growing to like his pupils and wanting to help them. Moreover, he found it galling that some Peruvians might be getting rich on the back of his charity. Notwithstanding this and several other criticisms, he was very positive about the Wisdom Programme.

While Samuel and Lynn took Lizette sightseeing, I filled up the week on business. Firstly, I negotiated with the government's ministry of art and heritage for an agreement in principle to incorporate an important state-owned collection of photos in our universal portal. Secondly, I finalised a deal to purchase a private collection of 19th and early 20th century Andean photographs, including several by the Courret brothers and Martin Chambi. The seller and I had agreed on a price and conditions, but, months later, the government intervened to prevent the collection leaving the country. It was my mistake. There had been no formal legal requirement to do so, but I should have sought permission for the private purchase directly with the ministry of art and heritage. At the very least, I could have informed them about my negotiations. I was on a learning curve: the <u>buying</u> of historically-important <u>art</u>, or access to same, required different negotiating skills from those I'd employed for decades in the <u>giving</u> of welfare-important development <u>aid</u>. From Lima, we flew to Cuzco, for various trips, not least to Machu Picchu where I secretly relived, for a moment or two, the excitement of my early holidays with Diana.

In São Paulo, where we stayed in an unmemorable hotel, Lizette insisted on a city tour. It included lunch at the highest restaurant in the Southern Hemisphere, truly high enough to fully appreciate ant-man's achievements. I had dined there 20-30 years earlier, with a Brazilian minister, but then it had had some class, now it was no more than an over-priced tourist guzzleshop. On another day, we sought out the Museum of Modern Art, where I rediscovered the beautiful wood/metal panels by Hector Julio Paride Bernabo I'd once seen in Salvador. We also went to the world famous science museum, Museo Biomass, which used scintillating displays and 3D-integration exhibits to demonstrate man's use of wood and other vegetation to provide heat and fuel, and, of course, to show off Brazil's pioneering role in the modern history of biofuels, such as Vivido. Mostly, though, we were in São Paulo so Lizette could meet up with a Brazilian friend who had done a PhD and some lecturing at Keele University, and so I could spend time with Arturo, Fatima and his children, my grandchildren.

Arturo had retired from O Futuro and sold his ranch in Goiânia. He now divided his time between a huge mid-block apartment and sky-garden in São Paulo and a villa in the hills overlooking Florianopolis on Ihla de Santa Catarina. I never went to the villa, but from the camclips Arturo sent me, it looked glamorous, like a billionaire's home. The apartment in São Paulo was richly appointed also, with dark marble corridors and columns and gilt wall cornicing, both of which gave the place an ostentatious feel. Arturo himself had the appearance of a man who had lived too long. He had grown fat. Cosmetic surgery on his face had long since decomposed the features. He wasn't yet grotesque, but a cartoonist would have required little imagination to sketch him. If I exaggerate, it is only because there was nothing left of my son or his life that I could engage with. When I enquired about his cloned daughter Alicia (as I had done by email without any answer), he said she had behaved very badly and disappeared years earlier. Disappeared!

Arturo had two main interests: golf and tropical fish. The palatial apartment was full of fish tanks, some of them built into the walls. When the screens weren't in use they showed soothers, live broadcasts of fish swarms swimming in coral reefs. Arturo showed me his proudest possession: a tank with a dozen unremarkable slender fish, each one about ten centimetres long with blue and yellow partial stripes. He told me they were called Brachydanio AM, and asked if I had any idea where the name came from. I did not. Nor was I happy to know when he told me. The species had been named after him, Arturo Magalhães, because the pattern of the partial stripes, looked at sideways, showed quite clearly an AM marking. I assumed this was an accident, until Arturo told me otherwise. He was the director of a specialised lab which genetically manipulated such fish to order. When I reminded him that independent genetic experimentation on animals for commercial gain was banned at the UN level, Arturo shrugged his shoulders and explained that the Brazilian authorities had deliberately shown no interest in enforcing the international law.

I learned, during my two visits to the family, that Fatima, who I had not met before except by camphone, was about to have her jaw and forehead skin restretched and her earlobes extended. She proudly trumpeted, using a mixture of Portuguese and passable English, the various enhancements she'd already subscribed to over the years, such as the sockets – they looked like moles – for cheek miniscreens which she only wore on special occasions. Without a trace of modesty, she also mentioned her vaginal muscle implants. I responded, without thinking and enough subsequent embarrassment for the two of us, that Arturo must be a lucky man. Fatima's quizzical expression suggested she hadn't understood my remark, or that I had missed the point.

I met Ignacio, the oldest child, only the once, at a family meal, to which I went alone without Lizette because I saw no reason to inflict Arturo's kin on her. He arrived late, dressed in skin-tight clothes like a cycle racer, and had the confidence of someone much older than his 16 years. After giving a mock bow to Arturo who was watching an American golf tournament on the wallscreen, he planted a sloppy kiss on his mother's mole-marked cheek. Fatima was grateful for his presence, not angry at his tardiness. He sat down and delivered a quip that caused his younger brother and sister to laugh. He turned to me and said something in Portuguese which he asked Tina to translate.

'Welcome to Brazil, to the land of dreams.' He was barely with us an hour, before he rushed away.

Juliano, 13 years old, spoke rarely either time I was at the apartment, preferring the company of his games console and the largest screen he was permitted to use at any given time. The closest affinity I managed with him was for about half an hour when I feigned interest in one of the football games he was playing, and used my earphones to get a bitty sense of his commentary. As for Tina, only ten at the time, she was strangely aloof from all that happened around her, and would often fail to reply when spoken too. She had no time for the tropical fish or for Juliano's games, but she did enjoy dressing up. On one visit, she took me into her bedroom to show me a cat, Salvatore (named after a current singer). He was sky blue, which I found very disturbing. I had grown used to jet black tulips, purple cucumbers, lavender-flavoured berries, and had seen, onscreen, illegal genetically-modified hamsters and rabbits, plus I was trying to get my head around the idea of fish species created to order. But sky-blue cats ... I would not have thought it possible. The sight of it made me feel physically sick.

I was not using the translator earphones at this point, partly because they functioned inadequately with children who could not or would not make the effort to talk more deliberately than usual, and partly because Tina had sufficient English to complement my inadequate Portuguese. Thus, I was in a state of moral consternation for a full two minutes before I comprehended Tina's explanation: she preferred Salvatore orange, the colour he was dyed last week. Then she gave me a comb and asked me to groom him, which I did with relief.

The day we arrived in Rio de Janeiro, 8 May 81, was the day two chemists from Pittsburgh in the United States announced they had created life in the laboratory, and could do it again. The media went berserk with the news, and so did Lizette. As far as she was concerned this was the holy grail of scientific research. She stayed in the Leblon beachfront hotel all day glued to the screen watching interviews with the two scientists themselves, and the debates with politicians, religious leaders and others. One of the traits I loved in Lizette was her endless enthusiasm for science and scientific developments. Barely a week would go by without her returning home from work bursting with news of some discovery or invention reported by the science media during the day. Despite my limited knowledge I would usually encourage her to explain more, to colour in the scientific picture for me.

On this occasion, though, I had to leave Lizette to her own devices since, as in Lima, I had pre-arranged appointments on behalf of the Project. The oldest Argentinian photographs (mostly taken by itinerant US photographers such as Charles DeForest Fredericks), and the only ones we wanted for the portal, were held in a private collection, and the owner Max Voll, a billionaire, had agreed to see me in Rio. We met at the Club Militar, a glitzy restaurant in Urca at the back of a beach, directly beneath the Sugar Loaf. As with most of our eventual collaborators, Max was keen on the plan but wanted to be reassured that the benefits would meet the costs, and that public screen access to his collection through our portal would not compromise the ownership security attached to the photographs (i.e. that they would not be directly printable or download-able). In terms of costs, all we asked is that the owners put copies of each of the photographs they had agreed to share into a database format that we would supply. On the benefits, I explained that we fully expected the portal to increase, not diminish, interest in the original collections, and that we would pass on 85% of the page view income. (The Project development board had already decided against free access and that our content pages would be billed on Solar's lowest mainstream charging level – close to 0.01 euros at that time.) I was not as technically knowledgeable as Max, but, having been sufficiently briefed by our technical advisers, I was able to provide confident assurances on portal copyright security.

Also that week, in-between day trips with Lizette to Petrópolis and Búzios, I negotiated portal access to the most important photographs owned by the Brazilian state, including several daguerreotypes from as early as 1840 by Louis Compte. And, miraculously, I was also able to buy, from Senora Maria Pedrosa, an archive of late 19th century Brazilian photographs for our collection which included 37 Ferrez prints! It is a negligible story but I cannot resist telling it.

I located Maria Pedrosa at the end of a trail which started with old auction catalogues. I had noticed a series of lots at one particular auction firm, spanning several years, which appeared to come from the same anonymous collection. I guessed there might be more. I contacted the auction house staff who gave me, somewhat unwillingly, the details of an agent they dealt with. Then, I engaged in a drawn-out email dialogue with the agent, who, eventually, set me up with a meeting. Maria Pedrosa, who was a similar age to me, had been a star of Brazilian soap operas in the 20s, 30s and 40s. She was very wealthy and lived in a mansion behind fortress-style walls in the Santa Teresa suburb of Rio. Four husbands had come and gone over the years. The last one, from whom she had inherited the photograph collection, died in the late 60s. She no longer ever left her home, but she did have a small army of live-in staff, and there was a constant stream of visitors. Not only were there many advisers and visitors wanting something from her, but there were the rich and/or famous who had once loved her on the screen and who petitioned to come to her weekly dinner parties. All this I had learned from the agent or my own research.

But she was one of the most memorable people I have ever met, both in body and in character. When I entered her opulent receiving room, she was standing seven or eight metres away with an elbow on a grand mantlepiece. She looked every inch a movie star, and could have been mistaken for half her age. Admittedly, my eyes were no longer very sharp. When we sat down in antique armchairs, she remained a good four metres away. At this lesser distance, her light-golden curly-haired wig looked real enough, but I could detect heavy layers of make-up designed to hide the age of her skin, and the clever way a slinky gold gown appeared to make her look youthfully slim and not agedly slouched. Whether she didn't care, or had no means to change it, her voice sounded croaky and old; and she farted constantly. The agent, a handsome dark man, around 40, impeccably dressed in a pressed white suit, sat in a third lounge chair. When Maria's English gave out, he translated; and then, later, when Maria and I had finished talking, he was the one with whom I finalised the details.

For nearly an hour, Maria quizzed me incessantly, wanting to know why I was in Brazil, what I'd done in my life, how old I was when I'd first had sex, how many wives I'd married and children I'd sired. She wasn't the least impressed by my career at the IFSD, although I could see she perked up when I mentioned my collaboration with Pam, the film director. She was very interested in the fact that I had a Brazilian son, and, when she enquired further about him, I told her, reluctantly, about his work. I thought she might kick me out – few other topics could elicit such violent reactions in people as cloning – but the reverse was true. She herself had a cloned son, she said, thanks to the O Futuro group; moreover, she thought she remembered meeting a techno-clinician called Arturo. When I enquired about her own son, she waved an arm (flashing inch-long purple nails) to dismiss my enquiry, as she had done with all my other questions. At the end of her inquisition she spent another half an hour giving me a well-rehearsed monologue résumé of her life story. Thus I learned that her mother had acted in a 1980s film, *Edu*, about the origins of cinematography in Brazil. On my request she asked her assistant to ensure I was sent a copy. It is a beautiful movie. I have it on Neil. Perhaps I can persuade Chintz to watch it with me this evening. I am missing Jay's near daily visits. I wonder if he would judge me as being too long-winded in this chapter. It is certainly taking me a very long time to write. I think my concentration is fading.

I realise that by naming certain early South American photographers, and Max Voll and Maria Pedrosa, I am giving them too much relative importance. Most of my negotiations for the Project were conducted by camphone or email, and I would certainly not have made trips, involving time and expense, to Lima or Rio without other reasons. The most important photographs and photographic collections we had earmarked for the portal were in Europe and the US, and therefore the only special journeys I made, during earlier years, were to negotiate portal access with the important curators and owners in East and West Coast United States, Moscow, St Petersburg (far too late for Alan or Anna), Warsaw, Berlin, Prague, Paris, Marseilles and Milan. By early 82, we had appointed a director, Giselle Dufkova, to take charge of the photograph museum side of the Project – to be called The Josephine Collection – and we had poached Leo from Bradford to look after the photographs themselves. This meant that, much to my regret, it was sensible to hand over most of my photo-purchasing role to Giselle. By early 83, we had also appointed a technical director, Lorraine Lomax, who was to manage all the museum's computer-based operations, including the portal, which was to be known as Portia for no other reason than that its official name, the Universal Portal to the World's Earliest Photographs was too clumsy for common use.

The success of The Josephine Collection and Portia was largely down to the dedication and skills of Giselle and Lorraine. But it was Josephine, with her special talent for enthusing others and making the impossible sound possible, who was responsible for finding and attracting both women in the first place. I feel sure that if I had been the one to approach either of them they would never have considered leaving their highly-respected, well-paid positions. Yet, there was also a point where Josephine's ability gave out, she lost patience with detail, and got angry if she hadn't found anyone to whom a task could be delegated. Thus, the courtship of Giselle and then Lorraine followed a similar pattern: Josephine wooed them to the Project, and I married them to it; she fired their imaginations and made them believe in the dream, and I showed them why we should, and how we could, make it a reality.

Both Giselle and Lorraine were exceptionally gifted individuals. The former, a quiet studious lady, had spent 25 working years at the Société Française de Photographie and was looking for a new challenge. She loved the idea, as sold to her by Josephine, of abandoning Paris and working in London. Unfortunately, the Société Française de Photographie resented her leaving and it wasn't until the 90s, long after I'd gone, that it finally agreed to allow its photographs to be accessed through Portia. An American by birth, and with a much livelier personality, Lorraine had lived in London most of her life. Recently, she had spent five years helping the Royal Horticultural Society and its international affiliates launch a series of themed portals for universal read-only access to all existing and relevant pre-19th century publications. The results had been much applauded in the media.

***

I have raced too far ahead, and need to backtrack to the months following our South America tour. In June that year (81), Diana died, from kidney failure. I went to the funeral in Amsterdam. Guido arrived just in time on a delayed flight via Miami, having left Mireille to cope with looking after Inti and their theatre's busy schedule alone. We sat in a row with our friends Peter and Rudy. Peter's wife Livia was bedridden and in a nursing home by this time, having been crippled by a stroke. I don't know where Rudy's sister Ulla was. Nearby were Mireille's mother, Helene (exquisitely dressed but undeniably old), who had travelled from Paris with an escort, and Mireille's sister Veronique who had come from Geneva. It was not surprising to see them there since all the Rocard family had been very fond of Diana, as a consequence of her friendship with Didier (who had died a decade earlier). Diana's younger sister Dominique, her partner Waltar and their two sons, Jurian and Lukas, with their wives and several children sat in front of us, as did Dimi, Diana's oldest sister, who was in very good shape for 90 odd.

A haggard-looking Karl gave a moving speech, but one which neglected the middle portion of Diana's life, the part during which she had lived happily with me, and during which she and I had raised Guido. After the service, there was a wake at Karl's house, but neither Guido nor I wished to go. Instead, we took the train to Leiden for a nostalgic stroll around the town and through Oldwijkgaarten. Nothing had changed. Centuries of architectural history had not been affected either by the wars or the Grey Years. Our old house and the surrounding gardens appeared the same, well-cared for, with children playing on the lawns, and colourful roses blooming in the borders. I would have been content to walk in silence, but Guido had a need for confession. He felt guilty about having emigrated to South America and deserting Diana, especially as he was her only son. He never meant to stay away a lifetime. She had resented his distance, he confided (for he had never mentioned this before), and wanted to know if I had too. I said I had missed him greatly, but I'd never resented his choices, especially since I understood that he was devoted to Mireille, and that they had found a fulfilling life for themselves. Your mother should have appreciated that, I told him, so don't think about her resentment as anything other than an expression of her love. It may not have been apparent at times, I said, but you were the most important thing in her life, more important than Karl, me or even the theatre itself. At which point he burst out laughing, and said 'now I know you're re-inventing the past'.

We met up with Peter and Rudy later and took the tram to Rudy's house in the Amsterdam suburbs. There we spent a melancholy and, for me uncomfortable, evening talking about Diana. Peter's memory had begun to fail, and he was unable to censor out of the conversation his memories of and anecdotes about Diana and Karl; either that or, when talking about Diana, he became confused between Karl and me. Peter had known Diana together with Karl long before I came to the Netherlands, and then, when they reformed as a couple in Amsterdam, he and Livia both remained friendly with the two of them. This had not affected my friendship with Peter and Livia since, by then, I was seeing them infrequently (they only came once to Taunton House), and, until recently, they had always been careful to avoid discussing Diana in any context that involved Karl.

As far as I could tell, Rudy's life had not been as rewarding as Guido's and, as a consequence, they had grown apart over the years – it wasn't only the geographical distance between them. Rudy had separated from his wife, who had taken custody of their child, Arnout. And, although Rudy had tasted success as a professional musician, his standard of living had fluctuated with the popularity of jazz.

Four months later, in October, Karl and Dominique organised a memorial service at a small theatre in Amsterdam, and I heard Rudy play for the first time in 20 years. He had such a sweet touch. There were other faces, familiar friendly ones who sang Diana's praises, or who acted out sketches, sad and funny, from her favourite plays. I was sorry Guido and Mireille had decided not to come, but they followed the event onscreen, and the three of us talked about it at length afterwards. I couldn't resist taking a personal swipe at Karl, for it must have been he who decided that the memorial service/show should include a two-hander sketch from Angelika Stockmann's *The Children's Land*. I asked Guido if he remembered, when he was about eight, being woken by his parents shouting at each other, and coming out of his bedroom to try and stop their argument. He did, along with a vivid recollection of being afraid that we might be about to break up, and that he might lose one of us. I explained that it was during the production of the Stockmann play in Antwerp that Diana had got back together with Karl, and that the secret relationship had been the root cause of the argument – although I didn't realise as much at the time. I was convinced Karl's staging of an exert from that play was no coincidence.

Diana's passing led me into sadnesses and regrets which went on, in one form or another, for weeks, and were then resurrected in the run-up to the memorial and in the weeks after that. The memories of her colourful, magical warm companionship could easily send me into a maudlin mood if I let them. And, obviously, I had regrets about the final years of our relationship, not only for myself, but also because of the possibility that our behaviour may have contributed, albeit slightly, to the decision by Guido and Mireille to leave Europe. But, although I felt truly privileged to have known her, to have spent part of my life in her orbit, and to have fathered her son, I could not regret our eventual separation, for then I would never have met Lizette with whom I experienced the most complete and rounded relationship of my life.

By contrast, I felt very little emotion at the news of Arturo's death. It was as though he had never managed to pierce his way through to my heart. He had arrived too late, when my emotions were already spread too thin. I tried to act as a father, and, I guess, he tried to behave as a son. A cynic might argue that for several years we played out our respective roles, one giving mock respect, the other providing financial support. Again, I am probably being too clinical in my assessment. While Arturo was here, studying, dependant on me, I'm sure I did care for him, as I do now – in a distant kind of way – for his daughter Tina, and his grandchild Maria.

Arturo died in 82, of skin cancer. I was too busy and tired to make the trip for his funeral, and so expressed condolences and made excuses to Fatima by camphone. She told me that Arturo was already suffering from the cancer when I was there, in São Paulo, but that he had not wanted to burden me with the knowledge. She also told me, nervously, that I had not been mentioned in Arturo's will. Before dying, however, he had proposed I might want a pair of his tropical fish, the Brachydanio AM. Fatima said she would arrange and pay for safe transport. I declined politely, as I did her offer for any other memento. She informed me the family would be leaving São Paulo and moving to live permanently at the property near Florianopolis, a place where her children's grandfather would always be welcome. I returned the offer, suggesting (as sincerely as I could manage) that she and her family should come to England one day and stay with us at Taunton House.

I cannot resist adding a short postscript to Arturo's story. When Tina was here a few weeks ago, she told me her father had left instructions for his ashes to be mixed with fish food and fed to the Brachydanio AM. Fatima had done as instructed, with a tear in her eye, but the fish died in transport to the villa near Florianopolis.

I could mention that, within three months of Arturo's cremation, the United Nations concluded, as part of the ongoing post war negotiations, a comprehensive, permanent and mandatory agreement on human and animal cloning. Concessions were made to the pro-cloning scientific and political communities permitting a greater variety of cloning activities and techniques than had been allowed hitherto under the previous UN code and by the AGCT. However, whereas the old rules were wholly inadequate (being neither mandatory or widely accepted), the new international law imposed such strict licensing and operational conditions, with punitive sanctions for non-compli-ance, that the commercial cloning operations in Brazil and China, for example, were finally obliged to close down.

***

Chintz has abandoned me. She declined to watch the old Brazilian movie, *Edu*, claiming that she hated all foreign language films; and she no longer pops in to see me when she's off duty. How can she be so fickle? Guido and Mireille have been and gone today, and Jay returns tomorrow. He will find me much weakened, and struggling to conclude this chapter.

However, he should be content to discover that I am skimming over his two year drop-out period, and the angst this caused Lizette who thought he would end up spending his life with the Noteks as Mercurio had done. On returning to Reading University (a move much applauded by Lizette), Jay continued with the same course, on 'The Information Interface', although he switched the focus of his modules away from scientific information towards social and environmental knowledge. Subsequently, he went to Birmingham to do a year's teacher training. Lizette was unable to suppress her disappointment at his career choice. Jay and I both had to cope, in different ways, with her infrequent, but nevertheless stinging, attacks over his lack of ambition and achievement. On the whole, by this time, Jay felt comfortable enough to spend some weekends at Taunton House (occasionally bringing boyfriends with him). But, if ever Lizette began to make snide remarks about his profession, he would engage her in argument for half an hour or so, then storm out and not return for several months. I tended to defend him, especially before any argument had escalated, and then after he had gone, but my interventions never served any purpose. Instead, they usually led Lizette into a semi-emotional attack on me, there being a surfeit of teachers in my background. Personally, I believe teaching is one of the most important and noblest of professions, and that Lizette was wrong to give her research undertakings far more value than her education work. Within a few days of such arguments, Lizette would find a way to apologise. In my case, where the apology was genuine, it was unnecessary. In Jay's case, the apology took the form of an unwelcome excuse without any trace of repentance for – what Jay rightly viewed as – her illegitimate judgement on him and his life.

My five years working on the Project passed all too quickly. In the preparatory stages, when Josephine chaired the development board, and we worked together as a small team, the meetings were often long and unstructured. And yet, such was the pleasure of Josephine's intensity and enthusiasm, and the nature of our endeavour, that I usually felt a touch of disappointment when she finally shuffled her papers together and said: 'Ladies and gentleman, enough. You have been so patient with me, and so generous with your time, I really must let you all go now. But we have made progress, haven't we, such progress.'

During 82, we acquired an interesting property near King's Cross (in Chalton Street, a stone's throw from the British Library), and, by 83, with Giselle and Lorraine both in place and formal committee structures operating, the implementation stage was well under way. Nevertheless, Josephine continued to be very demanding and involved, and this led to a spate of awkward arguments over minor decisions. Thus, wisely, Josephine agreed to step back leaving me to preside over most meetings. She continued, however, to chair the main development board which met to decide on key budget issues and the more important artistic questions, such as those concerning photograph purchases and the evolving parameters for Portia.

King's Cross was inconvenient for me, so, when the office refurbishment works were completed on the second floor (i.e. before the gallery areas on the ground and first floors), I planned to spend only two days a week there, with Bel organising my meetings accordingly, and to sleep over at a local hotel. When Josephine learned of this, she insisted I make use of the self-contained guest suite within her own apartment and join her for supper on a regular basis. Only when she advised me in advance that the suite would be occupied did I make alternative arrangements. Thus, we settled into a useful pattern, with the weekly supper together serving as our main point of contact.

Even with Josephine in the background, rarely a month went by without her causing one mini-crisis or another. Josephine, for example, continued to want everything done yesterday, while Giselle would not be rushed. She worked earnestly, kept long hours but became surly and uncommunicative if asked to speed up some action or other. The only effective way I found of dealing with this was to sit down with Giselle and look at the detail of the work required for a specific action. If I could demonstrate where a time saving was possible, she would accept it, and the surliness would evaporate. If I could not demonstrate where such a saving was possible, then at least I was sufficiently briefed to argue Giselle's case with Josephine. Another problem arose because of Giselle's dissatisfaction with Leo Vaughn. Having convinced the Collection's executive board of the need for a second curator to manage special exhibitions, she employed a compatriot, Henri Pouile, who was more than ten years younger than Leo. Thereafter, she began a very deliberate process of obliging Henri to encroach on Leo's responsibilities. Her idea was that either Leo would resign in protest, or Henri would end up taking charge of the main collections anyway. But Leo was no fool. As soon as he had sufficient evidence of Giselle's manipulations, he went straight to Josephine. She then came to me, insisting on fair play for Leo. I won't suggest it was easy, but, after three months, I did mange to persuade Leo to take the lesser position (i.e. curating special exhibitions). Moreover, I convinced Josephine that Giselle was right to have wanted to replace Leo, and that Henri was perfect for the job; and I gave Giselle a stern warning not to be so devious again. Much unpleasantness might have been avoided, I advised her, if she had only approached me early on with her doubts about Leo.

Although the Société Française de Photographie used the lame excuse of Giselle's defection to justify its obstructive attitude to Portia, I am certain its director, whom I personally went to see twice, resented our initiative. Britain's National Museum of Photography, Film and Television, in Bradford (which was only a few years away from its centenary) did not need the pretext of Leo's departure to precipitate stolid opposition, not to The Josephine Collection, which it fully supported, but to Portia. Arnold Cowerbridge, the museum's chief executive, argued publicly that the portal we were trying to build should be directed through, and launched from, his museum, a national museum with international credibility. Our venture, he told the *Guardian* newspaper, was doomed to failure. Even if we managed to launch Portia, he suggested, it should be called 'Partial Portia', he claimed, for it would not be able to provide access to a very significant number of the most important early photographs, such as those in the Bradford museum. When, in response, the *Guardian* came to me for an in-depth interview, I stalled, and went to Bradford to talk to Cowerbridge. He was an unpleasant looking man, half my age but equally tall, with a trimmed moustache, flary ears and a sneering mouth (not entirely disguised by the moustache). He smiled a lot, though, which improved his appearance and helped in conversation. His glass desk was devoid of clutter, and spotlessly clean.

I explained to Cowerbridge that Josephine Lock, who had pledged more money to the preservation and promotion of early photography than any other private donor in history, had been deeply offended by his remarks in the media, especially as they came out of the blue without any previous discussion. I reminded him that he had deflected all our approaches up until now. He smiled. Then I gave him a very brief résumé of how much we had achieved so far, leaving him in no doubt that we had made zero compromises on the scale of our venture and that we were on schedule. The smile drooped. Next I told him I had five important media interviews pending, but first I wished to clarify what potential if any there was for collaboration between his organisation and mine. Without giving him time to reflect on what I had said or to respond, I moved swiftly on to the second part of my pitch – a direct appeal to his vanity. I told him how much we admired and respected him and the museum, and that although Portia would survive and flourish without his support, this would be a pity, a great pity for those who used Portia and for Bradford itself. Which led me on, smoothly, to the substantial list of advantages for the museum of taking part in Portia. This was the same list as I had used on countless occasions with other archives, collections and museums: an additional revenue stream; a new and important service for the world (pompous I know, but sometimes pomp works) making the earliest photographs more available than they had ever been before; and improved exposure (so to speak) for each collection accessible through the portal. Only minor collections, I intimated, should be insecure about Portia, since their contributions would be outclassed by the larger institutions (such as Bradford) which held the most important early photographic items (such as Bradford's first negative). Nevertheless, I advised, without Bradford, Portia would not be Partial Portia, but 'Portia providing access to all the world's most important early photographs except those held by the Bradford Museum'. Naturally, I did not mention our difficulties with the Société Française de Photographie. And, finally, I closed the pitch with three offers, especially for Bradford, which had been agreed with Josephine and Giselle (we'd not yet employed Lorraine): a partnership on exhibition exchanges, allowing Bradford special rights, giving it temporary but regular gallery space in the capital city; a general effort in our signage, publications and websites to promote the importance of the Bradford archive and holdings; and, with respect to Portia, a specific acknowledgement of support from the Bradford museum.

Cowerbridge listened carefully to all I had to say, so carefully in fact that I suspected his refusal to negotiate earlier and his media outbursts were all part of a planned campaign to get as much out of us as he could. By the time I finished speaking, he was smiling again. He promised to think over my proposals. For the *Guardian* interview and others that followed, I trusted my instinct, making no counter-attack against him, and playing up the hopes of Josephine, 'our benefactor', that collaboration would lead to 'a fantastic new resource for the world of early photography'. A few weeks later, when Cowerbridge was in London, Josephine took him to one of the most exclusive and expensive restaurants in London, and, then, over the next three months Cowerbridge and I negotiated a substantial framework agreement (which is not to say that, subsequently, Giselle and Lorraine didn't have their own problems working with Cowerbridge's staff on the details).

On the whole, Lorraine caused me fewer headaches than Giselle. This was because, on the technical side, she was a wizard, and on the artistic side, where Josephine was more sensitive, she advanced no firm opinions. She did have a gratingly loud voice, and an abrupt manner on the phone. This was a considerable disadvantage because one of her principle responsibilities was to help make it as simple as possible for our collaborators to prepare their own collections for use through the portal. Where the collaborators were prepared to take advice and instructions by email, Lorraine was as patient as necessary; when they rang, though, wanting to sort out a problem directly, Lorraine's manner and apparent impatience led to a few complaints. I decided the best way to resolve this problem, which might get worse in the run-up to the launch, was to allow Lorraine an assistant, which she needed, and to ensure she not only took on a person with the right skills but gave him or her the technical liaison responsibilities. A more persistent migraine of a problem for me, though, was caused by Josephine's whimsical approach to Portia's development, and Lorraine's spiky reluctance to make apparently insignificant alterations to already agreed parameters. Mostly, I sided with Lorraine, much of whose work was more complex than Josephine or I could understand, and so I learned to try and divert Josephine from responding to my weekly briefings on Portia with impractical new ideas.

Steadily and unsteadily, smoothly and with hiccups, we moved towards the launch of The Josephine Collection in March 85. Using Josephine's millions we amassed a remarkable collection of 19th and 20th century photographs, books and other paraphernalia (although not equipment, this was a decision made early on) while Giselle and Lorraine, along with Henri, Leo and our other staff supervised the development of the facilities to house them. On the ground floor of the Chalton Street property we had three large galleries, and, on the first floor, two further galleries, a library/reading room and a meeting salon. The extensive basement was dedicated to storage, but, in addition, we had storage areas on each floor. With so many different photograph materials (papers coated with myriad kinds of chemicals, glass, metal, cellulose, ceramics, even wood and cloth) storage was a complex and technically-demanding business. After much heated discussion, and on Giselle's insistence (she nearly resigned over the matter) we had opted for an expensive storage concept which combined maximum light and atmospheric protection with compactness, flexibility and accessibility. From what I could tell, it paid for itself several times over within a few years.

Giselle and Josephine had two major run-ins prior to the launch, both caused by Josephine. Giselle was devoted to the concept of a launch exhibition entitled *War and Peace*. In a collection of Russian photographs I had purchased at auction, there was a stunning portrait of Leo Tolstoy. Giselle worked out, from the date, that Tolstoy must have been writing his great book at the time; and, from there, she developed the idea of using The Josephine Collection photographs to show contrasting images of the world at war and at peace in the 1850-70 period. In an uncharacteristic display of egotism, Josephine objected and said it would be more appropriate to launch with a special exhibition based on her own favourites from the Collection. (I suspected – Josephine forgive me for this – she may have been involved with a new man at the time, and wanted to impress him, but any such suggestion would have been way beyond the brief of my relationship with her.) In the end, we put on both shows, in separate galleries, thus temporarily reducing the permanent display area by one room. This was not so complicated since we had, in any case, planned to rotate the permanent displays every six months.

The second dispute came when we were beginning to make preparations for the launch party and the opening of the museum. Josephine turned up one day unexpectedly with a young black woman, Leona Sumani, so pretty she could have been an actress or model. She was to be the Museum's new public relations manager, Josephine commanded, and her appointment would be confirmed by the next meeting of the executive board. Giselle in a moment of stress, threatened to resign (again), whether because of Leona's looks or the way she was foisted on her, I'm not sure. She calmed down when I reminded her that she herself had been 'chosen' in much the same way, and that much of the museum's public relations would necessarily come through Josephine's personal connections. My own fury at Josephine's capricious behaviour dissipated quickly. The next time we were together in private (subsequent to Leona's sudden introduction) Josephine confessed to thoughtless actions and apologised sweetly. I doubted there had been anything thoughtless in her behaviour at all. Instead, I recognised an artful touch of dissembling combined with mock naivety. Nevertheless, I accepted the apology. The incident and my own sudden anger helped remind me how remarkable a person our benefactor was, that every cent we had spent had been hers, and yet, overall and relatively, she had been so uncontrolling, so undemanding, so uncapricious.

The opening of The Josephine Collection went better than we hoped. We held two launch parties. The first was for friends of the Project, who came from far and wide (such as Max Voll from Buenos Aires). The second was for the media and political and artistic celebrities. We – I should say Leona – streamed the invitations for both events over the course of a day each, so as to avoid crowding problems. Josephine, who never sought publicity for her own sake but who was fully aware of its usefulness, gave a handful of interviews to the most potent media, particularly those with strong outlets in the US. In addition, Leona farmed Giselle and me out to the lesser media, taking care to guide Giselle, who had a sloppy screen presence, to radio and print journalists (I knew this because Leona told Josephine and Josephine told me). We learned from the extensive, and largely positive, media coverage that The Josephine Collection was the first new major artistic institution in London since before the Second Jihad War. One commentator went so far as to say the opening of the museum presaged 'a reawakening of the city's cultural spirit', another called Josephine 'the Daguerreotype Angel'.

Several months later, a young and eager BBC-connected producer, Cos Williams, approached me (via Leona) wanting to make a quality documentary on the building of The Josephine Collection. I consulted with Josephine and the staff. We agreed on giving our full support, but on the condition that the programme only be broadcast or sold after Portia was up and running (we thought the opportunity of publicity such a programme would generate would be wasted if Portia was not yet operational). Cos agreed, and, thereafter, I spent one day a fortnight discussing progress and plans with Cos or being interviewed by his researchers in preparation for their further work with our staff. By taking such a focal position between Cos and the museum, I was able to direct, as it were, the director and help him to appreciate certain key aspects: above all the unique contribution of early photographs to our history, culture and society; but, also, Josephine Lock's unrivalled benefaction to early photography (on top of her humanitarian charity); the dedication of our staff; and the generosity of our collaborators without whom the development of Portia would not have been possible.

With her staff assistant and a dedicated team of knowledgeable, mostly retired, part-time volunteers, Lorraine managed to complete on schedule the detailed cataloguing and comprehensive search criteria for the tens of thousands of photographs in the Portia database. Whether originally positive or negative, whether albumen plates, salted paper or collodion prints, calotypes or daguerreotypes, Portia could display every photograph in a variety of forms, in real size and tone or enlarged to fill the screen, or, in the case of negatives or negative images, as a reversed image. A standard set of six buttons also allowed for limited tonal and textual adjustments. Accompanying catalogue information (date, size, subject, photographer, process, country etc.) was available onscreen with or without the photographs and could guide the viewer easily through the database to similar items. All the photographs (or information about them) appeared with a prominent link to their original collections.

Launching Portia, in February 86, was largely a virtual affair, superbly arranged and executed by Lorraine. We employed an external consultant to find us the net/email coordinates of relevant media contacts around the world, but Lorraine's team did almost everything else. Before seven days had passed, we registered a million hits, from nearly 50 different countries, three-quarters of them entering more than five content pages. Within three months, Portia achieved a weekly average of two million hits and an average income of around 60,000 euros, 50,000 euros of which was transferred automatically to our collaborators. More significantly, our collaborators all reported a doubling or trebling of interest in their own collections. In addition, we held a non-virtual party at Chalton Street, with attention focused, not on the exhibits, but on the wall and freestanding screens throughout the galleries. We all watched a display, programmed by Lorraine, showing off Portia's attributes and workings, and Josephine gave a short speech. She had a generous word to say about everyone involved with Portia and the museum, including me.

'And finally what can I say about Kip Fenn? He has been our guide, our leader, our commander, directing our travails with such foresight, patience and fairness that I doubt my dreams for this museum and for Portia would ever have been realised without him.' She stopped and looked around until she caught my eyes (I was standing with Lizette to the side and at the back, but I was taller than those around me). It was as though there were only two of us in the room. 'Thank you, Kip, thank you from the bottom of my heart.' And she blew me a kiss across the top of the crowd.

EXTRACTS FROM CORRESPONDENCE
Jay Sanderson to Kip Fenn and Lizette Sanderson

October 2079

I'm in Cumbria. In Caldbeck. I'm taking a year off uni. I should have talked to you about it, but I didn't decide till I went back to Reading last week. It hit me, all of sudden, that I needed some time to myself, some real time. I should have done it last year, before uni, but I can go back next October – I checked.

I know Mother will go potty when she reads this. I'm at a Notek community, it's bigger than Mercurio's, and makes money from Lake District tourists, but we're still rigorous, pre-electronic, like Stackpole Haven. I'm doing odd jobs, labouring mostly, but I'm learning fast, especially how the mill works. We buy in the grain (organic and certified Traditional, of course) from all over the place, and grind and mix different kinds of flour. There was a bobbin mill here on Cold Beck River once which had a wheel nearly 13 metres in diameter. It was said to be the second biggest in the world.

Brin is here too, he was the friend who came last Christmas and who Mother said must have been dragged through a hedge backwards – but then you said that about me too. Brin's graduated now, as an information officer at St Mungo's, the Caldbeck Notek Community Library. It used to be St Kentigern's Church. Kentigern, also called Mungo, was an early Christian missionary. I'm told, Kentigern means 'high lord' and Mungo 'my dear friend'. We live in an 18th century cottage, similar to the guest house at Stackpole Haven, made of stone. It's very basic, but homely.

Hope all's well with you. (How's the ankle Pa?)

November 2079

If you want to chastise or moan or argue, Mother, then direct your letters elsewhere – I won't be reading them.

December 2079

So sorry Pa not to be with you for your birthday, especially as you've reached the grand old age of 80. We're very busy, and, as always I'm very short of money for travel (no, that's not a beg – on your birthday that would definitely be out of order – you know I don't want any help). But I hope you like the tie, it's silk, and handmade by a friend. It'll look smart on you.

Love to Mother.

PS: We've a covering of snow, which should brighten up the trek to High Pike for midnight on new year's eve.

August 2080

Thanks for the prodigal son welcome. Not! I'll try again next year. As it goes, I've decided to spend a second year at Caldbeck.

August 2080

Pa, thanks for your letter, but sorry, I can't make it back again now. And I don't care if Mother 'doesn't really mean it'. But good luck with the photo project, sounds exciting.

November 2080

The wet summer was bad for our market gardens, and now the cold has come early. Much as I love this landscape, it can get very dreary at times. But I don't mind. Brin's taken over running the library. I'm his assistant, although I don't do much with books. I manage the Learning Exchange – did I tell you about this before? It's not much more than a card index which is used to put people wanting to learn a skill in touch with those who can teach it. And vice versa. It would be far easier with a computer (don't ever tell anyone I admitted that). It's the same principle as the barter markets, only with people's skills instead of their goods, and it takes a bit more managing. Yesterday, I had an enquiry from an accountant in Carlisle who wanted to learn calligraphy. We've two girls here into calligraphy, and one of them needed some bookkeeping assistance. It doesn't often work out so easily. If there's a lot of demand for one type of skill, then we try and set up a class. It could be here, or in Carlisle, or in Penrith, we're not as isolated socially as Mercurio's happy family. I also run the children's book groups (which I love doing), and organise the CMA (Church of Moral Atheism) meetings, which take place in the library. I hesitated for ages over joining the CMA (Brin hasn't joined), but most others here are members. Membership doesn't entail much more than a commitment to a decent way of living and sharing.

And did I tell you I do the school groups now. Once every couple of months, we get a school group coming to look round the community. I do a vote thing at the beginning giving them a choice of five out of ten possible places to visit (the mill, a farm, a market garden, the fish ponds, the library, a potter, a weaver, a beehive keeper, a herbalist ... did you know sticky willy is good for psoriasis?), and then, because they think they're being hard done by, they want to see more than they think they've been allowed. They press me for one more visit, and then another. I love the kids' enthusiasm, and the way they ask so many questions.

October 2081

Hi Ma, Hi Pa – surprise – I'm here at Reading, in a student pad with a couple of other lads, one who was brought up a Notek, and the other who's done a year with a community in Derbyshire. It was good to see you again. I feel bad about having stayed away so long. And I know it must have been dispiriting for you to watch me drop out and live with the Noteks (Ma especially – sorry). But, honestly, I feel the two years have done me a lot of good.

PS: I left the CMA. Brin never joined. He said there was something faintly homophobic about the emphasis on hope for future generations. I agree with that now. (He's left Caldbeck – did I say? – gone to Tierra del Fuego. But, as it goes, we'd split up by then. He'd become very introverted and antisocial.)

Chapter Ten
ALICIA, DYING AND CENTENNIAL THOUGHTS

'If I am asked to look into the future, which happens all too often (why do people imagine I have a crystal ball in my pocket), I close my eyes and shake my head. It is a comfort to find the darkness, for the future of mankind is far blacker. The 20th century was the blackest in human history, until, that is, the 21st century. I've no doubt that 100 years hence, man will be scratching his head and wondering why, despite being richer, cleverer and nobler than ever before, the 22nd century was the most terror-full and destructive in all history.'

Please don't ask me about the future in *The Tap Dancing Essays*
by Crispin Gregory (2086)

'One way of interpreting history is to see Homo sapiens in a constant struggle against his primitive, animal instincts. For the best part of 10,000 years, it has persistently sought to improve itself, through cooperation and civilisation, but until the 19th century, this effort was largely haphazard, guided largely by imagination and guesswork. While some philosophers, preachers and leaders pressed humankind forwards, in what we would now judge as a progressive way, others – many others – did not. Only with the understanding allowed us by the sciences of evolution, psychology and genetics, for example, can we begin to try and chart a deliberate route towards peace and prosperity for the whole human race.'

Survival of the Fittest in International Politics – *Towards a View of Progress*
by Zoe Bergmann (2082)

It is Thursday 3 December 2099. A memorable day, if such a term has any meaning to a man whose life and memory have but two months to go. This morning, my doctor, the gentle but direct Rupert Lipman, apprised me of the results from a sequence of tests carried out in the last few days.

'Fine, Mr Fenn, everything is fine.' He agreed to increase the dosage of some of my pills, in particular those which completely numb the pain in my joints, and those which ensure my neural alertness. (I've hardly written a thing during the last two weeks.) The tests, he said, showed that the increases were fully consistent with my planned death date, and that, with one more increase in four weeks time, I should be able to maintain my current well-being status through to the end of January – which is good news. Having completed so much of this manuscript ahead of schedule, and then having slowed down in the last month, I'm anxious to finish soon.

But now, for the first time since signing up for my deathday, I am having doubts about dying.

No sooner had the doctor, his assistant and Chintz all left together (a cheery, friendly word from Chintz would have been welcome), than another nurse came in to ask if I felt strong enough to see an unexpected visitor, one who preferred not to give a name. I expected a journalist or a researcher interested in my old friend Oakley or in the history of the IFSD or possibly in my 100th birthday vis-à-vis the forthcoming centennial. Any such person phoning me here at Willow Calm Lodge is given a number for Jay. Usually, he says I am very ill and cannot see visitors. Occasionally, therefore, those with chutzpah turn up at the Lodge and try their luck. Most of the time, I refuse to see strangers without an appointment, but this morning I felt more carefree than usual (and neglected by Chintz) so let curiosity get the better of me.

The woman who entered was tallish, with a dark-skinned face, light make-up, and long hair pinned back tightly into a pony tail. A chocolate-coloured roll-neck sweater beneath a beige fleece and light brown jeans lent her a stylish but modest appearance. She smiled in a warm, giving way, like a colleague, not a journalist trying to create an instant friendship.

'Visitors usually make an appointment. I only have ten minutes.'

'I would have made an appointment with Jay if you'd not been able to see me now, straightaway.' She spoke English with an amateur fluency and a strong accent, part American part Brazilian. And, then, as she sat down in the chair by the bed in front of me, I noticed how familiar her features appeared.

'Are you from Brazil? Have we met? Are you related to Arturo Magalhães, or his mother Conceição?' She laughed kindly, but sadly, for I could see hesitancy in her eyes and too many frown lines reflecting a life of troubles.

'Yes, yes and yes. For an old man – I hope it's not rude to call you old, when I'm old myself – you're sharp. I am Alicia. Alicia Magalhães, now Gonçalves. You held my hand once, and I showed you my bedroom. For years I had a camclip, but then I lost it.'

'Alicia. You're Alicia. I have that camclip.' All of a sudden, I was no longer carefree, but taken over by emotion. 'I was looking at it only a few weeks ago. I've been writing my Reflections, an autobiography of sorts ... Do you know that half a century ago, your father ...', I saw the lines on her face involuntarily tighten, and her eyelids flutter, '... Arturo surprised me ...'

'I know, he told me. Which is why I came like this.' She got up and leaned over to kiss me on the cheek. 'Hello Grandfather.'

'Alicia. Alicia. Alicia. I thought you were dead. Everyone – even Tina, your sister, who came here in September – thought you were dead. You disappeared 20 years ago.'

'I know. It's not true, though. What Arturo told you is not true. But I'll tell you my story. Not now, soon. I'm here for a while. I'll come every second or third day, and we'll talk. Will it be good for you? Now I must tell you one more thing. I have a daughter, Angela, who was 20 last month. She is married to Quasim and they have a son, Renato, six months old and as healthy a baby as you could ever imagine. We're all in Portugal, in Porto, where I live with João Gonçalves – not Angela's father. So, Grandfather, you are a great grandfather, and a great great grandfather. Now you see why I call you old.'

Alicia did not stay very long, but promised to return on Saturday when she would tell me more about herself. For the rest of the morning, I felt joy again – the first time, I think, since before Lizette fell seriously ill. Although writing these Reflections has taken me on an emotional roller-coaster ride, it has been by proxy only. I was tempted to call for an extra bath, or drift off into a dreamy sleep, one in which Alicia and I might stroll through the gardens, along by a river, hand-in-hand, chatting about old times, family parties, our shared history, as if we had known each other forever. Yet, after my chat with Dr Lipman, I realised I must press on with this writing.

There is little left to tell.

***

It is not only Alicia's arrival that is interfering with my ability to concentrate. The world is going mad with centennial fever. The nurses and doctors talk continually about their own and other people's plans for new year's eve; the media is full of programmes reviewing the century just gone, or previewing the century to come, or advertising centennial programmes; and I'm receiving more email than usual, invites from people I haven't seen or heard of for ten years or from organisations I've long since left behind. I have standard replies so it doesn't take long to deal with them. But the general buzz of excitement is distracting, and it will only get worse as the days tick by to the end of the year (and, 31 days hence, to the end of me).

The coming centennial has led me, as well as everyone else, to reflect on how life has changed during the century. I do not claim my thoughts are original since I've culled most of them from the media. I have no doubt, for example, like many commentators, that for an individual in the rich developed nations life has not changed anywhere as much this century as it did during the last one. (The very reverse might be true – i.e. more advances in this century than ever before – if one considers scientific understanding, industrial processes, medical techniques etc, but these are beyond my knowledge, and I am only reflecting on daily life for an ordinary person.)

During the 20th century, there were so many major advances. To list but a few: transport (the car and the aeroplane); health (sewage and fresh water systems, electricity, antibiotics, vaccines, organ and joint replacements);

communications (the telephone, the internet); the home (central heating, carpets, labour saving kitchen appliances, personal computers); more time and money for leisure pursuits (volleyball, television, holidays, eating out); and the individual's relationship with government (human rights, the vote for all, media freedom). If I take this same sample collection of categories (transport, health, communications, the home, leisure and citizenship) which affect the daily life of an individual such as me in Western Europe, it's not easy to identify any in which there have been changes as fundamental as those experienced by my forefathers.

In transport, the fuels and engines might have changed and the outward appearances may have gone through fashion trends (in the 40s Diana had a Fiat Klimt!; and, currently, Jay has an Archangel Flitter which, frankly, is a triumph of design over function), but we still use cars, buses, trams, trains, metros and aeroplanes. Yes, we learned to plug our cars into cables on returning home from a drive, or to 'fill up' on a journey by plugging in at roadshops, and we became accustomed to planning trips according to toll costs (with monthly toll bills) and to using dashboard congestion busters, yet traffic jams continue to blight our society. Despite commonplace fictional predictions, evident in my childhood, of traffic moving to the skies, there is no real prospect, even today, of a mass aerocar/aerohover transport system (for obvious reasons of safety, cost, fuel consumption, traffic management complexity etc.). But, at least vehicle traffic creates negligible atmospheric pollution and far less noise than in ages past (engines naturally became quieter with the switch over to the hydrogen fuel system, but it took decades for European Union laws to encourage improvements in road surfaces).

In terms of our health and well-being, I'm living proof of many advances. One hundred years ago, I would probably have died in my 80s or 90s; but who knows exactly how many years have been added to my life by better informa-tion on diet or by improved medical advice and treatment. Life expectancy certainly crept up during the first four decades of the century, but nowhere near as sharply as it did in the 20th century; then, during the wars and the Grey Years, it slipped back again. I am certain, however, that the quality, as opposed to the quantity, of life for older people, certainly in Western Europe, has improved significantly. If, a century ago, I had lived to 100 I would not have done so in comfort, free of pain, and neurally alert.

Certainly, there have been far-reaching developments in communications during this century (but few would argue they are more significant than the invention of the telephone, radio or television). Large wallscreens were not ubiquitous when I was a child in Surrey and a student in London. Moreover, then there were important limitations on computer memory and speed, and on digital information flow through the net, and these, in particular, restricted the way people accessed sound and moving images. And, although cams, for personal use and surveillance, were becoming more popular, these too were unsophisticated (limited by memory, quality and battery technology) and consequently the cam infrastructure (and the public debate on personal freedom issues) was in its infancy. Our relationship to computers and screens was thus immature at the start of the 21st century, and it took a while for the way we store and access information, of all kinds, and how we relate to screens to become more fluid and natural, more freewheeling. It was not until the 30s-40s that most of us were communicating with screens (using personal or installed computer consoles) to find information, access a film or documentary, or talk to a friend as smoothly as if we were talking to a librarian, a disc store attendant or a neighbour on the front porch. By then, of course, we could transmit and receive across the world (as easily as our forefathers made telephone calls) high quality private broadcasts, camclips or films of any event: a journey, a conference, a family reunion. For the running cost of a highly efficient light bulb, we could Livepicture our lounges or bedrooms with streamed views of Mars, Himalayan pandas, Serengeti giraffes, an Australian termite colony, a Red Sea coral reef, a Bangkok brothel, the latest volcanic eruption, Fifth Avenue or Tiananmen Square pedestrians, views from a friend's lounge or bedroom, Tokyo stock market transactions, abstract art images, and so on. What we do not have today, despite movie-inspired predictions in my youth, is three-dimensional screens. It seems our brains do 3D better and cheaper than any technology can.

In our homes, no change has been more evident than the use of wallscreens, but there have been many other not so spectacular (!) developments. Houses are far more energy efficient than they ever used to be, and I'm sure (no, I'm more than sure, I'm certain, because Lizette told me often enough) the materials for house construction, furbishing and decorating have changed a lot (s-glass is an obvious change, and now z-glass), but not so that you would necessarily notice. Lots of gadgets have come and gone and come again (various heat and recycling units for example). My personal favourite was the bath/shower thermostat that guaranteed a regular water temperature every time without fuss or fiddling. I first experienced them in hotels, but, unless you remained several days, there was no benefit since it took effort to calibrate the controls. I didn't have one in my own home until we moved into the Oldwijkgaarten house. Before then, now I am thinking along these lines, Harriet had a favourite gadget too: the intelligent microwave that reliably cooked according to barcodes. I could also mention the major changes in food packaging (one of Lizette's favourite topics), but I'm already spending too long on this deviation. What we do not have today, again despite 20th century fiction implying we would, is domestic robots. Most regular tasks around the house or garden are too complicated by far, and can be done much more efficiently by humans. Besides, we enjoy many of them; and they can provide welcome relief from sedentary occupations.

After several decades of increasing wealth during the latter part of the 20th century, the developed countries went on getting richer in the first half of the 21st century, and so we had more money and time for leisure. Nevertheless, I don't believe this century has given us anything truly new or important in this area. In the 1990s, the internet had already created international gaming communities, and it was only an extension of this that led to the gaming pubs which I used to frequent (unwillingly) in the 10s and 20s with my buds. Already by the end of the last century there was no corner of the globe left unexplored by intrepid tourists, and there was no action sport or adventure not available to those with the right amount of foolishness and money. As for virtual reality 'trips' into the so-called Matrix world, it soon became clear that very few of us wanted to sit around with goggles on all day, especially when the real world is so exciting as it is.

It is true that movie holidays did not take off until the 20s but they were no more than a repackaging of the kinds of experiences you could buy at adventure complexes (such as Disneyworld, and later Dracula Park, Bride's Galaxy, The Wild West) or on adventure tours (white water rafting, skyscraper climbing and game park trekking come to mind). I remember discussing this fad with Tom once. We had gone to a guzzleshop after seeing Pacciotti's glorious bio-flick *Garibaldi*. This must have been in the early 30s, for it was not long after our trip to Malta. Tom was so taken with the film and Vincent Mallow's performance (as the Italian hero) that he mused on whether he would be able to buy a Garibaldi holiday. Then he wondered if he would prefer to re-enact being the first real (as opposed to fictional) astronaut on the moon (Neil Armstrong), or the first (fictional) spaceman to encounter extraterrestrial life as in the film *Planet Sister*. For my part, I confessed that if I were forced to take a movie holiday I would want to be Manuel from the film *Trumpet Boy*. I said I would choose the scene where, having defeated the evil Reefland dictator, Manuel walks proudly into the main government building to address the country's parliament. Although all the establishment cronies are sniggering and joking, for they expect Manuel to act and talk without maturity, he wins them over with a powerful speech full of traditional ideals and practical suggestions for how to achieve them. A year later, Tom sent me a camclip of himself as Garibaldi (kitted out in red shirt, scabbard and beard – which was a shock because I had never seen him with more than two day's stubble) and a band of compatriots apparently engaged in a gun fight along the length of a Palermo back street. An attached note said: 'Didn't fancy having to wear a spacesuit, and, in any case, Fragrance hates all that space stuff.'

Finally, to finish off this digression, the only major innovation in terms of citizenship that springs to mind is the electronic identicard. Although the European Union introduced a standard format for identicards in the 10s (leading to a huge civil rights campaign in Britain and elsewhere), it was not until the late 20s, when faced with chronic and acute immigration problems, rising crime trends and the spasmodic chaos caused by First Tuesday Movement activities, that the Union began to enforce their use. By this time, identicards also had the ability to hold a vast amount of additional private information (medical records, for example, emergency telephones numbers, photos, written/voice signatures, Galileo position coordinates) accessible through most standard consoles via the card-holder's individual access codes. Over time, it has been shown, by research and public acceptance, that carefully-planned and regulated identicards provide, for society as a whole and individuals, far more advantages than disadvantages. Civil liberties may have been breached in many well-publicised cases, but the debate is no longer over whether we should have identicards, but whether one day the United Nations should agree on a basic harmonised (and, obviously, voluntary for the time being) format which could replace passports. Such discussions are part of the ongoing New Century Mandate, agreed at the 95 summit in Geneva (celebrating the UN's 150 year anniversary), which, by further strengthening the UN system, aims to maintain the momentum created during the last quarter century of peace

I must stress that this brief and flawed analysis is only valid from my perspective as a citizen in Holland and England. I understand only too well from a lifetime of business errands to every corner of the world that many of the major innovations and advances in the 20th century, so significant and life-enhancing in the developed countries, did not touch many in the developing world until the 21st century (with many more impoverished, ill and hungry yet to benefit). Thus a Brazilian or Nigerian or Chinese individual the same age as me might believe his world had changed far more during this century than it would have done if he had lived in the previous one.

When I think forward towards the next century, I am full of hope, but it is not a hope that paradise can be found tomorrow if only the right beliefs or policies are pursued. I believe history has shown clearly enough how idealism, whether religious or political, can be so very dangerous if not tempered with realistic expectations and a firm commitment to peaceful, humanitarian and sustainable principles. Nor do I dare hope that war or plague or famine will vanish, for they will not; nor do I hope that all men and women will suddenly take on a Zen-like calm and be more happy, for they will not. No, my simple (and wobbly) hope is based on only two cornerstones: one political and one religious.

The starting point for my hopes is the United Nations. Despite, or because of, the Jihad Wars it is far stronger today than it was 100 years ago. It has its own army with the authority to intervene in sovereign states in a few well-defined circumstances; a plethora of powerful and improving institutions which effectively redistribute five or six times as much wealth as they did in the late 20th century; a rudimentary justice system that may well be able, in the near future, to regulate aid, competition, trade and environmental issues fairly and effectively; and well-equipped and funded emergency response teams to deal with sudden disasters. Moreover, the New Century Mandate appears to demonstrate that all the fine words from the world's major regional groupings about further strengthening the UN will be translated into action – eventually.

The other foundation for my hopes is the Church of Moral Atheism. I would not have said this in the mid-80s when I retired, and when the Church was largely confined to the Notek and other alternative communities. But since then it has swept through Europe and the Far East, attracting millions of adherents, many of them writers, artists and intellectuals. Catholic and Muslim religious fervour is as strong today in parts of the world as it was prior to the First Jihad War, but now that non-religious social and political intellectual leaders have an alternative (apart from sport and celebrity-worship) to offer those needing religious-type passion or wanting religious-type guidance, it is possible to believe that the Church of Moral Atheism might forge a new way for man to mould his faiths and hopes.

I am in danger of preaching, which is certainly not in my nature.

***

Jay is in excellent spirits. All is well in his relationship with Vince. There were reasons, personal to Vince which I shall not go into, which led him astray. It is possible, Jay says, they may 'reaffirm' their marriage vows next year, on the tenth anniversary of their wedding. Normally, Jay is careful not to talk about the future, and especially not 'next year'. I wouldn't mind, but he thinks it would be tactless. On this occasion, though, his enthusiasm got the better of him, so I was tactful and did not say 'I'm sorry, I won't be able to come'. If I had, he would not have taken it as an offhand quip, a joke, a way of dissipating the ever-present tension about my death date. Instead he would have apologised – three times.

During his visit this morning, he cleared up the Chintz mystery. One of the other nurses, whom he chats to now and then, told him Chintz has a strict policy with patients who have signed up for a deathday: exactly three months before the day, she closes up, shuts herself off emotionally. It's the only way she can cope, or so her colleague told Jay.

As I've already commented, there is not much left to say about my own life. Lizette went through a tough period in the mid-80s. It began with a work row, in 83, over plans for one specific area of future research efforts. The department head, Sidney Jensen, had taken a neutral stance, leaving Lizette in dispute with Olive Norrington. One Sunday, Olive and her partner Marcella (a senior lecturer in psychology, and named, I presume, after the movie heroine) had come for lunch at Taunton House. It was already late in the afternoon, and we had all been drinking. I was showing Marcella some 19th century photographs through Portia, when an explosive argument between Lizette and Olive erupted in the other room. It stopped abruptly. Olive shouted through the house to Marcella that she was leaving, and we heard the front door slam. Marcella collected her things, apologised, and raced off after her friend. This argument, or whatever had caused it, left Lizette moody for weeks, but she would not talk about it. By the end of the year, Lizette had begun to consider leaving Surrey University. In the spring she told me there was a job vacancy at her old college, the Farnborough Science University which, having closed during the Grey Years, was up and running again. It would mean, she said, the end of her research career but a comfortable few years stoking her retirement funds. She also, finally, explained a few details about the departmental row, admitting that Olive had been in the right all along. In May 84, Lizette informed me she would be starting at Farnborough in October. This was not a moment too soon, since Sydney was about to retire as head of the department at Surrey University, and Olive would be taking over.

I semi-retired from my duties at The Josephine Collection immediately after the launch of Portia, in February 86, and then fully retired in December the same year. The staff organised a party at Farmer King's, a newly opened zini bar in the next street, to which both Jay and Lizette came. I was fêted with presents and mini-speeches. The night before, at a private supper in her apartment, Josephine had given me the most astonishing gift: an original Marc Ferrez photograph of Copacabana beach, wild and undeveloped. It was housed in a Perfect Frame, meaning I could hang it on a wall without having to worry about damage from light, humidity or heat conditions. It must have cost her well over ten thousand euros. When I tried to express my thanks, Josephine dismissed them saying the gift was only 'a very small token' of her gratitude for my contribution to the Project. I put it in a prominent position on a wall in the office at Taunton House (replacing an over-sized reproduction of Le Gray's Garibaldi which moved into storage).

The following year, 87, was the year the world held its breath, as it were, while the caldera in Yellowstone Park, United States, growled more loudly than it had ever done before. It was also the year Great Britain won the football World Cup for the first time in more than 100 years (alas I'm still waiting for GB to win any volleyball cup), and our neighbour, Sami, smashed the international record for a marrow size. According to *Guinness World Records*, the heaviest marrow was 55.1 kilograms, and Sami's was over 56 kilograms. I had been invited to inspect his specimens in early September, while the vegetables were still growing. He rattled off a list of weights and sizes, which I thought were village records. When he tucked a special set of scales under the largest of his marrows, and confided a dream that he might beat the world record, I thought he'd gone loopy. A few weeks later, the very same specimen hit the headlines. Journalists began arriving in their hoards, parking their strange vehicles in our lane, and coming to us and other near neighbours for additional comments and colour. Iona pranced around the village as if she were a queen, and, no doubt, dreamed Sami's marrow would give her more than 15 minutes of fame. Lizette, who had never liked the woman but tolerated her because I was Sami's patient (he was treating rheumatoid arthritis in other parts of my body by this time), began to loathe her. Fortunately, their brief celebrity status left Sami and Iona with such a long list of potential dinner party acquaintances that we were no longer in demand. By 89, they had moved, to a bigger house in socially-upmarket Hambledon.

My life during the later years of the decade – it seems like yesterday – was not only happy (apart from the deaths of friends) but peaceful. The happiness came from being with Lizette. Our partnership, nearly 20 years old by this time, was a rich one, full of enjoyment in each other's company and many shared pleasures (not least 'affection, tenderness and other pleasant things'). Lizette did have a sporadic tendency towards depression, and could be demanding at times, yet I never sensed or believed these difficulties were caused by me. Indeed, the reverse was true. She made it seem as though I helped her through the bad times, that I was a rock onto which she clung temporarily during the storms. In consequence, I always felt wanted, needed, loved.

And the peacefulness came from the fact, I suppose, that I did adjust to a routine without deadlines or meetings or responsibilities, my tenure with Josephine having served well to ease me into full retirement. Not that my involvement with The Josephine Collection terminated the day of my retirement. As an unpaid non-executive director, I sat on one of the advisory boards, which convened every quarter. Moreover, at Josephine's initiative, she and I met once a month for lunch. Less often, I saw others from the museum, usually Giselle or Belinda (who had become a highly competent administrator). In addition, there were certain photo-world individuals – Arnold Cowerbridge for one, and Max Voll for another – who considered me a friend and, when in London, would invite me for a meal or to join them at a gallery or auction.

I visited Jude Singleton, who had reluctantly entered a sunset hospice (not dissimilar to this one), and had opted for a medical regime leading to a deathday 18 months hence. But I think she made a mistake in telling everyone, for it made contact with her near the end awkward. I found saying goodbye on my last visit a very unnerving experience: I could not find the words, emotions, or actions to equal the occasion. One day, perhaps, when our society has become more comfortable with the notion of death, those of us with planned death dates will be able to have our parties before lights out, not after.

At Taunton House, we continued to receive guests regularly. Jay, who had taken a job teaching in London, visited fortnightly, sometimes with a friend; and during school holidays would stay for several days at a time. I enjoyed having him around (especially when Lizette was at work), he was helpful and companionable. Already by this stage he had begun to take on a paternal role with me, worrying about my health and prompting me to do more exercise or to try a newly marketed Chinese remedy for arthritis. He was less comfortable with his mother who, on occasions, would still let loose flurries of criticism (much as she had done on her husband Clint during their marriage – she confessed this once). They originated not so much out of disappointment with him, I came to understand, but out of a deep-seated inability to let herself accept the situation, because it would be wrong to do so. From what I learned about Mervyn Sanderson, her Pa, I suspect this tendency came from him through a combination of genes and the domestic environment which he dominated.

And now from preaching I've moved on to psychoanalysis, which suits my writing disposition no better.

Horace continued to stop over on his way back to Southampton. Tim had died in 84, leaving Horace devastated, uncared for and lonely. He appeared to lose all of his ebullience over night, as if he had been waiting for an excuse not to go on performing; and, at the same time, he developed a form of senile dementia. A doctor took nine months to find adequate medication. He became maudlin too, and would hark back to his youth and our days at Witley Academic. Then, in 86, urged on by his publisher, he completed a second book. It was published under the title *Uncommon Times* and promoted as 'a companion volume' to *Reflections of a Political Lightweight*; but it revealed nothing different or new. Consequently, the media ignored it, and this vexed Horace more than the meagre sales that followed. He hired a driver/assistant at his own expense and went on a gruelling book signing tour. Less than halfway through, at a lit-arcade in Exeter, he was seated at a table with his books piled high, waiting for customers, when a stroke saved him from any further embarrassment. He died the same day. His body was brought back to Southampton. One of Tim's children who lived not too far away and suffered his uncle better than others, organised the funeral. Horace would have been disappointed at the turnout. Too many of his friends had already died, and, others, especially those in the Progressive Party and other Conservative Alliance parties, had been alienated by his scandal-rich autobiography. I couldn't help wishing he had made it to 50 years as an MP, for the achievement might have given the media more to focus on in their obituaries than the secret affair with Terrance Spoon.

Our other guests at Taunton House were mostly Lizette's family and friends. Mercurio kept up his annual ritual, although age forced him to relinquish the bicycle for a car ('the scourge of post-Victorian man') adapted to Notek standards. Samuel and Lynn visited too. Gratifyingly, they often talked about how much they had enjoyed the experience in Peru. If they had been any younger, they both said, they might have taken another contract. We also saw Irene Sanderson, Lizette's niece, for she lived in south London, and would drop in to visit before or after an ice skating excursion to the sports complex in Guildford. She was curious about our interests, following Lizette into the garden to ask questions about the fuchsia varieties, or browsing with me through old photographs on Neil. When Lizette and I began taking mini-tours, she was full of advice: beforehand, on what to look out for; and, afterwards, on what we had missed. We never saw Saul and his family, or Mahonia, who had married an architect, given birth to twins and moved to the Shetland Islands.

Nor did we have any contact with Esos, although Mercurio kept us informed of his news. He moved for a while to a Notek community in Denmark, but, after three years, returned to Pembrokeshire. He is still there, at Stackpole Haven, with his father. Yewla showed up a couple of times at Taunton House, once when Mercurio was there; they argued the whole time. He hated that she had left the community and that she was happy working in the real world, for a company which made children's broadcast programmes. However, they must have patched up their relationship for, when the two of them came here to Willow Calm Lodge some months ago, they demonstrated a good rapport. (Having brought me a beautiful bunch of lemon yellow roses and sunset gladioli, however, they did have one argument – I couldn't tell whether it was testy or tongue-in-cheek – about the glittery vase on the windowsill: Yewla loved it, Mercurio hated it. I didn't dare tell them why it was there. Although much in tune with the bright and tacky end-of-the-century fashion, I think it's a ghastly thing in itself, forever trying to upstage the flowers that it holds, sometimes succeeding, sometimes not, yet how can I help but love it.) Mercurio looked very weathered, but retained an impish look around the eyes. Yewla was pregnant, visibly so, and, therefore, must have been with child already when she visited with Irene a couple of months previously.

418

As for Lizette's friends, I would say we saw Rhoda too often. She had retired, but rather than taking retirement as an opportunity to slow down, she speeded up. She was one of these middle-aged women who dress up and make up as though they were 40 not 60, and who not only delay the onset of the menopause with pills but deny it forever with self-psychology. She was always on the move, searching for a new man. I've no idea why she thought she would find one at Taunton House. Jay said she was a typical Maysie (middle-aged young, single, independent and exciting). By contrast we did not see Pete and Clarity often enough. By the mid-80s, Pete's health was poor. Since he refused to travel, and Clarity would not leave him on his own, Lizette and I made the trip north once a year, usually in the summer.

In the late 80s I lost Peter de Roo and his wife Livia. Livia went first, in 89. I travelled to near Leiden for the funeral, sad at Livia's death, but looking forward to seeing Peter. But he was a shadow of his former self, with grey skin, and a rake-thin and stooped body. Rudy played a beautiful tune on his sax – apparently Livia's favourite – at the funeral, and Ulla spoke some words I could not hear for her sobbing. Four months later, I returned for Peter's funeral, which was less depressing, probably because Guido was there. After the funeral, we spent a nostalgic evening with Rudy and Ulla and a few others at Rudy's house in Amsterdam. The next day, Guido and I together went to the old Oostlander family house in Utrecht to visit Dominique and Waltar, who were relatively fit and active (still are, I hope), to catch up on their news and the progress of their children. I hoped Guido would return with me to England for a few days, but he was obliged to fly straight back to Quito.

The peace of my retirement years was regularly punctuated by bad news. Barely a month went by without my finding an obituary of someone I knew. I became so accustomed to the idea of past friends and acquaintances dying that I regularly checked two obituary netsites, one dedicated to United Nations staff and the other focused on international politicians. The names and biographies triggered memories, and led me into reflecting back over my working life in a way I had not done before. Otherwise, I continued to play bowls in Tilford, once a week usually, but never very well. I became friendly with a handful of other players, and would stroll home with one or another of them for a drink and a chat. I continued trying to work my way through a teach-yourself bridge course. I would sit in front of the screen and play demonstration hands with three very attractive photo-constructed young ladies (I could choose from hundreds of composites), and the games would proceed as slowly or as fast as I wished. At any time I could stop the game, ask for hints or explanations; or I could instruct the screen to intervene whenever I played below a certain standard. I could even set one of a dozen styles of cross-table banter (which had a higher humour content than I ever encountered playing bridge for real). But learning was a pain: I could never recall what cards had been played and, however odd it might sound to others (and to Lizette), whenever I made a mistake, I could hear my father Tom calling me a 'stupid idiot' as clearly as if he were one of the players onscreen.

While Lizette continued to work, my life was relatively quiet. Somewhat whimsically, I called this period my yoga and yeast years. Jay teased me, saying if I lived any longer I'd turn into a Notek. The idea irritated Lizette, which may have been Jay's objective, but I found it intriguing, flattering almost, as though there were more to my personality than I had realised.

I had Sami to thank for the yoga. He suggested I take up the discipline soon after installing my new ankle, but I ignored his advice. Then, as the arthritis progressed, he urged me further to consider yoga as a natural way of keeping my joints as supple as possible for as long as possible. With the right commitment (up to ten minutes every day permanently), he said, I might need less pills to control the pain and keep me mobile. He directed me to a tailor-made course of exercises (onscreen, and demonstrated by an elderly man, not unlike me, with movements restricted in the same way as my own). Daily practice was laborious initially but, after about three months, the exercises had become as much part of my daily routine as breakfast, watching the news, or preparing a pot of Ceylon tea for Lizette on her return from work.

And I had Jay to thank for teaching me how to make bread, a skill he picked up in Cumbria, and for finding a shop nearby which sold fresh yeast, without which the process would not have been so satisfying. I liked that I could conjure up breakfast baps or olive bread with very little cost in terms of time or money; and, besides, kneading dough was good exercise for my fingers. Apart from the trips to London, the visitors, the bowls, the yoga and the yeast, and the onscreen auctions, there was plenty to read (I was partial to biographies), and I spent a fair amount of time listening to and extending my classical music collection. I also became attached to Alan's clinic in Bangladesh. As a significant donor, I was sent regular reports on its activities and budgets; and the administrative staff were friendly and forthcoming whenever I called by camphone.

***

Alicia has now met up with both Jay and Guido; and, Mireille and Guido have spent time with Jay and Vince. They all get on, or so they say, and intend to stay in touch. Mireille and Guido are coming tomorrow for the last time. Alicia visited a couple of days ago and told me more of her story. She grew up at Arturo's ranch in Goiânia, accepting that her natural mother, Edna, had died during childbirth, and loving first Luz and then Fatima as her own mother. But as brothers and sisters came along, Ignacio, Juliano and then Tina, her own position in the family became more tense: Arturo seemed to be permanently angry with her, and Fatima was too weak not to be prejudiced towards her own children. Alicia, like 'Cinderella' (her own description), was given far less spending money than her siblings, she was taken fewer places, and was given endless chores. At 14 she ran away, to Rio, and became a night club prostitute. By avoiding the drugs trap and being lucky with friends (including a man called Rodrigo whom she called Sao Rodrigo – 'without him I would have been washed away in the Rio sewers'), she gravitated towards the safer and more lucrative call girl scene. At the age of 17, she decided to make a journey home. It took a while to find her family because they had moved to São Paulo (this was about three years before Lizette and I went to South America). On day one she was welcomed as 'a prodigal daughter'. On day two, though, she had a violent argument with her father. A fish tank got broken, and she stamped on one of the fish floundering in a puddle on the marble floor. Arturo lost his temper and told Alicia the truth: she was a clone, and Edna was nobody, just a girl he had married for fun, who died from a drug overdose.

The news devastated Alicia. Immediately, she ran away again, back to Rio where not even Sao Rodrigo could comfort her. She felt 'worthless', like a 'freak', like 'nothing at all'. She told me she had known a few clones in Rio and they had all been 'messed up, more messed up than everyone else', and some had died very young. As a child she had seen documentaries about the terrible things that had happened to children cloned in Brazil (especially female clones from a male parent), and, although she saw other films and read books that showed how most clones were healthy, she gave more credence to the bad stories than the good. She decided to run further away, to Los Angeles. There she hitched up with a charity group ostensibly aimed at helping cloned individuals integrate themselves into society. This particular organisation attracted her and other foreigners because it offered not only clone counselling but help with work and residency permits. Alicia got sucked in for a while, until she realised it was a clearing house for slaves. All the instruction and help came with a persistent message: you are nothing, therefore expect nothing but be grateful for any mercies. After six weeks, she was offered a poorly-paid job as a domestic servant in the household of a rich Mexican family in Baja California, 300 kilometres from Los Angeles. She was pressed to sign a contract which committed her to the job for five years. She refused. The organisation threw her onto the street. She went back into prostitution, this time with as many chemicals in her blood system as she could get her hands on. More and more she came to believe all the clonist media hype, and expected to die at any time, from a defective organ, a failure to resist a virus, or from an overdose (because she was not psychologically strong enough to be alive).

While Alicia sat by the bed telling me this story, she appeared to grow more calm and self-confident. It was as though she was not telling me about herself, but about someone who had been in her care, someone she had cared for and guided to safety. Some of the time, when she was talking or responding to my questions, she took hold of my hand, as if it were me she were trying to lead to untroubled waters. She has promised to come again in two days time.

Tomorrow is the day I must say goodbye to Mireille and Guido. They do not know about my deathday. Outside of this hospice, only Jay knows I have scheduled my death. It was distressing enough to decide on a definite limit to my own lifetime, but then I had to make a decision about who to tell and who not to tell. My overriding aim was, and is, to give friends and family the minimum amount of sorrow, both before and after my death. To begin with, I considered whether I should tell Jay. After Lizette's departure he became my closest friend, and then my carer. I honestly did not believe his behaviour towards me would alter in any significant way if I told him. Indeed, having made up my own mind and before finally signing the papers, I discussed the idea with him in some detail. He objected vehemently (as any loving son would) using practical and emotional arguments, not least that such a course would be unfair to those who loved me. But anyone who loved me, I responded (trying to match Jay's tone) would respect my decision. It boils down to quantity versus quality, I concluded. I'd prefer to enjoy the days and weeks left to me than have extra time just to be a spectator at my own mental decay show. In time, he accepted my decision, albeit grudgingly and under pressure (as any loving son would). I am sure this was the right approach with Jay. He may have become slightly more over-attentive and condescending, especially as time is now running out, but, if I hadn't told him, he would have been very deeply hurt afterwards.

With Guido, my closest relative apart from Jay and my only living natural son, it is not the same. He may be pained when he discovers my deception, and then feel guilt at not having found more time to spend with me in recent years. But I am planning to speak to him by camphone on 30 or 31 January, and then, within an hour of my death, he will receive a letter. I have already written this letter, and Jay will organise its courier delivery. If I should die prematurely, then Jay will act accordingly. In any case, Guido will know from these Reflections that I believed it for the best to act in this way. It would have been an excruciating experience to have him, with or without Mireille, here for days or weeks prior to the end – excruciating for him and for me. We have been apart too long, and there is no easy rapport between us (as there was a long

422

time ago when we worked together on Ginquin) which would see us through the anti-drama of hours and minutes ticking away towards the final moment, the moment when I let the paradise poison-soaked disc of rice-paper melt slowly on my tongue.

Having sorted out my own mind with regard to Guido, it was clear that I would not tell anyone else either. But that was before Alicia. Such is my sudden and deep affection for her, and her apparent affection for me, we are as father and daughter, once estranged and now together.

***

This last chapter, these last few pages, seem to be transforming themselves into a kind of diary which is definitely not my intention. Perhaps I am losing my ability to concentrate, or perhaps I simply do not have much to say about these final years of my life.

Guido and Mireille, who departed yesterday, gave me all the news from Paris, mostly about the Rocard family (several distant relations of Mireille have become famous or infamous), but also about Guido's relations on Diana's side and his friend Rudy. They described their own plans for a centennial eve theatrical extravaganza in Plaza Chica, Quito, which they are to host, and which is to be given a major live broadcast. Guido promised to email me the relevant net details and times, and I promised to tune in; and when he went out to the loo, Mireille whispered (to imply she was telling me a confidence) that Guido was secretly planning to deliver, live on air, a special message for me close to midnight Ecuador time. There are not many presents you can give a 100 year old man who has no possessions other than those stored and waiting to be distributed to his heirs (in a room at Jay's house), and who rarely leaves his bed – but that might be one.

When Guido and Mireille walked out of the room, both of them smiled. They were confident of seeing me again – which is for the best. I felt sad, very sad for a few minutes, and then, astonishingly, I caught myself thinking of Alicia, and feeling happy again. This fickleness of human nature, in others and in me, never ceases to amaze.

Alicia, who came this morning, continued her story as follows. In 77, she fell pregnant and aborted the foetus without a second thought. But, thereafter, she could not stop wondering about being fertile. It gave her a fresh perspective on herself, one which included, for the first time in years, a sliver of pride. She began to believe that if she could give birth to a normal child, she could be normal herself. She weaned herself off the drugs, and chose her clients more carefully. And then, when the time was right, deliberately avoided contraception with one handsome regular client. When a pregnancy was confirmed, she packed her bags and flew to Lisbon to start a new life. Since she had managed to stay in the United States for over two years on the back of a month's visa, she hoped Portugal would pose no problem. And it didn't. Within weeks she had found a man, João, a carpenter, who wanted to marry, despite her condition.

When I nodded slightly, Alicia stopped and asked me why. I began to explain about how Lizette was already pregnant with Jay when we fell in love. But, having talked at length with Jay, Alicia already knew this.

'I'd like it to be the same, but it's not is it? I was desperate and I cheated my way into João's heart before telling him the truth. I had too many tricks. With you and Lizette it was different, no? An accident of fate? I was not an accident of fate, and nor was Angela.'

'But João didn't mind. You are together still, so the marriage must have worked.'

'I owed him too much. It had to work. I could never want anything different. Yes, I love him and he loves me. It was not easy. I thought Angela would be the end of my problems, and I would feel good again, as I did when I was a girl. I planned to go back to Brazil for a holiday with João and Angela, but I couldn't. I hated Arturo too much. I told myself, over and over, I'm normal, I'm normal. And then I discovered I was afraid again. This time not for me, but Angela. She wasn't a healthy baby and I kept thinking it was my fault. One day I was worried about her heart, the next about her liver, and then about her brain. I was – what do you say – a hypochondriac about her. João wanted a child of his own. I wanted one too – at first. But then this fear came, and I couldn't do it, I couldn't have another one. My unhappy João. He took me to doctors, and persuaded me to join another organisation to help clones, a proper one this time, but I couldn't change what was in my head.' She paused here. During our previous encounters she had looked at me hesitantly, but now she gazed at me intently as if trying to discover who was behind my eyes. It was such a strange moment, I don't think any girl – Popsicle comes to mind – had done this to me since my student days.

Feeling abashed, I broke the silence: 'You'd been through such a lot, it's not hard to understand.'

'It wasn't only that I was a clone, but how I'd lived, what I'd done.'

I could think of nothing to say, so we sat there silently for a few moments. Then, all of a sudden, she flicked to life, with a warm happy smile filling her face. She told me about her life with João and Angela, about how she trained to become a tour guide for American tourists (travelling up and down the Douro river twice a week, and spending more time in port wine lodges than with her husband), and how João became an artisan earning good money from making tables and desks to order. Angela filled out as a teenager, became healthier, grew taller than both Alicia herself and João, went to university, fell in love and gave birth to Renato.

'I never wanted her to get serious with a guy so quickly. I never pressed her to marry or have children. I didn't push my troubles onto her; she understood about my background, but not about the fears in my head. She went that way. She's an apple pie girl – not complicated. She cooks and shops and goes to the beach. She finished university with a degree in business, and was working in a big store. Now she'll go back in six months, when Renato's one year old.'

At this point, Alicia used my screen to access her private memory store so as to show me a collection of camclips and camstills of her family. When she pointed out Angela's husband, Quasim, I asked what he did for a living.

'Quasim. He's lovely. His parents are Moroccan. They run a large fruit and vegetable import company. Quasim works there part-time, but he's studying to be a town traffic planner. In one year, he'll be qualified. It is a good profession, it pays well, but if he gets a job, it might be a long way from Porto. We'll see.'

'Won't you mind?'

'Yes, of course, but things are changing for me too. My fear has gone. It's why I am here. After Renato was born, I went back to Brazil. With João. We tracked down my brothers and sisters, and this is how I found you. Tina had only just returned from London. This is not all. I have one more thing to tell you.' She leaned over and kissed me on the cheek, then took hold of my hand and said: 'I'm pregnant myself – nearly three months – with a boy.'

'Oh, how wonderful.' I am not very good at communicating on an emotional level, but I felt elated. 'João must be a very happy man.'

'He is. We are. And you know what's so strange? It happened in Brazil.'

A nurse interrupted us to make a routine check on my monitoring equipment, to remind me to take my pills (which I had forgotten), and to forewarn me that my lunch tray – salmon trifle and spinach wafers – was waiting.

'I should go,' Alicia said, 'I will check times with Jay and be back tomorrow or the day after.'

'I'll look forward to it.'

'It's good news, my Grandad, is it not? By July, you'll have another great grandchild. A boy. I'll bring him to see you, in September or October, I promise.'

***

Lizette retired from her academic career in July 90. The Farnborough University gave a splendid party, to which several of her past Surrey University colleagues were also invited. Sydney Jensen was there with a strange-looking woman who Lizette said was his sister. He had recently published a book on the history of the use of plastic materials in the transport industry (we had a copy in the house). Olive and Marcella were there too. Despite not having seen them for several years, we fell easily into a friendly banter, which, on this occasion focused on the writer Gregory. He had died a few months earlier, and the publicity had led me to seek out some of his books. Marcella hated him and his ideas. She called them pop psycho-history, and claimed they were nothing more than a concoction of bubbles and sugar.

There were plenty of young people there too, and it felt good to hear from them that Lizette had been a good teacher and popular. One of her colleagues, an overweight middle-age woman called Jane, who had been at the university ever since Lizette first worked there (having been laid off when it closed and then re-employed), was half-glossy and outspoken. She said this to me: 'I don't know why she ever went back to research, she is such a talented teacher.' On the way home, when I enquired about her, I discovered Jane was none other than Lizette's bête noire, the most troublesome person in her department, the one she referred to as 'Findzinski' or 'that Findzinski woman'. So then I quoted what she'd said, about Lizette being a 'talented teacher'. It was part of a pattern in our behaviour: she over-impressed by science and scientific discovery and undervaluing the job of teaching, and me arguing that education was as useful to society as science, if not more so. I thought I had partly won this battle when she went back to Farnborough, yet she could never rid herself of the idea that teaching was a job of secondary importance. I wish she had known my mother, Julie or, better yet, my grandmother Eileen.

Lizette planned to pursue several interests in her retirement, all of which involved me. I did suggest she might want to try wearing whites and playing bowls, but I never had as much success in persuading Lizette to share my interests as she did in coaxing me to share hers. There was the garden. We did a lot of digging, planting, potting, mulching, weeding; we browsed books (many of them from the 20th century – Lizette had a special fondness for Graham Stuart Thomas) and netsites; and we made regular expeditions to the Royal Horticultural Society gardens at Wisley.

There was also the bridge. Lizette had always been an aficionado. It was a family pastime, and we played when together with Samuel and his wife; Mercurio too enjoyed a game. In Brussels, Lizette had indulged twice a week. When we moved to Taunton House, she played only occasionally with friends, until, that is, she switched to Surrey University where she found a thriving bridge club. Once every few months, I was taken along for a 'social'. Then, with a playing partner, she joined the larger and more serious Guildford Bridge Club and rarely missed a Thursday evening session, when competitions were played.

I was rarely required. In retirement, though, she decided that she wanted to spend more time at the club, and so every Tuesday afternoon she and I played together informally against other mixed ability couples. It was fun, at times. We met some interesting and some not so interesting people. This is where Lizette began to employ me as a social crutch – I don't know how else to put it. She had always been proud of my achievements, particularly my career at the IFSD. To my knowledge, though, she had never boasted about me to friends or acquaintances, as she began to do at the bridge club during those Tuesday afternoon sessions.

Lizette's other burning interest was to visit parts of Europe she had never seen. Thus, for about three years, we embarked on a series of expensive, comfortable and well-organised mini-tours, lasting no more than three or four days each. Among other places, we visited Bergen, Corfu, Helsinki, Kiev, Linz, Porto, Rome and Zagreb, most of which I'd been to on business but not as a tourist. Some of our trips were arranged to coincide with bridge conventions. Lizette's playing partner (a woman called Carla Rawlins) would travel separately. While Lizette played with her in the formal tournaments, I would either watch or take in a few historical or cultural sights alone. On these trips, whether purely for tourism or for bridge, we met many people, and Lizette's incessant need to brag about me became a constant pain.

It was an incremental process. In the beginning, Lizette would use the chit-chat sessions at the bridge club to explain that I had been not only 'a UN official', which was how I described my past career to strangers, but a 'very important UN official'. I guessed she was trying to make up for my inadequate card play, about which I felt, if not guilty, then censurable. Within a few months, though, she had progressed to introducing me as if I was the most important UN official on the planet (never mind that I had retired 20 years earlier and that I had failed at director-general level). If this did not impress, she would move on to elaborate other achievements of mine, by mentioning REACH or The Josephine Collection. I began to worry there might be more to her behaviour than a crude attempt to compensate for my bridge skills. I wondered, for example, if she was embarrassed by my age. I thought to broach the subject with her but cowardice prevailed: I was painfully aware that, over the years, she and I both had often derided our ex-neighbour Iona, Sami's wife, for precisely the same kind of self-aggrandisement talk.

About 18 months after Lizette's retirement, Jay saved me, us, from this ridiculous predicament. I confided in him about my growing discomfort in going places with Lizette. Speculatively, he suggested that the behaviour trait might be connected with her depression. I had not detected any unusual symptoms of depression, nor had she mentioned any. A different person might have quizzed his son for more details, but I was reluctant to admit my ignorance, a habit acquired from too many years in meetings and negotiations. I did ask Jay if he might be able to persuade Lizette to see a doctor or psycho-counsellor. She didn't trust his opinions on anything, he commented, but he promised to try. One weekend, and without any apparent immediate cause, Lizette announced she had been feeling depressed and had booked an appointment with her local doctor, for whom she had much respect. When I probed gently, she refused to discuss the subject any further.

A week later, in the afternoon, Lizette came into the lounge where I was snoozing on the long sofa, with the Sony Reader I had bought her for Christmas on my lap. (Incidentally, I had always disliked reading on portable screens, such as the early Book-Mates and Palimpsests, and the later Shelfmans, Noveleases and Readers. I suppose it was because I had been brought up with hardback books and paperbacks. I was certainly at one with the Noteks on this. But I had to admit, at the time, that the new Reader was a pleasure to use, especially its soft leather mulberry exterior, and the smooth operation of the thin film page, that felt like parchment, and allowed one actually to turn a page giving the all-important sense of a book. Also, with my eye/spectacle combination losing tone and definition, it was more convenient to read larger type which the Reader does so well; and, I do admit, I did find it pleasurable to drift off to sleep in the afternoon with the Reader's dulcet tones reciting some Kolin Delvreux, Unwin Johns, John Betjeman or Walt Whitman.) She woke me gently, teased me about using the Reader, sat down by my side, snuggled up to my shoulder, all soft and giving, and curled her arm through mine.

'Have I been a pain?' I shrugged my shoulders. 'It's like I've been charging around through a fog trying to find something, or get somewhere. It's hard to explain. But I can think clearer now. The doctor gave me Chalaminth, only a mild dose for three months. It's working. She said my odd bouts of depression might have been caused by retirement. I had no idea. Did you notice?'

'I didn't know you were depressed, you never said.'

'No, I didn't really know.'

'You mentioned it to Jay.'

'Did I? How have I been difficult?' I could sense her thought processes working. 'How have I been difficult? Why didn't you tell me? You sod.' She mock punched me and I evaded the questions.

Chalaminth was the latest wonder drug, first released in the 80s. I do not pretend to understand how these medicines work, but, because of this one, Lizette developed the self-confidence to reflect on her own behaviour and feelings, and to talk them over with me. At the root of the problem – she worked

428

out – was the fact that she had staked too much of her sense of self and worth as an individual on her work and career. Thus, on retiring suddenly from a near full-time post to nothing, she had become insecure and vulnerable and sought to cover over such feelings with activity. Having acknowledged the problem, and faced up to it, Lizette slid off the Chalaminth more quickly than her doctor advised. She said she felt much better, more alive, more conscious than she had for months. And, because she became less determinedly busy and less manic, our journeys abroad were more widely spaced, I was hauled off to play bridge less often, and our social intercourse with friends and strangers alike returned to a more measured rhythm. For about two years, we continued our pleasurable jaunts to Europe. Then, in 94 Lizette had a horrible fall. We were walking through the botanical garden in Monte Carlo when she fell and broke her left hip. The emergency services were excellent, given the awkwardness of our location, but then we faced tedious administrative delays and other difficulties in organising the flight home. By the time Lizette had recovered from her operation and a new joint, she had lost all enthusiasm for further travel.

As I hope I've indicated, Jay remained an important part of my life, a regular visitor to Taunton House. The tension between him and Lizette invariably present to one degree or another until this time, had ebbed and flowed in response to Lizette's moods or Jay's life choices. There was a tense period after he chose to study teaching, and another when he opted for a secondary school post in Ealing, London, teaching pure geography (Lizette wanted him to teach one of the sciences), and yet another when he announced, in October 90, that he was going to marry Vince Wells, the advertising designer friend we had met several times. Lizette had accepted Jay's homosexuality better than she had done his teaching career, but she did not condone the idea of gay weddings in general, let alone her son going through with one. Jay claimed then, and still does today, that he wanted to marry Vince out of love, and scorns the idea that he wanted to spite his mother. He knows, however, that I suspect there was an element of filial revolt. Fortunately, Jay and Vince chose to indulge in one of those expensive wedding holidays, to the island of Bermuda, over Christmas that year, thus allowing Lizette to ignore the whole episode. In Jay's defence, I would say he has taken the marriage seriously, and it has lasted longer than many orthodox heterosexual marriages.

Things between Jay and Lizette remained tense and complicated after her retirement more or less until she went on the Chalaminth. Thereafter, we all got on surprisingly well. And then, after Lizette's accident, Jay began to recognise that Lizette had become old and fragile, and that, like me, she required more help and support. In 95, Jay won a much sought-after head-of-department position at a well-respected school in Highgate, in north London. It was only a small department, teaching sustainable balance, with three other staff, but Jay was so enthusiastic about the job even Lizette was full of congratulations. Today, Jay has five staff, and expects to be considered for deputy headmaster within a couple of years. He'll make it. Vince, too, changed jobs in the mid-90s, from advertising (the excitement of which had worn off) to product design; and the two of them bought a pretty Victorian terraced house in Muswell Hill. It had three bedrooms, a backyard and a permanent parking permit. As a house-warming present, Lizette took them six fuchsia plants, ones she had nurtured from cuttings and planted up in attractive glazed Spanish pots. She arranged them on the concrete steps at the back of the yard along a high wall, and she organised (and paid for) the installation of a reliable and automatic watering system. From then on, whenever we went to the Muswell Hill house during spring or early summer, Lizette took a bottle of plant food with which to feed the fuchsias. The last time I went to the house in summer, in 97, just months before Lizette's death, they were still dripping crimsons, purples, and violets.

I do not wish to dwell on Lizette's illness, which proved the most tortuous time for Lizette and those around her. It began with intestinal ulcers, and progressed towards increasingly serious attacks of peritonitis one of which ultimately killed her. In retrospect, I am far from convinced she had the best treatment. I suspect the first surgical intervention which should have relieved her condition, exacerbated it instead. When we moved, in August 96, she did switch to a different consultant but, by then, the damage – if my suspicions are correct – had been done. How can we ever know the truth of these things. There are so many cases reported of clear-cut medical malpractice and mistakes, what about those which are not so clear-cut? However sophisticated our equipment has become, doctors are only human.

But how unfair that modern medicine should have kept me in such good relative health to 100 years of age, well past my sell-by date, yet been unable to cope with Lizette's physical and mental deterioration. Lizette, herself, was a saint, there is no other word to describe her. She was stalwart and unselfish; she rarely complained (a characteristic which does not always serve an individual's best interests with the national health service) and she regularly tried to minimise the emotional and practical demands on myself and Jay. On the practical side, I was no longer able to drive or walk very far so I rarely accompanied her to the surgery or hospital for tests. During the periods when she was hospitalised, I went twice a day by taxi and used a hospital Swifty to negotiate the long corridors to her room. On the emotional side, I loved her too dearly to want to do anything other than talk through every nuance of her illnesses and treatments, and share as much suffering as she allowed. To my surprise (I confess this freely), Jay demonstrated how much he cared for his mother by visiting often, and making himself as available as possible to act as her chauffeur. Without his help, I don't know how we would have managed our move from Taunton House to a rented bungalow in Finchley, on a street called Meadowland View (but only in the imagination), not far, in fact, from here. The trauma of the move did nothing to ease Lizette's illness, but with my own mobility declining fast, we had no alternative. I guess Jay's readiness to help us out caused strains in his relationship with Vince, and may have led to Vince's first affair. But this is really none of my business, and I am only glad things are working out between them now.

Lizette died a week short of her 79th birthday in October 97. The funeral service was held at Golders Green Crematorium. Jay made all the arrangements. It was a busy funeral, with a reception held in private rooms at a nearby tavern. I was too distraught to take much part in the proceedings. Lizette's brothers (Samuel and Mercurio) and Jay all coped well with the social responsibilities. As it happens, it was the last time I saw several members of Lizette's family: Samuel's oldest son Saul (with wife and near grown-up children); Samuel's youngest daughter Mahonia (with husband, also an architect, and twins, not yet architects!); and Mercurio's son Esos (so similar to Mercurio when younger). I did not expect to remain much in contact with Samuel or Lynn either but, surprisingly, they made an effort to visit me in Meadowland View whenever they were in London. They were among my first visitors here at Willow Calm Lodge; and, since they are planning to come in January (Jay says) they may be among my last. (Which reminds me, I must ask them if they've heard any news of Liam.) After the funeral, I lost touch with Lizette's friends: Clarity and her daughter Joan went on extended sojourns to Kurdistan; and I don't know what happened to Rhoda (but surely she must have grown out of being a Maysie by now).

There was not much left of me after Lizette's death. We had shed many of our things in the move out of Taunton House, but we still had a bungalow full of possessions, many of which were Lizette's. Jay helped me go through them, and make decisions on their distribution or disposal. It was an unpleasant task. Within six months, I had a stroke that left me unable to walk, partially paralysed in my arms, and incontinent. Fortunately (or, as I thought at the time unfortunately), there was no damage to my brain, and I was as conscious of my disabilities as I was of Lizette's absence. Thus, in the spring of 98, I went into hospital where three months of treatment stabilised my condition. Then I moved into this hospice which Jay found. After extensive discussions with Dr Lipman, and a talk with Jay, I decided in October, 12 months after Lizette's death, to sign up to a deathday, and to spend my last year writing these Reflections. The journey – inspired by a letter from Lizette and made possible by Jay's unflagging support and Lipman's pill menu – has been exhausting but rewarding; painful and pleasant by turn, sad and joyful.

In these closing paragraphs, I will resist the temptation to pass any further judgements on myself or my times (not that I've been entirely unopinionated so far) with one exception. I have regrets, many of them to do with Crystal and Bronze, but there are other, lesser ones, such as not having gone to St Petersburg to spend time with Alan, losing Guido to South America, and having had minimal contact with my grandson Inti.

More generally, though, I can see now how I have lived most of my life on autopilot, not stopping to appreciate the taste, the colours, the feelings of life. I don't mean that I did not enjoy a good meal, film or political discussion, but rather that I did not enjoy the enjoyment – I'm not sure how else to put it. It is possible that there were good reasons for this during my 20s, when I was with Harriet, and when I was caught up with Caxton, but there were 20 years with Diana, mostly content, which drifted by in a haze of domestic routines, work deadlines and theatre society. I wish that I had been more conscious of my good fortune in being alive, and in being alive in a rich peaceful country, and through such a golden age of human history. It was only in the 60s that I began to reflect more on the pleasures and essence of being alive. I link this change in me to the First Jihad War and to meeting Lizette. The war was long predicted. I remember Alfred saying to me in 43: 'The IFSD is swimming against the tide. It's only a matter of time before there's a real war – five years or 20 – it's inevitable now.' But when it came, it still shocked the Western world out of its political malaise. And as for Lizette, her enthusiasm for the real (as opposed to Diana's imaginary) world, and in particular its scientific foundations, opened my eyes. Unfortunately, my conversion came too late – the best had passed. Yes, I was lucky enough to have found Lizette, and, yes, we had a good second half, as it were, together; but the world had fallen into decline, the golden era of oil and chips was gone. I – we all in Europe and the US – had been living through a great age, surrounded by a fairyland of riches, in a culture prosperous, free, full of art and science and invention and imagination, and we hadn't noticed how special it was, not until war tore us apart, and the sun's shine was taken away.

I am aware of a dichotomy here, a set of incompatible regrets. How can I reproach myself for not having luxuriated (enjoyed the enjoyment – I am at a loss for words) in the golden era when I believe it should never have been so golden, not with so much of the world poor, hungry or diseased? Having spent much of my life in the service of the United Nations trying to ensure a more balanced distribution of wealth, how can I not regret that we achieved so little, and that our failures led to such terrible wars, to terror, destruction and death, and, because the wars had left the world so deficient in resources, all of that terror, destruction and death multiplied tenfold during the Grey Years. But I recall Pravit Krishnamurty saying, of the development aid we were trying to negotiate in the 30s, 'You know and I know it is not enough' and, 'It will never be enough'. And I try to understand what common sense tells me: it could not have been any other way. As I have said, I tend towards Zoe Bergmann's view on this – although I certainly would not have done so as a young man. And, as I've also already said, I do have hopes for the new century, modest ones. Recalling (or paraphrasing) something Flip once said: if you look carefully enough at history you can detect a progression, not of nature which always has its own balance – and you'll have to go to a biologist for that – but in the civilisation of men and women, mankind and womankind. Since I've never had any difficulty in separating out the professional and quasi-political aims I espouse from the ordinary human actions I take, I do not really perceive any need to resolve the dichotomy.

***

This morning, before Alicia's visit, I spoke to Dr Lipman. I did not inquire directly about the consequences of delaying my own death, instead I asked him if he had had much experience of patients reneging on death date contracts, and deciding to hang on 'for dear life'. We had discussed this early on, but then I'd had no doubts about my decision or about my will to carry it through, and hadn't needed to pay any attention. This time I did. He told me that about a third of his patients change their minds in the last four weeks. Of these, half deteriorate very rapidly; a quarter take longer, a few months, to die and do so without comfort or dignity; and a quarter do get a tad more life, of acceptable conscious quality. But there are other factors, he explained. Most of those few patients whose pain and discomfort can be controlled longer than expected do not appear to benefit from the extra time because of the 'emotional confusion' experienced by the individuals themselves and/or their close friends and relatives. I had thought to close my conversation with Dr Lipman at this point, but I succumbed to asking him, without any further artifice, whether I might be one of the few that could hold on for a few extra months. I have a new great grandson on the way, I said, in June. He'll be the first born of my kin in the 22nd century. Dr Lipman's head nodded very slightly, he pursed his lips, as if about to impart bad news, and informed me that I was on such potent medical doses that, in his professional opinion, I'd be 'ga-ga or dead' long before the summer.

Since the day she arrived, I have scarcely been able to stop thinking about Alicia. I am a schoolboy again, daydreaming, but not of Melissa or even Gabriella. I have come to terms with saying goodbye to Jay. I assume this is because our relationship is mature, tidy. But I did not foresee Alicia's arrival, and if I had, I would never have guessed that I would adore her, or that she would tell me she was pregnant and wanted to return. So, when she came this afternoon, and after we'd spent 20 minutes or more looking at family camclips – hers and mine – I told her that I would be dying on 31 January, and why. She wept, which made me feel terrible. And then she stopped suddenly, as an actress might when a director says 'cut'.

'I'm so sorry, that was terrible of me to do that, to cry. That's so selfish. It must have been painful for you to tell me. What use is crying. I'm going home tomorrow. And in January, when all the centennial business has finished, I'm coming back. I'm coming with João, and Angela and Renato – they'll come, I'll make it work – and we're going to have a late fiesta for your 100 years. Is it good? Will it be good?' She was holding my hand.

'Yes, Alicia, it will be good. But please arrange it with Jay. He can help with the fares; please, please don't be shy about that. And, before you go I have something for you. I'm not giving it to you now because I'm worried I might die before you come again, because I won't I promise, but because I want you to have it now. It's under the bed. Don't open it. Take it home with you, and share it with João, and then, if you can, pass it on to your son.' In anticipation of Alicia's last visit, I had asked Jay to unbox the Ferrez photograph and frame and parcel it up in gift paper. Months ago, I had thought about giving it to Tina, but changed my mind.

'Then I too shall give you a present. I was thinking this already on that first day with you, and I've already talked to João. The name of our boy shall be Kip. Will it be good for you?'

'Yes, Alicia, it will be good for me.'

EXTRACTS FROM CORRESPONDENCE
Kip Fenn to Guido Oostlander-Fenn

31 January 2100
Once before you received important family news by letter, and now this time it is me choosing not to tell you something face-to-face. By the time you read this, I will have gone, and my hope is that I will be cremated quickly without any fuss, and my ashes will be buried near my mother's in a garden at Parsonville. If all goes according to plan, we will have talked on the camphone earlier today. You will have asked me how I am, and I will have said I am fine. But I have only been of sound mind, and relatively free of discomfort for this past year because I chose to fix a death date and take increasingly strong medication until then.

If you and Mireille had not planned to come in the autumn, I would have asked you to do so. I wanted to see you both very much, thus your visit was beautifully timed. But I did not want our last hours together weighed down by you knowing about my deathday. This was my selfishness, and I am apologising now as sincerely as I can. I did not want you returning to Europe just to see me die, not for you and not for me; nor did I want you to be conscious of me moving weekly, daily, hourly nearer the fixed date. I saw this happen to a friend of mine. You could say this should have been your decision not mine. But I took it anyway. Perhaps I was wrong. It is of no matter now. Jay was the only person who knew my death date for certain, and since I see him nearly every day, it was not possible to hide my decision from him. He has been a stalwart friend and confidant, helping me to organise my thoughts and write my Reflections. You will be sent a copy (in which I plan to append both this letter, some of those written by Diana, and some by you) and I hope you find my story interesting and accurate. As I write this I am thinking about those days we spent together on Ginquin, and I am wondering whatever happened to our boat. Perhaps if you ever come back to live in Holland, you will seek her out. Beneath her panels, she holds some of my very happiest memories.

Guido, I want you to know that you have been a star in my life, from your birth until my writing of this letter, more than 60 years, whether near or far, you have been a source of comfort and joy in my heart. It has been a privilege to be your father, to know and to love you.

Remember me to Inti, and to Mireille, and, above all, to yourself – take me with you into the 22nd century.

All my love.

Lizette Sanderson to Kip Fenn

October 2097

My darling Kip, if you are reading this then the worst has happened. I am so sorry for leaving you. It seems wrong and unfair that you should have had to look after me, and watch me slide away. It is 3 September as I write, you have fallen asleep on the sofa in the next room listening to one of your favourites, the Berlin Philharmonia playing Zanichelli. Tomorrow, I go to hospital again. I fear I might not have another chance to write this letter.

It's a silly letter really, a selfish one with three requests.

I'd like you to do that thing with my ashes, put them in a pot, a flower vase. It was Rhoda's idea, she read it in a magazine. Do you remember us laughing about it. Best of all, I'd like it if my ashes could be turned into glitter – it's possible, some potters (but please not the Noteks) have the equipment – and used for the glaze. I'm confident you'll appreciate why I'd prefer a flower vase to a plant pot.

Secondly, tell Jay how much I loved him; look after him, as I know he will look after you.

Finally, I want to say this: do not mourn my passing, rather hold on to life, on to what we had together, on to what you are – and set it down. I mean I want you to write your Reflections, Kip. You have lived so long, seen so much good and bad, joy and suffering, you have done so much for the people around you, for me, for Jay and for the world, even though I know you do not feel this. Write it all down. You've thought about it before, and I should have encouraged you, but I didn't – as usual, I was thinking of myself not of you. Do it, write your Reflections, don't let yourself be forgotten.

We had a good time, though, didn't we. It wasn't all plain sailing, but you kept your hand so firmly on the tiller of our sailboat that when the inclement weather came along I couldn't help but feel safe and loved and in love.

INDEX OF PEOPLE

440

This index lists people according to their surnames where mentioned in the text, otherwise by their first names. Only people referred to on more than one page are listed. For national leaders, dates for their period or periods of office have been noted (as listed in *Encyclopaedia Universal*, 2098 edition).

FAMILY RELATIONSHIPS

BACKGROUND

Evvie+Barry Fenn   Eileen (+Oswald Hapgood)   Percival

Tom Fenn+Julie   Alan (+Anna Mastepanov)

Neil (aka Kip) Fenn

PARTNERS AND CHILDREN

CONCEIÇÃO

Kip Fenn+**Conceição Magalhães**

Arturo Magalhães (+Edna)   + Fatima
(cloned)

Alicia (+João Gonçalves)   Tina   Juliano (+Eliane)   Ignacio

Angela+Quasim   Maria

Renato

HARRIET

John Tilson

Constance Tilson

Kip Fenn+**Harriet**

Crystal Fenn   *Bronze Tilson*

DIANA

Claudine+Anders van der Klein   Maartje+Eduwart Oostlander

Betje   Kaatje   Neeltje + Powles   Saartje +Anthony Nash

Kip Fenn+**Diana**   Demeter   Dana   Dominique+Waltar Meijer   Liam

Guido Oostlander-Fenn+Mireille Rocard   Jurian   Lukas

Inti

LIZETTE

Wendy+Mervyn Sanderson

Kip Fenn+**Lizette** (+Clint Tuohy)   Samuel (+Lynn)   Mercurio+May   +Andrasta

Jay Sanderson   Saul   Irene   Mahonia   Yewla   Esos